Tides of Fortune

By the same author

Novels
Let Me See Your Face
The Dakota Poject
Death of a Terrorist

Narrative History
The Chinese Opium Wars
An Open Path: Christian Missionaries 1514–1915
The Galleys at Lepanto

Verse
Aspects of Love
The Polythene Maidenhead
Twenty-five Short Poems

TIDES OF FORTUNE

Jack Beeching

HUTCHINSON
LONDON MELBOURNE AUCKLAND JOHANNESBURG

© Jack Beeching 1988

All rights reserved

First published in Great Britain in 1988
by Hutchinson Ltd, an imprint of
Century Hutchinson Ltd, Brookmount House,
62–65 Chandos Place, London WC2N 4NW

Century Hutchinson Australia Pty Ltd
PO Box 496, 16–22 Church Street, Hawthorn,
Victoria 3122, Australia

Century Hutchinson New Zealand Limited
PO Box 40–086, Glenfield, Auckland 10, New Zealand

Century Hutchinson South Africa (Pty) Ltd
PO Box 337, Bergvlei, 2012 South Africa

Phototypeset in Ehrhardt 11/12 pt
by Input Typesetting Ltd, London
Printed and bound in Great Britain
by Mackays of Chatham Ltd

British Library Cataloguing in Publication Data

Beeching, Jack
  Tides of fortune.
  I. Title
  823'.914[F]   PR6052.E315/

ISBN 0–09–170620–3

Note on Method and Sources

Historians who wrote about the period in antiquity – Zosimus, Orosius, Procopius – disagree almost more than they coincide. Secondary sources, the work over centuries of meticulous scholarship, also differ widely. Gibbon for instance gives a date other than mine for the battle of Pollentia, and in this novel the interested reader will notice other discrepancies. To reconstruct the fifth century in Rome with fidelity there are simply not enough facts.

Our most copious witnesses are Claudian, a poet, and Augustine, a theologian, exactly the kind of person that an academic historian mistrusts. They figure as characters. When there are no actual words to put in their mouths, I thought of the kind of men they probably were, so as to invent. But the novel follows what we know of them.

Paulinus of Nola is another instance. A persistent church legend speaks of his selling himself into slavery during the Vandal invasion. Academic historians cast doubt, because he would have been too old to be worth buying. So I picked on a likelier time. My narrative also differs from Procopius's account of the Vandal invasion of Africa – unfair to Boniface, whom we know about from his correspondence with Augustine. For his new-fangled armoured lancers – predecessors of the knight and tank – Stilicho needed stirrups, so why should he not have them, even though there is no reference to stirrups in literature until a century later? All this fiction, though, from beginning to end, tries to convey reliable information, and always has some basis in known fact.

Clearly there is another ambiguity. Whatever his scruple the historical novelist finds himself writing about his own time as well as the past – how could he not? There are barbarians at our gates too, though they no longer ride horses.

Part I

1

Gilda squatted on turf beside the muddy hoof-tracks, waiting for her breath to come back. Again she crouched and kicked, bare feet upwards. A little human tripod, she stood balanced on head and hands. Under her skull the ground thudded. Enormous stalks of grass pressed close to her face. The world was upside down, a throb of blood in her ears. She was squinting upwards, to catch sight of her own bare toes against the blue of the sky, when around the corner came armed horsemen.

Gilda could see them moving towards her in a distorted jog-trot, upside down, their horses huge. Best to run away – run away fast – yet so long as she stood on her head she was out of the dangerous world of men with giant moustaches, horse archers, and nothing could touch her.

The leading archer carried a short flagpole. A windsock blew out of it in the shape of a dragon, bloated, meant to terrify. One glimpse of this banner upside down, as if it were a real floating monster, and the strength went out of Gilda's arms. The little human tripod tottered. The second horseman in line reached down and made one handful of her ankles. Pulling her right off the ground he threw her limp across his saddle. The sweating horse rose and fell under her. She could see the little spurts of mud kicked up by its hooves, horse-sweat and man-sweat enfolding her. These jolting riders in helmet and breast-plate, these soldiers with large moustaches, were laughing at the sight of her. She was their captive.

The man who had lifted her off the ground shouted a joke

in pig-Latin which Gilda only half understood: *fur*, a poacher? On the forest road, but a long way behind, her mother appeared, breathless.

'Come back! Give her back to me!' As she screamed abuse at the disappearing horsemen the demented woman began tearing her hair, as if one pain might drive out another. None of the men looked back, but they fell silent.

The horse archers were barbarian mercenaries serving in Britain under the great General Stilicho. They were back from one of Stilicho's cavalry raids – he had driven a mob of plundering invaders from Ireland up against a line of forts and made mincemeat of them. Britain's invaders, Irish and Saxon alike, were being driven back to the benighted places they came from.

But, meanwhile, the Roman army lived off the country. The soldiers took farm carts without paying, used draught oxen for beef, stole the seed corn and called it requisition. They were keeping Britain in the Roman Empire but bankrupting the countryside. They were almost more feared than the wild and pagan enemy.

Towards sunset, with dark forest all around, the soldier who had lifted and carried Gilda off set her down on solid earth again. She was aching with stiffness. She pulled a long face so he took hold of her and threw her, like a flying bundle, to another soldier. This man, after throwing her up and catching her, turned round and tossed her towards another pair of hands, three paces off. Gilda had started to yell with helpless anger and that made them laugh even louder.

They began arguing among themselves.

'And if the girl runs away?'

'Don't talk silly. Where would she run to?'

'You could tether her to a peg,' a corporal said sarcastically, 'like the horses.'

They are only boys, Gilda told herself, loud, treacherous, laughing big boys. And fools. Knots and a peg are nothing. I can undo knots. What holds me here is not rope but the arrows that would come winging after me if I turned and ran. And the terrors of the wood – wolves, bears, demons. Even if I found my way home, what would be waiting for me? A beating from my mother.

The men were taking their ease, lifting off leather-lined

helmets, shaking back ragged, sweat-streaked hair, taking a drink from leather water-bottles, wiping long moustaches.

'Drink!'

The water in the bottle they passed her tasted muddy but she was glad of it. They were easing straps, smoothing wrinkles out of horse blankets, and rubbing down their chargers' sweaty rumps with handfuls of grass. They had begun talking to the four-legged beasts as if the horses were human beings.

'Catch!'

Something to eat was thrown at Gilda as you might throw a scrap to a starving dog – Army biscuit, hard as a plank. They cheered her for catching it, much as they would have cheered a dog for doing a trick. Using her teeth as scrapers Gilda grated the biscuit and sucked in the crumbs until she had a mouthful. She was hungry, her belly was empty, and what else mattered?

Next day the mounted archers reached their camp. They crossed the ditch by a plank bridge which reverberated surprisingly under their horses' hooves. They went through the gate and past the guardhouse, each man in the double column holding himself up smartly. Inside Gilda found a bewilderment of tents and huts, men, horses and smoke, stray dogs, braying trumpets, commands shouted so unexpectedly that they made her quiver. Yet in all this chaos she began after a while to make out a kind of order.

'Mounted archers, dismount!'

The soldiers will take you away and lock you up! Gilda's mother had sometimes used those words as a threat. But in the camp they treated her like a pet on two legs. She stuck close to the men who had first taken possession of her, the mounted archers. They were loud and strange men, hairy, boastful, quickly angry, but they knew her by name, Gilda, and gave her food and drink and made a joke of her.

Their leggy, piping-voiced, curly-headed captive was left to wander at will between the mounted archers' bivouacs and their muddy horse-lines. After dark, around the fire, they gave her beer to drink out of a helmet, and laughed uproariously to see her stagger. She was their pet. If any other soldier in the camp had so much as laid a finger on Gilda's bare shoulder, daggers would have been drawn.

Gilda soon had their simple-minded, pig-Latin jokes by

heart, and made them sound funnier. In a mood of mimicry that came upon her like a kind of madness new jokes kindled in her brain. She could make them laugh as easily as pouring water from a jug. She didn't know the meaning of half the filth they habitually spoke but she could twist the words around and provoke grown men's laughter. Jokes earned pats on the cheek and the best lump of salted meat. She was nearly eleven.

Had the girl they kidnapped been a year or two older and nubile the mounted archers would by this time have been squabbling over her, even fighting for her. She would have become the winner's girl until some centurion, ordered to clear out illicit camp followers, made him sell the girl to a dealer for cash. And no regrets either. Find them, fondle them, forsake them. Should she be pregnant – ran the standing joke – lucky for the dealer. Two for the price of one. But Gilda was young enough to be everyone's, and she had this natural gift for being funny.

So it went on for months. She was safe among the mounted archers until the campaign was over. Then they were being withdrawn to their depot in Gaul and thence to the threatened forts along the Rhine. They couldn't take her with them and her breasts were budding.

Stridor – 'The Squeak', named for the emasculated sound of his voice – dealt in anything a soldier might fancy: wine shipped across from Gaul, brooches enamelled to catch the barbarian eye, whetstones for weapons, dice that would always roll the big number uppermost. He would even lend a soldier money against his pay. He was a clever little mannikin, Stridor, who knew when to squeeze and when to let slide. Now he was waiting for Gilda to fall into his lap.

A long time ago Stridor had been a slave himself – a spayed towel-boy in a Roman brothel. To castrate a slave was against the Roman law, but it was a highly profitable illegality. By the time his boyish bloom was gone Stridor had made enough money selling his body on the side to buy his own freedom. He was now small, wrinkled, grotesque, and what he wanted to trade in most was the human riffraff swept up in the army's wake. When his throat was dry a soldier might sell the two-legged piece of property trailing at his heels for the price of a drink. There were always bargains. If you knew how to pick them out, fatten them up, teach them their business, and carry them to the best market, there was money to be made in slaves.

And from a clever little girl like Gilda with a pretty face, a singing voice, and the knack of making soldiers laugh, more money, perhaps, than might be expected. She was wasting her talents out here on the edge of empire. Stridor had promised himself Gilda ever since the mounted archers taught her to mock him.

'Hey, Stridor, why do you squeak? Dropped your eggs and broken them?'

The words had been put in her mouth, Gilda had no idea what they meant; but when she repeated the taunt she had seen that she was flicking the wrinkled little man on the raw. Stridor, now the girl was losing her protectors, stalked her like a fox with a goose. The child who mocked him would, one day soon, lower her voice fearfully if he so much as glanced at her. Those mounted archers were spoiling her. It was time she began to learn.

The day before breaking camp and leaving for their depot there was a drunken celebration among Gilda's mounted archers, maudlin farewells to Britannia with her drizzle and her skirmishes, and the beer had been provided by Stridor – good old Stridor! They had begun by drinking a brimming toast in their helmets to General Stilicho – good old Stilicho – and then had gone over their small personal exploits in drunken detail. They had seen action. They had seen the enemy run!

While living in camp Gilda had lost her awe of soldiers. She had watched them sob at a wound, groan from a hangover or at an unlucky omen. These very men boasting in the firelight of how brave they were could be frightened by a lightning flash. They are big clumsy children, Gilda told herself. I can play with them as I used to play with my doll.

Next morning – their last day in camp – Gilda caught a glimpse of General Stilicho himself, as he went off with his plumed and caparisoned guardsmen to begin his journey to Milan, to report to the Emperor. Except for his gilded helmet and his scarlet cloak he might have been a trooper in his own mounted archers – a huge man with bandy legs and the usual blue eyes and yellow hair. His beard, though, had been trimmed short along the jaw in brutal Roman fashion. He was Rome's best general, according to the archers – yet a Vandal!

'There he goes!'

They lifted Gilda high on their shoulders. The trumpets blared as the great man went by. Gilda looked at Stilicho, and what was he but a man like any other? She was sick of hearing so much about him.

When the procession was over the mounted archers felt sorry for themselves. A barrel of beer had been drunk the night before and there was the devil to pay. There could be no bilking Stridor. The centurion was his patron and there they were, both of them, coming their way.

'They won't let you take that girl where you're going,' the centurion said, shaking his head grimly. He had already come to an arrangement with Stridor.

'Suppose I took her off your hands?' the dealer squeaked.

'What do you need a woman for, Stridor?' asked a mounted archer jocosely.

'To mend my clothes,' he answered mildly. This morning there was no provoking him. ' To wash my dirty dishes.'

There would be pickets at the transports taking them to Gaul to turn away any camp followers. Were they to cast Gilda adrift on the waterfront like a stray dog, when here was good old Stridor, making them an offer?

'For the beer?'

'For the beer.'

'The beer, then.'

'Done.'

As hands were clasped on the deal, Stridor kept the smile off his face. Merely to deal was an intense pleasure to him – a victory of the impotent over the virile. The centurion, with Stridor's bribe already clinking in his leather purse, slapped his boot with the vine root that was his badge of office and nodded benignly. The soldiers thought they had done wisely, got off lightly.

Stridor stood there, a little downcast, as if they had been too much for him, but with his grip tight around Gilda's thin wrist. For Gilda, happening so suddenly, it had been an outrageous betrayal, the first of her life. Jogging in double file out of the camp towards the sea, the mounted archers were already beginning to forget her.

On the far side of the ditch was an untidy civilian encampment for whores, dealers, fortune tellers, boozing and gambling dens. Stridor lived in a hut there amongst his stock of wine jars and whetstones, with a crop-eared mastiff on guard. Against the hut was a lean-to stable which stank of mule droppings. There he housed half a dozen waifs, manacled at night to a long iron chain like a heavy snake, none of them over twenty. Britons any older than that were not worth shipping out. They would never learn.

Gilda went at Stridor's heels into the stink of that lean-to, telling herself that she would never trust him. She would never trust anyone again.

From a peg on the wall Stridor lifted the blackthorn stick which hung there as a warning and dealt sharp blows with it to left and to right. '*That* for fighting,' and, as he struck the least successful of the combatants, '*that* for having a black eye.' He turned round as he struck out a third time. '*That* for muttering behind my back.'

Gilda tried to shrink into her skin. She was the youngest, she would make herself small and unimportant, but it was unavailing.

'And you, girl. Broken eggs to you, girl.' Stridor had hold of Gilda by the scruff of her neck. He was forcing her down across his knee and laying on the stick. Some of the others laughed because it wasn't happening to them. Not enough to spoil her nature, Stridor told himself. Just enough to teach her. He was enjoying himself.

'Hear what I say?'

Gilda had known beatings before, at home, and she knew how to resist the hot shock of his first stroke. Her silence, though, prompted Stridor to lay on the next one harder. Her clenched jaw loosened, and out came the scream he was vividly anticipating.

'For you,' he said, 'no supper.' Hunger tames them too, he reflected. Gilda lay there in the half dark, screw-manacled by her left ankle to the chain, sprawled among the others as they fidgeted or whimpered in fear and pain, a hot ache across her buttocks, the gripe of hunger in her guts and murder in her heart.

Next morning, to her surprise, Stridor was uncommonly kind, he might have been a jovial uncle. That, too, was how you tamed a slave – make sure they never knew what to expect. He even made jokes Gilda could have made better, but timidly she pretended to laugh.

While they were crossing the Channel in a flat-bottomed boat full of soldiers, to Rotomagus on the Gaulish side, and the other slaves were as sick as dogs, Stridor, who liked the sea air, took Gilda on his knee, and began teaching her a patriotic song about the Roman army and its eagles, his squeaking voice blending absurdly with her pure girlish pipe. Army men lounging around, pleased with themselves for not being seasick, began joining in more or less discordantly. One of them gave Gilda a copper farthing – the first money she had ever earned. As soon as the soldier turned his back, Stridor took it from her. He was already day-dreaming of the money Gilda might earn for him, in Rome.

2

Bishop Decius, though an old man of great learning, was simple by nature and impetuous. He might take it into his head one fine morning to walk from one end of his diocese to the other, alone, using his crozier as a staff, visiting the little Christian communities scattered along the coast. He would arrive back unexpectedly at his little brick basilica in Noviomagus, covered with mud and often drenched through, but smiling. Then Lucas's holiday was over. Again the dictating would begin and Lucas would be kept hard at it, hour after hour, following the drone of the old man's voice, and making his fair copies.

Bishop Decius had never yet been attacked, so he said, either by wolves or bandits. The sight of his crozier, he had told Lucas, almost shyly, the sign of his sacred function as shepherd of his flock, was evidently enough to daunt them. But Lucas was more inclined to think that thieves left the bishop alone simply because he was not worth robbing, a poor old man in a threadbare cloak, plodding along with a plain wooden crozier which might well have been a real shepherd's crook. He often muttered to himself – working out the long theological epistles which later he would get Lucas to engross for him in fair penmanship.

The forest inland had its perils. Ruined men fled there and lived as cut-throats. But the coastal land east and west from Noviomagus – Chichester – was considered safe. Both the British shore and the facing coast in Gaul were dotted, these days, with Roman lookout posts and patrolled by small fast galleys. If they spotted a piratical intruder they could signal for a man of war. A Saxon raider from the east would have to run the gauntlet of these patrols, against the prevailing wind, and Irish freebooters in their clumsy leather curraghs could hardly get this far up Channel with anything less than a gale of wind in their favour. People on the coast would still talk of danger from the sea, but only to add a spice of excitement to their lives. So the violent way the old bishop met his death, wandering with Lucas his scribe at night along the fogbound shore, was all the more shocking.

Tall, thin, calm, young, courteous but unbelieving – in every way unlike the obsessed old bishop – Lucas had been taking dictation from him for three days and far too long into three successive nights. These letters were sent off by friendly officials who had access to the Imperial Post – not that the postal service in the Empire was what it had been – and replies would come eventually from other churchmen in Gaul and Rome and Africa. There had been a long letter to Ambrose, Bishop of Milan, about the Arians; and an even longer screed, on Manichaeanism, to Jerome in Bethlehem – a sarcastic man to judge by the letter to which Bishop Decius was replying. Looking up in the course of his droning onrush of long words, the bishop had noticed Lucas's look of mild astonishment.

'Do you suppose that there is no such place on earth as Bethlehem, young man?'

What had just then struck Lucas was the simple thought that he, Lucas, sitting here in Britain on a wet night, simply by pushing an iron pen across papyrus, could pour words into the ear of another man sitting in a monk's cell in the Holy Land on the other side of the world. Writing was a mystery, the Latin language a power.

'Bethlehem? Why not?' said Lucas, not quite respectfully. He was always uneasy when the bishop fired off a question at him, sometimes a difficult question, as if Lucas were not a mere scribe but a theological student – as though copying hour after hour were not hard work in itself. He would answer with the first thing that came into his head and then regret it when he saw Bishop Decius's forlorn glance.

Towards midnight the lamp flickered for want of oil and Lucas paused to rub his reddened eyes. The old man, in his impulsive, unexpected way, called for a break.

'A walk along the shore,' he suggested, 'and we shall come back refreshed.'

For Lucas, bed would have been more like it, but putting his ideas into words had raised the bishop to a state of high excitement. Though how could anyone get worked up, Lucas wondered, about Manichaeans and Donatists? It was splitting hairs.

'Pelagius puzzles you,' the old man declared knowingly, as if reading Lucas's thoughts.

'We go at such a rate,' said Lucas, though trying to keep any tinge of resentment out of his voice, for he loved the old man, 'that all I can think of is the shape of the letters.'

'No doubt a well-conducted young man like you is safe enough inside the church,' conceded the bishop, 'without bothering his head about Pelagius.'

'I am glad you think so well of me, my lord.'

Bishop Decius's remark had left Lucas ill at ease. He was not, for one thing, 'safe inside the church' and did not plan on so being. He was not even a catachumen. He was a scribe and a freeman, lent to the bishop by a well-to-do and pious friend in London, to help his failing sight. This was a job for him, not a vocation. Lucas sometimes wondered if he might have a piece missing in his mind – the piece that made other men religious.

'Womankind is a chief source of evil for a young man like yourself,' said the old man as if announcing an important truth.

'Woman – a temple built over a sewer.' Fog lay heavily along the beach, making their voices resonate.

'If you say so, my lord,' Lucas answered, a little too casually perhaps. After the dizzy girls of London the country girls down here did not amount to much, yet even so he had managed to get entangled.

The old man went on talking, half to himself, about Pelagius, following his own train of thought, as if in an intellectual dream.

'Pelagius for all his shortcomings – and I think we may as well be charitable and call them shortcomings rather than grievous errors – has a knack of putting a difficult thought like a proverb. *If I ought, I can.* That is the core, heart, kernel, essence of his teaching. If I ought, I can. Yes, Lucas, I agree with you. There is evil in the world, enormous evil, but not overwhelmingly so much evil that a convinced Christian, with God's grace –'

Was it on the third repetition of that word *evil*, Lucas afterwards wondered, that a screech of pebbles under a keel came to his ears like a warning portent, as a boat was run ashore? On such a night nothing good came out of the sea. The old man was still wrestling all unaware with his long sentence about evil. To run? Cowardly. And even had they both run for their lives as the keel struck the beach, the pagan Saxons would have been after them, and collared them. They were big men, but quick. They had been drifting quietly offshore under cover of the fog, listening for footsteps and voices. They were out for captives.

The Saxon captain had protuberant eyes, like the eyes of a deep-sea fish, set in a hairy slab of a face. Of the dozen fighting men who tugged oars in his square-sailed longboat he had the broadest shoulders. He held the steering oar and, as the boat's keel touched the pebbles, he had been overcome by the frenzy which came up on such pagans in times of extremity – a kind of mad exhilaration in which they neither understood danger nor felt wounds. This drunkenness was upon him now.

To have come impudently all this way down the coast, avoiding Roman patrols under cover of the fog, had been a wild risk, but the cruise so far had paid off. Like so many logs along the wet bottom of this undecked, clinker-built sailing boat, were his prisoners, wrists tied to ankles, mouths gagged.

The Saxons had ventured a long way from home, raiding the British coast for slaves to work their lands, so that they themselves could live at ease, as free as men should, feasting and drinking, quarrelling and fighting. The prisoners underfoot? Human cattle.

And loitering loud-mouthed on this pebble beach, here were two more.

The Saxon captain was over the side into the spume and running up the shingle, his long iron sword lifted against Lucas and the old bishop, almost before the prow of his boat had settled into place. His crew tumbled after him, the frenzy upon them too. By the time they had caught up with their chief the blood was spilled.

He had seen at a glance that the old one, scraggy and white-haired, would not be worth his rations. There was no work left in him. With a double stroke of his two-handed sword the captain, in a glee of berserk fury, did for old Decius. The downhanded stroke adroitly cut open his soft parts – paunched him like a rabbit from rib to groin. The second stroke, on the upward swing and delicately judged, bit into the old man as he was already tumbling, and ripped out his windpipe. At the sickening gasp – the old bishop's last breath – the Saxon captain laughed.

With that second stroke, the captain told himself, I could just as well have cut his head off. I have the strength. In my war-madness, who can resist me? But why nick iron blade on bone? The elegance of that second stroke – to the windpipe – went on filling him with joy.

The younger of the two unarmed British idiots stood there aghast, neither imploring mercy, as they usually did, nor attempting to flee, but stockstill. The captain could almost have wished that this tall thin youngster would run for it, so as to give his men coming up the beach behind him a little fun. Men cheated of action grow restive. The young man stood there, white-faced, as if his heart had stopped. All the better. He was able-bodied, he was young, he would be useful, and any such chase up the beach might have crippled him.

The captain took a last glimpse at the heap of dead flesh

down at his feet and his berserker rage drained away. No longer was he invulnerable, drunk on the wine of action, but lonely and sad and very nearly afraid. His left cheek had been touched by the first moist puff of a sou'wester – a salt whisper. His luck was changing with the wind. A little more and it would blow away the fog that had so far covered their audacious foray, and hidden them in the narrow seas from the Roman patrols. What chance was this devil-wind giving them of rowing their cargo of prisoners past the sacred island of Heligoland home to the Saxon shore? By now his men knew too. They were dragging their prisoner aboard as if time mattered.

If someone afterwards had obliged Lucas to swear as to how Bishop Decius met his death – his body turned to dogs' meat by a double stroke of a sword, while his soul flew up invisibly to paradise – he would have answered, with conviction, a demon. The Saxon captain, a great hairy demon, had come up out of the night like an emanation of evil. The world one lived in was full of such embodied evil and the old bishop's death was proof of it.

The Saxon captain had demons of his own to propitiate. He knew that to escape this unlucky wind he must give back to his men their potent fighting spirit, their manhood, by a sacrifice. They had a good catch of slaves on board. The womenfolk would greet them with smiles. All they needed now to dodge the Roman patrols was luck.

Instead of fleeing fast out to sea, the captain walked across the prone bodies of the prisoners in the bottom of his boat, counting on his fingers. The tenth man, when he came to his second little finger, was the man next to Lucas. On the faces of his crew, instead of fear at this worrying wind there were smiles of anticipation at the promise of a sharp and viscerally-exciting ritual for bringing luck.

The seamen, as they pulled the tenth man from his place, treated him with a strange kind of respect, almost joking with him as they spreadeagled him with ropes, high up on the cross-trees of the mast. The nails and the sword stab would come later.

The keen young commander of a twelve-oared Roman coasting

galley, painted the regulation blue and on dawn patrol out of Anderida, caught a glimpse on the horizon of the Saxons' oblong, homespun-coloured mainsail, then lost sight of it and wondered if he could have been mistaken. The dubious craft had been hull-down and heading for mid-Channel. The fog was still thick on the shore over the marsh, but out at sea it had begun to lie about in patches. The rising sun had caught that porridge-coloured mainsail only for an instant as it slid from one patch of fog to the next.

'A raider, sir?' asked the old bosun, who had no doubts.

A raider this far west? The young Roman officer wondered if he dare take a chance. If what he had seen had been the squared-off sail of an innocent trader crossing to Gaul, and he called out a warship, he would make a laughing stock of himself.

'Bosun – let's make sure.'

Orders were to keep a raider under observation and report her ashore, but only to fight her in an extremity. Man for man, the crew of this fast Roman galley might not be able to outfight the dozen barbarians aboard the raider they had glimpsed, but they could overhaul her. The lookout by the firepot on its platform of bricks in the bows was ready to send up his smoke-signal, but the young commander had decided to make certain. A merchantman would have a fat belly. A raider would be shaped like a knife. He was badly in need of another sighting – this time of her hull.

He had his second chance. The lookout in the bows sang out another 'sail in sight!' and the young officer, at that moment, saw her again, clear of the fog, and edging off-shore as if creeping away. The crew that made the first report of a capture took a share in the prize money, so the oarsmen were bending their backs with a will.

All at once the commander swore a gross oath by Hercules. Through hesitating he had lost his chance. The man in the bows was already putting green alder chips over the hot fire in the brick box, to make smoke, when from the lookout on the long-nosed chalk cliff ashore rose up a single, thin, smokey column, wavering in the early breeze, and slowly darkening and thickening as the fire was fed. The first signal had come from the men who never got their feet wet. The cadence of the rowing faltered.

'Bosun! No slacking!' The arrogant young voice was angry. Across bent shoulders a rope's end began to rise and fall as if picking off flies. This, though, was pique, and the men all knew it. Why row their hearts out when the job was done? Soon, from one side or other of the Channel, a warship would turn up, crammed with seamen and bright with weaponed soldiers. They would overwhelm the Saxon and bring her in, but all the prize money, not to mention the illegal pickings, would go to others. Across the sea from the runaway came a scream – so faint that it might have been the cry of a seabird.

The stroke oarsmen aboard the Saxon longboat had left their bench. Rowing would not save them now, more than ever they needed luck. Using sword pommel for hammer they were nailing their man to the mainmast crosstrees. All aboard, rowers and prisoners alike, as they turned their eyes upwards, could see the aghast expression on the pinioned man's face. Lucas would rather not have looked but his eyes were dragged round irresistibly. Strangely enough, in this other violent death there was no horror for him, but a surcease, as if the man spread-eagled up there, nailed and now stabbed with the long iron sword, might be taking all their doom upon himself.

The prisoner they were crucifying aboard the Saxon longboat had almost but not quite given up the ghost, when a big ship from the Gaulish side, running before the wind, bore down on her. Though the luck-ritual had failed it had hardened the men for the fight to come. A golden early morning, a Roman warship arriving to save them, and yet Lucas, as the ship approached, felt inexplicable anguish, as if his life had been torn up by the roots.

The fight between the dozen Saxon barbarians and four times their number of Roman regulars, armed with round shields and the stabbing *scramasax* – short and sharp as a cutlass – was savage but soon over. The broadshouldered pop-eyed captain – the last of the Saxons still on his feet – jumped into the sea, long sword held upwards over his head in both hands, rather than be taken. The sea around the frothy hole he had plumped into was tinged red with his wounds. Those of his men not quite dead had their throats cut, methodically, unfeelingly, one by one, by a soldier with a *scramasax* who had been told off for the job.

'That's tidier,' said the petty officer commanding the prize crew, in the tone of a careful housewife. 'Now tip them overboard and wash her down.'

Quickly their bodies were stripped naked, and everything in the longboat worth keeping was collected into one heap for the treasury official aboard the warship to value. The dead Saxons, lifted by head and feet and swung, were sent over the side to join their captain among the fishes. The dead man in the crosstrees was unpinned, and he went over the side too, but as the petty officer gave the order he crossed himself. A Christian, wondered Lucas, here at sea and ankle-deep in blood? The boarding party dipped leather buckets over the side, splashed water, scrubbed. Once the longboat had been cleaned up to the petty officer's satisfaction, Lucas and the other prisoners were scrambled aboard the warship. The prize crew took up the abandoned oars and headed for the coast of Gaul.

When his bonds were cut one of the prisoners had flung out his arms to embrace the man who freed him, but a push in the chest sent him sprawling.

'You – keep out of the way! –'

Gloom settled over Lucas's mind and it was confirmed when he heard the treasury official's first question.

He was a plump man, with thinning curls spread carefully to cover the wrinkles of anxiety across his forehead, and the first thing he asked was 'Any *honestiores*?' Now that so many people all over the Empire had citizenship, Romans were divided between *honestiores* – rich men who paid no taxes and escaped corporal punishment – and *humiliores*, who could at a pinch be flogged. The treasury official could see at a glance that the prisoners were a rag, tag and bobtail of fishermen and labourers from along the coast. He had not seriously expected any *honestiores*. Lucas himself was only a freedman.

This was not liberation, and the fact came home to the most obtuse among them when a squad of soldiers arrived carrying leg irons. *Honestiores*, even *humiliores* of acknowledge status, would need to be sent back to where they came from on the other side of the Channel – a source of trouble and expense.

About riffraff like this no one would ever ask questions. They could be held under duress and sold off at a profit.

All that was happening to him on this bright morning, out at sea appeared to Lucas as inevitably following on Bishop Decius's violent death, in the very moment when he spoke of resisting evil. There was nothing but luck, there was nothing but fate. In his bones he knew, as a soldier matter-of-factly began screwing on leg irons, that once in Gaul he would have no rights. When those who acted in the name of the law were becoming lawless, how could you expect sense and order from the world?

'Name?'

'Lucas –' and he was going on to give his *cognomen* in a clear voice, and state loudly what he was, a freedman of Londinium – freed at six years old on the day when his parents were manumitted – when the plump treasury official cut him short.

'Don't give me that. Your name from now on is not Lucas but Balbus. You are in Gaul. And in Gaul you are what you always were in Britain – a slave.'

'But the deed of manumission was registered,' Lucas foolishly persisted, 'in Londinium. I am *libertinus* – a freedman.'

'Lies,' said the treasury official as if he had heard all this before. His handwriting, Lucas noticed, could have been better and his face was pale. He was petulant because he was on the verge of seasickness. 'All you ruffians tell me the same thing,' he announced to the world at large. '*Libertini!*'

The warship was hove to and had been pitching and rolling at the same time. The treasury official had wedged himself against a bulkhead to write, but sweat stood out on his forehead and he was making hard work of pushing pen across papyrus. The breeze ruffled the little ring of curly hair clustered meagrely across his brow.

Lucas, thinking irrelevantly of Bishop Decius, could not keep his mind on his own fate. They would find the bishop dead on the shore and bury him solemnly by the altar of his own brick basilica. A martyr's crown? No doubt; and a martyr went straight to heaven. And that young man who had done the bishop's copying? Was he called Lucas – or Balbus? This world, where even your name was not your own, made Lucas feel helpless.

'Trade?' The treasury official had had to ask twice.

'Scribe.'

This answer caught the man's attention. 'Can you prove it?'

'Sealed of the scribes' guild in Londinium.'

Lucas, from a narrow pocket inside his salt-blotched tunic, brought out his tool of trade – an iron pen.

'Watch that!' exclaimed the corporal of the guard, striking the pen from his hand as if it had been a weapon. The pen clattered across the deck and the corporal put his foot on it. With the ship wallowing under him, the treasury official could hardly see to form his letters.

'Can you take my dictation?'

The soldier was smiling as he let Lucas pick up his pen, but not in friendship. On the market a scribe was worth ten times the price of a day labourer. There would be more prize money to go round.

'I am ready,' Lucas said. He was at work with a pen again, he had changed sides. When the treasury official paused and looked the other way he pumiced out that false name, 'Balbus', and wrote in his real name, 'Lucas'. He was himself once more, but only just.

3

Lucas could have been worse off. The treasury official's own name was Balbus. He lived in the treasury office on the quay at Rotomagus, a stone-built house with barred windows. Two tax-gatherers, morose but cunning men, with the legal right to call in soldiers if they ran into trouble, did all the outside business. All day they came and went, bringing in bags of coin to be checked off against receipts. The accumulated money was carried south in barrels every week, on muleback, under armed guard.

Downstairs were the office and the strongroom, neither in very good order, since Balbus was always behind with his accounts. In the thickness of the downstairs wall, next to the strongroom, was a cubbyhole. Lucas slept there, and his dreams

– fragmentary recollections of his old safe life as a copyist across the sea in Britain – were broken in upon all night by the crunching tramp of the ironshod boots worn by a sentry going up and down outside.

'You can stay here and work in my office for as long as you behave yourself,' Balbus told him. 'But at the first mistake, you go.'

The other captives had already been sold off and the money paid into the prize fund. But Balbus, glad of a helping hand with his arrears, hid the document concerning Lucas at the back of the old chest that contained his muddled archives.

Lucas was warm and dry and fed, and that was much, but the work was deadly dull and he had always preferred words to figures. From Balbus's apartment overhead a basket of fragments came down the stairwell to Lucas twice a day on a string. Their leavings, but the two upstairs ate well. To climb those stairs was forbidden, though no one could prevent Lucas from sniffing the kitchen smells that drifted down, or overhearing their afternoon noises from the bedroom.

Balbus kept company up there with a plump little slave girl with long curling hair whom he did his best to keep from everyone's sight. Lucas caught his only glimpse of her in the early morning, when she scurried off to the market and there bought only the best. The girl's eyes avoided his. She had been warned off him, and the hood of her cloak was always pulled discreetly over her head. She tiptoed back and forth through the downstairs office as if pretending to be a ghost.

When the sensual odour of grilling turbot or broiling lobster drifted downstairs at midday, Balbus, working at the desk opposite, would lift his little snout of a nose, run his fingers carefully left and right through what was left of his hair as if to arrange it, and moisten his lips with his tongue. Soon after, as if yielding to temptation, he would put down his pen, leave the rest of the work to Lucas, and stumble upstairs like a man in a dream.

And Lucas, if he chose to listen, could catch the rumble and squeak of their bed, accelerating at last to a rapid to and fro. The noise overhead would become too much for him, he would not know which way to look. He would sit there squirming, holding his pen tight between sweating fingers, but keeping very quiet indeed in the hope of catching her trilling little final scream. From Balbus at last would come a heavy groan as if he had been smitten down with a weapon. Then yawns, talk, the splash of water, and very likely it might begin again. Balbus would eventually totter downstairs because he must, but with a face more shocked than serene. The collectors would soon be back from their rounds. He would stand at his desk, fiddling with a pen, while Lucas kept his head down, not daring to say a word. Balbus would take another look at his quarterly returns and like them no better. His appetite for that girl upstairs was ruining him and he knew it.

'You just wait – he'll catch it' – the tax collectors liked to mutter on days when they arrived back from their afternoon rounds loaded with coin, and the master had not yet put in an appearance. The outside men were waiting gleefully for the day when an inspector of imperial revenue and his team of auditors would arrive unannounced. Then the fur would fly.

Balbus had begun by treating Lucas in a way that was almost comradely, explaining the work to him, even making little jokes, but this quick-witted young slave with the charming smile made him fell old, and jealousy was soon added to his other torments. At last he simply couldn't believe that, whenever he was called away from the office, Lucas would not go running upstairs. He began to set clumsy traps, sprinkling powdered chalk on the top flight of steps, or else arriving back in the office sooner than expected. Of course, Lucas noticed, and the jealousy provoked him.

To prove himself a man, and only by chance a slave, he began to accept the absolute necessity of going upstairs to have it out with the cook-maid who trilled on her back with her knees in the air perhaps three times in an afternoon. Lucas found himself looking with emotion at the dents her sharp little teeth had made in a discarded crust of bread sent down to him. When the endless tramp of ironshod army boots up and down the quay kept him awake at night, he would try to picture what, under that all-enfolding cloak, her body must be like: a plump kitchen goddess. He daydreamed of her coming down the stairs in the dark to his pallet of her own accord, astonishingly naked.

Lucas decided to write the girl a poem. Finding a clean squared-off piece of papyrus under the pile of accounts on his desk, he began to compose in elegiac couplets, a hexameter followed by a pentameter, clumsy for a love lyric, but elegiac couplets were what he had been best at in his class of rhetoric in Londinium. He was full of emotion but short of words – the poem was uphill work. He would put it in the empty basket under the earthenware platter. She would haul on the string and know who it came from.

Lucas had got as far as the seventh line when an obvious thought struck him. Was it likely that a girl who worked in a kitchen could read? He was beginning to detest Balbus for loitering in the office when there was plenty of work that should take him outside all day. Both their minds were not on work, but on the girl upstairs.

A brown-faced, bald-headed man came into the office one morning, the father of a family, to appeal to Balbus as boldly as he dared, against his tax assessment as a member of the guild of fishermen. Early in the day, before bed had softened him, Balbus could be ferociously official.

'You have a house, I dare say? Then sell your house.'

'We had a house at one time,' the fisherman said bitterly one eye on the soldier who had come to stand in the doorway, hand on his sword hilt. 'We sold it off ten years ago – to pay taxes.'

'Then where do you live?'

'Aboard the boat.'

'I will make it easier for you,' said Balbus coldly. 'Sell your boat to a willing buyer before my soldiers seize it. From a willing buyer you will get a better price. I am being merciful. That boat of yours could have gone to auction over a week ago. This tax is overdue.' Balbus said overdue – *iamdudum solvendus* – as if for anything whatever that his office might handle to be overdue were profoundly shocking.

'If I sell my boat, how shall I earn my living?'

'That is hardly the concern of the imperial treasury.'

'Those are the types who make so much extra work for us,' Balbus remarked as he put down his pen after the man had gone. 'In being stern,' he explained in a self-justifying manner, 'and there are times when it breaks my heart being stern like that – I need only remind myself that here in this office we are simply fulfilling our duty to the Emperor.'

'Of course we are,' Lucas mumbled, who had heard it all before.

'No revenue – and how can the soldiers be paid? No soldiers? The empire collapses. The barbarians rush in.'

'Taxes to pay the very soldiers,' Lucas flung out sarcastically, ashamed at not having felt sorrier for the fisherman, 'who flog them when they don't pay their taxes?'

'You must never over-simplify like that,' answered Balbus patiently. 'Have you thought what would happen if the barbarians took over the empire? Neither life nor property would be safe anywhere.' In some pigeonhole or other of his mind, Lucas thought, this man Balbus is provided with an answer to everything.

At last the day came round when Balbus was obliged to get up at dawn and go out in bad weather in a ship from the fleet, to check through merchandise taken from a captured pirate.

Lucas watched him go off, miserably, into the pelting early morning rain. He went back inside and blew out the lamp. In the dark he felt braver as if what he did next would be a continuation of his dreams. Go upstairs now. Catch her in bed, warm – and willing? Up he went, step by step, like a sleepwalker.

The girl had been heating soup in the kitchen to warm Balbus before he went out into the bad weather. There she was, outlined by the fire-glow, round and cuddly, leaning over her charcoal stove, crumbling bayleaf and thyme into a steaming iron pot. Her long and curly hair hung loose beyond her shoulders and trembled as she moved. She stirred the pot and the long ringlets of her hair, her shoulders, her whole plump body rippled and shook. Her haunches moved gently to and fro in time with the dabbling motion of the wooden spoon. She was secretly dancing.

Lucas could not keep his hands off her. Under his outstretched fingers the flesh of her opulent thighs began to twist and thrust as she pushed herself against him.

'What took you so long?'

She moved away, turning to face him. Towards Lucas's mouth she held the wooden spoon, and tilted it so that a sample of the hot soup dribbled inside him.

'Good?'

She was pretending to take what remained on the spoon into her own moist mouth, but she was taking the taste of his mouth into hers. She was smiling wickedly at him around the spoon and it cluttered to the floor as she swayed forward to offer him a kiss, pouting mouth coming towards him, not waiting for him. The long kiss melted both of them.

Lucas had some idea of carrying her in his arms to the bedroom, but she broke loose and scampered on ahead. Once naked and between clean linen this girl was no longer softly yielding. She took charge, as if love were a better kind of cookery, and she knew how.

'Slowly – *lente*. Yes, like that. We've got all day.'

Hands and mouth diligently appraised him. She took possession of his manhood as something to venerate, after what the pot-bellied treasury official had to offer. Her name was Flora. She particularly wanted to hear herself called Flora because Balbus always called her Balba.

Flora's hands smelt of the herbs she had been crumbling under her nails and a faint oceanic odour of fish. The armpit where Lucas nuzzled had the scent of charcoal. She was all juices and flavours. All morning, with the equinoctial rain beating outside they lay in the clean sheets that soon were a tangle – bewildered, entwined, enraptured.

'How little you know!' Flora would say, moving him into the position she wanted, or bridling his physical impatience. 'Slowly! Like this!' Perversities and enormities that she had learned from fat Balbus she passed on one by one to thin Lucas, as if they were recipes.

'I began to write you a poem,' Lucas said, trying to get his breath back. He recited his seven lines.

Flora giggled. 'Is that all?'

'There is this too.' His hands roamed over her, arousing her.

Out on the quayside a clatter of hooves could be heard, and a jingle of harness. Horsemen had arrived at the door of the treasury office.

'Balbus? He can't be back already,' Flora whispered.

'These are others. The soldier let them in. They are officials.'

When Lucas half rose from the bed Flora pulled him back. 'That is their business, not ours. We are only slaves.' But curiosity got the better of her. Tip-toeing to the barred window, stark naked, she looked out and laughed.

'A little surprise for Balbus. It's the imperial inspector.'

Men downstairs were talking in blatant official voices, not surprised to find the office empty. They would get busy and when Balbus got back they'd keep him busy too. Meanwhile, a swift look around the house mightn't be a bad idea.

Lucas whispered, alarmed. 'They're coming upstairs.'

Flora threw a smock over her head and found her sandals. She had even pinned back her dishevelled hair with a wooden comb before the first of the intruders had put his foot on the top stair. She closed the bedroom door behind her and went forward to meet them with a coquettish boldness.

The slave girl in charge of the living quarters? – and what could she do for them? Yes, her master was away for the day, with the fleet. What a slut she is, after all, Lucas thought. Long hours of overmuch pleasure had slightly disgusted him.

The imperial inspector had brought with him four hard-bitten auditors to rummage through Balbus's accounts, and the man who had come upstairs was one of them. Between thumb and forefinger he was holding the document about Lucas that Balbus had hidden away.

'And a slave called Lucas – did he go out with fleet too?'

Lucas came out of the bedroom, hurriedly clad but keeping his chin up. He would dearly have liked to do himself credit in front of Flora, but the auditor pushed him downstairs, nudging the back of his knees to make him stumble.

Balbus's archive – the wooden chest where he hid whatever he wished to postpone or ignore – had by this time been emptied and neatly docketed. Lucas could see at a glance that nothing in the office was any longer a secret. They were bringing a peremptory order into the confusion of the accounts. The imperial inspector himself, a large man with a broken nose and the impenetrable visage of an old and grubby city statue, was already making up his tally of Balbus's misdemeanours. It was clear that a sum of money – not in fact a large sum, and mislaid, perhaps, rather than stolen – was unaccounted for. But that was a crime against the Emperor.

In any criminal investigation the usual thing was to begin with the slaves. If the lost money could be pinned on the two guilty-looking slaves, so much the better. The imperial inspector would always rather incriminate a slave than a colleague.

'Strip him!'

Grinning, two of the auditors began taking off the clothes Lucas had only just put on. A naked pen-pusher, their faces said, a mere slave, is a contemptible sight.

Flora was unmoved by his plight and looked right past him. She was frightened. They felt through Lucas's clothing, even jokingly poked goosequills into unpromising bodily apertures pretending to look for the lost coins. They were enjoying themselves. Finally they cut up his mattress and searched with busy fingers through every inch of chopped straw.

Two of the men, at a nod from the inspector, went upstairs dragging the girl with them. Up there, a piece of skittishness that began with a giggle and ended in a scream made Lucas wonder what they could be doing with Flora. The scream was of a strange and fearful pleasure.

It had never occurred to Lucas to steal, so they found not one illegal farthing on him; and that displeased them. But to judge by the sobs coming down the staircase the others had been luckier with Flora. She had turned obstinate. One auditor was pulling her head downwards by her long curly hair while the other pushed her from behind. To bring her down again they had thrown a sheet over her nakedness. The other two auditors held Lucas tight, thereby doing him a good turn, since for a slave to offer violence to an imperial official was the equivalent of suicide. Flora was on her knees, long curls falling over her face, looking up at the imperial inspector imploringly.

'You've found something, have you?' he said, ignoring her. One of the auditors pushed across a leather bag which clinked.

'At the bottom of a sack of beans.'

With no particular expression his face the imperial inspector loosened the string and turned the bag upside down on the trestle table. Curving his hand, he stopped the coins from rolling off it. He was used to handling coin.

'Small copper,' he said derisively.

He put his cupped hand under Flora's chin, not brutally, but so as to look into her eyes. The sheet slid from one shoulder so he pulled it back in place with his other hand. She might have been his errant daughter. With his forefinger he stirred the heap of copper coin.

'Tell me, child, is this your private fortune?'

Flora was sulky. She was used to men who did what she wanted.

'Answer.'

Flora turned to catch Lucas's eye and still said nothing.

'Or would you rather go to the torture – both of you?'

Even slaves who were not incriminated but only witnesses could be tortured, and Flora knew it. Tearful words came pouring out of her. Those were odd coppers she had saved out of the housekeeping money and hidden in the bag under the beans.

'But why?'

'To buy my freedom.'

The hard-faced imperial inspector surprised them all by laughing out loud.

'Do you know how many years that would take?'

By the time Balbus himself arrived back, drenched to the skin, the four clerks had ransacked the treasury office from top to bottom and found no sign whatever of the money missing from the accounts. Lucas was so obviously innocent that they were particularly fierce and threatening to him. They would have liked to pin the default on this slave who had no right to be working in the office. He was not a member of the club of treasury officials. He knew too much. The sooner he could be got rid of, the better.

Lucas stood quietly in the corner, not replying unless obliged to, hoping most of all that he would avoid a flogging. There was not much to be got out of him, and after a while they left him alone. The imperial inspector and his four auditors found more amusement in cross-questioning Flora, in her master's hearing, about how she and Balbus had spent their long afternoons. Flora, having overcome her sullenness, was playing up to the inspector. What a slut she is, thought Lucas gloomily. And a little while ago she seemed so wonderful.

'You are his last asset, young woman, let me tell you. It all depends on how much you fetch tomorrow at auction. The only way he can fill this hole in the imperial accounts is to sell you.

As for you, old friend –' The inspector was addressing Balbus in a cordial tone, as if such a lapse from grace might happen to anyone, but Lucas could tell that a shock was coming. 'It's chains for you, and a nasty couple of hours in front of the prefect in Lugdunum – for which I don't envy you. Off you go –' he said to the youngest of his men, 'and fetch a blacksmith. The sooner my old friend here gets used to wearing his cold iron, the better.'

As the blow went home to Balbus the four auditors smiled like wolves. This was the exquisite pleasure they had been waiting for. To Lucas the imperial inspector's manner was suddenly peremptory. 'Now you. Is there something of your own here – anything that belongs to you?'

'The clothes I stand up in. And this pen of mine,' Lucas said, absurdly fearful that if they took his iron pen away they would have made him no different from any other slave.

'It's his pen, all right,' Balbus mumbled. 'I vouch for that. He had it when he came here.' The word 'chains' had made him humble, helpful. He had no real feelings left, even for Flora, but he was pleased with himself for being magnanimous about the pen.

'Take this young fellow to the slave dealer near the barracks,' said the Imperial inspector. 'See what he will give us to get rid of him. He should have been put on the market months ago. Get a receipt. The more we can pick up on trifles the better our report will look for everyone.' He slapped Flora's bottom playfully and pushed her upstairs to her pots and pans. 'And you, little girl, we've all worked hard today. See if you can cook us something worth eating.' Flora looked back flirtatiously over her shoulder at the inspector.

As one of the auditors dragged him by the arm into the drizzle outside, Lucas glanced back into the treasury office. No one was taking any notice of his departure. He had a pang of loneliness, as sharp as a bereavement. A part of my life is over, he thought. A part that seemed real enough while it lasted. Now all I feel is emptiness and loss.

4

A little, wrinkled slave-dealer with a voice like a door hinge – Stridor – was digging his fingernails into Lucas's muscles. He made the young man cough, then bend, to open up his crevices. No rash, no rupture, no evident vice. Healthy, thought Stridor – not that I intend to say so.

A mule on sale in the market might have kicked at such treatment; Lucas stood there stock-still, and let it all happen, as if he could not believe it was real.

Stridor had by this time a string of a dozen slaves, dragging along the highway behind him, each slave as he plodded onward carrying in his left hand a loop of the long slave-chain. Everyone but Gilda carried a bundle, and laggards were tickled up with a stick. They were also Stridor's pack-animals; he himself carried a leather pouch full of keys and coins, and never let go of it, day or night.

His plan was to get to Rome with his merchandise in good condition and there was always a demand for a penman, in Rome. But as Stridor began to chaffer, nothing showed in his monkey-face but dissatisfaction.

'Did he dip his hand in his master's cash box?' he grumbled to the treasury auditor who had been sent to sell Lucas.

No welts from flogging on this young man's back. Why then were the tax office so anxious to get rid of him?

'He dipped his wick in his master's mistress,' the auditor answered jovially. Stridor, not laughing at the joke, coolly offered half what the youngster was worth, even here in Gaul.

'And my heavy expenses?' Stridor said woodenly, when the treasury official expostulated. 'A dozen idle mouths to feed?'

The man from the treasury office was better at squeezing overdue tax-payers than bargaining in a market place. Stridor feigning unwillingness began turning his back, and the treasury official fell over himself to shake hands at the knockdown price.

Stridor scowled, as if even so he had been worsted. Always let the other man think he's had the best of it.

For the next day or two he watched Lucas carefully, and was pleased with his bargain. He was polite, educated, willing, and not yet marked with the slave's habitual sullenness. Stridor hated that sullenness. Why be sullen, when they were fed and looked after so well that they put on flesh? Sad? But he was young, he would get over it. There were even times when little Gilda made one of her jokes, and he smiled.

Gilda was usually left to run free of the chain. Though she took two paces to Lucas's one, when the other slaves began to grouse she would hop on ahead, shout 'Oh how my feet hurt!' and mime such mock agony that even those who limped could not help laughing. She had learnt not to let a joke drag on until it became a bore. Stridor gave her every encouragement to sing and joke, yet he was strict with her. Gilda was quite evidently his treasure. In Rome – went his daydream – she would make money for him, and he would spend his time as a Roman should, at the bath and the barber's.

Gilda's sexual attributes were growing, so that when she walked ahead of the gang she caught everyone's eye. For Lucas she was a little maiden, a nymph, yet the fascination Lucas felt was not the same as his obsession with Flora. Out of Gilda's mouth would come the filthy things the soldiers had taught her, but with a heart-breaking innocence.

As they walked inland up the valley of another great river, where ripening vines grew in long rows, Stridor watched both of them closely. At last he decided to let Lucas and the girl walk side by side unfettered, and talk together freely. He was taking a chance. But Lucas could teach Gilda her letters, and a smattering of literary polish – a few of the right quotations. In Rome that would enhance her value.

Stridor's own start in life had been as a spayed boy in a Roman brothel of the highest class, and he had always admired the readiness with which the best people quoted and spoke. Apart from slave-trading, commercial vice was what he understood best; he had plans of his own for Gilda's burgeoning sexuality. He would show her how not to lose her head, whatever the titillation – show her how to use her body, on his behalf, for riches and power. As Stridor made his way south and east, himself shabby, most of his slaves in rags, he lived on his ambitious dreams: he was in Rome, making a fortune from managing Gilda.

But to make her way in the theatre, Gilda must know how to read her parts. Making funny jokes in the pig-Latin of soldier and slave was all very well. She must learn how to scan verse, how to sign her own name – know how to speak to rich protectors in their own idiom. This young man Lucas could sketch in for Gilda at least some beginnings. Your eyes can't be everywhere at once, Stridor told himself. You will have to chance it that he might touch her up.

'Pantomime? He'll have her with a bellyful of arms and legs before we reach Lugdunum,' said one of the other slaves loudly, as the two of them walked free of the chain, their heads together in a continual mutter, Lucas stooping, the girl craning up to him. The slave who spoke, though standing with his back to Stridor, intended to be overheard. But Stridor was an old hand at slave-dealing, and not a man to bounce remarks off. He had been watching the pair of them. This tall, thin, thoughtful young man treated Gilda like a sister.

Lucas kept her hard at it – grammar, ciphering, the stumbling formation of letters, with a pointed finger in the dust, whenever they halted. And on the march, the memorising of verse. While he was speaking to her Gilda would never make jokes, even though a good one might now and then flash through her mind. All this was new to her, she was in earnest, and the speed of her brain thrilled Lucas. What she heard once only she remembered. She heard and understood.

The schoolmaster's strap in London had imprinted innumerable verses on Lucas's memory, and she took the scraps from his lips. This is Virgil. That was Ovid. Flora, though he had known her only for one afternoon, had left a wound. Gilda was the cure.

Further southeast, the country became hillier and wilder. They were in the heart of Celtica: the Auvergne. The outer edges of Gaul and its river valleys were fertile, the centre barren, the going harder. His slaves at the rate they went were eating up his money, so Stridor decided to risk a short cut to Lugdunum through rough country, and that was a mistake.

At Lugdunum – Lyons, a city where two great rivers met – his plan was to take a river-boat down the swiftly-flowing Rhône, and at Massilia – Marseilles – buy a passage in a coaster to Ostia, the port of Rome. And that would be all plain sailing, but the country Stridor had to cover once he left the smiling vineyards behind him was wolf country.

They were around the dying fire on their first night in the forest, sleeping off a hard day's march. The chain clinked and jerked as now and then a slave tried to turn over. Gilda was awake. Stridor, she could tell, was moving about. From the far side of the glimmering fire she could hear Lucas's snuffling little snore: asleep. So the hand that touched her thigh must be Stridor's. In the dark he was fingering down past her knee to the manacle, turning the key that freed her.

Gilda followed Stridor numbly away from the diminishing circle of the firelight. A half-burned log behind them made a noise as it broke open and glowed. Early October, and already the nights were cold. The wolves, as winter came on, would be howling and scratching at night outside the bolted doors of lonely farms.

Stridor took her to a beech tree, far enough away from the fire to be private – a bare space of small, dried leaves under the boughs. Gilda lay down at once in the posture she knew he would want, on her back, knees apart, beech leaves rustling under her. I am teaching you, Stridor had said, all the things needful for a woman who doesn't wish to be the slave of the first good-looking man who comes along. Be a slave who enslaves others – won't you like that?

Enslave Lucas? Gilda wondered. He might know the secret of words, but how much of all this did he know? Gilda found herself wantonly wishing that it were Lucas's hand, and not Stridor's, moving into the crevice between her thighs – Lucas, not Stridor, putting his clever little touch upon her.

The private place last night had bled, but the twinge of loss was over. Tonight, as Gilda moved woman-like, even voluptuously, Stridor gave a triumphant little laugh. It was happening: her body had begun to learn.

'Hold my finger tight. Not with your hand, little silly. With your own inside. As tight as you can. Doesn't it feel bigger?'

Gilda, as she found herself taking a grip on the eunuch's

finger with her tentative inward muscles, murmured 'Bigger', and that excited him.

'Hold it so tight that I can't pull it out. Good. And again. Now three times. As I squeeze your wrist. One. Two. Three. Talk to my finger with the inside of your body. Do you feel my other hand – my fist – there in the small of your back? Pretend it's an egg. You mustn't break that egg. Lift yourself up. Move. Don't break it! Press against the ground with your feet. My other finger is still there? Hold it. The egg is under you – don't break it. Now your little dance. Remember?'

Blazing with stranger feelings than before, which came in a crescendo, Gilda still managed to keep her head, as Stridor had told her she always must.

'Know exactly what you are doing, yes,' repeated his creaky, sexless voice, 'but always seem to others not to know. Play tricks on them.'

The unexpected thrill had faded, all this was becoming a game at which she was ready to laugh, when from the dying fire in the distance came yells and wild oaths.

Matter-of-factly, Stridor wiped his finger on the hem of Gilda's ragged skirt. His other hand he had already pressed across her mouth. Close to her ear he whispered, 'Men-wolves!' The hand across her mouth was trembling; he was afraid.

Gilda lowered herself slowly and without noise to the brittle carpet of beech-leaves. The egg in the small of her back had been make-believe – let it go smash. I should be as afraid as Stridor is, Gilda told herself, yet I am not. She felt sore, and dissatisfied. She was very alert.

There were only three of them, sprung out of darkness into the glow of the fire, but they were armed and knew what to expect. Against a dozen slaves on a chain, and their eunuch keeper, three armed men were enough. Their leader carried a long iron sword, and wore an old army helmet with a javelin-hole through the front. The helmet was too small for him, and he had tipped it jauntily to the back of his head. The other two carried iron pike-heads on the end of eight-foot poles. They glared ferociously, but they might have been farm workers, and those pikes their reaping-hooks.

Lucas, impeded by the chain, had staggered halfway to his feet, with some muddled idea of standing up to them, but a contemptuous kick from the leader's booted heel laid him flat. Slaves were merchandise, but slaves had tongues and might bear witness. Somewhere about lurked the master; he was the dangerous one.

'Take these slaves along to the barn, and bolt the door,' said the man with the helmet. 'If they give you any trouble, set the barn on fire, and let them roast.' He grinned mirthlessly, as a wolf grins.

Lucas was dragged away with the others on the slave chain, the side of his chin sore where the boot had struck. Looking over his shoulder he saw the ring of ash, and the first streaks of dawn come into the sky. The bandit with the helmet was making a cast like a hunter, his long iron sword naked in his hand. Cut the city-bred dealer's throat, and whom did those slaves belong to then? The man who took them into his possession.

Gilda by this time, at a sign from Stridor, had scrambled like a cat up among the boughs of the beech tree, out of sight under the leafage. She had carried up Stridor's heavy leather pouch for him. The little man had dipped under the flap, and taken out what looked like a handful of marbles and a knotted cord: a Balearic sling, which even in the hand of a eunuch could hurl a lead pellet with force enough to kill. Gilda from the tree watched this game of cat-and-mouse as if it were a play acted out for her.

The little eunuch had taken up a stance away from the trunk, where the boughs were high, and he had room to whirl his sling. Gilda, sick with excitement, could hear the other man approach from the left like a wild boar breaking through the undergrowth. Stridor turned to face his target. The hunter was hunted.

Though Stridor expected to have only one shot at his target, he put a second pellet in his mouth, for luck. He had become so motionless that Gilda, up in the tree, could hardly tell he was there. A prudent, cunning stillness – his eunuch's brain against the big man's bodily strength.

When the robber in the old helmet caught sight of Stridor he raised the long sword with both hands above his head, and with a roar meant to petrify ran full tilt at him, as if to cleave him down the chin at one blow.

Stridor let the man come on. He was waiting his moment. Gilda saw his arm go up, and the cord whirl faster than her eyes could follow. The helmeted brigand paused as he ran forward. He might have been hesitating. His pause became a drunken stumble. On his forehead under the rim of the old helmet as he fell was a blue mark, bloody at the edges.

Stridor took the sour-tasting second lead pellet from his mouth, tossed it in his hand with a kind of joy, and fitted it into the leather cup of his sling as he moved forward. The bandit lay there in the grotesque attitude of death, and no one else was coming. A long way off they could hear the noise of the slave column, being led away by the two men with pikes.

The dead man still held his long sword in both hands, reaching forward as if frozen, and Stridor at first began circling him, well out of reach. Then with a contemptuous push of his foot, he rolled the dead man over.

Gilda shifted the leather pouch higher on her shoulder, and began slithering down the beech trunk. Stridor with a little whimper of pleasure went on his knees beside the man he had killed, and fumbled inside his dirty jerkin.

Out came what he was after – a purse of pigskin with hair still on the outside, pulled tight by a drawstring. In the purse was a handful of coins, two of them gold *aurei*. Stridor poured the coins happily from hand to hand, smiling, as though they were the water of life.

He wrestled the brigand's sword from stiffening fingers, but left behind the useless, perforated helmet. The two of them walked away quietly, in another direction, until the noise of the slaves on their chain had receded into silence. I still have something, Stridor told himself, as he put the large sword across his shoulder like a boy with a plaything. I have Gilda and my money. But if they come back, I shall have nothing.

For three days the two of them made a detour through the tangled forest, away from the road, eating berries and autumn nuts and most often going hungry, until they came to the army post where the forest road met the imperial highway. At the crossroads was a statue to Quadrivium, the deity, but the statue was defaced. Paganism now was unofficial, even in Celtica.

The sentry, when he saw a wrinkled eunuch waddling towards the guardhouse with a long Gaulish sword over his shoulder, began to guffaw. Stridor left the long sword outside, leaning against the wall, and when he came out later omitted to take it with him. He had talked inside with the *decurio* – the corporal commanding the post – and got nothing from him. Were these soldiers likely to believe he had killed a man in single combat, and taken away his sword?

The *decurio* had faced up to Stridor brazenly. 'Oh yes, three days ago. Our patrol did report a party of slaves, moving up the forest road. If you can prove they are yours, and find them, and take them away from whoever has them, there you are. But you've left it late – they might be anywhere by now. Sold off the day before yesterday – that's the likeliest. And shipped down the river –'

Stridor had been doing business with soldiers and dealing in slaves for years. From the *decurio*'s facile answer he could tell there was nothing to be done. Somewhere, a bribe had passed.

The sentry's laughter had wounded him, his pride was hurt, but he accepted his loss and did the proper thing. He left the usual coin on the window-ledge, 'for wine, for the men of your squad,' and went into the October sunlight. Of his dreams, all he had left was Gilda. Her talent, he told himself, is my capital. I shall share her with others, I shall have to, but only for money.

At Lugdunum, with autumn rains begun, the Rhône was in full spate. Baulks of timber from some bridge overrun upstream, trees torn up by the root, dead cows, floated past the city, cannoning into one another, and spinning in the whirlpools. The two of them, Gilda and Stridor, waited at Lugdunum a week for the river to go down, eating away at their stock of money, until Stridor got word of a boat that would risk it. The boat starting down stream next day, was taking on board a barbarian princess, and her suite. The Princess Veleda, daughter of some barbarian king allied to Rome, impatient to go and indifferent to danger. Stridor caught a glimpse of her, tall and pallid, arrogant in the tilt of her head, yet not much more than a girl, with long, thick, flaxen hair in dangling plaits.

Passages downriver in the first boat going would cost Stridor more than he bargained for, but waiting would cost him, too.

'If you travel with a princess, you must pay for it,' the boat-charterer told him, trying to bend between his fingers the gold *aureus* Stridor had given him, in case it was gilded lead. Stridor bought two places – one for himself, one for the girl, whom for the last time since reaching Lugdunum he had tried to describe as his daughter. He never would again. They always burst out laughing.

Part II

1

In the heart of the city and surrounded by hills you came to the Forum, a huge piazza a little longer than it was broad. The Forum served the city in many ways at once: as its bread basket, as a souding board for gossip and rumour, and as the place where men came seeking justice or scholars went to read in one of the two great libraries. It was, above all else, the public open space where the victorious splendour of Rome's past was celebrated in statues and inscriptions.

The Forum was entered from the south. Around it on every side ran a colonnade sheltering loiterers from the breathtaking summer sun, or from the insidious drizzle of a Roman winter. Exactly opposite the entrance stood a large, five-storeyed building, the Forum market.

On the uppermost floor was the fish market. The fish on sale swam alive in two great tanks, one of fresh water and one of salt water – fetched up daily from the seaside at Ostia. The fourth floor swallowed up an endless queue of Roman citizens, each offering a small wooden tablet – a *tessera* – to serve as a food ticket. They stood in line, pot and basket in hand, for the wine, oil, bread and pork, given out free each month as a ration. No free Roman citizen had to demean himself by hard work if he chose to live frugally off the dole. Once the ration had been granted it went on for life. Two-thirds of the city's inhabitants ate and drank free, and were entertained at free shows in circus and amphitheatre. Bread and circuses kept them out of mischief.

The belly of Rome was catered for in the Forum – and so

were tongue and ear. From under the resonant porticoes came an unending babble. Lawsuits were being tried there, one after another: the Forum was full of litigants. Men came to Rome from the ends of the earth looking for justice. A hired mob followed each well-known and successful lawyer, ready at a small sign from him to hiss or to applaud. Less lucky pleaders shuffled and loitered under the eaves of the porticoes, hoping for a client, tongues for hire.

Other idlers drifted in and out of the two great libraries. One library contained Greek manuscripts, the other Latin. Under the shadow of the library colonnade Rome's shabby men of letters came and went, young poets on the lookout for someone patient enough to hear through their latest copy of verses, older men made sarcastic by neglect, spoiled by envy, but still hungry for fame. Men came to Rome for literary fame as they came for money or justice, and a few found it.

In an arc outside the library stood the statues and busts of the great Latin poets – Virgil, Horace, Tibullus, Ovid, Propertius, Lucan – a visible proof of fame achieved. The Forum was dotted with other statues – of generals and administrators and half-forgotten emperors – some of them gilded to catch the sunlight. The Emperor who conquered Dacia – Trajan – had enlarged the Forum, paying for it with plunder from Transylvanian mines. But Dacia was barbarian once more and the mines were lost. Armenia and Mesopotamia had gone long since. Barbarians were even filtering into civilised Gaul, and few men believed that unprofitable outlying provinces like Britain could be held for much longer. The gilt on the statues and inscriptions was flaking away.

Yet, to a casual observer arriving in Rome when the fifth century after Christ had just begun, the vitality of the Forum might seem inextinguishable. Here, in the Eternal City, under the rule of law, great wealth – rents and tax money – still flowed in from every corner of the Western Empire. The mob were fed and entertained. Culture was held in respect. Life had been going on like this for centuries – why should it ever cease to do so?

In the hot September sun beyond the shadow cast by the library arcade, three Roman workmen flourishing trowels, their blouses powdered with cement, were attaching a portrait-bronze to a brand new plinth. Under the new bust, in gilt letters, had been incised the name *Claudius Claudianus*. Here was a Latin poet, Claudian, about to be honoured as immortal in his own lifetimes. The inscription under the name said 'To the most glorious of poets'.

The workmen, once the bronze was in place, had another tricky problem to face – how to cover the bust of Claudian with a sheet in such a way that one tug on the cord would unveil it. A crowd of idlers, come to watch them, marked each of their successive failures by an ironic groan, until a man with the happy-go-lucky look about him of a sailor came forward, and offered to finish job for the price of a jug of wine. The workmen gave him the tasselled cord, and the sheet, and stood back ready to mock him in turn. But from the way that he folded the sheet across and made the knot it was obvious the sailor knew how.

'And the unveiling? Not the Emperor?' The sailor handled cord and sheet like rope and sail. A practice pull and the sheet fell off. The audience was losing interest.

'Princess Serena, the Emperor's half-sister. And her husband, Flavius Stilicho –'

'Yes, I've heard of Serena. And is she as beautiful as the poem says?'

The workmen guffawed. 'She never was.'

Serena had been the Emperor Honorius's guardian before he became of age. She was married to Stilicho, Rome's greatest general. She was a suitable person for a poet to praise, and Claudian had praised her beauty in a poem of which even the sailor had heard. But what she most resembled was a horse.

The sailor passed the tasselled cord over to the scruffiest of the three workmen. 'All right, dad. You are the beautiful Princess Serena. Now you have a go.'

The old workman approached the veiled statue on tiptoe, waggling his withered hams. A jerk of his fingers and the sheet fell off the new bronze bust, like the veil falling from a bride's face. Meticulously, the sailor began to put sheet and cord back the way it was. He had earned his jug of wine.

'Stilicho will have your guts for garters if this fails,' whispered the old workman in the sailor's ear as he passed across the money.

Under the colonnade of the Latin library, onlookers clustered. The poet himself, Claudian, had arrived a little sooner than he need have done. He was a dark-complexioned man, round-shouldered, plump. He wore his black hair lank and you might, at first glance, have taken him for a Syrian necromancer, eking out a living for himself by making predictions. This was his great day and, typically, the other literary men were cold-shouldering him. One or two were even sniggering, but that was because he had worn a toga. If I left this toga in the library on a peg, thought Claudian, those envious fellows watching from the shade would bombard me afterwards with epigrams.

She was coming towards Claudian as he stood alone, near enough to smile at him now, Serena, politically the most important woman in the western Empire, with her long jaw and chlorotic vacant face and her shrewd veiled eye, dressed as a great lady, in silks, walking slowly under a canopy carried by four little Nubian slave boys. What if I did lay it on thick, thought Claudian, when I praised her beauty? She looks like a horse but she always acts like a great lady. It was a good poem. No one else – certainly none of those sniggerers over there in the shade – could have written verse to touch it. In my poem, when there are none to remember her face, she will always be beautiful.

Striding behind his wife's canopy, overtaking her, moving ahead, came the general himself, Flavius Stilicho, looking around affably from his great height, noticing everything, the busiest man in Rome yet come to see his poet's bust unveiled. I praise him too, thought Claudian, Rome's saviour, and he deserves every word.

Stilicho had noticed the incongruous toga and carefully had not smiled. Faces were crowding to get a glimpse of him at the windows of the fishmarket, five floors up. Rome's general.

He went straight up to Claudian, taking him Roman fashion hand on wrist, greeting him as an equal. The literary men under the colonnade stopped their muttering, and began as by common consent to move towards the veiled bust.

Stilicho had saved Rome time and again from the barbarians and yet he was a Vandal. Claudian was the greatest living Latin poet and yet he was from Egypt. Now, on Claudian's day of glory, blue eyes and black eyes looked at each other and both smiled. Without a word being spoken they had both been struck by the incongruity of what was happening.

Serena had reached out an imperious hand. The black slave walking behind her, negligently carrying the laurel wreath, was a little behind his cue and she took it from him impatiently with both hands. Claudian, as Serena placed the wreath slightly cockeyed on his brow, sniffed the pungent odour and was instantly back in a Roman garden – or a Roman kitchen.

With a finger under his chin, clumsily affectionate, Serena tilted Claudian's head and put the laurel wreath straight, like one girl helping another to get ready. Stilicho looked on all this friendly, easygoing play with an air of amused approval. He detested the stiff, oriental forms of respect that were coming into vogue – the obeisance, the prostration. He did his own little bit, casually handing his wife the tasselled cord.

Serena stood there, the tassel in her fingers, breathing through her mouth, uncertain what came next.

'*Impetus Subitus*,' Stilicho murmured. 'Give it a jerk.'

Serena gave a tug. The sheet fell off the bronze and there it was in the sunlight, glittering, the gilded name CLAUDIUS CLAUDIANUS. Up rose a chorus of *vivats*. Even those who detested Claudian most grumbled him a *vivat*.

As the plaudits of the crowd died down, out strutted a high official to make a speech in the Emperor's name. He fancied himself as an orator. And speaks, thought Claudian, in language so embellished that he will soon get on my nerves.

Stilicho was only half listening. His eyes roved this way and that over the crowd like a soldier appraising a terrain... And there she was again! A shawl pulled over her head but there was no mistaking the way she watched him. He kept the smile on his face because this was Rome. There was always someone watching – to judge his hidden thoughts by his expression. He watched her. With his fixed and formal smile he looked right through her. The last thing I want, he told himself, is for some personal enemy to discover that that young woman follows me everywhere. What if it leaked back through Honorius's secret police, the *agentes in rebus*? The pious young Emperor liked mildly scandalous gossip about the general who until lately had been his guardian. But this was a hostage princess, and forbidden to leave the palace!

Cold blue eyes looked directly at him from under her shawl with a hero-worship close to obsession. Her name was Veleda. She and her kind were kept close in the enormous palace on the Palatine Hill, up there, beyond the Forum, and for political reasons must remain virtuous until the imperial diplomacy arranged a marriage. Or can I find a use for that besotted devotion of hers, wondered Stilicho, which will keep her out of harm's way?

Stilicho had until lately been too strong to jostle. He had controlled both the army and, through Serena, the Emperor. But young Honorius was now of age, a difficult boy, who disliked his guardians, Serena and Stilicho, and detested their unlucky daughter, Maria, to whom they had tried to marry him off. And the Christian priests had got hold of him.

One campaign too long-drawn-out, thought Stilicho, perhaps one lost skirmish, and my enemies at court will stand up to be counted. I have lived so far on victory, but what soldier can guarantee always to win? His rise in the great world – the son of a Vandal officer in the imperial guard – had depended on his knack of winning battles – and on Serena. She has her own splendour, he reminded himself, watching her swallow a yawn as the orator droned on. She may not be the beauty Claudian pretended in that shameless poem of his, but she understands court politics, and she lets me go to my actress without a word of reproach.

He looked suddenly, unexpectedly, at Veleda, and she dropped her eyes like a nun, excited by his displeasure, by the notice he had at last taken of her – pushing her way through the crowd away from him, returning before the crowd dispersed, up the hill to the palace she should never have left.

It was not easy to bore Romans with the sound of their own language, but this the orator was succeeding in doing. Then came the shock of a scandalously improper line, quoted from a poem Claudian was still working on –

'This is the City that Stilicho and
the gods guard!'

The line came out loud and clear and all the spies heard it. How had the palace official got hold of it? To read such words alone, in private, in context, was one thing. But declaimed aloud in the Forum – Flavius Stilicho equated with the pagan gods? Had this piece of malice been planned?

The general inclined his head close to the poet's ear. Claudian's eyes were moist with despair.

'Keep your chin up. Good. Look around and smile. And arrange a public recital soon of the lines in your new poem that particularly praise Honorius.'

The poet nodded. 'And no mention, good or bad, of Stilicho. I promise.' Between them a hint was enough. 'My opinion of you, however,' he added skittishly – he was getting his nerves back, 'will ring through the gaps between the words.'

And there he is, the great Stilicho, thought envious onlookers, watching the bland unchanging smile and resenting the private whisper, enjoying the sound of his own praises.

Claudian was alone in the Forum, his white toga folded across his arm, the laurel wreath in one hand. He was drifting through space like a man a little far gone in wine. The others had left him, the general and his wife, the literary loungers, the lawyers: they had all found something better to do elsewhere. Behind Claudian's back the new bust stared blindly, his name glittering, but I myself, Claudian told himself, am not yet turned to bronze, and all that really matters is the order of the words in the poem I'm engaged upon. I must set to work and praise the Emperor, or if not the Emperor then the imperial idea, for that is what holds Rome together.

Most Romans lived in an apartment block but Claudian had a private house on the Aventine, surrounded by its own garden. The literary gang from the library would go home at the end of the day to some garret under the tiles. Claudian began remembering his own first year in Rome, in just such a garret, seeing the sky through cracks overhead and obliged to go down eight flights of stairs to fetch a pitcher of water: a spur to ambition. No wonder they envied him.

He could not help turning for one last look at the bust, from a distance. The sculptor had taken it upon himself to square Claudian's shoulders, Latinise his hair, and curtail his long probing Levantine nose. He had falsified. Today they had immortalised a stranger. I'm still alive, he reflected. I am myself. They wanted to turn me to dumb bronze but they have failed.

A woman struggling with her loaded shopping basket came up behind him, a gap-toothed, smiling peasant from the Campagna. He offered her the laurel wreath.

'Crown me? Go on with you!' Her smile was broad.

'To flavour your soup.'

'It's yours to give, I hope?' Could this be a trick? Lovely fresh laurel, though.

'I'll think of you,' she said, 'every night when I dish up the first plateful of soup.'

And now, Claudian told himself firmly, to clear my mind about the public reading Flavius Stilicho has asked for. If the Emperor came, public opinion in Rome could be skilfully turned. Perhaps Serena would manage to drag him along – although all the young Emperor ever liked hearing read to him was theology. Christianity, Claudian thought contemptuously. A religion for slaves and hysterical women. But if their priests are warning people off me and making life more difficult for Stilicho? Very well, the Sunday before the reading I shall put in an appearance at St Peter's.

There are quick changes to make in the text, and here I am without a copyist I can trust. My publisher has a hundred, busy all day copying out my works – for him the profit, for me the glory. Yet if I ask him as a favour to lend me a scribe he'll send me some nincompoop.

The god, Claudian thought dismally, has this morning deserted me. The divine faculty that comes down upon me, almost daily, elating the mind, turning the scurry of my thoughts into measured verse pregnant with images, has sunk away to nothing. I was worried, I was self-conscious. How boring not to be inspired. An old thought occurred to him, but this time with the force of conviction: the god, perhaps, was also Rome. So long as there was a general to hold back the barbarians, a poet to renew her Latin soul, why should the age of greatness not return? Why should glory nowadays so quickly turn, as it had this morning, to shabby farce? Horse-faced Serena under her canopy, a household slave carrying a laurel wreath? Farcical. The toga – but by this time Claudian could not bear to think of his toga. Behind the large statue of a forgotten consul he let it slide from his arm and fall to the ground.

Under the toga Claudian had worn a modestly embroidered linen robe. He entered the market unnoticed in the crowd. At last, of course, someone recognised him. It was the auctioneer in the slave market, a man who made it his business to know everybody. Many of the slaves, male and female, on offer this hot forenoon were naked, a sight that flicked Claudian with a pulsation of sensuality. Look closer, though, he told himself, and you'll see what horrors they are, sullen and grotesque, lumps of muscle broken down by work or vice.

They were on a low platform, being turned round and led up and down like prize cattle, to show them off in the half hour before the daily auction began. Two of the slave girls, big-bosomed and in milk, were on offer as wet nurses. The auctioneer began provoking the few nubile ones to make them strike postures. They might catch the eye of some randy young man with money to squander. Or some feeble old man looking for a cheap slave girl to warm his bed. More likely, thought Claudian – the girls were unappetizing. Cooks and gardeners and craftsmen stood a little apart, with a take-it-or-leave-it air. They were being sold off not for their looks or their milk but for what they could do. They knew their worth.

'A scribe?' asked the auctioneer, after muttering the few obligatory words of congratulation – words that by this time Claudian no longer wanted to hear. 'That young man at the back, thin, tall, glancing this way? He might suit you. Go and have a word with him, if you like.'

The auctioneer failed to hide a small leer. He knew Claudian's taste in slaves: always boys.

'All I need is someone who can copy manuscript accurately,' Claudian answered stiffly.

'That I couldn't say. Ask him. He has got his wits about him and he strikes me as truthful.'

Truthful, thought Claudian. That was a cunning word to drop into my lap. Truthful here in Rome – a slave? I have baited the hook, the auctioneer thought, keeping his eyes on the poet's face

'Who is putting him up for sale?'

'A ships' chandler in Ostia – going out of business. And sorry to lose him, so he says.'

Lucas, as the poet came up to him, returned Claudian's stare not over-boldly nor timidly but calmly, eye to eye. Years had passed, he was no longer a boy. There were lines at the corners of his eyes from writing by lamplight. He had several times been bought and sold and now it was happening again. He had no particular fear. A scribe was a piece of property too valuable to abuse. In the past the mere fact of being exchanged had frozen his heart, but here he was looking a potential buyer calmly in the face and almost welcoming the change... Stale scent, eyes bright, lank hair: a Syrian or an Egyptian. Impossible to guess what business he was in. What did he want with a scribe?

A little too thin for my taste, thought Claudian. Good-natured, not stupid. Not unattractive. Or is all this only the itch of the flesh on a hot day – a day of excitement? Whenever you felt the impulse to buy him, any new slave looked promising, even ravishing. And later on your blinded eye began to see his faults.

'I want a scribe who can take literary dictation accurately. What did you do before Ostia?'

'Clerk to an almond merchant in Marseilles.' Lucas was laconic, not selling himself, but not depreciating himself. If this man wanted him badly enough he would pay the price.

'Have you ever copied manuscript from dictation? Be frank with me.' Claudian found he was waiting with a certain nervous excitement for the young man's answer.

'I was amanuensis once in Britain for a Christian bishop. He dictated, I copied. There were no complaints.' Into Lucas's face had flashed a reminiscent smile, quickly gone. And when did you last, Claudian asked himself, see such a frank smile on the face of a slave?

'Does that mean you are a Christian?' Claudian asked, who had no intention of buying a devotee who would only cause trouble with the others.

The young man's 'no' came out more bluntly than was prudent in a spy-ridden and nominally Christian city.

'You don't know who I am?'

'No, *dominus*.' Lucas's answer was deliberately polite.

'I am Claudian the poet. Let us see how much you know. *Arma virumque cano* – continue.'

'*Trojae qui primus ab oris* – but everyone who has ever gone through grammar school remembers that. The opening line of the *Aeneid*.' After making up bills of lading in the busy port of Ostia, Lucas thought, to copy for a poet might be a easy living. In Claudian's face – and slaves are quick to notice – there was avidity perhaps, but no mark of cruelty.

'*Formosum pastor Corydon ardebat Alexim*,' quoted Claudian, testing him with a tag a little more out of the way.

A poem, also by Virgil, but celebrating homosexual love. Lucas felt his insides clench. They had arrived at the hard truth of his condition as a slave. This lank-haired long-nosed man with the glittering eyes could simply put down a handful of money, the price of his body, and make away with him, possess him in any way he chose.

'Virgil, the second eclogue, I know that too. Though the theme, I might as well tell you, is not one that has ever appealed to me. Or ever will.'

His tone, thought Claudian with excitement, is manly, though of course in the end he would succumb. How can he help himself? And would that be good for me? A resentful lover with a taste for blunt truth who, when I hope to escape will keep bringing me back to myself? No slave had ever answered him with such a show of independence.

'A critic too, I see,' Claudian said sarcastically, 'as well as a scholar.' Slaves were either devious, complaisant, slack and in the long run disgusting, or else they were Christian, conscientious workers, yet always silently triumphing over you, since they were going to heaven and you were going to hell. This slave was neither. For some reason the rottenness of slavery had not yet touched him.

'Do you fancy me,' Claudian asked gently, 'as a master?'

'I am a scribe. I can spell. I can take dictation. I can copy verse.' Lucas answered civilly enough, but he avoided Claudian's eyes. Blood flushed up peony-coloured under the poet's swarthy skin.

'Your name?'

'Lucas.'

'I shall bid for you.'

People were assembling. The auctioneer was on his dais. Did he suppose, when I quoted the eclogue, that I might buy him and force him, Claudian asked himself, horrified at himself. Do I look such a beast? What has Rome done to me? Lucas was staring into space as the bidding began. We must feed him up, Claudian thought, make him plump. Love from a slave? Absurd. *Eros* perhaps, in some incandescent moment, but *agape*, the love of the soul? I fall in love with them, desperately, and they laugh at me. Always hoping that the next one will be different. With this one I shall be severe at first, then polite, then cheerful, companionable. The habit of willing obedience will grow upon him in the long run like a second nature. The love of the body and the love of the soul, both at once, in the same person? Not impossible.

There was one other half-hearted bidder; scribes were expensive. After the auction Lucas followed Claudian across town to his flower-bedecked house on the Aventine. I trot at his heels like a pet dog, Lucas thought with self-contempt. Once the deed of purchase had been signed, the poet never spoke. He was strict and cold, it was the best way, at first, with a slave.

2

His favourite staff officer, Marcus Curtius, stood in the curtained doorway so earnestly erect in manner that no one, these days, Stilicho thought, would ever guess his father was an old moneylender, who, after speculating triumphantly in army supplies, had bought his way into high rank. Nowadays in Rome we are none of us what we seem. Claudian is an Egyptian, I am a Vandal, and Marcus Curtius as he stands there looks every inch an ancient Roman. A bronze statue of the better sort cast from moneylender's copper coin. Clever as they come though – he gets that from his father. Yet his father was crooked and Marcus Curtius is straight.

'This Alaric business, *dux*. All here in writing.' Marcus

Curtius began in his brisk, almost conscience-striken manner. 'For our imperial mastery's eye, and written up accordingly – simple, in purple ink, with purple patches.' He then dropped his voice. 'A piece of gossip besides.'

Alaric and Stilicho had already fought it out once in Greece and Alaric had been soundly drubbed. As a sop to the half-Romanised mercenary whom the Visigoths had elected as their king, Alaric had afterwards been given the Roman command in eastern Illyricum – a country of wild mountaineers, and therefore a good recruiting ground. If only Alaric would learn to behave himself – this was the idea in buying him off – he might live in his buffer state, his ambition slaked. But Alaric was more than commonly ambitious and he was now getting restive.

When word first came to Marcus Curtius through his agents – most of them merchants trading through the Illyrian mountain country – that all the state workshops there had begun turning out weapons of war, the imperial court turned a deaf ear. Hence this second intelligence document cunningly built up by Marcus Curtius like a mosaic from a multitude of little indisputable facts. With this report there could be no arguing. Stilicho was familiar with the gist of it: Alaric would cross the Julian Alps this autumn, by surprise, and pounce down into rich and unprotected Italy. Those closest to Alaric whispered that he even had his eye on Rome.

Stilicho took the forty-page papyrus roll inside a purple parchment cylinder, written out in purple ink in large clear script for the Emperor's never-enthusiastic eyes. With this tube, as if beating time, he tapped the palm of his left hand. Will he let them argue, or will he act, Marcus Curtius wondered? If Stilicho began his war preparations without a formal imperial decision, he was risking all on victory.

'All my staff please, here, in this room, at noon.'

Marcus Curtius though happy to hear the order, trying to keep a smile off his face, felt an inward shock at Stilicho's boldness.

Bureaucratic battles are often as hard-fought as real ones, and here in the palace Stilicho had just won a victory that would help pay for his war. Throughout the empire pagan temples had been closed down and their treasures confiscated. Everyone wanted a share of the money but Stilicho, when he saw what was coming from Alaric, had claimed it for the army – a windfall that would not happen twice. 'Plant money,' he had told Marcus Curtius cheerfully at the time, 'and up spring soldiers.'

'A meeting in here at noon, but managed discreetly. Start a rumour to mislead the palace. Will you do that? By the way, Marcus Curtius, do you speak Gothic?'

'Not a single word,' said Marcus Curtius, as if washing his hands of something loathsome.

'Alaric does, alas, and so do all the Visigoths. I do myself as a matter of fact. All your best sources – your merchants – will soon be closed to us. What if we could put someone who spoke Gothic close to him?'

Unlikely, thought Marcus Curtius. He was having second thoughts. The more he considered the military situation the gloomier he felt. There were hardly any troops in Italy itself. They were spread out thinly along the imperilled frontiers. All very well to say that money bred soldiers, but where were they to come from when Alaric held the best recruiting grounds? Alaric could march his men into Italy and what was to stop him? Yet the old man sounded so calm.

'Well, no matter. Tell me your piece of gossip.'

'The court, *dux*, returns to Milan.'

'A possibility I had already heard whispered. You must have found out from some source very close to the Emperor –' If you force me to tell you, I shall, said Marcus Curtius's silent imploring glance, but I'd much rather not. An intelligence gatherer always hates to give away his sources.

The double-walled city of Milan, four hundred miles to the north, and a stronghold at the foothills of the Alps, had in recent decades been an alternative capital – a centre of government nearer the barbarian threat. To have the young Emperor close to the scene of action should on the face of it be good for morale and make for quicker decisions. Or would an intriguing court try to interfere in the working of the army? Were Stilicho's enemies moving to Milan to spoil the army's game?

'We shall have set the legions marching, Marcus Curtius, before the courtiers have finished their packing. But why move to Milan now? That is what intrigues me.'

He is pressing me to tell him how I found out, thought Marcus Curtius, but he is too good a soldier to ask me outright.

'Our imperial master is listening more and more to what his priests tell him,' he hinted. 'Therefore – Milan.'

'And how did you pay off your informant?' Stilicho asked with a broad smile.

'The payment has yet to be made. This priest has a nephew – let us be charitable and say a nephew – in the ranks of our infantry. Joined up, no doubt, on a sudden patriotic impulse or to get out of trouble. Now he would like a commission, please, but well behind the lines in some safer branch of the service.'

'You want him for a comrade-in-arms?'

'No.'

'Nor do I. Can he read and write?'

'Yes.'

'Second him to the Imperial Post. Any more?'

'Done. Nothing immediate.'

'Then I have one for you,' said Flavius Stilicho with a wry smile. 'A certain young woman here at court is madly in love with me. Old and ugly as I am. The Princess Veleda – ever come across her?'

Marcus Curtius drew in an audible breath and tapped his foot.

'Yes. Dangerous. A hostage princess, and expected to be chaste.'

'Such a scandal just now could do me no good. An actress might be forgiven me – but a hostage princess? She can go one better than you, though, Marcus Curtius. She can speak Gothic. Now – I'm thinking aloud – what if at our suggestion she deserted to Alaric and –'

'Could she convince Alaric?'

'She could but try. Such single-mindedness? A virgin in love?' Stilicho patted Marcus Curtius on the shoulder. 'As usual we have wasted time here chattering like this. We have just time before the staff meeting to arrange it.'

'You will begin by speaking to her yourself, *dux*?'

'Such was my intention.'

'Then leave the rest to me.'

I must take that girl off the old man's back, Marcus Curtius told himself grimly, even if for the girl herself it ends in disaster.

Each morning when she was at home, Veleda's father would dispense justice, often enough outside, under an oak tree. At night he sat under his own roof by a good fire, drinking deep with his boon companions. But many people in this enormous cluster of buildings which the Romans called a palace, of whom Veleda herself was one, had never so much as seen the Emperor face to face. The most anyone ever caught was a fleeting glimpse of him.

The young Emperor Honorius had spent all his life behind curtains veiled by yet more curtains, in a world of rumour and seclusion. Stilicho, when he had been his guardian, would have liked to see him manlier, but Honorius made no effort to break free – the life suited him. He made excuses not to attend the imperial games, because an accident in a chariot race – and what was a chariot race without an accident? – made his face turn white. The sight of gladiators fighting to the death disgusted him. He felt awkward on horseback. As the Christians now so influential at court liked to put it, their Emperor was a man of peace.

What most exasperated Veleda at the imperial court was the ceremonial. For any action or object concerning the Emperor's person there would be a special category of slave. Anyone lucky enough to be admitted to the imperial presence would find there two *velarii*, one on each side, who raised the curtain for him, an *ab admissione* who ushered the suppliant into the presence, while the *nomenclatores* called out his name. Every sort of dress the Emperor might need, from his nightgown to his full-dress uniform, and any small article he might ever wear, had a particular rank of slave to look after it. Honorius even had a specially appointed slave – *a fibulis* – to look after his pins.

Veleda had first come across Stilicho shouldering his way through the palace with a pleasant smile on his trimmed and bearded face, as though everyone he came across owed it to him and to themselves to be frank and helpful. But woe betide anyone who obstructed him. She overheard him dressing down a high-ranking civil servant – a man she herself considered a monster – and that won her.

She had been raw in those early days. After seeing him chide the civil servant she had actually blurted out in front of others, 'What an Emperor Flavius Stilicho would make!' There had been an appalling hush and no-one had wanted to look her way, until old Julia, who looked after the morals of the hostage princesses, and was too old and well-connected and kind-hearted and sly to fear consequences, leaned over to say in Veleda's ear, very low, 'He can't of course, my dear. He isn't suitable. He is a Vandal.'

Vandals spoke Gothic, they were cousins. Veleda was giving all her love to a great man fitted to be Emperor, but cheated of his destiny simply because, like herself, he was a barbarian. She learned by heart the poems Claudian had written in his praise – to learn Latin verse was highly approved. As the words resounded through Veleda's mind, her body fermented.

When the young aide-de-camp sent to fetch her marched into the hostage princesses' private quarters – barred to him at other times – and in Flavius Stilicho's name asked old Julia for the Princess Veleda, his mere physical presence fluttered them all. Even Julia was blushing. Stilicho has sent for me! Veleda cried to herself, but she stood up rigidly and her smile was cold. She was too clever nowadays to give herself away. She was remembering that terrible glance he had given her yesterday, down in the Forum as he stood by the poet's bust – a cruel message not to follow him or stare at him, and it had gone through her like a stab. Yet, after all, he had sent for her.

The room in the palace that Stilicho had chosen for his own was small for such an important and powerful man. He liked it for the brilliant view downhill, through a small round window, across the busy Forum. In the distance was the Capitol, with the Tarpeian Rock jutting from it, and a long stretch of Rome beyond, marble white and brick red, smoking in the autumn sunlight, and fringed by masts along the Tiber. In this secretive, treacherous palace, such a visual contact with the world outside made for sanity. Also, he had arranged the room so that it would not be easy for an eavesdropper to overhear what was being said inside.

'To save Rome', said Stilicho, 'I must know what Alaric is doing. You will be a vital part of me – my eyes and ears. The big facts, yes, when and where he marches, how many horse and foot, whether he takes his siege-train. But small facts too. Never neglect them. The sort of facts a woman can so easily pick up – camp gossip, how much fodder they have left, what his soldiers are grumbling at, how many have fallen sick –'

'I have heard my father speak of things like that –' Veleda began brightly. Then she stumbled. Almost she had gone on to say '– when we were fighting the Romans.'

'Before I go, one thing,' announced Veleda, and with such emphasis that Stilicho wondered if she might be now about to make some impossible demand.

'I think it would be only right for me,' said Veleda, her chin obstinately tilted upwards, 'to see the Emperor. All these years in the palace and I have never been presented to him. After all, here in Rome I represent my people –'

'An absurd oversight,' Stilicho answered blandly, getting to his feet and taking her arm. 'I shall present you to him now, this very minute. Though please, not one word about your mission. The Emperor should never be worried by things he need not know. What did you say your father's name was, again?' He led Veleda through the labyrinth that she might be seeing for the last time. Oddly enough, the firm grasp of his muscular fingers didn't excite her. They were on a different footing now. When you walked through the palace with Stilicho all doors opened and there were servile smiles.

Wicker birdcages had been stacked along three sides of a courtyard open to the sky. As their names were pompously announced by the *nomenclatores*, the caged birds twittered a ragged response. A pale young man of eighteen, with an immature face, sat unmoving on the ground in the middle of the courtyard, as if stupefied by a kind of guilty boredom, his right hand in a sack of corn. Around his neck was a silver crucifix, heavy enough, Veleda thought, to be a real burden to him. His robe was purple, the imperial colour, and his shoes red with red soles, otherwise she might have found it hard to believe that this insipid young man was indeed the Emperor Honorius. He would get pleasure from feeding those birds, she thought, yet cannot bring himself to make the effort.

Honorius, though married for four years to Serena's daughter Maria, had never yet gone to bed with her. This piece of gossip had set the more knowing of the hostage princesses all agog. Julia, the old lady-in-waiting, who had an explanation for everything, whispered to them that this might simply have been a political precaution – they were princesses, they must judge for themselves. In the old days there had been easy divorce. Christian marriage was for life, but the Church would never hesitate to dissolve a marriage that had not been consummated. That set the hostage princesses twittering and day-dreaming. What if his second choice should fall on one of them?

Honorius looks so hapless, Veleda thought, sitting there with his hand in his sack! A sick-looking, difficult boy. Let someone else be his Empress.

The pallid young man, ignoring the new arrivals, took a handful of grain and shook it out near the cock pheasants, his favourites. Their long and iridescent tail feathers were at their best in autumn. As they began to peck, the Emperor's face softened into what was almost a smile. Stilicho bided his time, respectfully silent, massive, and in the end there was no ignoring him.

Honorius glanced back over one shoulder, his face plunging again into boredom. Stilicho waited until he had turned and then made him as profound a bow as a man could bring off and still remain soldierly. Veleda, though with a tiny inward bonecrack of resentment, prostrated herself in due form. (Old Julia had taught them all their court manners). In a voice too low for her to catch, Stilicho went through an introduction. The young man mumbled a conventional reply, repeating her father's name, speaking of him as a 'friend of Rome'. Even while speaking Honorius glanced back at his pecking birds. Then, with a lift of the hand, he indicated to his former guardian that the audience was over.

Why had Stilicho bothered him with such a trifle?

When Veleda looked back on him from the doorway, he was happily scattering corn.

When the shadows across all the sundials in the palace courtyards were at their shortest – precisely at noon – Flavius Stilicho met with his staff, and he worked them mercilessly until the sundial shadows had stretched out wide and the sun gone down. Here in self-indulgent Rome some of them had got a little slack. That afternoon pulled them up sharp.

The commander-in-chief described to them the army's present situation, speaking for an hour without the help of a note, as if the strength and whereabouts of every unit in the Roman army were marshalled inside his head. He went on to issue a succession of orders so outrageously bold as to have some of them gasping. Stilicho intended to meet the threat to northern Italy by stripping Gaul and Spain of troops – even though Gaul, too, was threatened with a barbarian incursion from across the Rhine. His orders were to reduce the garrisons along the Rhine to a token force, and concentrate every man they could call upon at Milan. He had weighed the impending dangers and made his own choice.

'Forced marches? Yes. Move them briskly. But they must arrive at Milan well fed – in condition to fight. I want their rations – *cibaria* – held in readiness at halts all down the line of march. The harvest in Gaul is in by now – and the best of that food is for my soldiers, even if Gaul itself goes hungry this winter. Quartermaster-General – there is to be no commandeering and then selling it back to civilians at a price. Peculators in army supplies are to be strung up at crossroads, where everyone can see and take note. If they are men of rank, court-martialled, stripped of their property and sent to a small island. No mercy. Provost, you are to verify in every case reported to you that this is done.'

'But general, what if this winter the Rhine freezes over?' An old general called Mucapor had spoken, in his day an intimate friend of Stilicho's father, now Inspector of Cavalry. Mucapor had put Stilicho astride his first horse – and in meetings like this was privileged to put into words what others might think but hardly dare express. 'What if a horde of barbarians manage to cross in their wagons and raid Gaul?'

'They may get their wits and their wagons together in time to do us damage in Gaul – yes. That danger we must accept and I will tell you why. Those will be sporadic raids, impulsive – not an organised invasion by a barbarian army trained in Roman tactics, poised within striking distance of the imperial capital.' Mucapor waved a clenched fist in acknowledgement, as if he had lost a boxing bout on points. 'Late next spring, after victory here in Italy, our legions will be back in Gaul, chopping them up, easing them out, pushing them back to where they came from.'

Stilicho has become so accustomed to victory, the younger

men were telling themselves, that he does not even stop to consider what will happen if he loses his battle.

Marcus Curtius said bleakly: 'And if the Alemanni come over the Alps into Italy before the legions from Gaul arrive?' The Alemanni too, as well as the Visigoths, had this autumn made threatening motions. The Alemanni were a rag-tag-and-bobtail, but Marcus Curtius had documented the threat they represented, and it would be unwise to ignore them.

Stilicho laughed as though the Alemanni were a great joke. 'If the legions have not yet arrived I shall lead out the palace guard against them and terrify them into submission.' At the back of the room someone whistled through his teeth, and at that irreverence Stilicho knew that he had won them. His strategy – of stripping Gaul to defend Italy – was not the mad gamble it might at first have sounded, but logical and necessary. By this time they all saw it.

'Let us get down to detail. Aquileia.'

He was speaking of the fortified city that stood where the road through the Julian Alps met the plain at the head of the Adriatic – for Alaric, perhaps, a stumbling block.

'You will of course, my dear Mucapor, reinforce Aquileia with cavalry to the limit. At least three hundred of your best light horse and ample fodder. Quartermaster-General – you have noted the fodder? All useless mouths moved out of the city with no exceptions. Send them back to Milan. If they feel like complaining they may take me to law. Knock flat all suburban buildings –' He was speaking now to the commandant of his engineers, a clever Macedonian. 'Nobody's summer-house, please, obstructing our line of fire from the walls. Those who accept a bribe to allow a building to stand, Provost –'

'– Strung up at the crossroads!' murmured the same irreverent voice at the back.

'With a little luck,' Stilicho went on, repressing a smile, 'we may hold Aquileia until the first of our troops show up at or near Milan. A city full of cavalry across his lines of communication will make Alaric think twice. My belief – and I know him as well as I know you – is that he will pause for the time it takes to neutralise Aquileia. That is what the general of a real army would do, and that is how he likes to think of himself. You think so too, gentlemen?'

They thought so too. Enthusiastically they had entered his mood and were of one mind with him.

Later the mood was a little spoiled by an ugly outburst concerning the Quartermaster-General – and quartermasters are notorious for feathering their own nests. In answer to a question about the shortage of entrenching tools the man spoke without thinking, making the excuse he would have made elsewhere.

'But general, what you ask might not be possible. The military budget –'

Stilicho's temper flashed. 'If this army of ours is to save Rome – and save Rome it will – my soldiers must have everything they need. Even entrenching tools. If funds this year are lacking for entrenching tools you may draw on my private fortune.' Stilicho paused, like a man about to make a lethal stroke with a heavy blade. 'Or on your own.'

Everyone in the room held their breath. The Quartermaster's face had gone bloodless, as if being strung up at the crossroads would, at that moment, have been a welcome relief. Stilicho held his eye for a painful count of five, then nodded understandingly as much as to say, 'Even so, you rogue, I still trust you, because who else knows your job as well as you do, if only you put your mind to it and let nothing stick to your fingers?'

All afternoon Stilicho drove them, firing their willingness, piling on work. Impossibilities were one by one reduced to mere difficulties, and what were mere difficulties? Sleeves wiped sweat from foreheads, the room grew offensively hot. As time went on Stilicho noticed with a spasm of happiness that they were even beginning to talk of his daring proposal to move the legions out of Gaul and into Italy as if they had thought of it themselves.

When they had come in and taken their places they had all been so well groomed, but Stilicho had already worked them at full stretch through the sacred hour of the siesta – when every self-respecting Roman was found either in his barber's or at the bath. Now this office, crowded with men, began to smell like a fox's earth. By the time the sun's last rays had angled into that bright little window which overlooked the Forum, and vanished, they were becoming restless. There was no more to be got out of them.

'Any last comments?' Stilicho asked. There was a tension of complicity in the room, as if they were boys in school once more, daring each other not to break the silence.

'Then off you go. And no gossip. Keep the army's secrets.' Stilicho had caught the eye of one staff officer in a particular hurry. 'Don't even tell your mistress.' There was laughter.

As the room emptied, Stilicho put a hand on Marcus Curtius's shoulder and detained him. This afternoon's vast exertion of his will which had drained the others had revitalised Stilicho. Tonight there was no need for him to join Serena in the matrimonial bed, broad as a burying ground and about as lively. His girl was waiting.

'That other small matter?' he asked.

'The girl who speaks Gothic? All arranged.' Stilicho's nod was meant for a dismissal but Marcus Curtius stood there blank-faced and almost inhumanly erect, as if bracing himself for a possible outburst of justified rage.

'May I make a submission to the general?'

'Not a long and discursive one, I hope.'

'Simply that as things are, with Rome so full of Visigoth slaves, and Alaric's agents active among them, the general should not go out in Rome after dark on a moonless night alone.'

'By the great gods!' Stilicho exclaimed, pretending to be enormously angry because such a reaction would be expected of him. His mind, though, was moving smoothly and fast. Marcus Curtius knew of his rendezvous with his actress. Well, it was his job to nose out secrets. The threat of assassination, though, was that real? A treacherous *sicarius* lurking with his dagger in some dark alley? Can Marcus Curtius be hoping to gain an ascendancy over me by enclosing me in a circumference of fear? If so, our friendship is over. This must be settled on the spot.

'I don't believe in your assassins. Though tonight, if it will amuse you, you may come and guard me.' Stilicho's voice was grim, though his mind was tending to move in Marcus Curtius's favour. 'I warn you my appointment is private, and will last all night. Are you going to mount guard in the street, or would you feel more at ease on a stool outside the bedroom door?'

Marcus Curtius's lips twitched as if he would love to answer that one as it deserved, but the habit of discipline checked him.

What he could not bear was to be suspected by the great man, if only for a moment, of double-dealing. Stilicho smiled, a frank, friendly smile, and for Marcus Curtius it was as though an immense weight of guilt had been lifted from his back.

With drab cloaks over their soldiers' garb, cowl pulled down so that faces could hardly be seen, they blundered through the noisy dark of the city night, now and then pressed against the wall to avoid the delivery wagons, dragged tumultuously by horses through the narrow streets. Wheeled traffic was allowed inside the walls of Rome only after dark, and the grinding of wagon wheels on paving stones kept everyone awake at night.

Not far from the seven-storey apartment house which Stridor was by this time renting with what Gilda earned for him on the stage and in bed, the general had a narrow escape when someone from a top floor window let fall the contents of a chamber pot. Marcus Curtius, not so lucky, took the brunt of it across his shoulders. Stilicho wondered whether to keep the joke to himself. Behind his proud manner Marcus Curtius was sensitive, he had already been discomfited tonight and a loud laugh might wound him. But the stench could not be ignored. Stilicho said 'Keep close, but not too close.'

'I promise, *dux*, not to stand to windward.' With this answer Stilicho knew that they were friends again.

The apartment building reared above their heads in the gloom like a cliff. Stridor and Gilda were using the luxurious ground floor for themselves, and letting off the floors overhead in single rooms. There was only one doorway, and outside it the two men paused.

'Are you going to mount guard? Or go home and change your clothes?'

'*Dux* – the dangers are real. Alaric has plans to organise the Visigoths in Rome.'

'So are the dangers on a battlefield real. Suppose you let me take my chance with both.'

Stilicho went inside abruptly, leaving Marcus Curtius standing on the doorstep telling himself that he had handled that badly. The general should have been told at some other time, in some other way. But Stilicho dead? Worse for Rome than a lost battle or a lost campaign. And does Gilda wear a dagger in her garter? That, he thought, is another risk the general must take by himself.

The little wrinkle-featured eunuch, Stridor, was hovering in the background, over-dressed and over-barbered as usual, and he came forward to offer the golden beaker of choice, cooled wine, with all the high polish, Stilicho thought contemptuously, of a master of ceremonies in a fancy knocking-shop.

'But Stridor owns me, body and soul,' Gilda had told him on their first night together, when she and Stilicho were still feeling their way with each other, and coming to explanations. Gilda had never been more carefully serious in her life before. She had felt from the first that Stilicho might be her doom. 'I mean literally owns me – I am his slave. But I'm also his invention. When he bought me I was a little girl in a ragged skirt.'

And the eunuch, Stilicho had thought angrily, will never sell her. And would I buy her? How can you own, as a piece of property, the woman you have begun to love?

'Though here, while we are together,' she had gone on to say, giving Stilicho a glance, a touch, that took away his breath, 'I am your slave, body and soul.'

She said it again, another way, as a reminder, tonight, this time in Stridor's hearing, when Stilicho told her: 'First I must have a bath. I have worked all day without a break.'

'Then I shall be your bath slave.' Gilda was going towards the *balneum*. 'Come when I call you – not before.'

'Masters call to slaves, not slaves to masters.' She laughed.

The little eunuch was refilling his goblet without being asked. And whereabouts in Rome, where everything was trafficked and faked, did this scallywag manage to find such real white wine?

'So the imperial court is going back to Milan?' attempted Stridor in his squeaky voice. He was fishing for information and he deserved a snub but Stilicho hesitated. How far over Gilda did this little monster's power extend? Stridor might have his private ways of making her suffer. The most powerful man in the Roman Empire in the West smiled at the eunuch vacantly, pleasantly, and though making no direct answer went on chatting with him.

'Who actually owns this *insula*?' These apartment blocks in

Rome – called 'islands' – were hurriedly run up, rack rented, and often in danger of tumbling down. Here, on the ground floor, there was abundant piped water. Overhead, in the single rented rooms, there was nothing but the wind blowing through the shutters, and if someone emptied his chamber pot out of the window rather than carry it down flights of stairs, who could blame him?

'Renting out this *insula*, *dux*, is my principal investment so far. Nothing to you, I know. It is but an insignificant part of the patrimony of the real owner, Pontius Meropius Paulinus – a magnate indeed.'

'His wife is even richer,' Stilicho said curtly, though the wife's estates, he reflected, were mostly in Spain – a Spain soon to be stripped of troops and nothing then to stop barbarians trickling in. A whole structure of wealth and property – the actual everyday life of Rome – depended on their victory. All they had done together that afternoon was necessary, vividly real.

'Actually I rent this *insula* from Paulinus by the year – for thirty thousand pieces.'

'And let it out for more, of course.'

'And of course, we live rent free,' Stridor said brazenly. 'Since I have no children it will all go, in course of time, to Gilda. I have made arrangements.' Stridor's face was folding into a beatific wrinkled smile. He was about to confide his private dream.

'Pontius Meropius Paulinus and his wife are selling off all their property, piece by piece. Did you know that, general? It will take a long time, of course, because there is so much of it.'

'A very long time.' One of the great consular fortunes of Rome, Stilicho thought, waiting impatiently for Gilda to call him.

'Twenty years purchase is what they will ask – but actually ten, if you stop to think, the way I manage this property. At the very most, six hundred thousand pieces.' He mumbled the sum of money like a sweetmeat in his mouth. Stilicho had begun to think of the cities he had seen go up in flames.

'But what is forcing Pontius Meropius Paulinus to sell off all this property?' murmured Stilicho, as if asking the question of himself. Paulinus was one of Rome's more conspicuous rich Christians, a man of no vices.

Into Stridor's face came a look of horror. 'He and his wife are giving it all to the poor.' Stilicho's laughter shook the room.

From the *balneum* came a clap of hands, palm struck loudly against cupped palm, a mistress summoning her slave.

Gilda's brown hair was down to her shoulders, and moistened into ringlets by the steamy heat of the marble-floored bathroom. A gown of cashmere from India, costlier than silk, clung to her figure. She had put aside all her jewels. Not hers, either, by Mithras! Stilicho thought. Those, too, are Stridor's. I have not been giving them to Gilda but to Stridor, helping him buy this building! But then, they gave her pleasure.

Gilda was confronting him with a diabolical simplicity, her hands held up, palms towards him, as if he had disarmed her. The thin Indian stuff clung – he could see her nipples and her navel, and as she leaned towards him, submissive, the dimples in her thighs. Gilda was unclasping his belt, lifting his sword on high and carrying it away as though it were a sacred object in a ritual. She was hitching, hauling his soiled shirt over his head, a tug that sent Stilicho's mind drifting back into childhood. Some other woman had managed his shirt exactly like that. He was happy, yielding himself up to her.

Gilda could be witty, gaudy, mondaine, crude as a camp follower, but in one respect she never changed. When her hands were upon him, touching him, Stilicho forgot all else ... the unremitting anxiety of his great office, the flickers of doubt, even of fear that came on him at times like birds of prey. Her touch could heal all that.

Gilda had laid him flat, chin down, and was beginning with subtle fingers to take the knots of muscle out of his thick neck. Why, he was sleepily asking himself, are there never enough soldiers? You bought and trained barbarian mercenaries – Romans had forgotten how to fight – and soon after they turned into enemies: Alaric. Her clever hands were loosening the rigid column of his spine. He could hear his vertebrae click like dice. Not enough soldiers. In this voluptuous ease, he could feel his sex stirring, snake's head lifting. He had been waiting for that. He rejoiced.

Uncommonly brave in all other ways, Stilicho's secret fear

was of impotence – that some night he would be flaccid, even with Gilda. Money bought soldiers. Taxes for soldiers, but taxes throttled trade. He was suddenly angry at the thought of that eunuch speculator out there coining money from all he touched. His anger made his sex lift and Gilda laughed merrily. No soldiers meant no Empire, but could the Empire afford them? Alaric thought he could take Italy by the throat. We shall give him a shock. Soldiers. Legions. Money. The big man smiled as he yawned and turned over at Gilda's nudge.

Gilda had begun to flatter with her fingertips. With gentle touches she was exploring the scars of his old wounds, as if with mystified reverence. The sabre-cut across his ribs, given him blindly, accidentally, by a runaway man on a runaway horse at Thessalonica; his little souvenir from Britain – an arrow-hole through the left shoulder.

'Wounds – and all in front.' Gilda was pouring soldiers' flattery onto him like ointment.

'The arrow also left an exit-wound in the back,' he grumbled. He knew what she was doing, the trick of it, and yet happily accepted her words. Gilda was dropping kisses, ignoring his sex, as if his wounds were more important. Gilda was a soldier's woman. He was sure in his heart that she cared for him.

'Shall you need me up there, my lord? I mean, if everyone goes to Milan. Think before you are angry with me for asking. To serve you I need to know.'

All afternoon there had been life and death decisions, and now Stilicho hesitated to give a simple answer.

'Gilda in Milan might shock the Emperor's strict morals,' she answered for him. 'Or your soldiers might be jealous? Oh, yes, I know soldiers. But if you find you need me, lift your little finger. Stridor may get an engagement for me in Milan anyway. The theatre here won't be doing much business.'

Out of the corner of his eye Stilicho saw Gilda reach for his sword, one hand on the shiny pommel. Had this been a trap? Would she now lift it and plunge the short heavy weapon deep into his flesh? All his old wounds ached. Roll away, off the rubbing slab, he told himself. Pick up that three-legged stool and defend yourself. Though if you are wrong you will have made yourself ridiculous.

What she was doing, in point of fact, was setting up a new mime – using his sword as a stage property.

Gilda had been a costly harlot, and then his simple slave girl. She was turning herself now, sword in hand, into a soldier in the awkward squad, never mind her impudent breasts and plump flanks. When Gilda made a soldier of herself her female attributes were not what you noticed. The raw recruit at his sword exercise – Gilda had seen them in Britain, in Gaul – making one mistake after another, and driven to worse incompetence by the rebukes of an invisible centurion. Stilicho began to laugh, a huge spasm of laughter, an eruption, coming from his barrel chest.

'That will do?'

'That will do splendidly.'

'And another act, a new one – one I have just thought of –'

She lifted hands to forehead, wiped them magically across her face and she was an eighteen-year-old boy so haunted with scruples that he had never once slept with his wife. The Emperor Honorius? Horrifyingly dangerous. But the instant supposition had been a trick of the mind. Stilicho could now see that Gilda was a young muleteer.

'The Court,' she announced, 'goes to Milan.'

She was a young muleteer – and yet also the Emperor – loading birdcages against the flanks of his beast – a resentful animal that could stand on one leg and kick with three. The mule kicked. The cages fell off. With a saintly, stupid, bored patience, the young man loaded them up again.

'Where have you seen him?' asked Stilicho in an awed whisper. Honorius was never on public view and she was portraying him exactly.

'I have been nearer to him than you might think,' Gilda said, breaking out of her act and giving him an impudent pirouette. Then once again she was the muleteer emperor.

The mule kicked. The cages fell off. With the long-suffering patience of a saint or a fool the young man picked up the birdcages. They were all in place. He was reaching across to tie a muleteer's knot, under and over and the twist of an invisible tightening-stick. When, yet again – and a theatre audience would have been on their toes waiting for this – the devilish mule once again kicked out. The cages fell. One had burst open. The birds! Birds! There were two, there were three! Birds everywhere! Flying in every direction!'

'Enough!' Stilicho said, choking with laughter. 'But, Gilda, this is sedition. The *agentes in rebus* will tear you to pieces.'

She had been watching his face, hands dangling at her side – a little girl who had tried her best and failed to please.

'No?'

Stilicho felt like a grown man whose foot had trodden on a little girl's favourite pottery toy. He remembered warning his staff officers against betraying army secrets. But this next thing had to be said.

'Listen, Gilda. I will tell you something you should not repeat. Very soon there will be a war. Yes – with Alaric and the Visigoths. Overnight the mood of the Romans will be patriotic. A mood that never lasts long, but at such a moment it would not be funny and it would certainly be dangerous to undermine the confidence we all ought to show in the Emperor.' He had managed to put it safely into words, a little pompously perhaps.

Gilda found from somewhere deep in her throat a tone of touching simplicity. 'It doesn't matter. I can easily think of another.' She gripped one of his great muscular hands with both hers, and lifted him to a sitting position, a little girl heaving up a giant. She sat in his lap and put a soft cheek against his naked chest.

'This war of yours,' Gilda said, delicately reaching across his shoulder to touch the arrow's exit wound, a dried leaf of skin under her finger. 'Be brave. You always are. How could you not be? But remember – I love this body. Do not be reckless with it.'

'I shouldn't have spoken of the war.'

'I know. It doesn't matter.'

Stilicho dumped her from his lap on to her two bare feet. 'Bed.'

'Bed,' she echoed, leading Stilicho across the room with one hand on his nodding phallus.

'That hurts.'

'Then don't hold back,' she said.

The hairs all over his body began to prickle, like a thousand little fleas.

3

In the gloom at the back of the basilica, Marcus Curtius was standing behind a pillar, his cropped soldier's head piously bare. The cloak over his arm had an odour of fuller's earth where a domestic slave in his father's house had washed the acrid smell out of it.

Many came into church whom he knew, but most avoided catching his eye. Here to St Peter's came three types that he could identify, fervent believers of good family, many slaves whose presence here on terms of equality worried Marcus Curtius, even though from his point of view this morning as a gatherer of intelligence, slaves hardly counted. And thirdly, more and more people tepid in their beliefs, paying only lip service to Christianity, who with a Christian Emperor on the throne saw public piety as a way of advancing a career.

Most baffling to Marcus Curtius, were the true believers. They were often rich. Some of them he had known all his life. What was there about this religion which could bring such an extraordinary change?

For someone using St Peter's as a listening post, it was hard to tell, standing there half-hidden by a pillar, which of them up there at the front near the altar were repentant millionaires, come here modestly clad, and which their slaves in their Sunday best. For Marcus this equality between slave and master was odious, simply not Roman, though of course one should treat one's slaves decently.

They are here to worship, thought Marcus Curtius uneasily; I am here to spy on them. He could not help feeling slightly ashamed.

In the days of Honorius's father, the great Ambrose when bishop in Milan had roused the passions of Catholic Christians against the Arian Visigoths by writing hymns to sing in church. Here in St Peter's they were just beginning an Ambrosian hymn. Might that signify?

Splendor paternae gloriae
De luce lucens proferens
Lux lucis et fons luminis
Dies dierum illuminans

An Ambrosian hymn – a hymn to the dawn – a straw in the wind. I ought, Marcus Curtius told himself, to know much more than I do about this religion, for professional reasons. Even though Stilicho might laugh. Visigoths for example call themselves Christian, but to Catholics they are only Arian – heretics unsound on the dogma of the Trinity. But what is the dogma of the Trinity? How can I inform Stilicho efficiently of the mood in Rome and Milan unless I know? I will get up Christianity, he promised himself, as a lawyer gets up a case.

During the hymn there was a disturbance at the front which made even the meekly-submissive Christian women turn their veiled heads. Into the basilica, a little late – but does not a well-known public figure often make his entrance a little late? – came a lank-haired, over-dressed man, not in his first youth, followed by a tall, thin young slave with a calm face, carrying his cloak.

As if unaware of their consternation, Claudius Claudianus was easing his way expertly to the front, looking out for a good place. He stood close to the altar, nodding affably to those he could recognise, even though they might not respond. This might have been some kind of public recital, a poetry reading even, where one need not give excessive attention to the performance. At least, thought Marcus Curtius, trying to repress a smile, he has not worn his laurel wreath. The most notorious pagan in Rome, and what was he doing here? Claudian, with a poetry reading of political significance at hand, had evidently come to curry favour with the Christians. It had not yet struck him that, with the court moving to Milan, no one in Rome would care, one way or the other.

As the Ambrosian hymn came to its quavering end, Marcus Curtius left his lookout post by the pillar, to slip away through the double doors. He had gathered up his little crop of gossip and surmise. The Christians would not oppose the move to Milan. For them, the Visigoths were still heretics. And he also had a story that would make Stilicho roar with laughter –

Rome's most famous pagan, blundering about on Sunday morning in St Peter's. Of course, a great poet, and Stilicho's encomiast and crony. The men had ideas in common – an exalted idea of Rome. They even in a strange way loved one another. Though why need Claudian always be so undignified?

In pagan days, thought Marcus Curtius in perplexity, as he moved out into the sunlight, there had been any number of gods who died and rose again. Power over death was what you expected of a god. But why crucified – a punishment handed out in its time and deservedly, to bandits, mutinous soldiers, rebel slaves? 'I feel crucified' was a common cant phrase, meaning, 'This worry will be the death of me.' The symbol of the crucifix nagged Marcus Curtius like an aching tooth, not least when alone in the small hours, always his worst time.

If a god was made to endure the death of a public criminal, and then rose again from the dead, all idea of legal retribution lost its force. An enemy of the state, once killed by form of law, should stay dead and buried. How dare he rise again, as a god? If enemies of the state rose again, and were worshipped, then the safe and solid world was coming to an end. Marcus Curtius as he walked away from the basilica towards the Tiber could feel the points of nails entering the soft palms of his hands. The symbolism of the cross was approaching his very body. Against his side was the prick of a spear point. He was unbearably thirsty, as men are after wounds. A god suffer that?

Lucas, who from boyhood had been familiar with the Christian liturgy, and could recognise a bishop when he saw one, was being made acutely uncomfortable by Claudian's behaviour. The gesture, coming from a slave, was improper; some masters might even flog for it, but he tugged at Claudian's sleeve, and lifted a warning finger to keep his Levantine tongue quiet. A brave act, which Claudian acknowledged with a hard stare.

Lucas after only a week of taking dictation from Claudian was beginning to understand him. Though such a blunderer in everyday matters, Claudian was preternatually sensitive – the lifted finger had been enough. That face he was pulling hid his agony at having gone astray.

Like the Levantine copycat he was when he was not remembering to be sternly Roman, Claudian in self-defence was taking up the reverent attitude of people close by. The Ambrosian chant:

Aurora cursus provehit
aurora totus prodeat
in patre totus filius
et totus in verbo pater.

ended. And neatly turned, thought Claudian, whatever it may mean. Ambrose was not illiterate.

Someone with the resonant voice of an orator began to recite in Latin what Claudian had at first taken for some other piece of versification. He listened carefully, and the passage did not scan. Then he guessed what it must be, Jewish literature, disproportionate, overstrained. He had read Jewish literature years before in a Greek translation that was knocking about Alexandria: a grotesque rhetoric, that worked by parallel and repetition.

The suffering servant who is numbered with the transgressors and bears the sins of many.

And exactly what, he would have liked to ask the more cultivated among his intently-listening neighbours, has poetry or for that matter literature in general to do with servants or suffering or sin? Should Latin ever be self-pitying?

Yet despite the clever arguments his quick mind was devising, Claudian was deeply perturbed. He had ventured too boldly among the enemy. These people made him nervous. All around, recognising and yet ignoring him, were those whose meek beliefs and mediocre language had debilitated Rome – members of great families aping humility and indistinguishable from their own slaves.

Dies dominica, announced the bishop – the Lord's day. Anyone out there on the street would have said *dies sol* – Sunday. At the new and mealy-mouthed form of words, Claudian's soul cringed within him. He would have liked to shout aloud into their very faces those good old valid Latin words, *dies sol*. But the massed ranks of these meek Christians were moving close, to crush him. A slave, Claudian's inward voice affirmed, is always a slave – a two-legged animal of servile mentality. Yet how could he overlook that tug on his sleeve? Was Lucas to be an exception? No, there could be no exceptions, or the argument fell to the ground. Should the authority over inferiors that had made Rome great crumble into compromise? Servitude had been written into that young man's stars.

Claudian looked furtively sideways at Lucas and his face was calm, even noble. That is only, Claudian argued with himself, because the work he does for me is ennobling. Transforming. The words go in his ear, he responds, and thus becomes my extra arm, extra hand.

Claudian whispered, 'Do we stay to the end?' Uneasy with embarrassment, Lucas shook his head. The sermon had begun: *What shall it profit a man if he gain the whole world, and lose his own soul?* Though the theme he developed was a piece of nonsense, full of fallacies, Bishop Innocentius was such a good Latinist that Claudian felt a certain pleasure in lingering.

Lose his own soul?

How could a man lose his own soul, except at death, when all that made life living would be over, anyway, and the little that remained of one, the twittering residuum

animula vagula blandula
hospes comesque corporis

went down to the boring shades. What actually survived death, Claudian allowed himself to remember, was literary fame – glory more enduring than bronze. Stilicho shall win victories as he has won them in the past, but the unborn will remember them only because the god puts memorable words into my mouth to praise him.

They were almost at the final business with the bread and wine – their central mystery – when Lucas with almost impudent urgency muttered, 'Time to go.'

Claudian's curiosity was piqued. He was tempted to stay, and even join in, but standing nearby were important people whom he knew, staring stonily. Turning his back on them, Claudian walked towards the double doors rather slowly, as if admiring the architecture. Lucas, cloak over arm, followed a pace behind, clumsy with embarrassment.

Lucas during this last week with Claudian had worked harder than ever before in his life. At times he had almost begun to regret his old job as shipping clerk, diving in and out of warehouses to make up bills of lading, and check cargo. At Ostia there had been hot afternoons of gossip and a cup of wine, in company with a flock of chattering girls, who lay in wait for seamen off the incoming ships. As Claudian's scribe there had never been any such break. The tension of mind and body was incessant.

Anyone looking over the wall to catch a glimpse of Claudian as he fidgeted up and down his garden on the Aventine, and not knowing him for a famous poet, might have taken him for a madman. As he muttered under his breath, his features would be gripped by spasm. Sometimes he might pause to groan and hold his head, as if a man guilty of some appalling error. Then his eye would light up – he had hit upon his form of words. A finger lifted to Lucas, waiting tensely – and out they would tumble.

Almost before Lucas had time to scribble the first draft with iron stylus on wax tablet, Claudian would begin to make changes. Some trivial turn of phrase would be impatiently shuttled to and fro in the sentence, the scansion wrenched about, until to Claudian's hypersensitive ear the words had begun to sound inevitable. Lucas kept pen and ink and an unrolled papyrus at his elbow to fix the final version. Yet hardly would he have lifted his old iron pen, charged with ink, to make a fair copy than Claudian, testing the phrase for one last time on his tongue, would hold him fast.

Dictation was dictation: you had been trained in the scribes' school in Londinium to take it down impersonally. You were accurate, obedient, you wrote down what you were told. While Bishop Decius went on dictating to Pelagius, his scribe had managed to keep his distance and detach his mind. But Claudian's blank despairs, his bouts of frenzy, his desperate meticulousness, were catching. Lucas had found that he too began to swing like a madman from gloom to excitement. When a phrase came out right he rejoiced. Once or twice he had even found the right word, there on the tip of his tongue, a moment or two before Claudian himself, but had had the sense not to utter.

The poet had his privilege: out of his mouth, directly, would come the right word, like a gold coin flung into sunlight.

All through this week of close quarters and hard work Claudian had never once pestered Lucas. Dalliance evidently was for hot afternoons in the intervals between poems – Claudian's sensuality was at a low ebb when fitting words together. There was also his fear that if he made the wrong move – this new slave Lucas was anyway too tall and thin and sobersided – that might spoil him, and a scribe like this was harder to find than a catamite. But as the work went on, a kind of intuitive tenderness grew up between the two of them. Even against his will, Lucas began to develop an exasperated affection for this pretentious lank-haired Alexandrian, with his odour of stale scent and his miraculous obsession with language.

On their way back, that Sunday, to the flower-bedecked, marble and brick house on the Aventine, Claudian had changed. He was clear at last that the Visigoths were coming. He should have known, but when in the throes of composition he dropped out of the world. Therefore this was no time for the reading of old poems in Rome. His place was north, at Stilicho's headquarters. (Why had Stilicho not sent for him?) Already a poem about the Goths was making itself felt. In his mind's eye, as he walked home, with Lucas one pace behind, the cloak over one arm, Claudian could visualise them: hairy savages, heretical, bestial. He sought for words, imperfect as yet, to set them at defiance:

> The richer we were heaped with heartening hopes
> The poorer grew the Goths, who brushed the stars
> Crossing the Alps, and thought they'd won the world
> At last unchallenged. But they saw instead
> Our kindling youth, our instant infantry . . .

Our instant infantry! And broad-shouldered Stilicho riding steadily at their head, magnificent on horseback!

Claudian had a house in Milan too, but much smaller, so there was no point in travelling north with his entire household. Lucas, while the decisions were taken, sat in the library, twiddling his thumbs and wishing for work – a strange frame of mind for a slave. Claudian walked to and fro, making his travel arrangements in a curt, clipped voice – inside his head he was commanding armies. And if I take Lucas with me, he had decided, a scribe almost too quick and clever at following my thoughts, may I not be tempted to begin the new poem before the gods find it propitious?

'You, Lucas, will for the time being stay here. Keep busy on the library catalogue. I shall send for you in due course, from Milan. Never fear.'

'But, master –' Lucas felt a pang of disappointment like a long fall through space.

Claudian at the head of his imaginary legions raised an imperious hand. 'When the god touches my lips I shall have urgent need of you. Meanwhile, wait here and set an example. I don't want this place turned into a den of iniquity the moment my back is turned.'

In a household full of ill-conditioned rejects – slave boys no longer so lovely in Claudian's eyes as once they might have been, cooks who ruined any dish they touched, useless slaves that some clever dealer had palmed off, Lucas was the odd man out. Since the master had not seen fit to take his new scribe to Milan, the others decided that he must be safe to torment.

Lucas could defend himself most easily with words – the one thing a slave dreaded more than a whiplash was a sarcasm that stuck for ever in his mind. He kept them off him with the lash of his repartee like a crowd of curs, until he began to feel ashamed at how easy it was.

They soon learned to leave him alone, and since there was hardly any real work to be done on the catalogue, Lucas began to read avidly, passionately, in solitude, and that was his solace.

Part III

1

No one was being admitted to the imperial highway without a pass. The needs of war had crammed the Via Aemilia, proceeding through Modena towards Milan, with too much traffic. Military baggage trains made up of hard-mouthed mules and loud-mouthed soldiers jostled wagons filled to the brim with government archives, sewn in sacking against the rain. The influential rich had passes, and moved amid a concourse of their slaves and other portable possessions, getting in everyone's way, and sometimes running Lucas off the road as he made his slow way north, tugging at the bridle of a bad-tempered donkey.

There were hardly any legionaries or cavalry to be seen on the road as yet. Italy was empty of fighting men. To Lucas the traffic that jostled him on the splendid highway might have been a fashionable migration from one imperial capital to another rather than the onset of a war.

Claudian had very soon taken into his head that he needed Lucas. Since in years gone by Claudian had been given by Stilicho a nominal government position – all salary and no duties – which allowed him the privileges of the Imperial Post, sending Lucas a pass north was no problem. To speed him on his way, Claudian's steward in Rome, a malicious man, had bought Lucas the worst-tempered donkey he could find. With satisfied smirks on their faces the steward and all the household slaves had watched him go.

Lucas had dragged and goaded that complaining beast over the Apennines and past Modena. As if succumbing at last to the brutalities of a heartless master, the donkey had only just now stretched itself out at the roadside near a milestone, lifting all four feet in the air, and given up the ghost.

Lucas was beginning to sort out the possessions the donkey had so resentfully carried. He was packing the strict essentials into a smaller load for his own back, strapped with the bridle, when a fancy Roman palanquin came waddling up the highway borne by four well-matched slaves, and with another four marching behind, as a relay. Lucas when the *lectica* went past could hear two high-pitched voices nagging. There were worse ways of travelling, he told himself, than alone with a shoulder pack. Now that the donkey was dead he felt liberated. The *lectica* had gone another fifty paces when a woman in a coloured wig poked her head past the leather curtains, and yelled, 'Lucas!'

She vaulted to the ground without even waiting for the dumbfounded slaves to pause and lower. She had thrown her wig inside as a nuisance, and was running towards him, stumbling over her skirt, arms outstretched.

'Lucas!' The girl was so close he could feel her sweet breath on his face. But who was she?

'You don't know me? I am Gilda!'

Gilda herself had recognised him at a glance, sitting disconsolately at the roadside by a dead donkey – he might have been a character in one of her theatrical sketches. But she might not have run so fast to greet him had not Stridor who was in a nagging mood forbidden it. Latterly he had been growing jealous, like a half-discarded lover.

'I shall sell you!' he had threatened, as they moved north in the palanquin.

'Whatever I cost, Stilicho will buy me.'

'I will sell you to an African brothel.'

'No more ropes of pearls, then.'

On the highway, cheek by jowl, they had never stopped scoring off each other, like man and wife in the last days of a bad marriage. The name she had shouted – 'Lucas!' – at first meant nothing to Stridor. Then he remembered. And could he be another?

Gilda? thought Lucas, trying to bring to mind the muddy little tangle-haired girl of times past. There was no resemblance.

'Going to Milan?' she asked breathlessly.

'By easy stages.' She looked down at the dead donkey, and laughed, and it was Gilda right enough. That is how she would have laughed in the old days, at a comic disaster.

What might have been a hornet whipped over their heads, to make a metallic splash on the milestone just behind. That angry, over-dressed, red-faced dwarf jumping from one foot to another with a sling in his hand could only be Stridor. Who these days, thought Lucas, actually has slaves to carry him. All eight *lectica* porters were moving up ominously behind their master, as Stridor refilled his sling.

'He's jealous.'

'You mean he would kill you?'

'I am worth too much,' said Gilda. 'He is only trying to frighten me.'

As another lead pellet whizzed near them Lucas put his own body protectively in front of Gilda's, and held her tight. 'Don't ever let go!' she murmured. If only I were not a slave, thought Lucas. If I had a right to wear a sword. I would face up to Stridor and he would pay for this.

Utterly safe for the first time since the distant day when the mounted archers captured her, Gilda clung tight, whispering, 'In Milan will you come and see me?'

This trustful clinging had awakened in Lucas sudden memories of the little girl who once had trotted so many miles at his side. 'How shall I find you?'

A third pellet skipped venomously near their feet. Stridor's eight slaves wore unpleasant grimaces. They were evidently all longing for an order from Stridor to give that impudent slave with the dead donkey a beating, and bring back delectable Gilda by force.

'They still call you Gilda?'

'You have never even heard of me?' At any other time Gilda might have felt chagrin. What was the point of fame? Then a happier thought occurred to her: not for my fame but for myself. Fame is the life I lead with Stridor.

Her manner as she then went back to the *lectica*, dejected, defeated, was a masterpiece of acting. Gilda's impromptu performance of herself as repentant did not quite convince Stridor, he knew her too well, but it pacified him. The hot bitch coming back at her master's whistle with her tail between her legs. Years ago on the road, thought Lucas, she was like that, too – play-acting her defence, as vituperation is mine.

'If that had gone on much longer you would be sorry,' screeched Stridor.

'But I am sorry.'

As for Gilda, she was hugging to herself an indelible memory that to Stridor would mean nothing, Lucas's arm tight around her, not to possess her but to protect her. We are both slaves together, thought Gilda, smiling at her own paradox, and that makes us free. If Lucas does not now come and see me in Milan, then there is no faith in humankind.

New arrivals were stuffing Milan to the very walls – the famous double walls that made the city the fortress of the north. But as a bitter wind rolled down on Milan from the nearby Alps, the magnates of the imperial court all regretted Rome.

Some had even found urgent private reasons for returning to the softer climate of the Bay of Naples. Others wished they could invent business in Sicily, or, better still, in Carthage, second city of the Western Empire and capital of Africa, a province cut off by sea and desert that had never yet seen a barbarian. But most stayed, because of what they might be missing. Wherever in the empire Honorius had his court was the focal centre of money and power.

The city of Milan was overcrowded, but except for eight hundred or so imperial guard the army barracks were empty. All veterans, those guardsmen, and magnificent soldiers in their days, but nowadays employed more often in ceremonial drill or palace sentry-go. Occasionally they were sent to crush a city riot. That was their only excitement.

On this cold morning the imperial guard had been drawn up on the Field of Mars in full marching order, highly polished, rigidly erect, many with blue noses, while the Emperor Honorius inspected them on horseback, with Flavius Stilicho, as commander-in-chief, walking his own charger a couple of paces behind. The Emperor, in dress uniform as *Dux Imperator*, also wore scarlet boots and the newfangled imperial diadem. Since arriving in Milan Honorius was indeed no longer boyish, as if the imminence of danger were bringing him one step nearer some kind of manhood. He was growing up petulant, no doubt, and too prone to notice those who whispered timidities in his ear. But manly enough, this bitterly cold morning, thought Stilicho, despite his bad horsemanship, as to make not a bad impression on the guard.

An almost imperceptible nod from Stilicho to the watching centurions – they knew him well – and a deafening and to all appearances spontaneous cheer broke out across the parade. Honorius flushed with pleasure.

Most of the old sweats who picked up the signal to cheer had already fought campaigns under Stilicho's command. If he chose to prise them loose from their soft billets so as to lead them on a wild-goose chase into those implacable mountains on the northern horizon, they might curse and grouse. But old Stilicho knew what he was up to. He was a lucky soldier as well as a randy old devil.

Officially Stilicho was marching the guard out to confront the Alemanni – a tribe of odds-and-ends who fought on foot and were pouring down to Lake Como over the Engadine, the Alpine pass that would take them by the shortest way to Milan. They were much nearer than Alaric – they were an immediate danger. The Alemanni were opportunists. Stilicho's gamble was that he could deal with them before Alaric arrived.

One or two guards officers with good political contacts had other private doubts. Who or what, after all, was Stilicho, his military reputation apart? A Vandal. He had made deals with barbarians before. How ambitious was he? Was he perhaps no longer satisfied with being the power behind the throne?

Marcus Curtius had ears everywhere, and some of the rumours about Stilicho that had lately come his way were foul. All the treasure from the pagan temples squandered on the army – and no soldiers at Milan? Into whose pocket then had it gone? A fortune embezzled and a secret deal with Alaric – and after? Those who set such rumours going did not, as Marcus Curtius well knew, necessarily believe what they were saying. They had some good reason, financial or political, for speculating on a military setback. A disaster – even a stalemate – would drag Stilicho down from his eminent position here at court, and thus give them room to move a little further up the ladder themselves.

If something goes wrong, thought Marcus Curtius, then the

best death for both of us – for him and for me too – would be on the battlefield. Yet on this cold parade he was disinclined to think too much about death on a battlefield. Better to brood over roaring log fires and mulled wine.

Many of those young guards officers are only toy soldiers anyway, thought Marcus Curtius contemptuously, as with others of the staff his frozen body was marched on frozen feet off the parade ground in the wake of their mounted general. Stilicho was apparently impervious to cold, but the young Emperor by his side looked as peaky as a frozen bird, even though before bringing him out here on this ceremonial parade they had padded his uniform with wool. The prestige of a Roman Emperor still counted for much – his presence here in Milan, claimed Stilicho, was worth a couple of legions. So long as Honorius kept his nerve!

If they want to make themselves useful, thought Marcus Curtius cynically, let the Emperor's priests pray for a thaw. Let this snow melt into the tributaries of the Po, so that Alaric finds flooded rivers to ferry his wagons across, all the way from Aquileia to Milan. He was a fool to come on campaign with those wagons. Exercising his mind on this little problem kept Marcus Curtius's brain from freezing solid too. He reckoned up thirteen rivers between here and Aquileia, thirteen difficult crossings, and tried repeating their names to himself, as an encouragement. Tilaventus, Meduaeas, Athesis. No, he had missed one. But Alaric would find it. Let the snow thaw in time to flood them all!

Before marching his guardsmen north to Como, the commander-in-chief had a private word with Marcus Curtius, walking him beyond the city walls and into the open, clear of eavesdroppers. To an onlooker they were two military men, standing amid the frost-bound market gardens, warmly clad, perhaps gossiping about girls. The news I have to tell him these days is so gloomy, thought Marcus Curtius. How does he always manage to smile?

'Aquileia?'

'Will hold out for perhaps a couple more days. They have a *testudo* going. But may well have fallen by now.'

'That excellent girl of ours?'

A crumpled handkerchief stinking of horse-sweat had come in from Veleda in the middle of the night, and been decoded.

'She is almost as good as you are, Marcus Curtius. And a princess too. Why don't you marry her?'

'General, is that an order?'

Stilicho's loud and genial laugh exploded, but not for long.

'The latest on the Alemanni?' He may try not to show it, thought Marcus Curtius, but the Alemanni have him worried.

'Their scouts are in the pass and coming downhill. Nothing to stop them but the walls of Como, and our little flotilla on the lake.'

'You have not revised your earlier view – your considered view – that this is only a raid in force? Not a stratagem of Alaric's? They are not secret allies? He is not trying to outflank us?' The questions came like hammer blows.

If my intelligence appraisal has gone amiss, thought Marcus Curtius, feeling both important and dismal, then both Rome and Stilicho are doomed. In stiff-lipped military fashion, in a voice devoid of emotion, he answered, 'Only a raid in force, general.'

A straight answer to a straight question, thought Stilicho. How often these days does a Roman give you that, even in the army? And what could be better?

'This, then, is what I propose,' said Stilicho in a voice so brimming with confidence that for a moment Marcus Curtius, who loved the man, was taken in. But he is hiding his profound anxiety, Marcus decided, at the chance he is taking. 'I shall lead my eight hundred veterans up the lake in the fast galleys of the Como fleet. Pray that they are not all seasick. I shall use them not to fight but to confront and dazzle the Alemanni. It can be done, you know. Frighten the silly wits out of them. Provoke their enthusiasm for Rome in all its splendour. Recruit the best elements of our would-be enemy into the imperial army –'

Stilicho rattled through all this as though the task would be easy, indeed, a great joke. But suppose it doesn't come off, wondered Marcus Curtius. What if Alaric is nearer than I suppose?

'Stick very close to that young man in the diadem,' added Stilicho in a more earnest tone. 'My wife, the princess Serena, will give you all the help she can. Wherever he moves – and I think that some of those around him will encourage him to move – you follow. You are to become the Emperor Honorius's military shadow – yes? If you are given no choice in the matter you may even pretend to repudiate me. I have already spoken to Serena. We spent last night together.' Stilicho shuddered, and not entirely because of the cold wind from the mountains. 'A coded despatch to me by courier or pigeon every day. The good gossip and the bad. Since I know how much you like coding –'

You think the Emperor will run for it? was what Marcus Curtius had almost asked, but what was the point of putting what they both dreaded into words?

'*Dux*,' he said instead, 'I wish I were coming with you.'

'A glorious death on the field of honour?' asked Stilicho brightly. 'Yes, I have thought of that, too. But not for intelligence officers. And not for general officers, either. We have to accept the consequences of our actions. You will serve Rome best by sticking close to Honorius.'

The two men shook hands, military fashion, each grasping the other's wrist. Betrayal, thought Stilicho, is everywhere imminent. The court is going corrupt like a bad apple. Marcus Curtius is a man I assume I can trust to the bitter end. Yet, by contrast, his rich old father? Rotten. Serena was saying so last night.

Serena had been brought up as a girl at court in the old triumphant days at Constantinople, when her father, the Emperor Theodosius the Great, ruled the empires of both east and west competently. When Theodosius died, seven years earlier, the empire had been divided up between his sons Arcadius and Honorius. With Honorius, a simple-minded boy doomed to be Emperor, Serena had tried to take the place of a mother, yet in recent years Honorius had begun to resent her and, now he had come of age, new voices were encouraging Honorius in this resentment. Serena still had her own ways of pricking his sensitive conscience, even at times of knocking a spark off his dull intellect. But she could feel her influence over him begin to wane. There were too many others these days busy at the political game of isolating Stilicho.

There had been the significant incident when Stilicho took

his formal farewell of the Emperor. Just as he went down on one knee, in an abbreviated obeisance, Johannes the Emperor's confidential slave, black-fringed, heavy-eyebrowed and impenetrable, began to whisper in Honorius's ear. Down on one knee, said his glance, was not prostration. At a stare from Stilicho, who saw and heard all – *a slave, to come between himself and the Emperor?* – black-avised Johannes had slithered from the room. Stilicho's eye could still deter, perhaps frighten. But by such whispers damage was done, and Rome's best general undermined.

In a lonely corner of the palace, with the wearisome day's work behind him, and all his guardsmen preparing their battle-order equipment so as to march out at dawn, Serena, with a little smile like an amorous signal in the old days in Constantinople, had cornered him.

'Your last night, I think.'

Stilicho grunted. He could guess what was coming.

'I want you to spend it with me.' She might as well have jabbed him hard in the ribs with the hilt of a dagger.

'I claim, after all, only what is mine by right,' Serena went on calmly, her long upper lip twitching like a rabbit's with pleasure at his discomfiture. 'Suppose, Flavius, this night is destined to be our last together on earth? *Absit omen.* But if it were, would it be seemly to spend it with someone else, however lubricious?'

Gilda is here in Milan, and simply waiting, thought Stilicho, for a word from me. Serena must be spying on her.

Now that she had her great man in a corner, outmanoeuvred, into Serena's heavy-lidded eyes came tolerant affection. Since they first met in the imperial court by the Bosphorus, both young, both able to make good use of the other, they had gone through so much together. They were a team.

In Serena's room was no perfume or brazier or silk robe, no warmth, no funny red wig. There would be no preliminary massage either. There would be cold water for an ablution, the stone-cold mountain water of Milan. In the midst stood the broad matrimonial bed, with its moulded bronze knobs and claw feet, its heavy white blanket. This bed was an exact replica of the one in Rome. A sacrificial altar, thought Stilicho wryly. And I am the sacrifice.

A meek little bronze lamp proffered a flame as big as a thumbnail. Before she undid her clothes Serena modestly blew it out, as if once again a trembling youngster in love with her Vandal guardee. She would rather not have me see how she is ageing, thought Stilicho. But I am ageing too.

In the chilly dark Serena was placing her long boniness against him, all knees and elbows. Marriage rites. Yes. His duty to her. First though, since theirs was a political marriage, would come political conversation. He waited for Serena to begin.

'You observed Black Johannes? That malicious whisper? In some way that I can only guess he has wheedled himself into the Emperor's confidence. You can control him with your eye, yes – but when your eye is not there? Luckily for you, Flavius Stilicho, your enemies are my enemies too.'

'It comforts me to hear you say so, Serena.'

'Now – these other women of yours.' Here it came at him, straight as a javelin. Not for nothing was Serena an Emperor's daughter. 'Or to simplify our conversation, shall we say, this other woman? What you or anyone did in the dark was at one time a private matter. Your infidelities did not enchant me. But everyone went on pretending that the commander-in-chief slept every night with his wife, as a good Roman should, and you were happy enough I think to go along with the pretence. Except that times have changed. Here in Milan, the Christian priests who find it suits them to take their tone from Black Johannes are already muttering the deadly word, adulterer. Not an amusing peccadillo any more, you may be surprised to hear, but to them an enormous sin. And how can a sinner – a sinful barbarian – win a battle for Christian Rome? Of course if you eventually win your battle, Flavius, as you always have done before, that will shut them up. But what if you don't?'

She had put the question that must never be asked.

Stilicho lay there rigidly beside her boniness, more furious than penitent. What concern was it of these nonentities – these insects? His anger waned as he reminded himself that at least from Serena you got the truth. Might there be danger in it, though, for Gilda? Were they planning to make her a scapegoat?

Now that Serena had managed to land her blow, her voice grew more generous.

'I understand you, Flavius, better than anyone. Another

woman – a younger woman? Of course, all the time, that is the kind of man you are and always have been. This one they tell me, vulgar though her profession, at least has style. She would not betray you, they tell me, or disgrace you. I should hardly care for a young woman who might disgrace you.'

Stilicho, all at once bone-weary, said 'Is this your idea of a suitable conversation for our last night together on the eve of battle?' From old habit he had begun stroking her breast, a withered handful, the dug of an ageing wolf, a caress, though, that had always comforted her, as it did now. She eased herself closer, held him muscularly tight, as in the days of her first pregnancy, unlucky little Maria – anxious as she had been to present him with a son, and yet so terrified of death. Her voice in his ear, though still political, had become an endless intimate murmur.

'Flavius, listen. The court is no longer the court that we knew when we were young, in the time of my father, the divine Theodosius. They are madmen. Those whom the gods would destroy, they first make mad –'

She stumbled over the quotation as if uncertain whether these days to say 'God' or 'the gods.' The Emperor Honorius's court might be rigorously Christian, but the old gods were still somewhere about the place.

'They think first of themselves – never of Rome. They expect everything to go on as it always did, and with no effort on their part. They have adopted a religion of peace, haven't they? So why should they not be left in peace? I have heard them say, outlaw war. But who is going to enforce that law? So that they may go on enjoying their power, their pleasure?' Serena groaned with pleasure herself at the touch of his hands, but went on talking politics as if politics for her were a carnal pleasure too. 'They think of barbarians as a sort of demon. They see barbarians everywhere. They see a barbarian at the head of the Roman army –' Serena was holding him with a maternal passion, as though she would give her heart's blood to protect him. 'Their wicked tongues are making a pattern out of it, Flavius – a crazy pattern, not the true mosaic. They whisper that you have made bargains with Alaric before –'

'And shall again, perhaps next week,' said Stilicho around a heroically stifled yawn, 'if I consider it in the interests of Rome.'

Tonight in bed with Gilda there would have been laughter and pleasure, delicious make-believe, the cut-and-thrust of sex, a night which would have charged him with confidence for the coming battle against the Alemanni. If there were to be a battle. There might not be.

'My victory over Alaric,' said Stilicho gruffly, 'will shut their mouths.' Victory bought time, a year or two at least, and thus the life of Rome went on.

'The gods grant it,' said Serena piously, and Stilicho chuckled. This time she had come down on the pagan side: *the gods*. She liked it when he laughed.

'Serena, it is getting terribly late, but listen. The young man who wears a diadem is not quick-witted, but he is not a fool. Contend as best you can with his resentment. Cajole him, bully him, shame him. Try to keep him here in Milan. He should be encouraged to think of my victory as his own victory. In the minds of simple men – millions of simple men – the Emperor signifies Rome. His is the face on the coin. So long as he stays at his post, and is publicly identified with victory, the army's morale –'

'I failed with him,' said Serena, in a regretful, womanly voice. 'When he was little I must either have been too strict with him, or too indulgent –'

'Not you but fate perhaps.'

She had been both strict and indulgent by turns, but Honorius was unpromising to start with. Nothing that I know of, thought Stilicho, would have made a man of him. What was Black Johannes's hold over him? Too late at night to ask.

With a shamefaced eagerness that turned back the years for him, Serena came awkwardly closer. There was no mistaking what she expected. This too I do for Rome, thought Stilicho, as easing her elbows out of his ribs he reached for her buttocks.

Serena had giggled. She was no longer a matron but that young girl again, in Constantinople, meeting her lover on the sly. When Stilicho came down upon her with all his weight, Serena could have fainted. Her young guardsman still – yet older, even larger, his body covered with wounds. Like being taken – she thought – by incarnate power. She shut her eyes and waited passively for what always came at last – the punctual little bliss.

To one side of the road winding into the mountains from Milan to Como, on a little hillock, was a shrine, long since defaced, to Mercury the messenger of the gods. These days no one posting along the mountain road would pause to leave a honey cake or some flowers as Mercury's refreshment, and some fervent Christian or naughty boy had knocked off the divine messenger's nose. The pagan gods these days had it hard.

Gilda arrived at the shrine that morning on a riding mule, before the soldiers of the guard had marched that far, and she tethered her mule out of sight. She intended to stand up there on the mound where they could all see her as they passed by. Only a blind man would miss her. She had dolled herself up in a white headdress of ostrich feathers which shivered barbarically in the wind, and she wore a cloak of Sarmatian furs, opulent, extravagant, falling below the knee. The fur cloak had been a peace offering from Stridor. Only Gilda could make an appearance so well-covered, and yet below the hem of her furs, above the booted ankle, offer you a suggestion of nudity, a glimpse of all she had. They would think, rightly, that underneath the furs she was naked.

Around the corner came at last the gilded eagle of the regiment of guards, borne aloft, and after their glittering eagle, the leading files of guardsmen, stepping it out. Many of them had known Gilda in Rome by repute, if not by sight. As the whisper of recognition went down the ranks, from the first few men rose in chorus one of the Roman army's lewd marching-songs. It was a spontaneous response to her presence. The tune was picked up without prompting all the way down the line, until it reached the muleteers at the back with the ambulance wagons.

More or less in limerick measure, sometimes rhymed for comic effect, occasionally sentimental, often ineffably obscene, such songs as they were now singing had for centuries been the Roman soldiers' commentary on life as seen from the ranks. A new song would become roaringly popular, no one knew why, then sink out of sight when some unknown genius in the ranks set going a more topical one.

This homage to Gilda, their song of the moment, had gone the rounds in Milan, prompted by Stilicho's desperate stroke to the north, and hinting as ever at his sexual reputation. Gilda was not ready for it, and the words pierced her ears like a flight of arrows.

>   A l a r i c
>   has only GOT! ONE! BALL!
>   *Alemanni* – NONE AT ALL!
>   S T I L I C H O –

and the song, made thick and three-dimensional by crashing male voices, went on to celebrate the magnitude of their general's genitals, and his insatiable night-time prowess. A posy for Gilda.

The whole long procession of them, armed men marching past, had set themselves to make her blush – to acknowledge them for what they were. And sure enough, a peony-coloured blush rose across her face. Gilda simply could not help it. Watching her expression they roared with delight. The first files were stepping past the shrine, heel and toe, eyes stiffly to the front as if on imperial parade, yet each of them watching that girl in the ostrich feathers from the corner of an eye.

As if alone on stage, Gilda raised her arm upwards and above her head in one vast blessing, the furs falling back from naked throat and wrist, the white feathers trembling. They were marching, these hard-bitten soldiers, away from the love of women, towards ice and mountains. She was giving them her voluptuousness. The song roared in her ears to a crescendo. Their general's girl – and good soldiers share. She was their girl, too.

>   S T I L I C H O
>   fucks like a B I L L Y G O A T

Halfway along the column, the general riding at the head of his staff was reining in his bloodstock mare, containing her to the marching pace of the troops, horse and rider as usual superbly one. Stilicho heard the song and identified the woman ahead of him in the ostrich-feather headdress. He at once began to ride as if parading on the Field of Mars, his features impassive, eyes straight in front. He is going to ride by and not even spare me a glance, thought Gilda, in despair. He detests all this. I have belittled him.

From old-soldier instinct, the guardsmen marching behind the general, seeing the stiff-backed way he rode, had by now begun muting the words of their song – which might turn out to be not a tolerated joke but a breach of discipline. All eyes in the flagging files were on the cropped nape of the general's neck. What would Flavius Stilicho do when he reached her?

In the leading files the bawdy song was working its way round yet again, but had become only a half-hearted affirmation.

Alaric
    has only GOT! ONE! BALL!

As horse and rider passed the shrine, the volume of singing shrank to almost nothing. You could have heard a man cough.

And then, when Gilda was exactly opposite, as if she were his empress and he in duty bound to present his troops, Flavius Stilicho turned his head sharply, in an impeccable yet quite impersonal salute. He was stonily all soldier. Their eyes met like a clash of weapons, and Gilda's heart leaped. After having faded for that one cautious moment, the song roared up like a forest fire, until the last soldier had gone by her, singing his lungs out.

Once they had all marched past Gilda, and each man had had his brief sideways glimpse of her – raped their general's wonderful girl with voice and eyes – the joy went out of that particular ditty. As if they had just been reminded where they were going and why, the files up front picked out a song for a different mood, a sentimental favourite of the Roman army's, going back centuries. The well-known words, the softer tune, spread down the line:

I've lost Britain and I've lost Gaul
I've lost Rome, and worst of all,
I've lost Lalage.

Lalage, thought Stilicho, as the horse moved under the pressure of his knees, changing step. Not Gilda now, but Lalage. A girl who belonged to some legionary long dead. What an instinct they have for the truth! Picked men from every legion in the list; veterans of every war fought by Rome in my lifetime; guardsmen. They better than anyone know the chances I am taking – they march as if to a wedding.

I've lost Britain? Yes indeed. After the legion I have withdrawn, XX *Valeria Victrix*, marches out, the blond Nordic pagans and hairy pagan Celts will swarm in from north and east, and what's to stop them? *I've lost Gaul?* How long before my kinsmen decide to thrust their way across the Rhine? One year? Five? As many as ten? There is only a ghost army to oppose them, what makes them hesitate is the Roman reputation. *Rome?* Not lost yet, no reason why it should be. The object of this exercise is to make the loss of Rome unlikely. And so long as Rome holds, what is lost can one day be reconquered.

... worst of all, I've lost Lalage ...

For Lalage, sing Gilda. Serena condemns her, is working against her. And I did wonder if I had lost her. But no. Not yet.

Serena was exacting a price for her political support. *How can a sinner win a battle for Rome?* Serena intended to cut Gilda out, and it would not stop at that. Brilliant Gilda, here this morning like an empress, to salute those about to die. The common soldiers' empress. But when news of her magnificent whim, thought Stilicho, gets back to Milan, I shall have to pay a price. Or she perhaps will. Last night when I was told to give up Gilda, it crossed my mind that if I did, I might lose my knack of winning. But this morning, simply because she came and stood there, foolish and imprudent perhaps but all-glorious, I know I am still good for something.

Gilda, not warm even inside her new cloak of furs, and yet delighted with herself, was riding back hard on her mule to Milan. That one clear stern glance had paid for all. If she lost him, she lost him, but he would not have thrown her away. No word from Stilicho last night? Affairs of state he could not cancel? Then when her disappointment was at its most intense a message had come from Lucas, scratched on a wax tablet. Gilda could read plainly written letters well enough, a little slowly perhaps. But the rapid sideways scratches on wax which a literate used for quick notes were a conundrum, and no one in Stridor's house could be trusted to tell her what the scratches meant.

Gilda went out into the street and picked a likely passer-by, elderly and pleasant-looking. With a twinkle in his eye he told her that the message said, 'My love, Claudian needs me in Como,' and looked quizzically at this elegant woman with a fur coat slung over her shoulders, vaguely familiar to him, who did not know enough to read her own love letters.

Gilda, turning away, held the wax tablet under her furs against her breast, as if to take Lucas's hurriedly scratched words into the warmth of her own body. In writing 'my love' he had used the poetic word 'flame', signifying, thee for whom I burn. That pleased her more than a necklace of rubies.

The more far-sighted people in Milan were by this time getting out. Seeing the backs of the guardsmen as they were marched into the mountains had for many been the last straw. Stridor caught the mood, and in his high-pitched voice began arguing the wisdom of moving south to Rome if not further.

'But we have only just got here.'
'And when Alaric hears there are no troops in Milan?'
'The theatres are full.'
'The Christians will close them,' Stridor sneered.
'Meantime I am pulling crowds. Let us wait until it happens.'

Stridor could only see the house he owned here in Milan if not his *insula* in Rome put to the sack, set on fire. Barbarians were those who destroyed a man's property. Her jewels, though, were a fortune he could carry under his arm to some place where property was safe.

'Carthage is safe. There is a theatre in Carthage.'
'Carthage is provincial.'
'Provincial but safe,' he reiterated obstinately.
'You go there, then,' said Gilda in a simple, self-sacrificing tone that was meant to gall him. 'Take my jewels. They are yours, anyway. And get things ready for me there. For me to leave Milan just now would be a mistake for both of us.'

Carthage was all talk. He would go to Rome because Rome was what he knew.

'Why a mistake?' Out of his wrinkled little face, Stridor gave her a cunning sideways glance.

'The legions will arrive; Stilicho said so, and they are my best audience. They would never forgive me if I ran. And what is the worst that could happen to me here? To be raped by some Visigoth?' She laughed, and this laughter told Stridor that she was being false to him. Or planned to be, once his back was turned.

'Listen, master. Apart from my talent – and there are always others with talent coming along, pressing hard – the one thing of real value to you that I have is my reputation. I am the soldiers' sweetheart. And what will they think of me, now and hereafter, if I run away to Carthage?'

'You have a lover here,' said Stridor in a petulant voice that was close to a scream.

Like a woman making an obvious confession, Gilda spoke calmly. 'I always have a lover and I hope I always shall. I play the game you taught me – remember? And another thing to consider. If I leave Milan now, in time of danger, will Flavius Stilicho ever have me back? How much money have you made, in this way and that, out of Flavius Stilicho? Suppose you let me take my own small gamble on his coming back in triumph?'

That confusing half-truth, flicked towards Stridor, won from him a grudging, 'Very well.' Meanwhile, one word in Lucas's scratchy handwriting sang at the back of her head. *Flamma* – my love for whom I burn!

These slaves, thought Stridor – they are all the same. She has some underlying reason that she would never admit to me, even if I put a hot iron to her breast. The sickening thought that he might, one day, if he chose, disfigure her, destroy her value on impulse, was like a luxurious dream to him.

'Die like a heroine, then,' he said scathingly. 'Up on the walls of Milan, with a helmet on your head and a pitchfork in your hand.' She is losing her old fear of me, thought Stridor. Once again she has somehow got the better of me. She has made of herself a public face – Stilicho's mistress. How can I drag her back to Rome by the hair? She wants me to go, and leave her here? Very well. But she is still my property, and Roman law has a long arm. (If the Visigoths arrive, will there be any law, any property? Stridor felt dread.)

If he goes, thought Gilda, and I think he is going, he has gone off at other times, chasing money, then he will set a spy on me. As if there are no ways of evading spies. I shall stay in Milan with Lucas. And if Stilicho comes back, with Stilicho. I shall stay here with the Emperor – with all three of them – a gorgeous thought.

'This poky place here in Milan which you bought so cheaply,' Gilda was saying to Stridor with almost contemptuous matter-of-factness. 'You wouldn't get what you paid for it; it's been terribly neglected. I shall have it done up. Simply leave me the money when you go. Decorators just now will be looking for work – I promise you a bargain. When I am resting I am never idle. And I shall have new acts to rehearse. We have been living too close to one another, Stridor. I have been getting on your nerves. I am fond of you – you know that. Don't worry your dear sweet old head about the Visigoths. Once the raping is over they will want to be Romans, and Romans love the theatre –'

'They are zealots,' grumbled Stridor. 'Arian heretics. Why should barbarians want a theatre?'

She has a lover here, and would say or do anything rather than admit it.

'I have quite a lot of new material about the army,' said Gilda briskly, pretending to ignore him, now that she had won her way, renewing in her mind's eye the memory of what had happened that morning on the hillside near the shrine of Mercury. 'If Stilicho should bring back a great victory, as I am sure he will, that kind of thing should be extremely popular.'

'A victory?' said Stridor. 'You must be dreaming.'

2

Como, a small walled city two days' march into the mountains, and an advanced Roman military headquarters, was squared off in a shape reminiscent of an army camp, with a gate set in each wall, and an octagonal defensive tower at each corner. The long, narrow, lead-coloured lake stretched northward towards the pass that came over the Engadine. The pass itself formed a funnel down which barbarians could pour. A *classis* of fast-oared boats, not unlike the fleet of galleys on the Saxon shore, was based on Como, and kept up a lake patrol as a lookout against raiders.

There, in Como, with a raw, cold wind skipping off the lake water, Claudian, tremulous as a schoolboy, waited in the unheated anteroom of the large town house which the general had commandeered for his headquarters. Today Claudian was not feeling particularly Roman. The climate up here in the Alps froze him to the bone. Yet in spirit he was greatly elevated. The mood in this little fortified town, with guardsmen in battle order swaggering the streets, all of them cockily confident though blithely aware of the odds, had borne him upwards like an eagle.

Claudian had waited among the crowd in the anteroom for an hour or more, yet the time passed for him with a vivid swiftness. Bubbling into his mind came turns of phrase provoked by what he had been seeing in the streets. He was already mentally stammering out rough-hewn hexameters, possible images, and half-turning to scribble down reminders, while others in the room eyed this lank-haired, slightly over-dressed man as though he might be a spy. Rough notes, scaffolding, upon which the great poem on this campaign might take shape and form.

Local civilians who obviously thought themselves of great importance were beginning to resent the long wait in this anteroom, but for Claudian it had been like having one's finger on the pulse of war. Shepherded in by a harassed-looking aide-de-camp, and ushered into the general's room ahead of everyone else, had gone a mud-splashed cavalryman, staggering with exhaustion. Out a moment later came that white-moustached old general of cavalry, Mucapor, a friend of Stilicho's father in his early days, his face so preoccupied that he actually failed to recognise Claudian, though he admired him. What did that matter? Mucapor was on his way to the wars. A confidential buzz went around the anteroom not long after that the Alemanni vanguard had met Roman light horse, and clashed with them, touch and go, at the far end of the lake.

Flavius Stilicho was badly off for cavalry, yet on the intelligent handling of the few dozen horsemen he could send out ahead of his eight hundred guardsmen, everything would now depend. Claudian understood that much. Old Mucapor's first duty would be to screen Stilicho's guardsmen, conceal their small numbers. But in carrying out this difficult duty Mucapor must make his weight felt, probe enemy positions aggressively yet avoid costly skirmishes, be seen, yet never involved to an extent which might betray the Romans' real weakness. The cavalry were the eyes of the army. Though so few, they must be everywhere.

Up from the lake shore as they waited in the anteroom came an insistent sound of hammering. A flat-bottomed barge, intended for shipping corn, was hastily being fitted with sweeps and a mainsail. Everything on Lake Como that floated and could carry men or supplies was being pressed into service. As soon as Stilicho himself arrived to take command, the guardsmen would move up the lake in the fast galleys of the *classis*, in battle order, with their rations and *impedimenta* limping along behind.

Among the files of armed men getting chilled as they stood waiting near the galleys, a saltily blasphemous joke that someone or other claimed to have overheard Stilicho making had gone the rounds.

'But general – if the lake freezes over?'

'My men will walk on the water.'

'And if the ice is not thick enough?'

'We shall dig our way out with our entrenching tools.'

The army's notorious shortages – everyone blamed the speculators – had already become a subject of grim mirth. But walking on the water? If the Christ of the Christians had known how, why not Roman guardsmen? To pull off this bluff would need some kind of miracle.

Across the anteroom rippled a stir of expectation as the general himself came through the door, a public smile fixed on his lips. The impression Flavius Stilicho gave everyone that morning was of solidity, physical and moral, as if his actual grizzle-headed body were generating the energy that set everyone else on the move. He looked around at the many who were waiting, at a glance identifying more than half the people sitting there as time-wasters. Even those who were not must forgo their turn. The time for departure was close.

'No one else, alas,' he said with a courteous, disarming shrug. 'Except of course our great poet, Claudius Claudianus. The imperial guard will be going into action almost at once.'

There was a gasp of almost palpable envy as the poet stood up when all the rest were sitting, and crossed in his awkward gait like a sleepwalker to the general's door. The crowd in the anteroom began to disperse, chattering angrily. Every single one of them had business of more importance than Claudian's.

'One request, *dux*.' Claudian would dearly have liked to evoke a military bass from deep inside his chest, but his voice piped out like a schoolboy's. 'To be allowed to come with you and your men across the lake.'

'Out of the question,' answered Stilicho, with the broad smile of an indulgent father refusing a favourite son a piece of evident foolishness. 'We may none of us come back. Then who would be left to immortalise us? Listen – there is very little time. You have begun to write?'

'The first premonitions perhaps,' said Claudian, excessive in his modesty, but his radiant smile gave him away.

'This campaign is the Emperor's. Need I say more? If you can do so with dignity, praise Honorius. Even though he does not fight in the field, let it be taken for granted that he inspired us. Since for Rome – do I need to say? – the Emperor, the imperial idea, is our hearthstone.'

'And if the young man's nerve should crack?' Claudian, in a whisper, was asking what must not be said.

'We must distinguish, must we not,' said Stilicho gently, like a wise veteran giving a hint to a young hothead, 'between the office and the man. A mere human being may on occasion lose his nerve. Poor fellow. A Roman Emperor? I don't think so.'

The two men grasped hands, and Stilicho was gone.

The Alemanni – a rag-tag-and-bobtail of miscellaneous Teutons – had come down in arms from their mountains under the sway of a materialistic dream. They lived a hard life, pasturing flocks up and down the Alps as the weather changed from summer to winter, living off milk and meat when times were good, often going cold and hungry when the deep snows began. Rome for them was not only the plenty but the peace and law-and-order and entertainment that as mountaineers their own lives lacked.

With snow deep outside and a log sputtering in the hearth, old warriors who years before might have done time in the imperial service would sit around, yarning about Rome's immense empire. They would speak of the unbelievable carnal pleasures of life in great cities – Rome, Constantinople, Milan. The circus! The gladiators! The women!

The younger Alemanni, who had never yet seen Roman service, affected to despise Rome for living soft. Down on the fertile Italian plains were all those good things the mountains never saw. Alaric King of the Visigoths might wish to inherit Roman civilisation. They themselves would be happy with the crumbs of plunder.

Grab what might still be going: jewels, luxuries, women, gold. Why leave them all spread out down there for Alaric? In their idle, hungry, first months of winter, the younger Alemanni in their mountain huts had sharpened weapons – the dagger, the long sword, the terrible throwing-axe. But should any such raid be seriously discussed as a proposition, some veteran would be sure to remind them, insufferably, 'You may not know it, living in these mountains all your lives, but Flavius Stilicho had already beaten Alaric into a cocked hat, there in Greece.' Over the plundering raid of which the younger Alemanni daydreamed, and to which even the older men were becoming reconciled, Stilicho's name was a question mark, a permanent shadow of doubt.

The first of the Alemanni, carrying their sharpened weapons ostentatiously, came down that morning in not bad order towards the lake. Roman cavalry, continually observing them from afar, had never yet closed up for a fight, and this had encouraged the younger men into thinking that the fight when it came would be a walkover. The older men came on more stolidly, knowing better. The Alemanni as they came down the hillside were beginning to bunch and separate, the hotheads coming foremost. Old sweats who had tried to keep good order were being pushed aside. They will soon be more of an armed mob than a fighting force, thought Stilicho, watching as they came into sight. There are a lot of Alemanni coming down on us, but they are not all of one mind.

As they came on through the morning mist, the Alemanni saw, drawn up on flat ground, with the lake at their back, eight hundred superb soldiers, the imperial guard, Rome's best. They had been deployed in a triple line, centre advanced and wings refused, as if they were playing out a mimic battle-order on some parade ground.

Covering their wings to left and right was that handful of disconcertingly ubiquitous cavalry, snuffing, pawing, neighing, yet their lines as precise as if drawn with a ruler. Although the Romans had their backs to the lake, as if disdaining retreat, they had in fact a way of escape: the galleys of the *classis* were moored offshore. In war as in life, Stilicho was careful never to leave himself without a way out. The Alemanni had come down from their mountains for easy plunder. They had not bargained on a fight with troops like these.

Stilicho in command at the centre of his little host felt the excitement of a gambler when the dice yet again have fallen right for him. Warfare meant planning, supplies, timetables, discipline, self-control. But there came at last that sublime moment – action – when what counted for a general commanding was the instinct of a gambler. My luck this morning, thought Stilicho, has not deserted me. What I now have to do is perfectly clear in my mind.

Those Alemanni coming down the misty mountainside to the lake shore must outnumber us five to one. In any kind of fair fight, five Alemanni could easily overwhelm one Roman veteran. But a fair fight, thought Stilicho, is not what I have in mind. The trick with antagonists like these it to engage not their bodies but their minds.

The silence, the perfect immobility of the imperial guardsmen were unnerving. Bristling with weapons, like workmen arriving to a field with edged tools, the disorderly Alemanni moved closer, the young men well ahead of the mass, and shouting defiance.

Conspicuous under the gilded eagles, Stilicho lifted his hand. A trumpet spoke. At that brazen command the Roman skirmishers stepped out of line and moved ten paces forward. Halted. Opened ranks. Moved forward another fifteen paces.

Grounded javelins, as if on a parade ground. The mob from the mountains was facing a machine.

If I am wrong, and Marcus Curtius is wrong, and this does happen to be a deliberate little war of Alaric's making, thought Stilicho – if the men approaching us are secretly his allies – they will attack now without hesitation. If they have pledged their word to Alaric, they will charge. Teutons are loyal. I am a Teuton myself. We must in that case stand with our backs to the lake, and make them pay for their effrontery. We must maul them before pulling out, even if it costs us a few guardsmen, and then take to the boats: a fighting retreat to Milan. But if they are only here for plunder, now that they see our formation they will hesitate.

Having worked themselves up to a frenzy, in twos and threes the younger Alemanni were coming on headlong. Those square-headed, sharp-pointed Roman javelins, thrown deadly straight, would punch a hole in a man's skull. A word of command broke the silence of the Roman line. Javelins whistled from the skirmishers – not a great many, but enough to make men pause and think. Over like selected ninepins went the foremost of the Alemanni hotheads, before they had come close enough to throw their own axes. Those still alive hesitated.

In that moment of hesitation, out from the Roman ranks came a trumpeter, – a herald, asking for a parley. The host, pressing down the mountainside, held back. Like most Teutons, the Alemanni prided themselves on proper behaviour. A parley now? But tradition demanded respect for a herald. What might the Roman general have to tell them?

Stilicho watched a tremor pass through them as they halted their onrush – a shudder of indecision, as if the many-headed barbarian mob were but a single invertebrate creature sharing one rudimentary brain. Their moment of hesitation won the day for Stilicho. Once having paused, even the fiercest of their young warriors could not easily be got going again, and only a furious charge would push the triple rank of the imperial guard into the lake. I have them off-balance thought Stilicho. And it's their throw of the dice now.

Five men, their chiefs – three of them greybeards and one a former Roman mercenary, a good fighter, whom Stilicho with his long memory recognised – were coming forward with dignity but without enthusiasm.

A lift of the forefinger brought up Stilicho's charger. Stilicho borrowed a javelin from a man in the line, and with it vaulted into the saddle, light-cavalry fashion. Not every man of his height and weight would wish to do a trick like that, with so many eyes on him. The soldiers loved it.

Flavius Stilicho began to walk his horse quite slowly to cross the gap between the confronting enemies. When he was very nearly halfway, employing a gesture that went right home to the hearts of the Alemanni chieftains, he unbuckled his jewelled sword-belt, lifted it on high for all the battlefield to see, turned in the saddle and let it drop. Encounter his enemy unarmed? Why not? He trusted to their honour. Welling up from the ordered ranks of the guardsmen came a mutter of high approval, instantly repressed.

The space between the motionless enemies, where their confronting leaders now looked few and small and alone, might very well have been filled by this time with mutilated men, and everyone knew it. The scattering of impetuous youngsters transfixed by Roman javelins, ugly, prone, immobile, was a reminder. Dismounting, Stilicho let his bridle trail. The charger whinnied, as if aware if the excitement, hammered one hoof, and then stood still.

Stilicho, a disarming smile on his face, went right up to the man who years before had fought in the Roman army, as if to greet an old friend, taking his hand, greeting him correctly by name and rank.

'Many years, old friend, since we two saw service together. I hope you have not forgotten all your Latin?'

Gratified, confused, the old mercenary broke out with a few words of soldiers' pig-Latin. It would have to do.

'I am a Vandal myself, as you all know, so apart from Latin I know only Gothic. But I was sure when I came here that I would have no need for an interpreter. Among your chiefs there was bound to be one of my old comrades who understood good Latin.'

Around Stilicho's interlocutor the other chiefs hung and buzzed like wasps, while he explained what was being said. Not all were pleased, and there were clear signs on two of their faces of a readiness to embark on a Teutonic argument. Keep the initiative, Stilicho warned himself.

'So you are bringing your young men down here to serve Rome as soldiers?'

While that simple but flabbergasting proposition was being translated for them, Stilicho watched their expressions. He went on, at the right moment, 'We shall pay them well – as we always did. There is no wine in your mountains, I know. But down in Como we have full barrels, waiting their arrival, to pledge their promise of service.' The point about wine in this cold weather raised smiles. 'There is more to be gained by serving Rome than by fighting her – eh, old friend?'

The Alemanni were exchanging mutters, and from one of them, a man who had been ready to argue, came an embarrassed laugh. Stilicho went on talking in the tones of friendship, saying not very much but enough, and there it was, all laid out for them. The great general had come to meet them, unarmed. They had him in their power? No, he was their guest. Now as ever, he talked like a man who did not understand fear. He had made them a liberal offer. Stilicho, as they wavered, raised the tone.

'Rome needs soldiers and Rome rewards them well. Look, gentlemen, what Rome has done for me – a Vandal, a soldier like yourselves, my birth obscure. And now as you see, a general, commanding armies, and my daughter married to the Emperor.' (Poor little Maria! thought Stilicho, as he always did when he remembered her). 'And let me tell you I am not the only one. Over there is old Mucapor – remember him? And who was he, before he became Rome's Inspector of Cavalry? Well now, let us get on – it's cold up here in your mountains. Down at my headquarters in Como I have silver and gold ready waiting.' (The plunder of our pagan temples, he thought wryly – another time you might not be so lucky). 'Today your young men will eat the Emperor's bread and salt, and drink wine, and draw their first pay. As their fathers did before them.'

The simple idea that it might pay better to fight for Rome than fight against her, repeated first in one way then in another, at last went home to them. Turning their backs on Stilicho, putting their heads together secretively, the five chiefs were talking slowly, knowingly, and like simpletons; but in their own tongue they were coming to agreement. The time had arrived for Stilicho to keep quiet.

With barbarians there is eventually no point in wasting words – eloquence will not serve you. But Rome, Stilicho told himself, means the power of language – Claudian's language. And these are classic Roman tactics too – divide and rule. If only there were some equally straightforward way of buying off Alaric! But Constantinople has already tried buying off Alaric with a principality – and Constantinople has failed. Foxy ambitious Alaric, who by this time would probably not be bought off with anything less than the imperial diadem.

The Emperor Honorius lay between sheets of purple silk, loitering on the languorous frontier between sleep and waking. Two old woman – dream caricatures of the two who last night had presumed to nag him – were still shouting intermittent phrases in his ear. He lay there until the last echo of their voices had faded. Roman Emperors never do this! Roman Emperors never do that! But how could they tell? They were not Roman Emperors. They were grey-haired women.

Serena and Julia, the two old bats abhorred in his childhood, had dared to come into this bedroom last night, pushing their way past the guards. They might even have come, thought Honorius with a shudder, to kill me. Orders would be given right away to Black Johannes – it must never happen again. They caught me alone and parroted Stilicho at me. They implored me to stay in Milan. And if Milan turns out to be a trap? Black Johannes thinks it very well might.

Johannes must have come and gone in the night, about his confidential duty, because the silken sheets of the bed had an odour of girl. I am a man now, thought Honorius, I am aware of myself, as Emperor. I remember almost nothing of the one last night, except that she was certainly not that first and most marvellous girl. I should remember all about her if she had been. Black Johannes says I must never have her again, lest she put a spell on me, get a hold over me. Some girls, the most marvellous ones, are like that so he tells me, and he must know.

Since I never saw the one last night, and hardly remember, Honorius debated with himself, do I need to confess her? No name, no face, only the silken sensation of her coming all too close, as in a wicked dream. When I confessed, after a clumsy fashion because I was bewildered, to that first girl, the marvellous one in Rome, the priest told me she was only a *succubus*, dreamed without evil intention, and if she came back to haunt me he would exorcise her. How little he knew. Some priests know much less than others. I told Black Johannes, he knew better, and now we have arranged it so that all the women he brings me in the dead of night are *succubi*. When he comes with her into the room he hardly wakes me. And if you don't see her, how can you name her?

With quite another part of his mind – a part as yet not clouded by daydream, drink, orgasm and theological surmise – the Emperor Honorius knew perfectly well that some real and actual girl was adroitly slipped into his bed from time to time by Johannes, a girl of flesh and blood who had been warned to hold her tongue. Done in broad daylight, all that must be confessed, but always it was done in the dark, with eyes shut throughout the act, as if in a dream. Honorius would have liked to be simple and honest. He would have liked to look into the girl's eyes. He was reaching the limits of his mental confusion.

The eye of God saw all. Even in the dark. Could God be cheated?

Honorius had sworn, and with good reason, that he would never sleep with Maria even though now she was big enough. Was he always to be beholden to Serena and Stilicho – tied to them for life? He had never wanted to marry their daughter Maria in the first place. Black Johannes saw the point, and had warned him. Maria was a political trap for him, but the girls who came in the night could do him no harm. He could never cast off Stilicho – the general whom the soldiers cheered louder than they did their Emperor. Was Stilicho's grandson to be Emperor in turn?

Impatiently, Honorius shouted, 'Johannes!'

Here he came, moving sideways through the curtains, prompt and fresh, his thick black hair cut in a fringe across the forehead, and heavy black eyebrows just underneath that gave to a face otherwise shaved smooth a look, in Honorius's opinion, of distinctive integrity. Truthful eyebrows, those.

A year earlier, Johannes had been appointed the Emperor's *lector* – his reader – the man who spared the imperial eyesight by reading out the gist of official documents. A post for an intelligent and honest man, since so much might hinge politically on what was emphasised and what omitted. Johannes had been born and bred in the palace, and that bland face, those heavy eyebrows, helped his reputation for veracity. But his study for years had been the Emperor Honorius himself, his whims, his weaknesses, for in the end what else mattered? Here in the closed world of the palace, if you had the ear of the Emperor you had everything.

As Johannes a year before started reading out the official reports, Honorius was at first distressed to find how much had been kept from him when Serena ruled his life. Johannes worked conscientiously until he was sure that the Emperor trusted him. After that it hardly mattered how much was edited. Since Johannes had the Emperor's confidence he also had control.

As soon as it was well understood that Johannes controlled the state papers that came under the Emperor's eyes, men of the greatest importance began paying court to him. He was appointed, confidentially, to a high rank in the *agentes in rebus* – the secret police. Except for an occasional dosage of unpalatable facts to add verisimilitude, Johannes these days told the Emperor only whe he might want to hear.

The next step in achieving domination had been to organise the Emperor's guilty dreams. His first success had been in Rome with Gilda – Johannes picking her out on the principle of choosing for the Emperor the woman who most appealed to himself. But after gratifying the Emperor – plucking his boyish maidenhead in a way that he could never forget – Gilda had refused the thick-eyebrowed slave. Johannes got rid of her. There were other women, less expert perhaps but less dangerous, who would hold their tongues and do it for money.

Johannes this morning was taking from the imperial cup-bearer – *pocillator*, an official who knew better when dealing with an imperial favourite than to stand on his rights – a gold cup of spiced wine against the chill of the morning. Wedged between full cup and warm wine jar was a stack of documents.

'The usual dreams?' Johannes murmured. Honorius frowned, as if the luscious encounters of the small hours were something of which it was improper to remind him.

'If I don't remember dreams, do I have to confess them?'

'Of course you don't.'

'I thought not.' Honorius put both hands around the wine goblet. Hands and lips sucked in warmth. He hated the cold and this helped so much. Wild dreams, warm wine. Honorius these days though never visibly tipsy was never quite sober. That was no sin, either, as Johannes had pointed out, and therefore need not be confessed. What was Our Lord's first miracle? Turning water into wine. What does St Paul tell us in his Epistle to Timothy? Use a little wine for the stomach's sake. And what else but that was Honorius doing?

'These are our urgent reports?'

Reports for the Emperor were written in purple ink and inserted in cylinders of purple parchment. Honorius looked at them blankly.

'But Johannes, if you have already gone through them, why need I? Give me the gist of them' After the warm wine, colour was flowing back into the young man's cheeks.

'In brief, then – there is almost universal acceptance, my lord, of the view you have yourself adopted, as to the unwisdom of staying in Milan. Who can ever forget how after the battle of Adrianople, one Roman Emperor was cut down and killed by the Goths? Or that another Emperor was captured and died in an iron cage –'

'– like a bird –' murmured Honorius, who had heard the story before.

'– as a prisoner of the Persians? God forbid that you, *imperator*, by accident or design, should ever fall into the hands of Alaric.'

Honorius could be agonisingly slow in making up his mind, but once he had done so, that was that. He raised his voice, so that the slaves beyond the curtain could hear. 'Bring me my travelling clothes!'

The Emperor's unexpected order sowed panic among the slaves of the wardrobe. The men in charge of the *a veste privata* or palace clothes, the *a veste forensi* or city clothes, the *a veste castrense* or undress army uniform and the *a veste triumphali* or full-dress parade uniform had all been behind the curtain with their garments impeccably pressed and brushed, in case today might be their turn.

The slave who looked after the clothes the Emperor was expected to wear to the gladiators – *a veste gladiatori* – knowing full well that Honorius never went to the gladiators, was dicing in the corner with the slave who looked after the travelling clothes. Honorius had only just arrived in Milan – he was not expected to go travelling, either.

Johannes had been a palace slave all his life. He knew what the panic scramble on the far side of that curtain signified. He cleared his throat loud enough for them to hear, and the fuss grew more desperately intense: delicious power! The travelling clothes were forthcoming.

Efficient Johannes had already stage-managed the Emperor's departure. At an unusual speed compared with the way these things usually went, the travelling caravan that was to take the Emperor out of Milan was set rolling. He was gone from both palace and city before Serena discovered it. Arles, near the mouth of the Rhône, was considered a safe destination. All the Emperor's needs on the journey had been catered for. His confessor was travelling, so were his tame birds. The confessor had some interesting new reading matter, a manuscript of *Contra Faustum Manichaeum*, in case the Emperor might like to be regaled, as sometimes he did, with difficult theology in superb Latin. He might understand only imperfectly, but then, this was a body of thought – theology – as some flatterer had once told him, that everyone, even the great Augustine, only understood imperfectly. The knowledge of God. Though what could be more important, for an Emperor?

The caravan lumbered off, hardly doing twenty miles a day. So long as they were not obstructed by rivers in flood, Alaric's cavalry could do a hundred. And behind them, the Visigoth wagons, floated by pine logs, were moving every day across one or more swollen rivers. Each day the enemy came closer.

Lucas had seen Honorius leave Milan. He was trying to enter the city gate with his sick master when the lumbering procession of horsemen, slave-borne litters, wagons, moved out and blocked the way. He was held up in a two-wheeled farm cart outside the western gate for more than an hour, while Claudian, stretched out on straw and covered with sacks and a cloak, moaned and sweated and gabbled verse in his fever.

Lucas had found Claudian in frozen Como transformed into a madman, voice stammering, eyes preternaturally bright, drunk not on wine but with excitement. At bedtime, Claudian had called Lucas to his room, to 'help him undress.' Apprehensive of what might come next, Lucas went in, knowing his master to be in a state of gabbling exaltation close to madness.

My body is myself, Lucas reminded himself as he lifted the bedroom latch. I am my own. Am I to have no property in myself? Or in my soul? – for when he enters my body against my will, he will also pollute my soul. If I refuse him, will he have me flogged? (But they all said, in Rome, that Claudius Claudianus had never yet sent a slave to be flogged.)

All naked before a roaring fire, the great poet was a pathetic sight. Bony legs sustained a little pot belly, chest was sunk under rounded shoulders, and however recently Claudian's hair had been dressed, it always looked unwashed. The warmth from that fire was all going up the chimney – light without heat – and the night was bitter. Claudian, having displayed himself, reached shivering for a woollen robe.

'You don't like me?' he said in a piteous voice. 'Does the sight of my body fill you with repugnance? I know I am not exactly beautiful. Few of us are. Even you, my dear Lucas, are too thin, too bony, for the canons of male beauty, which I take to be Greek: plump, like a little Greek.' He sighed. 'Though I always supposed until I saw your face just now that you felt something real for me. Some true emotion.' Claudian put a hand on Lucas's hand – his fingers were clammy. With a sad leer he tried to place the young man's hand on his own rump.

Lucas moved his hand away, and placed it instead on Claudian's forehead. Male flesh, no thrill. The man, though not admitting it, was in a fever.

'So it's my brow you love best – my laurel-crowned brow?' As he spoke, Claudian's teeth began to chatter. He brushed away Lucas's hand, and pulled the robe closer around himself.

'Listen, master. This is the beginning of a fever. Let me also wrap you in this blanket. Sit closer to the fire, while I go to the kitchen and fetch you something to drink. Hot wine with spices?'

'Hot milk,' mumbled Claudian. 'Mingled with honey for my throat. But not goats' milk.' His poetic fever had been overtaken by a real fever. From now on there was no more of his grotesque flirtatiousness – he did Lucas's bidding like a sick child. Later Claudian began to cough, and he coughed all night.

Next day, sunk in the bewilderment of fever, Claudian gabbled verse, and the verses were meaningless. Lucas from then on did everything for him, fed him by spoonfuls, washed his stinking body, sponged his forehead. Claudian particularly liked a cool sponge on his forehead. On the third day, meaning began to enter the verses, and Lucas as a sacred duty copied them down, only to find later on that they were all by other men, dead poets, Virgil, Horace, Lucretius, Propertius.

When the farm cart reached Milan the house steward called in a physician, who muttered about Fire and Water overcoming Earth and Air, and made Claudian take a nauseous dose to restore the balance. Lucas after watching Claudian and listening to him had formed his own opinion. This fever would last as long as the military crisis Stilicho had to face. Lucas was beginning to feel for Claudian a tenderness in no way amorous. My soul and his soul? Lucas wondered. Even though he is my master? But in his writing he disregards the soul, as if the body were enough for him, genitals, brain, the sound of his own eloquent voice.

The household slaves in Milan took over Claudian and his fever entirely, ousting Lucas as an interloper. Up in Como by mere neglect – said their accusing glances – Lucas had almost killed their good master.

After sorting out a pickle of notes that Claudian had brought back with him in the farm cart, Lucas had no more duties. He could no longer keep the thought of Gilda out of his mind. Two days after the Emperor Honorius ran away, their love affair began.

Gilda lay on the bed in the bare, hired, upper room, shaken body and soul, and for the first time in her life, by this patient but inexperienced lover whose hard cheekbone nudged uncomfortably as he slept against the soft muscle of her arm. Gilda eased Lucas's head down closer to her breast, and his lips moved of their own accord, poutingly, against her nipple. This was not erotic but tender, and tenderness was a feeling that, until they began to share this bed in this room, Gilda had hardly more than guessed at.

Lucas as he came out of his sleep still held her close, as though the physical differences between them had merged and melted. The act of love was over yet they were still one. Gilda was not Stridor's any more, nor was Lucas Claudian's. In this room, this bed, they belonged to one another.

The city of Milan that week was masterless – everyone knew the Visigoths were approaching – and they had spent almost every moment of the fearful time in this bed together. They had walked out of the world into this room. They had escaped.

The theatre was closed, and in the city market there was every day less to buy. Stridor had long since gone scurrying back to Rome, carrying her jewels, leaving Gilda's ear ringing with good advice, and Gilda as she watched him go had admitted to herself how much she hated him. On the street the poor people of Milan were much in evidence; with so many rich running away the city was theirs. A few big houses were looted, and when plunderers were arrested sometimes the mob rescued them. People were rapidly discovering that they had barbarian forbears, and practising to say 'Hail, Alaric!' in Gothic. It was a great time to fall in love.

Lucas once awake could not lie idle in bed for long. He was up and around the room, doing simple chores. Gilda, more indolent – in her profession she saved her energy for her performance – loved to see him moving about like this, with only a blanket across his bony shoulders. British, and hence in other people's eyes some kind of savage, impervious to the cold. But my own imaginary elder brother perhaps. I love him more than any brother. (She had never had a brother.) And I should be doing all that myself – pulling the blanket up to her chin – that tidying and fixing. Am I not his woman? Instead she stretched like a cat, smiling, because she understood that from sheer fun Lucas was being her slave.

'Hardly enough food,' he announced (her slave!), 'for today and tomorrow.'

'Money will always buy food.'

Lucas laughed. The idea of being rich enough not to care was new to him.

'Come back to bed,' commanded Gilda.

'What if the day after tomorrow we go hungry?'

Down in the street, poor people were standing in line to buy food. Those who had hoarded foodstuffs in good time were making fortunes.

'I am hungry now. But for something only you can feed me.' Gilda let the blanket slip from her as she reached for him. 'Come over here,' said her nakedness silently, 'let me gobble you up.'

Lucas, ignoring her stoically, was squinting inside the waterpot. 'Just a minute – there is no more water.' And when he saw her angry face – mock anger, actress anger, 'Gilda, darling – *mellita, amatrix, flamma* – afterwards you are always so thirsty.'

'Very well, then. Go down to the courtyard with your waterpot. Put your tunic on first, though. I am jealous of what the other girls might see. Be quick.'

Lucas had been gone for longer than anyone simply fetching water should have taken. Up from the street in his absence was coming a different kind of roar. Gilda was pushing anxious thoughts out of her mind, but with that noise from the street they began crowding in.

After this with Lucas, could she go back to other men – the men to whom Stridor pimped her? Even Stilicho, dear splendid Stilicho, was just now a little more than she could bear thinking of. That other kind of profitable love was a theatrical act of which she was sick. Lucas for some inexplicable reason shook her to ecstasy, and that was real.

Think happiness, she told herself fiercely – invent a wild possibility. Become suddenly rich. Buy Lucas and free him – free yourself. Go away together to a quiet place – a villa by the sea.

Having made some private arrangement with the barbarians to leave us alone? And another private word to the tax collector? And the secret police? (She had snubbed Black Johannes, rebuffed him, and was proud of it, but ever since she had been particularly fearful of the secret police). Stridor hobnobbed with certain *agentes in rebus*. Anyway, Stridor would never part with her, not if she offered him a million. You are not only, she told herself, Stridor's prize possession. You are his reason for living.

Gilda lay there, impatient for the sound of Lucas's feet on the stairs. Don't spoil it with Lucas, she warned herself, by growing angry. But she was angry. She was humiliated by the thought of her own helplessness. The world had moved closer, like the four walls of a prison.

Lucas came in not long after, with the filled waterpot on his shoulder. The bed where they had slept together was empty, a tangle of bedclothes. He saw that first, and felt a crazy pang at the thought that Gilda might be gone. But she was crouching in a corner, naked, squatting with her back to him, like an animal easing itself.

'What are you doing?'

'Never you mind.'

This was another thing. To prevent the child that she and Lucas might make together, using the method Stridor had taught her, was more than she could bear.

'You took long enough. What was the noise out there?'

'Flavius Stilicho is back from the mountains – the Alemanni are our allies!'

'What do I care about the Alemanni? Come back to bed.'

Lucas, in Gilda's arms, warming his cold feet on her cold feet, warming both of them, waiting for their love to ignite, went on talking.

'At first the people on the street were sure that the Visigoths had arrived. You should have heard the women screech. But the imperial guard are back, strutting like gamecocks, and with them thousands of mercenaries. Since you might be interested I went and asked – they are opening the theatre. In the distance I saw Stilicho, on his horse –'

'Do you suppose any of that interests me?' said Gilda.

'With a touch of your hand like that you could raise the dead,' he told her.

This is what matters, thought Gilda, to be filled with him.

Early next morning the first of the legions marched in from Gaul. Through the phantasmagoria of broken sleep the two of them heard a voluble, ragged cheering come up from the street, and the stamp of iron-shod boots. In that one night the common people of Milan all swung the other way. Stilicho was everyone's hero. Nobody complained any more at the way he had gambled with their lives. His gamble had come off. Some of the rich, when the news reached them on the imperial highway, turned round and came back. They too wanted to be on the winning side.

They will very likely come looking for Lucas tomorrow, thought Gilda, drenched in the sweet melancholy of her third successive ecstasy, unless he goes back to his master, Stilicho's great friend, of his own accord. A runaway slave. He will go if I tell him that he should, he has his own sense of duty, he is never quite a slave. Would I have him, otherwise – could I love him? I have been sanctified by all this. Because of Lucas, whatever happens, I shall never quite become a *meretrix* – a whore. She folded her hands complacently on the belly where Lucas's child might have been planted.

I shall let him go, Gilda decided, before I actually have to. A woman who lives a life like mine known when to let a man go. When he hears that the danger is over and they are opening the theatre, Stridor will come racing back. Stilicho may send for me. This is nearly over.

Part IV

1

Early on the Thursday before Good Friday – which in the 1155th year since the founding of Rome, AD 402, fell on the third of April – the hostile armies were close enough for the smoke from Alaric's cooking fires to be clearly visible, thin, blue and wavering, along the river valley where the Roman legions were grouping. That morning a picket of regular cavalry attached to XX Legion *Valeria Victrix*, not long marched in from Britain, went on patrol between the two armies, and caught a young Arian priest, cloaked and cowled, trying to pass into the Roman lines.

Luckily they were regulars. A pagan barbarian in the Roman service – a Hun for instance – might very likely have speared the young priest for the fun of it. Gothic mercenaries fighting for Rome – Arian in their faith – might with equal likelihood have turned the young priest around and told him to run back where he came from. But the cavalry attached to *Valeria Victrix* did the proper thing. A prisoner was a source of information and should be sent under armed escort to squadron headquarters. A trooper picked up the frightened young priest by the scruff of the neck, dropped the limp body across his saddle, like dead venison wrapped inside a loose cloak, and rode off, lance erect, head up, at the regulation collected trot.

At squadron headquarters, a military tribune from staff was ruling the roost. He had been sent to warn these new arrivals that there would be an army inspection. This military tribune, both clever and ambitious as they all are on the staff, was called Olympius. He was rough with the young Arian priest, dragging back the cowl that covered his face, tugging to pull him backwards until he staggered. Olympius would never have treated a Catholic priest like that. He was one of the new breed in the army of ostentatious Catholic Christians. Arians were heretics and he meant to show it.

A pale, womanish face emerged – blonde hair growing out of a cropped scalp raggedly. The Visigoths had not even known how to disguise their spy convincingly – hacked hair but no tonsure. In arrogant Latin, which hit Olympius like a smack in the face, the young priest exclaimed, 'I am here at some risk to myself to see Marcus Curtius, on the staff of General Flavius Stilicho. Take me to him at once.'

The military tribune, after being spoken to like that, was well aware that the troopers stood around were watching him. Could this be an opening move in a complex game of treachery? Marcus Curtius – who had deserted from Stilicho's staff to run for his life with the Emperor Honorius? Olympius spat over his shoulder, to mark publicly his opinion of Marcus Curtius.

'Who put you up to it?'

The young priest raised his beardless chin, imperiously. 'I demand to be taken to him. I insist upon it.'

'Marcus Curtius isn't here. My name is Olympius – military tribune. I am in fact equal to Marcus Curtius in rank, and I too am on the staff. Suppose you tell me what you would have told him.'

'Then I will see General Stilicho. He knows me well – he will vouch for me. You I have never seen before.'

For this piece of effrontery in the hearing of the common troopers, Olympius would dearly have liked to order the heretic priest a flogging. But a Christian, he reflected, is one who controls such impulses to his own ultimate advantage.

'Search him for weapons, you men.'

As the cavalrymen laid hands on Veleda's body, they began to look at one another with sheepish, incredulous smiles. The roughest of them had a hand on each breast when Veleda pulled herself away from him, and vomited. Incessant anxiety had stretched her nerves; she began to shudder.

Veleda was urged under the tent flap, a man with a drawn sword keeping a grip on her shoulder with his left hand. Not another would-be assassin? thought Stilicho with wry smile. When Veleda has last seen Stilicho, his Vandal hair though flecked with grey was yellow. His head since then had gone entirely white.

A wave of his hand ordered the armed soldier outside. Olympius standing officiously just by the tent flap was casting a shadow on the canvas, so Stilicho poked his head through and gave the military tribune too his marching orders. No eavesdroppers!

'Tell me anything you may know of what will come to pass in Alaric's camp tomorrow.'

'On a Good Friday? When you know that all we Goths are Arians?'

'A religious service? I see.'

'Early, soon after sunrise,' Veleda went on, 'because Arians fast for it –'

'Catholics too, so I believe,' he murmured, gently amused. She had become more than ever a Goth.

'On Good Friday, then, while they are still fasting, Alaric's entire army will have a service – a mass –'

'To bring them luck?' Stilicho asked with false innocence, as if making out that he did not quite understand the meaning of a mass. To mask his excitement he was teasing her. Did this big, smiling, white-haired man, wondered Veleda, as he tried to charm her, suppose she was still in awe of him – besotted? I have grown past Stilicho, she told herself. It was like coming of age.

'And everyone will attend – the whole army?' prompted Stilicho.

'Except sentries and orderlies and the sick parade. We Arians –'

Stilicho's laugh rang out so robustly that it might have been her own father laughing.

'What makes you laugh?' asked Veleda bleakly.

'Because such piety delights me. If only my own men here in the Roman army were as intent on their own religious duties. But they would rather fight than pray.'

Tomorrow, at daybreak, he was thinking, and all Alaric's Visigoths on their knees!

'Last night, when Alaric was drinking the last of the October beer with his womenfolk, I overheard him boasting –' The sour, malty taste of Visigoth homebrewed rose in her mouth as she spoke, and Veleda stopped short. Might not her father have said, of a time like this, that though not lying, she had no right to betray?

'Alaric boasting,' prompted Stilicho. 'Yes, I know him. He does boast, doesn't he? Quite a man, though – larger than life. How do you get on with him? I get on well, myself – you can believe what he says. Then when you had heard what he had to say, you dressed up as a priest, and came through the lines to warn me. Isn't that it?'

Veleda's voice rose to a screech. 'They will kill you – every one of you. Alaric says he outnumbers the Romans three to one. And Visigoths always mean what they say.'

'If he says three to one he is not far wrong,' answered Stilicho cheerfully. She had let him drag that one all-important fact out of her, and now she began to shiver – the onset of hysteria.

At her loud screech, the head and shoulders of Olympius, who had been loitering self-importantly as close to the general's tent as he dare, pushed back the flap. He had no business to be hanging around, he had been told to go away, but at such a moment, decided Stilicho, one military tribune was as good as another.

'Call my surgeon, will you?'

Olympius who had quite expected to make a name for himself by saving the general from a would-be murderess hesitated in surprise.

'The Princess Veleda is to receive every attention due to her rank, but you are not to let her out of your sight.' The title 'princess' brought an instant change in Olympius's demeanour. 'When she is a little more herself – but waste no time, do you hear? – escort her yourself to Marcus Curtius, keeping her all the time under observation. She is not to speak to anyone, except Marcus Curtius. When you leave her with him, give Marcus Curtius my warm regards. You will find him with the Emperor, behind the walls of Asti.'

I am being asked to take this Princess to safety at Asti – on the eve of battle? said the look of histrionic disappointment on Olympius's face. That disappointed look has been put on for my benefit, thought Stilicho. And I have a hundred other things to do, besides consoling an ambitious military tribune.

Olympius was looking at Veleda more respectfully, and wishing he had treated her better. Stilicho left the pair of them, and went out with relief into the moist spring air, the tepid Ligurian sunshine. Horsemen were grooming their chargers as if for a parade. Legionaries squatting beside their improvised bivouacs – a cloak on a taut string, and a blanket under – were busy putting an edge on their swords with whetstones that went to and fro, whimpering.

That brave and silly child with the cropped hair had been right. The odds against him were ridiculously disproportionate. Yet my intimate daemon – my luck – Stilicho told himself, insists that I should fight it out. I sought this battle, and here it is. I planned all this last autumn in Rome, unaware that the legions I could call on for use against Alaric are no longer what they were, Dwindled. Changed for the worse. Well, I must make the best of them.

A Roman legion should have numbered six thousand men or more, but none ever did. You would be lucky these days with a nominal roll of two thousand. Stilicho had begun to walk his charger steadily along the third side of the vast hollow square formed by drawing up his army on parade. On the right, at attention, stood XX *Valeria Victrix*, named *Valeria* from that tract of barren land in Britain between Tyne and Forth. Time was when we fought a lively campaign across Valeria, the Twentieth and I, thought Stilicho, against the painted Scots. More of them, in those days, and they were better men.

XX *Valeria Victrix* had gone downhill. The legionaries were parading this afternoon in three ranks, not six. Only the front rank was equipped in traditional legionary fashion, with helmet, breastplate, shield, javelin, stabbing sword. In the second and third ranks, the men of XX *Valeria Victrix* wore swords but no armour, and they were carrying heavy bows, meant to outrange the barbarian enemy's mounted archers. Their job now was to protect the single armoured front rank from cavalry charges. Barbarian horsemen dominated the battlefield, and since the legions under the Emperor Valens had been defeated by Gothic cavalry, Rome had gone on the defensive.

They call that a legion? Stilicho asked himself, as he leaned from the saddle to speak to a centurion he might very likely have known in the old days, when serving against the Scots.

'I know you, don't I?'

'Yes, *dux*, the time when we –'

'Was there enough food on the march?'

'Yes, *dux*. Ample rations at every halt.' The centurion as he answered looked sternly to his front, impeccably an old-style legionary on parade.

'In my campaign against the Scots, I rather believe.'

'Yes, *dux*, when we –' The old soldier's harsh though immobile face was melting.

'Yes, old comrade – how well I remember.'

Stilicho rode on. A good guess like that did no harm. There used to be more faces like that – tough, regimental, impersonal, self-effacing. But take a look at the younger faces in the ranks, plump, discontented. How it upset them to leave their well-established camp at Chester, with its little comforts and little rackets, and make the long route march south! XX *Valeria Victrix*, like so much else that flourished in its day, had gone to seed. Or is it merely, Stilicho asked himself, as he turned his charger's head away from those meagre lines of infantry, that I am getting old?

The big-boned mare under him whinnied as Stilicho's knees forced her closer to the irregular cavalry, fur-clad, wild-looking and apt to disobey. Plenty of cavalry on this parade, thought Stilicho. Enough I dare say for two simultaneous flank attacks, which if pushed hard enough might buckle Alaric's undisciplined centre. Worth trying? On a battlefield, the Visigoths had never been much good at keeping formation.

As Stilicho walked his nervous mare closer, the long block of cavalry began to shuffle and mutter among themselves, some even brandishing their weapons as if in welcome. Mercenary irregulars, their discipline never quite up to the mark. Good at heart, though this waving of weapons was going too far. The first contingent he rode slowly past, his presence daunting them, were Goths – blue eyes set in whiskery blonde faces. Did it concern them that they would soon be fighting their kinsfolk? Their faces gave nothing away, but in battle their heart and soul might not be in it.

When Stilicho walked his charger by the Alemanni, his newest recruits, they gave him an outright undisciplined cheer. They had been drinking Roman wine. They were ready to fight anyone whatever, and the sooner the better. Stilicho did his best not to smile.

From over to windward drifted an acrid stench from Rome's least civilised barbarian recruits, fur-capped, scar-cheeked Huns. They spoke no Latin, they had no sentimental links with the enemy. Those then are the men, thought Stilicho, for my first attack – the ones I shall depend on to knock Alaric off balance. And what a good bodyguard the best of those Huns might make – if only I could learn to put up with the smell! The Huns stink, they speak no Latin and everyone detests them. In consequence, none of my enemies at court could tamper with them. All other soldiers on this parade they despise. I shall get Saulus their commander to post some of his men, tomorrow, when the battle begins, behind those disreputable legions, with orders to stick a lance through the first legionary who turns and tries to run. They will do it, too.

Next came a regiment of mounted archers, mud-splashed, disheartened. They had made forced marches day and night, from Gaul. Stilicho's voice, unexpectedly bellowing high, was enough to split eardrums.

'*What are those Godforsaken scarecrows?*'

Chargers not groomed?

Mud on parade?

The mounted archers' commander rode forward with a hangdog air. He knew what was coming. Stilicho had beckoned him much closer, so that the terms of his rebuke would not be overheard, but its ferocity could be measured by the way the delinquent officer blenched.

Stilicho, when that part of it was over, raised his voice so that all could hear what came next. What exactly, he now wanted to know, was that outlandish banner the mounted archers were flaunting?

'The pennon by means of which my archers judge wind deflection.' Plummily the answer filled the commander's mouth.

'No unit under my command flies Draco!' exclaimed Stilicho to all the army, as if explaining a self-evident truth to the weak-minded. 'You know the reason? You don't? Because in the confusion of battle they might well find themselves rallying to some other unit which also flies Draco. And that, since we are fighting Visigoths, who also fly Draco, might be an enemy unit. Is that clear to you? It is? It should be. Let then fly the *labarum*. You hear? The *labarum*. See it done. See that your banner bearers know. That goes for all the army. The *labarum* –'

Stilicho wondered if his vociferous display of anger had perhaps been overdone, but the chance had been too good to miss. The *labarum*! he thought, with a private smile. The mystic Christian symbol under which Constantine the Great had fought – a sop for all the priests great and small who nowadays clustered around Honorius. They too would have their spies here, they too would have heard.

Alaric's much larger though less organised army was only half an hour's gallop away, a thickening cloud of smoke and dust northward across the alluvial plain. With the spring sun at a low angle one could even catch from time to time a glittering flash from their weapons or armour. Constantine fought under the *labarum* and won by a miracle, thought Stilicho derisively. And a miracle is all I need. Across his falsely-angry face came a more affable look.

'I will now address the men.'

Only the front rank of those men, on horseback or on foot, were likely to catch what their general might have to say. But those who heard would pass it on. In the minds of that decisive handful Flavius Stilicho intended to fix an idea so simple – so acceptable to the troops – that it would spread through the army like a passionate conviction.

'King—Alaric—of—the—Visigoths—has—made—one—big—mistake!'

Stilicho beat out his words slowly, one by one, in an enormous voice. The legionaries were no longer shuffling. They were all listening to that bell-metal voice of his, above the faint jingle of horse-harness.

'He travelled with the wagons you will find over there.' Stilicho pointed a contemptuous hand towards the enemy. Hundreds of front-rank heads turned as he pointed. And turned back his way as Stilicho slowly let fall his arm. He had them in the palm of his hand. 'Those wagons will be the death of Alaric.'

In Rome's great centuries, Stilicho told himself, an appeal

like this on the eve of battle would have been patriotic. What a speech Claudian could have written for such an occasion – in hexameters if need be! But Roman virtue no longer signified. Only two things could move such men as these – cupidity and lust. Very well then – he groped around in his mind and found the right words.

'Listen. In those wagons are his womenfolk – more Gothic virgins than Hercules could deflower.' A titter went down the line. Gothic chastity was a stock joke. They are listening on tiptoe, I have them, thought Stilicho, a little disgusted with himself.

'Gothic virgins and even more. His treasure. Alaric has kindly fetched all the Visigoth treasure here to Pollentia. Some of the plunder from Greece, where, you remember, we trounced him before. He got away from the battlefield with his treasure last time. Are you going to let him get away with it again?' Gilda would have known, he though ruefully, how to put that one across better. But then her audiences aren't standing in long straight lines under discipline. Let's hope I have at least stuck the idea in their heads.

'Over there, I say, are Alaric's wagons. His women. His treasure. And to dip your fingers in that sweetness you have only to defeat his army.'

Stilicho broke off abruptly – soldiers liked short speeches, and so did he. Now that the end had come, there were ragged cheers, and Stilicho noted carefully where they came from. The Huns cheered him with wild ululating cries, though having no Latin they could not have understood one syllable. The Goths – good-hearted Teutons – cheered a man they admired, a Vandal in the service of Rome. They hadn't grasped much of the speech, either. They are not wholehearted in this campaign, he decided, but they will fight as they are ordered. But the legionaries – the men who mattered, whose cupidity was being tempted – were particularly slow off the mark. That hooray was being dragged out of them only by dread of their centurions. The legionaries are not the men they once were, but then, ruminated Stilicho, what about yourself?

One day you are in the prime of life, the Emperor your nephew and Gilda as your mistress. A little while later, your hair turns white, and you talk to a girl like that Gothic princess as if you were her father. Those infantry faces were truculent, as if they knew very well that everything worth having, from imperial taxation to the imperial purple itself, dangled on the point of a sword.

The army with which I now find fault has been my life, reflected Stilicho, as he rode back with slow dignity to rejoin his staff, keeping everyone waiting – ceremonial at times is serviceable. And was I wrong? No one can relive his own life. The Christian church claims to be one great power in the civilised world. I, like Claudian, have always seen the Roman army as the other. And a power more actual, because an army operates according to the circumstances of the everyday world – human reason expressed in discipline, control as a function of force. There on the faces of my legionaries, as if military virtue is a religion that has failed, are the marks of corruption.

That is what comes of trying to live up to Claudian's high poetic idea of me, thought Stilicho, amused at his own grim joke. Who but he would choose a Vandal assimilated to Rome, to exemplify Roman virtue? Am I real or Claudian's invention? Is Claudian perhaps his own invention? Will I live except through him?

He was trotting his chestnut mare towards that large and conspicuous pavilion in the centre of the Roman camp where his banner was flying at the flagpole. Behind his parade-ground face, and hardly aware of his surroundings, Stilicho had begun to brood. Recognising his frame of mind, aides-de-camp kept their distance. Tomorrow's battle had begun to form a valid pattern in the mind's eye of the general.

He told off an aide-de-camp to fetch the Hun commander to his tent. Saulus was a small and wrinkled man, with flattened nose, Tartar eyes and the characteristic scarred cheek of a Hun. On the day of his birth a male Hun, before he put lips to his mother's milk, was marked across one cheek with a hot iron. Male children who survived that branding were Hun warriors, and Saulus himself had been particularly disfigured by the birthmark. Saulus had hired his personal following for the time being into the Roman service. Huns were heathen, they believed in a cruel magic. They were not exactly broken to Roman discipline, and never would be, but they had learned to now to respect Stilicho, and they would follow Saulus anywhere.

*

A heavy mist across the plain of Pollentia early on Good Friday morning was a piece of luck for Stilicho.

The Visigoth host were kneeling by the thousand, a vast concourse of dismounted warriors, growing more distinct as the Romans came closer through the mist, their stacked lances tufted here and there against the dawn sky. The Visigoth rank and file formed a semi-circle around their, priest, as if in an open-air theatre, but that was to their advantage, since a half-moon was also their battle-formation. Beyond the lines of men, at the wagons, stood a crowd of women with scarfed heads. The Arian bishop had begun to intone from the gospel of St John.

'My peace I give unto you, not as the world giveth I give unto you. Let not your heart be troubled, neither let it be afraid.'

The kneeling men might hear no more than the ghost of a text drifting over their heads on the April air, but this vast congregation knew the words by heart. Like the preliminary shudder of a great gale, a multitude of uplifted voices began to mutter the first words of the response, when out of the mist broke a black cloud of riders, spewing arrows: Saulus, heading the Hun cavalry, their bows twanging incessantly, their lances lowered.

As the fur-capped, unwashed men with scarred Asian faces galloped down on the worshippers, a tatter of screams rose up from those women near the ring of wagons. They turned and ran for cover. Their screams and the stamp of Hunnish hooves drowned out the priest's voice.

Men lurched upwards from their knees and ran towards the stacks of lances scattered here and there amid the congregation like wheat stooks in a field. The quickest had already reached their tethered chargers, spear in hand, and were vaulting into the saddle, willing to fight, but not sure which way to turn. On Alaric's left wing, where Saulus and his men had ridden out of the mist to strike their cynical blow, the Visigoth host was in disorder.

In this confusion, Alaric showed himself a King.

Calm on horseback, making himself conspicuous, uttering brief, clear, loud orders amid the blizzard of arrows, he sent word to his brigadiers in the Visigoth centre and on the far flank. He set himself to sort out the disorder on the flank the

Huns had struck. No one would have supposed from Alaric's sanguine demeanour that this was first blow in a battle that could win or lose him Rome.

The Twentieth Legion, *Valeria Victrix*, with her sister legions to right and left, were advancing in a long triple line. They had broken through the mist at marching place, and were moving implacably to challenge Alaric's intact centre, They had been drawn up in battle order since the first glimmer of light, and were glad to be on the move. The veteran legionaries went onwards like men going to a rendezvous. The many untried soldiers in the ranks felt hollow as they braced themselves for their first glimpse of lowered lances. They had heard frightening things of Visigoth cavalry.

For most of the Twentieth, to risk their lives like this, cold-bloodedly, against an enemy that outnumbered them, was a moral shock. They had lived an easy life in their cantonments on the river Dee, with an occasional punitive foray, always a walkover, against the impudent Welsh, and at the worst some garrison service up in the cold drizzle along Hadrian's Wall. Inside their iron-shod boots their feet were still sore after their long march south. They would be buying back this morning, perhaps with their lives, the great privileges they had hitherto enjoyed as soldiers.

As the trumpet blew, halting them to await enemy cavalry – luring the Visigoths into a charge – one or two of the nervous ones glanced back over their shoulders the way they had come. Pickets were walking up behind them, sinister fur-capped riders on plodding ponies, lance lowered, their typical stink wafting ahead of them. Huns! XX *Valeria Victrix* was being herded into line by barbarians who did not even speak Latin!

'Virgins for you in those wagons, lads!' shouted an old centurion, who after twenty-five years' service was still in high spirits at being recognised yesterday by his general. Virgins somewhere up in front, but Huns at their back, and other lancers were now looming up in front of them, Visigoth chargers with long and untrimmed mane and tail, riders with long moustaches, long sharp lances, moving towards the legions at the walk, but not for much longer. They began to bob up and down through the remnants of mist as they broke into a trot.

Three bowshots from the advancing enemy the legionaries

were brought to a halt. Stilicho out in front, on horseback, could not help noticing as they halted that their triple line was crooked as a dog's hind leg. Where the line bent it might break. But the centurions were already moving along, dressing their men into place with painful flicks of the vine-root. The front line came straight quicker than he ever expected, the second and third lines following suit. At the sight of the commander-in-chief, out in front and sharing their danger, even the malcontents felt better.

To right and left was a hammering of hooves. Stilicho's irregular cavalry would by this time be engaging Alaric on both flanks. After their surprise attack, the Huns on the left were keeping up the pressure, thrusting and pig-sticking, work they would relish. On the other flank the Roman heavy cavalry, mostly Gothic mercenaries, had conscientiously borne down on their kinsmen, but without wild enthusiasm. Stilicho, listening intently, heard them go from walk to trot, through a canter to the brief gallop of their final onset. They had at least charged home, even if in the noise made by their brief charge Stilicho could detect no fillip of reckless gallantry.

Both Alaric's flanks were under pressure, and the squeeze was already visibly confusing the Visigoth centre. As they approached closer to the stationary legions, the horsemen of the centre were shoving, jostling, overlapping. At every pace forward they grew less like organised cavalry and more like a barbarian horde. Battlefield tactics, thought Stilicho, have done for us what they could. Now only one question remains. Will the Roman infantry hold?

Stilicho had halted his legions on the near side of a shallow ditch running across the plain, where the foremost Visigoth horse might stumble as they charged. On an order from their brigadier the bleak triple-line of foot soldiers plodded fifty yards closer to the ditch, as if making a direct challenge. This time as they came to a halt, their dressing was better. They could not yet be called hot-blooded, but their morale was picking up. Some of them even look cocky, thought Stilicho. I can trust them at least to drive back Alaric's first charge. And by then their blood may be up.

To the brigadier at his elbow – an experienced but unimaginative military tribune who would soon take over direct command here – Stilicho spoke in a matter-of-fact voice as if they were out together for a day's peacetime manoeuvres.

'Our front line should stand the first onset. When the Visigoth cavalry break off – you know how Goths fight, touch and go – the front line of legionaries but only the front line will charge them as they retreat. A sharp charge but a short one. Disengage in good order. Retire at discretion, and reform into line, as they are now. Each Visigoth onset as it arrives thereafter will be met before it can be pressed home by just such a short hard charge. After the first line is used up – as it soon will be – the second line will charge. As the second line wears down, the third –' (and after the third, thought Stilicho, hearing his own words ring hollowly in his ears, the gods come to our aid, for Rome has no more legions).

'Charge, *dux*?' repeated the brigadier, a literal-minded man who wondered if he had heard correctly. Offensive action by infantry against cavalry? But foot soldiers in recent years had never been used like that. 'The third line too?' The army's duds were hidden back there, in the third line.

'The third line have swords, don't they?' said Stilicho, his impatience breaking through. Alaric's centre was already massively on the move towards them. 'A chance to blood them – eh?'

Since their shameful defeat at Adrianople, twenty-four years before, Roman infantrymen, grown accustomed otherwise to easy victories over badly-armed tribesmen, had developed a respect for Gothic cavalry which at times amounted to fear. At Adrianople the Goths had boxed in the best legions of the Roman Empire, and systematically massacred them, killing the Emperor Valens. The lancer on horseback had ever since been considered the lord of the battlefield.

Today is their chance to learn another way of war, thought Stilicho, hardening his heart. Those who don't learn quickly enough will die. Duck under the lance-point, hamstring the charger. Stab the unsteady rider in the armpit so that his lungs fill with blood, drag him down. While your comrades, the archers, cover you overhead with flights of arrows. As Alaric's cavalry charge time after time, wear them down. What other option do they have, these legionaries, with my Huns stalking up behind them, except learning quickly to be heroes?

Flavius Stilicho on the night before battle had slept well, though he had opened his eyes in the small hours to find his old wounds aching as reminders. His mind was joyfully lucid: this was the day he had been born for. The shape of the battle – its probabilities and eventualities – had been as clear as daylight in his mind's eye before the first lance was lowered.

But now, with fighting begun all along the line, something in his plan was going amiss. Pressure from the left flank on the Visigoth centre was not being kept up. The Visigoth riders as they massed for their charge had begun to regain formation. Saulus's Huns must be in trouble.

As Stilicho watched the shrinking space between the armies, a splendid charger went caterwise, riderless – it had been his own gift to Saulus. A groom pelted after, trying the grab the trailing bridle. Saulus had been knocked out.

Beneath the thickening hail of arrows, as if every Visigoth archer were using him as a living target, Flavius Stilicho spurred his chestnut mare diagonally across no-man's-land to rally the leaderless Huns. The legionaries as they turned their heads to watch him thought he had gone mad.

Between a Hun chief and his men the bond was personal. Saulus's followers, disheartened, had begun wheeling away, drawing off. The chief they would follow everywhere had been knocked out of the saddle, stone dead. A shouted order to hold their ground, especially in Latin, would have left them cold, but their eyes were caught by Stilicho's wild courage as he rode towards them. When this old Roman general whom they knew for Saulus's friend, a fringe of white hair apparent under the rim of his helmet, came hurtling towards them on his big-boned chestnut mare, the Huns grouped themselves around him like bees round a Queen. Stilicho found himself out in front of them, breathing in their friendly stench, impelled onwards by bloodcurdling, ululating war cries in a barbaric Asian tongue, actually leading their next charge.

But this is absurd, Stilicho told himself with a blissful smile, as rhythmically between his knees the whinnying mare moved up from her trot to a long canter, and his jewel-hilted general's sword, sharp but never used in combat, protruded heavy and threatening in the same line as his outstretched arm. What right have I to be here and enjoying it? I am Consul, commander-in-chief, father-in-law to the Emperor, and here I am, heading a cavalry charge.

For the first time since word came of Alaric's invasion, Stilicho was entirely happy. No more decisions, all plain fighting. The battle had anyway gone from his personal control, and from Alaric's too. How Alaric himself, he thought, would like to be where I am now!

Everything on the battlefield depended hereafter on the outcome of one man with his weapon encountering another. The key to victory lay with that withering line of infantrymen at the centre, as their mounted Visigoth antagonists, confused, to their own surprise driven back, turned their chargers out of range and rode down on them yet again, incredulous that a Gothic charge should have been broken by men on foot. If the legions hold their ground – if they dare to push back – then, thought Stilicho, victory might tilt our way. If they break and run it is all up with Rome.

Though now, this moment, with my Huns closing up at the gallop, what difference does it make? What does anything matter?

Stilicho, his big horse pulling him out in front, was screwing up his ageing eyes against the morning light, picking out one enemy face for his own – a target once they came in striking distance to receive a Roman salute from the edge of his sword. And if that young man I have chosen is quicker – sticks his point in first? The thought of death, exactly as he prepared to make his own sword stroke, filled Stilicho with an unanticipated joy. With a yell on his lips which echoed the Hunnish warcry, Stilicho led his frenzied men smack into the line of faces, and turning adroitly in the saddle thrust with his sword. The blow he had planned struck home, and after came cut and thrust – with his own skill dominating, a delicious bloody madness.

The general came out of the prolonged melee without a scratch, though covered with blood from the wounds of other men, some his victims. Death, Stilicho reminded himself, as his Huns, cleverly disengaging, wheeled in good order at his signal and trotted clear – death anywhere but here on the field of honour is not a glory but a humiliation. Today I have learnt something. No doubt that clever fellow Claudian knew it all along. Death creeps up on one, shamefully, in the murk of night at Gilda's doorway. Or by fever. Or as one bows the neck, kneeling to an executioner's sword. Death, just now, in action, would have been apotheosis.

The wave of approval – a battlefield promotion and no words spoken – towards Saulus's second-in-command, an impenetrable man with a raw sword slash across his branded cheek, and the Huns had a new leader. They were in high heart, and already grouping, spontaneously, for yet another charge. Stilicho on his lathered chestnut, hardly conscious of the fresh bloodstains that disfigured him, went about his proper business at last, and began to be severe with himself for having been tempted to join in what, had it failed, would have been counted blind folly.

His legions at the centre were still hotly engaged. They were doing better, though, than hold their ground. They charged hard with sword uplifted, and charged again, a reiterated butchery, until legionaries had their tongues hanging out, from thirst, exhaustion, bloodlust, stifled fear. The centre of the battlefield was piled high with dead soldiers from both sides, and the carcasses of horses. The line of that shallow ditch could be exactly traced where horse after horse had stumbled.

Yet the Visigoth cavalry still came on, for one more time, though Stilicho judged that they were losing heart. The second line of legionaries – with no body armour – were engaging like veterans. From the corner of his eye Stilicho saw one legionary bowman, during a lull in the fighting, kneel down, drag a breastplate from a nearby corpse, hurriedly buckle it on. Then raise his own sword with both hands, rather clumsily, and run forward.

Into battle along the worst-hit part of the front was coming the third line, their arrows spent, their comrades dead, their seldom-used swords drawn and shining. Rome's last throw. They charged home, they broke off in good order, copying the men ahead of them who by now were dead. The single frail line of foot soldiers, when enemy horsemen drew off, went back, formed up, and waited. There were not so many of them left, but they were good for one more charge.

King Alaric was a general of experience. As his weary horsemen returned to form line once again, and lose yet more comrades in another charge against that thin fence of cold steel, he reminded himself that unlike the Romans he was not here at Pollentia to fight to the last man. So long as the Visigoths as a people kept their army intact they would have a second chance. Alaric decided to sacrifice his wagons – they would delay the oncoming Romans and perhaps save his womenfolk. He would fight a delaying action, and then move faster than an ox-wagon off this battlefield.

Alaric sent instant word to the women that they were to quit what the Visigoths in their own language called their *carrago* – those wagons, laagered in concentric circles behind the army like a little fortress. Abandon the wagons, take the spare horses, ride for their lives down the valley of the Po. The old men and boys who had guarded the *carrago* were to be their escort. They should ride fast out of Stilicho's reach.

All the Visigoth women did what they were told except Alaric's own family, the frizzy-haired, opinionated minority who lived in the wagons grouped around the treasure. They had the long-standing habit of disagreeing with their lord and master. While the common women – the cowards! – fled, they stayed on.

The discipline holding Alaric's army together was not military so much as tribal, traditional. Visigoths might take it into their heads one day to hoist some such victorious fighter as Alaric over their heads on a shield, and announce him as their new king. In a combat that was clearly heroic they were willing to die around him one by one, as his companions. But the Visigoths as a people had come to Italy to enrich themselves, not to fight pitched battles. They were here to better themselves. They had never bargained on getting themselves chopped into dog's meat by foot soldiers.

Stilicho, as King Alaric decided on retreat, was pondering a similar question. At the price being paid, could he afford to win?

Here on Good Friday at Pollentia he was slowly defeating Alaric by sacrificing the lives of his own legionaries. But those were the legionaries who held the menaced imperial frontiers. There were not many of them, they were all Rome had. When his enemies at the court heard how the battle had gone they could accuse him of throwing them away, and they would not be far wrong. If this blood-letting went on to the bitter end the battle of Pollentia might be won, but the Empire lost.

Flavius Stilicho could see that some of the mauled Visigoth cavalry were pulling out of the shambles, and had begun to drift away over the edge of the battlefield, across the skyline, like hurt animals. The disheartened cavalry were following closely in the tracks of a multitude of women on horseback, two to a horse, with streaming hair and abominable seats in the saddle, some with children in their arms.

He had a trumpeter sound for the regrouping of his own cavalry, making it easier for the mounted Visigoths to escape – and a hint to foxy-faced Alaric, if he wished to take it. A barbarian enemy can be defeated only by being destroyed, and how can you destroy a whole people, especially when you recruit your own cavalry from among their cousins?

Alaric must know what is in my mind, thought Stilicho, as I sit here astride my charger, and watch the chaos of the battlefield. He has already sent away many of his womenfolk. Some of his men are losing heart. King Alaric, if I read his mind, would dearly like to cut his losses. By calling back my own cavalry I have tacitly signalled that I will let him go. They will blame me for it. Later, at court, there may be a price to pay. But for Rome, any price I am made to pay will be less than that of the utter destruction of her legions.

As the late afternoon sun eased its way lower down the sky, making the shadows longer and the firmament lurid, Alaric, as if accepting Stilicho's offer, sent one mounted unit after another off the battlefield, cowed, tired, some of them still showing a kind of defiant shame in their demeanour, but all in passable order. For the Visigoths this battle was becoming one vast rearguard action. Nor shall I try, Stilicho told himself, to chase Alaric on horses worn out by charge after charge. I know him of old. Alaric will find a clever way to turn and maul me. He is well aware that he has been thrown back by a force that he greatly outnumbers. He knows I have no reserves – no fresh cavalry that I might order up to attack and pursue. But the Romans stay in possession of the field. We did not annihilate them. We never could. This, though, is our victory.

Alaric had hardened his heart and sacrificed his treasure. To withdraw at the pace of those heavily-laden wagons? Impossible.

On the other hand, he well knew that nothing on earth – not even Stilicho and his staff officers blocking the way with their drawn swords – would hold back those Roman legionaries from plunder. They would stick fast at the treasure wagons until the last of his own men got away.

By the time the sinking sun touched the misty horizon to become huge and red, haggard survivors from the triple line of legions were tossing handfuls of gold coins in the air, and dragging Visigoth noblewomen this way and that, one man to each heel, and skirts pulled over her head.

In the description of the battle that he wrote afterwards – though he himself was a long way off, that Good Friday, in Milan, and had to work from hearsay – Claudian gives an account of Alaric's treasure: heaps of gold and silver coin, massive bowls in precious metals from Argos, chryselephantine statues from Corinth. He worked no doubt from the official record of the plunder. There was a great deal of it.

One trophy the soldiers came across, which in their simple-hearted way they looked upon as an insult – a personal affront – was the purple robe which had been stripped from the cross-eyed Emperor Valens when he and two-thirds of his army fell to Gothic cavalry at Adrianople. Iron shackles, wrote Claudian, were struck off the ankles of the hostages that Alaric had taken prisoner on his way here – hostages with whose lives he would have bargained had Stilicho ever pinned him in a corner. When freed they wept for joy.

Nothing though was written about the rapes. As they were bundled about from one avid, blood-bespattered soldier to the next, the Visigoth women were paying with screams and brutal raptures for having been on the losing side. Nor did Claudian mention Stilicho's one last unpopular action, which from that day on lost him for ever the love of what remained of XX *Valeria Victrix*.

Legally, as spoils of war, the plunder from Alaric's wagons was the Emperor's. An army was a costly toy; after such a campaign as this, the military treasury would be drained dry. Yesterday, on parade, Stilicho might have let his men suppose that the Visigoth treasure would be theirs for the taking. But he had not actually promised they could keep it. And the law said otherwise.

Worn out by violent action and debauch, the infantrymen came back from the wagons smiling broadly, like threshers after a day of toil, staggering under leather sacks of coin as heavy as wheat sacks, with jewelled rings all the way up to their fingernails, and precious necklaces hung by the half-dozen around the throat. The looters walked straight into a ring of Hunnish pickets.

Large, barbaric carpets – the fringed carpets with which the Visigoth women floored their wagons – had been stretched on the ground at the picket line as a place to dump the rifled treasure. Each single valuable object that the soldiers had filched was taken from them. Clerks to the military praetor, non-combatants, were kept feverishly busy, listing and valuing the precious objects piled on the carpets. No-one got through that network of pickets with so much as a single gold coin hidden under his tongue. By the time night fell, the legions hated the Huns, and detested Stilicho too.

Immensely rich for a few glorious minutes, and physically satiated, the legionaries went off in gloom, empty-handed. The law had been observed, the Emperor reimbursed. They should have known what would happen. In the old days, thought Stilicho, still on horseback, watching from a distance as by the light of guttering pitch pine torches the laggards one by one were stripped and sent away, a shrug and perhaps even a knowing laugh would have been the end of it. Legionaries nowadays were resentful because they were money-minded. In the old days they never had been.

They had won for him – for Rome – a necessary victory. But who grows fat on victory, except the birds of prey, already beginning to flop and hover across the darkening battlefield? To win the battle of Pollentia, the frontiers had been stripped of their defenders. And victory could not bring back the dead.

'A victory?' reiterated Honorius, tipsily.

Victory was in its own way good news – a proof of God's blessing. And no need to scurry along highroads any more – he was safe! Was it true, though? The Emperor's mind was just then in a more-than-usual muddle. He had been snatched from feeding his cage birds, to be told the news. The birds knew him and were grateful – much more sincere than courtiers. If you fed the birds at proper times they got to know you. They pecked their corn and glanced their thanks, and hopped away without a word. No sitting on a dais to listen to their flattery, and then racking one's brains for a reply. Birds never haunted your dreams with their insistent nagging voices. They were content simply to be beautiful.

The God who watched over the fall of a sparrow watches over them. And over me too, thought Honorius, obscurely comforted. As for war – did not war put at nought the very words of Jesus Christ? He who takes up the sword shall perish by the sword? What was all this about a victory? On his dais, the Emperor hiccoughed.

Honorius had never cared much for soldiers – men who were harsh even when trying to speak to you civilly. As they looked your way soldiers never quite hid their silent accusation that as Emperor you were hardly ever brave enough. The soldier who had brought news of victory was, however, a better type. In his obeisance he had gone right down flat, as everyone should in the Emperor's presence.

He also knew the right way to speak to an Emperor who had just been feeding his friends the birds, and so felt taken by surprise. No shocks. From his turn of phrase – regretting the bloodshed, giving the credit to God – he too was evidently a Christian. With surprised pleasure Honorius thought, but this is a soldier, a military tribune, who likes me!

'And Flavius Stilicho – not killed?'

News of victory at Pollentia had overtaken Olympius on the road, while he was escorting the Princess Veleda to Asti, and sent him galloping onwards full tilt. The girl knew how to keep her seat in the saddle, she rode like the devil, and just as well, for here was the chance of a lifetime. The bringer of good news is a man to be smiled upon.

Olympius, when the Emperor asked him that question about Stilicho's fate, had no idea – on the road they had spoken only of a victory – but his tongue soon found a form of words.

'All men, *imperator*, say of Flavius Stilicho that he fought most bravely.'

The fleeting frown that went across the Emperor's face brought to Olympius an illumination that changed his life. Stilicho's glory as victor, even his merely being alive, were secretly repugnant to the Emperor. Here at court a man aware of that great secret, who built upon it cleverly, might make a personage of himself.

And here came the face of one who by his scowl declared himself a rival – a palace slave with a heavy black fringe cut across his forehead, who had entered the imperial presence unbidden, and was so sure of himself that he dared interrupt a military tribune by whispering in the Emperor's ear. That must be the notorious Black Johannes.

When listening to this slave of his, the Emperor wore a submissive look. Enslaved by his own slave? I have now discovered, thought Olympius, which way to strike. He talks to the Emperor, that slave, like a pimp who has become a little too sure of himself. The Emperor obviously needs at his elbow a decent soldier – a declared Christian – a man who would minister to his small vices with better discretion. The slave is handing him a goblet? Drink is evidently one of them.

Given half a chance I can do better, thought Olympius, already living his future role as he made another low obeisance and withdrew. I could touch that young man's soul – and with a conscience-stricken young man like Honorius, what goes to the heart will always be more potent than what titillates the flesh.

As Olympius went backwards through the enfolding curtains, the Emperor looked up to smile on him, as if promising him a future reward for bringing him good news. Black Johannes, lingering, happened not to notice that smile, and just as well, for these days he brooked no rivals.

In the walled garden of another house in Asti – a house falling into ruins – Marcus Curtius and Veleda walked side by side, scrupulously not touching so much as a fingertip, but talking incessantly. Marcus Curtius had brought her to this quiet place to learn all she knew.

With the battle of Pollentia fought and won, all Marcus Curtius felt was shame at not having been in action. He had done his secret duty, obeyed Stilicho to the letter, stuck close to the runaway Emperor – and thereby besmirched his own good name as a soldier.

Before the month is out, thought Marcus Curtius bitterly,

the Emperor Honorius will have forgotten that he ever ran away – just as Stilicho will never be fully aware of the sacrifices this girl Veleda, for instance, has been making for him. The great ones use us. And is the answer simply to become powerful? When power also uses up its possessor?

My face at court will be a reminder to Honorius of a cowardly episode – one he would rather forget. And now that I have this black mark against my name, shall I continue to have a career in the army? Certainly not, if Stilicho falls from grace. And from what I have been overhearing at court, he may.

Rome once demanded of us probity as well as courage, he told himself, as he listened to the girl talk at random. But in the Rome we know – my father's Rome – how can probity and courage prevail against corruption and evil tongues? Do I in any case have battlefield courage? It has never been put to the proof.

'So there it is,' said the tall, pale, incongruously-dressed creature at his side. 'I have told you why, and thank you, Marcus Curtius, for listening. But the confusing fact is that I feel neither Goth nor Roman.'

Veleda had on a linen tunic lavishly trimmed with gold thread, which had been pulled over her head hurriedly by old Julia when she snatched away that priest's robe. The dress was too small for Veleda, and down her thigh a seam had split. To hide her short hair she had been given a scarf, but the scarf had already slipped back from her forehead, and a cockscomb of ragged hair stuck up. Unselfconsciously, the Princess Veleda put fingers under the edge of the scarf, to scratch herself, and Marcus smiled. In Visigoth wagons there was no escaping fleas.

She said, 'Did they tell you what had happened to Flavius Stilicho even before the battle?'

'No?'

'His hair has all turned white.'

Veleda's voice as she spoke was a ghost voice, like wind sighing through a tunnel. She too, like me, thought Marcus Curtius, has been driven a little mad by all this. It never occurred to me before that warfare wounds mind as well as body.

'Stilicho looks more than ever like my father,' Veleda added quietly, as if confiding something that deeply embarrassed her.

'Why not tell me a little more about your father,' Marcus Curtius suggested. Anything to keep her talking – so far she had spoken only about herself. He had some way yet to go in this conversation before out of her mouth Alaric's secrets would come tumbling.

'My father?' Into Veleda's dismayed voice came pride. 'My father was a friend of Rome's. So the Emperor himself told me.' Marcus Curtius waited patiently, and she began to expound at a tangent, in a tone of voice not quite her own, telling him the history of her nation.

'We Goths were all one people when we left Scandinavia to sail across *Mare Suevicum* – the Baltic. That is a sea very far to the north of here, and on its shores they find amber. We Goths began our great journey south, to the shores of the *Euxine* – the Black Sea – because we needed land. There were too many of us for the barren lands of Scandinavia. We have multiplied since, and now we need even more land. And our search for land split us up, led us in different directions. The Ostrogoths. The Visigoths.'

'Some of them I have even met,' said Marcus Curtius. (Though never yet, added his rebuking private voice, on the field of battle.)

'Then you must have heard of the *Gepidae* or Torpid Ones – called lazy because they were last across the Baltic in their boats? Well, I am a Torpid –'

Veleda giggled. Marcus reached quickly for her hand, took it in his own, accepting the risk that his touch might send her from giggles to screams. But she went on expounding as if nothing had happened to interrupt, her hand inert in his as a dog's paw might have been.

'The *Gepidae* – the least important of the Goths. And a quiet people until the dirty filthy Huns came riding out of Scythia, chivvying us onwards into the forest lands –' Veleda shuddered. In Stilicho's camp – not far from his tent – she had actually seen one of the evil Huns her father had so often warned her of, and what her father had said about them was all true. They were squat and ugly and scar-faced and they stank.

'The Huns pushed us across the river into Roman territory. Though against our will. We Goths never wanted to be enemies of you Romans –'

'And this is the kind of thing they have gone on telling you night after night in Alaric's wagons?' Land hunger, no wish to harm the Romans – this was an old tale in the mouths of Visigoths.

'Over and over.' Veleda yawned, like someone wakened too suddenly from a dream. 'Their women told me stories about our people that I already knew, but over and over, just as you say. The point though is this, Marcus –'

Veleda pressed her own hand closer to his. She had never called Marcus by other than his full formal name before. 'They told me those things, and I believed them. They told me the glories of our people, our travels, our courage, our victories. Yet all the time I went on working for you. Their stories did not deflect me. For you and for Flavius Stilicho. Did I tell you that his hair had gone white? All this must have been terrible for him, too. So now, as I have been trying to tell you, I feel neither Goth nor Roman, and what is to become of me?' She was holding his fingers tight.

'The great service you did Rome will have earned the Emperor's gratitude.' Marcus Curtius repeated the usual formula as if consoling a political simpleton. 'One day he will arrange a happy marriage for you.'

Veleda dragged her hand away, appalled. Her voice fell to a whisper – a palace-bred habit, and she looked around circumspectly before she replied.

'What has the Emperor Honorius to do with it? Or marriage either? That halfwit in his courtyard with his cage birds? I served Stilicho.' Veleda looked Marcus Curtius right in the eye. If she goes on talking in the palace, he thought, as she has here, just now, she will make trouble for all of us. Even though what she says is true.

There was an easy way to distract her – a crude option that Stilicho himself had once joked about. But when Marcus Curtius inveigled a hand around Veleda's waist she whirled away. She was all at once muscular, self-possessed, aware of herself, an adversary. She was real – a woman. What he wanted to do with her was suddenly no longer tactic but desire.

Veleda, at arm's reach and out of his grasp, spoke calmly, like someone making the best of a personal deformity. 'For some reason I don't understand, there are times when I can't bear a man to touch me. Even by accident. It never used to matter. Though I find, you know, that I can put my hands on a man's body of my own accord. For instance, if he is wounded.'

'The wounds I have after Pollentia don't show. They are hidden, like yours.'

Why had he said that to her when he always preferred to think of himself as a proud and self-sufficient soldier? A man like himself should simply grasp a woman in his arms, and then, afterwards, put her back on the shelf with a silly smile on her face, gratified. By admitting to his own hidden wounds Marcus had somehow established their equality, as victims.

'Look at my hand,' he said. 'A human hand – there is nothing odd about it.'

Veleda gazed down, because he had told her to, at the five-fingered thing that could shake her to the core merely by touching her. 'Well? What are you waiting for? Be brave. Take hold of it.'

Her own hand was large, but Marcus's long, broad muscular fingers were strong enough to overpower her. Veleda under his provocation twined her own stiff fingers in between his up to the very roots. 'A brave Goth,' he murmured. 'A brave Roman.'

'Now kiss my hand,' Marcus Curtius said sharply, as if giving a military order, 'and I will kiss yours.'

Mastering her distaste, Veleda touched his hand with dry lips. A token, she told herself, of gratitude. Marcus turned her own palm over, and lingeringly kissed the soft middle. His upper lip this morning had not been shaved closely enough. That roughness made her tremble, but she bore it.

'Now the lips.'

'Oh no!'

But this had become child's play, and Marcus Curtius took her as if they were two children, amiably wrestling. Lips pressed against lips, man held close against woman, her own strength gone. Their lips opened, moistened, and they clung to one another like people drowning, her breath coming in sobs, his too, as if both trying to tell the other: No more! This is folly! Yet all the time taking and giving more.

With a royal hostage? What greater imprudence! thought Marcus with a last, lingering, reflective flash of his mind, as, like a man helpless in a dream, he lifted up Veleda's tight tunic and sought the soft skin. An entanglement, an embrace to destroy me! This thought was exultation, and Veleda the battle he had avoided, his own physical destruction. A crazy gawky Goth, not quite sure how to hold herself so as to offer her inwardness to him, yet fully willing. Marcus Curtius laughed, and Veleda laughed, too, gaily, as his hand touched deliriously all that hitherto had been forbidden, impossible, sacred.

You are losing something and gaining nothing, Veleda told herself, reproachfully, a voice out of a past she had already rejected, as the sword-thrust entered her. The pain she had braced herself against was less than anticipated, a small and justified punishment. An interlinked dance, a spiral of joy, swept the pair of them upwards.

Except that others, thought Veleda, as she wept her tears of entangled pain and happiness, are bound to find out, and then what will happen to us? Yet even as she told herself this, she sensed that the enormous pressure of her anxieties was gone. Obscurely she wanted this man – this good man – to hurt and salve her again in the same way, but Marcus Curtius was for the time being all quiet tenderness.

'And your father too,' Veleda said, as though asking Marcus Curtius about his father might bring him back the more easily to the real world, 'is he anything like Stilicho?'

The last person of whom Marcus Curtius proposed to speak was his own father. 'Stilicho is finished – do you know that?'

His answer, as crazy as her question, had burst unexpectedly out of him. At any more normal time, Marcus Curtius would never have allowed himself to put the terrible thought into words.

'How can you say such a thing?' exclaimed Veleda. 'Hasn't he just won the Romans a great victory?'

'Blasphemously. On Good Friday. Wait and see what the Bishop of Milan will have to say about that. All the priests are aware by now that Stilicho has lost his control of the Emperor.'

'But compared to Stilicho, does the Emperor matter?'

The Emperor Honorius was an obtuse and tedious young man, but also the greatest landowner in the West, and the source of all legal authority – politically the centre of everything. Of course, she knew that, everybody knew that. She was talking wildly – saying what both of them secretly thought.

In a low and guilt-ridden voice Veleda said, 'I was the one to tell him about Good Friday.'

'And I led the Emperor a dance across country for him. Stilicho has used us.'

'Yes,' she said judiciously, a grown-up woman at last, 'he has used us.'

She did not even care. Her mind was singularly clear – would always be clear after this. 'Not that it matters.' She was holding one arm tight around Marcus Curtius's waist, as if ready to share all his misfortunes.

'Or rather, to put it better,' said Marcus Curtius, easing away, 'Rome has used us.'

After sex, so the poet Ovid tells us, all living creatures are sad. They had both been used by Rome. Either you use power, or power uses you. But this can't go on, thought Marcus Curtius. I am changed, and she reminds me that I am changed. Perhaps my career as a soldier is at an end. A love affair with a hostage princess could destroy me. And if it did, would I mind?

It was simply not possible that this female Goth with her large strong body, her innocent ideas, could be a new beginning. What was she but a small and unimportant name to use as a counter in Roman diplomacy? She is admirable, Marcus Curtius told himself, but she is foredoomed. She let me enter her as though it were a holy rite. I have only, now, to hold on to her, and she would never let me go.

Or could we not go away together? wondered Marcus Curtius, succumbing to what in his profession he sedulously avoided, daydream. There would be a scandal, but scandals are eventually forgotten. Only, where could we go? Leave civilisation behind, cross the frontier, live with barbarians? In a month we should be driving each other crazy.

'If we were born again,' said Veleda, her thoughts moving oddly parallel to his own, 'I would like to be born a man.' She gripped his arm. 'But only if you were born as a woman.' To his own surprise, Marcus in his languid affectionate mood did not resent her fantasy. Born again was what the Christians said. And what was it supposed to mean?

She wants to penetrate, ejaculate, thought Marcus. She wants to possess me as I have her. She wants us one.

'Are you listening, Marcus? I know what comes next, and there is no need to spare me. You have your own work to do – your duty. Your little questions. I know all that. Well – what little questions do you have? What answers do you need?' Veleda smiled, calmly, as if to reassure him that never mind what they had done and said, she was still a woman in the service of Rome.

Nearer the house, across the neglected garden, something moved. The canes growing thickly in the corner near the wall shook their feathered tops.

'Over there!'

A slap of a sandal on the threshold! The spy had seen and gone, and might, thought Marcus Curtius, have been anyone: a prurient-minded boy, at the luckiest. Veleda was blushing before his eyes from the roots of her cropped hair down to the soles of her feet, tingling, shrinking, her modesty outraged. She asked outright the question that was in his mind too.

'An imperial spy?'

Had they been tracked here? What else had they done that made them vulnerable? The vast sticky cobweb of court intrigue settled over their heads as they stood there, stronger at that moment of alarm than Vulcan's iron net.

Marcus Curtius looked at Veleda, and she might have been any young woman, tall, blonde, gawky for her age, her sea-coloured eyes coming close towards his own, her ugly unwomanly short hair an affront. She touched her hair with both hands, as if made aware of it. She was pulling that scarf tight, to hide it. The gold-embroidered skirt was scandalously torn.

A woman of Gothic origin, for the time being in the intelligence service and so at his orders, whose maidenhead he had ruptured. Like Hercules. Veleda looked back at him, coldly, straight in the eye, the same mood upon her. He was a man, a military tribune, the son of a Roman senator, standing consciously erect now as if to efface the liberties he had taken with her. Of their passion nothing was left but a trickle of blood on his thigh, a trickle of seed on hers. How could she ever have borne to let him come so close to her, body and mind? If only we could trust one another, thought Veleda. But in this world we inhabit, who can?

2

Claudian, still coughing his heart out, kept Lucas pinned hour after hour to the writing desk, as if the battle against Alaric would not have been properly fought and won until Claudian's poem on the theme had been polished to perfection. Lucas could manage to slip away now and then, but not often. With Gilda performing almost every day it was never easy to coincide with times when she was free.

One afternoon, at a loss for words, Claudian decided to take Lucas with him to the theatre. Claudian needed to see soldiers again, hard-faced veterans, and overhear what they might be saying, and these days the theatre in Milan was where you found them. Lucas had never seen Gilda perform, and disliked the idea. In their room she was his. In the theatre she made a gift of herself to everyone.

The open-air auditorium that afternoon was filling to the brim. On the highest and cheapest stone seats were men back from Pollentia, blueing the last coins of the Emperor's donative. Lower down with a better view of the stage sat the *honestiores*, less rowdy, more critical. Lucas folded the cloak he had been carrying against the chill of early evening, and made a pad for his master to sit on. Claudian began, but stifled, a gruesome cough. There are times when I would even do the coughing for him, as well as the penmanship, thought Lucas, and this is one. People were turning to stare – Claudian supposed it was on account of his fame.

'So thoughtful,' the gratified poet murmured as he eased himself on to the folded cloak. Why do I get more pleasure these days, he asked himself, from the company of this austere young slave than from any of my plump and pretty boys? Am I becoming Platonic?

The soldiers in the rows behind them, clearly audible, were impatient for their first glimpse of Flavius Stilicho's woman, virtually their own woman now. By paying the price of admission they had all bought shares in her. Lucas did his best to close his ears against the lewdness of what they were saying.

The act just before Gilda came on was not quite good enough to hold their attention – a ventriloquist with an ape on his knee dressed as a little girl, who to all appearances was telling dirty stories. The soldiers, their attention wandering, amused themselves by bawling out the lank-haired civilian down there with the hacking cough. An Egyptian, wasn't he? A Levantine, anyway.

'Try a dose of olive oil.'

'Hold his head under.'

'Come on, lads, let's cork him.'

'Go home to the Nile, you Egyptian, and cough yourself dotty.'

Claudian hunched up at their raucous cries, as if shrinking into himself. Yet in their threats was a certain pleasure. Lucas left to himself might have stood up, turned to face them, tried to wither them with a superior brand of sarcasm. But not when Claudian wore that crushed smile on his face.

The poet turned to Lucas and whispered, 'I can't stand Milan. I'm leaving. Tomorrow at the latest. Today let us enjoy ourselves. Did you suppose those rowdy fellows up there would drive me out of my seat? It is only their high spirits.'

'You intend, *magister*,' asked Lucas, his heart ready to freeze at the news (leave Milan? leave Gilda?), 'to follow the Emperor to Ravenna?'

The imperial administration was at sixes and sevens. Terrified by the dangers his timid mind had suggested to him on his flight to Asti, Honorius had chosen as his future capital the safest place in all Italy – the naval base of Ravenna, on the Adriatic, protected by lagoons, surrounded by impassible marshes, and served by only one road, across a causeway. If the barbarians ever did come uncomfortably close to Ravenna, a fast trireme could take Honorius to his brother in Constantinople. Ravenna in Claudian's opinion was not so much an imperial capital as a place for the Emperor to hide his head.

'Ravenna? That mosquito-ridden hole? I am going back to my house in Rome.'

The furry baby on the ventriloquist's knee had attempted one last inept obscenity and been swept off-stage. Now here came Gilda, the one they wanted, dancing out on the balls of her feet, light as a feather. That lyric agility of hers was made all the funnier by the bloated, artificial belly floating up and down like a trophy before her. She slapped her make-believe pregnancy, and all the soldiers got up to roar her a greeting before she had said a word.

Claudian closed his eyes to slits and tried hard not to cough. If this was the famous Gilda's theme he did not propose to enjoy it. Pregnancy: a blatant function of womanhood that particularly offended him. Was not a poet himself pregnant, eternally pregnant, and of something nobler than mere flesh and blood?

Staggering out from the wings came a giant dressed as a Roman legionary. His costume made him even more enormous – boot-soles raised on platforms, shoulders immensely padded, a helmet as big as a tub and a sword particularly gigantic. He came on untrussed, as if around the corner out of sight he had been relieving himself up against a tree. The soldier turned to face his audience, and in front of him wobbled an artificial phallus so long and large that to move towards Gilda he was obliged to lift it up with both hands.

Gilda from modesty hid her face with spread hands, but everyone could see she was appraising the size of him between her fingers. The prospect overcame her. She fell flat on her back, heels lifted, belly wobbling an obscene invitation.

The soldier came close enough for Gilda to measure the size of his phallus with her outstretched hands. Yelping 'Not inside me! Not likely!' she scuttled off, hitching up her artificial belly and cherishing it as she ran.

In a high and clear voice that took off a Gothic accent to perfection, Gilda told her audience, 'I'm Alaric's sister – I've been done by you soldier boys already.'

The vast howl of laughter from the soldiers massed in the high seats made the stone theatre tremble. Laughter went on reverberating through their chase-me-Charlie up and down the stage, giant legionary in hot pursuit of pregnant woman, almost caught that time but got away, a piece of theatrical precision raising obscenity to hysteria. Then Gilda tripped. Sooner or later, she had to.

Would she miscarry? But the pregnancy like the phallus was imaginary, the stuff of fantasy, her dramatic groan was a joke.

Gilda had rolled over on her back in the very place she started from. She lifted her feet. She wobbled invitingly. An easy rape: Alaric's sister could never have enough. The cackles from the buffoon were echoed in the high seats by all the soldiers who had been at Pollentia.

'All right, young man.' Out again came Gilda's Gothic accent, crystal clear. 'Put it in, Only don't wake baby.'

This, thought Lucas, is sickening. There was just enough of Gilda herself, in her gestures and that pose to remind him.

The couple on stage were desperately trying every posture, including one or two that strained credulity. But they could never achieve a fit. Their attempts were a crazy anthology of human copulation. They lay wrestling with one another on-stage amid gales of laughter, grotesque yet innocent lovers, bewitched into a kind of shameless impotence.

And obviously enough, in all that, thought Claudian, she displays a kind of theatrical shrewdness, even of pathos. Should I disdain the famous Gilda, when the soldier boys so obviously adore her? Stilicho too, by all accounts. No doubt she is less vulgar with him, perhaps quite different. She is clever enough to be very different. The simple fact is, Claudian told himself, you are jealous of the effect she is having. Enough then.

'Are you enjoying this?' he asked Lucas.

'Not in the least, *magister*,' answered Lucas, white-lipped.

'You must not be too censorious,' said Claudian, like someone removing a piece of rotten fruit from his own mouth. 'Some of her little touches, now. Plebeian wit?' Bouts of coughing had reduced his acid voice to a whisper.

Lucas would have liked to believe that the pantomime actress on stage with her orange-coloured wig and her blown-up belly was not Gilda at all, but someone different and worse. Yet in a vulgarly exaggerated way Gilda was playing herself. Those larger-than-life erotic gestures were indeed her own gestures, he knew her and could not help recognising them. Some of the jokes had even been bawdy little items from their lovers' intimacy, chaff about his size, her size, another posture, but made loud and crass.

With a couple of fingers pulling each corner of her lips, Gilda offered to the crowd the biggest mouth ever yet seen on a human countenance. The mouth I have kissed, thought Lucas desperately, as if in thrall to a demon. And was trying now to take that gross male protuberance between her gaping lips, but the piece of slithery meat was too big for the pot. Do you want her to touch you like that, Lucas asked himself, ever again?

Claudian's departure from the theatre before the end of Gilda's act was not popular with the rank-and-file on the higher tiers. To move away was lacking in respect – though they were at least getting rid of the man who had coughed. Lucas jockeyed his master through the crowd, merciless with any civilian who got in their way. He could still hear her comic, ringing, Gothic tones, but never turned his head.

'The other Roman soldier got it in. So why can't you?'

'Oh, did he? Who was he?'

'He went on having me and having me –' pause '– until his hair turned white!'

The seats higher up responded with an exhilarating whoop.

'*S t i l i c h o !*'

The plebs up there were cheering even louder than the soldiers. Those are the voices, thought Claudian, who seldom missed a nuance, of the poor of Milan. Stilicho's victory saved their little dwellings and workshops from wreck, their daughters from rape. As for the blasphemy of fighting on the anniversary of the Crucifixion, the people up there don't give a damn. This year Stilicho is their hero. But next year? Soldiers and plebs soon forget.

Though the *humiliores* – listen – are shouting louder and more wholeheartedly than the soldiers. The legions have not forgiven Stilicho the blood-letting and the loss of their plunder. Gilda and I – and how I envy her such closeness to her audience – have this much in common. We both speak up for Stilicho.

Someone in the back with a compelling bass voice – had he been planted there? – broke in with the first line of a song. The soldiers all took it up – and would forget for the time being, as they sang, their lingering resentment. Iron-shod boots were stamping out the time.

A l a r i c has only GOT ONE BALL!

Gilda heard him coming up the stairs, she saw the wooden latch lift on its string. She was impatient with waiting, was tapping her foot against the floor. She had dressed to come here with false simplicity, in plain linen, veiled, and holding in her hand a bunch of heavily-scented wild hyacinths, bought out on the street. She was playing the decent matron.

Lucas's nostrils as he opened the door were filled not only with that wild flower perfume, but with a faint underlying odour, the heavily sensual scent that only Gilda wore. Lucas had quite expected to find her different, changed, but the actual change she had made in herself surprised him.

'At my performance this afternoon, weren't you?' Still jangling from her work on stage, Gilda lifted the veil. The spy in the street outside had not been looking for a woman in plain linen, with a veil, holding a simple bunch of flowers. She had hurried here. Her face under the veil was still painted as for the stage, white and red, with exaggeratedly blackened eyes.

'I thought you never went to the theatre?'

'I had to keep my master company.'

'The thin man with the hair and the cough, Syrian, isn't he?'

'Egyptian.'

'He was of course the one I first noticed, not you. Sitting up straight as you were, like a good boy in church. We always notice coughers. I might have worked his cough into my act, I often do, make him think twice. But as you must have seen for yourself, today it wasn't that kind of act.'

'Claudius Claudianus – a friend of Stilicho's.'

Under this high-bred woman's nervous rant – for Gilda was acting what she wore, her veil, her simple dress, despite her cosmetics – Lucas looked in vain for a glimpse of the Gilda he had known as a little girl, running merrily beside the slave caravan.

'Not the great poet?' Gilda asked, only waiting for Lucas to say, without thinking, yes, the great poet, so that she could pounce and mock. Quote some of his lines with a humdrum intonation – the certain way of putting down a poet. But Lucas, seeing her in a mood for ridicule, said nothing.

Gilda's painted face was a distant travesty of her naked face. She had let her veil drop to the floor – under one veil, another. But even her naked face, as Lucas now knew, was a veil.

'Well – what did you think of it?' With a touch of their old comradely tone she then answered her own question. 'Horrible, wasn't it.' The painted lady had spoken at last like a slave girl.

'Not in the least what I expected.' Lucas's whisper was a distant echo of Claudian's hoarse whisper.

Miming childish contrition, yet unable to hide a smile at his innocence, Gilda said, 'Were you very ashamed of me?' He found he could not look her in the face.

'And what did Claudian the great poet think of my performance?' She added, impatiently, 'I notice that he left halfway through.'

'Plebeian wit was what I heard him say.'

'As distinct no doubt from the patrician wit of the great poet.' Astoundingly, she began to cry.

Though very likely, Lucas told himself, resisting an impulse to take her in his arms, an actress like Gilda can cry at will. Her face with its ruined paint had become absurd. He reached out a tentative hand.

'You may want to touch me even less, once you know.'

'I don't see why.'

'You will be like all the others,' said Gilda with a strange, clairvoyant frankness, the after-effect of tears. 'You will want me to get rid of it. You will give me the usual good reasons, and turn your back, and go down the stairs, and leave me.'

Into her remarks was coming a cadence which though Lucas had heard it before he could not identify – she was talking to an invisible audience. Her manner rose to a histrionic fury. 'What a fool you must think me, letting you take me time after time, like the town bull. Or are you going to say I should have it – keep it – make Stridor a little present? Hasn't he ruined enough lives already?'

'But Gilda, what are you trying to say?' asked Lucas, almost beside himself with confused emotion.

'I've let myself become pregnant, you fool – *gravida*.'

There was a long and deadly silence.

'You know it's yours, don't you,' she said meekly. 'No-one else's. You tempted me into it.'

'Yes.'

Lucas wanted to prove that he was there beside her, that he admitted it all, that he was hers, by taking Gilda into his arms at last, but her manner did nothing to encourage him. They were looking at each other without touching, like wary combatants. With Stridor her legal owner, thought Lucas dismally, the child is his property too. Or would Gilda be more profitable to him childless, and able to perform? No doubt, as she was saying, he will want her to get rid of it. He must now make up his own mind, and the necessity enormously depressed him.

Few Roman women from the highest class to the lowest went to the trouble of child-bearing, unless they were pious. The fashion for a pleasure-loving infecundity – one child or none – had spread downwards gradually through society, until in Italy there were hardly enough Roman citizens left to man the legions or plough the fields. And slaves had an even more cogent reason than free citizens for not bringing another little slave into the world.

And she knew she was pregnant this afternoon, on stage, thought Lucas bitterly, at the very time that she was pretending to be pregnant, to make those soldiers laugh.

'I shall tell Stridor no,' muttered Gilda, avoiding his eye. 'This child is mine, I have a right to keep it.'

'Ours,' suggested Lucas, almost too gently for Gilda to hear. But she glanced up under swollen eyelids, her eyes brilliant, and Lucas knew that his one word had gone home.

'What was that you said? And I thought you despised me, for going on stage like that, with my big mouth, and a bladder glued to my belly. If the act goes on being popular, I soon shan't need a bladder.' Gilda grimaced at him, exactly as the funny little girl in the slave convoy might have done, and at last Lucas crushed her to him. Gilda this time made no effort to fob him off, she let him hold her, but as yet there was no response. He held in his arms a simple supple body covered with plain linen, like a prisoner.

Lucas said in her ear, 'If Stridor tries to force you, I shall kill him.'

Gilda pulled herself away, and looked him earnestly in the eye. That was a dangerous thing to say, even in a whisper.

'A death he would deserve,' Lucas added, as if trying to convince her.

'And yet you know what that means – a slave killing a master?'

Behind her reproving face, Gilda was jubilant. The father of her child, himself a slave, and yet striking this attitude of a sword-bearing free man and her protector. He meant it, though she dare not let him. When a slave killed a master, every other slave in the house could legally be made to pay for it, either by torture or by death. Under the apparent tranquillity of Roman domestic life lay terror.

Gilda tried the water in the earthenware bowl with her finger, and it was cold. From a little pocket under the hem of her gown she brought out a green phial as thick as a man's finger, and went to work on the wreckage of her make-up with the oleaginous liquid, but scrupulously, like a craftsman. Her own face emerged, damp and nude and naughty. By pulling a funny face at him she did her best to make Lucas laugh, but he was past laughing.

'I suppose, after seeing the way I earn my living, you won't want me.'

'You mean there is still room inside?' The bawdy answer had come quite of its own accord to his lips.

'You put it there, in the first place,' said Gilda complacently, lacing hands across her belly. 'It's all your doing, this.'

'Come here.'

'Don't be in such a hurry.'

'You mean, be careful?'

'That too.'

They made a curious sort of love, without urgent passion, and yet the ultimate bliss was intense. Then it was over and done with, and they were safe in the same bed, arms around one another, an old married couple. Lucas had quite forgotten in all this to tell Gilda his bad news. Claudian was carrying him off to Rome. Tomorrow. But she took it calmly.

'Stridor won't keep me hanging about here much longer either,' she said, as if minor setbacks could make no difference to them now. 'The legionaries you saw this afternoon are down to their last coppers. When they don't come to see me any more, and the Emperor moves out too? And that will happen soon. What is this place in a swamp he is taking everyone off to?'

'Ravenna.'

'Milan will be dead as a doornail. Stridor will have me back in Rome, because Rome is where the money is.'

'You are not afraid of him?' Lucas asked, in a small voice.

In the old days, walking side by side in the slave gang, the little hand inside his own had trembled whenever Stridor, lifting his stick, had turned back to seek out a culprit.

'I may have been once,' Gilda told him, 'but not any more. He taught me how to manage men – and now I manage him.' She nudged Lucas. 'You too.' Then she laughed. 'What if I let him believe that the child I am carrying might be the Emperor's?'

'And might it?' But Gilda avoided a straight answer. Some secrets were a mortal danger.

'I just say the Emperor for argument's sake. As I might with even better reason say Stilicho's. I know how Stridor thinks. He would never get rid of the child if there were money to be made. Though he might grow sentimental, and that would be awful.'

Lucas said with an odd smile, 'Then you are asking me to spare him?' As he spoke those words, Lucas had made an involuntary violent gesture, like a sword thrust, and the mere sight of it made her heart turn over.

'Put your clothes on lazybones, and go quickly.' Gilda spoke as if this time she meant it. 'Look up and down the street for a tall, bald man who wears his sandals cross-gartered. He's clever, but I know how to dodge him. If you see no sign of him, whistle. That vulgar London fishmonger whistle of yours –'

A fashionable, red-painted *lectica*, carried by four slaves, had been plumped down bodily on the setts at one end of the causeway which linked the naval harbour at Ravenna, called Classis, with the fortified city a little distance inland, called Caesarea. All four *lectica* porters were big and blonde men who took pride in their extravagant moustaches. They had quiet tongues and observant eyes, and were leaning in the shade against the harbour wall, as if brooding with pleasure on the swish and wash of the sea. Nobody could come past the four slaves without being noticed from a long way off, and then if need be, deterred.

The curtains of the red *lectica* on the side facing out to sea had been opened. The woman lounging inside on shot silk cushions was watching half-naked slaves at the oars of a single-decked government galley out on the tossing water, as the galley was rowed away from its berth. The muscular oarsmen were vigorous in the sun, and watching them gave her a languid pleasure. That galley carried despatches; by sunset it would be a long way down the island-strewn Adriatic, those naked men tugging more wearily at their oars, past the blue and sun-defined capes of Greece, to the cold, enclosed waters of the Bosphorus, thence to Constantinople.

Years before, as a girl, the woman watching the galley slaves had lived in Roman Constantinople – a city better governed nowadays than Roman Italy, and much safer. Yet she was aware in her heart that she would rather be here in Italy, amid the frightening risks, than there, in Constantinople, where life was made boring by ceremonial.

A second figure, in the black cloak and discreet veil of a rich widow, was tottering along the flagstones of the causeway, as if come out obstinately to take air and exercise in the afternoon heat. She was small, and though her face was hidden by the veil, also evidently old. The four porters let her pass. As the little old woman in the cloak ducked vivaciously inside the *lectica*, the larger woman at the same instant reached to draw the curtains, and block out the seaward view.

Hidden behind curtains. Two ladies, past their first youth, one bonily large, like a horse, one small, like a sparrow, and they were conspirators. Here at the end of the harbour, no one in Ravenna could overhear them. Those four porters, leaning against the harbour wall, were their sentries, to keep them from surprise. Serena and Julia, friends since childhood, looked into each other's eyes and laughed, as if these conspiratorial precautions, which might indeed by a matter of life and death, were also fun.

'A little present I see, from the commander-in-chief?'

'My porters? They are his Vandals. So you noticed! Aren't they well-matched. And speak only five words of Latin. I give them my orders in Gothic.'

'You speak Gothic as well, Serena? How clever of you!'

'Only so as to follow what my husband might be muttering, when he talks in his sleep.' Old Julia laughed.

'I too find it an advantage to know a little Gothic,' she went on complacently. 'My silly girls may think of it, some of them, as their private language, but I can usually follow what mischief they are up to.'

Julia undid the opal brooch at the throat of her stifling black cloak with a sigh of relief. On forehead and down withered throat she dabbed the refreshing scent that Serena offered her. And hardly room on that face of hers, thought Serena, for one more wrinkle. When little Julia was so pretty once. That indoor life of hers, at court, and far too many false smiles. All written in her skin. We of the imperial family are not obliged to smile quite so much. Julia has not worn well, but then again, she is my oldest friend.

After her ten days in treacherous, spy-ridden Ravenna, only here, alone, in Julia's company, did Serena feel moderately safe. The two of them had been testing the mood of the court, for Stilicho. Julia was still passionately loyal to him, as she had been all her life. Serena had never quite forgiven Julia for once having tried to carry off Flavius Stilicho – but everybody in those days tried, he was the handsomest man in the guards, and Julia had her looks then.

In those days, thought Serena, Julia had her wits too, as well as her looks. The most fascinating woman at court, let's be frank, but I had the imperial effulgence. I meant for Flavius the certainty of power. And my dull old face has lasted better, after all. Look at poor Julia, how copiously she sweats, in this heat.

'Gossip first,' suggested Julia. 'I am so bored with politics.'

'You are simply bored with Ravenna,' Serena told her tartly.

'Bored? With our famous marshes, which keep the barbarians from ravishing us? With our no less famous mosquitos?' Julia scratched herself, to add point to her remark, but not Serena, though she wanted to scratch. 'A provincial hole like this – for those of us who in our younger days, my dear, have watched the sun rise over the Golden Horn! Ravenna,' she went on with disgust, 'where the only local dish is eels, and drinking water costs more than wine. I swear a sip of tolerable white wine hasn't passed my lips since the day we were all fools enough to leave Rome.'

'If Stilicho gets his way, some of us will be back on a visit,' announced Serena, tossing the juicy morsel of gossip to Julia as if to an impatient lapdog. 'You will have all the good white wine you can drink. After Pollentia he is planning a nice, old-fashioned Roman triumph. There hasn't been one for years.'

'You consider that wise?'

'To present poor young Honorius to the people of Rome as the real victor of Pollentia? It's all slightly ridiculous, of course, but I certainly don't see why not.' They were safe from eavesdroppers, no safer place in all Ravenna, and Serena was politically the most influential woman in the Western Empire, yet she had dropped her voice almost to vanishing point when she uttered the imperial name. 'Don't giggle like that just because I said victor.'

'He won, all right,' said Julia. 'Look how he has got his way. The young man is happy here. He has found his perfect place. In Ravenna he lives in a dream, and all the toadies encourage him. He sits in his own imaginary world, full of cage birds, and supposes he is governing the Roman Empire. We are all his cage birds now.'

'Now a piece of really juicy gossip from me,' said Serena. 'You will laugh even more.'

'Yes, please.' Julia settled her little legs so that they were not quite so much in Serena's way. 'Laughing is all life has left me.'

'Claudius Claudianus is getting married.'

Julia went into a peal like a screaming cockatoo. 'Picture their wedding night! Claudian trying to turn her upside down. Poor girl – is she anyone we know?'

As tears of merriment came into Julia's eyes, a little trickle of black underlining crept down her left cheek. That's ruined Julia for the afternoon, thought Serena cheerfully – should I tell her? But friendship was friendship. She leaned forward with a fine linen handkerchief, dabbing the trickle away, and as she did so explained the marriage.

Stilicho years before had fixed Claudian up with a couple of sinecures – nominal posts as notary and tribune. The revenue from them enabled Claudian to live in comfort, with handsome young slaves to look after him, while he got on undisturbed with his poem. Not daring as yet to attack Flavius Stilicho – yet willing to inflict pinpricks on his friends – Black Johannes had one day dropped a poisoned word in the Emperor's ear. A notorious pagan, receiving a stipend and doing no work for it?

Simply to have deprived Claudian would have caused an uproar in good society. So he had been moved to a post appropriate to his rank, but demanding incessant work. To make matters worse, the poet wasn't well.

'So I have fixed up a nice little marriage for him, with an heiress, a widow. A big woman, so they tell me. But what would Claudian make of youth or beauty? Or slenderness? Rich and lives a long way off, well out of harm's way. Which will take a weight off my mind, and Stilicho's too, things being as they are, since Claudian, though our dear friend and a very great poet of course –'

'Great indeed!' echoed Julia solemnly. In their intimate circle, Claudian's greatness was an article of faith.

'He can also be an old silly at times. He has fits of trying to be heroic, and these days it doesn't do. He can be so indiscreet – sometimes he forgets that we have enemies.'

'Where does this heiress of yours live?' asked Julia.

'Somewhere in Africa, I believe.'

'Where exactly?'

'Somewhere far beyond Carthage, quite out of reach.'

A silence fell between the two old women. Each could hear the other breathe, and each knew what the other must be thinking. Serena began to make her apologies.

'Claudian came back from the Alps with such a cough. The climate out there will be good for him. His enemies can't reach him, or worse still, get at us through him. Why shouldn't he be as busy and happy with his writing out there, as he is here? A rich widow to look after him? At least he won't starve.'

'Gilded exile?'

'Better than actual exile – an uninhabited island, a desert oasis. Which as you know, has been happening often enough. We can't protect our friends as once we could.' Serena's mouth, Julia could not help noticing, had the bad habit of closing up these days so tight that the lips disappeared. That in Julia's opinion was ill-considered. A woman at court however awkward the political situation should never stop smiling. Julia put on an encouraging smile to keep in practice, but thinking about Claudian's fate made it less than easy.

'Scythia, wasn't it,' Serena inquired, pretending not to notice

Julia's death's-head grin, 'where our imperial forbear the Divine Augustus sent the poet Ovid? You always know these things.'

'Scythia,' agreed Julia blankly. 'But Scythia wouldn't do for Claudian. Scythia is beastly cold.'

'There you are. Hence Africa. Hence this heiress. And now to business.' Serena's long and horsy face, Julia noticed, was growing a little too much like the face of a man.

'To bring it off, we need,' Serena said coldly, 'a swordsman – but with brains enough to hide the fact that he has real brains. Loyal to Flavius Stilicho – that goes without saying. Yet not too obviously connected with him. A man who when the time comes will not hesitate to strike the blow. Any suggestions?'

'Who better at one time than Marcus Curtius?' Julia had dropped the last trace of frivolity. 'But did you know? There was a rumour that he had got religion. Anyway, he has disappeared. His father is spending a small fortune to find him.'

'Disappeared? You know what that might mean.'

'One might suppose that even Black Johannes would think twice about dropping a man as well connected as Marcus Curtius in the marsh. But there it is. He became disputatious, and was of late a little too openly disgusted with life at court. That won't do, will it. Now he has gone, but there is a new man on the scene, more circumspect, who might do quite as well. Served as military tribune under Stilicho, a Christian but ambitious –'

'So many of them are,' said Serena. 'What happened to the unworldly ones we used to meet years ago?'

'Olympius is just the sort of Christian for our purpose. He is such a good Christian of the new sort that Honorius gets on quite splendidly with him, even though he follows the trade of a soldier.'

'Would he stab a man in the back, this Christian soldier, and have no pangs of conscience? Not even ask why?'

'Olympius? When a slave like Black Johannes is standing between him and the light? He loathes Johannes – yet hides his loathing so cleverly that no pair of eyes less sharp than yours or mine would ever notice. His scruples of conscience are under excellent control. He is yours if you need him, Serena.'

'I'll take your word. Can you hook him for us?'

In answer, Julia smiled a stabbing smile. Once the business

arrangement had been silently clinched, Julia plucked up courage to go on and ask Serena her own last private question.

'In Rome you intend to have it out with her face to face? You are going to squash her?' Julia made the thumbnail gesture of someone breaking the back of a flea.

Even to such an old and tried friend, a dangerous question. Julia had been prompted to it by thinking, with a pang, Serena has had Stilicho all her life. Has had his children, shared his bed. For me in all those years, no more than a smile, one of his smiles, whenever we pass in a corridor.

Julia's rash question about Gilda provoked not anger but floods of tears down Serena's cheeks. And looks her age at last thought Julia, sorry and yet not sorry. She can no longer keep up that severe look of hers, like a man's. What everyone knows is happening – Stilicho's mistress pregnant – had mortally wounded her. But I need to know what she will do.

'This woman Gilda has put a spell on him,' whispered Serena. 'Woman did I say? Demon. Since that glorious achievement of his at Pollentia she has found a way to tie him in a knot. He is good for nothing, Not anything. I mean physically. And you know what a man he was once.' Here in this *lectica*, with the curtains drawn, they could after all these years admit to one another that they had both had Stilicho, because now they had both lost him. 'Yet the old fool is still dangling after her. It's witchcraft.'

Gilda's pregnancy was not a stage joke any more, but an important political fact. Those in the know said with a wink that of course the child was Stilicho's. Had not Gilda herself as good as said so, on stage, up in Milan, to a theatre full of soldiers?

But going the rounds was another and far-fetched possibility.

Many years before, when working in a chic Roman brothel, Stridor had hit upon an obvious truth – that it was better to work for the *agentes in rebus* as an informer than be suspected by them. When he came back to Rome and began to pimp Gilda, he renewed his old connections. So it was to Stridor that Black Johannes had applied, when looking for a first woman for the young Emperor.

Honorius on that memorable occasion had been a little too smitten with Gilda, so that Black Johannes deemed it safer not to have her back for a second time. But in a palace vibrant with rumour, Julia had penetrated the little secret that Stridor and Black Johannes shared. They had been tampering with the young Emperor had they? Then the actress's unborn child might be his!

Any courtier could explain the political danger. An imperial bastard, even by a slave girl who earned a living as a *mima*, was a living threat to the dynasty, especially a dynasty as precarious as this one. Was Honorius ever likely to have a child by his lawful wife, Maria? He had a younger sister, an uncommonly strong-minded teenager called Galla Placidia. Was the man who happened to win Galla Placidia's heart to be considered automatically as next in line for the purple? And what if Gilda's child were a son – a focus for discontent?

Imperial blood legitimises, and Emperors had before now adopted their successors. A boy bastard, manipulated from birth onwards, as a potential heir, by Black Johannes? In all this fierce gossip there were improbabilities, but the black-browed slave who had found clever and covert ways of dominating the Emperor was coming out of it badly, and to Julia and Serena that was what mattered.

'This swordsman of yours,' asked Serena, 'will act at a nod?'

'Olympius,' said Julia stoutly, 'will allow nothing whatever to stand in the way of his future career, though if you heard him talk you might never think so. Butter wouldn't melt in his mouth.'

'I would so much rather it had been Marcus Curtius. Such an upstanding manly fellow, and devoted life and limb to Stilicho.'

'And now for all we know to the contrary, rotting somewhere out in the marshes.' Old Julia also could sound hard.

'That actress's child, even if it be Stilicho's,' answered Serena, 'shall not stand in the way of any child my daughter Maria might have.'

'Oh, the babies I have sent sinless to heaven over the years,' said Julia with a laugh like a cackling hen,' when my virginal young ladies have lapsed from grace. Though this one has been going rather long. Do you need my help?'

'I will see to it myself,' announced Serena, her face again adopting the unpardoning look.

The *lectica* by this time was stuffy with stale air and scented bodies, and Serena had given herself a fearful headache. Pulling back the curtains she uttered a sharp word in a strange tongue. Sea air came in upon them like a benediction. The huge blonde Vandals, rousing themselves, took hold of the leather loops that held the poles. Off they went together, Julia and Serena, at a pleasant, sexy, swinging pace, invisible to the world at large.

'Splendid men, aren't they,' breathed Julia.

'Enormous. Vandals. Sometimes they even remind me –'

'Yes, I know.' And Julia took Serena's hand, like a sister.

Marcus Curtius, at one time a military tribune but known to his workmates these days simply as Marcus, was busy making criss-cross scratches to and fro with the point of a small iron pick across an unplastered wall. He was ludicrously happy, as if scoring the wall this way and that with a simple tool were bliss. He had managed to translate himself, body and soul, into another world.

His uncut hair was white with stone dust. His dirty workman's blouse was held by a rope at the waist. When the working day was over his hands at first had been blistered where the tool rubbed, but since then he had grown calluses. And at the same time, he told himself gaily, as the tool went to and fro and the stone dust rose into his nostrils, stripped away the calluses that for so long had covered my soul.

They were in a new building on the outskirts of Nola – a small town near the bay of Naples – and across this long wall the three of them were at work. Marcus, the clumsiest, had been set to roughening the surface of the wall so that a polished surface of plaster and marble dust would stick well to it. Felix, a Goth and once a slave, was their plasterer. He went through the same procedures every day, his mouth moving slightly as if talking to himself. He was praying in Gothic: as he worked he prayed, to concentrate himself. He mixed lime-mortar and marble dust with obsessive thoroughness, then with an oblong iron plasterer's trowel fetched up a length of the long wall to a meticulous flatness. Not a dent, not a scratch. To work is to pray.

Felix would turn rapidly away from his own wet plaster as soon as the painter begain transferring his cartoon to the wall, as though painting were none of his business, only plastering, and begin working overhead, from a ladder, on ornamentation, florets and lozenges, inconspicuous works of art up in the ceiling corners.

Felix's name had been Athanaric until he took up work here at the shrine. As a sign that he was abandoning the Arian heresy – which thought of Jesus as a man, not a God – Felix had taken as his own the name of the saint to whom this was the memorial. The original Felix, son of a Roman legionary, had been a local hero in the persecution set on foot a hundred and fifty years earlier by the Emperor Decius. Felix had rescued the bishop, eluded capture and the painful death they had in mind for him, and ended up afterwards at Nola as parish priest. This fresco was to show the Bishop of Nola's miraculous escape.

The painter himself was Theodorus, a Greek-speaker from Syria, whose real name, thought Marcus, is very likely not Theodorus either. We are all here to make fresh starts – do they perhaps think I too borrowed a new name, from Marcus the Evangelist? Theodorus and Felix this morning were helping one another apply the cartoon, that was unusual, Felix stretching the pasted-up fragments of papyrus across the wet surface, while Theodorus pricked rapid holes along the outlines of his drawing with a stylus dipped in lamp black. On the plaster those dots would guide his brush, but the colours and ordonnance of the mural were already held fast in Theodorus's head. He follows the vision in his mind, thought Marcus, and there are no false moves. He finishes each day's work exactly, before the plaster dries.

Once in a while, not often, they might ask Marcus to hold one end of the papyrus for them, if it happened to be an awkward shape, but usually they hesitated, because Marcus made mistakes. He was just as happy, scratching across the wall with his pointed tool, or carrying a hod of wet plaster up the ladder, or even fetching one or other of them a jar of fresh cold water. Theodorus with his bladders of pigment, his brushes arranged in a fan, had begun applying his paint in flicks and strokes with his usual astonishing quickness. Every touch signified.

Today's section of the painting, though evidently radiant in the artist's mind, would not make much sense until joined up with tomorrow's. There was today a foot and a soldier's boot in it that had no connection with anything. What informs that brilliant, kingfisher-rapid hand of his, thought Marcus, and no less guides my own clumsy hand as I scratch this wall, is God. We all work not to gain money, but to the glory of God. Even my breathing, our breathing, is therefore a prayer. From Marcus, the least handy, the clumsiest, this prayer. I breathe out. I breathe in. My breathing a prayer to God. Along this wall, though, we are all equal.

Equality in a Christian sense – *aequalitas* – was an understanding that had only lately grown upon Marcus Curtius, and as he worked he hugged this new thought to himself, and considered it. Not *aequalitas* in rank, years, wealth, or any kind of formal equality that could be overthrown in a court by a phrase of legal Latin or a trick in rhetoric. *Aequalitas* meant equal in the sight of God. Equal, therefore free: *liber*. Equal and free. All of us along this wall are free. Felix, in the days when they called him Athanaric, had been captured in some frontier war, and enslaved. His master had him taught the trade of plasterer to enhance his market value.

Pontius Meropius Paulinus, a Roman magnate until he became priest here at Nola, having overhead the mutter he made when mixing his plaster – his prayers – had bought him and manumitted him. Still plasters walls, but here, in the shrine at Nola, as a free man. Theodorus had been a painter all his life – of rich men's seaside villas, in fact often painting, as he had once admitted with a schoolboy's blush on his middle-aged face, salacious pictures in bedrooms. He was free of that now. He was equal, he was free. He had come here of his own free will, with his brushes and bladders and his wonderful hand and eye, submitting to the discipline of the shrine. He painted drapery and faces and hands for God. He imagined what it must have felt and looked like to be a persecuted bishop, so that people in the centuries to come would have a true idea. Turning his head slightly, Marcus watched Theodorus with a flick of the wrist add a tassel to a curtain. On which rich man's wall, wondered Marcus, did he first learn the trick of that sumptuous drapery? Perhaps some man I know.

Or knew.

And the third man on this wall? Though legally no slave, I was then subject to an invisible slavery, and this is *libertas*. Slave to the ambitions which my father thrust upon me ever since I can remember, but to which I consented, so the blame is mine. Slave to my pungent little vices, to those hot matrons, to those tender little gullible girls. A slave to my professional habit of manipulating others. Which I told myself I did for Stilicho, yet found pleasure in. Then, in the midst of all the pointless pleasure, the dumb guilt, struck with lightning, smitten by God.

And how did it happen? I can only answer, by the grace of God. My old comrades will ask why. The Princess Veleda, if she still remembers me (but of course she remembers me, they always remember their first) will be baffled. Freed by no process of law, as in ordinary manumission. Freed by accepting symbols that signify states of mind and soul. Redeemed by the indelible blood of a God who chose to be crucified, taking upon himself the death of a thief or a mutineer. Baptised in water as a sign. A God who went down to hell, to save me from hell, the hell into which I was plunging my old self. And rose again. Here too, he told himself, we are also brothers. *Fratri*, kinsmen, brothers. I am brooding too much, I am neglecting the work. I am making mistakes.

Marcus – an only son, to whom brotherhood was a novel idea – went back patiently along his line of work to a patch of wall his hand had missed. What other remissness had slipped by, while his mind was running away with itself? He concentrated, stroke after gritty stroke. Criss. Cross. This wall is scored criss-cross, to the glory of God. Nothing slapdash.

The bell rang, though Theodorus to all appearances took no notice. On the fourth stroke of the clapper, however, his brush made its last triumphantly opulent twist. Then, because their painter had finished, the others too set down their tools. They were there to serve him.

Theodorus sighed, as if after a great physical effort, and looked critically at what he had done. I watch the other two closely, only to understand them, thought Marcus. I am an observer. That is my nature. I used to watch others so as to have power over them. Now I look at things and people, and contemplate God, so as to understand.

The cluster of buildings stood on the tipping edge of pleasantly wooded ground that overlooked the white walls and tiled roofs of Nola. They stood foursquare around an open space, the shrine of St Felix, and at right-angles to it, two low-roofed blocks of cells, one for men, one for women. Facing was the basilica, its walls lined with frescoes and with heavy silver vessels on the altar. A library across the way, and the plain, severe refectory. Everything here, thought Marcus, even that clanging bronze in the campanile, is an object made for a purpose, the service of God. Here in Nola, to left and right, are the last material traces of the immense inherited fortune that Pontius Meropius Paulinus and his wife Therasia once shared between them. All the rest but this had gone to the poor.

They bought slaves their freedom. They gave money, more or less ineptly, to the poor. Cunning men pounced on them, like carrion crows, helping to strip them, until towards the end there was just enough left to create the nucleus, here in Nola, of an alternative to the established ways of imperial Rome.

At Nola, Paulinus worked hard, his heart and soul were in what he was attempting, but he was more poet than saint, and sometimes, thoughtlessly, more of a grand gentleman than was entirely prudent. He could be impulsive and wrong-headed, but no one at Nola ever turned against him, because what other way of life was there, once you had tried this?

Members of the community were lining up in the basilica to right and left, men on one side, women on the other. Marcus ever since he first got here had made a particular effort not to interest himself in those women, sisters though they were – no surreptitious glances. That they were not all plain and saintly he was by now well aware.

Here, in the unceasing war between the sexes, a truce had been declared, which ran counter to the lifetime habit of both Marcus and Paulinus himself. The Rome of inescapable provocation and meaningless amours was behind them both. Sexual neutrality, Marcus tried to remind himself, is good for the soul. Until to you those women are neutral – are sisters – you will not be a Christian.

Heads up, their faces dusky in the gloom, they had all begun to sing a verse from Prudentius's Hymn before Sleep.

Fluxit labor diei
redit et quetis hora
blandus sopo vicissim

The seductive soaring of the women's voices made it more difficult not to glance at their forbidden faces. The differing characters of these women, severe, innocent, sensuous, hearty, naive, came ringing out in the timbre of their voices. The sound of one particularly cold pure voice made Marcus tremble.

A shuffle of muscles easing went through the basilica as Paulinus, standing at the rail which marked off the altar, began to read from a papyrus roll held out between his two hands.

'*Pater noster qui es in caelis sanctificetur nomen tuum. Adveniat regnum tuum fiat, voluntas tua sicut in caelo et in terra –*'

This newfangled translation of the gospels into Latin had been made by Jerome in Jerusalem, and a copy sent across the sea to Paulinus. Not everyone was used to it yet; older people resented the unfamiliar form of words, yet by daily repetition Jerome's 'paternoster' was entering the mind.

And the church, thought Marcus, standing for the moment outside all this and in the skin of his old, observant self, has brains. Not the pestilential Christian lobby around the dim-witted Emperor Honorius. The faith might be better off without that. Brains. The handful of exceptional men, Jerome and Augustine, Prudentius and even Paulinus, scattered around the Mediterranean, the inland sea, centre of the civilised world. Men to whom God has given intellect and literary power.

Paulinus, up there by the altar, was a man over fifty, and his hooked profile gave him an inherited look of arrogance, which Marcus when first he came here had misinterpreted, until he saw how Paulinus tried always to soften his accosting stare with a deliberate smile. And all of us here, thought Marcus, can watch him struggling with his own imperfections, at the same time as he observes us wrestling with our own.

The service had come to an end. With a gesture of his right hand – one Roman patrician signalling amiably to another – Paulinus invited Marcus to attend on him in the sacristy while he disrobed. Marcus helped Paulinus off with his vestment, as a matter of course, though outside Nola any such menial service would have been a job for a slave, and derogatory, and both saw the humour of it.

'By the way,' Paulinus told him, 'you have a visitor from Rome.'

Marcus felt at those words like a wild creature lured by a

ruse into a trap. Someone here asking for him, from the world he had renounced? Had Veleda tracked him down?

'Your father,' added Paulinus, taking care in the way he spoke to make out that this was nothing extraordinary. 'I think he wants you back.'

'And do I go?'

'He has the legal power to compel you,' said Paulinus, formally, yet both knew that the question was being left open, for Marcus to answer as he chose, but according to the spirit – the *ethos* – of Nola.

As a Roman, Marcus both in law and by tradition had a duty of obedience to his father. He might until lately have been a brilliant staff-officer with the rank of colonel, yet a father had much the same dominion over his son as over his slaves.

Even before he knew his father for a money-lending upstart, persistently shouldering his way to ever greater wealth and influence, the old man had made Marcus cringe. Even as a boy he had tried to live by some different model – to form and follow his personal idea of what it might mean to be a Roman.

The expensive life he had led as a fashionable young officer, the commander-in-chief's personal friend, had of course been paid for out of his father's pocket. Of this he could never be unaware, yet even so Marcus had tried in every way to live differently from his father. Stilicho, with his joviality, his amours, his guile, his devotion to the army, though hardly the perfection of manhood (*Christ was that!*) had been his living model in those days. And I came here to Nola, thought Marcus, seeing his way through all this, to leave the world of money, and break that last golden link. Now he will forge it again.

'You are waiting for me to say that by now I have another father,' Marcus suggested to Paulinus. '*Pater noster qui es in caelis* – Our Father who art in Heaven.' Paulinus's arrogant face relaxed – delight at this answer was shining in his eyes. 'But in any case,' said Marcus, 'he has *potestas* – legal power over me. I must see him and explain.'

'Perhaps even have an effect on him,' answered Paulinus sententiously. 'Try to bear in mind that your father, Octavian, is a man too like other men, and with a heart which may be touched. I put him over there, in my cell – and getting bored with waiting, I'm quite sure.'

Priest though he may have become, Pontius Meropius Paulinus still considered old Octavian Curtius as a rich parvenu, who had used his money to marry into a family too good for him: it showed in the curl of his lip.

The first thing anyone noticed about Octavian Curtius's face was his bulbous red nose, which made him look like a comic drunkard – an unjust disfigurement, that nose, since as rich Romans went, Octavian was temperate. Nor was he in the slightest bothered by the grossness of his nose, he would tap it significantly, he would stroke it. Marcus as a small and lonely boy had got firmly into his head that money itself must be poisonous. He saw his father every day run money through his fingers, heard him talk of it incessantly. Was money what made noses swell and then turn red?

Marcus rapped knuckles on the door of Paulinus's cell, and pushed it open. The nose, the sarcastic voice, would be waiting for him. His father to pass the time had been taking a quick look at Paulinus's private business. He shoved a rolled papyrus hurriedly into a rack, and turned to face Marcus with a shameless grin.

'I hope they are giving you a better room than this,' said red-nosed Octavian, lowering himself, like a man not used to such discomfort, on to the plank edge of the pallet-bed.

Marcus tried to keep every trace of rancour out of his voice. 'What have you come for?'

'Don't worry, my lad. I'm not here to give your little game away.'

'My little game?'

'I see what you are up to,' said Octavian Curtius, wagging his finger with mock severity. He could now, thought Marcus, bringing to mind the past, turn either way. His mock severity could become real severity – *potestas*. Or he could pretend – which is almost more clever of him, but more horrible – to be my true friend.

'There was a nasty rumour that Johannes had got rid of you – pitched head first into the marshes of Ravenna, a feast for the eels. Why couldn't you trust your wise old father? I worried about you. When you decided to disappear, why not tell me? Do you suppose you are the only one clever enough to spot how things are going?'

'Clever enough?' No one had spoken to Marcus like this for a long time. He could not follow the idiom.

'Go on, play the innocent if that amuses you. So nothing more was to be gained in the service of Flavius Stilicho? That much I grant you. His day is over. The Christians –' Octavian gave a long, low whistle. 'At the imperial court? Thick as fleas. If I were a younger man with my life before me I would join them myself, only everyone would laugh.' The old man held out a hand. Marcus took hold of his father's hand – infected, no doubt, he thought, with a suppressed shudder, from handling all that money – and deliberately passed the infection on to himself. His father's handshake was as usual the firm, sincere handshake by which men of business were so often deceived.

'How did you find me?'

'Olympius pointed me in the right direction. There is not much these days that your old comrade-in-arms fails to notice. And what a career he is making for himself at court! He has the Emperor's ear – but you know that. And a Christian, too. But of course, he got in early.'

Octavian held his protuberant nose between two fingers, and gently caressed it, as though its redness, its largeness, were a private charm. He did that only when he was very pleased. 'Christians?' Octavian went on, and began to shake with silent laughter. 'Don't give me Christians! Play the saint with others, my boy – not with me.'

The old man dug Marcus teasingly in the ribs, as if the two of them had met by accident on some hot and idle Roman afternoon in a fashionable brothel. 'I shall spread the word. Discreetly, of course. Even pretend to disapprove if you like. Yes, that would carry conviction. But, Christians! Though look here, Marcus. Saint Marcus, if you like. You're my son, and the time has come for us to talk seriously.'

'If you think,' answered Marcus simply, though here, now, in front of this once-dreaded face, of what use was simple sincerity? 'that anything you might say would alter in the slightest –'

'Money any use?' Octavian cocked his head sideways, and the small eyes on either side of his huge nose twinkled. 'Paulinus and his wife are fools where money is concerned. I've never seen a couple in such a hurry to get rid of it. Listen. The time may well be coming when they would be glad of a little more of the same. And then's your chance –'

'I've put all that behind me,' Marcus told him, but in a voice denuded of conviction. Touch this ugly old man's heart by confiding in him about one's father in heaven? I might as well still be a naughty little boy, waiting with hands behind my back for a thrashing. The commandments bid me honour this ugly old man. Very well, then, honour him. Tell him. Speak what is in your mind. Slowly Marcus began telling his father how he was living here, what he was doing – working with Felix and Theodorus on the wall.

'Work with your hands? On the buildings? So they told me.' Octavian dropped his voice confidentially. 'Humiliating for people like ourselves. I know. But what cleverer way of getting them to accept you? I see what you are up to, my lad.'

'I have another father now,' Marcus Curtius began expounding, uncomfortably, as if repeating a lesson not learned well enough.

'Your father in heaven? I heard all about that, just now, from Paulinus. You would never suppose to look at Paulinus now, so mealy-mouthed, that years ago he stabbed a man.'

His voice when he said that had been raised loud enough to be heard at the end of the corridor. Can this be the devil, wondered Marcus despairingly, come here in familiar shape, as my father? Or has my father all my life been simply the devil in human form?

'You don't like what I say? But it helps,' said old Octavian cheerfully, 'to restore your sense of proportion. Don't worry, you are doing all right. Only bear in mind my little offer.' He made a gesture as if counting coin. My hands are too much like his, thought Marcus. And will my face be, soon?

'You had better go,' said Marcus. There were footsteps in the corridor. The old man nodded, as if they had become fellow conspirators.

'Oh, and another thing –' Mischievously Octavian Curtius had again raised his voice.

'Yes?'

'What do you do here for cunt?' The last word rang out like a clash of cymbals.

'You wouldn't understand,' answered Marcus hoarsely, as if

his face had been smeared on both cheeks and across his mouth by foul fingers.

'You think so? I saw whole flocks of them, trotting demurely into that church of yours. There's some nice pussy there, my boy.'

He slapped Marcus on the back. And if only, thought Marcus, I were a boy again, and that heavy slap the first of his blows, ever increasing in savagery and meant to bring on tears. Then since Romans do not cry, the tears too must be punished. More blows. After the fist, the strap and the stick.

'*Si non casta, cauta*. I know your Christian cant. If you can't be good, be careful. Just so long as you never take a turn the other way,' Octavian Curtius said, in a parting voice now deeply serious. 'Boys, you know. I will stand for most things but I would never stand for that.'

3

There was once a time, Flavius Stilicho felt bound to remind himself, as he stood bareheaded before the Emperor, when to ride two hundred miles down a Roman highway, with a dress uniform in a parcel on the crupper, and a groom tagging on behind you, killing horses under you, would have been exhilarating. Why then, today here in the throne room, do I feel so stiff?

His bow to Honorius had hardly been more than a painful jerk of the body. That piqued the boy on the dais, with his pout and his diadem and his red-soled shoes.

The black-fringed slave Johannes, perpetually by the Emperor's elbow, had lately been making sure that in the imperial presence all ceremonial was kept up in the smallest detail. The less real power here at court for that young men, thought Stilicho, the more humbug. Stilicho as he came erect, bones creaking, saw Johannes start to whisper a sarcasm in the Emperor's ear.

No more of that, thought Stilicho.

The moment had come.

Gilda, alone before a rapt audience, could hardly have improved on the single gesture with which the heavy-bodied, white-haired man, accustomed all his life to the army way of prompt obedience, raised a finger. He pointed straight at Black Johannes's face – the pinning-down gesture that makes any slave writhe. In a clearcut voice few anywhere would care to disobey, Stilicho said simply, 'You. Go a long way off, and don't come back.'

From his throne, would Honorius speak up for his slave? That was Black Johannes's only chance.

But Honorius had been hearing that tone of voice from Stilicho since boyhood, and dare not. The young Emperor's mouth hung open, his vacant eye was pretending to be many miles away. From long obedience, and from wine-stupor, the words he might have said were stifled in his mouth.

The black-haired slave was taken aback, but had not yet begun to obey. He was still waiting for a word from that vacant-faced young man. Everyone in the palace now feared Black Johannes. The simple, confident, arrogant order from this terrible old man had taken him by the throat. Still gazing into space, the Emperor said nothing. I had better simulate obedience this time, Johannes told himself in dark anger, and trap that old man later.

Stilicho put his right hand casually on the jewelled hilt of his dress sword, and lifted it an inch as Black Johannes hesitated. The slave no longer dragged his feet, but hustled through the curtains. Slavery is fear, reflected Stilicho, bred from birth into the flesh.

Johannes as he left the presence-chamber was passing among self-important menials, *nomenclatores*, *ornatores*, not even glancing at his fellow-slaves, his palace-bred face impassive. I shall let him win this one, Johannes decided, because I have to. This morning we all thought that Stilicho was in Rome, not here in Ravenna. But this time is the last. He shall never take me by surprise again. I shall dig a pit for him.

The palace guard had been posted around the throne room, and were watching Black Johannes as he hurried away. As Stilicho went in to see the Emperor, hand-picked men moving at a nod had been backed into recesses along corridors, or placed quietly behind curtains, or set on make-believe sentry-go outside empty rooms. The guardsmen were under the direct command of Olympius, who had beforehand promised a gold chain to the man who struck the first blow, a gold coin for each man who took an active part, and instant death for the first to speak out of turn.

'That cry?' asked Honorius, closing his vacant mouth as if roused from a dream. He was alone here, with formidable Stilicho, and a man screaming like that meant violence.

'Olympius on my orders is punishing one of your household slaves.' Stilicho might have been mentioning a domestic matter of no consequence. 'The punishment in this case was death. So that all the posts your man Johannes held under the Emperor are now vacant.'

From under his dress uniform Stilicho brought out a glass phial full of purple ink, with a gold pen, and a roll of papyrus from which an authenticating lead seal already dangled. Honorius, though he had not quite taken in about Johannes, felt apprehensive. They were always after him to sign things.

'Here, *imperator*, is a commission to appoint Olympius – an honourable soldier for once, and not a slave – to all the posts now vacant, including command of the *agentes in rebus* –'

The gold pen was in Honorius's hand. How had it come there? Stilicho, on one knee and not even caring how much the posture hurt him, had uncorked the ink bottle, and was holding out the pen. He unrolled the blank end of the papyrus, making of his own knee a rough-and-ready desk, as if this were not the palace, but an encampment. Honorius's eyes were fixed on that dangling lead seal. His simple signature added to a document with that seal attached would give it the force of legal authority.

And would refusing to sign bring Johannes back to life? This terrible old soldier had no right to affix the lead seal first. That was disrespectful.

'And if I won't?' said Honorius petulantly. But Stilicho remained there, impassive, as though he hadn't heard, and already, as if of its own accord, the gold pen had written a purple H, two verticals, a small horizontal. The imperial signature, his very self in fact, going down there letter by letter on the papyrus held ready. His name as Emperor was himself in the highest degree. Then why, Honorius asked himself tipsily, do I always hate signing things? Why am I writing down the letters of my name, one by one, against my own will?

Stilicho wiped the gold pen on a square of clean linen, exquisitely hemmed in purple thread, since even a small drop of the Emperor's ink had importance. Now came the less-than-honest but no less necessary part. Honorius himself, before his own thick ideas became clear, must be implicated.

'*Imperator* – today you have done a great deed. By this time they are fastening a weight on your slave's ankles. They will drop him in the marshes, where he has already sent so many victims to feed the eels of Ravenna. You have had a very lucky escape, Honorius. You have acted just in time.' He used the Emperor's name familiarly, as if Honorius were a boy again. 'Today you have saved both your throne and your life. You have survived a terrible threat, and all Rome will be glad.'

Most of the time we are honourable truth-tellers, Stilicho prompted himself. But only so that in such an emergency as this our lie may be believed. Serena, Julia and Olympius had put their heads together, and insisted that what he was now about to say must be uttered in the Emperor's presence, word for word. The Emperor if not won over must at least be confused.

Stilicho went on to tell the dramatic lie, and even to make it ring true.

A harlot, introduced into the Emperor's bed by a trick, was claiming now to be with child. Johannes's plot was simply this: to have under his thumb an imperial bastard – a pretender to the throne. You must mention Gilda by name, Serena had insisted, though not looking at her husband as she spoke, thinking, that will finish her off. Stilicho had said coldly, no names. But could the infatuated young man – this was the thing to find out, have known that the first time he ever had a woman it was Gilda?

Honorius told him at last, unwillingly, petulantly, 'They came one after another, as in a dream. I told my confessor about the first, and a dream, he told me, was what she must have been. The first never came again, she was wonderful, she showed me everything.' Hearing that said gave Stilicho a twinge of insupportable resentment. Share Gilda with this hobbledehoy? Yet with how many others had he shared her? And never thought twice about it? I am getting possessive about her, he told himself – and what does that signify?

'My confessor merely said it was a *succubus*. I was to fold my hands on my chest as I went to sleep, and think of Christ on the Cross, and say my prayers. If I missed out a single word, I was to go back again, from the beginning.'

'If your confessor is right – and of course, he must be,' said Stilicho gravely, 'then, as I suspected, you have been a victim of witchcraft.' He spoke in a paternal tone, as if he, too, were a confessor, a shrewder and more worldly one. A hint of witchcraft, once passed on, he was thinking, would set all the priests by the ears.

Into Honorius's immature face had come a vindictive grin. He was eager to wound. He let fly with words someone else must have put in his mouth – Black Johannes? – like an urchin flinging a stone.

'What is it like – to be *impotens*?'

Stilicho's hardbitten face, to the Emperor's chagrin, gave nothing away, though inside he went as brittle as ice. An insult was an insult, even from an Emperor. Stonily he ignored the question, as though it had never been asked.

'The other thing is a sin, anyway,' muttered Honorius, dropping his eyes. 'Perhaps I also should be *impotens* – for the sake of Jesus Christ, you know.'

'Not *impotens* – *castus*,' said Stilicho, thinking with sour amusement, here I am, teaching this young dunderhead the rudiments of his own theology – the distinction between impotent and chaste. In the course of nature, everything comes to an end. Why should that particular natural loss be held so shameful – a topic for mockery? And leave me so devastated?

Strike back, he told himself. Another way to poultice your pride. On the young man's breath was the habitual odour of hot spiced wine.

'And what has the slave who for his witchcraft is at this very moment going down headlong, to burn in hell, been giving you to drink?' These, thought Stilicho with weary bitterness, are the victories that now I win. Verbally, over a weakling.

'Wine,' mumbled Honorius.

Black Johannes was dead, and here, watching him, was the

dominatingly obsessive masculine ghost that had haunted his childhood.

'Did it taste like wine?'

'It tasted better.'

'There are opiates that sorcerers use,' went on the old man, mock-solemnly. 'I implore you, Honorius, from now on touch no wine. Whatever your priest may try to tell you that St Paul may have said – I know the arguments – wine is the worst witchcraft of all.'

Tomorrow, thought Stilicho, he will wake up with dry mouth, and reach for a goblet of wine that is not there.

'You will crave for it – but pray for strength. Resist the temptation to drink wine, like a man – like a Roman Emperor.' The recollection of Serena's bony old body had come into Stilicho's mind – a body now abhorrent to him. Had Serena's demands on him made him impotent? For her he was doing this dirty job. Yes – but also for Gilda.

Honorius sat there, sullenly gloomy. The terms of his life had changed so quickly. Johannes was dead, in hell. On the difficult journey to Asti some of his cage birds had died – not even a Roman Emperor could alter the fact of death. For Honorius, there was nothing worse that death. Whenever like a black bogey it entered his mind, he would send for his confessor, and plead to be told yet again about the Resurrection.

Stilicho wandered through the corridors of the palace, avoiding his fellow conspirators, that word *impotens* echoing uncannily in his ears. For a Roman there could be nothing worse – to be flaccid, to be passive. You have lived by facts in the past, Stilicho told himself sternly, and this misfortune is a fact.

In course of time, would even Gilda mock? A public woman, who slept with men for money? When the pregnancy was over, at the time when she might have less need of him, would she turn away from him, laughing?

And the other question, that even I cannot answer – is this child mine?

A child who might cost me my neck? Do I want this child? Was it to make this child that I entered with such eagerness, time and again, Gilda's appetising body?

In public, on a stage, Gilda had made an open jest of his

fatherhood. And would she have done that, Stilicho asked himself, if the child were not mine? Yes, thinking how Gilda had stood at the roadside, in her ostrich feathers, when he marched against the Alemanni – yes, she might well have done. A woman both fearless and unpredictable. She would dramatise.

He was moving rapidly past gilded columns and purple curtains. The guardsmen once hidden there were gone. Here I am, thought Stilicho, a white-haired and once all-important man, walking down an empty corridor of the palace, scratching my head and laughing to myself. They will think I am going senile. In this dry old age of mine, I am evidently becoming what as a young man I thought I might like to be, only father opposed it. A philosopher.

In a downstairs room of Claudian's house on the Aventine, Lucas stood at a ledge-desk, fair-copying a manuscript. The narrow, latticed window on his left had a view across the garden – rose arbours and clumps of carnation, and a dribbling, moss-encrusted fountain with an old, pot-bellied garden-god exhibiting his phallus.

Not far off was the Tiber, a row of masts, and, on the far bank, busy workmen, who in the Emperor's name but at Stilicho's urging were beginning to repair the old city wall, neglected through all the safe centuries.

Lucas turned his head from the window – the glimpse of green, the distant animation, had been a relief to his eyes – and went on conscientiously copying scroll after scroll. His one idea was to finish this copying and slip away, surreptitiously, into the heart of the city, in case Gilda might be able to meet him in their upstairs room.

She was by now heavy-bodied, the skin stretched tight over her face, her vivacity gone. They met in a room on the seventh floor – the safest place to hide, Gilda has said, because Stridor's spy dogged her only when she left the *insula*.

Gilda's obstinate silence about the father's identity however was making Stridor morose. How could he do his best for her unless she would tell him? Halfheartedly, since she was too valuable to damage, he had even threatened Gilda with a prod from his lead-weighted cane – enough to break a bone. Or even, he warned her, to make her child miscarry if he poked her in the belly. Out of me, though, he got no names, Gilda told Lucas afterwards, reliving what had happened and even exaggerating it. Lucas could have gone downstairs, there and then, to strangle the little eunuch with his bare hands.

Lucas obsessively watched Claudian's measured words come neatly, one after the other, from the iron tip of his own pen. He told himself: I am Claudian's other pair of eyes, his other hand. He and I between us are giving this sequence of Latin words its ordered excellence. His effort one way and another is greater than mine, but mine, too, is essential. Is this my hand, or his? Are those his words, or mine? Lucas paused very briefly, to improve the shape of a serif. Would Claudian himself ever have bothered?

On the other hand, as Lucas well knew, when a scribe starts thinking, self-consciously, about the shape of a single letter, mistakes creep into the copy. He lifted and flexed his hand, took another and this time longer look at the view. Army engineers with measuring rod and long chalked cord were marking out a line. Barbarian pioneers had begun mortaring into place a huge stone, perhaps fallen out of the wall a century since. Precautions, they said, against Alaric. But surely Alaric had been defeated?

In through the door as Lucas stared through the window, and smiling with benign self-importance, came Claudian. He was usually distraught when he pushed his way in here, his mind full of necessary verbal changes. But today with a smile he led into the room a stranger carrying a white rod, an official. Lucas wondered at first if he might be some kind of army engineer with a very short measuring rod, but of course he was a *lictor*, and that rod his *festuca* – his symbol of authority.

Claudian gestured Lucas to get up from his work and come closer, then began to speak, but in such a formal and distant voice that Lucas's heart sank. Had he been spotted on some nightly foray to that hired room? Would this turn out to be punishment? If so, why the smile?

'This man is Lucas, son of a freedman in Londinium. Lucas asserts that though born a slave he was freed in Londinium, at the same time as his father, when he was six years old, and was in due course lawfully received as a freedman into the scribes' guild there. He was sold into slavery by an act of injustice, and here in my hand are the written proofs of what I assert –'

Claudian had all that part off pat, he was waving a scroll – but how had he got to know? He must, thought Lucas, have done it very laboriously, through the imperial bureaucracy – the all-pervading justice-machine. He must have sent questions to Londoninium and to Rotomagus, and insisted on an official reply.

'I Claudius Claudianus, tribune and notary, am his *assertor libertatis*. I hereby assert that my slave, Lucas, should be free.'

The truth of what was happening to him dazzled Lucas's eyes like a flash of summer lightning. Not punishment, but the dreamlike piece of luck he had seldom even dared dream of: manumission!

Raising his white stick the *lictor* hit Lucas over the head, sharply enough to hurt. The blow was meant to come as a shock. And that, officially, will be the last blow, the last indignity, ever to fall on me unresented, thought Lucas with great joy. By that symbolic blow the *lictor*, concurring in what the *assertor libertatis* told him, had acknowledged Lucas as a freedman.

Like being born again.

A smack on the head from a white stick by a state official – was freedom that easy? No, there was more to come. With a smile of generous complicity, lank-haired, haggard Claudian slapped Lucas on both cheeks. He then spun him around, as in a child's game, until he was giddy. These actions of the former master meant nothing legally, but were a bit of traditional fun, meant to impress on the mind of the freedman the importance of what had happened, by bewildering him.

Lucas had felt for one crazy moment that he was the toy of these two men – a puppet, being manipulated. As Claudian smacked his face – but Claudian until now had never laid hands on him – Lucas even began to fear the change. Since they kidnapped him on the Channel shore he had grown used to the life of a slave. Freedom was lost by the flash of a sword, as when the pagans killed the old bishop. And regained, in this present instance, by the tap of a stick!

'Your name from now on,' announced the poet, his solemn announcement muffled with a cough. 'is Lucas Claudianipor.' *Por* for *puer* – boy. Claudian's boy. That new surname was another traditional touch, hinting at a claim to loyalty that would be almost filial.

The *lictor* was allowing himself a brief smile as he began to note down details of this manumission on the three papyri drawn up in advance – copies for the owner, the freedman and the imperial archives. He went off cheerfully enough, his fee in his pouch, giving a little twirl to the *festuca*, as if his white rod had done a good day's work for him.

'Come upstairs and join me in a meal,' said Claudian, the smile of complicity fixed on his face. 'Let us eat and drink and talk at last, in *aequalitas*, like two old friends.'

Lucas as he trod the broad staircase, with its ivories in alcoves, and its long mural painting – *The Rape of Proserpine*, a clever piece of perspective down the concavity of a wall – was in a turmoil. He had always until now gone up these stairs respectfully, one pace behind Claudian. Today Claudian was purposely walking at his side, and had placed an affectionate hand on his shoulder. Never let me forget, Lucas warned himself, in my changed condition, that the true centre of my life is not here, in this house, with its books and paintings and trophies of great fame, and bad-tempered pretty boys, who will hate me all the more for what has happened. But across the city, in that seventh-floor room in Stridor's *insula*.

What kind of day would it have been for Gilda? Lucas felt obliged to ask himself, as he climbed the stairs one by one. Had she been giddy or breathless or sick? Would she be there waiting, in the attic – if only he could slip away?

Claudian's domestic slaves began to serve the meal, coming and going with dishes and wine, keeping their faces straight at this unwonted novelty, the flute-player performing his discreet music and never once looking Lucas in the eye. They must have talked it over among themselves, decided Lucas, and decided that the best insult was indifference.

Claudian had noticed, of course, and pulled a face, and began ignoring them in his turn. Lucas as he drank glass after glass of a memorable wine tried to find answers to Claudian's civilised chatter that were not too stupid. They had something to celebrate, yet this was not quite a celebration. At last Claudian judged that the wine might have begun to warm Lucas, that odd and stiff but excellent young man.

'Come closer – I have things to tell you.'

The idea of liberating Lucas from servitude had come upon Claudian like a splendid inspiration. Some men, held Aristotle, were by nature slaves. And that certainly goes, thought Claudian ruefully, for any other slave I have ever bought. I lead them home from auction, vibrant with hope, only to find that they are silly, boring, stupid, vicious, and that I am stuck with them.

One should treat them, even so, and bad as they are, not as animals but as men. That was the teaching of the Stoics. Just now, polishing his verses on Pollentia, Claudian fancied himself as a Stoic. Was it Stoic – was it just – to have Lucas linger on in a slavery that was contrary to his nature? His scribe as a freedman, virtually an equal, perhaps even a friend, had been a singular temptation.

There would be one great practical advantage, too.

'I would like to make it clear from the start that I have set you free from motives of affectionate gratitude,' announced Claudian, when the slaves who had served the meal were gone. The two of them were lying there, Roman fashion, taking fruit after the meal, stretched out beside one another, each with an elbow on a low table – and Lucas on slightly closer physical terms with his patron than he might have wished. Claudian had given him, stalk foremost, a pear exactly ripe. The juice trickled down his chin.

'You are free, of course, to choose for yourself. You are free in every way. But I should particularly like you to represent me on a confidential mission.' Claudian reached for Lucas's hand.

Lucas had been thinking, tipsily, of Gilda struggling out of breath up seven flights of stairs and waiting, on the offchance of finding him. She was beginning to look like her own stage caricature. She was gross.

'If you care for me,' said Claudian, as if he were not seducing but discussing some abstract consideration, 'and I believe that you do care for me. Then why not love me? Love, yes. But in another sense a small and not disagreeable bodily action – a service rendered no different from any other.' When Lucas stolidly said nothing, Claudian added in an impatient voice, 'What is so disgusting about it? Even if you think you won't like it – and you might like it very much. You did far more horrid things for me in Como, and never once blenched.'

Claudian, whom the wine had much affected, rose from the couch, and took a fold of his gold-threaded tunic in his left hand. He placed one foot forward, in the stance of an orator. He is displaying himself in front of me, thought Lucas, like a peacock. Lucas knew the poet's foibles well. Under the double influence of wine and fever he was imagining himself a living statue, all glorious. The attitude was broken when Claudian was bent double by a cough.

Outside in the corridor sounded a titter, from eavesdroppers. Did Claudian hear? Lucas wondered angrily. Have they drilled a peephole?

Claudian was meanwhile strutting to and fro, an unappetising body, a stale odour and an epicene demeanour obscuring a sublime mind. Thought Lucas, excited by this new insight, Claudian is making signals – offering to be my slave instead.

Like an old whore, selling herself in the half-light of an alley to a casual passer-by, Claudian flipped up the hem of his silk tunic, to show a flashing glimpse of his brown bottom, and giggled. Lucas, although there were watchers and listeners, found that he too had giggled.

He tried, it was not easy, to keep in mind Claudian's long days of intellectual labour, when he himself had been a mere accessory to this man's tongue and brain. There is no one quite like him alive, thought Lucas, as a human consciousness, a soul. Pathetic when he exposes himself like this. But without the pathos perhaps he would not be human.

Lucas went on sandalled feet across the marble floor towards Claudian – whose feverish face as he came closer grew bright. Lucas whispered in his ear, 'Outside the door they are all listening. Perhaps looking, too.'

A shudder went through Claudian. Lucas put a reassuring hand around his shoulders – let the eavesdroppers think what they chose – and led him back to the couch. After that it was straightforward. They sat, half-reclining but not touching. Lucas filled Claudian's goblet with watered wine, dabbed at his clammy forehead with a napkin. They were talking calmly. Almost like friends. And why not entirely? Lucas wondered.

What lies between us – the shadow of an obligation that Claudian himself was perhaps trying, momentarily to overcome

– was *obsequium*, the tradition of obedience due by a freedman to the master who had liberated him.

Claudian, thought Lucas, is solitary. Except for Flavius Stilicho, what like mind does he have? And Stilicho can never be his intimate friend. He has this solitary vision of Rome as Rome should be. He is lifting both hands to sustain the weight of a falling world, by words and will alone.

'You won't simply take me in your arms,' suggested Claudian roguishly, 'because, despite all you say, you are a Christian.'

A waspish tease, and old ground between them. Claudian had never let Lucas forget that once he had copied for a bishop. He knew perfectly well that Lucas was no Christian.

'I am a philosopher,' said Lucas, with a confident smile that Claudian had never seen on his face before. Freedom changes men very quickly.

'You? A philosopher?'

'On this topic, anyway. What does Plato say, in his *Laws*, of the diversion you had in mind for me?'

'See what comes of learning Greek!' said Claudian, with mock indignation. 'I too grew up with a head full of Greek, but found it too slippery for the verse I had in mind. I grew up in Alexandria, you in Britain. What do they speak in Britain? Tell me again.'

'In Londoninium, we all, more or less, speak Latin.'

'An Egyptian if you like to call me that, a Briton, and Latin has made us Romans. I wished to write in the language of the civilised power that has kept peace in the world for four hundred years! Never before in world history has there been world peace! And perhaps never again! Latin, my dear Lucas, is not only the words we use but the way that they lead us to think. Justice. Duty. Integrity. Seriousness. *Justicia. Gravitas.* What have we Romans to do with the complicated philosophical notions of quarrelsome little city states, who could never manage their own small affairs without endless civil war?'

'The mistress of the civilised world has lost her grip – ask them in Londinium,' said Lucas promptly. He brought to mind what for years, here, in safe Rome, he had been trying to forget: pagan pirates on the Channel coast, brigands infesting the forests of Gaul. All that mindless violence, coming closer.

'Mistress more than ever,' Claudian retorted. 'Mistress of

the world in the realm of the spirit. Every barbarian who assails us – even Alaric – wishes in his secret heart to be Roman.'

'Even the Huns?' asked Lucas, and Claudian laughed, throwing up his hands, like a fencer hit. The presence in the city of a few dozen Huns, recruited for Stilicho's guard, men with no respect whatever for civilised values, had set tongues wagging. Smiling indulgently after that snap answer about the Huns, the poet added.

'Well, Lucas – what did Plato tell us in his *Laws*?'

'*Magister*, what you were inviting me to, Plato forbids. Saying, so far as I remember, this. *A law which permits the sexual act only for its natural purpose, procreation, and forbids homosexual relations, in which the human race is deliberately murdered* . . .' Lucas thus far was pleased with himself, but how did it go on?

Claudian with a corpse smile broke in, 'Not quite correctly quoted, but even so –' He paused, his sick chest croaking with excitement, and as he spoke, his eye swivelled towards the door. They had spoiled it for him. There might have been no pallid quotations from Plato but for those beastly slave boys. In the morning, Claudian told himself, I shall order whippings. I really shall. There is a first time for everything. Yet he knew that however dreadfully his boys behaved, he could never have them whipped.

'And you will have to leave me right away,' said Claudian plaintively. It might have been the wine, or perhaps the fever, but there were tears in his eyes. Lucas got up to go. There might still be time to see Gilda.

'Not leave right away, not now, you silly. *Fatuus*! I don't mean this very minute. Dare one call one's own freedman *fatuus*? Do you resent that I call you *fatuus*, Lucas Claudianipor?' For the first time since the ceremony, Lucas heard his new name spoken aloud. *Claudianipor* was someone else, as yet a stranger.

'Ah – you mean this commission you spoke of.'

'You must anyway go away from here – from this house – without delay, because if you stay much longer the others will poison your soup. They are beginning to hate you.' His voice dropped, so that no one outside the door could possibly have heard. 'I too am compelled to leave Rome, though don't tell anyone else, I implore you. The great Serena ordains, the great Stilicho concurs. Unprotected by them, here in Rome I am nothing. And they admit that they can no longer reach out a hand to save me. Does that surprise you, Lucas? The times are changing. What grows must decay. My health, too – I really should try a better climate. And my wealth – my potentially enormous wealth. Yes Lucas,' he said brightly, 'I am going to be rich. The widow they have found for me has numerous properties. Near Zama. There is nowhere else in the civilised world, you know, as safe as Africa.'

'Even after Pollentia, you think Rome unsafe?' asked Lucas in astonishment. Had they not just spent weeks polishing the verses that celebrated that great victory?

'*Pollentia, take my song's eternity*,' Claudian tipsily intoned.
'*Your splendid name that chimes eternal joy*
Earth of our fated victory, and grave
Of savage hosts! Your fields have deeply learned
The doom that falls on all who menace Rome
– splendid, no doubt, but is it true, my dear Lucas? I mean, historically. Everyone would dearly like to believe the truth of it, and it has poetic truth. But is it true, as prophecy?'

'So long as we have an army, the Roman legions, a great general –' Lucas suggested.

'Alaric is still king in Illyricum, and the mountains of Illyricum are the empire's best recruiting ground. He will have a new army before we can collect our wits. Meanwhile pray tell me where can Rome recruit an army? I mean, without recruiting barbarians. From the demoralised mob, here in the city? And tell me something else – a very simple question. Who is Rome's best general, if you don't count Flavius Stilicho? I would like to hear you name him.' Claudian was uncovering sentence by sentence, the pessimism that in his public verse – written for the sake of Rome – resonated underneath but never came quite to the surface. 'In an underhanded way, the legions are being turned against their general. Everything is going to pieces.' Claudian pulled a face. 'I have been Stilicho's friend, his spokesman – trumpeted his fame,' said Claudian. 'And – yes – he has protected me. As things get worse for him, they will strike at him through me. They have tried already. Now do you see why my two patrons say so firmly that it must be Africa? And you are the man I need, Lucas, to prepare the way for me. No-one else will do.'

'Africa?' muttered Lucas. Africa was just a name – the distant place from which the grain-ships arrived. Himself to Africa – and Gilda here in Rome?

'To introduce me there. To represent me,' said Claudian, with a formality that showed he was also making an appeal, and one Lucas could scarcely deny, to his unwritten right of *obsequium*. 'Tell me the facts. Warn me what to expect. Lucas – simply think of it! Not since I first got away from my mother have I ever contemplated marriage. Could you yourself bear the thought of living in the same house continually, with any woman, were she ninety years of age? Perhaps you can – but I am terrified. Here in my house on the Aventine there isn't a single female of any description, not even a tabby cat, and while I live there never shall be. This bride they have found for me – this Cornelia. To judge by the portrait they have sent me, she is no small size.'

He went to the sideboard, where a woman's likeness on a small, thin panel of elephant ivory had been turned to the wall. Claudian showed Lucas the portrait with a limp grin, as though it were intrinsically lewd. 'You observe the tricks the painter has used to shrink her dewlap cheeks, her double chin, and still keep a likeness?' he said to Lucas with a nudge, as if sharing with him a boyish secret. On Cornelia's forehead was a girlish cluster of little black curls like a bunch of ripe berries. Her complexion was dark – in real life, perhaps even darker – and she had thick lips, as if a creature meant by nature to taste and suck and swallow.

'African,' remarked Claudian, as if that said all.

'She may be fat, but she looks good-natured.'

'Oh – you think so?' said Claudian, as if grasping at that much hope. 'You see, then, why you must go? I too would rather stay here. I like my view, and I shall miss it. But I too have obligations. I am Stilicho's man just as you now are mine. We are Romans, all,' he announced, as if deriding his own rhetoric. 'Lucas, having become a free man, does not therefore instantly become one with the demoralised city mob. Don't you feel more than ever a Roman, Lucas, now that I have so carefully explained all this to you? Apart from anything else, let us also be practical. I need my library packed into boxes, and carefully conveyed to this woman's house, or we shall neither of us have anything down there to read.'

'Barrels,' Lucas interjected.

'Why barrels?'

'Sailors find them easier to handle, and most of all, they are watertight.'

'How much you know that I should never think of!' Claudian took Lucas by the wrist, at last in earnest. 'I need to hear, from someone I can trust, what she is like, what the place is like. What my new life will be. How to prepare myself, Lucas – how to protect myself. For the sake of my work, I must protect myself. And who but you understands the necessity?'

The imploring note that had come unwontedly into Claudian's voice was choked off by an atrocious fit of coughing. Once again Lucas was Claudian's nurse, spreading him out on the couch in the posture that he knew from experience made breathing easier, drenching a napkin in wine to bathe his temples. The poet was screwing up his eyes against the light of the silver lamp that Lucas had brought close. The fit was over.

'You consent?' Claudian asked, in the ghost of his usual voice.

'I obey.'

'But you do *agree*?' Claudian's voice had a tinge of irrepressible irony.

'I obey and I agree.' The imminent loss of Gilda had at first seemed greater than any other consideration. But impulsive tenderness prompted Lucas to add, 'I consent.'

With a throaty chuckle of pleasure at getting his own way, the poet lay back, relaxed. His breath after a while came with more regularity, and, getting up, he went across the room to a locked chest in the corner. From under folded clothes and stacks of papyrus he fumbled out a small leather bag.

'Catch!' Claudian tried to throw it across the room, but had nowhere near the strength. The leather bag hit marble: a metallic clash: those were coins.

'Lucas Claudianipor, free man as you are, the law no longer obliges me to feed you and give you shelter. From this day forth you live at your own expense. Others have learned how to hire themselves out to best advantage, and if ever you leave me, so must you. The money in this bag is to pay your way to Africa.

Spend it prudently. Remember, there can be no freedom without money. More's the pity.'

The papyrus recording his manumission had been rolled as tightly as it would go inside a hollow piece of cane, sealed by wax at each end and sewn inside the lining of his tunic. Around his waist next the skin was a body belt, with the gold and silver coins from Claudian's bag, and the poet's first present for Cornelia – a thumb ring, cut entire out of a large, flawed, Egyptian emerald.

The ring had been wildly expensive, an extravagance that Claudian no sooner committed than he regretted. But after all, he told Lucas cynically, I shall soon get my money back. There was a couplet engraved inside in tiny letters, which could just be read if the ring were tilted to the light.

She mingles hues. The stars with gold she dowers,
Purples the sea and gems the shore with flowers.

Claudian, instead of composing something new, had simply taken a couple of lines from the manuscript nearest at hand, his unfinished *Rape of Proserpine*.

Lucas in preparation for a long journey, much of which must be done on foot, was wearing leather boots that came halfway up the calf. Inside the right boot had been sewn a hidden sheath for a knife, and the hilt of the knife pressed against his leg, as if to remind him that a freedman was not forbidden a weapon.

The sword-smith from whom Lucas bought his knife had worn a bullhide apron, and the skin of his face and bare arms was pocked by a lifetime's exposure to live sparks. Against the folded-back door of his booth under a colonnade near the Pantheon, enviable new swords were hanging in a row from hooks. From inside came the gasping puff and glow of a forge. When Lucas paused, to take a good look at the swords hanging there, the smith, speaking to him as if he were a slave, said jocosely, 'Not for you, young man. Do you want an old fellow like me to end up in prison?'

Since the day he was freed there had been other similar snubs, and they made Lucas angry. Did the mark of slavery never rub off?

'I am manumitted. I have the document in my pocket.'

'Manumitted – and the first thing you think of is a sword – am I right?'

Lucas did not bother to argue. This was obviously a conversation with a customer that the old man had had many times before. The old man rolled his sleeve higher and showed his brand. Workers in public factories were branded.

'Now take me. I'm manumitted too, a long time ago, and swords are my trade. But carry one? Not me. Swords I leave to bandits and gladiators. Even though I lose money by telling you this.'

'I can afford one, if that's what worries you,' said Lucas, though he knew there would be nothing for it but to hear out this spark-scarred old man, who so much enjoyed the sound of his own voice.

'You have money? From your savings? Then you can't, I take it, have bought your own freedom. Let me see – you were manumitted from gratitude, and now you owe your old master *obsequium* –'

Lucas was tongue-tied at the thought that his own condition should be so apparent. 'I am doing a commission for my master. My former master. To Africa,' he added, as though the distance he had to travel would put a proper value on his services.

The old man came closer, saturating Lucas as he approached with the smell of charcoal smoke and hot metal. 'Buy a sharp knife,' he whispered. 'Hide it in your boot. And if ever it comes to a fight with a swordsman, say in a tavern, that is where the fighting always starts, duck under the table and slash at his hamstrings.'

'Not exactly heroic,' Lucas remarked.

'Rome heroic?' said the old sword-smith. 'Was once, before my time – but no more. Of course if you would really rather buy one of those swords up there, and swagger round being heroic, the one you had your eye on isn't bad. Buy a sword, then, and make me that much richer. Get in a brawl in a tavern tonight, and be a dead hero, like the legionaries at Pollentia.' The old man uttered that piece of sedition with his jaw thrust out, as if denying argument, though in a mutter, and looking swiftly right and left, for spies. He then showed Lucas a bone-handled, leaf-bladed knife – a knife to throw, he said, a knife that would stab. 'The sheath will be extra but I'll throw in the workmanship – my old woman is a dab hand with a leather thong. Just give me your boot – no, not that one. The other – unless you're left handed.'

Lucas stood and waited under the arcade, balancing himself by touching one toe to the grimy pavement, and jostled by passers-by, while the whetstone the old man had taken from his belt brought up an edge on the sheath-knife faster than the eye could follow.

'Careful with it now. And don't be heroic – give him no warning. Why? I'll tell you. Because with a knife you can only ever get in one good blow.'

'What was it like in your case,' Lucas asked, 'being manumitted?'

'Hurry up with that sheath, old woman. This customer of mine hasn't got all day. Freedom is all very well when you can make ends meet. Ever heard of taxes? If happily you haven't, you soon will. I slaved as a swordsmith for thirty years – in the imperial arms factory at Lucca. Where they hammer out all the swords for the legions – did you know that? Shields at Verona, breastplates at Mantua, bows at Pavia – spread out across Italy like that so that tearaways can never arm themselves simply by seizing one factory. My father was a sword-smith at Lucca before me, and a slave all his life. Then Flavius Stilicho manumitted a whole lot of us, older men, made us a speech, and I can remember his words: I am rewarding the best among you with your freedom. Doing us a favour? He certainly thought so. Freedom, you think, and a nice little business of your own. Home at night, hand in hand with my old woman? Yes, if the tax gatherer ever gave us a chance to breathe. But he never will. And another thing. Listen to this. A slave who is old and worn-out goes on getting fed, if only on horse-beans. A master must show *pietas*, it's expected of him. But a freedman? A man like you – a man like me – when he's too old to work will be thrown on the scrap-heap.'

Out of the shop came the old woman, carrying the boot with the hidden sheath.

'There you are. Tuck your knife away out of sight. Sharp enough to shave with. And ready to cut your own throat, when you are too old to work. What did you say your trade was?'

'Scribe.'

'Not a bad trade. You can go on pushing a pen longer than you can swing a hammer. Only, don't ever lose your eyesight – or get palsy.'

The tricky time for Lucas was when actually entering Stridor's *insula*, because now and then, as Gilda had warned him, the little eunuch would take it into his head to stand on a stool and look out through the spyhole in the door. Once on the stairs, Lucas was safe. So it came to him as a shock when at the top of the first flight he was hit in the ribs by a fist. The punch doubled him up, and tumbled him all the way down into the hallway. Worse than being winded by the blow was the humiliation.

He could see two men up there on the first landing, blocking the way, and looking down on him as if he were nothing. They were big men, with long, fair, untrimmed moustaches, and on their shoulders they bore the leather patches of *lectica* porters. Lucas picked himself up again. There was no eyeball at the peephole – no sign that Stridor had been roused by the noise.

As he got to his feet, Lucas felt against his calf-muscle the pressure of that bone-handled knife, but there were two of them, and they were big men, so though his fingers were itching to grasp the knife-handle he decided to conciliate them. As he climbed the stairs he began speaking to them quietly, in the simple-minded Latin that people like himself used when talking to barbarians, telling them that he was only on his way to his room upstairs.

Though they heard what he was saying, their faces did not change. The other *lectica* porter lashed out this time, and landed on the side of Lucas's chin the blow of a trained boxer. He went tumbling downstairs again. Then they both laughed.

And if I rush at them with my knife? wondered Lucas. Though what if, for years, they have been practising with knives, as they obviously have with punches? They can't stand there, blocking Gilda's stairway, for ever. Better to wait a while and see what happens.

He took the cloak from his pouch, put it over his shoulders and hid his head inside the hood. Squatting there near the main door on his haunches, he looked to passers-by like one of Rome's mendicants, getting ready to pass the night on the street. On the first day of his independent life, the start of his travels, Lucas was simmering with rage. The longer he waited on the pavement, the angrier he grew.

When Stilicho arrived in Rome to supervise the Emperor's triumph, he might have done better to ignore the presence of Gilda in the city, instead of deliberately seeking her out. She was pregnant, and what use is a mistress who is pregnant? But he could not shrug her off. Echoes of Gilda's wit came to his mind, to torment him. And what if the child were his, as so many were saying?

Flavius Stilicho earlier that afternoon had come up to the attic room, unannounced, alone, plainly dressed. He came into the room, smiling at the sight of her, like a man of no importance. I smile back, I can't help myself, thought Gilda, and he is glad of that. Every pair of eyes in Rome would know him for Stilicho if he wore sackcloth. Gilda was an unfamiliar shape by now, but as she crossed to greet him she bore her weight on her two legs, like a dancer, and spoke as if they had parted scarcely an hour before.

'I know you have been busy. But what kept you?'

He laughed at the tone she took, and tried to kiss her. Gilda, passive, let him buss her cheek. Complacently she lifted her swollen belly with cupped hands, as if making him a present of it.

'Here you are then. It's all yours. And I won't be this shape for ever.'

Two slaves in love, and on a dim afternoon in Milan, a flash of lightning makes them one. A small private happening, thought Gilda, a moment of joy, and then all this fuss. Stilicho however, watching her closely, saw Gilda as carrying round inside herself a small being likely to be his, concentrating herself protectively around something invisible and precious. He sat at first like an old man, a family friend, with his arm around her shoulder, careful to say nothing, but at last grew impatient.

As if his awareness of his own power had suddenly taken possession of him, Stilicho came to the question bluntly, fingertips feeling as he spoke for the pulse in the nook of Gilda's shoulder. If she lied he would feel it beat faster. He had learned that trick as a subaltern, interrogating prisoners of war.

'You can swear, then, that it's mine?'

'And if it were?' Gilda answered, her pulse as unhurried as her answer. 'Why aren't I lounging about on purple silk, with slaves to wait on my every whim?'

'You mean you are up here in this paltry room because Stridor has cast you off?'

'I am worth even more to him pregnant. He will never cast me off.'

Whatever the eunuch might ask for her I would pay, thought Stilicho, with the inner excitement of a man who has placed a big bet.

'Downstairs in Stridor's place I get so sick of luxury. I come up here from time to time to be myself. Simple. Poor. Domestic. The woman you hardly know.' He did not believe a word of it.

And where was Lucas? Late – on his last day? And if he came barging in? The truth would be admitted, thought Gilda, and I must put up with its disadvantages. Lucas would never dissemble.

'Apparently everyone in Rome is itching for me to tell them whose baby this is.'

Stilicho's face wrinkled in an uneasy smile. 'Have you told Stridor? I mean, told him the truth?'

'Not even when he pulled me around the room by my hair,' Gilda boasted, 'and threatened with one tap of his lead-loaded cane to break my collar-bone.' Stridor had wanted her to admit that the child was the Emperor's. 'One thing you can be sure of,' she said with a merry laugh – a stage laugh, 'the father can't be Stridor.'

'And to make you swear to the unequivocal truth, I must pull you by your hair around this room, and break your collar bone?'

'Come here and kiss me properly Flavius – you have earned it.'

Stilicho's firm mouth with its bristling fringe of clipped white hair was on her own soft mouth greedily. A kiss that would lead nowhere. Here we are, the two of us, thought Gilda, in a new role – younger sister, older brother. A good man, this, who will look after me and the child too, in case of trouble. I have to deceive him, a pity, but that is because trouble will so soon arrive. I am alone. Lucas is free and I am not. He is going to Africa. I stay here, and go on being somebody's slave.

'You help me, Flavius, I shall need it. And after this is all over, perhaps in some way I can help you?' Gilda said this last with a rising inflection and a cock of the eye. She has noticed, thought Stilicho. She observed that her kiss – such a kiss – did nothing to rouse me. She noticed and is not laughing. Stilicho nodded consent to their bargain, unashamed, her equal at last, stripped naked and at Gilda's mercy – but she was a good woman, and merciful.

'In only a month or so,' said Gilda with a lopsided smile, 'if you can wait that long.'

As they sat there, Stilicho with his arm paternally around her shoulders, Serena burst through the door, uttering an outraged scream. That scream brought neighbours' heads out of their doors along the landing, but when they caught sight of the two other Vandals, waiting at the head of the stairs for Serena's orders, they ducked away and latched themselves in. Nobody wanted trouble.

This was all play-acting, and Gilda was used to stage fury. With Stilicho's thick arm unmoving and heavy on her shoulder, she felt safe.

Serena's self-discipline has never lapsed, Stilicho was thinking, in thirty years: always the hard-headed, court-wise princess. And now, up here, she makes this display of herself – putting me in mind of the wild mare who shared my bed all those years ago in Constantinople.

Or is she going mad?

'Slave! Strumpet! Witch!'

Gilda, pulling clear of Stilicho, raised a forearm to protect her eyes as Serena reached to claw them. As the older woman lost the grapple, out came the last and worst accusation of all. '*Mima!*'

Serena as Gilda managed to push her away uttered a long, cold, shrill cry of disappointment. Stilicho had by this time moved between the two of them, a great shouldering bulk of a man, standing with his back to Gilda, and stonily facing down his wife.

Pulsating veins stood out on Serena's forehead. A thread of saliva trickled from the corner of her mouth, but the sight of

Stilicho's stern face, so near, forced her to take better command of herself. Like a tide going back visibly, quickly, across flat sand, her fury shrank. Instead came sarcasm.

'Everyone in Rome, but everyone, has had his go at her. You know that, I suppose?' She half turned so that her sardonic glance took in Gilda. 'And if you decided to carry this child – so unlike the women of your profession – because you think it will make your fortune –'

The callous voice went on and on, striking blows at Gilda, question, accusation, and getting no answer of any kind. Serena was waiting for indignant answers which could cleverly be turned – she was here to shake Stilicho's belief that the child might be his.

'*Venefica!*' she screamed at Gilda's deliberate silence. 'I will have them put you in a sack with a mad dog and a snake and drop you in the Tiber!'

Gilda lifted her arm at last, as if indicating that her turn had come to speak – but it suited Serena better to take gesture and half-enunciated words as a physical threat. She shouted in Gothic. In from the stairhead came her two Vandals.

On a battlefield amid masses of men, Stilicho rarely made a wrong move, but here, in this shabby, crowded bedroom, he mistook where the real threat was coming from. He tried to obstruct Serena, moving to block her violence with a quickness unwonted in a man so large. He meant to save the child.

This time, though, Serena went directly for her husband. She had a grip on two handfuls of his white hair, and bore down his obstinate head to her level, clinging against Stilicho in a frenzied parody of love, as if only the clutch of her body, his wife's body, could save him from the enchantment of this witch.

Stilicho, blinded by her closeness, heard Serena shout the terrible Gothic phrase: 'Throw her downstairs!'

The heavy old woman, strong as a horse, held him tight as he strove to pull loose. He was dragging her weight along behind him bodily, but too slowly.

'Down that flight of stairs!'

The two Vandals, one on each side, had taken Gilda up off her feet, and were edging through the door with her, lifting her high over the landing rail. They flung her without emotion into the stairwell. She might have been rubbish.

Gilda as they lifted her had not even struggled. She was a girl again, these were archers. Crouch in a ball, she had told herself. Cushion the life within – but already she was falling. This was the end – the final change. She was flying downwards, as if into hell. That scream in her ears must be her own.

At the turn in the brick stairway two flights down, Gilda struck, paused, and rolled lethargically past the edges of the next few stairs. She knew she had fallen, and struck a hard edge, and after, red, cruel, blinding, came the pain. *The pain!* How could there be so much pain, and the mind still aware?

Lucas as he crouched against an outside wall saw Serena, a woman of the upper class and vaguely familiar to him, walk out of the doorway head high, but her grey hair coming loose. She had trodden without a glance across Gilda's bloodstained body as she came downstairs, and her bloodstained sandal when she moved away made an ever-diminishing mark on the pavement. The two men from the first landing, the Vandals, were following her like dogs.

The atrocity of what these two barbarian slaves had done was clearing Stilicho's wits. Gilda was down there, dying – but might there not be time to save her child? As neighbours crowded once again to their doorways, he gave them orders with a force which they had never before heard. They and the Vandals scuttled to obey.

Neighbours were crowding across the hall of the *insula*, carrying between them someone wrapped in a bloodstained blanket. As they passed Stridor's door, Lucas observed a quick flicker of an eye at the spyhole. Then they went by where he was waiting, and Lucas caught his glimpse of Gilda's white face. Close after her, and with a smitten look, as if convoying the injured woman under his protection, came the white-haired man whom no one in Rome could ever mistake.

Lucas rose up to stammer out a question, but Stilicho shouldered past him as if not hearing – as if this intrusive bystander simply did not exist. Blame Stilicho? wondered Lucas. But he is suffering, too. Blame Stridor!

And where are they taking her? I must know that.

Up and down the narrow, noisy, darkening streets of Rome,

Lucas tracked them, a young man in an old cloak, inconspicuous. Out from the slope of the Quirinal protruded Stilicho's mansion, flat-roofed, marble-faced, and colonnaded on all four sides. Around the walls, picked men from his bodyguard of Huns were prowling like wild dogs.

Women slaves came running out of the house, their tongues clacking with concern as they carried Gilda inside. So she must still be alive! But once taken inside that house, would he ever see her again? They were carrying Gilda past the line of guards, into that forbidding house with its colonnades and tall, green-fingered cypresses, a house too much like a tomb. The house of a Roman patrician, but so watched-over and guarded that it might as well have been a robber's den.

Huns had been taking notice of Lucas; two with drawn swords, strangely curved swords, were moving towards him, and he slunk off, his mind concentrating on revenge.

Lucas went back in a sick dream the way he had come, retracing crowded streets, jostling impatiently past those who got in his way, his rage having tipped him into a mood of madness, so that he felt himself insubstantial as a puff of smoke. Find and strike home, nothing less. And then he might feel real again.

In the little hinged spyhole high on the panelled door, an eye appeared. Stridor had clambered again on his stool, and was peeping out.

The idea came to Lucas, with cold glee, of an arrow through that spyhole – an arrow driven with force through the eyeball into the skull. But instead, with sober face, Lucas raised a hand to greet the man who owned the staring eye, and ask him for entry. The leg of a stool scraped, the door opened, and there was Stridor, small and absurd, beckoning Lucas inside.

The little eunuch wore a long-skirted dressing-gown of heavy brocade, gold figured on blue. His hair, freshly singed by hot tongs and piled up in kiss-curls, had been drenched with perfume. A cane in a cover of plaited leather dangled from Stridor's left hand. It might have been a swagger stick, and Lucas thought it was, but Gilda could have warned him that Stridor's cane was loaded with lead, and heavy enough to break a limb.

Stridor was a little perplexed – in one way and another it had been a perplexing afternoon – but here was Claudian's confidential slave, and Claudian was Stilicho's friend. Earlier, noticing Stilicho arrive, he had gone out, bowing from the waist, to greet him, only to be brutally shouldered aside, as Stilicho went headlong up the stairs. My own house, thought Stridor, and I dare not follow him.

Later, and again Stridor knew better than to intervene, they had carried Gilda, bloodstained, out of the building. Since then, under the busy hands of the barber, instead of being consoled his perplexity had grown out of all proportion. Perhaps this young man, Claudian's scribe, someone he had in fact bought and sold years ago, would know the answer.

'And what does the great poet want of me?' the eunuch simpered.

Lucas looked at him without answering, and Stridor recognised that implacable gaze for a threat. With any slave you had once known, a time might come, often years after, when he turned on you.

Stridor pointed his leather-covered cane like a long finger, his epicene voice high-pitched. 'You know what they have done with her?'

Lucas, not answering, was fanning his rage to the point of action. A man who had killed before, and knew how, would have struck sooner.

In the old days, in Gaul, on my slave chain, thought Stridor hysterically, they were taught to give prompt answers. One tap on the shoulder from this stick of mine would open that Briton's mouth. Do it quickly, Lucas was telling himself, before the household slaves come in.

Stridor, brothel-bred, saw the angry-faced young man crouch, as he reached a right hand to his boot. That stance was an old warning. Stridor took one pace back, out of reach of the blade, and poised his cane. He shouted for help, but nothing more worthwhile came out of his mouth than a squeak.

Lucas lifted his knife, but the wrong way around – for a downward slash, not the deadly jab upwards, under the ribs. As he heard the young man exclaim dramatically, 'Down with her, then – to the shades!' Stridor smiled. Here towards me comes a man, he thought contemptuously, who has never yet thrust his knife into another man's body. He signals his attack, and when he tries to strike, I shall have him.

The cane swung, a bone in the clenching fingers splintered, Lucas's knife skittered across the marble floor.

Stridor laughed, a self-indulgent laugh, high-pitched, depraved, and he lifted his cane high for a blow that would crack the young man's skull like a walnut. Claudian tomorrow would need to buy another slave! Lucas had heard that same whinnying laugh in days long gone by, whenever Stridor gave a slave on the chain a taste of his stick. That laugh blotted out the pain of splintered bone. His own left hand was still good for something.

Lucas wrenched at the eunuch's chicken-bone wrist, lifting the perfumed little creature sideways off his feet, like a large doll, and tossed him down. He hit a slab of marble and lay there, prone, the cane beyond the reach of his hand.

Biting his lips with pain, Lucas groped left-handedly across the floor, and touched his leaf-bladed knife. The faces of household slaves had begun crowding in at the far doorway. Should they not go to their master's aid, the law would hold them culpable, yet they were enjoying what they saw. They were holding off, to see what else happened. Lucas could smell Stridor's perfumed hair. Blade found jugular – the deathstroke was as easy as slicing meat. In small pulsations, the little eunuch's blood began to seep across the patterned marble floor.

The bolder slaves were pushing their way past the curtain, as if to enter the room and justify themselves. Lucas found his wits.

Suppose the body of their master disappeared?

Lucas wiped the knife, left-handedly, on the blue brocade dressing-gown, and sheathed it in his boot. He fumbled his one good hand into the bag hung by a string from his neck, and sent a handful of coins rolling and racing across the floor. The nearest slaves scrabbled to pick them up. The dressing gown had fallen open, and inside, the little eunuch was naked, like a shaven monkey, his sex a cropped appendage. With so much blood drained out of him, Stridor was white, like veal. Which makes me a butcher, thought Lucas wildly. For Gilda's sake, I have killed him, like an animal.

Lucas hoisted the limp corpse one-handedly to his shoulder.

The appalling pain in his right hand made him excessively strong. Slaves as he left the room with the mortal remains of Stridor began moving in, half-heartedly, some still bending to pick up money. The boldest followed him to the outer doorway, and stood there, looking, but soon lost Lucas in the dark. They were slaves. They would wash the floor clean, agree on a story, rush off to the authorities and hope to be believed. But what was a homicide without a *corpus delicti*?

And if one of those household slaves, wondered Lucas, as he staggered down alleys under his naked dead burden, knows me by face or name? Claudian's scribe – a murderer? Less than a week of freedom, and his life not worth a copper coin. I am free, Lucas told himself. I carry a weapon. I have killed once – I can kill again. He felt ashamed.

Lucas found the garbage-heap by its smell, foul and yet rotten-sweet, dog-haunted, rat-infested. Here unlucky Roman women exposed the babies they did not propose to feed, and, less often, a childless woman would lurk about, to snatch up an abandoned baby before the dogs got their teeth in. Tonight, thought Lucas, let any such woman snatch up Stridor and press him to her bosom – see if she can revive him.

A dark night, with no moon glimmer, and nothing visible but the carrion dogs, snapping at his heels. Lucas let his lost, dead orphan drop, and stumbled off, towards the river. The pain in his right hand had become enough to make him sick and giddy. He had money in his belt, he would take the first boat down the river to Ostia. Then Carthage, that was easy, a passage in some grain-ship or other returning in ballast. As he staggered along, the gold and silver in the money-belt was inordinately heavy around his waist. The sense of shame grew deeper.

Part V

1

Eventually the historian Zosimus was to describe Olympius as 'one who under an appearance of Christian piety veiled every sort of wickedness.' But that was later on, when Olympius had been found out for what he was. Just at present he was universally popular. He had played a bold part in bringing down Black Johannes. 'He was a man that day!' declared old Julia, who afterwards had a soft spot for Olympius for longer than most.

Olympius himself, coldly appraising behind his ever present smile, had decided that the next step to personal power was to drag down Flavius Stilicho, and Serena with him. The Emperor plainly detested his old guardians, and they were beginning to dislike one another.

The Emperor enjoyed hearing the latest savoury details of Stilicho's depravity, but though one of the general's confidential slaves had been bribed by Olympius as an informer, there was not much to pass on. Up there in the gloomy columned house on Rome's Quirinal, the actress and the general were to all appearance living like brother and sister. Her child had been born dead.

The spy was confident of his facts because he had caught a glimpse of a newborn baby, gorgeously attired and awaiting burial. This piece of evidence had in fact been stuck under the spy's nose, on purpose, by Stilicho himself. The child was a boy, born prematurely, and without fingernails, but alive. Gilda had never suckled him, nor even seen him. Into her bewilderment of pain had come one child's cry, but the cry might have been a dream. Stilicho had thought at first glance that the little boy would be a cripple, but the only thing the matter was his head, set awry. Since he had to be called something, Stilicho decided to call him Iynx – Wryneck.

Just before the child was born a woman slave called Sara, at one time nursemaid to Maria, had brought Stilicho a letter from the steward of an estate of his in the mountainous countryside of Samnium. Sara made a good messenger in a confidential matter because, though highly intelligent, she was both illiterate and dumb. With the stump of her tongue – cut out years before by bandits – she could make noises which Stilicho though almost no one else understood. He had been overheard to say that he wished all his slaves were as silent as Sara, and as faithful. The dumb nurse looked after Gilda during a travail in which the mother was hardly ever conscious, and if afterwards Gilda asked a question she was answered with a grunt.

To have stifled this little boy before he drew breath, Stilicho tried telling himself, would have made good political sense. But once that first little birth-cry had echoed in his ears, the general felt for the child as an old-fashioned Vandal would have done – to Vandals, the newborn were sacred. A long whisper to Sara, some gutturally grunted replies, and the child was swaddled and carried off. In Rome, to procure a dead infant as a substitute was easy. Next day there was a convincingly secretive funeral, and to keep tongues wagging Stilicho had the corpse laid out in imperial purple.

Escorted by a mounted Hun, the nurse Sara left the house after dark, carrying Iynx swaddled in her arms. Stilicho had given her a corner of parchment with the four letters, IYNX, written across it, and the little boy's horoscope. He would grow up at Samnium healthy, on goats' milk and mountain air.

When she could get up and walk about, Gilda never dared leave the house on the Quirinal. Her place of safety had become her prison, because Stridor, in his last days, when he lost patience, with her, had hit on a clever revenge.

He had always told Gilda that she would be his heir. 'You make all this money for me,' he would say, sentimentally. 'I think of you as my child. Who else would I leave it to?' But when Gilda's pregnancy caused a scandal, and she refused to tell him who was the father, Stridor like other Romans discontented with their heirs had changed his will, leaving all that he possessed to the Emperor. When he was stabbed, Gilda overnight became imperial property. Inside Stilicho's house, no one dare touch her. But once out on the street, and with Olympius out to trap her, she was likely to be picked up, and might be sent, anonymous and helpless, to some imperial property on the far side of the world.

'The difficulties are greater that you might think,' Stilicho was told by a quaestor in the Treasury, who had always been his friend. He hinted that the invisible obstacle was the Emperor's new favourite – and this was the first time that Stilicho discerned Olympius, clearly, as his secret opponent. Because he himself had promoted Olympius, he tended to underrate him.

Olympius, with the giggling connivance of Honorius, kept Stilicho dangling for three weeks, until Honorius lost his nerve, and hit on an argument which justified giving way. Had not the church expressed formal disapproval of theatrical performance? 'These spectacles of uncleanness, those licentious vanities,' as the great Augustine called them.

'I hardly suppose, *dominus*, that he is keeping her up there on the Quirinal to teach him how to sing and dance,' commented Olympius. This was the sort of cheeky joke about his old guardian that Honorious usually enjoyed. But Honorious could only keep one thing in his mind at a time, and at present he was asking himself whether a Christian Emperor could, in conscience, own a *mima*.

'Or if you would rather, *dux imperator*, you could have him pay a fine – for bad morals.'

He mentioned casually a price for Gilda that would have been excessive for half-a-dozen top-flight gladiators.

'A fine for bad morals,' the Emperor agreed gravely.

Stilicho made his way to the Treasury, followed by five of his strongest slaves, bent double under the weight of leather sacks filled with gold coin. The gold had come from a walled-up hoard in the cellar, and he had dipped into it without consulting Serena. At the Treasury, Stilicho kept a cheerful face, as though for him such a payment were a matter of indifference. This nonchalance of Stilicho's, when reported to Honorious, spoiled the joke for him. Olympius, though, was not so easily put off. Through his suborned agents he set another useful rumour going. Why was the legionaries' pay in arrears? Because Stilicho had dipped into the military treasure chest to buy back his mistress.

'Now at last I am your thing – and a very costly thing too,' Gilda had said ruefully, when Stilicho told her with a selfconscious laugh of the price she had fetched. 'Though you never treat me as a thing – I must say that. And I hope you never will. Even now that I have cost you so much.'

Stilicho who had been expecting more conventional thanks digested that remark slowly. Only here, he tried to tell himself, in this marble-floored room of hers, overlooking the formal central courtyard with its bleak statues of famous dead Romans, was he never flattered, never deceived. Or do I deceive myself, he wondered, by thinking so? Gilda was thin; under her radiantly luminous eyes there were hollows. She has changed, he told himself, she is different. Sincere now. She is devoted to me. With Gilda, even living as brother and sister, he felt happier.

'You feel like that for me – even when I hold you in my arms, and nothing happens,' he said at last, dubiously.

'You want me to flog you with nettles?'

'I too have read Petronius,' he answered gruffly. He would rather she did not make a joke of it, his impotence, a misfortune he himself took seriously enough. But Gilda, whatever the risk, went on jokingly, dragging what Stilicho hated to admit into daylight.

'Stick a hot peppercorn up your fundament?' Even Stilicho had to laugh at that soldierly proposition. 'For the man who twice conquered Alaric,' asked Gilda, 'might that not be lacking in dignity?'

'Defeated – not conquered,' he muttered.

'Or I am sure some dancing girl from Gades would sell the great Gilda a spoonful of her little flies – crush them up in your food, make you insatiable – '

'I have heard too,' said Stilicho dryly, 'of the tricks of the dancing girls from Gades.'

'Stridor trained me in all this and much more, and Stridor knew everyting – '

' – except how to duck a knife-fighter.' Had Gilda sent in

that man with the knife? Once or twice since, Stilicho had wondered. A costly knife-stroke, that – five leather sacks of gold coins! Gilda for her own part was sure the blow had been struck by Lucas. Had he not promised? Only where was Lucas now? On the other side of the world. And what use was that?

'Or simply take my body, my dear – this old thing of yours, this possession. The most expensive provocative in Rome, at one time.' When at that he merely stared, Gilda added, 'Well then? Don't you find me provoking?'

'Very.'

'Or another woman, for a change. Someone simpler and fresher and plumper. Yes, dear, I have even thought of that. Sitting here in this room alone. I have not much else to think of, except how to cure your misfortune. And have at last decided – '

'Yes?'

'No remedies, no provocatives, no clever little tricks – not for us. We must somehow manage this matter by being ourselves.' At his look of perplexity, her tone changed abruptly. 'You know you have a spy in this house?'

'I know. I have begun to use him against the man who pays him.'

'And I thought I was the clever one,' said Gilda, pulling a face.

Stilicho had eyes just then for nothing but the disposition of her limbs, the witty radiance in her eyes, the way her mouth formed words. She fascinates me, he told himself – but why? On the stage she fascinated everyone – indeed, my whole army. Serena would say the fascination was witchcraft, but I know better. Stilicho was in a dream about her. So the next words that came in all innocence from Gilda's mouth particularly stung him.

'Flavious – *amator* – this impotence of yours – '

As if hit full in the chest by an arrow, Stilicho caught his breath, and waited tensely to hear what she might next have to say.

'You are tied in a knot – but not by potions. In my opinion – and I know you better than anyone – you have tied this knot yourself. You have thought too much about the weakness of the army. The weakness of Rome. And weakness is not in your nature.' Gilda paused, wondering if she had trespassed too far into a world that was privately his.

He stood there, silent, thinking his thoughts, waiting for Gilda to tell him what next to do.

As both Stoics and Christians admitted, there was an invisible part of any slave, the soul, which could never be bought or sold. And how exactly, Stilicho wondered, can I touch her soul, as she has just touched mine?

'No provocatives,' Gilda was going on to say, 'and no incantations either.' Stilicho, as he stood waiting, had been muttering, and from that she took her cue. 'If you want to pray, then pray this afternoon, with your body. You are my God, Stilicho – the god of my religion. And with my body I shall pray to you.' The most extravagant of flattery, this, and sounded so emphatically sincere because Gilda as she spoke the words had been filling her mind with the thought of Lucas. How else would she have brought out the right intonation?

Bring this old man to ecstasy, she thought. Now if ever. And hereafter he will be my slave, not I his.

In Rome when the Emperor made his elaborate toilet there were no longer gulps of spiced wine to enliven him, but a golden voice behind a curtain, which lulled the imperial mood by reciting passages chosen by Olympius from some theological work in good Latin. Honorious was surprised to find how much cleverer he felt, now that he had Olympius to turn to.

The theme set germinating in the Emperor's mind this morning was a Christian's attitude to gladiatorial games, something else that might turn him off Stilicho, who was insisting on the Emperor's presence. Augustine's vividly sonorous Latin was telling Honorius of a young man who forswore gladiators because the church condemned them. Then his friends jollied him into going to the arena for one last time. He began by shutting his eyes to blot out the horror, but at last looked down, and was trapped.

'He saw the blood and gulped down savagery, without knowing what was happening he drank in madness, he was delighted with the guilty contest, drunk with the lust of blood.

He took away with him a madness which would goad him to come back again.'

At a cue from Olympius – a slightly-raised forefinger – the reader's golden voice fell silent. Slow at taking in, Honorius was silently mouthing the phrase, 'without knowing what was happening, he drank in madness.'

Drank in madness had struck him. Did not that describe how it had been for him with Black Johannes?

'If the games are a sin for a Christian,' he asked Olympius hesitantly. 'what about today?'

'But the plebs have come to expect them, *imperator*,' said Olympius briskly. 'Flavius Stilicho warns us that after an imperial triumph the mob might riot if there were no gladiators. Are they a sin, though? Your chaplain, *dominus*, is the man to ask. I, though a Christian, am a plain soldier. Personally I never enjoy them. Your great forbear, the Emperor Constantine, decreed gladiators illegal – oh, ages ago.'

'Olympius – nobody told me. But why?'

'You have heard, *dux imperator*, of the days of persecution? Because in those bad times, so many Christians were martyred in the arena. In Constantinople where your brother reigns they don't have them – '

'Then why here? Am I not Emperor, too?'

Honorius was aware this morning of being dressed up to go to a show that he hated. Once in his father's lifetime, up there in raw Milan, he had been obliged as a small boy to watch gladiators. A man's severed head with staring eyes, which had rolled across the sand like a plum pudding, still appeared in his nightmares.

'Put it that we are in Rome,' said smooth-cheeked Olympius firmly, not sorry of a chance to talk on both sides of the question, in case someone else's spy overheard. 'Gladiators are essentially Roman.' There would be no need to press the point. In the Emperor's mind, the seed was sown.

Only in Ravenna, the dream city amid the marshes, did Honorius feel safe. In little Ravenna the Emperor was all-in-all – here the mob had to be pandered to. Rome's million inhabitants would be out on the streets today, shouting sarcasms, breathing garlic, tippling too much of their free wine.

(And why should wine be free? Wine for the mob – and not for the Emperor?) The physical immensity of Rome with its Senate and Capitol, its rambling warren of a palace, its mansions and tenements, its monstrous Colosseum, had always frightened Honorius.

And his dread this morning was the sharper because the theme of the triumph Stilicho had organised was essentially false. The Emperor Honorius as the victor of Pollentia? Stilicho yesterday had tried massively, patiently, to convince Honorius that in a certain sense he was.

'The decision that you now so much regret, *imperator* – to leave Milan – was not strictly speaking made by you, but by Black Johannes, who then exercised a power to which he had no right.' Stilicho's voice when he said that had been hateful – severe though pretending to be kind, the identical voice that in boyhood had always been teaching Honorious lessons for his own good. 'The staff officer I sent with you, Marcus Curtius, kept me closely informed. You were always in my thoughts, *imperator* – and everything turned out well. Alaric fell into the trap you thereby set for him, when strategically, believe me, he would have done better to head south and strike for Rome itself. That was what I had most to fear – never bringing him to battle. But he followed you, and there he was. You yourself to this extent saved Rome – and Rome is grateful. Only the imperial presence, Honorius, could have lured our enemy to the place where the legions were waiting to crush him – Pollentia, your victorious battlefield.'

Should I blush at what I am telling him? Stilicho had asked himself. Is my cheek still capable of a blush? How else though do I convince this silly boy that to go on being Emperor he must agree to look the part in public? If Alaric one fine day came back to Italy at the head of a newly recruited army, the last thing Rome needed would be doubts of the Emperor or disobedience to imperial commands. The only sensible tactic was to unite behind Honorius.

Poor old Claudian – with a cough between every word – had in these last weeks been knocking out another of his amazing poems, in which the Emperor was not forgotten. People on the street were already quoting snatches from it. Everything helped, but particularly the authority of a great poem. Even the clothes the Emperor wore through the streets today would help.

They were dresssing Honorius now.

The designated slaves were pulling over his shoulders the *trabea* – the consular robe. As the title of Claudian's new poem was reminding everyone, Honorius had been made 'Consul for the Sixth Time.' In the thousand years and more since the city was founded, such an honour had been awarded only thrice – once to Honorius's father, Theodosius the Great, and before that, to Constantine the Great. As the Roman mob cheered an Emperor it seldom saw – and Consul for the Sixth Time! – let the comparison sink in. Should war break out again, Honorius would need the Roman mob behind him.

The *trabea* was jewelled – an innovation that the stern and frugal consuls of Rome's republican days would have deplored. They were fitting a diadem on Honorius's brow. (A consul in a diadem? Julius Caesar had been assassinated for rather less). The slave *ab ornamentis* was clipping around the Emperor's neck an emerald necklace. Another slave – an *ornator* – had begun expertly colouring the Emperor's cheeks, applying carmine with a little brush and a swansdown pad until pallid Honorius looked the picture of health.

Yet really, thought Olympius, as he supervised all this, what a poor specimen he is – even in robe and jewels, even in paint. Low forehead, that long yet feeble nose. He looks too much like his dim-witted mother. Why did the great Theodosius ever marry her? On the other hand, were he more of a man, I could never hope to control him.

There had not been a triumph in Rome for a hundred year.

In the courtyard of the Palatine, imperial ostlers were pulling and pushing gilded processional-cars until they had them standing the right order. Honorius was to ride in the first car, splendidly attired, with Stilicho discreetly at his shoulder. The second car was for the Empress Maria, seldom seen, who would ride attended by her brother Eucherius, Stilicho's son. Eucherius like Honorius was a son who belied his father, an undistinguished youth, who had risen in the Civil Service only to the third-rate place of Tribune of the Notaries. He would be dressed as a Tribune of the Notaries, and today the Romans could see for themselves that Stilicho was not giving his son undue promotion. In the third car would follow the Emperor's vivacious younger sister, Galla Placidia, together with her lady-in-waiting.

The mob liked what it had seen and heard of Galla Placidia – the one member of the imperial family thoroughly popular. All the brains, toughness and imaginative quickness of the great Theodosius were Galla Placidia's portion. But she was a girl – a mischievous girl of thirteen, with sparkling eyes – and how could a girl rule Rome?

Galla Placidia was squared-off, blunt-nosed, quick-witted – no beauty, though combining blue eyes with raven hair in a bold style that would soon have ambitious young courtiers glancing her way. She spent too much time – they said – poking her nose into books that did not concern her role in life, or playing alone in a walled garden in the palace, pretending to be a boy. This triumph was her first public event in Rome, and already there was talk of a husband. The Emperor's younger sister was a valuable piece in the game – and one of old Julia's happier inspirations had been to put forward Princess Veleda as her lady-in-waiting.

The vital, dark-haired little girl had a passion of her own. She adored barbarians, and could never hear enough from the Princess Veleda – beautiful Veleda – of her adventures at the court of Alaric. Galla Placidia thought Veleda brave and wise as well as lovely. And apart from wishing that she too could have lived with the barbarians, so much less boring than Ravenna, living in a wagon and eating roast beef with your fingers, she wanted most of all to have a bust just like Veleda's – small, firm, high, perfect, instead of one that as it bulged forward was beginning to make her look like an obstinate little black cow.

Galla Placidia would tease a palace guard until he repeated to her some Gothic phrase or other that she wanted to learn, and then sit alone, under the almond trees in the Palatine garden, repeating the words like a private spell. Or she would get Veleda reminiscing again about Alaric's women – the gold carcanet a husband made his woman twist around the neck, as a sign of submissiveness, the patterned carpets with long fringes that covered the wagon floor, their home-brewed beer. Here in Rome Galla Placidia had begun to make out that wine disagreed with her, and that beer she must have. Was it generations of barbarian beer that made your breasts grow small and firm and high like that?

'Stand still while I fasten these diamonds.'

'Wear some yourself, Veleda. There are plenty.'

'I must be inconspicuous.'

Galla Placidia sighed, and once the diamonds were fixed, bobbed up and down in front of the silver mirror that Veleda held for her, until she could see her own reflection.

'You are lucky to be dark,' said Veleda. 'Diamonds make you splendid.'

'You mean I don't look like a small black cow?'

'Today some unfortunate young man, very handsome but quite unsuitable, who would never be allowed to marry you, or even speak with you, will catch one glimpse of you and fall suicidally in love.'

The snort Galla Placidia uttered was pure scorn. Veleda was well aware of the plot sponsored by old Julia, to marry Galla Placidia off to Eucherius. Politically it might help Stilicho and Serena – that, anyway, was Julia's idea.

Galla Placidia did not openly dislike Eucherius – nobody disliked Eucherius. He was a nonentity. She despised him a little for not being brashly gallant, like the other young men at court who had the daring, already, to pay her compliments. He was disproportionate. He was dull.

'If they do force me to marry someone,' announced Galla Placidia, pulling the pout of a girl choosing sweetmeats rather than husbands, 'let's hope he will be a – '

'Barbarian?' Veleda slipped another bracelet on the girl's arm. Galla Placidia disliked bracelets, they got in the way, but the order had been to cover her with jewels. 'Don't even say the word. Even if I do. What if this barbarian husband of yours should turn out to be a Hun?'

'But how *could* he be? Huns believe in *devils*. He would have to be a *Christian*! At least an *Arian*! And *royal* – like *you*!'

'Do you want me to pinch you to remind you?' said Veleda in a stern, low voice. 'There are people in this palace who would have us both locked up if they were to hear you so much as whisper that word Arian.'

Galla Placidia bent her head. She really had gone too far.

She was a good Catholic, and had eagerly learned by heart the texts – from John, from Solomon, from Acts, from Matthew, from Corinthians – proving that Arians lived in error. One day she might find herself disputing her faith with a barbarian king! And, of course, saving his soul. But Galla Placidia's impulses of shame never lasted very long. Raising her head she went on tiptoe, to give Veleda an audacious kiss from a pouted mouth like a strawberry not yet quite ripe.

Stilicho had allotted Gilda two seats, good ones, for the triumphal procession and, afterwards, for the gladiators. Rash though it might be, he has begun to flaunt me, thought Gilda, pleased that Stilicho should still wish to. But she took her own womanly precautions against his rashness. Few who had applauded Gilda on stage would recognise her, on this day of festivities, as she passed by in the street.

She had dressed as for a part in a play, demure, no wig, no cosmetics, but a fine veil – a well-bred widow, emerging into life again for this important state occasion after her stipulated time in mourning. They would need to be clever, thought Gilda, to know me today. Get there early, Stilicho had said to her, make sure of your seat. He had so badly wanted her to see his cataphracts.

Gilda arrived in good time, on foot, escorted by a broad-shouldered household slave, who carried a stick to clear a way for her through the jostling crowd. She was so successfully the inconspicuous widow that nobody at all looked at her, and that even became irksome. Look, here is Gilda, she wanted to cry out. You applauded me. Remember? Look this way, and I will make you laugh.

On consideration, she decided that playing at being anonymous was almost funnier. Today, she told herself, I am the audience. This is the day for the others, the non-professionals, to perform. Stilicho, the imperial family, all of them actors, and Rome their theatre.

A gasp went up when the Roman sun, burning down from a blue sky, glinted on the gold leaf of the cars, as one by one they emerged from the Palatine, and came downhill. In earlier times – as Gilda's neighbour, a very old gentleman helped along by two sticks, tediously explained to her – the Senate had had to walk in front of the Emperor's car, as a mark of subservience. Honorius had graciously abolished that obligation. 'Or I should be hobbling along down there,' he said. The old man was a Senator, and wanted her to know it. 'And these days so many of us patricians suffer from gout, y'know, or have put on too much weight.'

A blinding glint, the clatter of caparisoned horses approaching. Here came Honorius.

And really, thought Gilda, they have done wonders with him. Honorius will never make a leading man, but he is trying his best, standing straight, holding up his head, not blinking or twitching. I took that awkward young man's innocence, she reminded herself, and perhaps he is the better for it. The cheers for the Emperor were real cheers.

After Honorius came some Visigoth prisoners of war, with long moustaches and shaven heads, and nooses dangling from their dejected necks. They were all convinced that as an item in today's entertainment they were to be hanged. The nooses were in fact only symbolical. As the Emperor began to ascend the Capitol steps the prisoners were to be freed, thus showing Rome's magnanimity to subject races.

Next came the gilded car bearing the Empress Maria – a poor, pale thing, not in the least an Empress – with her brother, Eucherius, more boring than ever, wearing his low-grade civil service uniform as though it were a joke. And was that dimwit, Gilda asked herself, really Stilicho's son? Might my son had he lived have turned out just as dull? Her eye was then caught by little Galla Placidia's diamonds, her plump, braceleted arms, a well-set up blonde standing self-effacingly behind her. They made a pretty tableau, and went down well with the crowd.

As Eucherius, the notorious pagan, went by, a dozen well-dressed youths on the stand near Gilda sounded the first discordant note. They began to chant, in unison, a tag from Claudian's latest poem, which was becoming a watchword for the fashionable malcontents in Rome.

Winged Victory, guardian of the Roman toga, coming herself to her shrine.

Their chant, thought Gilda, could have done with more

rehearsal, they did not quite keep time, young Roman bucks were always disorderly, but all the more important people heard. The recitation was meant to be politically shocking, the more so since on Eucherius's lips could be observed a faint smile, as though he secretly approved. He would have done better, Gilda knew, to keep a straight face.

The statue of Victory, a pagan statue but the ancient guarantee of Rome's military prowess, had been removed from the Senate by order of the young Christian Emperor. How could Rome win wars if Honorius spoiled her luck? As Stilicho up ahead, at the Emperor's shoulder, in the first car caught the chanted words, his blood ran chill. A plot! Everyone would think he had put that blockhead Eucherius up to it!

Elated by their first success, the dozen young bloods were about to repeat their chant, when Flavius Stilicho turned. At his glance, full of threat, they fell silent in mid-repetition, like cowed schoolboys. From the crowd came a half-cheer, but whether for them or for me, thought Stilicho, who can tell? And the spies in the crowd will now report that the young men reciting Claudian were under my control. I looked, they stopped. I had better not catch Gilda's eye – she is somewhere hereabouts. That would be another blunder. The sooner poor Claudian sets off for Africa, the safer for us all.

Galla Placidia in the third car, though Veleda had impressed on her to look ahead, could not resist the occasional glance over her shoulder at the soldiers marching close behind – the smartest cohort in the smartest legion in Italy, here to represent the Roman army that had been victorious at Pollentia. If only all our legions, thought Stilicho, were like that one show-off cohort! They have been drilled until they glitter.

A legion was good if its centurions were of the old sort, regimental, and its officers Roman gentlemen, devoted to the profession of arms. And where, wondered Stilicho, as the Emperor got down self-consciously from the car and began climbing the symbolic steps alone, does Rome find men like that? Either my officers think of nothing but money and pleasure, or they are sick with political ambition. If only I had a hundred like Marcus Curtius – but see what happened to him.

After came the cataphracts – sixty men in column of three

on horses that were seventeen hands to the shoulder. In full body armour, and with grim black iron helmets, shut down across their faces, they walked their chargers in procession, heavy, taciturn, ominous. The irreverent Roman crowd was by this time ready for a bit of fun. What caught their eye were the newfangled stirrups.

'They weigh so heavy,' exclaimed a shrill gutter-voice, 'they have to rest their feet!'

The laugh was bigger, thought Gilda, than the joke deserved. Then a woman threw a half-chewed cucumber, and it bounced off a helmet.

'Feel that, did you?'

'You can feel mine, if you take your iron drawers down.' added a deep bass voice.

'A fig for a cucumber!' screeched the woman, and at that hackneyed bawdy pun the crowd roared. If I tried that joke in the theatre, though Gilda, they would hiss.

'Can't bear to show us their ugly faces.' The last voice was distinct, commonplace, but it expressed what everyone felt. The crowd fell silent until the last of the cataphracts had passed by.

And are those the horsemen Stilicho believes so fervently could save Rome? Gilda asked herself. Today they look like actors too, their iron armour painted cardboard, their costumes a theatrical exaggeration. Nothing today here is real.

Gilda's slave, once the procession was over, began wielding his stick on nearby plebs with judicious jabs at ribs and little cuts at calves, easing his mistress through the jostling crowd as though she were a patrician. Gilda caught his arm.

'Not to the Colosseum.'

The broad-shouldred slave looked at her with his mouth open. But she had a ticket to one of the best places! Today she would see the most famous fighters in Rome (and so would he). But Gilda in her mind's eye had seen a little gladiator paunch a big one, so that his tripes dropped in coils around his feet. They would all be sitting there, these patrician mountebanks, these treacherous self-indulgent faces. Flavius Stilicho was obliged to be there. Not she.

'Gangway for the Christian!' remarked an upper-class young man sarcastically, as this good-looking widow in expensive grey, the veil half-lifting from her face as she walked, was conveyed by her slave against the trend of the crowd. He was one of the gilded youths sitting near her who had made a battle cry of that line of Claudian's. They were all moving the other way through the crowd, the dozen of them, high-spirited, and as they went past Gilda caught a snatch of their talk.

'You say he will pay us?'

'I'd have shouted it for nothing.'

Their ringleader – the youngster who had been sarcastic about Christians – turned and answered in a browbeating tone. 'As the Divine Vespasian remarked, *pecunia non olet* – money does not smell. Why not take what is offered?' They were swallowed up in the crowd.

A little titbit for Stilicho, thought Gilda – my day has not been wasted. They chose and timed that line of Claudian's – they were paid for it. But who paid them? What had sounded like high-spirited upper-class paganism was underneath a sordid little conspiracy.

Gilda soon became weary of the enormous crowd as it flowed like a river against her, one drowning face after another gone by too quickly. She was longing already for her quiet apartment in the bare and severe house on the Quirinal. In time gone by, a crowd like this would have charged her to the brim with theatrical excitement – she had made this mob dance to her tune. Not any more though, the feeling was not there. Am I finished – she wandered – with the theatre? Is that possible?

So the cataphracts had been a flop? Tonight she would strive to make Stilicho forget it. She would mime the funnier parts of today's procession, one man her audience, and that was enough.

Galla Placidia had never seen the gladiators. Veleda, though, knew what to expect – Roman beastliness. The seats the two of them had been given were just under the conspicuous raised dais where Honorius sat, raising a hand to steady his diadem, with white-haired Stilicho erect and affable at his shoulder.

Galla Placidia on her first public occasion was wild with excitement. Unlike the rest of the imperial family, and most of the patricians sitting in rows along this side of the arena, she had no fear of the mob confronting them on the far side. The Roman crowd sensed it in her, and loved her for it.

Sunwards, on the skyline, agile men were busy with ropes and spars and sails.

'Veleda – what are they doing?'

'No need to point – they are sailors putting up an awning. Or to stick your elbows in my ribs either. If something out of the ordinary interests you, glance quickly and then look away. Over there they are all watching you.'

The crowd in the popular seats along the far side had seen Galla Placidia's pointing finger, and was roaring out good-natured laughter. Any little novelty was better than nothing in the wait before the real fun began.

'Observe what is happening, but *be gracious* – '

Be gracious was a standing joke between them, a sardonic echo of old Julia's advice to her young hostages, especially, thought Galla Placidia, to the ones who were clumsy donkeys. Galla Placidia knew very well that she had been doing little things that would stir up the crowd for the thrill of having them react.

As hot gusts blew, the canvas awnings bellied and flapped. If a few seamen fastening ropes get her so excited, thought Veleda, then I dread what effect the bloodshed will have. Galla Placidia, child-like, had taken her hand, and was gripping it hard as the procession of gladiators marched out, and made their formal circuit of the arena.

'Aren't they splendid!' But Galla Placidia was careful not to clap her hands. She was doing her best to be dignified.

The sun blazed down on the gladiators' gilded helmets, on their gorgeous armour. Tubas blared, fifes shrieked, the big water-organ uttered pompous notes like sobs. Nearly all of them marched, as Veleda noticed, with defiant smiles on their faces. Cunning, cruel, brutal faces she told herself, debased male faces, half of them doomed to die. Yet, even so, as they swaggered past, they were eyeing the women.

'*Suspirium et decus puellae!*' sang out a lady of the court, sitting not far behind, to her favourite. 'Pin-up and heart-throb of the girls!' The big brute, in acknowledgement, lifted a hand, as if she had been throwing him flowers. For the jaded appetites of the fashionable women of Rome, those gladiators were a last resource.

The gladiators – men about to die – were parading in a line

now, just below the imperial dais, leering upwards. In loud voices, and keeping better time with their words than the young aristocrats had done, they gave the Emperor his ritual greeting.

'*Ave, imperator, morituri te salutant*!'

At *morituri* – 'those about to die' – the crowd fell still, drew breath. On the far side of the dais, Maria and Eucherius were sitting awkwardly together, with nothing to say to each other. Honorius, prominent and visible, had gone pale under his cosmetics like a doll. Flavius Stilicho, at his side, was singularly calm. Stilicho nudged the Emperor gently, and Honorius raised a hand, to return the gladiator's greeting.

The games today were to begin with not death, but fun. While the last of the Roman mob went filing into the five thousand standing places that had been provided, the earlier and more important arrivals must be kept amused. A crowd of mock gladiators had swarmed into the arena – whip against stick, or wooden sword against wooden sword, all dressed ludicrously, in derision of the men who would later pair off and fight to the death. This was dumb play, they were making fools of themselves. Galla Placidia was entranced.

If only I dare, thought Veleda, take a scarf and bind her eyes, so that this much is all she will remember! For the mob over there, one attraction was to watch how the imperial family took it – hope to see them wince. So how – wondered Veleda – will Honorius get through the day, undisgraced? In Rome, the mob drag us all down to their level.

Out trotted a dozen of Stilicho's cataphracts – an exhibition bout. They were fighting each other as *andabata* – horsemen charging with sword and lance, but blindfold because wearing helmets with no eyeholes. They were fighting a skirmish in the pitch dark, and Galla Placidia grunted anxiously when an accidental blow landed heavily, knocking one of them out of the saddle.

The stirrups, Stilicho decided, make all the difference. With his feet braced, a horseman could stand impact yet stay in the saddle. Some of them down there, even though blindfold, were learning the new game fast, using their brains. One or two were lost. Let Alaric's spies here take note. Let him think that if he came back to Italy, these are the armoured horsemen he might have to meet. Not many of them yet, but enough to awe barbarians perhaps.

The cataphract knocked clean out of his saddle was being dragged, as all casualties were, to the edge of the arena, by men dressed as Hermes Psychopompus – Mercury, conducting dead souls down to the shades. They found him a heavy weight.

Honorius was shocked. Everyone else here apparently took Hermes Psychopompus for granted. To Galla Placidia he was a man in fancy dress, and this was all pantomine. But Honorius was still concerned about the line of pagan poetry those young men had chanted in his hearing, at the solemn moment when he climbed the stairs to the Capitol alone. In his muddy mind he was hunting for a pretext – trying by striking a moral attitude to swamp his fear of the hand-to-hand fighting yet to come.

He would have yet both to watch and to judge, maintaining through all the bloodshed a judicial face, the one man with the power over them of life and death. A man with his blade on his antagonist's throat could appeal for a decision to the Emperor – and if the Emperor's thumb went down the man would die.

The Emperor's anger at the appearance of Hermes Psychopompus had been a lucky fluke for Olympius. From his seat a little way off he could see the look of distress come across the Emperor's face. Would Honorius fall into the clever trap that had been laid for him?

The *probatio armorum* was soon over. As soon as the fighters' weapons had been scrutinised, to make sure that all had killing edges, lots were drawn. The gladiators were faced with their antagonists. The first serious fight this afternoon would be between two Samnites – large-shield men wielding long swords, both well-known names, and survivors of many previous combats. A fight to a finish between two wily veterans – and highly popular with the crowd, who had been kept waiting for the real thing long enough.

'Watch them hack each other to pieces!' announced the excited society woman somewhere at Veleda's back, who had so loudly called out to her heartthrob.

The enormous crowd, warmed up by the joke-fights, were ready for something juicier. As the Samnites with their long swords swaggered closer to one another, menacingly, the crowds all round the arena fell miraculously silent.

The surprising hush made a sob rise up in Galla Placidia's throat. Two big men with long swords were going out to fight for her – for her brother, the Emperor, but also for her. They would go on fighting, never flinching, until one of them lay dead. Like a dead lizard, or a dead bird. The knowledge of death had never until today come very close to her. Every movement of their limbs as they circled each other, out there on the clean and dazzling sand, swords poised, was made so significant by this inevitable doom that Galla Placidia could hardly breathe.

The silence was being broken here and there by a few impatient yelps of encouragement. Most of the crowd, though, was still holding its breath, when down from the topmost row of seats came one huge, indignant cry – a cry so compelling that it dragged many eyes away from the gladiators, and upwards.

A man stood against the skyline, very tall, thin and stark, arms raised, his monk's garb a batwing black. There were even Romans in the crowd who recognised him: Telemachus, a Syrian monk and a fanatic. Soon to be a martyr, reflected Olympus, trying to keep all traces of a satisfied smile off his plump, smooth face. At my suggestion he chose martyrdom, and how he is enjoying it! A Christian martyr, punctual to his engagement.

The gladiators too had heard the astonishing cry, but dare not turn their heads. They went on circling one another, glaring, feinting, professional enemies who would take advantage of any upward glance to strike a death blow. The eyes of the crowd, though, were straying. Heads turned to watch as Telemachus bounded down the crowded terraces, leaping enormously from one level to the next as if on a stairway, and shouting in a voice all could hear, '*In the name of the Lord*!' *Dominus* – the Lord Jesus Christ – could also these days mean the Emperor. Which did he mean?

Flavius Stilicho leaned forward, to whisper in Honorius's ear. He wanted permission to call out the guard, but knew he had not been heard. Honorius was in the grip of a splendid vision: this holy man, this monk, was doing and saying all that his own bewildered heart had hoped for. Down to the sanded arena had come an avenging spirit, an angel in black – in the conjoined name of Christ and Rome's Emperor.

Telemachus had already leaped the barrier. Inside the arena he was visible to all. With one long stiff arm he thrust away contemptuously a Hermes Psychopompus who tried to drag at his robe. The pagan went down in the dust. *As they all should*, thought Honorius excitedly. *We are Catholics, and nothing can withstand us.* The Emperor's heart beat painfully, as if he himself were one with that symbolic black figure, striking down pagans.

Exasperated by the inattentive crowd, the gladiators had at last clashed. The Samnite who had the advantage was lifting his long sword for a decapitating blow, when with a cold courage breathtaking even in the gladiatorial arena the tall Syrian monk leapt between them. As the sword was about to fall, he raised windmill arms outward as if nailed to an invisible cross, forbidding them.

Galla Placidia was baffled. Were the gladiators always like this, with black-clad monks dropping from the sky, to spoil the fun? She turned back to look at her brother, on the dais, and he sat there with his mouth dropped open, stiff as if paralysed, giving no sign.

Honorius now has the chance – but will he? Under his unruffled surface, Olympius was desperately concerned. He clenched his right fist until the fingernails pierced his palm. The next few moments meant everything. Would Honorius do the obvious – make one clear sign of prohibition? He had the power.

The crowd was disconcerted. A busybody had cheated them. The first hurled sandal flew in an arc above the space of sand, and by an outside chance hit Telemachus full in the cheek. He jerked back, as if he had been slapped in reproof. He was raising a crooked forearm across his face, as if to protect himself from whatever might be coming next. He had asked for it. Objects of every kind were falling upon him from all round the stadium. If five or ten thousand aim at the same mark, hits will be scored. The tall monk staggered, his ragged cloak fluttered. A whirling waterpot struck him on the back of the head, and he fell to his knees.

A few daring plebs were clambering the barrier itself, to get to grips. No one was stopping them – they were in a mood to tear the spoilsport limb from limb. Turning his back on the stupefied Emperor, Flavius Stilicho half rose to get attention, over there on the far side, from the tribune of the palace guard. Olympius as he saw went stiff with rage. He had planned for the Emperor to assert himself – and now would this old man again take control?

The white-haired commander-in-chief raised his hand. A bugle sounded, and guardsmen, buckling their red belts tighter, began to move out across the arena with drawn swords.

Telemachus, struck time and again by flying debris, had tried to rise but was staggering. The Samnites had backed away, and were putting up their swords. They were not paid to die disregarded.

The plebs had their hands on the monk, and were tugging him this way and that, scragging him, twisting limbs at impossible angles as though he were a dummy. Telemachus screamed. They were dislocating and by now dismembering him. The crowd were out for blood, even if they had to spill it themselves.

Honorius watched, in a fascinated stupor, and only when it was too late to save the monk did his bewilderment clear. The crowd saw the Emperor rise, on his dais, extend his hand in rebuke. From those who saw came a groan of disappointment. Were all to be chastised for the misdemeanours of the few? Words Honorius might have said did not come, they were stuck in his throat. But what did it matter that the Emperor had not found words? He had given a signal. The palace guard were enfilading confidently across the arena, helmets well down, striking with the flat of the sword, riot tactics.

Olympius's heart was hammering with brilliant excitement. The scheme had worked. Independently of his commander-in-chief, the Emperor had acted. One small gesture had been enough. Whoever else gained advantage from this day's triumph, it would not be Flavius Stilicho.

Honorius and his suite withdrew, deliberately, not too hurriedly, Stilicho himself setting for them a dignified pace. The guard had the enormous crowd boxed in. Though Galla Placidia found it all very exciting – her first riot – there was in fact no danger. They disappeared from sight through the Emperor's private exit and thence under escort up the nearly Palatine Hill to the palace. More guards were coming downhill at the double to help shepherd the disappointed crowd out of the Colosseum, and back where they came from. Tonight the city would be patrolled.

The body of Telemachus, torn limb from limb, lay like rubbish on the sand, but when a Hermes Psychopompus, used to this kind of thing, began clearing up the pieces of corpse-like litter, Christians of the imperial household came down pell-mell, and formed a protective ring, shoulder to shoulder, around his remains, the relics of a martyr, and under imperial protection. They began to sing a hymn. A martyr goes instantly to heaven – the soul of Telemachus was flying straight upwards.

Honorius, afterwards, hardly needed Olympius's advice to prompt him. That same night was promulgaged in Rome the decree that had been exacted from Constantine in AD 326 by the bishops meeting at the Council of Nicaea. The interdict was valid in Constantinople, but never thoroughly enforced elsewhere. No more gladiators.

At crack of dawn next day, Honorius and his family left for Ravenna. To her intense disappointment, Galla Placidia had to go too. She had loved Rome – everything about it. She wanted to come back soon. She found Ravenna deadly dull.

Politically Stilicho too might have done well to return to Ravenna, so as to contend with his hidden enemies. He managed to persuade himself, though, that for the time being his presence was more vital, here in Rome, to work on the city's neglected defences. From a military point of view, he was no doubt right. Alaric had burned his fingers once, at Pollentia, but Stilicho could read his mind. Next time he would march south, for Rome – strike at the heart.

Those in the know at court were not convinced. Serena was in Rome, Stilicho once there would find it hard to avoid her, and she would have none of him. Most took it for granted that the old man was staying in Rome to be near Gilda. Sensing what might be said to his disadvantage, Gilda had in fact urged him to go to Ravenna, and, even though she herself had a dread of the place, offered to share his life, there amid the marshes.

'I think I shall stay in Rome for a while,' Stilicho told her. 'Do my duty, and be happy.'

He had never been openly concerned about happiness before. That one word – *felix* – was like a jewel to her.

2

The fisherman who had landed him, alone, on the small uninhabited island of Cuneus left Marcus Curtius on the shore and headed off towards the larger island from which they had come – a small purple smudge in an easterly direction. Marcus watched them from the shore, until the faces and the hull and the oblong of the mainsail had dropped out of sight.

Whenever they had a good catch from nearby waters, the fishermen and his mates would put a string of fish ashore for Marcus. He was helping them fight the devil – they owed him that much. Their holy man turned out not to be very practical. They had to show him how to bait a line, how to dry fish by splitting and gutting them and sticking them up in the hot wind like gloves on the branched fingers of driftwood.

By Easter the flour he brought with him had run out. The fishermen turned up with a sack of barley to surprise him, and a quern to mill it. They showed him how a seed of fire may be kept alight under ash. Marcus would say his prayers while rolling the quern to grind flour, laborious work, and anywhere else in the world, woman's work. *Laborare est orare.*

Like a man inventing unleavened bread by the light of his mother-wit, Marcus made flapjacks under the hot ash of a fire he now knew better than to let go out. He had begun to realise that, even though at Nola he might have worked with his hands, there, as in the world outside, most of the chores had been done by others, usually by women. Peasant women in the villages around Nola had ground flour for the community's bread. There were cooks to do the cooking, someone else washed the clothes. On Cuneus, everything had to be done with one pair of hands, and he must also pray. Prayer here, continual prayer, was the other fire he kept alight, even if only as one bright spark under ash.

For the first few days the absolute loneliness had been a horror, which Marcus tried to cancel by prayer on his knees until they bled. Prayers and incessant work helped him in the end to feel closer to God. His prayers were an unending mutter from morning till night, Latin running through his head even when his lips no longer formed the words.

He might have been a soldier, sent under discipline to carry out a severe and solitary duty, except that here life had begun to flow as a river of feeling. Nearness to God was also a strange joy. A Latin New Testament, in the translation of St Jerome, had been his splendid parting gift from Paulinus, and this he read and pondered like a man reading a message which meant more than the mere words. He had given to his day a strict framework, and that kept him going. He said the prayers of the church at the stipulated times. Despite all this, during his first year on Cuneus, Marcus's mind was often off its leash.

His Latin muttering should have been a dialogue with God, but far too often Marcus might find himself arguing with an intruder. Arguing, disagreeing, defending himself against a bulbous-nosed apparition who would drop sarcasms on him, withering down to dung and dross all the good he had striven for.

On Cuneus some food or other always came his way, though there was never enough of it. Marcus's ribs corrugated his skin, his beard came down to his chest, his robe was a beggar's. One besetting dream in the early days, as well as a difficult temptation, was of a Roman bath. After you had allowed the thought of warm water to enter your mind, then women sidled in. Once the dirt had, in dream, been sweated out of his pores, then soft lips approached to touch his own, and delicious in the palms of his hands was the weight of young breasts. All this filth began whenever cleanliness, or the mere memory of cleanliness, superseded prayer.

Women from the past whose names and even faces Marcus could hardly recall came back as apparitions, each with some particular remembered attribute to torment him – a kiss tasting of pomegranate, an inner thigh like silk. These women rising up in his mind were not actual women, old friends, but evanescent, devilish creatures, reminding him of what he would rather forget, and always one step beyond the touch of human hand.

Sometimes he slept in the hut, on the ground, under his blanket, more often under the stars. And why should there not also be a place here, a habitation, dedicated to God? One day he took his tools and set to work on a clumsy shrine – drystone walls, a sloping roof of the flattest stones he could find, overlapping on driftwood rafters. Two timbers drifting on to the beach from a wreck had been conveniently mortised. By sawing off three short ends he was able to make a wooden crucifix, large enough to be visible out to sea.

There was some vegetation on Cuneus, not much. Here and there grass grew in pockets of soil, only to wither, later on, when the hot wind blew. Capers had spread invincibly across the barren rock, the buds acrid. Apart from the smell of drying fish, and the smell of Marcus himself, the island's most insistent smell was caper. At the right time of year, instructed by the fishermen, he picked his capers, squatting low across the hot rock, and cured them in brine. There was a market in Sicily for capers, and he now had something to give the fishermen in exchange for what they brought him.

Prayer, work, unending preoccupation, in the course of time calmed down the effervescence of Marcus's nerves. Women had virtually disappeared from his mind. Had he, with God's help, subdued the flesh? Or would the subtle demons arrive back in some other form? At least, he told himself, as he grew stiff crouching to pick capers, I no longer live off others. (Was that the sin of pride?)

On this unpromising island, as a gaunt and hairy man in rags, Marcus had come into a different relationship with nature – but with nature as the dictionary of God. Prayer was almost always dialogue, fewer days were blank and sad. The devil less often came in the semblance of his father, to corrupt him. God would be somewhere near. There were intuitions, and even, at times, answers.

One of the Roman grain-ships, a two-hundred-and-fifty tonner, bound from Carthage to Ostia, ran in a night as dark as pitch on to the reef offshore, and all the crew were drowned.

Marcus stood with his back to a rock in a wind that blew his rags around him, aware of the disaster, and helpless to act. He began as he stood there to pray for the repose of their souls, but without conviction, and stopped before the prayer was finished, his throat choking on salt air.

A waterlogged carcass of a wreck, drifting inshore next day, rammed its bows into the beach, and toppled on one side. For the poverty-stricken fishermen of the archipelago, who began arriving through rough seas at the crack of dawn, this was a splendid day. They stripped the wreck of every useful thing before the authorities could get to hear, and send soldiers and officials. They took away boat cargoes of soaked grain and wet sailcloth. They stripped the dead sailors of what they wore – clothes were hard to come by in the archipelago – and left them tumbled on the black volcanic gravel, destitute, naked and swelling up in the heat of the day. The fishermen did all this with a passion like lust.

Hitherto they had dealt generously by Marcus, and he thought well of them. Now he began to see what involuntary poverty had made of them. As they stripped the corpses, they had avoided his eyes. At last Marcus raised his voice, pitching what he needed to say in an officer-like, upper-class tone he had not used for years. Those men over there, he told them, are our dead brothers.

An impulse towards dominion over others was the worst of temptations, but what else could he do?

'Take my spade, my pick. You over there – start digging a trench.' He might have been giving orders to legionaries. 'No – up higher where the tide won't reach them. Let's get it all done before dark.'

I am not serving Caesar, he tried to persuade himself. I am not using my moral authority over them to my own advantage. I am serving God. The grain they are taking is government property. In the eyes of the law they are thieves. But I say not one word about the stolen grain. These fishermen are only ever one step away from hunger, and look at the thieves in government – more thieves than honest men.

One's duty to God, simply that, requires at least a grave for those dead sailors, and a prayer over them. They too were men, brothers, with souls to save, not mere dead things cast aside to rot.

As Marcus began to say his awkward prayer, in Latin, for the repose of the men's souls the fishermen left their work. A tempting piece of plunder might be just within reach, might fall to another man, but plunder depended on luck, and this prayer too had to do with luck. Not that most of them understood what Marcus was saying, the Latin was too much for them; word-magic. Someone handy with a codline lashed two short, straight pieces of driftwood into a small crucifix and hammered it into the gravel of the common grave with the back of the iron spade. The dead men will wait there, Marcus had told them, until the day of Resurrection.

Marcus, though he scrupled taking any of the grain they offered him, had just seen a use for the great iron fire-basket which had stood in the bows of the wrecked ship, inside a casing of bricks, as warning-light and cook-house fire.

'Where do you want it put?' the fishermen asked him.

'Up there.'

When Marcus pointed to the top of the cliff they took it for a joke, and laughed, but he got them heaving, and at last they had manhandled it to the highest point on Cuneus. Today he had an ascendancy over them. When they asked him what for, he said, confidently, 'After you have left me here alone on the island, you will see.'

Another way to serve that was an inspiration direct from God!

Next day Marcus spent piling driftwood above the tideline, and when it had dried in the sun and wind he began hauling it in corded backloads to the top of the cliff. Inside a pot of ashes he carried a core of fire, and at sunset built a driftwood blaze inside the iron firebasket.

By day it gave smoke, by night he would have a blaze. A pillar of fire by night. Let all ships who came this way give the reef off Cuneus a wide berth.

A warning beacon would mean fewer wrecks, but though a wreck came as a windfall to the local fishermen they showed no resentment. They were proud of their hermit. Not everyone had a hermit, or a fire on the cliff after dark. When night-fishing, so long as they could see the glimmer on the clifftop at Cuneus, they knew where they were.

3

The tendon in the longest finger of his right hand still hurt when Lucas tried to write. Another splinter of bone was working its way through, and his penmanship as yet was nothing to be proud of. He took pains, though, with his letter to Claudian.

Cornelia was large and healthy and well-fed, younger than Lucas had expected, her smooth skin filled to bursting, like a sausage-skin with flesh. She was good-natured. She kept coming breathlessly upstairs while Lucas wrote, and popping her head in at the door to make suggestions. Tell my betrothed that we can get good fish here. Tell him I have a slave who can play the lute.

Claudian misses nothing, Lucas reminded himself, as he looked out from the upstairs loggia at the flat terrain around the manor house – corn crops and olive trees, and here and there across the landscape, defensive towers. He will read between the lines, and notice what I am omitting. He knows at once when I try to humour him.

Magister et amicus, the voyage from Ostia to Carthage was pleasant, the winds favourable.

True enough, thought Lucas, so long as one makes no mention of that first night at sea, my back against the steerage bulkhead, deafened by the screech of the rudder-oar, the knife in my left hand. And that bloated seaman with the gold ring in his ear, the bully, who had come aft to amuse himself with me, seeing the blade and backing off. Kill a man once in your life and it will show.

Describe the port of Carthage in a few distinct sentences. An artificial harbour, implanted by Roman power. Circular, built of dressed stone, with a quay all round protected by a parapet. Flanked by columns, so that the berths where sea-going ships were hauled up for repair looked like a portico. Not bad. Claudian will recognise Carthage when he arrives!

Pouch dangling from shoulders, Lucas had left the circular

quay behind him and walked uphill to the city itself – in size the second city of the Empire, in atmosphere so different from Rome. As soon as he entered the seaward gate, an obvious newcomer, up had come performers, pedlars, harlots of both sexes. Not only were they a little too vulgarly prosperous, these Roman Africans, too coarsely pleasure-loving, they were provincial. They wore clothes, they sang songs, that were out-of-date in Rome.

Lucas sat finishing his first meal on dry land, anchovies, olives, bread and a black wine he found too sweet – all African wines were too sweet – when from some place at the heart of the city had come the baying whoop of a riot. As Lucas, at a loose end, moved towards the noise, a man going in the opposite direction shouted to him, 'The same old thing!'

The whores had marched up from the port, a vociferous multitude, to join their sisters inside the walls, no less noisy, no less reckless, and try yet again to force open the bronze double-doors of the temple of Dea Celestis. For the past few years the temple had been shut up, on the orders of the Christian Emperor, Honorius. Before her name was Romanized, Dea Celestis had been a Phoenecian fertility goddess of great antiquity – and favoured by the public women of Carthage because she sanctified their profession. Now, they were locked out from the gates of pagan temple and Christian church alike. They were despised and rejected.

Louder and more blood-chilling came their screams as Lucas arrived near the temple forecourt. He took cover in an archway and watched, as to his ears came a reverberating clang. The first stone had hit the padlocked bronze door.

The gaudily-clad women who crowded the open space before the temple were squawking like birds of prey, pushing one another out of the way, shaking out the loose, flowing hair that was the mark of their trade, and, as if in self-humiliation, smudging their own painted faces. The ringleaders were up against the door, and wrestling incompetently with hasp and chain. If they know they intend to riot, wondered Lucas, why not bring along a cold-chisel and a file?

The crowd behind, as they waited impatiently, had began tearing open their robes, baring their breasts, in honour of the goddess, stripping to the waist, swaying in unison, their top-clothes dangling from their girdles, working themselves up to a ripe hysteria.

The whoops and yells that had first brought Lucas here to the forecourt were yielding to a rhythmic moan – as if these women were all speaking with one voice – which sounded like a threat to all mankind, and made him shudder. They were in a mood to crash themselves to death against the bronze doors, they were maddening themselves, when behind their backs, at a trot, arrived a *manipulus* of soldiers, shields lifted, drawn swords a-glitter.

The soldiers were men from the city guard, and they acted as if they had been called out on this job before. Matter-of-factly they began driving the whores like two-legged cattle to the other side of the forecourt, pushing here at a particularly impudent one with the boss of a shield, there threatening another tremendously with the flat of a swordblade, though never actually, Lucas observed, laying it on. The least combative of the whores were soon squeezed out through the double arch that was the forecourt's main entrance. They put their clothes right quickly, and went off to earn a living.

Lucas could see that the city guard were not keen on this work. Those girls or others like them – since soldiers were not encouraged to marry – would be their night-time sweethearts. Many had gone, but an obstinate minority, still remained scattered across the forecourt, screaming insults, lifting skirts to show the soldiers their bare backsides. Yet as they screamed they were laughing. Against the soldiers they showed no vindictiveness. All this they had a right to. The temple of Dea Celestis had, in the old days, been the one place where the whores had status – they were the women the goddess preferred. And now, simply because the Christians were powerful at court, the bronze doors of a place once their own had been locked in their faces. They had nowhere else to go in the world but the brothel.

The soldiers of the *manipulus* had done the last of their job half-heartedly, backing off before the forecourt was quite clear, and forming up in front of the temple gate. Lucas as he stood there had been trying to put into the right words, vivid, sardonic, a description for Claudian of the whores' battle for Dea Celestis, when a sacrificial victim tumbled into their arms.

A tall man, thin, not old, and wearing the black robe of a

Christian religious, stepped through the left-hand arch, as if intending to take a short cut across the forecourt. The women converged on him with a whoop of joy.

'Pluck the black crow, girls! Let's see the colour of his skin!'

The man in black was one of Augustine's community, and so, to the harlots, a temple-closer, a natural enemy. To come this way was imprudent, he had left it too late to get away. The *decurio* commanding the men of the city guard looked on with smug indifference. He had been sent with his maniple here at the double to protect the temple. And hadn't they? The temple was safe. If a fool in a black coat got himself entangled with a crowd of irate women, whose business was that? The soldiers settled down complacently to watch the fun.

The man in the black robe made no attempt to dodge or run or strike out. A dozen clawing hands had taken hold of his black garment and were tearing it to shreds. An absurd martyrdom – Lucas had been trying as he watched to find the right phrase. But would not Claudian think all martyrdom absurd?

Women were clinging to his elbows, and kicking behind his knees, so as to make him stumble. A tall, gaunt old whore, the stepmother of all the Carthaginian whores, with dyed black hair in rats' tails to her waist, her eyes smudged with black cosmetic, was forcing her mouth down on his in a kiss that was more like an attempt to wound. He turned and twisted to avoid her, but had at last to yield, because behind him another pair of hands had begun holding him by the ears.

They were stripping the last tatters of his black robe from him, until he stood amid them, thin, lanky, flesh-coloured, ludicrous. The women who held the ring had begun to clap and chant. They were swaying their hips in a dance – the libidinous dance that not so many years before had been performed across the way, in the temple, before the goddess. Lucas, watching all this, saw to his amusement that the man too was moving, though not very much. Against his will he was becoming one with all the others.

The long-haired woman's turn was over. She had yielded up her tall, naked dolly to a plumper companion, more succulent, who was rubbing the man's face between her bobbing breasts, and laughing as she did so at the way his head turned and twisted as if trying to escape. She had jammed his unwilling mouth against her nipple; he was her child. The moaning dirge became interspersed with shrieks of laughter, but the dance went on.

And there, on display in the midst of them, was his naked manhood, risen up and rigid. Augustine's black crow was no different from other men. Faces at the back were craning through to gape, to get a better view. From the women came a yell of derision. This was a man who closed temples – and their power over him was greater than his power over himself.

At a safe distance, the men of the *manipulus* ranged by the temple door were watching with coarse grins. Shall I order them to draw their swords? the *decurio* began to wonder. Some such action might look better in the report. But no. Those women are good-natured. No bones broken. He can't stand much more of what he's getting. All this will soon be over.

In the midst of the swaying ring, half a dozen women had taken physical possession of the victim. They had their fingers and their mouths all over him. One had even lifted a foot, to tickle the bare sole, so that he hopped on one leg. The other onlookers, fallen silent, were watching his face gravely. What this man might have to give they would offer to their goddess.

At last came the helpless twist of the clerically-severe features, the spasm. Those nearest broke out laughing. They had no more use for him, or for any other man they had reduced to that state. With the abrupt frivolity of light women they were turning their backs. Off they went, arms linked, and still laughing, having left the man there naked, his pride humbled.

I must cross this forecourt and go to him, thought Lucas, naked as he is. I must take the chance. As Lucas walked closer, the man turned away his face, rigid with self-disgust.

Rolled across the top of his leather satchel Lucas still carried the old cloak. He stood behind the man holding the cloak out in front of himself, opening the hole with both hands spread wide, and put it over his head as if clothing the nakedness of a child. The man pulled the garment down on his shoulders, and tight around his neck, like someone unsure what clothing really was. His feet were groping around for his sandals; Lucas bent down and retrieved them. Clad, and with the reassuring feel of leather under his feet, the man said, 'You are not by any chance a Samaritan?'

That was a word Lucas had heard somewhere before, though never quite understood. Evidently it came from the Bible, and the Bible was not his favourite reading.

'A freedman. A Briton.'

'Walk back with me as far as the Augustinian house. I have a change of clothes there, so I can give you back your cloak. And thank you for what you did, by the way. Not everyone in Carthage would have done a thing like that. A Briton, you say?'

Lucas in the room Cornelia had given him put down his iron pen, and went across to close the louvred shutters. Gusts of hot wind were coming in from the desert, as they did every day, at sundown. He was glad of a pause.

After Italy, a monotonous scenery, flat, diversified by green crops and endless rows of olive trees. *What was he doing here?* Lucas called a house slave to bring him a lamp. To give orders to a slave was still a novelty that he would rather avoid, but letter by Greek letter, all this must be finished.

And I met the famous Augustine, not a large man, except in reputation, and not quite as black as a Nubian, nor as handsome as Ganymede, but with fine eyes, an amiable nature, and delightfully eloquent. He explained to me the Christian theory of grace, information I did not ask him for and, alas, have already forgotten.

The man who had borrowed his cloak invited Lucas to share their uninspiring meal of vegetables – raw lettuce, boiled turnip. The wine served had been excessively watered, or as Lucas's neighbour jocosely described it, baptised. When the little middle-aged African with dark features and glittering eyes had come to table, and taken a vacant place with an apology, like any late-comer, Lucas had had no idea who he was. But once Augustine began to speak it became instantly clear that he was the intellectual master of all present.

His voice had a provincial accent, and at one point he had turned to the lay brother bringing in a dish and spoken to him, without turning a hair, in fluent Punic. Augustine had the face of a peasant you might pass in the street, hauling along a donkey piled high with produce. But whenever he had something worth saying, the words came out articulated in marvellous Latin, distinct as a lamp on a dark night, and yet with a subtle throb of passion.

'They were rioting in the city, and I lost my clothes,' the man had explained curtly, when his turn came to receive Augustine's attention – carefully not making himself out, Lucas noticed, to be too much of a martyr. What was the virtue in a ridiculous martyrdom? 'Lucas here lent me his cloak.'

'Lucas?'

One word – his name inflected as a question – and a single penetrating glance from those eyes, and Lucas found himself telling Augustine about his journey. Lucas Claudianipor, he told him, a freedman, here in Africa on a mission of trust for Claudian the poet. About his forthcoming marriage.

'Ah, but you have hurt your hand.' Lucas had quite forgotten the pain in his right hand. 'Do you leave Carthage soon?'

'Tomorrow.' And he mentioned the estate, south, beyond Zama.

'They say that wounds – small, physical wounds, like yours – heal quicker down there in the desert. The wounds of the soul? I don't know. Why shouldn't they, since the desert is large and empty, and God omnipresent? But cities are what a Roman knows better. You are a Briton – but from Londinium: a city. I have never lived in a desert; have you? Our Lord did, for forty days. Jerome has. The Egyptians monks do. No doubt it is salutary. A Christian?'

Lucas hesitated – not that he was abashed, but from intellectual scruple. The man who had brought him here, seeing a chance to shine broke in to say, 'Like so many Britons, a demi-semi-Pelagian. Lucas, confess, isn't that how you would define yourself?'

'In coming here we had a difference of opinion about the saying, *if I ought I can.*'

'And you believe that saying?'

Lucas found that in reply he had given an almost imperceptible nod. If I ought I can? Why not? In this man's presence he was discovering his own beliefs.

'And because of that saying, and all that goes with it, you gave a stranger your cloak, in the midst of a riot? Perhaps not, though. Perhaps you simply remembered that tag from Pelagius as you might remember a line from one of Claudian's poems.'

'I am coming to think that I do believe it,' said Lucas a little timidly. 'I mean that we must take a self-reliant effort in this life.' He could sense the thronged table change, as he spoke, into a concourse of theological tigers, all waiting to spring. But Augustine protected him.

'At least a demi-semi-Christian act, wouldn't you say, Drusus? Or don't you care to admit them? *Anima naturaliter Christiana*? And Lucas, when next you write to Claudian, make sure you tell him that much as I may regret his paganism, I admire his verse without reserve. As who could not?'

'I think he knows that. You wrote as much. And it gives him great satisfaction,' said Lucas, grateful at having been extricated from the mess about Pelagius.

'Then Claudian reads me – as I read him,' said Augustine with a disarming smile, and skilfully he turned the conversation towards the homily they had all been waiting for once the name of Pelagius had been mentioned – about divine grace.

' – the fact that those things make for a successful progress towards God,' he said, lifting up a spoon as though to look at his own face in the back of it, and then putting it down gently, 'should cause us delight.'

Delight? Lucas wondered in astonishment. God to him had never meant more than a set of sombre prohibitions. The religious feeling Augustine was speaking of might be no different from the emotion engendered by a young face, a wrist well-sculptured in marble, a line of superb verse.

' – delight is not acquired by our good intentions, earnestness, and the value of our goodwill – but is dependent on the inspiration granted us by God.'

In the same way, thought Lucas, striving for insight, a line of Claudian's verse that I happen to be transcribing may at one time go dead on me, at another come amazingly to life.

'Delight!' Augustine affirmed, looking directly at Lucas, as if entering his mind, his thoughts, and then turning his head the other way. His time here at table had to be shared out fairly. With a quick epigram which made everyone laugh but which Lucas did not quite grasp, he answered someone else's long-winded question about the Circumcelliones.

And who or what, wondered Lucas, are the Circumcelliones? It would take me too long to find out.

The second great man I have ever known, Lucas decided, when the trance was broken, and he wandered off into the encroaching night, the cloak over his arm. More of a piece – less incongruous – than Claudian. I could so easily have got involved, thrown away my liberty, learned all about Pelagius, the Circumcelliones, the Donatists. About this Delight of which he speaks. Lucas had accepted the plate of vegetables, and their watered wine, but declined the offer of a night's lodging. Sitting there, amid pious talk and would-be saintly faces, he had made up his mind to a deliberate act of lust – much as one blows out a lamp. He had money in his pocket, and, out there, waiting for him, was Carthage and its multitude of women.

He turned under a low lintel down some steps into a tavern, and ordered hot meat on a skewer, with a jug of wine. The sweet, dark wine of this country, unwatered. Claudian's was the cult of the body, Augustine's of the soul. Across the room, a girl with straight, dark, smooth hair caught his eye. Attractive because in appearance quite different from Gilda. Picking up his half-emptied jar of wine, he went across to her.

On the imperial highway going south Lucas met with his first Circumcelliones. They carried no passes, but they were people no sentry would dare stop. When they came near a strongpoint they rattled their iron-bound, seven-foot poles and shouted their unnerving *Laus Deo*! Praise God! – which might as well have been a battle cry. They had taken Lucas for a solitary freedmen tramping the roads looking for work, and invited him to join them.

They were field-workers, itinerant day-labourers, vigorous, arrogant, simple-minded men with a primitive Christianity of their own invention. That night at the fireside the Circumcelliones shared their bread with Lucas, flaps of damper as big as a dish, unleavened, and heavy on the stomach unless you had previously done a day's tramping or field-work to raise an appetite. As the fire flickered and sank, and the stars overhead intensified – the desert night is bright and burning cold – they taught him, line by line, one of their hymns, which began with a Beatitude, and ended vociferously with the poor inheriting the earth. Here, yes, but in a tavern? Lucas asked himself, as he heard the shocking words come out of his mouth. I should be arrested. The idle mob in Rome – menacing enough – were at least not rebels. These men meant all they said. He decided not to mention the Circumcelliones to Claudian – they would only alarm him – and at the crossroads they parted.

The air here is good, Lucas assured Claudian *and wounds heal quickly*. His own right hand at least no longer festered. Into Lucas's mind had come more than once the old sword-smith's warning. The injured hand was not palsied, not quite, but would he ever write a perfect page again? I must keep close to Claudian, he decided, make myself indispensable. I must make friends with Cornelia. On his own, a free man may starve.

Lucas had been trying to keep Gilda out of his mind, as if a line had been drawn across the page. If Gilda lived Stilicho would have her. She had been Stilicho's woman before, and boasted of it, on stage, in front of a thousand spectators. Did I fail her? I stuck my knife into Stridor, and Gilda might have guessed who did it. Could I help it that my master sent me to Africa? Yet, still he felt guilty.

When Lucas arrived at the manor house, dusty, with a broken sandal strap, a shabby pouch at his side, a little too much like a vagabond, but well able to assert himself, he had begun as he meant to go on. He browbeat the household slaves into taking him right away to Cornelia, and what her past must have been with her first husband, Lucas could see at a glance, skin tight across her cheekbones, face puffy, large lips protruding as if to taste and swallow, body exaggerated like a schoolboy's dream of a desirable woman. All the food she had eagerly eaten since her first wedding night, as a surrogate for passion, the meat, the fish, the fruit, the bread, the sauces, had metamorphosed into a mass of human flesh.

Cornelia from the first made a great fuss of him, and Lucas soon found out that she was no fool. She had learned perforce how to run the property, and that occupied her loneliness. She went out of her way to find him a well-lit room with a table steady on its legs, and sent one slave off for ink, another for that rarity, papyrus. She then began questioning him, vivaciously but not foolishly, about her future husband.

By a lucky chance, Claudian's ring fitted exactly on the fourth finger of her left hand, which as everyone knows connects directly with the heart. The words of the inscription – Lucas read them for her – she found enchanting. And Claudius Claudianus had written them himself – for her? An emerald ring! Emerald protects chastity, makes child-bearing easier. Portents!

At dinner that night there was another guest, a centurion, who from his line of talk thought of himself as very much overdue for a rise in rank. 'A centurion still – with my responsibilities?' He was forty years old, with a cavalryman's big belly, and a face like a slab of cold pork. At one glance Lucas silently nicknamed him Inimicus – The Foe – and stayed on the alert.

The cook, a Galatian like so many of the best cooks, had done wonders. Inimicus and Cornelia put their food away as if tomorrow they might find themselves starving. Then between a belch and a breathless gasp they exchanged little disquisitions as to whereabouts the cook might have fallen short.

'Not enough musk in the sauce,' was Inimicus's blunt military opinion.

'And you, Lucas Claudianipor?' asked Cornelia, wiping her greasy mouth with an exquisitely embroidered napkin. 'Enough musk?'

'In Rome I have even known them use less,' said Lucas, only wishing he knew of some instant way of getting the flavour or perhaps odour out of his mouth. The most decadent Roman cookery was not only spiced but perfumed.

'Possibly you did not dine at the best tables,' said the centurion complacently. 'This master of yours – '

'Master?' asked Lucas coldly. The calf of his leg itched at the place where the seam of his knife's sheath had worn its own callus.

'I am surprised you have never heard of him,' said Lucas firmly. This greedy military man had better learn from the start where he stood. 'He is close to Flavius Stilicho, and went with him, as indeed did I, on the campaign to Como against the Alemanni. And famous all over the Empire among literary men for his account of Rome's great victory at Pollentia. You yourself were not, I take it, at Pollentia?'

Two such home thrusts should be enough, thought Lucas. Think of the tongue as another sharp knife and no less wounding.

From then on Inimicus had less to say for himself. He went

away on the plea of duty as the slaves brought on the second silver bowl of fruit.

'Take some with you,' said Cornelia gaily. He paused, scrutinised, and took a double handful of the best.

'Is he sick?' asked Cornelia, once alone with Lucas. She meant Claudian. She had guessed. Why should an important Roman be coming all this way to marry her?

'Very sick, but no doubt the excellent air down here will do him good.'

Cornelia nodded, and her double chin trembled. The new husband they had wished on her was to be no improvement on the last. She sighed deeply. 'The lady Julia, at court, and the Lady Serena, are my mother's old friends. Claudius Claudianus has been chosen for me, they would not choose unwisely, and anyone who is a tribune and a notary and a friend of Flavius Stilicho's can do what he likes down here. The centurion knows that, and it upset him.'

Cornelia had gone on to ask, in a resigned voice, over her last cup of wine, without any false shame, 'Will he be any good to me, as a husband?'

Avoiding her eye, Lucas answered, bluntly enough, 'None whatever.'

You have swallowed, he told himself as he heard his own voice, one bright gold cup too many of this dark, sweet wine.

'Does Claudian have his own house, there in Rome?'

'Yes.'

'A big house?'

'Not the largest, but yes, quite big.' Lucas was seeing Claudian's house in his mind's eye, flowers, statues, laurels, cypresses, the view over the Tiber. He felt homseick for his own life in Rome, even as a slave.

'The centurion will send a man for that important letter of yours to Claudian, in a day or two,' she said, 'and forward it by the imperial mail. And now that all the writing is done,' added Cornelia, a fat and sentimental woman, yes, but a woman used to organising the world around her, 'you must give this poor injured hand of yours to the *medicus* at the oasis.'

'*Medicus?*'

'The cleverest man in the world at healing. Go the day after tomorrow, because tomorrow there is no-one else coming to dinner, and we can eat our Friday fish together. They send me a decent-sized fish up every Friday from the seacoast – '

'From the coast? A hundred miles? Won't it stink to high heaven?'

Cornelia laughed, 'Our Friday fish comes alive, on camel back – in a barrel of seawater. Perhaps in Rome you don't have camels.' Then, conscientiously, she went on to inquire, 'Does Claudius Claudianus like fish?'

'Very much. If it's fresh. And not in a musk sauce. But when he is hard at work he is just as glad of a dry crust, dipped in olive oil.'

'Work?' she asked quickly, alarmed at the word. Only inferiors worked.

'Writing.'

'Ah – writing. I don't call that work. And does he eat meat?'

'He eats meat.'

'Even goat?'

'He eats simply.' Cornelia nodded. Here was something she would bear in mind.

When Lucas said that he could just as well walk to where the *medicus* lived, Cornelia told him scornfully that only sharecroppers walked – or rode donkeys. Perhaps he would rather ride a donkey? But Lucas never wanted to ride another donkey in his life. She lent him her own horse, gelded and broken in, she boasted, by a man on her stud farm who knew how to teach any horse manners. The gelding stood in the courtyard proudly submissive, flickering its intelligent eye while the saddle girths were tightened.

With the stable hands watching, Lucas managed without disgracing himself to get from the mounting stone into the saddle. Stirrups had not yet reached Africa, and he rode off, bobbing uncontrollably, the well-bred beast wearing a look of quiet resignation.

The military road southward petered out eventually to a stony track. Olive trees gave way to clumps of date palms – tall, shivering trees, and fewer as the desert slowly came to predominate. The only signs of Roman life were the occasional defensive tower or distant mounted patrol.

The air was singularly dry, the sky enormous. The well-bred

gelding followed the track at a comfortable amble, as if knowing the way. He was heading for water. As the sun overhead grew more insensate, a tuft in the heat haze to the south became a panache of fluttered leaves, and soon emerged as tall palm trunks, tilting away from the desert wind. Lucas's sight was refreshed by a patch of cultivation, bright-green young barley, ripening melons, a long, hump-backed mud hut, and beyond, under the trees, five desert men in dirty, homespun robes, watering their camels, halter in hand, at a large, muddy hole like a half-dried-out farm pond.

The *medicus* – dressed exactly like the others – came forward with upraised arms, 'I expected you!' he announced knowingly.

But how could he? – wondered Lucas. No horseman bringing word was sent by us, nobody overtook me on the road. Does this man practise magic? He looks as if he might.

The physician had impenetrable, ironic eyes, a hook nose, thick lips, a face all creases. He could have been a Roman money-changer, shrewdly aware of values, sitting at his bench near the Porta Flaminia with piles of foreign coins stacked in orderly rows in front of him, a man who lived off quickly-reckoned small differences. He wore a desert man's robe with a certain style, as though it were fancy dress. A Syrian, wondered Lucas? No, a Jew.

'That hand of yours? Well – don't be shy. Let me have a look at it.'

His own hands, however, were not those of a money-shuffler, but large, well-shaped, muscular, stained, as if he had done skilled work with them. The physician gently explored Lucas's sore tendon, and palped the fingers.

'A fight, eh? Though some time ago. Before you left Rome?' Lucas nodded in reply, confused at this man's being so cocksure that he had come from Rome. 'What did he use on you, to produce this unusual effect?'

'A lead-loaded cane.'

'A nasty weapon. I hope you killed him for it,' the physician remarked lightly. He is tempting me, thought Lucas, to brag.

For the first time since dropping the little naked body of Stridor on the dungheap Lucas began to ask himself, soberly, what killing the little eunuch had amounted to. Should he not feel ashamed of that, too? But no, there was no shame, no guilt.

Astonishment, perhaps, that a man like himself, a penman, should have been equal to it. And killing had been so easy.

'Yes, I killed him,' he said flatly.

This man who had come to him, decided Jacob, was no ruffian to be patched up before his next affray. But then, from what I knew already, I never supposed he would be.

'Is it really true,' asked Jacob, compounding the mystery, 'that Claudius Claudianus might come to live down here? Of all dead ends?'

Lucas hedged. 'You mean Claudius Claudianus the poet?'

'Oh – at one time I knew him very well. In Alexandria we sat side by side, on the same school bench. He wrote poetry even then; so in fact did I. At that time in Alexandria all we young fellows wrote poetry – mine was considered better that his. You smile. But anyone in Alexandria at the time will vouch for what I say. Thereafter I was attracted by other things. Philosophy, Medicine. Take a grip on yourself. This will hurt.'

Jacob's long muscular fingers as he gossiped and boasted had been unrolling a linen hold-all to pick out implements. Most were probes or small knives, clean and extremely sharp. After making a decisive small cut, Jacob took up the tweezers. How did he come here? Lucas wondered. Why does he stay? Did he really know Claudian? And how does he know my name, and so much about me?

A spasm of pain blotted all such questions from his mind.

'You stood that rather well,' said Jacob, rubbing his chin appraisingly, as though he were making a collection of individual reactions to pain. 'Not as well as the desert people – they are perfectly Stoic. At times one might almost think, insensible. Odd, when you consider the air they breathe. But for a city-bred man. Where are you from?'

'Britain, Londinium.'

'Cold and heavy air. Could account for it. Italians – their air is mild and warm – are apt to yelp. Egyptians have the best climate in the world – and have you any idea how much noise an Egyptian will make if you only scratch him? Here is the little thing that made your life a misery.' Jacob held up a splinter of bone hardly bigger than a fishbone. 'A piece of yourself,' said Jacob ironically, 'and I was just going to throw it away. I don't want to be accused of stealing a piece of yourself. I am in enough trouble already. Do you want this piece of yourself back?'

'I can manage without it,' said Lucas gravely, and Jacob answered Lucas with his first frank, unclever smile.

'Keep the hand clean, need I say that? And now let us hope,' said Jacob, again covertly knowing, 'that your handwriting will improve. Since that is your profession.'

A Christian hermit? wondered Lucas. But these demonstrations of mind-reading were magic, and Christians abhorred magic. No – a political prisoner?

'A great poet though, no doubt of that,' said Jacob conventionally, as if this were not a desert oasis but a statue-bedecked garden in Rome or Alexandria, and the magnificence of Claudian's verse had been tacitly agreed on as a topic of conversation. 'A man of enormous talent, Claudius Claudianus, and even as a young man, beautifully tolerant – of Jew, Copt, Greek. Not of women, though – never of women. None of us could ever quite make Claudian out, because he so easily became the mirror of the person he was talking to. I suppose poets do. Protean – is that the word? He insisted on calling himself a Roman, and in the end to Rome he went, and there became more Roman, to judge by his poetry, than any real Roman. If there are any real Romans left. If you suppose I am a Jew, then you are right. We were all at each other's throats in Alexandria, Jew, Greek and Copt, pagan, Arian, orthodox. Well, the Christians have come out on top, and that, let me tell you, is why I am stuck here on this oasis for the rest of my life. Alexandria is no longer the tolerant place it was when Claudian and I were young poets together. A wonderful city, though, in the old days –'

I am drowning, thought Lucas, in all this loquacity, and he still had not told me how he comes to know as much about me. He is amusing himself. Of course he is lonely here, with no one to talk to except desert men and palm trees.

'I made money – from surgery, mostly. But they mulcted me of my fortune with an exceedingly well-judged fine, and shipped me off here to this oasis. Don't bother to tell me – comparatively speaking, I am lucky. Others have it much worse. Think what happened to Hypatia.'

'And what did happen to Hypatia?'

'Monks from the desert scraped the flesh off her bones, with sharp shells. She was, it so happened, rather beautiful. And therefore, to them, a temptation.' Jacob laughed. 'The charge against me was Gnosticism, and in Christian Alexandria that was even worse than being a teacher of pagan philosophy, and also beautiful. No, for your information, I am not a Gnostic and never was. I have a few Gnostic texts here though, if you are interested. I keep them with me from pure defiance. Would you like to see a Gnostic text? A book that can bring a man's social life to a sudden end?' He might have been offering Lucas a bunch of roses.

He ducked into his mud hut, and came out unrolling a papyrus, and began to read, in a sonorous voice, mimicking those who read the Law in the synagogue.

'The males on the right are frog faces and the females on the left are cat faces. Put a square milk stone on the base of the turquoise tablet and write the name in hieroglyphics. O my son you will do this when I am in Virgo and the sun is in the first half of the day and fifteen degrees have passed by me. Make anything of it?'

'Who could?'

'A kind of marginal idiocy. A certain heavy-handed poetry though. I thought so then, I think so now, anyway, they charged me with it. Astrology was another one they threw at me. Well, I can cast a horoscope as well as the next man, perhaps a little better, but reflecting on astrology out here at the oasis where the stars are so much in evidence, I have begun to wonder. Take the case of twins. Identical horoscopes, widely differing destinies. Hermetic philosophy of which they also disapprove, these orthodox Christians, and which then fascinated me – still does – would you believe it was not even in the charge? The search, I mean, for a medicine which one day will cancel out death. I don't mean the blood of the lamb, either. Are you a Christian?'

'No. But those were opinions, not crimes.'

'Opinion can be the gravest of crimes,' said Jacob, his eyes glittering, 'for a Jew in Christian Alexandria.'

Lucas asked impulsively, 'And some day could you teach me how to cast a horoscope?' As he stood there the useful notion had struck him that these days fewer people than ever wanted books copied for their libraries, but almost everyone was anxious to know their future fate. Astrology as a second trade? Why not?

Jacob went on speaking rapidly, as if he had not heard. As for the young man's request, he was thinking it over carefully. Might what he had asked turn out to be a clever trap?

'My crime was being different. And yet, in Alexandria when Claudian and I were young, everyone was different. The city boiled with ideas, like a cauldron, until the monks came into Alexandria from the desert of the Thebaid and took over. They carried clubs, and hit dissenters on the cranium to make sure that everyone in the city thought the same. The water here at the oasis gives me constipation, but apart from that one small inconvenience I find plenty to occupy me, I read and meditate and practise my art. The desert folk bring me their sick. Next time you come over, will you bring me some wine? I still like a drink as the sun goes down.'

'Teach me to cast horoscopes and I will bring you a full wine-skin.'

'You never give up, do you? Did you think I would never stop talking?'

'Well?'

'Bring your wineskin with you next time, and meanwhile I will consider,' answered Jacob with a strange kind of cautious innocence. Now and then the *agentes in rebus* sent a convincing-looking spy to a political exile, to sound him out. But was this thoughtful and agreeable young man a spy? Jacob was not inclined to gamble that he was not. He had not reacted in the least to the giveaway Gnostic quotation. 'Now you would like to know,' he went on with a look of ineffable cleverness, 'how I found out so much about you. Of course you would. Don't pretend you wouldn't. I knew far more about you than you ever expected. Let me make one thing clear. If we are to lead a reasonable life here in this dismal place – we murderers, we Gnostics, we astrologers – then, my dear fellow, hadn't we better begin by trusting one another? I have no great love for the Roman army, which in its day sacked the city of Jerusalem, our city you know, with particular brutality. Unlike my old friend Claudian, I do not care to serve Rome, even in the smallest way. And nor, I somehow think, do you. I have decided to trust you. I will give you proof. Come inside – '

Having drunk the pond dry, and tugged inordinately at their halters in the hope of getting at the young barley, the camels were ready to move off. Jacob turned to shout words of farewell to the desert men in their own strange language, then ducked more again under the mud hut's low and narrow lintel.

On the trodden floor were a blackened cooking-pot and a pallet stuffed with barley-straw. On a bench along one side were other pots which certainly were not cooking pots. They were ranged around a charcoal furnace, and stank of strangeness, mercury, sulphur, antimony. On the far wall hung a wooden honeycomb filled with papyrus rolls.

'The books they would be looking for – hermetic and heretical texts – I keep over here in this big flour jar.' Jacob put one hand deep in the flour as if for a lucky dip, and brought out Hermes Trismegistus. 'See how I trust you, Lucas? Yes, here in this wilderness, people like ourselves should trust one another. I know you better than you imagine. And what else have we here? Surprise you? Your own handiwork I rather think.'

The flour-encrusted papyrus roll that Jacob handed Lucas was the letter given yesterday to the centurion's messenger, and addressed to Claudius Claudianus, tribune and notary, in Rome, Lucas had written the Latin in Greek letters as a precaution.

'That overweight centurion who dangles after Cornelia ordered me to translate it from the Greek for him. But how can I?'

'Inimicus?'

'Your nickname for him? Good. Inimicus has been set to work by the *agentes in rebus* – but Claudian for his own peace of mind must never be allowed to suspect that we know. And Claudian seriously proposes to marry this woman?'

He talks about trusting me, thought Lucas, yet keeps on adding question to question. Shall I answer?

'Claudian is moving as far away from Rome and Ravenna as possible, on the advice of his friend Flavius Stilicho.'

'Entangled in politics at last, poor fellow? That makes another of us, down here at the end of the world. As the cities decay, oases grow fertile. Desert islands too, so they tell me. Now what can we do, the pair of us, about this indiscreet letter of yours?

Here is an inkhorn – oh, you have a pen of your own? Good. Now, suppose you dictate to me, in Latin, such a version of the letter you hold in your hand as will set their minds at rest. No sedition, and above all, no wit, for wit is sedition. Write something innocuous to Claudian, and your real letter you can show him later, when he arrives. What a vivid letter you write, Lucas – less pompous than Cicero, spicier than Pliny? No, I mean it. If the epistolary art survives – I doubt if it will – you may yet make a name for yourself. Do look out carefully, by the way, for that pig-faced centurion – but I am sure you will. He has ideas of his own about the widow. He will do Claudian an injury if he can. Pass me that iron pen of yours, will you? I am ready to take dictation. Ready? And how shall we begin? Ah yes – *magister et amicus* – '

4

Flavius Stilicho, in his audience with the Emperor in Ravenna began with a quite unexpected remark. 'Honorius, I cannot live for ever.' He was using with Honorius the fatherly tone which he and nobody else could adopt – the Emperor was often impressed by it, though sometimes exasperated.

'After I am gone, the Roman army, which guarantees *pax Romana* as well as your *imperium*, will look to only one man – '

Pax with Honorius these days was a pregnant word, for was not the Christian church a church of peace? Should not a Christian Emperor therefore be a man of peace? Just now Honorius had this simple notion firmly fixed in his mind.

'You mean Olympius?' asked Honorius, innocently.

Stilicho grasped his chance. 'This man Olympius is no doubt a capable servant, or you would never have decided to make him your Master of the Offices. Sitting at a desk he would no doubt do very well. But as a commander-in-chief? You and I know exactly where he was, on the day of Pollentia.' At the thought of having, eventually, to report this answer to his master, the spy hidden behind the curtain shuddered.

'No, Honorius – no, *dominus* – ' To indulge the boy, Stilicho was deliberately using a form of address – *dominus* – that usually he scorned. 'The only man who can impose upon the soldiers of Rome, legionary and mercenary alike, an unbreakable loyalty is yourself – their Emperor.'

A sad political truth which when put tritely into words hardly bore thinking of. The Emperor in person held the Roman system together – and just look at him!

'I would not expect you to travel very far from here – not to Africa or Spain or Gaul. But if you left Ravenna for a while on a little excursion – a tour of those army units which defend the approaches to your capital?'

Honorius had been sure from the start that this audience with Stilicho would end, as they always did, by forcing on him some unpleasant duty.

'Give your soldiers a chance to see and cheer aloud the man they must ultimately obey.'

Pax – the word struck Honorius like a nudge in the ribs. He nodded.

Olympius had been sure until now of his success in turning the feelings of the army against the man who commanded them. With Stilicho busy licking into shape an army that soon might have to face Alaric, life these days for the legionaries of XX *Valeria Victrix* was little else but weapon training, field exercises and pack drill. They were ready to give a hearing to any clever grouser.

Their traditional rivalry with the cavalry was being blown up to a hot and active resentment that made the barbarians themselves uneasy. The barbarians served Rome for payment, as mercenaries – there were thirty thousand of them in Italy alone, and without them Italy could not be defended. Once their time had expired they were free to go – a foot-soldier was tied to the legion for life. But in the meantime the mercenaries had yielded up their families as hostages for good behaviour. These women and children lived in Italian cities unguarded.

Stilicho too could sense the bad feeling that Olympius's agents had been whipping up – sedition in the air. When the trouble was traced unmistakably to Olympius he could hardly believe it. Would a former senior officer, a man now in authority at the heart of things, play such a dangerous game with military discipline, merely from ambition?

His answer was that of a simple soldier. The way to counter all that nonsense, he told himself, is to let the soldiers see their Emperor. That may steady them. And if not, I shall have to act sternly, and strike hard.

The light of earliest dawn flooded up, duck-egg blue, and pink, and clotted-cream, fingering the sky from seaward. A single dove like a promise of peace flew urgently across the marsh towards the somnolent city of Ravenna. The dove's poised wings had flashed as it turned to follow the line of the causeway. At the shore-line the bird checked, wheeled, turned away from the blue Adriatic, circling sagaciously to seek out a particular house.

New patrician palaces of raw white stone had been built everywhere in Ravenna since the little marsh port had become an imperial capital. With a flap of wings the dove descended to the flat roof of a mansion standing apart, near a square, and opposite a little basilica, landing there on the hinged platform of a wicker cage, as if coming home.

A hollow cane the size of a little finger had been tied with twine to the pigeon's leg. The young officer rolled the strip of papyrus, spindled inside the cane, around a rod of the same diameter as the rod the officer sending the message had used. The edges of the letters joined up, and there was a message to send him running.

Iron-shod boots went helter-skelter down the stone stairs from the dove-cote on the roof. The clatter woke the household. Flavius Stilicho might indeed be in his room, taking his pleasure with his woman, and leaving orders not to be disturbed, but this he must see at once. Made outrageously bold by his sense of duty, the young officer hammered his knuckles on the bedroom door.

'Under the sheet!' whispered Stilicho to a flagrantly naked Gilda. The man on watch would knock like this only in dire extremity.

Gilda's face, small and toylike amid a sprawl of hair, had sunk into a large, soft pillow. Her delectable body was already covered. Would the young officer spare her a glance? When they met by accident on the stairway, he hung his head like a girl. Unable to help himself, he looked her way, and Gilda winked behind Stilicho's head as she pulled the sheet over her own head. She could hear the rumble of their voices, but the words were just too low to catch. Stilicho was responding to the news as if set on fire. His voice rose, and she could hear the orders he was giving.

'Go down and call out the guard. Not the palace guard, I shall need cavalry, not toy soldiers. My Hun guard – every man jack of them, boots and saddle, full battle order. I intend to lead them out of here in person as the sun comes up. Each man to be leading a remount. Strip the stables. Have your own charger mounted – I shall need you along. But now, listen carefully. I shall also need a good, small horse, one of my Samnium ponies, saddled up and left in the courtyard. Clear? Good. And as to where we are going and why, not a word to anyone. Anyone. Not a hint. Or I shall have your hide in strips. Understand me? Any questions? Good man. Now – go!'

Gilda as she brought her head out of hiding could hear the young officer's boots clatter all the way down to the courtyard, like a schoolboy let out on holiday.

The fine woollen robe with which Stilicho covered his nakedness was dropped around his feet. He stood there enormous, alone, and tipped cold water over his body. As it ran down his skin to make a puddle on the floor he gave an elephantine gasp of satisfaction. He has washed my smell off him, thought Gilda, my touch, my influence. That cold shock has washed away all tenderness. For this, which is his active life, he does not need me. Why should he?

Stilicho pulled on his parade uniform and put his feet in his boots with a quickness Gilda would have thought possible only back-stage. He glanced around, irritably for something not exactly to hand – and she knew what.

'Your sword is where you hung it last night – on the peg beside the door.' Gilda had by this time tumbled out of bed, the top sheet like a thin toga around her shoulders, but had been keeping her tongue still until he should need her.

'If an enemy ever came in here, one dark night,' he grumbled. 'I might need that sword of mine in a hurry.'

'Then put it closer,' she said, 'put it under your pillow. Put it under mine. Let me mind it for you.' He was about to expostulate, and then laughed. She had broken the tension for him. She had done it on purpose.

'Trouble?' asked Gilda. He would only tell her if he chose to.

Flavius Stilicho took her so harshly by the shoulder that his grip bruised through the sheet. Vandal blue eyes as cold as stone were looking straight at her.

'For all I know, the beginning of the end.'

'Yes?'

'And if the worst should happen, the horse they are saddling in the courtyard is for you. Have all the money I have given you hidden under your clothes, and a satchel packed. Meanwhile stay in the house, stay alert, judge the situation for yourself, and who knows? The day after tomorrow we may be in each other's arms again, and laughing at all this. You are an actress. Don't get bottled up in Ravenna. If you judge the time has come to leave, be someone different, because my enemies will also be your enemies. I suppose there is no one in this city you can trust absolutely?'

With a pang of regret Gilda thought of Lucas. And where was Lucas? Somewhere in Africa, in another life altogether.

Her smile was falsely radiant. 'You are the only one I trust.'

Out in the courtyard ostlers shouted, horses whinnied. An auroch horn blurted its strange note, and as if magic were summoning them from their lairs squat, hairy Huns came stamping out of quarters, buckling on accoutrements.

'What is it, then – can you tell me?' asked Gilda, adjusting his sword suitably along his belt, as if Stilicho were a comrade in the theatre, soon to make an entrance on stage. He looked down attentively from the window at his men assembling in the courtyard, as if in no particular hurry to join them. He would keep clear of the preliminary fuss, and choose his moment.

'How much wood will a small fire burn? A Christian joke, I believe. Or a pagan riddle perhaps. Do you say that in Britain – or is Britain too wet for a small fire to burn down a forest? It has begun in Bologna, of all places – and if it spreads? Things may go wrong suddenly, and if they do, get out of Ravenna before Olympius's blackguards block off the causeway – '

'A fire? What kind of fire?' She liked straight answers.

As he slid back the bolt of the bedroom door, Stilicho with a face like stone, turned, and told her with a whisper, 'Mutiny!'

The first city the Emperor Honorius went to visit on his tour of inspection was Bologna, where the garrison should have been orderly, peaceable, loyal – not troublemakers, like XX *Valeria Victrix* in Ticinum. As commander of the imperial escort Stilicho had sent a quick-witted and ambitious military tribune who clearly understood what he was there to say and do. But inevitably the man was a better politican than a soldier.

Sleepy, prosperous Bologna, at a road junction where the fertile valley of the Po edged up against the Appenines, was then a military town, streets squared off like an army encampment turned to brick and stone. In Bologna, reflected Stilicho, as he rode out at the head of his Huns, only garrison troops – and their pay was overdue. But what else had they got to complain of? They all knew very well that after an imperial inspection they would get a donative, to spend in the wineshops. Somebody must have been tampering with them.

'Have some of this Bologna sausage,' the generous stranger might say, 'chopped up fine – like Stilicho's infantry at Pollentia.' Or, 'This cheese stinks worse than Stilicho's Huns.' Once he had the soldiers laughing or grunting consent, the patter could move closer to the mark.

'What's wrong with the great man these days? Doesn't he trust his own infantry? Look at that civilian going down the street – the one with the bad case of piles. He walks as though Stilicho had just put a Hun up behind him. Remember that? Oh – you were at Pollentia too? Well, old comrade, did you get away with much plunder that day? Nor did I.'

Or he might take a different and more thoughtful tack. 'You have kids by your old woman? Haven't we all. It's natural – why not? A boy, eh? Takes after you – and I bet you're proud of him. There should by rights be nothing to stop you marrying her – except that there is. Army regulations were not drawn up for your benefit, but theirs. And what chance has your son or mine to better himself? Straight into the army – isn't that the law? Mincemeat for Stilicho. You'd be better off as a barbarian. What's that you say? Of course they do. And bring their wives and children with them, and married by their own priest. Take up quarters in our cities – in houses where we ourselves might be leading a proper family life. I'm a family man myself, I feel it keenly. You there, another jug of wine. What's that you were saying about Stilicho? Don't make me laugh. You know exactly what he is as well as I do. A clever general, I grant you. But not one of us. Not a Roman. So what do you expect? He looks after his own.'

Olympius's hired mouthpieces in Bologna happened to have done their work a little too well. Keep hammering on the same nerve, and what follows? Strange and formerly unthinkable thoughts come to the forefront of the mind. Who wants discipline? What wants battle? Why go out of your way to seek death?

Many of the listeners were army brats, born in cantonments from some irregular coupling. They were being turned against Flavius Stilicho, the white-haired father of the Roman army, as if against a real and despotic if only half-remembered father. Obscure resentments, buried in the mind for many years, were breaking loose. A few of the rank and file grew thirsty for the strong wine of disobedience. With all else falling apart, why should only private soldiers stand up straight and take the brunt?

That noontide on parade, some of the malcontents were not exactly sober, and the centurions knew it. Honorius kept them waiting in the noon heat a long time, and the troops did not love him for it. The disagreeable thirst of men who have over-indulged in wine was growing upon them. Their tipsy geniality was turning to exasperation.

At last Honorius arrived, ill-at-ease, even though his horse was quietly biddable, and followed by a well-fed and important-looking gaggle of his own kind. Troops will stiffen when they catch sight of the dignitary who is to inspect them, but this time some of the line visibly went slack, until tickled up by their centurions. To the military tribune who rode at the Emperor's side, that should have been a sufficient warning.

One small, incongruous detail got the tipsier soldiers going – the Emperor's red boots. But a Roman Emperor always wore red boots – and with red soles, too. Some others took particular exception to the diadem – a white brow-band, set with pearls. Others, far gone in wine-inspired incredibility, even wondered if this flabby creature, uneasy on horseback, could really be their Emperor, and said so aloud.

Honorius was a personage known to them only by repute. As Emperor he was the living symbol of all-powerful Rome – the man whom even Flavius Stilicho obeyed. Bouncing about on a palfrey, hanging on to a gilt bridle, in red boots with a purple cloak, with a diadem? It takes more than that to make an Emperor.

From amid skulkers in the third rank, one tipsy voice yelled out, 'Here comes poll parrot!'

That spitting, derisive Latin sound – *psittacus*! poll parrot! – was taken up joyfully by even the front-rank men, the best soldiers, and armed in the old Roman fashion with sword, shield and javelin. 'Poll parrot! Poll parrot!' went down the line, until even Honorius could distinguish what they were saying. The troops in Bologna must somehow know he liked cage birds! Could this be a soldiers' joke, intended to do him honour?

Voices from the rear rank, however, in parrot screeches, were saying more.

'We like our red bootikins then?'

'Did we paint our pretty cheeks this morning?'

'Poll parrot! Pretty polly! *Psittacus! Psittacus!*'

The carmine artifically livening Honorius's cheeks stood out against his pallor, as he moved down the jeering line, like the blobs on the cheeks of a clay doll. Though mystified – Roman soldiers could have strange ways of showing their loyalty – Honorius as yet showed no fear.

'What about our pay, then?' spoke up a voice of a different timbre, harsh, manly, urgent. This cry was echoed up and down the line by men who were sober and had hitherto been quiet.

'Our pay! Our pay! We don't serve Rome for nothing.'

The least popular centurion, turned viciously on the nearest front rank man he could reach, and started to lay on hard with his vine plant. The centurion happened to have picked on a man, an exemplary soldier, who had been standing rigidly to attention with his mouth shut. His comrades to right and left were the smartest of the front rank men in Bologna. Nor had they said anything untoward, whatever they might have been thinking.

And here was their comrade, being knocked about like a naughty child. The absurd injustice of being hit with a vine root for the shouts and cries of others went home to them. A veil that all through their army service had blinded them fell away. If you stopped to consider, the reckoning-up was obvious. For any one centurion, like this one, there were a hundred soldiers, and they all had swords.

In regulation fashion, the front-line soldier who had been picked on, an Epirot, drew his sword from the scabbard exactly as if an order had been given. At any time but this his comrades to right and left would have clung to his arms, to stop him making a fool of himself. This time they let him go – he was acting for them, too. The sword lifted and fell, cutting the centurion across the side of his sunburned and muscular neck, the proper jugular blow.

The centurion staggered, his punishing vine-plant fallen to the ground. Blood spouted, death was certain. The Epirot picked up the vine plant, and started hitting the almost dead man, as if there were no other way to get rid of his rage.

The first blood had been spilled, and that was what sent them wild. Their parrot cries, their shouts for pay, had not so far sounded menacing, but as Honorius went on placidly with his inspection, their individual voices changed to a mob roar; the mark of mutiny.

To every outward appearance Honorius was responding rather better than the officers of his staff. Though puzzled, he did not fully grasp the danger. He happened not to have been looking that way when the soldier killed his centurion. The red-booted Emperor rode to the end of the front rank at the same clumsy pace, lifting a hand not so much to check the roar as in a strange and wrong-headed way to acknowledge it, as though the terrible noise coming out of their mouths were applause.

They were his own soldiers, he was their Emperor. Honorius for as long as he could remember had been obeyed in things great and small. Why should they disobey him now?

In turning, Honorius caught his first glimpse of the corpse halfway alone the line – a vivid splash of blood on the dusty parade-ground, and all the other centurions turning that way to stare. They were all ranker-officers with an old soldier's nose for trouble, and they could hardly believe their eyes. They too, no less than the Emperor, had always been obeyed, and obeyed at once, with no question. They were stupefied. Had they all moved at once, they might have broken the mood of the roaring mob, but they stood a little too long, waiting for orders.

The moment had come – and all this happened very quickly – when, even though blood had been spilt one cool-headed man, high enough in rank, might have taken the mutineers in hand, and quelled them. There were plenty of soldiers who knew they had gone too far.

Most conspicuous on the parade ground, after the Emperor himself, was the charming, articulate military tribune, chosen for this job by Stilicho. At ingratiating himself with Honorius this high-ranking and ambitious young officer had so far done well, but this mutiny had been moving so quickly under his very eyes that his will became paralysed. The regimental officers were looking his way for a word of command and it never came. The military tribune could already see his career in ruins. He knew well enough what an officer ought to do next in this crisis – rally the men who might still be loyal, sort out the ringleaders. But what if he tried and failed?

If only one single stone were flung at the Emperor's head, he might find himself for the rest of his life doing outpost duty in the deserts of Mauretania. The military tribune looked at the Emperor. Honorius was pale, puzzled, calm, but he gave no indication either of what he wanted done.

Honorius at last appeared to have made up his mind to press on. He had wheeled his horse into the second line, as if to continue the inspection. He ought not to take that risk, and the military tribune saw his chance. Grasping the gilded bridle, turning the horse's head, he galloped the Emperor off the field. Later on he would argue – and even he believed – that he personally had saved the Emperor from men who might have killed him. Indeed all the officers there would afterwards exaggerate the violence and the danger.

The headlong departure of the man in red boots, the personage of whom everyone was supposed to be in awe, was to the soldiers as good as a victory in the field. Some of them – a minority – broke ranks and moved forward to threaten their own officers with drawn swords.

Only a few of the younger officers had dabbled in sedition, and for this reason were hesitant. The best of them, even though outranked by that military tribune and greatly outnumbered by the mutinous soldiers, knew very well that they should be taking some initiative. They had missed a great chance of distinguishing themselves under the Emperor's eye. Everyone could see by now, as the men who had drawn their swords advanced, that the soldiers of the garrison were being swept off their feet by a discontented few. Even those with lifted swords did not seriously meditate more bloodshed. They were chiefly amazed at what they were being allowed to get away with.

Anxious to do his best, now as ever, but slow off the mark, and somewhat too ponderous and sedate for the decision being thrust upon him, the garrison commander had been anxiously seeking his second-in-command's advice. The second-in-command was hesitant to commit himself.

And what might all this – the shrewder of the junior officers were beginning to ask – signify politically? From those who knew there had been hints about Eucherius usurping the Empire, and a great change coming. Would they do better to join the mutineers?

From the mutineers was rising up an outcry against Stilicho and his mincemeat – whatever that might mean.

'Draw your swords!' exclaimed the old garrison commander at last, to his officers. 'Die to the last man!' But he had left it too late. Not a sword was drawn, and they all ran away, even the centurions. The garrison commander as he too went away pushed his own sword shamefacedly into the scabbard. As they scurried off the soldiers cheered and paused, as if they had dropped a heavy weight from their shoulders. Then they too sheathed their swords.

The military tribune who dragged Honorius away from danger was no fool. He had the wit to send off a message at once by pigeon – a message justifying what he had done by making much of the danger to the Emperor. The responsibility for restoring order was passed on to the one man whose oppressive paternal authority they would all, even Honorius, have liked to throw off their backs: Flavius Stilicho.

The cadence of hoofbeats as Stilicho and his Huns thundered down the paved road over the Appenines began hammering home to him, as if in muttered chorus, the bloody work to be done when he got to Bologna. The eyes of the men around him were alight with glee at the speed they were going, and the usual stink came from them, Today, thought Stilicho, that bad smell encloses us all, like a fog of evil. Though I feel intensely lonely amid my Huns, where would I be without them? A Hun just in front who had broken the wind of his charger by riding uphill at the gallop changed saddles in a vault, Hun fashion. The pace was tremendous, but to Stilicho, no longer exhilarating. He could not keep out of his mind the task that awaited him.

The worst collective punishment inflicted in the Roman army – inflicted only for arrant cowardice or outright mutiny – was decimation, the cold killing of one man in ten, and to have effect it must be done at once, before rebel blood had cooled.

Soldiers were men trained to kill, men prepared to die. Their disciplined aggressiveness was held in check by an invisible net of moral obligation, duty, tradition, self respect, fear of their centurion, affection possibly for their general or their Emperor. Legionaries, after such a breakdown in discipline could be restored to their sober senses – or so the officers of the Roman army had always believed – only by the shock of fear.

Decimare cohortes: surround the defaulters by loyal troops. Compel every tenth man to step forward and bend his neck to the sword. What pagan Saxons used as a shocking ritual, Roman generals kept in hand as a punishment of last resort. As in the blue distance the squared-off walls of Bologna came into sight, Stilicho had begun to mutter to the tempo of hoofbeats, *decimare cohortes, decimare cohortes*, without even a questioning inflection, as if he had convinced himself.

The addle-pated Emperor would never understand decimation – or forgive it, either. This would be much worse than the death of men on the field of battle – and that was bad enough. Death brought close, in a lottery that would strike the wantoning imagination of the rank-and-file – what else would restore to the nine-tenths who survived that quick obedience without which Rome might succumb? Stilicho hardly needed to repeat to himself the arguments. The fact that he did not quite believe them made him cling to them all the more.

'Take nothing to drink – except water!' had been his last order, as the Huns dropped from the saddle and slackened girths. Huns who tasted even a cupful of wine made beasts of themselves – but they would obey strictly an order to abstain.

Off into the back alleys of Bologna, where wineshops and whorehouses clustered, the Huns went like terriers digging out vermin. Their ugliness, their recklessness, their stink, their imperviousness to Latin argument, gave them that day a terrible authority.

The mutinous spirit in Bologna was by this time on the ebb. The more thoughtful men had been asking themselves what to do next. Seize the Emperor? But they had lost their chance, the Emperor had escaped. Better still, elect a soldier to rule them? But what could a soldier Caesar do for you? Double your pay of course. So long as he had the money for it: twice nothing was nothing. Give you your discharge? Then there would be no army. The hotheads were sounding foolish, and waverers had begun to cool off.

The mutineers were pushed in droves back to the parade ground by little knots of Huns whom they much outnumbered and could easily have overcome. The splash of dead centurion's blood on the place where he was cut down and flogged had been sprinkled with sawdust. Out in front of them they found Stilicho, immobile on his weary charger, alone. As yet he gave no order.

They fell into line under his mordant eye because they had the lifelong habit of falling into line; they had been rounded up by the Huns like stray sheep. The parade ground had fallen intensely silent, each man separate from his neighbour, alone with his poignant anxieties. Let them wait thought Stilicho, hating them for what they were obliging him to do. Wait and wonder.

To the jarring note of a trumpet, an open wooden coffin was brought into the field, borne on the shoulders of six Huns. Without a word, the Huns who bore it tipped up the coffin, to display to all present the body of the dead centurion, the sword cut across his throat concealed by a scarf.

Stilicho turned his head to one end of the line, and began looking down it slowly, as if to examine every face in turn for guilt. The soldiers who had done least were bracing themselves for a speech from him – a severe paternal chiding. Most of them had not done much. At an almost imperceptible signal from the general, the Huns drew their own swords, and went along the lines, lifting the sword from the scabbard of any soldier who had come to the field armed. Most had, since without his sword a Roman soldier felt ill at ease. These confiscated weapons were piled in a stack on the parade ground well out of reach.

Stilicho, still silent, raised hand and arm. The soldiers held their breath. Some in sick horror had guessed correctly what was coming next, others were hoping against hope that it might not happen. He said only one word, but very clear, very loud, and everyone heard it.

'Decimate!'

There was for any man a ten-to-one chance of escaping death, long odds, and this kept the mutineers paralysed. The Huns with little fixed stony grins on their hideous faces, went along each line, counting on their fingers, pushing every tenth man forward. One or two in the front line, when they saw their turn coming, stepped forward smartly, and of their own accord. Let Stilicho see that they at least were legionaries to the last.

Each picked man was made to bow his head. Along the line from right to left, over and again, a sword rose high and fell. When a sword edge was blunted on neck bone, a sharper weapon was fetched from the stack out in front. From the front line of the condemned there was not a murmur. except here and there a gasp, until a scallywag in the rear rank lost all control, and started raving. Even those who knew they had to die were glad when that one voice was silenced.

Will anyone speak to me, or even care to look at us, after this? wondered Stilicho. Will the Emperor? Or Gilda, when she gets to hear? Is there anyone left who understands the absolute necessity?

The worst of it was, they had all looked so much like sheep.

Honorius was off on another tour of inspection, to Ticinum. This time, it had been decided behind Stilicho's back that Olympius, the Master of the Offices, would accompany the Emperor. In Ticinum was stationed the discontented legion, XX *Valeria Victrix*. After losing men at Pollentia they had remained on duty at Ticinum to recruit, train hard, and defend Milan in case Alaric's army ever came back. Meanwhile the barbarian commanders in Rome's employ had all forgathered in Bologna's semicircular theatre, the shape of a bowl cut in half with tiers of stone seats looking down on the oval stage. Blonde heads choosing their seats across the open-air auditorium much outnumbered dark. Well away from the places taken for themselves by the Visigoth officers, and in the highest row at the back, sat a veteran nicknamed *Meles* – Badger – black hair sprinkled with white, the captain of Stilicho's Hun guard.

He was a clever man with a permanent grin on his repulsively scarred face. Meles had only rudimentary Latin, and was the solitary Hun. No one sat near him, and some turned round to look at him as though he had no right to be there.

A hot August morning. Even so, the younger Visigoth officers were following the fashion set by Sarus, flamboyant leader of Rome's mercenary cavalry and the Princess Veleda's acknowledged lover, even though Sarus might have wife and child tucked away in some garrison town. A coloured cloak and an enormous brooch were becoming marks of personal allegiance. These young men in cloaks moved upwards to their place with a swagger, shouting to one another as if calling across country. Nowadays, decided Flavius Stilicho, gazing up at them from his seat on the stage, our young bucks play at being barbarian. In my day we played at being Roman. And there at the top, looking down on us all, Meles, with his cat-grin, alone, noticing whatever I notice, watching me, outnumbered by men he does not trust. As am I. He looks confident, though.

The morning session ran over its time. On the broad and dusty open space outside the theatre fringed by big trees. Gilda had arrived and was waiting for Stilicho. She shuffled her feet through the dust, she caught a leaf as it fell. Barbarian troopers, also at a loss for something to do, were hanging about, playing simple-minded practical jokes on one another. Some of them had earlier helped the cooks to stun and flay the ox that amid sputtering fat was being roasted whole, over an uncomfortably hot charcoal fire.

The smell was tantalising. The soldiers were waiting for the hot meat to be cut off in slices. Their impatience reminded Gilda of days gone by, her troop of mounted archers, jovial, always hungry, unpredictable.

Flavius Stilicho may preen himself on passing for a Roman, she told herself, remembering the exuberant mood he had been in that morning, but underneath what is he? Only a special kind of mounted archer, a type I have always known how to cajole. I did it then, in the old days, as a flat-chested little girl. I still do. And how long will all this last?

The cooks had run an iron spit lengthways through the carcass. Under it the hot coals sloped, so that the basting fat dripped clear of the fire and into the pan. Even so, now and then the fat caught fire. The spitting smell was too pungent to escape.

'Hot enough for you over there?' Gilda sang out, unexpectedly, in a vibrant stage-voice. The cooks began laughing, wiping sweat from their brows in dumb play. A childish thing to have said, thought Gilda, but then, all this reminds me of being a child. Easy to make such men laugh.

Gilda had dressed this morning in a loose saffron robe with a long blonde wig held across her brow by a Gothic fillet, not so much imitating Gothic women as guying them. The soldiers, though, had recognised her for what she was, Gilda the *mima*, Stilicho's woman.

A new arrival had turned her head abruptly, nervously, when she heard Gilda's call: the Princess Veleda, extravagantly visible in white silk. She paused as if not certain what to do, began walking towards Gilda, and then hesitated. Scandalous person that I am, thought Gilda, she has recognised me in this wig, and I worry her. Immaculate gown, gold carcanet, braided hair – the Princess Veleda is dressed as a bride.

She is here to flaunt her love for Sarus – who then is the scandalous one? Or perhaps you could say that this morning she is dressed for sacrifice. But she has a question to ask, and would rather speak to another woman, even a *mima*, than to one of those soldiers.

Veleda made her heroic decision: she was walking towards Gilda. For Veleda, too, the smell of roasting beef was bringing back her past with a rush. She was, in her own mind, a gawky young girl again, in Alaric's camp, and secretly betraying him.

'Has Sarus come out yet?'

Gilda shook her head, and gave a glittering smile. 'Nor has Stilicho.'

The question had been asked and answered. The conversation faltered. They stood there, looking at one another.

Impossible now, thought Veleda, to turn my back on her. Stilicho's woman, and not quite as beautiful – as seductive – as they led me to expect. Why is she dressed in that ridiculous fashion?

'A wig, isn't it?'

'Yes, a wig.'

Sarus with his stature, long hair, dashing clothes, had today been the most visible of the three high-ranking officers on stage – indeed, a little larger than life. Flavius Stilicho's white hair was unfashionably cropped, and he had worn his regulation uniform. Old Mucapor, Inspector of Cavalry and for so many years the spokesman of the mounted mercenaries, had grown decrepit.

In the spring of this year, Sarus had fought a brilliant little campaign in Gaul against the mutineer Constantine, bottling him up for ten days in Valence, shouldering him further away from Italy. Thirty thousand barbarian cavalry now looked up to him as a political as well as a military leader. In any sharp crisis they might very well turn their backs on Stilicho, and follow Sarus. This then was a day for Sarus to emphasis his leadership. Both the women waiting outside knew that much already. The caution with which they were treating one another was an echo of the rivalry within.

As she waited ill at ease, at a distance from the roasting ox, words ran through Veleda's head in a gabble. Sarus, she was thinking, is first and foremost a gambler, though it took me time to find that out. Gambles with dice, and with his own reputation. Gambles with mine. Sarus claims to admire my father, likes to hear him spoken of. But how different he was, my father, from any Goth I now know.

Nor did my father hide himself away from his people like that pathetic creature in Ravenna, living in a marsh like a frog. He sat each morning under an oak tree with his dogs and his weapons and his wise men. They had long beards and clear blue eyes. My father would have cut down any man seeking justice who tried to fob him off with a lie. That much I know for certain.

Yet the sad fact is, since knowing Sarus, I can no longer

remember my father's face. The shape of his beard, yes. The colour of his eyes. But his face?

Sarus with the coloured cloak flung back from his shoulders emerged from the theatre, amid a crowd of other officers, and Flavius Stilicho close by him. The two women began to walk towards their men, taking no notice of each other until they found they had converged. Stilicho, his back towards them, was chatting with affable ease in Gothic to the half dozen troopers who had been kicking their heels in the shade of a tree, waiting for the roast meat. From the spontaneous way those men laughed, thought Gilda, when the general made his joke, no one would suppose that not long ago, in this quiet city, he ordered a massacre.

Flavius Stilicho had turned his cropped white head, and was moving nearer to the women, telling himself, as he approached, with a smile, that if these two became friends, that would be no bad idea. That girl won my battle for me, though she will never know it. To have followed Sarus here so openly is brave, but will have done her damage at court.

The morning session at the *consilium* had gone much as expected. Sarus spoke up at the very beginning not for the government but for the cavalry – a hot-headed and unexpected intervention which drew cheers. And their shouting, thought Stilicho, pleased him – he is easily pleased – and then I stole his thunder. I had come ready to settle out of hand, several little matters that I knew irked them – promotion, renewal of treaties, compassionate leave – any improvement in their lives that could be made at small expense.

As the discussion began to go my way, Sarus changed his tune. His public manner became almost embarrassingly filial. He is impulsive. There are times when he sincerely feels like that, but he is a bad son, who would like to topple his father. Ambition inflames him, and he thinks only of himself. Was I like that once? Probably. My father thought so, anyway.

Stilicho's gesturing hand had included both women in the same greeting, one tall, white, blonde, one smaller and witty, in a Visigoth-looking wig. Sarus's treasure and my treasure. Except that no Visigoth woman ever dare look so impudent. And as Sarus must by now be aware, treasure is what we lack. My little concessions this morning have emptied the bag.

'Veleda! Princess!' exclaimed Flavius Stilicho, as if in frank delight at encountering an old friend. Veleda, though, had no eyes for him. She was gazing almost drunkenly towards Sarus, who for the time being was deliberately ignoring her. With one broad hand at each waist Stilicho began gently steering the two women towards the roasting ox. They might have been his daughters. Veleda, he thought, has great style these days. I feel her body under my hand, all supple muscle. Though Gilda – pulling a jealous mouth, I see – has more devil. There is really no one in the world like Gilda.

'At some time in your lives you have surely, both of you, eaten roast meat straight off the hot carcass,' said Stilicho jestingly. The ox, the charcoal, had been bought at his expense. He knew what would best amuse the Visigoths on a day like this. So these two have known each other before? thought Gilda. Before he took up with me – or after?

Veleda broke out into a loud, selfconscious laugh when she saw Sarus, with a large lump of hot roast meat on the point of his dagger, come towards her as if to offer her a share. His once silky moustache was now greasy, and Veleda was herself no longer a woman finely bred at court, but a barbarian, her mouth watering. A creature all appetite nowadays, thought Stilicho, as Sarus bore her off, arm at her waist, tempting her to a bite. Veleda snapped at the huge, half-raw gobbet like an elegant tigress. Gilda was nudging Stilicho to cut slices for them too, since the men were waiting about, masking their own appetite until the generals had been served.

In the long run, thought Stilicho, feeling sad at the way the other two were playing the peacock and the swan in front of one another, he will treat Veleda badly, go too far, try to use her as he had already used others. Such is his nature, absorbed by power, used up by it, as a candle is used up by the flame.

They are incandescent now, though – just look at them. Gilda and I, in comparison, hacking and sharing our modest pieces of meat from the carcass with this borrowed dagger, are a sedate old married couple. Flavius Stilicho hit cautiously into the half-cooked meat, wishing his teeth were as sharp as once they were.

Stilicho had things to say. He was moving Gilda well away from the others.

'That man would like to step into your shoes,' warned Gilda. She missed very little that might concern him.

'As no doubt he will,' answered Stilicho. 'Best of all if it happens by common consent. So anything social between the four of us – your friendliness just now, and mine too – is no bad thing.' Gilda bit her lip; Stilicho was cajoling her. She did not feel particularly friendly towards that creature in white. Stilicho, having taken notice of her twinge of jealousy, was placating her. She smiled; she would listen. 'He has campaigned well, Sarus, in Gaul, how he would perform in a pitched battle against a competent general is anybody's guess. But Rome needs a younger commander. Of course if you make friends, they will try to learn our secrets.'

'Let them,' said Gilda. 'I am even better at keeping secrets than you are.' He pressed her small hand in his own large grasp, to confess his faith in her.

Many others by now were clustering around the carcass of the ox, and stripping it to the rib-bones. I can hardly throw this meat to a stray dog, thought Stilicho. Some busybody will be looking my way. But neither can I chew it.

'More trouble than you bargained for?'

Gilda took the meat from his hand, and made it disappear like a conjuring trick. 'What you lack now I dare say is a toothpick.'

'Or I could use the point of my sword, like a true barbarian,' said Stilicho, picking his teeth with his fingernail.

'How did it go?'

'The *consilium*? Dragged on, because this morning everyone who felt himself important had to show his face and have his say. I held my own though. This afternoon there is trouble coming, from these young fellows in the cloaks. They can change sides in the flicker of an eye.'

'Exactly like the mounted archers I knew as a child,' Gilda told him. 'One day you are their pet. The next they have sold you into slavery. Will it be bad trouble?'

'To judge by the signs, worse trouble than I had bargained for.' He gave a small inward groan, and that was unusual. And he will now go on to tell me, thought Gilda, what I probably know already. How he hates to put warnings into words!

'If real trouble should start – I mean today, and very likely it might – they will be looking for a woman in a blonde wig, and first you must get rid of it.' Under the wig Gilda's hair had been cut short, like a lad's, as a precaution: instant disguise. He was gripping her shoulder, as if to convince both of them, by physical contact, that all this was real.

'Head across the mountains to the coast. The little horse I bought you is up at the house, saddled – '

'Perhaps it may not be as bad as you think,' said Gilda gently. It had cost him something to tell her all this, yet again – admit in advance the possibility of a dire defeat. His voice was gruff.

'Mere precaution.'

Stilicho had made her bring all her property here to Bologna, the dagger in its encrusted sheath, the boar spear with its crossbar, in readiness for a part she might never need to play. Money in a lined leather bag. The embroidered tunic of a well-to-do young fellow, fond of his clothes, and carrying arms – the youngster you do well to leave alone, because he has powerful friends.

She already saw this other self in her mind's eye, and could slip into character at a nod. She had thought of everything – even a wide band of linen to wind around and flatten her breasts. She had ridden here at a jog-trot, on the biddable little horse, like a barbarian woman, and was still sore from it. All this to please Stilicho. Until he spoke just now, she had thought of these things as toys.

Stilicho repeated what he had said before. 'They will strike at me through you.'

'They won't,' she told him, putting actress-conviction into her voice.

Ever since the decimation, Stilicho when alone with her had by fits and starts been severe, exasperated, sometimes silently grimacing. Gilda could sense his spirit at such times, moving away from her into a world inhabited by demons. She took his hand and whispered. 'Your own plan for escape. Don't you have one?'

'Suppose you tell me where I can go,' he said brusquely, as if she were his enemy, or an irritating simpleton. Beg for employment from Alaric, if Alaric would have me – and why should he? I have eaten the salt of this Roman Emperor and his father for more years, Gilda, than you have been alive.'

Bitterness like that, she told herself, should be answered with a smile. But what kind of smile? The mounted archers scooped me up, and I lived afterwards in a world of vivid action, practising smiles. I am sure of this man without using false smiles.

Since the carrier pigeon brought word of the mutiny, Gilda's daydream had been of a place, far off, where if things got worse they might go together. The lost land to the west, Atlantis, or some island in Ocean with golden apples and a climate of perpetual spring. A place – an impossible place – without anxiety.

'The fools here,' he was muttering, 'will only remember the wig.' Stilicho was beginning to repeat himself – there had been a time when he never did that. These thoughts must be going round and round in his mind, obsessively. 'If things turn out badly, go at once. *Impero*. An order. *Impero* was what an officer said to a soldier, a master to a slave. The word was no sooner out of his mouth that Stilicho wondered if it might be a mistake, yet to all appearances Gilda was not resenting what he had said. He had manumitted Gilda, she was no longer anyone's slave. She stays with me because she wishes it. And when I die, she will be a rich woman. Stilicho told himself. Let Serena, sulking in Rome, makes what she likes of it. Though if Olympius scrambles to the top of the heap, no testament of mine in Gilda's favour will ever be honoured. He and his pack will be after me and mine like winter wolves.

'That's right,' Gilda was saying, with a wry smile. 'Give me orders as though I were one of your legionaries.'

'The very last of my legionaries,' he said, with the flattering candour of the lifelong courtier,' and the best of my friends.' He then went across with a smile to join Sarus, and chatting amiably as if they too were the best of friends accompanied him inside to the amphitheatre.

Any self-respecting Roman city had an amphitheatre. The one in Bologna was small and badly designed. Perform in that little cooking pot? had been Gilda's scornful thought. I could play to the back row with my eyelashes.

For this conference of barbarian commanders, however, it served well. They could spread importantly, lounging with their coloured cloaks on the stone seats, one man occupying the space of two or three. They could easily make themselves heard – in a place of more importance, their individual voices might have been diminished. An amphitheatre, thought Stilicho, a half-circle of stone seats rising away from the three of us here on stage: another symbol of Rome.

City life meant civilised life – only a city can support a theatre. In the old days, when Visigoths came into a theatre they were overawed, but not any more. Stilicho was put out by the way they sprawled and talked loudly, without decorum, as if the city were at last their conquest. They were not fit for it.

Sarus opened the afternoon debate a little more provocatively than he need have done. To a growl of approval from the auditorium his spoke the as yet unsanctioned word.

Stipendium?

Summer thunder, their growl, reverberated overhead into the cloudless blue. To that cry there was no rational answer, either. The mercenaries could shout for their pay as loudly as they chose. The military treasury was starved. Flavius Stilicho had an empty purse. He could not even make honest promises. Of course, Sarus knew this.

We begrudge them their pay now, had been Olympius's reasoning, and afterwards they will cease to obey Stilicho. Gaining consent had been easy – it was done in the name of peace. *Pax* would always win a nod from the Emperor. They will always obey the man who pays them. Olympius told himself. They are mercenaries. We ourselves have only to pay them again, in due course, and they will obey us instead. How else can civilian officials, he had argued at the Treasury, defend themselves – and the state – against the presumptions of the military?

I know the military treasury is empty, reflected Stilicho, and I know why. So does Sarus, though he pretends otherwise. But how can I stand up in front of all these angry men, and tell them the simple truth? How could I make them believe me? Yet tell them something I must.

Play on the irrational? The blood we share? Our glorious past victories? Teutons are sentimental. A few such phrases would bring tears to their blue eyes, and he knew it.

Yet Stilicho hesitated. With his trenchant claim for pay – *stipendium*! – Sarus had mingled a few sharp remarks about the way their women and children were being treated lately in the garrison cities. Insulted here, violated there. Angry shouts had gone up and down the steeply raked seats at each reminder. Play too much on their sentimental side, thought Stilicho, and they may take fire. They will rant all afternoon about the treatment of their womenfolk – and who can blame them? – then burst out of here in an incoherent rage. I shall lose them. Rome too might lose them, and with Alaric poised to attack.

From this day on, he thought, watching the effect the orator was having on them, Sarus is their man. For how long though? They are choosing a chief because he says what they want to hear. But there is more to being a leader than making yourself popular. Sometimes the necessary truth is what no one wants to hear, and it has to be said.

Flavius Stilicho rose to his feet amid the last of the applause for Sarus, and as he stood there, groping in his mind for effective words, the noise fell away. Down on the stage, diminished by distance, they saw a famous white-haired man, not so old as Mucapor, but a man from the past. Stilicho heard his own voice bombinate, and despised more than a little the arguments he was using. I am calming them, he thought. I am gaining a little more time. But I am coming to the end of the road.

Outside, under the dusty horse-chestnut trees, the two women waited, standing at first a little apart, as if to acknowledge that inside those stone walls their menfolk were rivals. Gilda made the first friendly gesture – a smile that would have melted a bronze shield – because Stilicho had told her to try. Veleda, the hint once given, was the first to speak, as though she had been keeping the words ready in her mouth. Perhaps Sarus had asked her. (To find out our secrets? wondered Gilda.)

'Your wig – it is a wig you are wearing, surely. Yet it looks so natural!'

'I had the whim of dressing as much as possible like a Visigoth.'

'Didn't someone tell us,' said the Princess, 'that you were a Briton? She made 'a Briton' sound like a second-rate Goth. Though if it came to that, thought Gilda, Britons were Celts, and Celts were generally acknowledged to be the more civilised.

No doubt all this was difficult for her: public conversation with a notorious *mima*. Gilda produced another brilliant smile like a conjuring trick, and was amused to see that, after all her years at court, the princess, though words might not flatter her, was melted by a smile.

'A Briton – yes. Though when I was very young I lived for a little with your people, and no doubt picked up a Gothic tone. Like this.' Gilda in the flicker of an eye was a small girl, mimicking the turns of phrase of horse-archer mercenaries, their loud Gothic, their bad Latin – a subtle theatrical performance for an audience of one. Veleda could not help but laugh, and once she had laughed she lost her stiffness.

Gilda went on to tell her how she had made her way to Rome, a slave girl escaped from bandits. I can make her laugh, she thought, I can make her sad. I can do that with anybody. And if I told her how Stridor sold my body for a free passage from Marseilles? The Princess no doubt would turn her back. Though what is she, now, with Sarus? A strumpet, like myself.

Hooves raised dust. Both turned their heads as a man arrived on a gasping horse, a Roman officer, bare-headed. He fell over sideways from the saddle with an exhausted lurch, and stumbled away as if blinded. From a slash along his hairline, blood had dribbled downwards towards his eyes. He smeared the wet blood across his face with his sleeve, and went towards the theatre, dragging his horse behind him, and looking gruesome, a Messenger in a tragedy.

The bloody-faced officer held out his reins to the Hun standing guard at the entrance. But the Hun was no groom. He had been put on the door as a sentry. He tried to bar the bloody-faced officer's way into the theatre with his sword – that was his duty. The man drew his own ornate dress sword and stabbed the Hun under the ribs, as if sudden death were the only conceivable way past any such hindrance. Tripping over the prone body, he stumbled inside.

Veleda thrust her fist into her mouth as if to stop words from coming. This was trouble, a terrible sign, and inside the two generals might no longer be friends.

The wounded officer paused on entering the theatre, and looked around him like a man striving to come round from a bad dream. He first recognised Mucapor, seated a little to one side, and was stumbling towards Mucapor when his eye also took in Stilicho and Sarus. He could scarcely control either the movement of his limbs or the pitch of his voice, he had pushed himself to the limit. When in the clear acoustics of the theatre he gave his message, head bent, in horase confidence, everyone heard.

'Mutiny – in Ticinum. The Emperor Honorius has been killed.'

Sarus did all he could to look shocked. He tugged his moustache his face became grave. '*XX Valeria Victrix*,' he muttered to Stilicho. 'What more can you expect?' The tone of voice though, in Stilicho's ears, had been complacent.

From the corner of Mucapor's left eye a slow tear was falling which might have been a trickle of old age. Stilicho's face was like stone.

XX *Valeria Victrix*? he wondered. If they mutiny Milan is defenceless. We should not be here debating. We should be riding full tilt down the imperial highway, every officer at the head of his man.

Out of Mucapor's lips were coming muddled words, some half-forgotten prayer or invocation, certainly not Christian. Sarus too had taken in the consequences, but the bad news suited him. He could hardly keep excitement out of his face.

Some high-spirited Visigoth half-way up was clashing his sword against the marble seat in front of him, and everyone else who could not think what to say or do began copying him. Soon no single human voice could be heard through the metallic crescendo of clashing swords. The noise was not only an instinctive barbaric mourning, but anger, an assertion of readiness.

Stilicho and Sarus sharing the same thought, exchanged glances. Honorius dead? And what followed?

Honorius had no obvious male heir except his brother in Constantinople Theodosius the Great's other son, a ruler almost as feeble. With invasion imminent, thought Stilicho, for there to be no Emperor was enough to make even Sarus pause and wonder.

Would a woman be unthinkable? Galla Placidia? If the right man marries her? I like the girl, Stilicho told himself.

Sarus for her husband? Might Sarus be thinking that too? Yes, obviously: the face of a cat licking stolen cream.

Sarus already had a Visigoth wife and family tucked away somewhere. Well then, a legal annulment? A state marriage to Galla Placidia? A bargain that might end all this rivalry, and secure for Rome a soldier who is at least competent. It would of course break Princess Veleda's heart, but the survival of Imperial Rome was worth a few broken hearts. If only Serena would be willing to make herself effective in Ravenna – to annul and contrive and work the priests and the court, and enjoy every moment of intrigue! But Serena was in Rome, an embittered old woman.

In Sarus's face, as he tried to milk more detail from the wounded officer, nothing was to be read but satisfaction. Thirty thousand barbarian cavalary, the army of Italy, and all my men – up to a point. I know very well that if Flavius Stilicho got up now, and put himself at their head, the fools sitting around us would roar out to have him for Emperor. The spell he puts upon them is not yet broken. And I myself would give way gracefully – for a price. To begin with, commander-in-chief. Later we should see.

Sarus's excitement was shown by the way he was indulging in a tick he could never control. He had begun rattling three dice in his cupped hand under cover of his cloak. The hard square edges, the click of the dice, were an infallible consolation. Lady Luck was coming to his aid. But this broad-shouldered, white-haired man sitting beside me, Sarus told himself, is an old-fashioned Teuton, true to his salt, like my own father. He would never stand up at a moment like this, and tell them to make him Emperor. For the scruples of the great general Sarus had mingled admiration and contempt.

The noises had gone on rising until it became impossible to think. Stilicho held fast in his mind to the one real question: was the news true? Hardening his heart he took the wounded officer by the wrist to drag him away from Sarus, and shout in his ear, 'Tell me, *praefectus*, on your honour. Did you see it yourself?' As he asked the question the sound of clashing swords began to wear itself out.

'With my own eyes?' The bloody-visaged man stammered, affronted at being made to say the same thing twice. How much longer would they go on doubting his word? 'Yes, general –

with my own eyes. The Emperor was walking the streets alone, after dark, clad in his *paludamentum* – '

'You had seen the Emperor before?' asked Stilicho.

'From a distance. On parade. Once. Anyway, I knew him by his *paludamentum*. A drunken mutineer run him through with a javelin – and that I did see with my own eyes, though I was not near enough to help. As the Emperor fell I saw the mutineer seize the purple cloak – '

He has memorised his story, thought Stilicho. He is repeating it by rote.

Promenading alone, after dark, through the streets of Ticinum, dressed in a ceremonial cloak? That did not sound much like Honorius. Yet this wounded officer had been so circumstantial. He was an eye-witness. And once he knew the Emperor was past help he had done exactly the right thing – brought the bad news here at the gallop.

Sarus showed his teeth in a smile and gave Stilicho a nod, but his mind's eye was turned inward. He could see himself – prophetically ' on a dais wearing a diadem of pearls.

If the old man disdained to take power for himself? Then someone else might try. The three dice under Sarus's cloak, his oracle, clicked together in the palm of his hand. the dice were speaking the language of audacity.

Stilicho stood slowly, wearily, to his full height, and faced the men. They had been waiting long enough.

As though a spell had been cast, the clattering of swords came raggedly to an end. As he paused for silence, Stilicho caught a glimpse of Meles, alone, in the top row, the only man there who had not joined in the clatter. Meles was vigilant, as if approaching a possible ambush.

I myself don't understand this any more than Meles does, thought Stilicho as he groped for words, except that Olympius over there in Ticinum has evidently gone too far. Poor Honorius, never cut out for the job he inherited, yet in his own small way he had done his best. When in doubt, begin with a commonplace truth.

'All of us here,' he said, in a loud, clear, simple voice, 'as soldiers of Rome are loyal to our salt.' They had been hushed, expectant, awaiting a call to arms. But Stilicho was giving them another kind of speech: mourning. The Visigoths began to stretch their legs.

'All of us here – Sarus your general, and my old friend and comrade-in-arms, Mucapor, for so long Rome's Inspector of Cavalry – ' Teutons respected age, though Mucapor was hardly looking impressive, ' – your commander-in-chief, in no way differ in our loyalty from the youngest trooper in the cavalry who joined his father's squadron only last week – ' Up came the pleased grunts of Visigoths responding with pleasure to a sentimental touch. Their sons!

'We have all – fathers and sons alike – taken an oath of loyalty to the Emperor – our *sacramentum*. We respect our *sacramentum*, we abide by it. And let me remind you that the legionaries, too, have sworn their own *sacramentum*. That is what unites us, all soldiers of Rome. Even the men of the Twentieth Legion, stationed in Ticinum, who are guilty now of the heinous crime of mutiny. They too have sworn – and this oath they swore stands at the apex of a Roman soldier's life. By his oath – his *sacramentum* – he lives and fights and dies. Let it therefore be noted in time to come that when others failed, we, the proud barbarian mercenaries of Rome, have stayed loyal to our oath – '

From top to bottom of the auditorium ran a gratified mutter. They were being praised, they did not quite know for what.

Stilicho raised his voice so that it rang out.

'The wounded officer here at my side asserts that he did with his own eyes witness the death of the Emperor Honorius – slain in the public street by a mutinous legionary, who stabbed our Emperor with a javelin, and stripped from his shoulders the *paludamentum*, the emblem of his rank – ' He said all this loud and clear, as if he believed it to be true. Someone was tugging at his elbow. He shook off the importunate hand, but it came back and took hold of him again. He was capturing his audience – this was not the moment to break off.

'The Twentieth Legion, imitating the wicked example of the garrison of Bologna, has defiled its oath and murdered its Emperor.' Then, exceedingly loudly, he added; On behalf of the violated sacramentum, let us march to avenge his death on the mutineers.'

They were rising to their feet, clashing weapons, raising strident voices.

Stilicho turned round, exasperated, to see who it was that still dared tug at his elbow. A face he knew but could not put a name to, an old soldier, a promoted ranker, veteran of the British campaign and of Pollentia. A centurion of the Twentieth. The man's face was caked with dust, and through the dust his seat had made dribbles. His reddened eyes were staring. Another one who had ridden hard.

'General! Not true! What you have just said was a mistake – the Emperor lives – '

'Wounded?'

'Not a scratch on him.'

Sarus too had heard. His face was aghast, as if insultingly smacked. Like a man retreating for help into a world of private dream Sarus lowered his cupped hand under cover of his cloak, and let his three dice fall on the marble floor. He glanced down.

Three sixes.

The most fortunate cast – none higher! The throw called Venus! He scrabbled up the dice with his fingertips, as if he had dropped them by accident. Out in the auditorium they were too animated to notice.

Those sitting closest had overheard the centurion's denial. Heads were turning; in whispers the news began to pass up the slope of seats. When Stilicho next raised his hand to call for silence, the noise that met him was defiant. Already these overimaginative barbarians were riding headlong across country, lance in hand, to revenge themselves, with at last a decent pretext, upon the hated legions. The death of an Emperor? What better reason could you wish for? But this centurion – this legionary – had come in and was trying to cheat them.

'The news of the Emperor's death is false,' Stilicho declared with all his strength.

There was a disputations growl. Why should this famous old man now want to block off their vengeance?

'False, I say!' Stilicho cried in tones more peremptory than joyous. 'The Emperor Honorius lives!'

You could at one time stake your life on the word of an old centurion in a frontier legion. Very well, he would stake his. Stilicho went on shouting at the top of his voice, though aware they were hardly bothering to listen. He might have been standing alone, arguing with a mere human voice against a tempest.

When Sarus also rose, kicking a heel at the dangle of his coloured cloak, and came close to him, there was sudden quiet. In a cold voice meant for everyone to overhear, Sarus declared to Flavius Stilicho. 'Even so, we ride to Ticinum.'

We should get out of here, the pair of us, and talk it over elsewhere, Stilicho told himself. The auditorium had fallen silent at this difference between the leaders. To argue a matter as intricate as this in public is futile, but Sarus intends to force me to it. Then I must answer what he says in front of them all. I must stand up here and do all I can to dissuade both him and then.

'Attack the Roman army, Sarus? Are you mad?'

'The Roman infantry are mutineers.'

'Not every legionary is a mutineer. Rome's loyal legions can clean their own house. Sarus, you have never yet won a battle. To win the next battle against Alaric, Rome must save what infantry she can. Or would you rather start a civil war?'

'We barbarians,' Sarus had no need to raise his voice, he spoke with insolent confidence and all in the theatre were waiting to hear his challenge, 'will do what we know is right. We will ride to Ticinum.'

Meles – Badger – the commander of the Hun Guard, may not have followed the argument too clearly, but he saw that this turn in events meant trouble for Stilicho. Without waiting for any signal he rapped out orders in the Hun tongue that to the Visigoths was almost as offensive as the vile Hun smell. A bunch of squat men with scarred faces came scuttling in, and occupied the exit nearest to Stilicho, standing closed up there, hand on hilt. They were already in a blind fury about their comrade on sentry duty who had been stabbed.

Another such squad with swords drawn was wedging a way on-stage. Noting all this, but pretending to ignore it. Stilicho meanwhile went on speaking to Sarus in a voice for all to hear if they chose.

'March to Ticinum, Sarus? When the Emperor is there, and alive, and in command? Such an act is neither righteous nor expedient. *Nec probus nec utilis.*' As he spoke these words, he looked intently into Sarus's triumphant and yet contemptuous face. What he had just said meant nothing. *Probus? Utilis?* Civil war? For Sarus the warning words he had used were mere words. Men like Sarus no longer cared about discerning and elucidating moral or political realities, so as to act accordingly. Sarus let the dice decide.

As his Hun bodyguard pushed closer – to rescue him from those who should have obeyed him – Stilicho knew that power had gone from him at last, like breath from a dying body. There was Sarus, the false son, his face made incomprehensible by ambition, dressed flamboyantly, with the long hair and flowing moustaches and conspicuous clothes of someone who willed himself to be from choice not Roman but barbarian.

My words, thought Stilicho, mean nothing to Sarus because he no longer has Roman ideals. *Nec probus nec utilis?* What am I but an old man who stands in his impatient way? Stilicho ran the tip of one finger along his own clipped moustache, as if to feel the difference. He smiled as he accepted the simple truth. Sarus no longer cares to be a Roman, nor do any of them. He has used me hitherto as a help to clamber up. From now on he will kill me if he can.

Part VI

1

His Huns swept him out of the amphitheatre like a piece of living debris. Once in the open, Stilicho broke loose from them. He made a detour to take Gilda by the arm and drag her away, leaving Veleda open-mouthed. The Huns following enclosed the two of them in a fog of stink like the breath of a demon.

Stilicho had shouted to Gilda, angrily, when he saw her standing there, 'But you know you should have gone!' As the words came out of his mouth, and Gilda flinched, he knew they were unfair. How could she have known? Gilda and Veleda would have seen two messengers arrive, one after another, and not known what they would be saying, once inside the walls. Stilicho as if to prove that he trusted her let go her arm, though it made no difference, since the Huns were bustling both of them along.

'For only a little while longer are you are safe with me,' he told Gilda in a more gentle voice. 'Not for long.'

Gilda did not like being pulled about by men, never had. She had instinctively hated Stilicho's grip, his anger, his tone. But now he was trying to make it up to her. She had to move fast to keep up with him.

The house in Bologna that Flavius Stilicho and Gilda had been occupying was solitary, with four blank outer walls built around a courtyard, and a solid oaken gate – a house that could be defended. And if I look, Stilicho asked himself, into Sarus's mind? What will he try to do next? Gain possession of me, I think, as a convenient symbol that when the time comes can be thrown away.

To the Huns crowding the courtyard he began speaking, through Meles, in language that might have been used to a pack of hounds – rough-and-ready Latin mixed up with Hunnish military jargon. Gilda did not need telling that the crisis had come. She stood there, trying to make herself helpfully invisible.

Meles was turning Stilicho's large and simple orders into small and detailed ones. Under Gilda's eyes, like the transformation of a stage set, their dwelling quarters were made ready to withstand a violent attack. Three paces inside the wooden gate a barricade went up, in case Sarus managed to break his way into the courtyard. Archers took up positions on the roof behind improvised cover. Outside, at a distance from the walls, piles of brushwood were stacked, to be fired by flaming arrows, so as to light up the action should Sarus attack after dark.

In a semicircle outside the gate they were hammering in stakes, and sharpening them, to make horsemen think twice about charging up close. All these preparations were so quick, familiar and urgent that Gilda began to feel ill-at-ease among these men, superfluous. What was she doing here, a woman – an actress? Was all this crisis anything whatever to do with herself?

Once he could see his orders were being carried out, and he could afford a pause, Stilicho very calmly and with what she knew was meant for a reassuring smile turned to Gilda and told her, 'Be ready to leave as soon as the sun goes down.' He might have been reminding Meles of some incidental detail. At his casual tone Gilda flared up.

'And what if I would rather stay here with you – take the same chances?'

Stilicho's face went stiff and white. Not rage, she knew him better than that. She knew his intimate nature – that look was shame. He had a confession to make.

'Why wait here with me only to die,' he said gruffly, 'when you have someone else important to live for? No, I don't mean myself.'

Is he merely trying to tell me, wondered Gilda, that all this time he had known about Lucas? A love affair with a slave, and long ago, too? He is not the man to care.

'If you want me to take notice, I think you had better tell me exactly what you do mean.'

Gilda had been listening all afternoon to Veleda, observing her, and the words came out a little too much as if a princess had spoken them. Stilicho recognised the copycat tone – so typical of Gilda – and smiled. The smile helped him to bring out what he had to say, as though it were the most natural thing in the world.

'Your son.'

'You can't mean –'

'The child was born alive.'

'A son!' Gilda had crammed her fist into her mouth, to hold down her sick anger. 'And you have known all this time, and not told me?' His face was utterly blank. Was there anything else that they had lied to her about – robbed her of? 'If you know for certain he is alive, then where is he?'

Having uttered what was so difficult for him, Stilicho was avoiding her glance, telling himself, I have to tell her. This may be the last chance. In a flash of intuition he had decided that it would be a night surprise: dare Sarus face him in daylight? He caught sight of a Hun, at work on the defences outside the gate, hammering in a stake so that it sloped the wrong way. Stilicho shouted and the man grinned sheepishly. Huns were violent and smelly children, but not fools.

'Well?' said Gilda at last.

'Hidden.'

'Hidden where?'

'Safely hidden.'

'But why?' Her voice was almost a wail.

Flavius Stilicho turned his heavy, weary body Gilda's way, giving her at last his full attention, letting his Huns get on with it by themselves. As if to mitigate her suffering, he began to account slowly, scrupulously, for his actions.

'Soon after he was born I sent him to my estate in Samnium, to be watched over by the shepherds. I put him in charge of a dumb nurse called Sara – a woman unlikely to betray us.'

'I remember the nurse,' Gilda told him. Stilicho had brought back to mind the night of her long agony: a dumb nurse, grunting like an animal as she went about her excruciating midwife duties. 'But why?'

'Both Serena and Johannes had already done you harm. Innocent newborn babe though he was, they would also have done your child harm. Your son.'

Gilda said slowly, 'Does this son of mine have a name?' She was trying to pluck out his duplicity like a thorn or an arrowhead.

'Iynx.'

'Wryneck?' She pounced on this clue. 'Are you trying to tell me he is deformed?'

Stilicho went on remorselessly, 'And if Olympius had known where to lay hands on him? A male child? Under my care? Born of the Emperor's mistress and an unknown father?'

Ever since Stridor first pimped me to this famous old soldier, thought Gilda, our life together has, of its nature, been deception upon deception. Stilicho was supposed never to have known that I once shared Honorius's bed. Yet he has known all along. And how much else?

'I asked you if my son were deformed?' Gilda spoke in a voice that would have filled a theatre. He answered with rebuking quietness.

'A boy, so I hear, of exceptional grace and bright wit. His head – yes – is a little pushed to one side, not quite perfect. But active and brave and in every way splendid. Not in the least like Honorius. I have even allowed myself to wonder if he might take after me.'

His last remark drew from Gilda a laugh so close to hysteria that a couple of phlegmatically-indifferent Huns working near turned to stare. They would rather not have this woman here, distracting their master with her gabble and screech.

Stilicho wondered gloomily, have I lost her by telling her? He said, 'I promise you, I have taken great care of him.'

'Men!' answered Gilda with an unnecessarily public laugh, harsher this time. 'Can none of you count up to three hundred? He was conceived when you, Flavius Stilicho, were off performing heroics on the field of battle.'

'So the father is neither –'

And if I tell him the truth? wondered Gilda. But the truth must be told.

'A slave. We came together, he and I, in the unpremeditated

way that slaves do. Have you any idea, Stilicho, what I am talking about? The love of two slaves?'

Stilicho turned his back, bored by her tone, doubting the truth of what she was telling him. Could the child after all have been Honorius's? And taking after, not the dim father, but the splendid grandfather? He shouted an unnecessary order to Meles about water barrels. When next he turned to Gilda his voice had become not unkind, but impersonal, peremptory, making clear who was the master.

'The horse you rode here from Ravenna is over in the stables, fed, watered, saddled. I want you out of this place before Sarus makes his first hostile move. He is a superstitious fool. This afternoon in the theatre, when he thought no one was looking, I saw him roll Venus. If he is convinced that Lady Luck rides with him –'

'And what reason have I to run away from Sarus?'

'The boy is your reason. Do you need any other?'

He had her cornered. With Stilicho in the end you always obeyed.

'You could have let me go to Samnium months ago –'

'When Olympius is having the place watched? As well as having you watched, Gilda – particularly you? One slip, even now, and you are in his power. There are questions about me to which he would dearly like answers. Why do you suppose that lately –'

'I would tell Olympius nothing.'

'Under torture?'

Slaves, though not freed women, could legally be questioned under torture. Who could trust Olympius, though, to make any such law-abiding distinction? Tell her more, thought Stilicho – she has the right, I may never see her again.

'Anyway, Iynx is no longer in Samnium. When things began to go wrong, I sent him a long way off. As I am sending you.'

And if they catch her? wondered Stilicho gloomily. Down in Olympius's cellars, sooner or later everyone talks. Even so, she had a right to know.

'You understand the danger to the boy of the slightest lapse?'

'Do you take me for a fool?'

'My brother-in-law, Bathanarius, at present commands the troops in Libya. He knows nothing whatever of this secret, and should never be told. For my sake though, in case of trouble, he will befriend you. And Africa is the last safe place. I have sent the boy there.'

Even amid the din of preparation, shouting, hammering, and in the hearing of many fanatically loyal to him who hardly understood a word of Latin, Stilicho as he parted with this secret lowered his voice to an almost inaudible whisper. 'Claudian's betrothed, a woman called Cornelia, has an estate a long way beyond the town called Zama, in Africa – a long way to the south. His nurse was told to take the boy there – I trust she has done so.'

Iynx, Zama, Cornelia – the names she needed.

'I have but one regret, Flavius Stilicho – and I hope after what you have told me that it is your regret, too,' Gilda told him, happy and yet not happy at the astounding news, deeply angry and yet no longer hating him. In a small way she was trying to make amends. 'And it is this. That all the times we went at it hammer and tongs, I never managed to make you a son.'

That put a smile on his face, the smile of a happy young boy. How quickly an old face turns time back, and becomes a boy's face! I am glad I said that, thought Gilda, true or not.

'Now, my dear – go!' he murmured, with only half his mind on her, and his animated glance already moving elsewhere. He was reckoning up what still had to be done before nightfall. 'You are clever – do your best. As you take the road out of Bologna, be quite sure nobody recognises you. My protection is no longer worth having. At sunset, go – but I would rather not see you go. Do you mind?'

'Even now, Flavius,' she began softly, meaning to thank him, 'with so much else depending on you – ' But Stilicho was hardly listening. He was concentrating his mind on the night attack.

Upstairs in the bedroom they had briefly shared, having changed clothes and slicked her hair boy-fashion, Gilda, as always before a performance, took a last glimpse at herself from head to foot in a silver hand-mirror. Yes, quite in character – a rich man's spoiled son. She envisaged a bandit trying to stop her, and held the boar-spear as if she meant business, asking herself, would I be man enough to run him through? She practised a lunge, and found herself hesitating to drive the point home, and laughed. Iynx, Zama, Cornelia. Three names never to forget.

At the bottom of her heart – where Gilda seldom cared to look – a little more had been added to her stock of sadness, a piece of her life had ended. As if an audience were waiting in the courtyard she walked briskly downstairs, head high. No sign of Stilicho, but as if his magisterial eye were upon her she checked the girths, climbed the mounting-stone, and from there astride the saddle neatly enough, like a boy. She rode out, head and heart high, hands and heels low, as if for a riding lesson. In the twilight the Huns opened the oaken gate for her, and all they really saw was short dark hair, fine clothes, a boar-spear. The blonde woman who had been talking for so long with Stilicho, interrupting him, had vanished.

Sarus's clever watchword that night, to men who might be of divided mind, had been: *rescue Stilicho!* Those Huns have put a spell upon him – we must save him. All Visigoths were convinced that Huns were pagans and enchanters. Save Stilicho, he told his men – but put all his Huns to the sword. Stilicho alive would be a useful bargaining-counter – at least for the time being.

There should have been a full moon for his night attack, the luscious moon of the Italian August, but during that day the hot sun had sucked up the omnipresent black cloud of an electric storm. As the first thunderdrops came heavily down on his cropped head, Stilicho by a blaze of lightning caught one giveaway glimpse of dismounted cavalry, stumbling this way and that as they tried to surround the house. They were ill-at-ease at having to attack the house on foot, in the thundery dark.

'He has brought enough with him to pull this house to pieces, brick by brick,' Stilicho said to Meles, who stood at his side, sniffing the thundery air like a wild animal. Had Meles taken in the remark? Probably not. But he had taken in the odds – they were extreme.

'I shall break out of here with four of your men,' explained Stilicho, speaking this time with slow care. 'Go straight through their line before they have their wits about them. Understand, Meles? Four men. I want you to keep the Visigoths busy here only for long enough to give me a decent start.'

'How long?' asked Meles. He had understood.

'An hour.'

'An hour,' the Hun promised, smacking his hands together with cheerful satisfaction. Unlike most of his men, Meles had a clear idea of Roman units of time, those clever alternations of twelve hours that made up night and day. Dividing up time was a new idea for Meles, and it intrigued him.

'At the end of the time, parley if you have to. Pretend to strike a bargain for your lives. Sarus will refuse – so be ready to cut your way out of here, and follow me to Ravenna.

Meles nodded. He had never expected his general to be so stupid as to let that man with the long hair and the bright cloak trap him in a house, but it had happened. It had something to do with his woman – a woman like that was bad luck. Forked lightning staggered brilliantly across the sky for emphasis. Meles shuddered. The only thing in the world he feared was lightning.

Olympius and the Emperor might very well be in Ticinum, with the rebellious infantry, but at Ravenna was the organised government. Within which, even though Olympius has been doing his worst against me, thought Stilicho, I must still have friends. And can perhaps with their help win my own rearguard action. At the worst, strike a bargain for my life.

Gilda has gone, a good thing too. We were friends towards the end, but with the world I know falling on my head, how could it have lasted? Despite the clever and consoling things she would say, her generosity with her body, did she even love me? The mistakes of a lifetime, decided Stilicho, can always be seen more clearly once it is too late to put them right. The simple mistake here was that I could never bring myself to treat her as an equal. How could I? She was a woman. A loose woman. Had we been equals we might have been friends for ever, in this world and the next, if there is one, but how could I? Until I freed her she was a slave. *Aequalitas*. Equality. For a while I even tried to treat Sarus as an equal, almost as a son. That failed too. He is not a man to whom the Roman virtues ever meant much. Under his skin he is a barbarian.

That sally on horseback from the courtyard gate, full tilt, with four good Huns crowding him knee to knee, his naked sword held out to strike, and the storm rain beating on his face, had been as excellent for Stilicho as any strenuous moment in his life.

Stilicho himself had crossed swords, briefly, with a young Visigoth, and afterwards, as he galloped off scot-free, was sad at having struck him down. The aftermath of killing that boy was too much like the sadness that comes after taking a woman – yet the youngster's own swordsmanship was at fault. No one had ever shown him how to counter a sword stroke from the saddle. Too late now.

Stilicho wiped the wet blade on his horse's mane, and ran it back into the scabbard, unable to shake off this increment of sadness: a young Visigoth sworn to serve Rome. Perhaps even the son of a man he knew. Why then – wondered Stilicho – should I be obliged to treat him as an enemy? Only because to answer the wrong stroke of a blade with the right stroke was inbred experience – the only way to survive.

Not so long since, thought Stilicho, as his charger, once clear of Bologna, settled down to the easy cadence of an extended trot, Gilda too must have ridden along this highway, a boy in a tunic, boar-spear in hand, out hunting for pleasure. Up in the mountains, wild boar were plentiful, and her disguise would carry conviction. Not that she would pause for wild boar. He had told Gilda to ride for one of the ports along the Ligurian coast, Genna, Portus Delphini, even Luna, and there find a ship to Africa. The last safe place, he had said, and so it was. Gilda was well out of it.

The years had withered Julia to a diminutive female monkey, but her eyes still glittered. Women stand up to old age in their own way, reflected Stilicho, better than we men. Their faces go, their bodies survive. We have poured so much of our own strength into them; perhaps that. I, at one time, mine into her. I had strength to waste, in those days.

'But Flavius – *carus* – ' Julia was whispering caressingly, as if this were Constantinople in years gone by, and she young and fresh at court, and Stilicho the dazzling young guards officer – the overwhelming lover – aiming for the Emperor's adopted daughter, but not reaching out for her yet, and taking, meanwhile, everyone else in his way. 'Exactly what do you mean by that word of yours, *amici*? Here in Ravenna, how many friends do you think you have, apart from me?'

All their lives, Julia had shared him with others. At last she had him to herself.

'Among the serving soldiers – no friends?' he asked incredulously.

'After Bologna? I should be surprised.'

She did not say – Julia's subtlety – whether by 'Bologna' she meant the cavalry uprising, or the decimation.

'But the common people. The plebs.'

'No doubt the mob in Rome would always come out to cheer you, if you happened to march by; they always did. But here in Ravenna we have no mob. In Ravenna there are no common people to take into consideration – only intrigues and illusion and dreams.' Julia smiled. 'And if you are looking for friends among those who count for something – the *honestiores* – those who wield power of some sort, or think they wield power? None whatever.'

'Surely, Julia – '

'Listen to me. There are men here whose careers you made in days gone by. Once your friends. Almost without exception they will turn against you, if they have not turned already. Men to whom you have done a practical kindness? Believe me, at this very moment they are speaking ill of you. And you know what they whisper? Flavius Stilicho is a falling star.'

Julia was right, and he knew it, though this was not what Stilicho wanted to hear from her, and it stupidly angered him. He struck his own forehead with a clenched fist, as if to teach himself hard truth by self-inflicted pain. Julia sighed. What fools men were, especially if they still had a touch about them of the barbarian. Patiently she tried to explain.

'Here in Ravenna we have lost the habit of putting our thought into words. No one dare speak out, and most dare not even think. We have the habit they have lost – you and I – of thinking, and expressing our own thoughts. Now let me tell you. Had you only plotted – and I mean this seriously – to make yourself Emperor. Or even that dunderheaded son of yours. As they are all beginning to pretend you had. No, listen to me, Flavius, I know it is false. I know. Hear me out. With a little help from me, you would by now have all the friends you could wish for. A party at your back, and an army of thirty thousand horsemen, and General Sarus at your right hand if you still wanted him. Every man who detests Olympius and despises Honorius, every ambitious and even slightly honest man, would be backing you. But as it is – '

Julia was tempted to say, you are dying, Flavius Stilicho, my Vandal friend, of your own Roman fidelity. Why be witty, though, at his expense, and break your own heart saying it?

'The last thing Rome needs at a time like this,' Stilicho told her with a simple obstinacy that Julia found touching and yet appalling, 'is a conflict of loyalties – a civil war.'

'Well then, what does Rome need? What follows?'

'As well as obedience to her Emperor? Rome needs an army that can fight.'

Julia sighed, a coquettish sigh, an intimate echo in his ear of the night nearly forty years distant when after going politely through the motions of rebuffing him, Julia made him believe he had been too much for her, yielding to him eagerly, inordinately. What a girl she was then, thought Stilicho, all glitter, cleverness, bright fire. Her own way to make at court, by her wits, just as I had. And she made it.

'*Carus – carissimus* – nobody talks as you do any more, about what Rome needs, except in the faint and unlikely hope of deceiving the gullible. Nobody looks on Rome as you do – as a mother, as a mistress. Yes, don't pretend – I know very well. All your life you have preferred Rome to me. Serena personified Rome. But should she waver, you preferred Rome even to Serena. Claudian was the very last of us to think and talk as you do. And he, poor fellow, has taken ship for Africa, coughing his heart out. Listen, old friend – ' At her every word, Julia tapped his broad chest with her ring-bedecked finger, like the pecking of a parrot. ' – you – are – out – of – date.'

Oracles, sybils, pythonesses, thought Stilicho – women such as this wise woman who has just touched me – are believed to know truths hidden from mere men.

'Tell me why all this came to pass,' he commanded, as if to an oracle; an order that Julia scarcely knew how to obey.

'For me it is simply this. That I can no longer believe,' she told him in a strange, wan voice, her private voice, 'that the world I see around me is real any more. Nothing has the flavour of the real – nothing I can see and touch – only memories. Or words in a book by some dead man or other. Some great man in the past. Ravenna is not real; but then it never was. They are all here, crowded in, the rich and powerful, simply because Ravenna is the last safe place in Italy. And now that they are safe, they live in a dream. One by one, the great provinces of Rome – Britain, conquered by the divine Claudius, Gaul, conquered by the great Julius Caesar – are wrenched from us. Your kinsmen, the Vandals, have gone through Gaul from one end to the other, and are off to found for themselves another kingdom, so I hear, in Spain. But I am telling you what you already know – '

'All we really need, when you come down to it,' said Stilicho, and as he heard his own voice, he demanded of himself, but could this be your own private sick Ravenna dream? 'are good drill-sergeants, a corps of officers with courage and common decency, and, above all, the money to pay our troops. Is that too much to ask?'

'The money. Ah yes. The money vanished first. People have always considered you a fool about money – did you know that? I mean, considering the opportunities you have had to amass a vast fortune. Oh indeed, people like old Curtius still have plenty of money. They have sucked in other people's money, mine and even yours, for all I know. But nobody, not even red-nosed old Curtius, knows the secret any more of how to make money breed and replenish. The money they have and lend does not lead to prosperity. They may sit in the Senate, but they have the minds of brigands. They only understand plunder. The Roman army? A band of mutinous brigands. There you have it. We are done for, Flavius, and you had better simply admit it – '

Stilicho could have wished her to leave it at that. What she said was bitter and repugnant, even though he was prepared to accept it. But Julia, being Julia, went on to put into words certain thoughts she had until now forbidden herself to express.

'Look below the surface. Here in Ravenna we still have a Senate, the old Roman ranks and titles. Not the real power, though. Hardly a shadow of the real power. Yet one man will destroy another – destroy Rome if need be – for a title which once meant something considerable, and now means nothing.

They are ghosts, my dear, gibbering bloody-minded ghosts. And they will converge to kill you, these ghosts, if they can – if you let them – because you are a real man, and cast a shadow – '

Julia pressed her two small hands fingertip to fingertip around Stilicho's thick upper arm, an old intimacy of theirs, her two hands together just touching around his arm, like a bracelet. Stilicho, though, for the first time she could remember, pulled away from her, and sat down on a chair, heavily, like an old man who has stood up for too long. All his life, when he had need of her, Julia had given him affection, insight. Why was she stripping herself bare, and him too?

'What shall I do?' he whispered.

Stilicho's head had sunk to his breast, as if become too heavy. Fascinated Julia watched him, after a moment's reflection, lift his clipped and bearded chin by an effort of will. For that Roman gesture she loved him.

'Will Flavius Stilicho the Vandal,' she asked, 'perhaps one day go over to the enemy? I mention only what others have begun to wonder. Ah – so it has passed through your mind, too? Change sides – like Alcibiades?' Stilicho as he shook his head had fixed her with his eye. 'Rather not? I see. We used not to think much of him, did we, when first we read about Alcibiades?'

Death, she thought, is certain. Yet how much we both cling to life, he and I! Must I say to him, out loud, in so many words, die like a Roman – as if I were giving instruction, in years gone by, to my hostage princesses, my ducklings, in Roman virtue?

'Julia – what went wrong?'

He had asked the question, in a private mumble, as if not requiring an answer. Julia tried to give him one anyway, as if one of her girls had been asking.

'You mean no money? No army? No brave gentlemen? What we Romans lack, if you ask me,' said Julia, 'is faith.'

'Growing religious, I see, in your old age.'

Stilicho smiled at her, ironically, but with affection. I could try to kiss him, thought Julia, but that would break the spell – his bristly white beard, my withered lips.

'I've always been so self-indulgent,' said Julia, in a sprightly court-lady's voice. 'Or if you are to accept what the Christians say, so wicked. A fornicator myself, given any slight opportunity. And trying to save my girls' reputations by malpractices. Though all my life I have at least tried to see clearly what was staring me in the face. We always tried to be honest, did we not? Oh yes we did. Not in anything you can see and touch – a corps of officers, a heap of gold. But in the invisible and omnipresent Rome – justice and peace – the Rome that we knew. You can't have forgotten, Flavius. When we were young, and Theodosius the Great was Emperor, this that I speak of was in the very air we breathed – '

Late that afternoon, as Flavius Stilicho stood in the courtyard of his own mansion, taking the air, a man with his arm in a sling who rode a stumbling horse one-handed came up to him, and dropped, clumsily with weariness, from the saddle.

'Meles reporting, general.' An exhausted grin, an expiring voice.

Stilicho turned abruptly to a slave waiting nearby.

'Take him inside. Have my surgeon see to that arm.'

'No time,' interrupted Meles, who now as ever spoke his Latin in fragments, 'You have soldiers? An army?'

'Your four men,' said Stilicho dryly. 'And now you. Five with you, Meles. Six with myself.'

'A man with a roll – ' Meles, not knowing the word he wanted, was making with his left hand, awkwardly, the unlikely motion of writing on papyrus. 'A roll? Not far behind. From the Emperor. Death.'

An imperial death warrant?

Meles, thought Stilicho, must surely have it wrong. Would Honorius knowingly sign any such thing? Burden his conscience for the rest of his life with the guilt of being virtually a parricide?

Meles was groping in his memory for a name – Roman names did not come easily to him. 'Tall.' He lifted his one good hand to show how tall. 'A smile that is not a smile. Never your friend.' At last he dredged up the name and in weary triumph out it burst. 'Heraclian!'

Blood was dripping gently, as if from a small leak, down Meles' arm and finger to the courtyard flagstone.

'Surgeon!'

Stilicho had turned head and body, his voice was urgent.

The *medicus* came running, and began to bind up the wound as Meles, ignoring him, went on speaking.

Of Heraclian, Stilicho was ready to believe anything. A commanding officer too hard on his men, a court blusterer, whose one topic was how he had been denied by the commander-in-chief the high promotion that was his rightful due. There were too many in this safe city like Heraclian.

'How far away, Meles?'

'A mile. Not more than two. Many with him – a troop.'

And if he does carry an imperial warrant, signature in purple ink and the lead seal attached, then you must certainly submit. Stilicho remembered with a twinge how one fine day he had cozened just such a death warrant out of the Emperor, for Black Johannes.

A priest and his acolyte had been busy around the altar, but when Stilicho opened the church door, letting in a broad shaft of light, and advanced open handed towards them, they scuttled off like mice. My near neighbours thought Stilicho they know my face well. Christians, but I have never done them harm. Is everyone in Ravenna scared to be seen with me?

This was not the fashionable basilica in the centre of the city – large and new and used by court notabilities – but a little church built years before, where local people came, the baker and the market gardener, pious old women and those household slaves from Stilicho's mansion who had taken it into their heads to be Christian. Small, unimportant, but here, as in any Catholic church, so long as Honorius was Emperor, the altar was sanctuary.

That little priest has gone scurrying off, thought Stilicho, to tell his bishop. So the court will soon know where I am, and Heraclian too. That no doubt is to the good. The church around him, calm, still, was as empty as if the priest and his acolyte had made him a present of it. I do not believe in this religion of theirs, Stilicho told himself, but I do not disbelieve it either.

When an outright choice, pagan or Christian, was for political reasons forced upon me, I would always equivocate. Why not? The Visigoths, the Vandals, are Arians, and none the worse for that so far as I can see. Claudian insisted on declaring himself a pagan, a little self-consciously perhaps. Myself? Not Arian and not Catholic either, whatever the precise distinction may be. And not pagan. Neither believer nor disbeliever. Today, here, I am simply using against my enemies the weapon that comes readiest to hand.

If they want me, they must come and take me. I am standing here alone, in a sanctuary – a sanctuary vouchsafed by the Emperor I serve – to see what happens next. If I had a brain in my head, I would have brought some rations. There is nothing in here, not a drop, not a crumb. When did I last go an entire day without water? The Peloponnesos, was it not? One hot midsummer.

A hiss behind his shoulder – an alley boy's hiss, as to his accomplice in mischief – had Stilicho moving round alertly, one hand touching his sword hilt. The acolyte was standing there in the gloom, with both arms full. He had brought Stilicho one of those large, round, coarse brown loaves that market women fetch in from the country, and the upper classes disdain. And a large and pungent earthenware wine jug. Or put it another way, thought Stilicho gaily – cheerful since food and drink meant he could hold out. They are giving me their sacrament, their mystery. Well, I thank them for it. The boy screwed up is eye in a guttersnipe wink, as much as to say, not a word!

Night came on. The gloom intensified.

Stilicho drank very little of the wine – in the long run, wine makes you thirsty. He broke off bits of country bread in the darkness, and made sops. His Vandal nurse had at one time done that for him. What was she called? He had forgotten. No doubt that dumb nurse, Sara, made sops in wine for young Iynx.

Stilicho began to run his past life through his mind, as though it had been someone else's life, recalling not so much his prowess as a lover, or his great victories, but things he had done as a boy – the boy who ate sops in wine. And a young devil too! He tried hard to recall to mind the day when Mucapor had put him astride his first horse. The fact had been mentioned so often by Mucapor that by this time the memory itself was dim, as if speaking of it so much had worn it out. Nor could he bring to mind how Mucapor must have looked at the time; young and splendid, no doubt. He could not expunge from his mind's eye the withered, petulant face at Bologna. Time had caught up with him, as with us all.

The open space outside the church was quiet no longer. A clatter of many hooves arriving, voices giving orders, and, beyond the door, an angry answer, an altercation. Despite his wounded arm and his orders to lie low, Meles must have been out there, silently mounting guard. Stilicho could hear his broken Latin, spoken loudly and with natural authority, like fragments of bronze falling on marble. Four swordsmen with him, thought Stilicho, and ready by the sound of it to take on Heraclian's entire troop. Brave men, but they are dead men, even as they stand there defiantly.

A scuffle followed, weapons clashed, a man groaned, and no more was to be heard of Meles and his Huns. Heraclian had swept them aside. His troop of horse would be taking up positions all around the church. There is no way out, thought Stilicho, and nothing but the symbol on that altar to deter them from laying hands on me.

How much in fact, he asked himself, are men like Olympius and Heraclian in awe of their God's altar? In Ravenna they talk a little too much about God. They manipulate the church for their own political ends – granted – but in their hearts do they believe, or only make believe? They will think twice, and I know it, that is why I came in here, before dragging me away from this altar, this symbol. A table with a cross above it – a Roman gibbet – at which a symbolic meal is eaten? What exactly does it signify?

As their guest in this place, a fugitive, a suppliant, should I kneel? If only as a token of respect? Thus far in his life, Stilicho had never knelt to anyone, unless to enter a woman. The half-hearted obeisance he would give in the throne-room had been a court joke, until it became a scandal.

From an overwhelming sense of propriety, coming close to awe, Stilicho knelt, telling himself as he did so, this is the custom. He is my host. He deserves a reverence. Into his kneecaps came twinges of pain. And before him, not the soft, enveloping body of a desired woman, some Gilda, awaiting his embrace, not this time, but a vast emptiness.

Was that emptiness God?

Old Julia too was evidently being tempted by their faith –

this altar, this image – though she pretended to shrug it off. Always, thought Stilicho, the most intelligent of us. And what kind of life, mine, had I married her? As so easily I might have done. She attracted me. Married to a court nobody, and my father a Vandal mercenary? Lucky to have been made military tribune. I might be living now on some small country estate, breeding horses for army remounts, grumbling at having been passed over. Or at court, making the petty mischief of the disappointed man, like Heraclian. So difficult to accept, at the end of one's life, that one's destiny could ever have been other than it was.

His kneecaps were hurting a little too much, but a soldier does well to ignore small pain.

You have never, Stilicho reminded himself, prayed in all your life. Why go on kneeling like this, once you have made the necessary gesture? Then old moments of past peril came into his mind, when words which could only have been some sort of prayer had been torn from his lips.

All around the church the troopers were audibly impatient at having so long to wait. In the stillness he could hear the fidget of hooves, the clink of harness. Death? He had seen far too many die. And condemned others to sudden death with a simple motion of his hand. Man to man, face to face, inflicting death with his own right arm, and not so long ago, either. With the edge of this very sword, hung heavy from the sword-belt.

What, though, was death like? I who have seen so much of it, thought Stilicho, have never stopped to think.

A darkness.

Sleep?

The flames of hell? The Christian hell? A tale to frighten children.

Some similar vast emptiness?

He said aloud, as if to an interlocutor at the altar, 'Help me die like a man.' To his own amazement, he had prayed.

Prayer, he told himself humorously, is a thing one no doubt gets the knack of. Should I go on? He felt very inclined to say aloud, *I am sorry for the evil I have done*, then told himself that there was in fact no need to put it into words, the thought would be enough.

His knees were hurting excessively. Stilicho got clumsily to his feet. Prayers over.

Evil.

The decimation was wrong, even though any other Roman general in years gone by, when faced by such a mutiny, would have decimated. To strike down one man in ten along the line marked their minds with a necessary terror – a compulsive obedience – but it was indiscriminate, and therefore unjust. The idea of Rome, he told himself, is the idea of justice.

And mercy? Christians talked too much of mercy – to his mind, womanish, Magnanimity? Yes, magnanimity was Roman.

Though with Gilda I went even further, he insisted, then *magnanimitas*. Towards the end I tried to act with loving kindness. If I have ever considered her unthinkingly as my slave, then I am sorry. In certain ways – physical ways – I was her slave too, and she knows it, though scrupulously she never brought it home to me. Whatever law and custom or the sneers of onlookers might imply, we were equals, she and I, towards the end, anyway, though at the time neither of us would admit it.

The law of property is the essence of Roman law, and now they will strip me of all property. Though since not everyone has property, that is a law of unequals. The dead have no property, they cease to possess. We are equal in death. Why should Gilda ever have been my property? There should be another law, of justice and magnanimity. Even loving kindness, I will grant loving kindness. A law of equals.

Stilicho as he blundered into this line of thought recalled with some amusement what he had for years pushed out of his mind – the time long ago, as a youth, when his father, then in the Imperial Guard, was pressing him hard to become a soldier, and his reply had been that he would rather become a philosopher. A serious enough whim at the time, though not allowed to flourish long. The rule in Rome was that son followed father.

In the queasy hours before dawn Stilicho felt less philosophical, and became ill-at-ease. This was the time of night for surprise attacks. The troopers outside had settled down, as if half-asleep in the saddle. A charger would at times stamp or neigh, or shake its bridle. He could hear infantry marching up to reinforce the troop of cavalry: the tramp of boots.

And if at dawn, Stilicho asked himself, they break in here and take me by force? Do I turn around from this altar, one man alone, and try to fight them off? Oblige them to kill me – take some of them with me? Force my own death upon them – spill blood in a house not my own? All through this life of mine I have taken violence with me everywhere. Shall I bring violence here too?

Help me.

Help me to die a good death.

Not entirely clear why he was doing so, but obscurely convinced that this would be right – a fitting act – Stilicho unbuckled his sword belt. As if carrying out a ceremonial drill he went forward, to place the weapon, with belt and scabbard, flat on the altar. Without the weight of a sword at his hip he felt less than himself. He yawned. He was glad to have saved most of the bread and wine. This was not a day to face on an empty stomach.

Stilicho mumbled at a hard crust to keep himself awake. As a boy, he had liked to eat hard crusts. In those days, his teeth were sharper.

A little after sunrise, a rich old lady with a silk shawl demurely across her face came through the church door, and made way for a priest who seemingly was a man of some importance. Could they by mistake have come here for an early service? Only as the woman lifted her shawl and smiled did Stilicho recognise Julia, old friend, old intriguer. The priest she had ushered through the door was the bishop of Ravenna.

'But you have food already!' she exclaimed. 'They would not let me bring you any.'

Stilicho had been trying to recall how you addressed a bishop. Ah, yes.

'My lord bishop?'

'A document has arrived here in Ravenna from our master the Emperor Honorius', began the bishop, not coming as close as he might have done, and speaking in too distinct a voice. He is here because I have sought sanctuary in a church, thought Stilicho, and because he is bishop of Ravenna. The matter has become official. He is being careful not to appear too friendly. Not as eminent in their hierarchy as the bishop of Rome, or even of Milan, but able, supple. Some people might even add, honest, which in Ravenna makes him exceptional.

'A warrant for my death, perhaps?' asked Stilicho with a cheerful indifference that made old Julia shudder.

'Outside, they declare not,' she interrupted. A bird voice, he thought – the cry of a seabird. 'They gave us a glimpse, the bishop and I – though only a glimpse – of both signature and bull. That was all, but Heraclian says he is ready to swear, here at the altar, in the presence of my lord bishop, that the warrant he showed us but would not let us read is not a warrant for your death.'

'He would swear to anything,' answered Stilicho.

'To his own damnation?' asked the bishop.

Julia made another sceptical, seabird noise. Getting up early did not agree with her.

'If his warrant bears the Emperor's name and seal,' said Flavius Stilicho with calm emphasis, 'then whatever it says must be done.'

'Buckle on your sword, my dear,' whispered Julia. Was it like him to confront then unarmed?

'I would rather leave it where I put it, than hand it over hilt foremost to Heraclian.'

As if responding to this second mention of his name, in walked curly-headed, coarse-featured Heraclian, head up, undaunted by place or occasion, with an iron-shod half-maniple of infantry crunching the flag-stoned floor behind him. They crowded the church to the doors. He had on his face the cocky look of a man of low tastes enjoying a personal triumph.

Olympius, Sarus and now Heraclian, thought Stilicho. All pups from the same litter. For an army which bred such men as they turned out to be, is there any hope?

The bishop took charge, however, and did his business well. Taking his stand at the altar, and turning to face them, he quelled the soldiers with one glance. The awed silence of the rough-and-ready men at his back checked Heraclian. His grin of self-satisfaction became frozen grotesquely on his face like the simper on a statue. Let us at least hope, thought Stilicho, that old Julia can manage to hold back her tears. She had been looking up at him with bright, moist, intimate eyes as if come to say a last goodbye.

'I swear before this altar,' declared Heraclian, not kneeling – though the bishop had motioned him to do so – but holding the rolled papyrus in its case of imperial purple out in front of him, as though it were a baton, 'that this warrant here in my hand is an imperial order for the arrest – but not the death – of Flavius Stilicho.'

He could not forbear throwing a triumphant sideways glance at his victim, and that angered the bishop.

'Give me the warrant.' He held out his hand.

Heraclian would have liked to refuse. That roll and seal made him the most important man here. But the gloom of the church, the awed silence of his soldiers, the single, withering glance of contempt that Stilicho had so far allowed him, and the calm authority of the bishop, standing erect with his back to the altar and his arm held out, overcame him. Reluctantly he handed it over.

Turning so that he was in the shaft of light from the narrow east window, the bishop slid the papyrus from its parchment case, and began reading to himself as he unrolled it, his mouth silently forming the words. Then he turned to Stilicho with an encouraging smile.

'Just so. The Emperor hereby orders the arrest of Flavius Stilicho. He is to be kept in honourable confinement, without bonds. This order is not for his death, but only that he be put under guard. And the purple ink, the imperial signature, which we all recognise – '

Flavius Stilicho as the bishop spoke had been keeping a quiet eye on Heraclian. That grotesque, stiff half-smile had slowly changed to a grimace of ill-concealed triumph. He was up to some dirty trick.

'Soldiers outside,' whispered Julia, in his ear, 'but also friends – *amici*. Armed.'

And how many *amici* would I need, Stilicho wondered, to break out of this place – this marsh-surrounded trap – and escape even as far as a gallop down the causeway? The other question is, where to? The army will not welcome me. Shall I take up arms against the Emperor, at my age?

He had pulled himself clear from Julia, and was speaking to her so that all could hear.

'Go to my friends outside. Say I thank them, as I must, for

coming here at such an early hour, to support me. But I shall not resist. A commander-in-chief, like any other soldier, must obey. What we have just heard read out is an order from the Emperor – '

The soldiers scraped their feet. They had expected a quick but famous fight, a walk-over – that was what they had been promised. Heraclian is looking at me now, thought Stilicho, as if I were the biggest fool he has ever known.

Perhaps I am.

Stilicho would have liked another mouthful of wine, his thirst was a craving, but this was not the time. At a word from Heraclian, two *decurii* with drawn swords came and took Stilicho, one on each side, to march him outside, into the daylight, an officer under arrest.

In the doorway, as the *decurii* crowded him closer, Stilicho paused, making them wait, turning his head.

'My lord bishop, I thank you. Julia, *delecta*, goodbye.'

The morning light had, for the moment, blinded him. The open space outside the little church was crowded with armed men. Jostling Heraclian's troops were perhaps a hundred of his friends, most of them barbarians. They had come, after all.

He raised a hand, palm outwards, in Roman fashion, and announced to them in a loud voice, 'Friends, I yield myself up of my own free will to the Emperor.'

'You do? I am glad to hear it.'

Heraclian's voice, just at his back, gleeful with triumph. Stilicho turned. From inside his military cloak, Heraclian was bringing out a second papyrus roll.

With a fixed smile he unrolled the document, and began to read to everyone in a loud voice, though obviously he knew the words by heart and was gloating.

'... *his crimes against the state are judged deserving of death* ...'

Somehow or other they must have tricked poor Honorius, thought Stilicho. He never did look carefully enough at what he was given to sign. How he will suffer when he gets to hear! Anyway, there it is. At least as legal as that death warrant I procured for Black Johannus.

Glad to get this over.

I wish I were less thirsty. Does it show in my face? Does anything show? Let's hope not. How good a swordsman is Heraclian? I see he is about to do the job himself. So long as he does not botch it – were Stilicho's jumbled thoughts as he stepped forward two paces. This took the *decuri* guarding him by surprise – they had been waiting for an order to hold him down by force. He bent his head, voluntarily, to the sharp sword that Heraclian was already pulling with undisguised eagerness from the scabbard.

'*So died*', wrote the historian Zosimus, when he described what led up to Stilicho's death, and what came after, '*the man who was more moderate than any other who bore rule at that time.*'

The day was 22 August, AD 408. Rome itself would fall in the same year.

Olympius had already made plans for what was to come next. A law was rushed through that all who had held office under Flavius Stilicho were to forfeit their property to the state. Stilicho, in his will, had enriched Gilda – the will was set aside. Two imperial eunuchs, Arsacius and Terentius, took Stilicho's children prisoner. His son, Eucherius, was put to death. The sister was sent under guard to her mother, Serena, in Rome. For these services the two eunuchs were rewarded with the post of grand chamberlain and marshal of the palace. Stilicho's brother-in-law, Bathanarius, who held high military command in Africa, was killed out of hand. His post was given to Heraclian.

The Emperor Honorius, by this time, was unsure in his own mind that he had ever knowingly signed a warrant for Stilicho's execution. Arrest, yes, but execution? He had never been willing to believe that there might be a plot to make Eucherius Emperor. His cousin, Eucherius, interested only in clothes? Honorius was beginning to ask for evidence, and he persisted. This was the one idea now in his mind, and he held to it: evidence.

Only evidence about Eucherius's plans – he said time and again – would set his conscience-stricken mind at rest. Eucherius had been killed too quickly to admit his guilt and ask for forgiveness. Stilicho, too, had been killed, and were there no evidence of his guilt, that would be parricide.

There could be no evidence of the kind Honorius was asking

for, because there had been no plot. Olympius knew this, though he tried to convince others and even himself, that the plot of which he had spoken so much was real. A plot of some kind or other there must have been. And evidence for it must be found, or what was the point of power? Olympius like a man morbidly obsessed went to work, to make illusion conform with reality.

He could see clearly enough that Gilda was the weak link, to be wrenched and made to give. A woman of bad morals, an actress, once a slave? Stilicho's mistress, then his heiress? She could be made to admit whatever she might be asked. Gilda was sought everywhere, but she had disappeared.

Word had already reached Olympius of the wry-necked child, being brought up in secret on the estate in Samnium. But Stilicho had been far-sighted, his precautions were thwarting Olympius, even after death. Long before the *agentes in rebus* arrived in Samnium to arrest them, both child and nurse too had disappeared, no one could say where.

Though what were these disappearances but additional proof that there must have been a plot? Olympius had all Stilicho's household slaves put to the torture. They contradicted one another, but they all talked, and Olympius learned a great deal, much of it amusingly scandalous, some of it far-fetched, about Stilicho's private life. The child who disappeared had certainly been born to the *mima* Gilda in Stilicho's house in Rome. And Gilda had once shared the Emperor's bed. But would Honorius want to be reminded?

All this, so far, was gossip, not evidence, and the Emperor with the obstinacy that was becoming increasingly typical of him continued to insist. Excitable talk about unaccountable disappearances was not enough, particularly because the people concerned did not really matter – a *mima*? a dumb nurse? Olympius struck out at men higher in rank.

Those *honestiores*, once Stilicho's friends and clients, who had already been dispossessed of their property, were put to the torture one by one. They broke without exception, and babbled pathetically, but gave away nothing to the point, because there really was no plot.

Mucapor died of a stroke, in the arms of a pretty little girl, the night they came to put him in chains. Pretty little girls, it turned out, had been his ruin. Old Julia met her death hung upside down by her heels, her back flayed bloody. She was old and frail. She had a lifetime of political intrigue behind her, and it was too late to save Stilicho, anyway. About others who might be involved, she did not greatly care. Olympius came down to the cellar himself to interrogate her – a question between each stroke of the rod. Julia would certainly have given him the answers he wanted had she only known what they were, but for all her cleverness she failed to guess exactly what was in Olympius's mind, and between one question and the next her heart stopped beating.

At the sight of the old woman, hanging there in front of him, useless, like flayed meat, Olympius felt neither thrill not horror, only a faint, exasperated disgust, as a man obliged on a hot day to pick his way on tiptoe across a butcher's yard. And disappointment too, of course.

Part VII

1

Men working on the wharf were rolling Claudian's barrels of books ashore, one by one, a fat-bellied dozen of them. On deck, stretched in his *lectica*, he watched them being stacked against the harbour wall. Claudian had spoken cheerfully to the men, and paid them well. Afterwards, they shouldered his litter down the gangplank, with him still in it. But then they put the *lectica* down with a bump at the end of the row of barrels, like any other piece of cargo, and went away, ignoring his breathless cries.

There he was, left alone, abandoned, a thing not a man, with nothing to look at but a blank wall. As they went off, the men were chaffing one another, almost as if admitting, thought Claudian, that they had played a practical joke.

'Turn this thing around! At the very least!' he cried to their departing backs – but they were talking coarsely, loudly, about women, and his own voice was almost extinct. Not heartless, though, simply thoughtless, he tried to tell himself. And such splendid physical specimens. I paid them well, I smiled at them, why have they done this? No doubt I was a lot of bother. I know quite well I was, on the voyage.

The mistake had been to take a passage from Rome in a ship that was too small. As well as not to be met on arrival, thought Claudian sulkily, as he gazed at the harbour wall, the rough surface of rectangular stone, the slanting marks left by the mason's adze, the white pouts of mortar squeezed out by the weight of the dressed block, the grey incrustations – it might have been lichen – left by the spray of last winter. Of many winters.

He watched a little spider make an enormous journey from the foot of the wall to the high rim. Up from hell?

'Like Proserpine,' he told himself grimly, 'I myself am now in hell.'

Claudian groped between the cushions for the parchment-cased rolls enclosing the draft of his latest poem – *The Rape of Proserpine* – announced prematurely by his Roman publisher, as if fearing that the poet might never finish. Part of it even read in public there by a professional actor, since Claudian himself could not but admit that his own voice was gone. What mannerisms, though, that actor. How little did he understand the meaning of what he had been given to read! How unappreciative of his great privilege! And why this hurry to complete – to publish? Claudian asked himself, gazing in a trance at the wall. Except, of course, that even from an unfinished poem, if it were his own, the publisher would make money. Is my poem perfect? (Is any poem, ever?) Are there not lines, even in the portion read aloud, that I can still improve?

Proserpine – who lived half the year with her husband, Hades, in hell, and afterwards escaped upwards for a year, like a flowering plant – or like that spider – into the sunshine! Claudian's eye took in words on the unrolled papyrus.

> My burning mind now bids me boldly sing
> The chariot horses of Hell's raping King,
> Darkening the stars, the gloomy bride-array
> That claimed the Maiden. You profane, away!
> The frenzy sluices my mortality,
> I am the God's, his presence breathes in me –

Rough and ready, but he could bring to mind again the emotion, still more or less rendered in these approximate verses. Shall I ever, he asked himself, again feel thus? Claudian pushed his roll of rough draft out of sight into its case. There was work to be done on it, and here in the litter facing this blank wall was not the propitious moment.

If only I had in this hand of mine simply a broken pomegranate, Prosperpine's pomegranate, thought Claudian, one ripe red seed to press moistly against my tongue. Juice for my throat, juice of any sort. That huge basket of Roman fruit – my cook carried aboard in triumph, when all the household trooped down, some red-eyed, to the bank of the Tiber to see me off! That basket of fruit! Long since nibbled, chewed and sucked down to pips.

I gave away far too much of it, thought Claudian pettishly, to the sailors. Splendid physical specimens though they may have been, it never does to spoil them. See how these others have left me, a man who smiled and paid them well, his fruit gone, his water-jug empty. Am I supposed to lie here uncomplaining until I die of thirst?

Perhaps this is not Carthage, but hell. Am I already dead? People pass from life to death in the flicker of an eye.

When my slaves carried me down from the house to the river, I was coughing enough to summon Charon. Farewell, my wicked, lazy boys, farewell my garden with its flowers. At least my books have arrived, that's one to the good. How clever of Lucas to insist that we pack them in barrels. Not that books will be any consolation to a man about to die of thirst. If not dead already. No books to read in the underworld – what a dismal thought.

Or is this hell – dead in the night, books just out of reach, in barrels. Am I condemned to a perpetuity of watching a spider climb a wall? There he is, at the top, brave fellow, and now – pitiful allegory of human life – he must spin a web to catch a fly, or starve. Hell for me is a spider up a wall. Hell for a spider is up a wall with no flies. Hell for a fly?

What kind of web shall I manage to weave around myself, here in Africa? Gilded exile – and with a wife? Time, let us hope, to work longer on *Proserpine*. *Labor limae* – the last fine strokes of the file. With a poem in their honour will the gods not grant me time and breath? Proserpine and her mother Demeter sent their poet fair breezes off Sicily. Those warm and halcyon days did me good.

But the winds off Malta! A little tub, wallowing helplessly in ballast because, though Carthage is obliged to send wheat and oil to Rome, what in return does Rome send Carthage?

Demands for taxes, he thought, and chuckled. Bills for rent, demands for taxes.

Civilisation, of course, his other self responded primly. They get an invisible return for their money, their oil and their corn. They get law, order, peace – my poems! Who would live in a mansion in Carthage when he might live in a garret in Rome?

Where in the name of all that is sacred is Lucas Claudianipor?

So thoughtful, when a slave; conscientious and punctual. Never wholeheartedly affectionate, but one can't have everything. The affection for which I crave was simply not in his nature. Yet in his own way, I am sure he was fond of me. Not everyone would have nursed me as he did. Where is this man to whom I so foolishly gave his freedom and a purse of money? Chasing after some little girl! Does he think I don't know. I have smelt the odour of girl on him, before this, and been revolted.

And my dry bones – are they to be encountered here, in the port of Carthage, by posterity? Famous poet. Died of thirst. And to posterity's immense surprise, within easy reach, my manuscript – my masterpiece. But bones are anonymous. Incomplete alas, my masterpiece. Almost Claudian got the manuscript out again, to pumice out and rework that appalling line, *A frenzy sluices my mortality.*

The workmen, after carrying Claudian ashore, had in fact gone off to look for Lucas.

'*Ave*'! hailed the voice of Lucas Claudianipor, '*Magister* – '

' – *et amicus*,' said Claudian crossly.

'*Magister et amicus* – ' the voice of Lucas chimed back, as if accepting the correction and yet smiling at it. There was his face. Smiling. Plumper. In his hair the first threads of grey. At his age? But it comes to us all.

'They simply dumped me down here like baggage, with nothing but a blank wall to stare at – ' began Claudian peevishly. Then, a little ashamed at his own thoughts, he began to mock himself. 'Would you like to know all about this wall? In sapphics perhaps? How many stones? I have been counting the cracks. Some are vertical, some horizontal, yet each is different. My water jug empty, and all my fruit eaten by those greedy sailors. *My throat!*' His last expiring words were like a fingernail scratching a taut piece of silk.

Lucas disappeared with the empty water jug. While his back was turned, half-a-dozen swarthy faces peeped into the litter –

muscular countrymen, Berbers, Cornelia's slaves, who had trailed here in farm carts to trundle Claudian and his possessions back to her.

'The water of Carthage is hardly the water of Rome – ' announced Lucas, passing him the wet, cool jar.

'For one thing, it does not taste quite so much of lead,' riposted Claudian after swallowing a little too much of it, and choking.

The Berbers moved the litter around neatly enough, lift and turn, and at a word from Lucas moved off with Claudian as if they had been carrying sick poets in litters all their lives.

By turning his head, Claudian could at last see the port, a symmetry of masonry, the semicircular quay, the ships hauled up slipways or turning at their moorings, and the slap and suck, that, he thought, describes it, hold tight to the phrase, of the imprisoned sea. They were going uphill, towards the city gate.

'My books?'

'Safely stowed away in the lady Cornelia's carts,' said Lucas reassuringly. What a comfort he is, thought Claudian. So practical and so good-natured. I had quite forgotten.

'You spoke to the bearers just now in – '

'Punic. They understand hardly any Latin.'

'It sounds like Hebrew.'

'It is,' said Lucas. 'In fact, very like.'

'I knew some Hebrew once,' said Claudian thoughtfully, 'But the literature is hardly worth the effort. You should encourage them to speak Latin.' Lucas is so much freer in his manner already, so much more amiable, thought Claudian, than when my slave. My magnanimity towards him is abundantly justified. Let us hope we can go on being friends. That he does not yearn a little too much for the full use of his freedom, and go off. Or I shall be damned lonely here.

'Men who don't understand Latin can't eavesdrop,' said Lucas gravely.

'That I suppose means you have some bad news to tell me.'

'Just as well, as things are, if I avoid even saying his name. A name so famous that even they might recognise. The great man whose victory over Alaric you celebrated in a poem.'

'Yes – I see.'

'Is dead.'

Flavius Stilicho gone before me! was Claudian's first unuttered reaction. I never for one moment expected that. He had lately been reconciling himself to leaving the world before any of his friends.

'What took him off, do you know? A cough? A fever?'

'The edge of a sword. A death warrant, real or false – there are two opinions, here in Carthage – but signed by the Emperor.'

'Lucas, are you quite sure of your facts?'

'The news reached Carthage by the day-before-yesterday's packet boat, in a secret despatch. But that kind of secret can never be kept for long – not in a port. I have worked in the port of Ostia, and I know. There are too many ears and eyes –'

He does not seem to care, this freedman, thought Claudian, that Rome's one great man is dead. Or is he hiding his grief, to spare me? Dead, poor Stilicho, and, unlike Proserpine, no resurrection.

Lucas had noticed that Claudian's face was twisting into a cold half-grin, like a death mask. Not self-satisfaction, though it might have been mistaken for it, but intense unhappiness. He is thinking, Lucas decided, of his dead friend, groping, perhaps, for the first words of an epitaph.

'And what is your own opinion of the news?' asked Claudian, but cautiously, as if, personally, what he had just been told were of no great concern. For the time being, thought Lucas, he is in that barren mood when he does not trust anyone. The time when his world is full of enemies. And if they have killed Flavius Stilicho, so it will be. Lucas did his best to smile back frankly.

'Rome will be another place without him. And Ravenna too.'

'Almost it scans – and would do on a tombstone,' said Claudian, relieving his feelings by sarcasm. 'A provincial tombstone.'

Malice: he is feeling better already, thought Lucas.

'Let me tell you one thing,' Claudian went on. 'But perhaps you have guessed already. Rome will be dangerous without him. For all his old friends, and the friends, Lucas, of his friends. Even you. And Carthage will not be safe now, either. The rats and carrion crows will come out of their graves, to eat his flesh and ours –'

Lucas turned aside without answering, to buy plums and

pears for a copper coin from a hawker at the city gate. Carrion crows – here, with the salt breeze blowing full in his face, off the sea? Fruit here in Carthage, he announced, as if that were information altogether more important, was better and cheaper than in Rome. Claudian filled his mouth eagerly with the juicy pulp, and swallowed. A benison that did not last. Melancholy returned.

'They will drag us down one by one,' Claudian predicted. 'We ought not to linger, here in the city. How soon do we leave?'

'If, dear master – '

' – and friend.'

' – dear master and friend, you can withstand the fatigue, we can eat supper tonight a long way south, on the road out of Carthage.'

'Six hundred years ago, Scipio and Hannibal fought at Zama,' said Claudian with a certain pomp, 'to decide the fate of the world.' He had at last found one small thing to say in Africa's favour.

'Anywhere south of Zama – and we are a long way south of Zama – is a lost place these days,' Lucas assured him.

'So – let us hurry off and lose ourselves.' Claudian's eyes were hotly burning but his voice had grown less hoarse. Lucas made a joke in Punic to the porters, and they laughed, as if to carry this sick man two weeks' journey south were for them a great joke. How nice, thought Claudian, settling back on the cushions, to be once more looked after by Lucas. In his own simple way, he reads my mind. With his plums and his pears, and his jokes to the porters, he has been diverting me from my sorrow. Regret for Stilicho – and it will be huge – will come down upon me tonight, in the dark. I have all this highly-coloured African life going on around me, distracting eye and ear. I can do no more than simulate mourning, and consider dangers. We who live in the imagination may sometimes give way to imaginary fears. But also, we may discern, where others are lulled or deceived. Is the dear boy quite convinced, as he should be, that there is risk to him too?

'Do they know who did it?'

'All blame Olympius, though the death blow was struck by a soldier called Heraclian.'

'I know the name. I even know the man. A brute, like all the others.'

One of Lucas's cart drivers came uphill towards them leading a saddled pony.

'You ride horseback now, Lucas Claudianipor?'

'To do you honour. The lady Cornelia insists that I no longer ride a donkey.'

'Are there bandits?'

'Except near the actual frontier, Africa lives in a peaceful slumber.'

'That's a comfort, anyway. Now lean down from that gigantic beast of your's. Closer. Whisper, because those men are hers. What is she like?'

Lucas was a Briton, and Britons were not adroit at telling lies. To Claudian all women were voracious, insatiable. 'Very large indeed, so I understand,' he prompted.

'But not gross,' Lucas answered quickly.

He was defending her. Did he like her? Will he perhaps, wondered Claudian cynically, manage to keep her quiet for me? 'Go on – tell me more.'

'Goodhearted. A simple person, but not a fool. She is aware that you are very ill.' Claudian winced at that. Why should one's state of health not be private – a secret? 'And so was her last husband,' added Lucas insensitively, 'so she knows.'

'Knows, you mean, how to look after people?'

'Just at present, she is looking after a little boy.'

'A little boy?' Claudian's voice went shrill with indignation. 'I read the marriage contract with great care, and nothing was said in it about a little boy.'

A brat! What he needed to finish off *Proserpine* was not the nursing of a fat woman and the screams of a little boy, but absolute peace and quiet.

Lucas darted a glance at the Berber porters. Impassive, but his voice dropped low. So even here, in smug Carthage, thought Claudian, men are careful what they say.

'Arrived one day, unannounced. On a donkey, in fact, along with a dumb nursemaid. Sewn into his clothes was a scrap of parchment, a horoscope. Which means nothing to me – but I did wonder if it might be a message to you.'

Rome and its intrigues! thought Claudian, with an affected

weariness, and yet an inner excitement. They have followed me all the way here.

'The nurse is dumb, you say?'

'*Muta.*'

'No doubt to keep the secret. It would be a political secret.' Claudian waved a feverish hand towards the bearers. 'Stop them. Get down from that horse. Come closer.'

'Lucas,' he whispered, with the urgent pathos of a man on the edge of fever. 'I know you are free. I admit you are free. I made you free. But don't leave me.'

'Leave you all alone, Claudius Claudianus – in a house with a woman and a child?' Lucas pretended to make a joke of it.

What is happening to the Roman world, wondered Claudian, that once we knew so well? Olympius. Heraclian. An insatiable fat woman. A noisy child. In Ravenna they will by this time be having their nasty little revenges.

Lucas, this fat woman – do you like her? was what he would have liked to ask, but the words were never enunciated. Imprudent, that question, humiliating, and incidentally, there was a great deal of property involved.

The bearers again took up their burden, and started a Berber song, on five notes, which, as the monotones passed by and returned, got on Claudian's nerves, but he lacked the heart to forbid them. He fell into a lewd dream, and when he woke up, unrefreshed, it was open country, scattered white buildings, fields full of crops.

Night found them in a roadside tavern, eight miles south. In the crisis of an overwhelming regret for Stilicho that descended on him in the small hours, Claudian called out aloud for Lucas. Claudian had begun to trickle blood from his mouth. Staunching the haemorrhage delayed them two days, and Lucas, to Claudian's delight, nursed him tenderly, as he had in Como. Anything was better than being nursed by that fat woman. But he must brace himself to accept what would be her privilege.

'There is a good doctor, living not far from the estate,' Lucas told him, 'a Jew, from Alexandria.' Claudian responded to the word *Alexandria* with a glare, so Lucas said no more about Jacob the political exile, this *medicus* who claimed to be Claudian's schoolfellow. Suppose they turned out to detest one another?

As they moved off along the next stage of their journey south, Claudian was plunged into black pessimism. The haemorrhage itself did not make him fearful – this slow corruption occurring inside his own body, though intriguing him morbidly, did not frighten him. The soul, he had come to believe, was quite other than the body, and would escape. Down to Hades? Hades would be a bore – no books – but perhaps not so big a bore as Africa. He had that morning been wounded to the heart by something the landlady said inadvertently, as she brought them their fruit and milk and fresh bread, before departure.

Word of Stilicho's death – no longer an official secret, if it ever had been – had spread like hot gossip down the main roads, and the landlady was full of it. She told her important guests with excitement in her voice that Flavius Stilicho had been killed as a traitor. Claudian, feebly angry, asked her how she could be so sure, and the woman had answered with bovine simplicity. 'If the Emperor said General Stilicho was a traitor, then he must have been, mustn't he?' Against stupidity, thought Claudian, the gods fight in vain. If this is Africa I should be better off in hell.

The legionaries had not yet finished with their insurgent madness. Once having freed their minds by one mutinous action or another from a lifetime habit of unquestioning obedience, they looked around for some larger chance to assert themselves. Their rivals – now their enemies – the barbarian cavalry greatly outnumbered them. But the families of the cavalrymen, women and children, living apart in married quarters, were there to be struck down.

Soldiers marching in military formation descended on the Visigoths' married quarters one midnight with all the resolution of an armed force carrying an enemy city by storm. After diverting themselves most of the night with rape and torment, until they had raised their own bloodlust, the legionaries began at last putting women and children to the sword, one after another, matter-of-factly, like trained butchers.

One of the few women lucky enough to escape – though her children were lost in the slaughter – was Medara, Sarus's wife, a bad-tempered woman made almost maniac by the loss of her young ones. Medara was close bloodkin to Ataulf, who was

King Alaric's brother-in-law and the Visigoths' best general. When word of the massacre reached Alaric through Ataulf, the King hardened his heart. The crime was a blasphemy. To Visigoths, the family was sacred.

Ataulf meant the Father of the Wolf – a Teutonic name surviving as Adolf. In brains and in ruthlessness as well as in appearance, Ataulf did have a touch of the wolf about him. He was small for a Goth, quick on his feet, ready with his tongue. His intelligent face, which might at one time have had an aspect of nobility, was marred by a vulpine broken nose. He was not only the Visigoth's best general but their shrewdest politician, and King Alaric listened to him attentively. In one considered sentence, pronounced in the Visigoth war council, Ataulf damned Sarus utterly. He was an adulterer, who had not cared enough to safeguard the families of the men who trusted him.

Meanwhile, in a red fury, and without waiting for orders Sarus's cavalry had gathered up the few survivors of the massacre, and were riding out of Italy to join Alaric. Sarus's embittered wife, Medara, biding her time, watched gleefully as the thirty thousand horsemen who had until lately been the source of her husband's power melted before his eyes.

Sarus would have done better to abandon Veleda the moment the bad news arrived – even take up again with Medara, a shrew but a woman of influence – and ride north with his men, so as to present himself to Alaric as a general to be reckoned with. But while one of his officers after another, enraged, unprompted, took the decision to change sides, Sarus prevaricated.

He could not quite bring himself to give up Veleda, even though she had been growing impatient with him to the point of rejection. By this time Veleda saw through him. Moreover he was still obsessed with the idea of persuading Galla Placidia to ride north too. What a hostage she would be – and what an opportunity! Was not her passion for barbarians notorious? Thus, in the days after the massacre, Sarus lost everything, as if Lady Luck had deserted him.

'One word to your important kinsman Ataulf,' Sarus insisted to Medara, the last time they spoke together, before she too departed, 'and I shall soon be commanding troops again.'

'Mine is the voice Ataulf listens to, not yours,' Medara answered scathingly, 'and you can be sure that by this time both

Ataulf and King Alaric know all about your Roman harlot. And that at heart,' went on the big-boned, bad-tempered woman, relishing her vengeance, 'you are a Roman. At one with those who killed our children. A Roman whore and a Roman heart. Ataulf already knows about you, because I sent him word. Now you would dearly like to know, wouldn't you, what message my kinsman, Ataulf sent me in reply'.

Sarus tried to ask in a dignified way, 'What then does Ataulf want of me?' but could not keep the expectation out of his voice.

'Ataulf has but one message for you, Sarus, and he asks me to pass it on. "Your husband," he says, "from this day on has become my *arbifijandsof*." '

Sarus felt his blood congeal. *Arbifijandsof* – sworn enemy – meant a life-long blood feud. General Sarus, gambler and womaniser, may have fought well enough for the Romans in Gaul, his wife's high-pitched voice went on to reiterate mockingly. She was repudiating him. She, like Ataulf, like King Alaric, had finished with him. Had he not, Medara asked him, betrayed Flavius Stilicho – an enemy the Visigoths had always respected? A man who once plays false can never again be trusted. And what, she asked, about chastity? Visigoths thought highly of married chastity – had he forgotten? What about his gambling? What about his bad reputation? What about his whore?

Sarus as he lingered in Ravenna had several times sent Veleda cleverly tempting messages, each in her opinion more insulting than the last. Even after Medara was known to have left the city there was not a word from her in reply.

At last Sarus, by a trick, forced his way into Veleda's secluded apartment in the imperial palace. He walked past curtains and down corridors, a tall man, distinctive in his coloured cloak, fearsome and charming by turns to the domestic slaves who should have barred his way. He came abruptly into Veleda's room – where no man had any business to be – with the face of a cunning stranger.

Veleda was in fact running a considerable risk herself by staying in Ravenna. She was Galla Placidia's lady-in-waiting but she had in turn been Julia's handmaiden, Stilicho's agent, Sarus's mistress. For those who did Olympius's dirty work, the

Princess Veleda was an ideal victim. In her present mood, feeling herself betrayed by Sarus and with a heart like ice, Veleda even courted the risk.

Were I now to cry rape – just one loud scream – thought Veleda, as she looked up and saw Sarus come through the door with one of his smiles, that would damn him for ever. I have only to open my mouth. But, instead, I shall turn my back on him, stare at the wall, refuse to say a word. He deserves only that much of me.

'Very well,' said Sarus, after a pause, 'if you dare not face me, you can at least listen to what I have to say.'

Veleda as he spoke pushed her large hands into her braided blonde hair, to cover her ears. So long as he did not take this silence, this refusal, as a sign of fear. Or of love!

'I will talk to your back,' Sarus was saying, 'your beautiful back.'

He was beginning to tell her, pitiably, of the horror his life had been, lately, with Medara. He went on to make Veleda one glib and impossible offer after another, like a cynical huckster. But Sarus knows he will never do what he says, Veleda told herself with bitter determination, as his words boomed inside her deafened head. He is showing me, unaware, that other side of his nature – the side I once did my best to ignore. All this time, he has had his eye on Galla Placidia. As he speaks he is making a monster of himself.

All I want is for him to go away. But dare I say it? No – stay silent.

At long last, humiliated by her unbroken silence and run out of words, Sarus walked off, telling himself as he walked away that she had turned into a viper. She pretended for so long to adore me, but look at her now.

With a mere three hundred followers – scallywag Visigoths, all of whom had some pressing reason for not going home – Sarus rode into Rimini, taking over the best houses there by force, living off the countryside, compelling the peasants to victual him until they began to hate the very sight of a coloured cloak. He was waiting for his chance to intervene in Gaul, where a fighting man – a freelance – might build his own good fortune on the collapse of Roman power.

*

Veleda was twenty-six when she cut Sarus out of her heart – almost too old for one of the diplomatic marriages for which the hostage princesses were bred up. And would anyone take her, with her good name gone, as well as her freshness? Yet whatever Veleda might do or say, Galla Placidia protected her.

Galla Placidia had by this time a mind of her own. She was intensely conscious of being the Emperor's younger sister, and when she went to Olympius and warned him to his face that the Princess Veleda was not to be touched, she was testing her own strength. Galla Placidia had come out of childhood obstinate and yet alert. With sardonic enjoyment she was already beginning to play the political game, though in her own fashion.

The many who abhorred Olympius were even beginning to look on Galla Placidia as the one member of the imperial family who might still be trusted. But Galla Placidia had no intention of being used by others; she kept conspirators at a safe distance. She had never in fact outgrown the effect on her of those romantic conversations in years gone by with the Princess Veleda. She hugged to herself one secret hope for the renewal of Rome: the barbarians. They were all that Ravenna was not. This hope of hers Sarus had cleverly discerned, and tried to play upon, but Veleda and Galla Placidia together had been too much for him.

Sarus had made himself detestable to Galla Placidia by his egregrious affability. He had, as she saw it, betrayed Veleda not because he was a barbarian, but by not being barbarian enough. Barbarians were honest. They were big, brave and virile. Less immoral than the courtiers here in Ravenna, not such hypocrites. At times even the distant sight of one of them could make Galla Placidia's heart beat faster. She was inexplicably sad when the last of the Visigoth cavalrymen had saddled up and left Ravenna for ever.

2

A ship's boat, submerged almost to the waterline, came wallowing in over the reef. The hull struck, an evil interruption, which brought Marcus running from his hut to the shore. The waterlogged boat rose and fell on the white water, and up came another wave, carrying it so far forward that the keel grated on black volcanic sand.

Marcus dashed in knee deep, to take the painter with both hands, bracing himself against the suck of the retreating wave. He turned the rope over his shoulder, to drag the boat a palm's breadth further in at each brief interval of slack water. On Cuneus, any wreckage gone loose from a trading ship was worth having, but he had not so much as turned his head to see what the wrecked boat might contain. When the boat was grounded, safe from incoming waves, he dropped the painter, exhausted, and then took a better look at what he might have fetched ashore.

Bilge water slopped from end to end across a human creature, puffy and blistered. Dead from exposure, and Marcus supposed at first glance, an overgrown boy: short hair in rats' tails, tunic ripped from hem to throat.

What at first he had taken for filth, at the twist of the legs, was a brown stain of dried blood. A wound? The clenched hands, too, were bloody. Waves lapped up greedily from the reef as Marcus stared, but were arriving short. The boat and its castaway were his. He had saved them both.

Marcus found himself staring at the anemone between her outflung legs: *Mater Omnium*, the mother of us all; the female *pudenda*.

What Tertullian once wrote of the female body came into his mind: *a temple built over a sewer*. Almost he could have justified pushing the boat and its sodden female body back into the sea whence it had come to trouble him. No witnesses. But God is always a witness. And that, Marcus told himself, as he took another look at her puffy and disfigured face, is what waits for me too, the death of the body, its corruption.

Marcus took Gilda out of the boat as he might have lifted a dead animal, a lump of water-soaked flesh, limbs dangling, a weight that dragged his own arms from their sockets. Finding she was too close to the advancing sea in the first place that he dropped her, Marcus dragged her by the heels to the black sand well above the tide mark. As easy a place as any other to dig a grave. The posture in which she had fallen was indecent, so he knelt to pull legs straight and cross arms over chest, and as his hand tightened on her wrist he felt a faint pulse.

Marcus waited, horrified, not daring to let Gilda's hand drop from his grasp, as if simply by waiting long enough the pulse might fade, and death reclaim her. How could she not be dead? He was conscious at the same time of having been saved as by divine intervention from a great sin. To have let her drift back into the sea? A temptation of the devil's. Thou shalt not kill.

Marcus had once seen a fisherman work the trick with a comrade rescued from drowning: patiently squeeze the water out of the lungs. Rolling her over face downwards hid her shame, those nippled breasts, the bloodied flower. To the tempo of his own breathing Marcus compressed the rib cage again and again. I am bringing to life, he thought, what I least want here: a woman. Is God testing me? From habit as he pressed and released her ribs he began to pray, as if not to pray whenever he had the chance might be a wicked waste of time.

Just as he had begun to wonder if all this might be of no avail, Gilda vomited up a mass of bile and salt water, agonisingly, as if turning herself inside out. To distract his mind from the shame he felt – to help her – Marcus decided to anoint her cracked skin. Olive oil here was a luxury, but his oil jar was still a quarter full, and as if to deprive himself Marcus tipped oil and smeared it wherever her skin had suffered, using it extravagantly, his hands moving with the indifference of one athlete greasing another. A woman at death's door, he told himself, is no real temptation. Seabirds went screeching over his head. After months of not noticing the birds, Marcus heard their quarrelling noise, and all at once it was like conversation.

Daylight would soon be gone. He had touched her everywhere, and thought nothing of it; indeed, liked himself the better for what he had been doing. His calloused hands were suave with oil – he rubbed his own wrists and throat with the very small pool of oil that was left in his cupped palm. Her burnt skin had been soothed, she was visibly breathing, but it was sunset – time for prayers and the lighting of the beacon.

At the makeshift shrine he went rapidly through the evening prayer, then scampered up the cliff face just in time to blow into life what was left of last night's fire, spark under ash, and heap on kindling. The driftwood in the iron basket sent up its usual volume of smoke before the first flame broke out of it under the lift of the night breeze. Marcus as he fanned the fire burnt his hand. The heat of the noon sun on your skin in a drifting boat would be worse. And thought – you fool! You forgot to give her water!

He went recklessly down the cliff face, filled his waterpot at the cistern, and put a hand under Gilda's head, to turn her unwilling mouth uppermost. He would have dribbled into it the benison of fresh water, but at the touch of his hand she cringed away, and put her bloody fists between her loins.

Around the coats of Britain, on the extreme edge of Empire, lawless violence might very well arrive from the sea. But in *Mare Internum* – the Mediterranean – Roman peace was as yet undisturbed. A ship of war had hardly been seen or used in the Mediterranean for centuries – since the distant days of Pompey the Great, piracy was unthinkable. But this control, on sea as on land, was breaking up at last.

The four seamen – or was it five? – who had possessed themselves of Gilda as of a plaything were not exactly *piratae*, not yet. They were seagoing men with trade at a low ebb, and alert for whatever might come their way. A well-dressed lad, alone and on the run, who turned up one bright morning and offered them money for a passage to Africa? Too much of a temptation.

The least law-abiding, when Gilda did her best to defend herself, took the boar-spear by its crosspiece and twisted it neatly out of her hand. One successful act of violence led to another. Their half-deck was no place to handle a boar-spear, but Gilda had somehow managed to cut him across the knuckles. That made the man furious, and with his good hand he knocked her down.

Villainy was a novelty to them, but not mere carnal temptation, they were seamen. As Gilda lay stunned, head hanging over the edge of the half-deck, her body sprawled, they soon discovered her purse and her sex. She could hear them as she came to, egging each other on.

'And cut the back of my hand wide open – look!' shouted the ringleader over his shoulder, as he knelt down and pushed her knees apart. 'What does she think she is – travelling in disguise?' After the first man had his will of her, with the others looking on, as if they all felt a certain shame on his behalf they joined to drag Gilda from the forecastle, where people coming along the wharf might see her. The man with the cut hand, having had his go, worked sheet and oar overhead, shouting bawdy encouragement down into the hold, while out of sight, in the dark, amid the smell of carob beans, they had her by turns.

When they had all done enough, and needed a breather, they went on deck and scrupulously shared out her money. Easier, she heard one of them say, than working for it. Had there been four of them, or five? There was no way of telling from the voices. And would they all come back, pile in again? Gilda meanwhile had time to consider, as she felt the wind on her stripped body, and heard the creak of the big sail, filling and pulling.

It is only my body, she began by telling herself. Who can touch my soul? Stridor when she was a very young girl had taught her the knack of saving herself. They think they have me, yet they have nothing of my real self. Once at sea, though, and out of sight, having had time to brood on possibilities, they came back with clever ideas in their heads, until pain and even almost a willing submission to their lust became inextricably mingled, and the very pain they practised on her was at times a shameful pleasure. She could hear them laugh together, when, at last, they left her alone, curled in a ball, making little whimpers of self-loathing.

As later on she tried to piece herself together, body and mind, Gilda could overhear them up there on the half-deck, discussing how and where they would put her ashore, and what she might fetch. Up above, by this time, were stars, shining down into the open hold like bright, small, unsympathetic eyes. They were heading for Sardinia, fever-ridden, ill-governed, an island where political prisoners were often sent. Though slaves fetched less in Sardinia, fewer questions were asked.

When the mountainous coast of the island was in sight, they forced Gilda down into the ship's boat, and made her lie flat, out of view, as they began to moor the trader fore-and-aft. They had their arms full of mainsail when the squall hit. A half-decked vessel, when it capsizes, fills and goes down quickly. Lying flat in the boat, Gilda heard all their voices cry out together. Stricken by the hand of God. The squall took the little ship's boat clear of them, tossing it out to sea like a cork, and though in the boat there was nothing, neither oar nor sail, neither food nor water, the gale of wind that followed sent Gilda a long way southward.

As Gilda winced away from the sight of his haggard, hairy face, from the pungent male smell of his body, Marcus tilted the waterpot a second time, and made a cooing sound, like a man with a shy animal. The huge craving for water overcame her fear. Gilda opened her mouth as if submitting – paying the price. He gave her at first only a little water, a trickle and a pause, as though from a spring running dry. Gilda choked on her first drop, but was passionately eager for more.

He shook his head, and said, in good clear Latin, 'Be patient!' Such a wild man, a savage, uttering a prudent remark in Latin came as a shock. Gilda, once she had tasted water, hated him for not giving her more of it. She would have liked to soak in it – drown in it. Her body craved fresh water as it had never craved men.

In a pause between small drinks, Marcus asked himself aloud, 'What could they have done with you?' Here on Cuneus, living alone, he often asked himself questions aloud, was hardly aware of it, and did not expect responses. Into Gilda's eye, as he watched her, came an incongruous tear, which moved lopsidedly down her scorched cheek, as if her dried-out body had, at last, been given back enough liquid to create one tear.

'What men always do to us.'

A woman's body – why had it been so surprising that she should give her answer in a woman's voice?

Marcus had turned away. Gilda's thought was, my God, I have driven him off, and he is taking the water with him. When Marcus came back with the blanket from his hut Gilda's eyes were closed, as if, while his back was turned, she had died. Marcus flapped out the blanket to cover her. And better if she were dead – peacefully dead. Something restrained him, though, from covering her face. To his chagrin she was sleeping like a child. Marcus carried her into the hut, wrapped in his only blanket, and went out to spend the night on the sand.

Next morning, after his dawn prayer, Marcus glanced into the hut, apprehensively, as if he had no business to be there. Gilda, shoulders against a corner post, was trying to push herself upright. Her ravaged clothes, the remnants of boyish finery, hung open in rags. Marcus flung an old piece of sailcloth across to her, keeping a prudent distance. Gilda stooped for it, smiled, and with fumbling hands draped it around herself. He watched covertly as she pulled and straightened it, each time biting her lip as if not satisfied, then tore off a strip for a belt. She had improvised a sailcloth robe. Gilda stood there, with one hip thrust out, a woman in a new dress. Light-minded vanity, Marcus told himself, and was annoyed that she should laugh at the set look in his face.

There was corn left in the sack, but not much. Once a week Marcus ground a couple of handfuls into flour, to make flapjacks. Gilda, craving bread, and best of all hot bread, counted the days until Sunday; the rest of the week they were fed, after a fashion, from the sea. Fish broiled on the coals if Marcus had been lucky with his hook and line, sun-dried salted fish if not. There was a mussel bed out on the reef, and their treat when Marcus permitted it was mussels, boiled in sea water until they opened and changed colour. He would only collect a few at a time, though, to give – so he said – the mussels a chance to breed. And do I respect him for that? Gilda wondered. Would I ever have thought of it? Later on, he told her, as if hoping to make her mouth water, there would be gulls' eggs. Never a full belly, though, not on Cuneus.

There had, early on, been a morning of horror when she scrambled her way all round the island and discovered how small it was: not a place but a prison. They slept well apart, they almost never so much as touched hands. He was respecting her. Not that Gilda, in her own opinion, would ever want a man to touch her again, even by accident.

She had at first taken it for granted that this thin and hairy man must be a castaway too. Sooner or later would he pester her – even attack her? Gilda made up her mind to defend herself to the point of killing him – there was only one knife on the island, his, but she would snatch it out of his belt. Instead of making advances to her, though, and this Gilda found even more disturbing, Marcus though unremittingly considerate would sometimes look right through her, almost as if wishing that she would disappear.

Life here on Cuneus, as Gilda soon found, had a strange and not easily explicable logic. Marcus came and went all day as if he were obeying a sequence of unspoken military commands – prayer on his knees at the little shrine, reading in the rolls of his book with eyes cast down and lips moving, the ritual of the nightly beacon-fire overhead.

She woke up one daybreak convinced that she had been sent to a hell for a luxury-loving *mima*. Dried fish to eat, sailcloth to wear, and a man, handsome under his neglected savagery, who ignored her. Panic grew as she found that, in her nightmare, she had lost the three names given her by Stilicho – they had dropped entirely out of her mind. Gilda lay there in dread. In hell – and lost her child. Her mind drifted in panic until the names came back to her: Iynx, Cornelia, Zama. I will say those three names all day long, she told herself – say them as he does his prayers. Then Marcus came into the hut as he did every morning, when he knew she was awake and dressed, bringing a full waterpot and something to eat.

Gilda asked him, 'Is this place hell?' and he choked as if on a bone, recovering to say gravely, 'Cuneus is very near to God.'

'I dreamt I was in hell.'

'Hell is the absence of God. You are close to God here.'

Marcus himself was in a continual turmoil. In pagan times in these waters there had been Sirens, and here at his side was a creature shaped like a woman who had been fished out of the sea to tempt him. She dreamt she had been in hell – but was it from hell that she came? A pagan Siren come from hell? A temptress, sent here by the Prince of Darkness? What else should a hermit expect? Here on Cuneus had he not, in the past, resisted valiantly, like a soldier of Christ, when those opulent similtudes of Roman women came to him in dream? Was the devil renewing his attack by means of a creature actually in the semblance of a woman of flesh and blood, standing so close he could reach out and touch her?

He had looked down one day from the clifftop, by the beacon, and there she was, naked. Thinking herself alone and safe, Gilda had let drop her sailcloth garment, and walked ankle-deep in her old enemy, the sea, to wash off the fish-smell. Or is she going back, Marcus asked himself, with a gust of almost lubricious excitement, to the place she came from – the devil who sent her? Foiled by my prayers? Yet felt a pang of misery at the thought of once more being alone.

This was a windless and illimitably smooth day in late summer, and, as Gilda dabbled her feet, ripples went outward. She was only washing, not escaping, and to Marcus came the thought, like me, she misses the Roman baths. And is she, as I might be, while she rinses her nakedness and remembers, thinking corruption?

Marcus came diffidently down the rock face, and by the time he reached her Gilda had the sailcloth garment tied round her, and with an intent look on her face was crouching over a rock pool, trying to make out her own reflection. She knew without turning her head that he was standing beside her. Gilda put a finger on a tuft of hair growing out above her ear, and said, 'That piece there. Has it really gone white?'

'You mean to say,' said Marcus, answering stupidly, 'it wasn't always white?'

Gilda in the past had prided herself on not crying even when Stridor beat her, but at this answer tears streamed down her cheek. It became difficult for Marcus to think of this woman with tear-stained cheeks as an emissary of the devil. To touch her consolingly, though, might be dangerous, so Marcus gave her what help he could, in words.

'But the body, you know, is corruption. Here on Cuneus I have never once wanted to look at my own face. No doubt I should hardly recognise myself. Only the soul is beautiful. And unlike the body, the soul is immortal.'

'I have no very clear idea of what you mean by all that,' said Gilda, 'but just then you answered me in the voice of someone I once met.' Here this man is, she thought, a Roman gentleman pretending to be a hermit. Inside the theatre and out, all men and women play parts. And what role must I play here? A nun? What kind of female companion is a hermit allowed? What kind of woman in fact does Marcus need? Gilda looked at him out of level, amused, self-contained eyes, and for the first time Marcus saw her as she was. Disregarding the incongruous clothes, the ragged hair, he too glimpsed the Roman demi-mondaine, and a foul gust of his own past rushed back at him.

'If you are who I think,' he said hoarsely, 'who sent you here? The devil?'

'Four or perhaps five devils,' Gilda said, screwing up her mouth as if yet again swallowing something bitter. 'Devils who looked like men. They did what they liked with me, and then carried me off in their boat, to sell me as a slave.'

The conviction once again came down on Marcus that here indeed was a demon arrived to tempt him.

'Who, in the name of the Holy Ghost, are you?'

In an infuriatingly casual way she answered, 'I was Flavius Stilicho's woman. Gilda, the *mima*. And one night, years ago, I saw you with him, in my hallway. Did you perhaps not see me? You must have done. I wore a red wig. I stood at first behind the door, and heard your voice, arguing with Stilicho about his own safety. Stilicho wouldn't have liked that. He would never listen to me, either, when I tried to warn him. Now stop being self-important, and tell me exactly who you were before all this began. Because that much I remember. And, placed as we are, surely neither of us can have anything to hide.'

'Let me do that for you.'

Sunday morning, and her words as Marcus rubbed the stone to and fro had not been easy for Gilda to utter. Coarse flour dribbled from the edges of the quern as he knelt to crush barley grains. Rubbing corn out like that, laboriously, was women's work anywhere in the world, even in the forests of Britain, but Gilda had not done it since she was a little girl. She was Gilda, the *mima*, and to grind corn would be a humiliating come-down. Deliberately though she had asked.

Marcus bade her with a wave of the hand leave all this to him, and as he rubbed out flour went on with the incessant mutter of prayer, like a half-heard chorus in a play – this praying, which took up so much of his time. Does he pray, she wondered, simply to keep other thoughts out of his mind? Thoughts of Rome – thoughts of me? Did he suppose I offered to grind the flour so as to stop him praying?

He is trying by all this prayer, she decided, as she watched him monotonously grind flour, to hold himself in check – never to be the kind of devil those others were. The thought touched her deeply. Yet he has just looked at me sideways as though I were the wild one. We have at the bottom of the jar a finger's breadth of olive oil. What if I take just half, in a clean shell, and one day along the beach find a sponge of the right size, and rinse the sand out of it?

Or, if I touched him in that way, the only way, Stridor always said, that matters to a man, might I destroy him?

Marcus was scraping up the last of the coarse flour with the back of his knife, as though it were gold dust. Gilda as she raked the fire for him thought of barley cakes cooking under hot ashes, and her mouth began to moisten.

As Marcus ran fresh water carefully into a clay bowl, to mix with his flour, Gilda said, 'And Marcus, I have remembered something else. One night Stilicho talked about you. He trusted you, and there were not so many he trusted. Me too I think. I hope so.'

Marcus squeezed the dough with his fingers, working it with unnecessary vigour until it cohered and felt like warm flesh.

'I must have been nineteen or twenty,' Gilda went on, 'Early days for both of us, Stilicho and me, and in those days I cared for nothing but pleasure. And gave more pleasure, believe me, than I ever got. I always have. It was the year of the great battle.'

As she babbled on, Marcus prayed for deafness. Each of her random words was hitting him like a flung stone. He rubbed his left foot to and fro in the black sand – like a nervous horse, thought Gilda – and his hands as she spoke went on making the dough into cakes. Uselessly, in the barking voice of a soldier, he asked her, 'Why did you come here?'

'Would it be wrong to say God brought me?' asked Gilda, maliciously, and to that there was no answer.

'I have been thinking,' she said. 'Those men who abused me – four, perhaps five – are at the bottom of the sea now, and eaten by the fishes. A gust of wind, and down they went, and I came here as by a miracle. So much sea, so few islands, and yet I landed here. God must have saved me for a purpose, don't you think?' She had said *God* – to Gilda an incomprehensible word – with sincere conviction, like an important word in a play. I am discovering, she thought, how to manage him.

'You are only trying to persuade me,' he answered obstinately, 'that you do not serve the devil.'

'I once served Stilicho, and so did you. Was Stilicho the devil?'

'He was a godless man,' was the best that Marcus could manage, as a riposte.

'He was a man.'

'Yes,' Marcus added, as if rebuked. 'A good man.'

They were at arm's length, still watching each other, and a little breathless, like boxers after the first hard exploratory round. With his usual scrupulous care, Marcus was placing the barley cakes, one by one, on the usual flat stone. As he put down the last he gave a sigh of despair. She was Gilda all right, a woman, no emissary of the devil: a woman of flesh and blood. The defences of solitude could no longer be maintained. Gilda watched Marcus as his real face broke through the mask of prayerful preoccupation. She took in his hair, his beard. A man at last, and yet hardly a sign left of the dashing staff officer. What had changed him?

'I can read, too, though not so fast,' Gilda told him, in a voice singularly calm and impersonal – the voice of a sister. And this is exactly how I shall speak, she told herself, until I know for certain whether I can bear this or any other man to touch me. 'Why do you never let me look in that book of yours. Are there secrets?'

'The secret of eternal life,' answered Marcus, but grudgingly, as if she had dragged this significant fact out of him against his will. 'Here. Take it. Read.' At this rate he would soon have no life left that he could call his own.

Gilda, always a quick study, could skip her way more or less correctly through Marcus's prayers – his potent private mumbles – after hearing them said aloud only once. Marcus himself had been able to fix them in his mind only by incessant repetition. And was finding himself obliged, moreover, to explain and defend everything that he believed – every word and phrase in those prayers, from end to end. Often he was at a loss, and Gilda would laugh.

'I wasted my chances of learning about all these things,' he admitted, 'at Nola. I put in too much time plastering walls, and being pleased with myself.' But the spirit of instruction soon got into Marcus, and he went on talking to Gilda, day after day, about the faith – a safe topic – as if her religious impulse must be at least equal to his own.

Often he found it hard to carry Gilda with him. His account of the Incarnation, God come down to earth to live as a man, and the Resurrection, a criminal nailed to a cross rising gloriously from the tomb – to Marcus the twin pillars of the Christian faith, believe them and all else follows – left Gilda dubious and wary. Affecting stories, certainly, but why believe them as the truth? They lacked probability. They went too far.

A God born of a Virgin? Who suffered and died? What kind of God was that – to suffer? And took upon himself our sins? Gilda's sins were in her own opinion insignificant, compared with the sins others had committed against her. Let the others crave forgiveness and repentance, beginning with the men. As if Marcus's religion were a personal rival, she went out of her way, subtly, to challenge and tempt him. The polite severity with which he treated her was discouraging, yet there were moments when Gilda felt a tenderness for him.

'You never got married?' she asked him one day.

'Never – and now I'm glad.'

His integrity was becoming a provocation. Her own invisible wound had taken long enough to heal, but her body no longer winced when he accidentally touched it. When black moods came down on her, she might live it all again, the tussle on the half-deck, the long misery in the hold, the consoling stars overhead, but almost as if the memory belonged by rights to someone not her present self. As soon as I lifted that boar-spear – thought Gilda – they must have seen I did not have the knack of it. What pleasure, though, do they get – men and even some women – from giving pain? From the humiliation of the weaker one? I know they do. I once thought I knew all about it, pain and pleasure – Stridor's knowledge. I know about whipping and stinging – a sin if you like? – but who taught me? And would Jesus of Nazareth wish to take such a sin upon himself? They whipped him. Yes, he would know. Were I to unlock and enter the citadel of Marcus's body – and I could so easily, when he glances at me in a certain undefended way – would that simply be revenge? Am I, too, planning to humiliate him, to destroy him, as those shipmen did all they could to destroy me? Really, here on Cuneus, is my good act to stay remote from him? Other women might find that impossible. But being the woman I am?

Gilda took him at last, rather in the way that a man might take a woman, at the end of one hard-working day, when Marcus's vigilance was relaxed, and Gilda herself had been on the island more than a month. They had been preserving capers and drying fish over the same fire, and between the two stinks there was not all that much to choose. With the day's work done, Marcus read aloud to her from Galatians, St Paul's condemnation of the flesh. And this, he told her, is exactly what is wrong with the world, outside Cuneus.

'Now the works of the flesh are manifest, which are these.' Marcus read fast, as if endeavouring by the cadence of his voice to race the sun, as its light drifted beyond the purple rim of the horizon. 'Adultery, fornication, uncleanness, idolatry, witchcraft, hatred, variance, emulations, wrath, strife, seditions, heresies, envying, murders, drunkenness– '

The Latin words as they clanged against one another -*irae, rixae, dissensiones, sectae, invidiae, homicidia, ebriatates* – brought vivid pictures to Gilda's mind of Rome, images of persons and happenings: Stridor's lewd giggle, Serena's voice, cruel in that upper room, Stilicho's ever-present awareness that he lived by the sharp edge of his sword. The Latin rolling off Marcus's tongue – wrath, strife, seditions, heresies – went out past the chill ripples of the darkening sea. They had come together, had they not, here, on this island, to discard such things.

'But surely, in the same epistle, doesn't it say,' Gilda protested, 'no, don't turn the roll for me. No need. I can remember. "For, brethren, ye have been called unto liberty, but use not liberty for an occasion to the flesh, but by love serve one another. For the law is fulfilled in one word, even in this, *Thou shalt love thy neighbour as thyself.*" Isn't that true, as well? By love, serve one another – I mean, even more true?'

'What you have just been saying is the other side of what I read,' said Marcus gloomily, as if weighed into the ground by the long catalogue: adultery, fornication, uncleanness, lasciviousness, idolatry. 'Some think it safer to emphasise one side, some the other.'

'One cancels out the other,' said Gilda, as if at long last she had begun teaching him. 'The law is fulfilled in one word. Love thy neighbour.'

That evening argument, with the wind rising off the sea, and voices in the dark become intimate, was Gilda's own private revelation. In the world they had both inhabited – still lived in and could never escape – there was love and love. One man after another had used her body, beginning with that ship's captain in Marseilles, the first of all, and she herself only a little girl. *Fornicatio* – twisting about with red faces to reach an ecstatic relief. And what always came after – always? *Irae, rixae, homicidia.* Lust led to horror.

Love then, whatever this other love the book speaks of may be, that is the love I demand, she decided, as at Marcus's side she watched the sunset wind flutter across the water, as if in chase of something invisible. His not touching me now, and I know he wants to, is even an expression of this other love, though a strange one. He treats me as he wishes I would treat him. Men in the grip of lust are devils – but we women are less likely to be their victims than their mercenary tormentors, and you, Gilda accused herself, have often enough been both. *Meretrix.* Prostitute. On this calm evening I deny neither word nor deed. I admit my past, but I reject it. By love serve one another. And if I now reach out and touch his hand, what does that make me? I should like, she told herself, to renew my virginity. I should like to give myself to him, as if for the first time. When Gilda touched his hand and involved her fingers with his, Marcus did not take his hand away.

'Time I went up and set the fire going,' he said, glancing up over his shoulder at the cliff.

'Later. Come here. No need to be awkward. Come here.'

Marcus's neighbours on the nearest inhabited island, the place that on clear days was a smudge on the eastern horizon, had begun to ask themselves, as they plied their nets within sight of Cuneus, whether there was one living creature there, or two. Could the hermit, whenever their backs were turned, have a familiar spirit there – an angel?

These days, Marcus never touched her, he was drifting back into his bad old habit of gazing right through her. They could tell the passage of time only by the shadow cast by the big crucifix at noon. Soon after the day when the shadow was at its shortest, the fishermen might arrive – Gilda meanwhile ate dried figs and made the best of it. The feast of Christmas was in those days a new one – a popular novelty. Anastasius, the last Pope, had won over the patriarchs of Alexandria, Antioch and Jerusalem to celebrating the birth of Christ on 25 December, and Honorius had persuaded his brother, reigning as Emperor in Constantinople, to do the same, so all through the Christian world there was unanimity at least about the date of Christmas. Marcus, on what he guessed might be the date celebrated the birth of the Redeemer a little selfconsciously, he and Gilda reading by turns from the gospel of St Matthew – the pregnant young virgin in the stable, the star in the east, the wise men, Marcus forthright as if addressing troops on parade, Gilda with dramatic expression, as if to an applauding crowd.

For the festive meal they added boiled mussels to their dried fish, and afterwards Gilda went, alone, to the far end of the beach, and was discreetly sick. So much for Christmas. And she came back along the beach hollow-hearted, but having made up her mind to amuse Marcus somehow. Gilda was swaggering towards him, a fat woman come with a basket of produce from the many-storeyed market in the Forum.

'Apples – juicy ripe apples! Lettuce to send you to sleep – fresh lettuce! New-made bread, all hot and soft!' As she cried her bread, Gilda pushed up her titties, saucily, as Roman market women always did – as much as to say, hot and soft like these of mine, and I dare you to touch. '*Ciceri* – chickpeas! The *ciceri* of Cicero!' At the gesture with the breasts, Marcus had tried to look disapproving. At the old joke about Cicero he laughed – a great patriotic philosopher called Chickpea!

'Marcus,' Gilda asked him pointedly, before the good humour faded from his face, 'is making other people laugh a sin?' He shook his head. But she had brought Rome back. There had been a Roman swagger. And her loud Roman accent – knowing, ironic, exaggerated, unimpressed by anything – brought painfully into Marcus's mind the face of Octavian, the red-nosed usurer who was his father.

Sometimes in the company of stiff-backed Roman *honestiores* who were beholden to him because they owed him money, Octavian would jocosely imitate the market cries, particularly the bawdier ones. A money-lender? What of it? A senator? But also a jolly old fellow, who had never lost the common touch. And has come back to me, here and now, thought Marcus, she has brought him back. From now on until I die, I shall never escape him.

On Epiphany, a calm day, bright and still, cold for these latitudes, the greatest number of fishing boats that Marcus had ever seen approached Cuneus. A man in the foremost boat stood up in the bows, and gave some joyous blasts on a conch. Scaring away the fish, thought Marcus, yet nobody seems to mind. This is a holiday.

'Stand where they can all see you,' Marcus told Gilda. 'After all, they are our friends. How could we live here, on Cuneus, without them?'

In the large boat that carried the conch-player, propped up amidships, was an old man, well wrapped-up. Dangling outside his cloak Marcus could see a heavy pectoral cross of enamelled iron. They were fetching over the bishop. The old man, despite the convivial mood, wore the pious look that everyone expected of him, but underneath, as Gilda could see, he was a good-natured but shrewd old peasant.

The fishermen liked their bishop because his Latin was no different from their own, hit-and-miss and peppered with dialect words. He could no longer see well enough to read, but what did that matter when he knew his Sacramentary by heart? His long sight, though, was as good as ever, and well before the keel grated on the sand he had picked out this woman confronting him on the beach. When they spoke so much about their hermit, they had not mentioned a concubine.

The old bishop stumped with his crook up the black sand, not sparing Gilda a second glance but holding out his hand to Marcus, palm down, ring extended, while the fishermen trailed up and fanned across the beach and looked on and took note. Several had brought their wives along – wives in the archipelago usually feared the sea – and among these women there were uncharitable whispers.

Marcus had almost shaken hands Roman fashion as if greeting a brother officer, but remembered in the nick of time that a bishop represented authority of a different sort. As a token of submission to the church – and yes, he told himself, entire submission – he kissed the cross set in the ring. Here on Cuneus the bishop of the diocese was his *dominus*.

'And your angel?' asked the old bishop quietly, in the moment when Marcus's head came down over his hand. Marcus, perturbed, stood erect a little too quickly, and looked the old man in the eye. The bishop was smiling indulgently, much as a grandfather chiding a boy who made mischief but was not irredeemably bad. 'Did she fall from the skies?'

'She came to me from the sea,' Marcus answered, not letting his face relax into any smile of welcome. 'Washed ashore,' he was telling them all, in a voice that carried, 'more dead than alive.'

Gilda noticed that this morning Marcus had dropped entirely the clerically-deferential accent picked up at Nola – she had never liked it – and was speaking out again like a Roman officer who expected to be believed and obeyed. Perhaps the old bishop did not much care for the forthright way he was being answered, but then, thought Gilda, you must take men as they are.

'You were at Nola, my son, with Paulinus?'

'At Nola.'

'We have heard nothing but good at Paulinus. And before that? A soldier, I am quite sure.'

'A soldier.'

The bishop nodded. He walked across to the little shrine, further away from the throng, beckoning Marcus to follow. The others kept back, the fishermen and their wives staring at Gilda, and a few edging closer to her, though none said a word to her. They are treating me, thought Gilda, as if I had been dropped here, on to this island, by stage machinery. I am on stage, and at the centre of attention, but the man who devised this comedy has forgotten to give me any lines.

How can I convince this important old man who ignored me that Marcus did good in bringing me back to life? The two men were talking in earnest, and it irked her not to hear. Whatever they were discussing would affect her too.

'You seek ordination?' the bishop had asked, extending one

plump old hand to touch the driftwood cross, as if to judge what kind of wood it was made of.

'I have sought nothing here on Cuneus but my own salvation,' answered Marcus, still a little too much the unbending Roman officer perhaps. 'But the fishermen over there have no priest, as you know, and feel the lack of one. The idea came from them.'

'And all the long while you have lived here alone, so they tell me, you have gone on reading the gospels. Gone on praying, despite the woman.'

'I also keep the beacon alight.'

'Ah yes. The beacon. A good work. And works, as well as faith, are required of us. Faith.' He cleared his throat. 'There is also grace, don't forget. Perhaps you are touched by it. Works alone, though good, are never enough. There has to be grace. And what did you do for them, over there, at Nola?'

'Plastered walls.'

And hark at the proud way he gave that answer, thought Gilda, who had moved near enough to be included, though the old bishop still ignored her. He is holding his head up, she told herself, on my account, wearing the armour of his rank and class, even though to the old man, a peasant but a Christian bishop, pride is a sin. She was by now so close that to give Marcus his answer, the bishop was obliged to stare blindly over Gilda's head at the blue sky.

'The canon against the matrimony of priests has been law in the church for over a hundred years. Though in more primitive times, not so, and in holy writ,' he pursed his old lips sadly, 'they even speak of married bishops.' Cornered by Gilda's approach, he decided to smile at both of them – the professionally tolerant smile of a busy priest used to dealing, every day, with weaknesses of the flesh.

'Even here, in this diocese,' he went on blandly, 'the canon is not universally observed,' and he looked with peasant slyness at Marcus's impassive face, 'or enforced.'

He needs a priest fit for work here among the islands. He is trying hard to give me, thought Marcus, a way out. But meanwhile is judging me, because the presence here of Gilda is a surprise. As priest here, and with a concubine tolerated by the bishop, I should be under his thumb. After this they would never have me back at Nola, not that Gilda could ever stand the life there, either. This old bishop is not only good, he is clever. Though what is he asking of me? Whether he knows it or not, I should be wallowing in sin.

The fishermen, though keeping their distance, could tell by now that Marcus and the bishop were not agreeing. Their womenfolk, after hearing so much in praise of the hermit of Cuneus, and seeing him now for the first time, ragged hair and beard, torn garment, and there, in front of them all, the proof that he was no saint, had begun turning against Marcus.

'Who is she exactly, again?' asked the old man, in an undertone? If he wants to know, thought Gilda, furious, why not address the question to me?

'As I said, a castaway.'

'There is also the question of vocation – or, if you like it better, of worthiness. I had heard you spoken of until now only as a hermit. Do you feel a strong call to be a priest? Here, in this wild place? With this woman, though. Because I think whatever happens that you cannot cast her off.'

He is cleverly making further life with me on Cuneus sound impossible, thought Gilda. Should I be glad? Do I love Marcus enough to cleave to him? He is an impressive man, and I admire him. Though when he has no island to play with, will he go on being the man I have known? They talk glibly, these two, of casting-off. But what if I cast him off?

The fisherman were beginning to shuffle. By the look of it, they were losing him, this man who kept the light going for them, and with his potent prayers fought the local volcanic demons.

'The answer to what you ask is not only mine,' said Marcus, to Gilda's surprise. 'It has to be hers.'

'And her name?'

'Gilda.'

'A believer?'

'You had better ask her.'

'Gilda – he says that is your name – do you want to stay on here?' asked the bishop.

'How can I say?' she answered elusively. 'Marcus came here to Cuneus of his own free will. So he must find his own answer. He must decide. And I am not going to lay claim to beliefs I may not possess, even to help him.'

She is honest, anyway, thought the old bishop. Not quite the slut I took her for. A castaway? That I find hard to believe – but would such a woman come to Cuneus of set purpose? Are they in collusion? That is the real question. She talks like a Roman. Did she know him before? They are fond of one another.

As these thoughts went rattling through his mind, the old man put a paternal hand on Marcus's shoulder. Whenever my own father did that, Marcus reflected – pretending, that is, to touch my shoulder with affection – I knew for certain that he was trying to trick me. Let me keep in mind that this old man is someone else – my father in God. He knows as well as I do that God is watching over all of us. In the presence of God, lies are meaningless, trickery is pointless. I must find him an honest answer. But what can it be?

'Yes. Stare at me as much as you like. I am an important man. I am a bishop,' said the old man with a twinkle in his eye. He might have been a countryman, telling a story at a winter fireside. 'And you, Marcus, have I dare say been even more important. A Roman officer? High in rank? You have the manner. I came here having in mind to ordain you, Marcus Curtius, by the laying on of hands. As sanctified hands were once placed on my head, and on the head of the bishop who ordained me, back to St Peter, who holds the keys of heaven. There are other sacraments too. Ordination is a sacred change in life, but not the only change. This is a holy day, a festival. Epiphany, a good day for a good deed. What if I married you?'

Gilda looked breathless with astonishment, as if ready to jump in the winter sea and swim her hardest to get away from him. From both of them. The bishop looked pleased with himself. He might have been a village boy with dusty knees, standing up and smiling after having won a game of knucklebones.

Marcus muttered, 'You must give me time to consider.' He would never, decided the bishop, make a priest on a small island, not supple enough, too craggy, too much himself. In an island parish, who wants a fanatic?

'Days? Weeks?' the bishop asked indulgently. 'The good people who brought me over would perhaps like to row me back before sunset.'

Marcus was never in fact given a chance to say in so many words that he wished or did not wish to marry, nor was Gilda. Word got about among the fishermen, and they began to make a feast of it on the shore, showing off the rarities they had brought with them, lobsters, a giant sea-bass, an octopus battered on a rock into tenderness. One reason for a festive meal was as good as another. At least, thought Gilda, if Marcus marries me, he will have to take me away from this place. I have never been married before; I suppose every woman should be married once. Gilda was looking at herself, scrupulously watching the way she behaved, and surprised by what she was doing, as though she was already someone else.

After the cermony, Cuneus was abandoned, the iron basket on the clifftop, full of ashes, left to rust. They rowed Marcus and Gilda – bride and groom – and their few possessions across to their own larger, inhabited island, a place with squat little houses hunched against the hot wind from Africa, and in and around their houses the usual smells, as in Britain, thought Gilda, of children and animals and household rubbish. The smell of their dried fish stuck up on dry branches clear of the dogs made her regret a sight she would never set eyes on again – of white spray coming over the reef.

With some jesting and blowing of conches the married pair were left for the night on a straw mattress in an empty house. Have I ever refused a man? Gilda wondered. I feel so distant from him. Now he can without guilt – now he has a right to – no doubt he will. But Marcus left her alone.

The simple fact is, Gilda told herself, as she lay there while he slept, he is a saint and I am a whore. I came between him and the life he particularly sought. Did I need so much to have him make love to me? I did it out of vanity, out of habit. Affection for him too, perhaps. And I wanted to show my power over him. If I never felt a man inside me again, would it break me? Can I live without love?

No, never – but, perhaps, some other kind of love.

A few days later, a trading vessel came in unexpectedly, blown off its course, and took on board a mixed cargo – dried fish, capers cured in brine, pumice stone, goatskins, decorative shells. Marcus and Gilda were given the chance of a passage to Carthage, and Marcus to Gilda's surprise did not argue but took it. He was stupefied by what had happened. He was letting his life take any direction that might offer.

3

'How many mouths are there in Rome?' asked Alaric of Ataulf, his clever brother-in-law. For information of this sort you always went to Ataulf.

'Men, women and children? They never have been counted. But say, a thousand a thousand times over,' answered Ataulf. A thousand was about the largest figure a Visigoth could grasp. There were a thousand horsemen in a Visigoth cavalry brigade.

A thousand thousand, thought Alaric, putting a great strain on his mind. He admired his brother-in-law all the more for being able to take in such numbers. He went on to speak, however, with all the cheerfulness of a man who in his mind's eye now sees it all clearly.

'And all these mouths open, like birds in the nest, for doles of food shipped across from Africa? The great walls of Rome, then, will simply keep the Romans from flying out of the city in their hunger, to search the countryside for food.'

Alaric in his time had seen a great deal of death. He did not really believe that a dead man could rise from his tomb – come back again out of hell, talk with his friends, and ascend to heaven, simply because he happened also to be God – and Arianism did not oblige him to. Ours, he thought with satisfaction, is not a religion for the sinful and the despairing. The assurance of eternal life means so much more to those dupes in Ravenna because their life on earth is coming to pieces about their ears. (Where had Ataulf gone? To count up shipments of African corn? No doubt. Alaric smiled grimly. The dog at his feet snapped at a fly).

Though if, the king decided, it is God's will that I rule over Italy, and most of them in Italy are devout Catholics, then as their ruler I can reach their minds only through their religion. I shall tolerate their differences from ourselves. I shall respect their churches. I am not going to offend them.

He shouted for Ataulf and his clever brother-in-law with the bright eyes and vulpine broken nose was not far away. Ataulf had known that this royal meditation though it might last an hour, would lead to decisions. Ataulf had brought in with him a small hinged tablet, made like a book, with four ivory leaves. The waxed surface of each page could be scratched with words.

'I have something here to make you laugh,' he announced to Alaric.

'Read it out to me.'

The Visigoth King could in fact read Latin well enough, both block capitals and cursive scribble, but Alaric had never quite overcome the notion instilled in him by his swordsman father, that reading and writing were womanish.

'*A decree of the Emperor Honorius, addressed to Olympius, Master of the Offices.* Honorius of course counts for nothing in this, Olympius is putting words in his mouth, as he always does. A spy brought this in at dawn. Listen and laugh. *We forbid those who are enemies of the Catholic religion to serve as soldiers in our palace. We will have no connection of any kind with a man who differs from us in faith.*'

'If Honorius has no Arian mercenaries and no pagan Huns either,' said Alaric, 'then he will have very few soldiers. What else? Was that the only joke?'

'Three imperial promotions to commander-in-chief. Listen to these. Cavalry, Turfilio; infantry, Varanes; household troops, Vigilantius. Ever heard of any of them?'

'No. Have you?'

'Nobody has, though I bet they are all good Catholics. Ataulf was prompting him to laugh again, but Alaric looked grave.

'Then my decision is right, and blessed by God. We bypass Ravenna, we make straight for the City. So much is clear to me. We shall take Rome, and squeeze it of its juice like a bunch of grapes in a press. Let us go now, and hear what our council have to say. And if they differ,' at last he laughed, 'tell them otherwise.'

Serena, for so many years the most influential woman in the empire, lived nowadays in Rome, alone, a long way from the centre of power. She had taken over what used to be Stilicho's mansion there, and seldom went further from the house than an evening stroll in the formal garden, with its statues and cypresses. Serena's world had shrunk to this one vast, bare, slave-infested dwelling. She shut her door in the face of all visitors, whether old friends, or agents of Olympius pretending to be old friends.

Through servants' gossip, news crept out of her lonely monologues, her tantrums, her blind rages. Those obliged to tell her of Stilicho's death had been almost too afraid to give her the bad news. As they spoke, they watched her face, but to all appearances the news made little impression on her, as if the famous soldier, the statesman, the unfaithful husband, had ceased to exist for her a long while before.

The figure in her past upon whom Serena sometimes brooded as she paced about her house and garden, and for whom in the still of the night she felt, at times, a sense of loss difficult to endure, was not Stilicho the general, the white-haired public figure, but the upstart young Vandal guardsman, who had not only won her heart but gained the good opinion of her father, the great Theodosius. She would bring to mind the days when she herself had been the Emperor's favourite child. He had taught her Roman virtue. He had taught her government.

As she grew older and more lonely, Serena changed around what she was bringing to mind of her own past, so as to forget what most had hurt her. She was not yet so mad as to inhabit a world totally inside her own mind, but if her slaves were to be believed she was moving that way.

She was in the eyes of all Rome, still the Princess Serena, a recluse, yes, but a woman great in her day. Official Rome however had of late begun to fear her. These were times when morbid fears might overwhelm all sober consideration: when craziness could become stark fact.

The hierarchy in Roman officialdom was strict. *Illustres* came first – officials of the rank of Olympius and those closest to him. Lower down the scale were the *Spectabiles*. With the Emperor Honorius in Ravenna, all the *Illustres* had gone there from Rome on one pretext or another, so as to be near the source of power. As Alaric's army approached and the crisis intensified, Rome the largest city in the world was ruled merely by *Spectabiles* – officials not of the first rank, men who has failed in life to climb the greasy pole.

Three of these mediocrities were in charge – Pompeianus, an ostentatious Christian, and known to take a poor view of Serena's paganism; Basil, the provincial governor, a silent Spaniard and perhaps a pagan himself, but cautious about admitting it – or indeed of admitting anything. In a bureaucracy a man can make a career out of having no ideas and never admitting anything. And John, chief of the imperial notaries, an efficient and small-minded little busybody.

All three were ruled by precedent; they waited for orders. Now, they found themselves governing Rome, with an enemy approaching, and no one higher in rank to tell them what to do next. Except Serena perhaps. She was an anomaly – a member of the imperial family, and once a great politician in her own right, who sat at home and took no part whatever in the life of the city. Pompeianus, Basil and John were aware of their own incompetence, and if they failed they wanted a scapegoat. They talked themselves into it.

And in one sense the danger they obscuredly feared was real enough. Inside the walls of Rome there were tens of thousands of slaves, far too many of them Visigoths. Among the slaves in Rome the rumour had spread that Alaric was coming to free them. Being slaves they would of course need a leader. Someone of rank, someone hostile to Rome's present government. Someone with known links to the barbarians – married to one, perhaps. Someone seeking revenge.

The Senate in Rome, though but a shadow of its historic self, preserved all its old titles and procedures. On the Capitol, there was a session to discuss the threat to the state. Many Senators sitting in the places once occupied by the great men of Rome's past must have known very well, as the three *Spectabiles* tried to pile suspicion on Serena's grey head, that they were listening to nonsense. Yet when the Prefect, Pompeianus, a man a little to fat for his height, rose to urge in quasi-Ciceronian sentences that Serena, adopted daughter of the last Emperor, be strangled lest she open the gates of Rome to the advancing barbarians, there were no incredulous guffaws. From Serena's one-time friends a deadly silence reached him.

Some other speakers – men anxious to rid themselves of disrepute – were aping what he had said, even copying this words and phrases. Should the gates of Rome be opened by a traitor? Not if they could help it.

Among those who sat ominously silent was old Octavian Curtius, the usurer. He was in Rome because in troubled times, values went up and down, there was financial business to be done. Fools in a crisis sold, and wise men who kept their heads made a profit. He was not disgusted at what they were saying about poor old Serena. If the fools now supposed that killing one old woman would save them, then, thought the old moneylender, let us have a human sacrifice and be done with it. But I for one will not sanction it. Before the vote was taken, he slipped away.

One of Flavius Stilicho's numerous freedmen, who kept a wineshop in the shadow of the mansion, and still had a duty of *obsequium* to the widow of his benefactor, brought Serena warning before the executioners had time to arrive. The old woman laughed in his face.

'Open the gates to Alaric – with hands like these?' Serena lifted up two old bony, arthritic hands, heavy with rings. 'Tell me, fellow, whch gate shall I open for Alaric? Pray instruct me in my new duty. The Porta Aurelia? The Porta Flaminia? From which direction is Alaric planning to arrive. Do you happen to know? Across the Apennines? Perhaps the Senate will be so kind as to tell me.'

The freedman, in his wine-stained apron looked uneasily at the old princess, not sure whether the irony he was hearing from her withered lips might not be madness. Then he reminded himself I served here as cellarman for years. I know them all. In the house there are no new faces. The lady Serena never goes out, never sees anyone – how can she be conspiring?

'They are all leaving the Senate in solemn procession.' Officials, soldiers, lictors. A Christian priest even – '

'Obliging of them. And when they arrive at my door, just inform them, will you, that I shall not want their Christian priest.'

'But mistress – *domina*. What I am trying to say is this – you still have time to escape.'

'*Quorsum?*' she screamed, as if the same idea had flickered in her own mind, as a momentary torment. '*Where to?*'

'You might be safer with your other nephew,' suggested the man from the wineshop, choking at his own audacity. 'The Emperor, I mean, who rules in Constantinople – the Emperor of the East.'

'Drag myself off as a mendicant to that wearisome young man?' Serena screeched. 'It's his place to come and see me. If they had looked after me properly, those nephews of mine, all this would never have happened.'

Serena's voice moved from sarcastic rage to querulousness. As if this freedman were her last friend on earth, she moved her head closer, and became confidential. 'You see, my good man, the simple fact is this. For me, for all of us, Rome was everything. If Rome goes there is nowhere left. The world is withering away, shrinking to nothing as I stand here. If all one asks of life is to escape, there is only heaven. And somehow I could never quite bring myself to believe in their heaven.'

'Or at least hide,' the man whispered, convinced by this time of her innocence, though he could not have explained why. 'Come with me down to the cellars. I know those cellars – they will lose themselves. I'll find you an empty wine-butt – '

He was our cellarman, she recalled, until Stilicho set him up in a wineshop. I remember. And a veritable barbarian, Flavius Stilicho, always manumitting the best of our slaves, as if he could not bear to see servile faces around him. If you have a good man in your service, I used to say, why be in such a hurry to let him go? And now he supples my domestics below stairs with their cheap table-wine. So of course he knows all about empty wine-butts. Serena was smiling, had already begun living in the past. And is a brave old thing, the cellarman was thinking. If only I could be sure of her keeping her mouth shut as the barrel was tilted and rolled, as it would have to be, I could even move her out of here. And none of them the wiser.

'Nothing undignified!' exclaimed Serena, in yet another voice, as if she were full of authority, and had made up her mind. The notion had sprung into her mind: my father, the Emperor! My husband, the great Flavius Stilicho! A generous fool, Stilicho, always manumitting slaves, and quite unfaithful. They would have stood here and defended me with their drawn swords, those two great men – two against all Rome. There are no such men any more. This man, this cellarman, was a good servant, loyal, but does he wear a sword? Am I to cower, thought Serena, indignantly, inside a wine barrel? And have them take off the barrel-head, and find me crouching, and stand around, jeering? Their faces!

'An Emperor's daughter – hide?' She wiped away the spittle, unselfconsciously, with the back of an arthritic hand, crooking her fingers carefully to avoid the scrape of rings against her mouth.

'Rome's new potentates wish to commit yet another crime? Do they? Then let them. They can hardly do worse to me, here in my own house, with their lictors and their priest, than they did to poor Julia.'

To the freedman's bewilderment, the old woman kicked an embroidered stool nearer, sat down on it – lower than her chair – bowed her head, and began to shed tears for Julia. At the courtyard gate there were voices. With their usual instinct for dodging trouble, the domestic slaves had vanished. The freedman, too, slipped off the way he knew best, through the cellars. She refused to help herself? Then why linger? Serena sat there waiting, alone, still sobbing for Julia.

Over and above the sound of her own sobs as they filled her head came the crunch of soldiers' ironshod boots on marble – a distinctive noise which had often enough echoed through this high-ceilinged mansion in the days when Stilicho had his headquarters here. They were opening the double door of her room, to push their way in uninvited. Serena, before these intruders could enter, began patting her cheeks with a piece of silk, so they would have no reason to suppose that her tears were on their account.

The man who had opened her door, a lictor, made way for the three city officials.

Serena, her wits sharpened by a lifetime at court, knew them at a glance for what they were – oppressive to subordinates, fawning on those in power. One after the other she looked them directly in the eye, and this checked them. John, chief of the imperial notaries, cleared his throat, and bade her stand up, as though sitting down in the presence of men like themselves were a breach of etiquette. Serena took no notice.

Since all this had better be scrupulously legal, Pompeianus read out the Senate's death decree, and with much the same emphasis, thought Serena, feeling remote from all this, even amused by it, as a little clerk running anxiously through his laundry list. In my day, she permitted herself to recall, at least Rome had style.

When Pompeianus with a significant glance under his heavy brows arrived at the words, *'in case she open the gates of Rome,'*

Serena made her first comment, a stagey laugh, but the laugh became strident and went out of control. From the looks they exchanged the three *Spectabiles* were trying to make each other believe that her wild laughter was a sign of guilt.

'Stand up, woman – stand up!' reiterated John, chief of the imperial notaries. Basil, prudently silent, was shoving his knuckles, as a timely reminder, into the ribs of the hard-bitten *decurio* who was to carry out the actual deed.

'Just tell me, would you, why should I?' asked Serena, in the voice of an arrogant but puzzled girl. Her hectic laugh had come to an end. She was wiping her mouth yet again with the back of her hand. The gesture – which she would never have permitted herself at court – had become a bad habit. When next she spoke, she was young again; the back of her hand had wiped away time. She was living, not here, but in ceremonious Constantinople.

'I perceive you are all officials low in rank. Not an *Illustris* among you! And I? Am I not the daughter of an Emperor? I know you are none of you familiar with the procedures of the imperial court. How could you be? But should you not be genuflecting? Here in my private room, I do not absolutely insist that you prostrate yourselves. It is not a throne room. But when men like yourselves come into my presence you should bow the head and bend the knee.'

Such was the power over their minds of the petrified system to which they had looked all their lives for promotion that the three officials yielded to the old woman's rebuke and bobbed their heads, before helping each other to push forward the *decurio*. He was a man all muscle, with a low forehead, and he came towards Serena with a half-smile on his lips like a sexual encouragement.

Wring the neck of an old woman? Nothing in it. Like twisting the neck of an old hen. He wondered if she might scream. That could be upsetting. He gripped the cord he had brought with him tautly between left hand and right.

As if to spite them, Serena went to her death in perfect silence, keeping command of herself to the very moment when her spirit fled. That dashed their spirits a little, but left them more than ever convinced that she must have been a traitor.

Roman weather had taken away the clearcut newness from

Claudian's bust in the Forum – everything new in Rome was rubbed down sooner or later by the humid winters. But the gilt lettering – CLAUDIUS CLAUDIANUS – had withstood the years and still shone out. *To the most glorious of poets*. Rome's last great writer; the Forum's last commemorative bust.

The literary men as they passed into the library may now and then have glanced enviously at this confirmation of his fame, but they were occupied these days less in scrutinising a text or appraising a contemporary as in finding some way or other to appease the gnaw of hunger. Under the arcade the shabbier of Rome's pleaders were kicking their heels and tightening their belts. They too were feeling the pinch.

The fish-tanks upstairs in the market were long since empty. Every scrap of trodden vegetable had been picked up by someone and made into soup. The market cats had disappeared into cooking pots, the scavenging dogs had themselves been scavenged, and the rats and mice were fast following them. One or two maniacs with wooden ration tickets would still turn up, and wait in patience to carry off the oil and pork and corn that had always been waiting for them. Blank-faced, simply unable to believe that the State, which had always fed them, should so abruptly be leaving them to starve.

Round and round the walls a myriad of Visigoth horse were endlessly patrolling, some of them clad in skins. Very little got past these horsemen. Corn-ships no longer came up the Tiber from Ostia. No produce-wagons or herds of beef cattle reached Rome from the Campagna. Even single messengers, moving cautiously at night, had been caught. The blockade would soon bite deeper, but already there was food only for those who had money, and today, in the open space in front of the empty market, rioters had assembled.

When soldiers came down, half-heartedly, from the Palatine, to break up the shouting mob, they were met with brickbats and sarcastic cries of, 'Go and fight the Visigoths!' The soldiers up to now had always enjoyed stamping on the toes of rioters and hammering their heads – a game which they were bound to win. But today, as half-heartedly they struck out left and right, they looked sheepish.

Rome was hungry, yet her two ambassadors, Basil the provincial governor and John, master of the notaries, did not admit to any such weakness. They dismounted halfway up Janiculum, since the Visigoth King had made it clear that he was to be approached on foot. As they walked uphill slowly, solemnly, their faces were set rigid, aping a confidence they did not feel.

Overtaking them, encircling, raising dust and clashing weapons as they came and went from Alaric's camp, moved barbarian horsemen, all subject to an invisible discipline, and in such masses that the ambassadors slowly became unnerved.

The pungent odour of horse manure, the rancid stink of barbarian sweat, were obnoxious to their well-bred nostrils. Worse still was the odour, drifting downhill to them as they plodded upwards, of roasting meat. Alaric was giving his guard a feast from an intercepted herd of bullocks. Though not as hungry as the plebs of Rome, Basil and John did not want to be reminded just now of roast beef.

With heads accostingly high, and walking a little more slowly than they need, the two of them came closer to the bannered pavilion, outside which Alaric awaited them, unarmed, unsmiling, with his councillors, headed by Ataulf, at a respectful distance, as if obliged to stand there but not expecting to be consulted. The ambassadors had been fearful, but their fears were ebbing. Alaric would surely respect them. They represented Rome.

Whimpering, but not yet starving, decided Ataulf, as he watched their faces come closer. As for King Alaric, he was looking at the two ambassadors as a man alone in a forest observes game. His great hound, Filimer, grumbled, and John, master of the notaries, who feared dogs, gave a visible twitch.

Enunciating with care, in case Alaric's grasp of Latin might be weak, Basil launched into his set speech – brief, but thought out for effect.

'The Roman people are prepared –' and Basil lifted one hand above his head in the rhetorical gesture that signified a measured generosity, ' – to make peace on moderate terms. But they are even more prepared,' and here he clenched his fist, 'for war!'

Ataulf, standing with the councillors, found it hard to keep a straight face. But King Alaric remained impassive.

Basil had raised his voice, as a school-bred orator should, to drive his main point home. 'We have arms in our hand.' His broad gesture reached outwards as if to take in the splendidly complete view of Rome from the vantage point of Janiculum – palaces, temples, gardens, apartment blocks, sprawled across seven hills: a million hungry mouths huddled within one encircling wall. 'And from long use,' Basil went on, a reasonable man at last, and opening both hands outwards to prove it, 'we have no reason to dread the result of battle.'

Alaric's deep, cruel, enormous laugh broke in upon the solemnities, and Filimer growled a canine accompaniment. So they had decided, had they, these Romans, to treat the King of the Visigoths as if he were a peasant idiot? Very well. To their condescending oratory, a peasant answer, one that would bewilder them.

'Thick grass is easier to mow than thin.'

Seeing the stupefaction on the faces of the ambassadors, and knowing why, from Alaric's councillors came an audible chuckle. These two nervous city-dwellers had never in their lives, used a sickle, or in all likelihood any other tool whatever, except a pen. Into Alaric's mind as he gave them their answer had come a consoling image, thick grass along the water meadows, the sickle blade swung, the stalks sheared off clean where they clustered thickest. Thus with many-peopled Rome.

'A moderate peace?' said Alaric, touching finger to chin, as if considering. 'You shall deliver up to me,' and he spoke in the reasonable tone of a man who meant to deal by the Romans fairly, 'all the gold in your city. All the silver. All the moveable property inside the circuit of the walls. Everything the city contains that I can carry away with me. And into the bargain – all your barbarian slaves. Do this at my bidding – right away – all of it – or the siege goes on.'

'But what are you leaving us?' protested Basil.

Alaric looked at them both in turn. Basil returned his stare with bold incredulity, but John, who had met Goths before, and knew something of their speech, felt the marrow of his bones dissolve.

'*Saivalos*,' answered the Visigoth King. As he spoke that one word, he turned on his heel. The embassy was over. The heavy curtain of his pavilion swung to and fro where it had been pushed aside by his broad shoulders. His councillors turned their backs on Basil and John, and followed King Alaric inside.

The two ambassadors stood there crestfallen. There was no one to speak to, and nothing left to say. Alaric had not even deigned to give his last answer to them – that one word – in Latin.

'What is he trying to tell us – what does it mean?' Basil whispered. He was frantic with fury.

'*Saivalos* means souls. He intends to take away everything material and movable that we have in Rome, our gold, our property, our slaves. But leave us our souls.'

Inside Rome, the last public stocks of food had long since been eaten up. No more food from private hoards was being offered, even at extortionate prices. The poorest and hungriest were dropping and dying in the streets, and there was no room inside the walls to bury them. Were the gardens of the rich to be turned into cemeteries? In narrow alleys abandoned bodies decayed. A stink filled the city, and pestilence broke out.

Yet when even the very rich were going hungry, there were others in the city, ruffians, who walked the streets by twos and threes, well-armed, plump of cheek and pink of face. Their mouths were greasy, their eyes furtive, and other men avoided them.

In the deserted Forum, against the wall where official market prices used to be displayed, some wag had nailed up a whitewashed board with lettering the colour of blood.

Pretium pone carni humanae
Set a price on human flesh.

Rome had written her own epitaph.

No army from Ravenna appeared astonishingly over the horizon. No miraculous balls of fire dropped down from heaven to incinerate Alaric, in answer to their prayers. But surely in the eyes of these barbarians, the Roman Senate still counted for something? The Senators went in solemn body out of the Aurelian Gate, and climbed Janiculum.

Once the Senators had finished their speeches, Alaric made them undergo a long royal silence. When he knew for certain that all were sweating, Alaric answered them tremendously. 'This, then, is what you will do for me, you Romans. First I will tell you what is to be your ransom. Afterwards I will tell you what political concessions my merciful attitude is to gain me from your Emperor. If my political demands are not met, then our treaty is instantly void.'

At the lift of a finger a young Arian priest, a good Latinist, advanced to a point midway between Alaric and the Senators, and began to read, clearly but without much expression, from a papyrus Ataulf had handed him.

'Five thousand pounds weight of gold.'

There was a gasp.

'Thirty thousand pounds weight of silver.'

This time mouths hung open. Could there be so much gold and silver in all Rome? The Senators, *honestiores* who seldom in their lives had paid taxes, were chilled by an ugly premonition.

As if privately he considered the next item frivolous, the priest's voice faltered.

'Speak up, man,' boomed Alaric. 'It says there, three thousand silk tunics.'

'Three thousand silk tunics.'

Both Alaric and Ataulf particularly liked that item. There were in the Visigoth army three thousand officers. Let their wives and their sweethearts go clad in silk at last, their nagging turned to momentary joy.

'Three thousand scarlet hides,' the priest went on, with an almost imperceptible shrug. All that expensive red leather? wondered the Senators. Crazy barbarians! But Alaric had in mind red tilts for the wagons of the nobility – a distinction that would please them enormously and cost him nothing.

'Three thousand pounds of pepper,' announced the priest more cheefully, as if anyway he approved of that one: spice for the meat slaughtered this winter by Visigoth families left behind in Pannonia. The folks at home had not been forgotten. And how they would like to laugh in my face, thought Alaric, these soft and civilised Senators, yet they dare not. Silk and leather and pepper are sops to my followers, but their gold and silver will be the sinews of my war.

'But I cannot bear Ravenna! Not a day more!'

Strewn near the tree were cushions, needlework, a ball, a book. From the sandy shore, amid the pines, the two women could see, far off, the tumbled spread of the parvenu city, important buildings of new white stone amid empty marshes.

The glimmering winter sun was losing its afternoon warmth, and across the flat marshland a wind had begun to blow. So long as there was sun to warm them, Veleda had read aloud in her grave and lucid voice from Tacitus, recalling to Galla Placidia's mind that, in days long gone by, other Romans too had resisted tyranny. The epigrammatic prose went only half-heard, because Galla Placidia had already made up her mind. Into everyone's life comes sooner or later a turning-point. She had said that she detested Ravenna, and she meant it. Smooth-cheeked Olympius was a despot for whose fate Galla Placidia the Emperor's sister no longer felt any personal concern. She hated life at court. If she could go away, she would.

The two women made these excursions along the shore not infrequently, and afterwards the *agentes in rebus* would ask Lugubris, their sad-faced but faithful Gothic servant, but what do they do? Embroider. And what do they read? Poetry. What do they talk about? Sweethearts, he had once extemporised, sensing that his other answers were not giving much satisfaction. And that had been a mistake, because over and again, with cuffs and threats, the question came back at him: what sweethearts? Veleda, next time, provided him the names of a few sweethearts he might as well attribute to her – men who did not matter.

'But doesn't Galla Placidia have sweethearts? they went on insistently, because this was the interesting question. The first male child of the Emperor's sister was likely to be the next Emperor. And if someone seduced her?

'Not that I ever heard tell of' And Lugubris stuck to his answer.

Galla Placidia's interest in men was, in point of fact, vividly alive, though in the spy-ridden court she hardly dare indulge it, for fear of ruining any younger man she became openly fond of. A woman at court must be circumspect – and so she was, though it went against her warm and impulsive nature.

'Walk the horses, Lugubris!' said Veleda, a little more loudly than was necessary. This was a private signal, master to slave. On to the mastiff jowls of the Goth came a death's-head smile, as he collected the bridles in one hand and began to move a long way off. What Lugubris never overheard – the politically dangerous stuff – he could hardly pass on, ever under torture.

'My brother Honorius won't let King Alaric have the hostages that were named in the treaty.'

Veleda laughed. 'Yield up the gold and silver, and refuse him the hostages? How typical. Well – and your other thing?'

Galla Placidia stuck out her lower lip. 'How can you tell there is another thing?'

'By the look on your face. When you would rather not tell, you screw up your eyes. Like this.'

Glancing back, Lugubris saw them pulling faces at each other, and smiled indulgently. Chattering, no doubt, about sweethearts, and had sent him too far off to overhear.

'It's this. You remember Alaric wanted to be Protector of Italy? He, after all, has an army, we don't, and much of his army used to be our cavalry. We can't defend ourselves – but Honorius says no. They are Arians, so he is not having them.'

'Instead?' prompted Veleda gently. In her present mood there would be no hurrying Galla Placidia.

'Did I squeeze my eyes up that time too?'

'You opened them a little too wide, hoping to mislead me. Same thing. Well then. Instead?'

'Oh, Veleda – I can't bear it!'

Galla Placidia's voice had trembled. She is feeling the strain, thought Veleda, just as I did myself when they sent me to Aquileia as a spy. From now on to be too gentle might endanger her. She is still hiding something – dare I drag it out?

'And the other thing – the thing that really upset you'.

If Veleda, thought Galla Placidia, can read my face as easily as all that, how can I ever keep a secret?

'You know Alaric declared that if my brother turned down his treaty he would renew the blockade of Rome, and this time be terrible?'

'I don't blame him.'

'Olympius has decided to send picked troops under Valens to relieve the city.'

'How many picked troops?'

'Six thousand.'

'*Six thousand*?' Veleda gave one of her old laughs, generous, unhesitating, abundant. Lugubris, holding their horses' heads a long way off, heard her laugh and was glad they were so cheerful. 'And Alaric with a hundred thousand horsemen at his beck and call? And Rome by the throat?'

'That's all,' said Galla Placidia.

'Let's go back, shall we, before it gets any colder.'

The lower edge of the over-large, coppery, Italian winter sun had come near the edge of the horizon, and spectres of damp were rising up from the marsh. Galla Placidia stamped her foot.

'No, Veleda – no! There is something else I've wanted to say all afternoon, and you've known it, and choked me off, and never given me a chance. I said it once, out loud, and you ignored me. *I can't bear Ravenna any more*!'

'I hate it too – you know that,' answered Veleda flatly.

'We work like this against Olympius. And afterwards, who will take his place? Another Olympius – you know it. We are playing the same dirty game as those we most despise. Aren't we ever going to stop and ask why?'

The girl is grown up at last, thought Veleda with a sad joy. The change has arrived. And from now on I must carefully bear in mind that she is my mistress. I have already pushed her far enough. I am conspiring out here on this cold evening to avenge Julia and Stilicho and even Serena. For me, as a Goth, revenge is a matter of honour. She waved to Lugubris: be patient. He had begun tightening girths – a hint to move back before dark.

Galla Placidia flung words into the night breeze, as if to disperse them recklessly all over Ravenna. 'And here is something else. The Visigoths are doing God's work. They have come to chasten Rome. Perhaps even to redeem it.'

Veleda could hear her own heart beating. In Ravenna these were the bravest words anyone could utter. She felt a surge of pure love. But for the most dangerous part of what she had to say, even Galla Placidia dropped her voice.

'I want to leave Ravenna. Go to Rome.'

'And die with the Romans? Splendid. But would Alaric let you past and let you in?"

Almost inaudibly the other one whispered. 'I shall go to Alaric himself. Go to him, stay with him. And no use telling me I can't. I have decided.' Galla Placidia reached to grasp Veleda's long thin hand inside her two pudgy ones, as if for reassurance. 'Go, I mean, to the place where we both belong. And won't you come too?'

The *yes* I must now give her, thought Veleda, will be the most perilous yes I have ever uttered. Once Alaric has the Emperor's sister, what other hostage will he need?

'If you are really serious, and have thought it all out – '

'I am! I have!'

'Then, yes.'

Veleda, to quell all thought of what might come her way now the dangerous word had been said, began to talk briskly of the practical side.

'I know a man who will do anything for me and keep his mouth shut – he will get passes across the causeway for us. In false names – mother and daughter perhaps. Unless you think I can't look old enough to pass for your mother?'

From Galla Placidia came a burst of nervous merriment. Veleda would know how to make it all come true.

'The sooner the better. Secrets leak out. We had better plan on leaving Ravenna the day after tomorrow. And not a word.'

'Not a word.'

'I know you would never speak, but what I really mean is, do not even act in an unusual way. Lugubris will see to the horses for us. I can find him a weapon. The other thing necessary is money – can you lay your hands on money?'

With the broad, girlish smile of someone offering to give a helping hand with a holiday excursion, Galla Placidia nodded. She had plenty of money. Honorius might have other faults, but never meanness, not with her.

Here they come at last, thought Lugubris, observing the two women from behind the mask of his sad and preoccupied face. Can they really have been talking about sweethearts all this time?

Part VIII

1

Once out of the house, this was the kingdom of Iynx at five years old: from the courtyard, with its solid double gate, as far as the white-washed water-tank, the mark he had promised Cornelia never to overpass. Beyond the white tank, the grey-green olive trees ran off dizzily for miles in endless straight lines, until they came to the desert.

Olives were trees he had promised never to climb, though the old ones were easy. Roving field-gangs of Circumcelliones picked the olives. They were ruffians – people to avoid. Cornelia spoiled him, and so did Sara, his dumb nurse, and both were full of fears. Claudian was wrapped up in himself, but easy, one way or the other. Lucas urged Iynx to be manly, and whenever he got into trouble for it, took his part, and sometimes even took the blame.

Sara had no ordinary way of speaking. She made noises in her throat that nobody else could understand except Iynx. Though Jacob, the *medicus*, who was interested in everything, had slowly been learning to make sense of Sara's odd way of speaking, too. Iynx had been with Sara since he was born, and her noises, to him, were a plain if secret language. Not that he would begrudge Jacob getting to know, because Jacob was a friend. If Sara yawned, and forgot to cover her mouth with a hand, you could see that her tongue was a stump.

Cornelia was smooth-skinned and perfumed and large; in her own house the centre of everything. To Iynx's annoyance she uttered her silly fears for his safety aloud, all the time, and to everyone. What harm could there be, in climbing an olive tree, or walking down those lines until one came to a nothing that went on for ever: the desert?

When the bottom of the cistern was nothing but muddy cracks, where did the eels go? Somewhere secret, of their own, because next year they came back. The immense sun making little holes of sunlight through his straw hat muddled his head, as Iynx watched one particular eel he had picked as his own. Both eyes and mind had dropped down there into the liquid green, so that he himself, Iynx, became that eel, twisting as it curved through the slime.

The granary was padlocked to keep the corn-jars safe, but cats flickered in and out through the small barred windows. The cats, too, so they said, had been brought here from Egypt. By the desert men. But I, so far, thought Iynx sadly, have never seen the desert men. Cats ate up the rats, that ate up the corn, that would feed the hungry in years when there was no rain.

Nobody's child, the *coloni* would mutter in his hearing. Not hers, nor his either, that other husband's. A child from nowhere, one of ours as likely as one of theirs, with a twisted neck and a dumb nurse, and a smile for everyone, the little darling. Understands Punic too.

Iynx made it a point of honour never to repeat in the house what he might hear the outside people say. He kept his worlds apart. Quick rattling Punic beyond the courtyard and its beetling arch; Latin in the quiet house.

Claudian insisted that for Iynx, Latin was the most important of all, plenty of time for Greek later on, but Jacob would make a hot case for Greek. The two men, doctor and patient, argued continually about the child's education as about everything else under the sun. The Greek-speaking Eastern Empire was intact, the Western Empire, Latin-speaking, was shaking apart already, so what of the boy's future?

Jacob the *medicus* was allowed to come once a week, by the unwilling permission of the slab-faced centurion, the man Iynx was by now well aware you must never call to his face, *Inimicus* A nickname. Though true.

'Iynx – are you sure you understand about nicknames?'

'Yes, Jacob. I will never call him Inimicus again. Even though it's true.' And Jacob had laughed uproariously.

Inimicus, these days, wore disappointment in his helmet like a withered flower. Over wine, elsewhere, he would tell regimental cronies how his almost certain prospect of enjoying Cornelia's ample charms and vast estate had been frustrated. First Lucas, the freedman, the penman, arrived and intrigued against him. How can an honest soldier contend with a penman? Except that when you get right down to it, the sword is what counts. Then that little brat from nowhere, Iynx, wormed his way into her heart. And then came Claudius Claudianus. It had all been fixed up at headquarters, in Ravenna, the place where they neglected the men on the frontiers, their pay and promotion. Sick he might be, Claudius Claudianus, and only a poet. But consider his rank and his connections. What chance did a simple soldier have?

When Jacob rode in past the cistern today on his camel and went towards the open gate, he gave Iynx no more than a small, private, disapproving shake of the head. Enough to say that he knew his small friend should not be playing there, but, even so, he would not tell. Jacob's arrival caused a flurry among the household slaves. One of them always had something urgently wrong with him, and would try to corner Jacob as he crossed the courtyard.

When Jacob had gone in and all was quiet, Iynx wandered back to examine the camel. He was interested in camels. Large feet like paws squashed out flat, neck swaying from side to side as if mistrusting all it saw, and on its face that camel-look, between a snarl and a sneer. But they could go fast across deserts.

The horses tethered on the courtyard's shady side hated the smell of camels. They were flirting their tails, stamping their hooves. But I, thought Iynx, am not a horse. I am Iynx. That smell is only camel-smell, nothing to be afraid of. He had his own eyes centred on the racing camel's bloodshot, swivelling eyes. As its long neck craned back and forth, the little boy's crooked neck swayed too. They glared at one another, camel and boy, not quite trusting each other, and yet becoming as one.

Cornelia, glancing down from the loggia's latticed window, saw the camel's snarling mouth come near the little boy's head. She was biting her knuckles, afraid to call out. Well aware he might be frightening her – though never once had he looked up – Iynx turned prudently away from the camel and strolled towards the gate. He gazed upwards at the two caryatids – naked women carved in stone – who carried on their shoulders the weight of the lintel.

Iynx stared up at the two stone women, their muscles enormous, their breasts bare. An eel might wriggle, a camel sway, but those statues were always the same. Only the light and shadow falling across their faces changed the look of them. They never moved, or grew old, or died. Iynx was awed.

Impulsively he ran away from the caryatids, and went inside, entering the cool of the house, a different province of his kingdom, where slapping to and fro on the tiled floor in sandals, the slaves had a different smell from the *coloni*, less earthy, more winey, softer. The household slaves would put themselves out to do things for him, often unnecessary things, but already Iynx hated being waited on, except by Sara.

All of them confusing my life thought Cornelia – I, like my caryatids, carry a heavy burden. A husband who could never be one. A child who is not my son, either, though his darling ways tug at my heart. Lucas – who might father me a child in Claudian's name, but dare I ask, or would he risk it, either? A grave sin, though, and Claudian if he got to know – and he doesn't miss much – would be insulted. Even if pleased to have a child who bore his name. Though would he want that? And a new arrival might spoil Iynx's chances. And is that what I would want?

Yet when he feels in the mood, Claudian can talk like an angel, make me laugh, make me forget. Hardly grumbles either, considering how ill he is. A great improvement on the other, the pompous one, as husband. The church says I should love him, yes, of course, women should love their husbands, except, what sort of love is this? How can I? I am grateful to God, though, for Claudian's good nature. He is quiet enough upstairs with his books, no bother. As for Lucas, he has an eye for others in the house, I know it, but what are slave girls for, except to help their mistress out?

Iynx, while these thoughts chased each other through Cornelia's head, had walked step by step up the long and narrow back staircase, the servants' staircase, so as to avoid hearing her say that he should not have played with the camel. He went down passages until he had arrived in Claudian's quiet room, the best room in the house. Claudian's books were there, and his documents, and his bed. Sometimes for days on end he hardly went further than the loggia that overlooked the courtyard.

The little boy pushed against the heavy bees-waxed door with both hands, until it moved back on its bronze hinges. Moved silently, since Claudian detested above all a squeaking door, and once a week an old slave not good for much else went around the house with an oiled feather, hunting for squeaks.

Claudian and Jacob were talking in Greek as Iynx entered; their private language. They had spoken Greek with each other in years gone by. In Alexandria, a city on the far side of the desert, *Icthus*, a fish, Greek; *pisces*, a fish, Latin. Today, *dies Veneris*, was the day Cornelia always had the big Friday fish, brought to her in a tank of salt water all the way from the sea. A fish was Christian, had been a secret sign, but Iynx was not certain he liked fish, because of the bones.

Iynx, having closed Claudian's door gently, stood there, still as a mouse, one little hand folded inside the other, to see how long they would be before they noticed him. If they never noticed him, he would know. Know, that is, the mystery of what went on in other rooms when he himself was not there. Men exchanging confidences in a language he was not supposed to understand.

When Jacob first turned up at the house, on camel-back, called in by Cornelia to treat his malady, Claudian had been dubious. A grizzle-haired travesty of a gifted young man he had known in years gone by. But not embittered, said Jacob's smile, as he first came in the sickroom. An Alexandrian Jew. There had in the old days been a million Jews in Alexandria, all busy, all gifted, and then the Christians began pushing them out. And Greeks who had remained pagan? Not many of those left, either.

If only I could have swallowed their nonsense, Claudian told himself, I might have been their patriarch by now, or their pope. Nor do I want this shabby, sunburnt Jew, moving closer towards me, to mention my mother, even by a whisper in my ear. This man Jacob has only to amuse himself by belittling me to others, and there will not be much left of the *persona*, that mask with a gap for the mouth, Roman, pagan, patriotic, out of which for all these years the poetry has come. I am not what I would like to be.

Mother always said my father had been a distinguished Roman officer, and though she would never tell me his name, she dropped hints. Pagan, brave, famous, I grew up with a picture of him in my mind. Mother in her raffish youth might well have had to do with a great many Roman officers. What if I bear the name of a man who never existed, and am therefore my own ancestor? Most poets are. And she herself? A manumitted Syrian dancing girl, who had scrambled halfway up the ladder before she lost her looks, and then fought like a wildcat to educate me. I had no looks, I had only brains, and how that puzzled her.

Jacob is close. Will he tell any of this? He looks on me, as he approaches not as a man he has known, but as a bundle of symptoms. I know myself. *Know Thyself!* Better than Jacob ever will.

Not male, nor Roman, nor a soldier, yet obsessed by all three. I have high Roman rank, Claudian reminded himself, when finally there was no avoiding the touch of the *medicus*. I am a master of Latin versification. My bust is in the Forum. If I am not Rome's greatest living poet, then who is? (In Rome, do they suppose by this time that I am dead? I rather hope so. I shall quite enjoy being posthumous. Long may it last). Claudian watched this revenant from his past take instruments from a case, pour a potion drop by drop, his intent medical smile unchanging. And told himself, with a certainty like the moment of relief from a nagging pain, that is an honest smile. He will not betray me.

Jacob, too, had been dreading this first encounter. But from the first, when Claudian muttered thanks, and produced his own smile, a spark of new friendship had been struck.

Poor Jacob, thought Claudian, in the old days the most brilliant of us. A polymath, driven into exile. Brighter than Greek or Syrian, funnier, more in earnest, indifferent to possessions: a Jew. He has no business to leave the oasis. Cornelia arranges it with the centurion.

Is stretching himself over my prone body while the boy watches – the sight will do Iynx no harm – ear against chest, his hair less grey than mine but no thicker, and he listens to this appalling noise I make when I breathe, as if it were intricate music. Even my own mother would have been less tender. Poor and an exile, yet he has not run to seed. Philosopher, mathematician, astrologer, alchemist. Poet? At one time he was proudest of his poetry, yet what did it amount to? Nothing much. Concentrated all of it into physician – medicine too is an art. And fritters away all he has in political exile. The way politics wastes men!

As Jacob raised his ear from Claudian's bare chest the two of them, taking no notice of the presence in the room of the boy, began arguing about Plotinus, immersing themselves in the argument as though they were were boys. These arguments, thought Claudian, vitalise. Plotinus was no philosopher for a physician, he tartly suggested – a man said by his biographer, Porphyry, to have seemed ashamed of being in the body.

'As indeed,' Claudian added, 'at times, am I.'

As Claudian made his joke about Porphyry, Jacob had been listening not to the words he used but to the difficult cadence of his breathing.

'Let me auscultate you again. Up with your tunic. Iynx, do you mind this?'

'No,' said Iynx. They always treated him as a man among men.

The touch of his ear, thought Claudian, pressing yet again the grey hairs of my chest, is done with such grave authority, that the gesture is not carnal but almost pious. For me, no more lovers. Would Jacob ever have reciprocated, even if only from curiosity? The answer is obviously no. His pleasure in touching, with such delicacy, this ramshackle body comes from seeking to make death wait in the doorway a little longer. As Iynx stands in the doorway now. Young life.

'Finished fiddling with me? Then tell me this. Did you ever take the Hippocratic Oath?' asked Claudian in a tone of breathless jocularity.

'Don't speak.' Jacob was tapping knuckles on one rib bone after another. Claudian tried to share what was happening by listening intently to his own breathing, but what he could hear was not encouraging. As Jacob straightened his back, he said, casually, 'Yes.'

'Yes what? Yes I shall live another week?'

'Yes, I swore the oath. On the island of Cos, actually, in the temple of Asclepios itself. You can't do better.'

'And yet,' Claudian tediously, breathlessly persisted, 'you read Plotinus and admire him – '

'Mistrust him,' said Jacob.

'You do not believe in Asclepios, or in any other divinity. Do you? Even in your mysterious Jewish divinity. Or in Hippocrates either for all I know. Much less in the sacredness of oaths.'

'Oh, if ever I give you my word that you will live till next week, you can trust what I say. If that is really what you mean. As for Hippocrates, certainly I believe in Hippocrates, whatever "believe" may mean. Hippocrates was not a God – whatever a God may be. He was a practising physician, before our time, of course, but he is mentioned twice by Plato – in *Protagoras*, in *Phaedus*. Of course you knew that when you spoke. And I don't want to handicap your argument – but try not to raise your voice.'

'Iynx – do you want something?'

'No.'

Iynx waited without a word. They were doing exactly what he wanted. This was marvellous – to know how men behaved when you were not there.

Claudian went on earnestly, 'If you discard the immortal gods, and are not even a Jew, much less a Christian what exactly do you live by? What are you looking for?'

'Call it wisdom,' said Jacob with a bitter smile, as if he had lately found wisdom to be not only a fickle woman, but a bitch. 'Then of course your problem begins. In Latin, *sapientia*, in Greek, *sophia*. And as we are both well aware, *sapientia* is not *sophia*, one tending towards the practical, the other towards the transcendental. Any truth – but you will never admit this – that happens not to be geometrical or scientific is seen through a *nebula* of words'.

And why throw in, wondered Claudian, like a garnish, the Latin for mist? An Alexandrian, use mist for a metaphor, after spending all his life on the edge of a desert?

Why am I arguing like this, thought Claudian, wasting my strength, when all that preoccupies me – the question Jacob will never answer – is how much longer do I have to live? Not that mere living matters so much, here, in this nowhere place, with every day so much like any other, and the last poems of all ranged on the shelf, corrected if not, as fools will say, complete. There are still a few other things to be done – it would simplify if one knew.

'Come over here, Iynx,' said Claudian, as loudly and cheerfully as his diminished voice allowed, in Latin. The resonant clarity of Latin. So splendid. No mists. 'Tell us what we two old men can do for you. Have you seen the camel?'

'Today I touched him,' said Iynx. He had pressed his finger, hard, against the camel's leg, and the camel had taken no notice whatever. 'Horses,' the boy announced, 'don't much like the way a camel smells.' The two old erudites glanced sideways at each other – Herodotus had known that, too. 'Claudian – do you know those eels in the tank?'

And I shall not, for once, thought Claudian, remind him that he is supposed to stay away from the tank. '*Anguilla* – an eel. Use the Latin word, not the dialect one. If you please. Yes, I know them. When I still went for walks I would look over the top, and watch them wriggle.'

'And their little ones,' said Jacob, softly. 'Like threads. *Filum* – a thread.'

'Where do they live when the cistern goes dry?' Iynx burst out. 'the *coloni* say they always come back with the rains – but where from?'

Before Jacob could launch into a scientific dissertation on the mysterious life of the eel – where does it breed? how does it renew itself? – Claudian suggested, 'Perhaps in the dry season they go underground. Like Proserpine – '

'Or, as we Alexandrians say, Persephone,' contributed Jacob naughtily, and tapped on the floor with his toe, as if about to break into a dance.

' – and who goes down deep into the earth, to meet her husband, the king of *hell*,' chanted Iynx.

Claudian in a sweet voice almost devoid of strength went on reciting from his poem, while Jacob and Iynx listened in a trance, as though the chain of musical words, one linked to the next, were binding them captive. The man might die as he spoke; the poem would go on sounding.

Claudian, looking down from the loggia into the courtyard, saw

Jacob hunch his legs across the camel saddle, and prod the squatting beast with a stick until it staggered erect. Claudian wanted to see Jacob go, in case this might be his last sight of him. Iynx was standing by the camel and, as the ungainly beast rose, Jacob put his hands under Iynx's armpits, to lift the boy high in the air. Iynx screamed as if Jacob were running off with him, but his screams were of pretence and delight. On a camel, and away into the desert! Claudian felt a double pang of loss. Jacob, Iynx, both going away? This disease of his exaggerated every small emotion.

Further beyond the cistern than strictly speaking he was allowed to go, the boy was dropped to the ground like a parcel, and ran off in the wrong direction, laughing and spinning, whirling his arms. As an olive tree he paused, to reach up a hand and pick one small, dark, ripe, prohibited fruit.

Claudian on his loggia smiled. The fruit looks particularly tempting, yet an olive plucked straight from the tree is bitter. Everyone alive, he ruminated, has to find that out for himself.

The Christians, thought Claudian, may try these days to claim Plato, even Plotinus – the argument with Jacob about Plotinus had left his mind trembling. But they shan't claim me. Even though I did stand up in that poky little Donatist conventicle across the way, and marry Cornelia according to their rite. How Roman high society would have laughed!

Lucky, though, that I did. So long as a Christian Emperor rules – if that lawyer from Zama is right – such a Christian marriage is virtually indissoluble. Men of my rank need not pay taxes even though her land is taxed. Why should we? We serve Rome in other ways. My rank will help my widow. So even when I am gone, I shall throw over Cornelia, and over Lucas as my adopted son, the protection of my name. The two of them will look after young Iynx. I can trust them for that. Or else the estate out there, so vast and tranquil – Virgilian and stretching for miles – would be so much plunder.

As soon as Claudian heard that Heraclian, Flavius Stilicho's murderer, was lording it in Carthage, the fear of being harried to death even down here, on the verge of the desert, had begun to invade his dreams.

Claudian had a clear enough recollection of Heraclian, a curly-headed, grinning army bully. We all know the type, he told himself as from the loggia, once Jacob had ridden away, the evening light began to collapse towards darkness. No Roman twilights here. Men of that type – I once tried them out, I have tried out most types – have never been fond of me. No imagination and no tenderness. They like to humiliate, and if I can't have imagination in a lover, I insist on tenderness. Or else give me a little harmless stupidity, louts, chopping-blocks, those slave boys racing up and down stairs in my house in Rome. Heraclian, though, is a tough, grinning brute. Poor Flavius Stilicho.

The last, slanting sunbeam illuminated briefly the crazily-dancing dust that rose from the courtyard, mingling with the stench of dung. And both are bad for me (life itself is bad for me!) thought Claudian conventionally, as he moved back into the cool stillness of his own room.

The boring thing about this endless, Virgilian tranquility was that you always knew what came next. That respectful knock, now, at the door, would be one or the other of them.

'Cornelia has sent me to inquire – ' began Lucas diffidently, well aware that Claudian hated to be asked.

'Jacob? Well, my dear fellow, he defended Plotinus with all the usual arguments, until I went for him.' The sentence was ruptured by a succession of coughs.

'I am sure he also said you are not to get worked up,' answered Lucas, gently imperturbable. 'Even not to talk too loud. And what else did he tell you?'

Claudian grinned crookedly. He gave a sensible answer, though, because he knew that Lucas would wait here, politely but persistently, until he got one.

'I am to avoid dust and the direct rays of the sun. Avoid dust – I ask you! Have you ever seen the courtyard at sunset, when the mules come back from the field? I must drink up my milk. Detestable goats' milk, of course. Not that I would like cows' milk any better – '

'Just as well then that he did not prescribe camels' milk,' answered Lucas, with such friendly sternness that Claudian smiled. He could not keep up this make-believe peevishness much longer.

'Anything you would like me to tell Cornelia when she asks? As she is bound to.'

'Oh yes. Of course. And thank you for taking the trouble. The usual things. Good hours. Deep sleep. Sweet dreams.'

'There is something else, perhaps,' said Lucas, and he stands there, thought Claudian, like one of the men my mother might have married, had it not been for me. From the way he pomps on at me these days, Lucas might as well have been my father. 'Something you might like to confide in me alone?'

'How is it, Lucas Claudianipor,' he burst forth, 'that though you are gullible in so many other ways, I can never hide anything like this from you?' Lucas smiled, as if he had just been handed an exquisite bouquet. 'Neither diagnosis nor prognosis would Jacob deign to give me, not in so many words. But he handed me a gift, which by some means or other he has procured from Luxor. And this gift has significance.' Claudian showed Lucas a squat, enamelled jar. 'Don't try to take it from me – don't touch. I am not letting it go. Yes, a sticky substance with a rather nasty smell. For the philosophical Jacob, you understand, this gift of *opion* – opium – is his simple way of admitting that he holds out no hope for me. A way out forbidden to a Christian – but luckily I am no Christian, any more than you are. He offers to ease my way down into hell with a diet of boiled goats' milk and sweet dreams. *Potio soporifera*. The dried juice of the Egyptian white poppy. But I, too, am an Alexandrian, and first stuck my inquisitive finger in the stuff at the age of fifteen. The most astounding dreams, dear Lucas, but let me warn you. The poets of my time who used *opion* very soon faded away – they used up in dreams their essential stock of metaphor.'

Holding tight to the jar, Claudian looked coyly at Lucas, as if this were his last attempt at seduction. 'We could try it together. Drift off to Lethe hand in hand. You are such a good companion on a journey. You could help row me across the Styx. Then in hell I should not be friendless.' A tear – but it might have been the involuntary meaningless tear of old age – had come into the corner of his eye.

Lucas took all this in, but answered matter-of-factly.

'And I don't tell Cornelia?'

'Is there any need?'

'I don't think so. What she would really rather know is, are you coming down to dinner tonight? A fresh tunny, baked whole, a stuffing of bread, herbs, eggs, a caper sauce. Washed down with boiled milk? Yes, I know. But in any case, don't you find African wine too sweet?'

'The white wine is acceptable. But no, I must be disciplined. Boiled milk. Tell her.' Claudian coughed, and wiped his mouth. 'There is just one last thing to nail down tight.'

'Your manuscripts? New corrections? You know I am here to serve you, day or night.'

Claudian made a gesture which affirmed that he did not doubt it. Poems though were over, must stand on their own in men's minds, without his further aid.

'I mean, make absolutely sure of the adoption before the wolves move in.'

Does my face, wondered Lucas, show embarrassment? Lucas had caught himself out in daydreams of being, not so much master here, who wanted to be a slave-master? But a man legitimately deferred to.

'Roman law is no longer a thing to boast about,' said Claudian. 'Bishops, for want of anyone better, are becoming judges, and frankly I would rather have even a Christian bishop to judge me than Heraclian. Wouldn't you? Everything that once was law-abiding and certain – secure – is hanging loose. Who in the eyes of a greedy world will Cornelia be, once I am dead? An heiress, and the widow of a man not well regarded in Ravenna. In other words, so much plunder. Listen. I have a secret to tell you, which possibly with your uncommon acumen you have already guessed. We know nothing of Iynx for certain, do we, except the horoscope sewn into his blanket – a detail than in my opinion is better not spoken of. If only that nurse of his could be made to talk!'

'Jacob has tried,' said Lucas. 'He even understands what she says. But she knows how to keep a secret.'

'*So long as the adoption is done properly*!' Claudian's voice had risen to a peacock scream, the petulance of a sick man near the end of his tether. 'Come closer. Listen. Jacob expounded that horoscope to me. He is an excellent astrologer, an excellent everything, a pity about his ham-fisted attempts at poetry. Jacob says the boy will have a turbulent life, with misfortunes, but a long one, and become a leader of men, making his mark on history, and come back here at last, to this very house. Personally I only believe in astrology when it tells me what I want to hear. But let me tell you something about that horoscope of more essential importance. After I die, there must be someone else living who knows, someone I can trust.'

His voice had fallen to a whisper. 'Not, I mean, as a document – a text. But simply as a piece of writing. The handwriting of that horoscope is itself an important message to me, and I am passing it on to you. I know the man who wrote it, as well as if he had signed it – '

There are some secrets, reflected Lucas, it is as well never to know. He raised his eyebrows interrogatively.

'You are sure you want to tell me?'

'Of course. When I am gone, who else is there but you? Listen. Do you suppose it was by accident that the dumb women brought the boy here, to Cornelia? The horoscope was copied out by Flavius Stilicho in his own hand. And that was to tell me, if the secret becomes known to bully-boys, the little one's life will always be in danger. Now the question is this. If I also adopt this child of Stilicho's, shall I make him too conspicuous?'

Marcus in their one sordid room in Carthage was just the same hard-working and considerate man that he had been on the island, but he had coarsened. And looks at me sometimes, thought Gilda, as if I were a fearful giant sundew, trapping men like flies. Marcus had become more ordinary, the acute and highly-educated staff-officer disappearing as if by an act of renunciation inside the working man. His work as a mason's labourer wore him out. The change – the choice – had diminished him.

What on Cuneus had been Marcus's everyday preoccupations, scripture-reading, continual prayer, the lips always moving as if he were a madman or a saint, to Gilda living with him cheek-by-jowl in one small room in a noisy street became infuriating oddities. The tighter Marcus's life was tied up in knots by a round of prayer and worship, the more Gilda craved spontaneity – to play a part in life of her own choosing. We were tied together, she told herself, by accident. In staying with him here, I am denying my duty to Inyx. She had never told Marcus about this other child, living somewhere far to the south.

'Nor, Gilda, is it easy for me,' Marcus stolidly told her, one evening, when, tired from work, he had seated himself on a stool, a papryus roll between his outspread hands, not reading but hiding behind it, until angrily she had interrupted him.

'Of course it is not easy for you, but why make it harder for others?'

Gilda as she spoke could hear an echo of her mother's ghostly voice, nagging at her father all those years ago in the hut in the forest. Marcus looked at her in dismay. When religious thoughts filled his mind, or doubts assailed him, Marcus craved to be solitary.

With the end of the world imminent – all Donatists were sure of that – the flesh sinful, and this present world no place to bring children into, there were other married couples too in the church who lived continently, for what they held to be Christian reasons. True marriages, theirs. But you promised in the hearing of God, Marcus reminded himself, to stay together for better or worse. If only Gilda were content to live as my sister.

Marcus had never supposed, either, that life in a city as a poor man could be so full of small injustices. Labourers on the city wall were robbed every day of their wages by fines for trivial offences, and no redress. Money earned by master masons was soaked away in tax. Blatant fortunes were being made by suppliers and their governmental confederates. The military engineer in charge of repairs to the wall was a blockhead. As Marcus went up the ladder carrying a hod, heavily dripping wet mortar, instead of occupying his mind by prayer he would sometimes find himself mapping out a siege of Carthage, and himself the enemy. Carthage had not withstood a regular siege for centuries. *Pax Romana.*

An afternoon came when Gilda, alone in their room, put a shawl over her head and went off, from curiosity, to find the theatre. Marcus would have said, a dangerous temptation, since in the neighbourhood of the theatre she was likeliest to be recognised. In fact she felt like running the risk – anything for stimulus.

Recklessly Gilda drifted along streets she had never before seen, like a cork driven by the covenant, bobbing down a stream. She gazed up at what once had been the great temple of Aesculapius, with its ascent of sixty steps, where nowadays the

African Senate met. There in the *praetorium* the proconsul of Africa, 'that murderer Heraclian' as Marcus had once called him between grimly unforgiving lips, now lorded it.

At her first whiff of the theatre, where the usual afternoon crowd were thronging the forecourt in anticipation, Gilda felt wildly excited. The warhorse heard the trumpet. She stood looking around her for a little too long, in those familiar environs feeling at last herself.

'Gilda!'

She was recognised.

No stranger had called her name like that for such a long time. Gilda turned her head, there was no resisting. A man was pointing his finger at her – a soldier of high rank, amid a crowd of attendants. He wore a polished breast-plate and a scarlet belt, his cloak hung dandy-fashion across one shoulder, a man of importance. Short and fair hair curled crisply above a coarse face, and the look on his face was knowing, possessive! She had seen him before, in Ravenna.

Heraclian?

The man who had recognised her was giving a quick order, out of the corner of his mouth, to a tough-looking little military toady nearby. Across the curly-haired man's face came the self-satisfied look of a gambler who has won. Gilda in one leaping heartbeat knew of her danger.

She could have hardly have explained afterwards why she turned so quickly and ran. Her own sudden move surprised him: she broke loose, she ran hard. The experience of her whole life since that wet afternoon when a mounted archer had leaned over in the saddle and grabbed her was consummated by an animal impulse to dive into the thick of the theatrical crowd, her own people. Not far enough behind she could hear the bullying exclamations.

'Gilda! Stop her!'

And then a trumpet, as if this were a hunt, and she the cornered doe. The trumpet was calling out soldiers.

All the young swaggerers of her time had known Gilda by sight, and even in her shabby clothes, that one glimpse had been enough for Heraclian. His mind, when his self-advantage was concerned, was quickly decisive. Gilda would be a trophy, a political bargaining-counter, since Olympius in Ravenna was still obsessed by this need to find one witness to cajole the Emperor. Stilicho's mistress? Who better? Since the Visigoth invasion, nothing had gone right for Olympius.

In his own heart – not that he examined his heart very often – Heraclian knew very well that there had been no Stilicho conspiracy. He like others had begun to despise Olympius, and he was even meditating a mutiny on his own account. Gilda, though, must certainly be guilty of something or other, or why should she try so insultingly to escape, when the proconsul of Africa himself shouted after her?

He sent armed squads to stalk up and down the waterfront. Pickets patrolled all the main roads into the countryside, and the proconsul announced that the man who first laid hands on Gilda would be paid a gold *solidus*. What Heraclian so generously stipulated he was soon provided with. One unlikely Gilda after another was dragged into headquarters for him to identify, and at each disappointment Heraclian's rage mounted.

The last woman they dragged in did, unluckily for her, have some resemblance to Gilda, animated face, dark curly hair. She even admitted to being an actress. The *decurio* who brought her in was in his own mind already beginning to spend the gold *solidus*. The woman herself was bewildered, but she would certainly be Gilda for these fascinating high officials, if only they would tell her more clearly what they wanted. She fawned on Heraclian; for a man of such importance she was ready to tell any lie whatsoever.

Heraclian did not need a second glance to tell that this was not the real Gilda. Angrily he ordered the woman to the flogging block, for prevarication. In a deeper, even gloomier rage he then countermanded his own order. She was a *mima* – and who could go lower? But this rotten cabbage-leaf might well have a prim sister who was a Christian. The day after tomorrow the bishop might call. The priests would be down on him. Disrespectful sermons might be preached. Here, in Carthage, even the proconsul of Africa no longer had a free hand. In Ravenna it was worse. And might they soon, in Ravenna, be whispering that Heraclian had let Gilda go for motives of his own? It was probably not even wise, thought Heraclian, when I saw her by the theatre, to have shouted her name aloud.

As, cautiously, she worked her way home again, Gilda encountered rumours. The soldiers were out on the streets, looking for Stilicho's woman. She had conspired against the Emperor. Here's hoping they catch her.

With the shawl pulled over her head, and the drooped shoulders and limping gait of an old woman, Gilda made her way cautiously down the narrow street where she and Marcus lived, moving on the shady side. She had made herself so anonymous that even neighbours passed her without noticing. She lifted the latch, and there was Marcus, in the gloom, back from work and dog-tired, splashed from head to foot with white mortar. Gilda hardly dare step across the threshold. The last thing she wanted was to drag this good man down with her.

His 'Where have you been all this time?' was a little more peremptory than Gilda cared to hear. These possessive habits of speech grew on men once you lived with them. But this was no time to bicker.

'In danger,' said Gilda, her voice dramatically low. He would hear all about it tomorrow, in the streets. 'So, Marcus, the time has come. I shall take what I think belongs to me – these other clothes. Do you have any money to spare? I shall be glad of it. Marcus, I am going away.'

His dog-weary expression hardly changed, and Gilda could not help saying, 'Are you sorry?'

Abruptly Marcus lurched up, still silent, to give her all the money he had. Not much, and she made him take some back, for bread, for the rent. He muttered a goodbye, a God bless, but did not look at her.

Yet the true blame, Gilda decided, as she turned away from him and from her life with him, a bundle under her arm, is mine. On Cuneus I tempted him when he was happy as he was. I could have done without it, too. With five men – five, and the last the worst – working their will on me, I had had enough. What is this madness that drives us to couple?

Gilda could see, as from the doorstep she glanced back, that Marcus was praying. For me? Gilda wondered. Or praying for himself? Perhaps he is praying for everyone who lives as we did. If in his prayer he is blaming me, I deserved it. The chances are, though, that he is blaming himself.

2

Gilda managed to pass through the market gate of Carthage towards dusk, when the vegetable-sellers were leaving the city for their villages. Soldiers at the gateway had been told to look out for a *mima*, and were picturing to themselves a woman covered with jewels and glitter. As Gilda went towards the gate amid the market crowd, a shawl like theirs over her head, a bundle under her arm, the *lectica* of a rich woman tried to pass. The soldiers were so busy poking their officious noses into the *lectica* – a gold *solidus*! – that they let the plodding old woman Gilda simulated go by without a word.

Iynx, Cornelia, Zama – Stilicho's three names. And now I have nothing else in the world, she told herself, to hold me back. Tramping the roads numbed the mind. She drank well-water, and ate stale bread and rotten fruit. The last coppers in her pocket ran out, and for two days she lived craftily, by stealing. The sole of her worn-out sandal had just begun to flap like a loquacious tongue when Gilda fell in with an exuberant band of Circumcelliones. They, too, were heading south, where the olive harvest had begun. They fed her. They were soon glad of her company.

Circumcelliones did not much mind where you had come from, or why you were on the road, so long as you respected their customs, despised the authorities and were companionable. After the first campfire night Gilda, a modest newcomer, even began, as she took her turn singing, to add verses. In her disguise of crack-brimmed straw hat, ragged gown, flapping sandal who would have known her? But from prudence she hid for a while under a nickname they gave her: *Clara Cantora*.

By degrees, though, one or two of her workmates found out that their singer's actual name was Gilda, and that for the Circumcelliones was an even better reason for liking her: Gilda was the feminine form of their great African hero's name. A dozen years before when Gildo the Moor rose against Rome, the Circumcelliones had all joined him. They had fought hard for Gildo, they approved of his rebellion. In their own way they were moral folk, with strange religious ideas by which they abided. A woman travelling on her own with the Circumcelliones had not much to fear, if she kept her wits about her.

'Cornelia? We know a Cornelia.'

'South of Zama?'

'South of Zama.' But, typically, none of them asked why Gilda – *Clara Cantora* – should wish to know about this rich landowner to the south, whose olives they were eventually on their way to pick. The olives furthest south ripened first. When the last of the corn crop further north was stacked and gleaned, yes, they would work for Cornelia.

Time passed, work and tramp and work again somewhere else, until one day they went in a gang, with their long iron-ringed sticks, through the town of Zama, and the citizens set the dogs on them.

In the course of her first morning's work on the manor estate, Gilda caught a distant glimpse of Cornelia, an ample-bodied woman, overdressed, but when she spoke to her field workers, businesslike and even cheerful. Later on, at the noon break, they all went under the shade trees, to eat the bread and cold lentils that that kitchen servants had brought out for them in baskets. Gilda, as she straightened her back, caught her first glimpse of the boy.

He had come out from the house alone, to play near the cistern. And should I go closer to him? Gilda wondered. But what if I frightened him? While her workmates portioned out the food, Gilda began to sing one of their songs. She knew small boys, the song would lure him closer. Iynx lingered guiltily near the cistern, the limit he knew he should not overpass, but the music was irresistible, and he came on closer. His head on one side, exactly as Stilicho had told her, but bright eyes. That small boy approaching with a shy smile must be her own son – who else could he be? I must go on singing, she told herself. I must not startle him. I must win him.

The day that Gilda arrived at the manor house with the olive pickers was the day that Claudian met his death.

Lucas had ridden off early, to argue on Cornelia's behalf

with a newly-appointed tax-collector about the road tolls he was arbitrarily and indeed illegally imposing on oil jars sent by wagon from the estate to the coast. The best way to deal with an awkward tax-collector was to bribe him.

Early that morning, Iynx had seen Lucas ride away, and with regret; Lucas was good company. On a short trip these days Lucas would sometimes take him along, but today, Lucas had said, there would be no fun. Claudian lay upstairs, helpless in the grip of what was to be his last fever, and sozzled with opium. Hardly had Lucas ambled out of sight along the highway when Inimicus rode in under the arch, a personage Iynx particularly disliked, bringing with him six mounted men.

Inimicus told Cornelia that they were here to collect some fodder due to the army, but as she was well aware, the centurion at other times had used her farm carts and slaves, and not his own soldiers. He had some better reason for coming here in force. Circumcelliones in the field, cavalrymen idle in the countryard, Lucas ridden off. Trouble might come of it.

Making use of today's mood of upset, Iynx had ventured deeper than ever he had dared, past the cistern and into the grey-green olive grove. The fearsome Circumcelliones were picking there, and someone was singing, and he wanted to see and hear them. If you stood quite still in the midst of the grove, so that straight lines of trees headed off in every direction, and then spun around, the lines of trees would move too, swivelling. He played this game for a while, but the woman singing tempted him closer.

Each verse ended with an enormous *Laus Deo!* – *Praise be to God!* – the pickers' battle-cry. Whenever they shouted their *Laus Deo* the men clashed the seven-foot, iron-ringed poles with which they tramped the roads and knocked down olives. The Circumcelliones were lounging around in the shade, eating from baskets brought from the house, listening to this ragged curly-haired woman, a singer, a dancer, dark-eyed, yet with one lock of white hair. She must be old.

Iynx knew she was looking at him too, she had caught his eye, and from then on it was as if she sang for him alone, as if to charm or convince him. She was one of them, though – one of the fearsome Circumcelliones. Their singer. In Cornelia's house they were called 'hands', as if the hands they used to pick up olives or to cut corn were the only bits of their bodies that mattered to those who paid them for their day's work. Hands – this woman? She was also voice. She was hands, arms, legs; she sang with her body entire. Iynx was held where he stood, enraptured by the pulsation of her voice. He took in her words as though they had been gospel.

'*St Cyprian has said and signed*'

With a dancer's stamp of her heel on the hard ground, for emphasis.

'*God's gifts are for all mankind*!'

Gilda's voice soared up, taking Iynx's heart with her, though his own voice was so far silent.

'*Laus Deo*!'

Then the poles all clashed, and the voices sang out as one, and Iynx thought, I could safely have said *Laus Deo* too. That can't hurt. That's a prayer.

'*St Ambrose these good words let falls
Mother Earth belongs to all
Laus Deo!*'

Cornelia had said last night at the dinner table that if you did not pay the Circumcelliones what they asked, when they arrived to pick your olives, they would set your stacks afire. They were fiends.

'Fiends they may be', said Lucas with a laugh, 'only we cannot do without them.'

It was therefore with great daring that Iynx after the second verse put his lips around the Latin words, *Laus Deo*! that these fiends sang. At least, to whisper what they shouted.

'*May the boss who trims our wage
Fall a victim to God's rage*'

Iynx felt a delicious shudder enter into him – he was betraying Cornelia – as he let himself be swept into their chorus, shouting this time with all his might, '*Laus Deo*!'

'*Let the money-lender RUN
God gave the world to EVERYONE*'

EVERYONE was the gesture of the woman's open hands, she gave away the world in handfulls to everyone around her, as if she were God's deputy. Cornelia lent money, too – and when she had lent it you had better pay up, but, *let the moneylender RUN*! And the thought of Cornelia being made to run, wobble-wobble, had him laughing so that he laughed his way right though *Laus Deo*. Gilda, watching him, was herself midway between laughter and tears.

'May the bully and the copper
Trip their heels and come a cropper
Laus Deo!'

He caught the chorus loudly that time.

'Like the day, the night, the sun
God's gifts are for everyone
Laus Deo!'

Her last verse came sadly, the words not quite echoed into rhyme, but fading away. Dying.

'God's gifts are for all mankind
Like being born, and then like d y i n g'

D-y-i-n-g, d-y-i-n-g went the voices, softly, and this time with no triumphal clashing of sticks, and softly yet again, L-a-u-s D-e-o!

The woman who sang was moving his way.

'Iynx!' she called. Her arms were held out for him. She wore a smile. But a man who had come up behind Iynx put a large hand on his shoulder, so that he broke out of a dream. A familiar voice, a friend's voice – Jacob's – spoke in the air above his head.

'Would you like to go for a donkey-ride?'

The singer hesitated, her attitude frozen, with hands held out. Then, for fear of going too far this first time – but she had spoken his name, he knew her – Gilda dropped her arms to her side. There would be a next time and a next time, she was here to make sure. Jacob looked her in the eye, as if not at all surprised that she should be trying to speak to the boy. Wait, his intelligent glance seemed to say. Show patience. Wait.

Sara with a bundle of clothes under her arm, some his, some hers, was waiting for Iynx there, on the shady side of the cistern, away from the house, where she could hardly be seen. Iynx dimly remembered, from long ago, the two of them arriving here at Cornelia's, after a journey together on a donkey, that had gone on and on almost for ever. Cornelia, as he knew, did not like her own people to ride donkeys. Only the *coloni* rode donkeys. Was that why Sara, sitting sideways, had hidden the donkey that was waiting for him, in the shadow on the wrong side of the cistern?

Jacob then spoke to Sara clumsily – though what he said made sense – in the language that until lately Iynx had always taken to be his own secret. Their private way of understanding each other. Sara understood Jacob though, although Jacob spoke as if he hardly knew how. She answered readily with the gurgle, the grunt, that with her indicated consent.

'Now we start our game of hide-and-seek,' said Jacob to Iynx, as, discreetly, he waved them goodbye. 'Duck your head, Iynx. Don't let them see you from the house.'

They headed south, Sara and he, towards the desert, the place he had never seen, the way he had always wanted to go, moving by little field paths beside irrigation ditches, well off the highway.

'But that little boy you were speaking to is the child of the house!' objected the tall, bony woman, with hair like a bush, Gilda's workmate, who had worked all morning at her side, and observed her, as she stooped for olives, looking back time and time again across her shoulder. When the boy moved past the cistern, Gilda's face had lit up. She had sung as no-one had heard Gilda sing before, until a man from the house came along to fetch the boy away.

'I tell you, he is mine!' announced Gilda with all her force. So long as her song lasted, Iynx's eyes had been fixed upon her in rapture, he had almost known her. When she called out 'Iynx!' he had answered to his name. He did know her!

'Don't think others haven't felt the same.'

Gilda knew that her workmate was taking her for one of those crazed women who, for lack of a child of their own, run off with someone else's. And who, she thought wryly, can blame her for thinking so, after what I have just confided. Was I a fool to tell her even that much? But she had been full to bursting with the splendid discovery.

'As bosses go,' the woman went on soberly, 'the lady Cornelia is not the worst to work for. I've picked this olive grove before. She pays what she promises, even though I've known her keep us waiting. But run off with that child – the child of the house – and you'll see. She will nail your skin to a barn door.'

'I tell you,' said Gilda with calm emphasis, 'he is mine.'

The woman was impressed by Gilda's tone of voice. She looked her quietly in the eye, and by that one glance was convinced. She muttered, more sympathetically, 'Or when next you get a chance, you could grab him. Take him and go – travel through the night. Keep running. We are not the only Circumcelliones down in these parts. Wherever there are ripe olives at this time of year, you will find our mates. Since he is yours, and he knows you. We would all say we hadn't seen you.'

The little boy, such a charmer, a pity his head sat crooked on his shoulders, might like so many stray children have been swept up by a slave dealer. It could happen to anyone. And was that why Gilda had taken up field work, and come looking? The woman went on, as if to participate in Gilda's bitterness. 'Rob us of our wages, yes, they try that often enough.' The big-boned woman laid a sisterly hand on Gilda's shoulder. 'But when it comes to robbing us of our children?'

Jacob, a man of an inquisitive turn of mind, had long ago made sense of those strange, guttural utterances of Sara's. Her native tongue was Gothic.

If spoken to in Latin, the language of command, she obeyed, though sometimes unwillingly, unless the order concerned the boy, on whom she doted. One day, from mere curiosity, Jacob had tried speaking to her in all the barbarian tongues of which he had a smattering, one after another – Celtic, Pontic, Nubian, even Hun. As he spoke his few words of Gothic her eyes lit up, and that was the clue.

For Jacob to listen for a pattern in her mysterious choking replies, until they had a small and sufficient vocabulary in common, was a game in which Sara had delighted. Having discourse with someone else, a grown man, was a stunning change. Iynx, at first, was not very willing to lend a hand – he would rather go on being the only one in the world who understood Sara, or could answer her. But the fascination of the game caught up with him, and whenever Jacob was at a loss, the boy would explain. To instruct a man as clever as Jacob? What could be more grand?

Jacob had summoned the mutilated woman out of her world of loneliness. Though Sara mistrusted all the others here on the estate, especially Cornelia, for Jacob she would do anything. That morning, after meticulous repetition, she had even grasped what kind of danger the boy might be in, and where to take him for safety. In their strange cryptic language Sara and Jacob had made their plans under Inimicus's very nose, and the centurion had not understood a word.

Jacob much earlier that day had arrived on a female racing camel as gawky as an old maid, and tethered her, as usual, in the courtyard until Inimicus led in his horsemen and at once ordered Jacob's beast outside the gate, since the camel-stink would upset the cavalry chargers. After obeying that piece of arbitrariness with a forced smile, – *but what in fact were soldiers doing here?* – Jacob went straight upstairs, unannounced. The old poet was stretched out on his day bed, breathing by fits and starts, his eyes almost closed.

'Claudius Claudianus. Can you hear what I am saying?'

Jacob's question exploded softly inside the lingering residue of Claudian's opium dream. He was glad of this interruption from without, for his dream was taking a deliquescent turn, as they sometimes did, and might at any moment turn to horror. The question came a second time, louder, and Claudian pulled himself up to the surface, for there would be no escaping Jacob. Anyway, he had something important to tell him. What was it? As he fought himself back into the land of the living, Claudian tried to remember.

'If you are happier snoozing,' said Jacob sardonically, 'I might go for a stroll, or read a book.'

A book! That was it. Claudian opened his eyes, to their fullest possible extent, eyelids propped open with fingers.

'I tell you – I have had enough.'

'Of my company? Already? Of my treatment? Of our conversation?'

'There is nothing in this benighted place, my dear Jacob, more reviving than your conversation. Even so, I have had enough. Of your conversation, and everything else. Particularly of myself, and of the world I am still obliged to live in. A book, did I say? Over there, on the clothes chest. I have left one out for you. A particular book, a precious book. Examine it inside and out, reflect on what it says with great care. Act as you think fit. As indeed shall I, the very moment you are gone. Can you hear them, down in the countyard, the soldiers? Their hooves – their brutal conversation? And now take the book, and please leave me alone.'

His voice faded away as he made this this determined effort at coherent speech, until it was a breathless ghost. Claudian had deliberately closed his heavy eyelids – a dismissal.

The book was an elegantly-written scroll, an odd volume from Claudian's set of Plotinus's *Enneads*, housed inside a blind-tooled cylindrical pigskin case. Why was he being given this precious odd volume, which would ruin the set? Under the leather tongue had been pushed a folded scrap of papyrus, as if to jam the fastening firm.

Out on the loggia, where the light was better than in the sickroom, Jacob unfolded the scrap of papyrus. Claudian had written a message for him in tiny Greek characters.

> Claudian and Iynx are on Heraclian's list, and in mortal danger. These soldiers are also looking for the boy's mother. I cannot discover what she is called or where to find her, but she is in danger too, and, so I believe, somewhere nearby.

Jacob tore the papyrus into the tiniest of fragments, and let the hot desert wind scatter them across the courtyard where the half-dozen cavalry chargers trampled and waited.

At bad news you should always put on a brave front. Jacob tiptoed away from the room, smiling as he passed household slaves, though later that day he was to reproach himself for leaving Claudian as he had declared he wanted to be left – alone.

Jacob went down boldly into the house, cornered Sara, and engaged with her in what other servants, glancing sideways and pulling faces, took to be some kind of comically barbarous and unnecessary love-talk. The boy's nursemaid was a slave – why did the *medicus* not simply take her? When Jacob later on that day, in response to Cornelia's hysterical cries, ran headlong upstairs, it was already over with Claudian.

The opium dream when Jacob had left the room and Claudian

shut his eyes again came on thick and rich, but soon began deteriorating. Grotesques came down on the old poet with a clap of dragon wings; emissaries from Olympius in the form of giant rats were trying to make a meal of him. He had only to open his eyes, though, in all likelihood for the last time, and they would vanish. But the real emissaries, the soldiers, were downstairs. With the muscular effort of a man opening heavy shutters on a windy day, Claudian again lifted his eyelids.

Coughing, shuddering in body but firm in mind, Claudian took his decision. He walked fumbling fingers across the bronze side-table, panting with the trivial effort, until he had tipped the lid of the enamel box. There was plenty left.

The stuff had the murky taste that had put him off when first he tried it, only fifteen then, yet into Claudian's mouth again and again went the little ivory spoon, and when it was all gone he held the spoon close, and licked the concavity. Death as a nasty taste in the mouth, and yet a pleasure – a deliberate, a voluntary pleasure. But then pleasures, Claudian told himself, clinging to the phrase and moving it around in his mind to consider, are born of conquered repugnances.

So much in life, lately, had disgusted him. For one thing, he was sick to death of the simple, painful act of breathing. He was sick of pretending, even to himself, that with Heraclian so close on his heels he was a heroic antique Roman. That *persona* no longer mattered. I was heroic when I pretended to be, thought Claudian, because it amused me. All my life I have conquered my repugnances, one by one, and in consequence had much pleasure. But this dream I now invite will be the last.

The taste on his numb and overwhelmed tongue was no longer so bad. A sticky mess, not in the least reminiscent of Egyptian poppies, big white poppies, nodding sleepily on mother's corsage. Dream now. *Nox est perpetua una dormienda.* Endless dream.

Cornelia who at much expense had found that rarity a milch-cow, so that Claudian should not have to drink the goats' milk he abhorred, not that he liked cows' milk much better either, brought him a warm, fresh bowlful not long after his breath had left his body, and found him there, serene. She had seen another old man laid out dead on this very bedstead, her first. Yet when her second husband, Claudius Claudianus, always such a good man to her, failed to reply, or to move, or to breathe, or even to wink at her, as he sometimes did, she simply could not believe it.

Cornelia began to scream for Lucas – but today, Lucas was not there. Then for Jacob, as if a physician could do anything for Claudian, by this time. The centurion came bounding upstairs, just ahead of the doctor, and he took charge.

Inimicus was extremely angry, and had difficulty in concealing it. His mission today was a secret one, so he could only relieve his anger by inflicting it on others. He had planned what he would do so cunningly, yet the boy, at other times always underfoot, was not to be found. His dumb nurse had gone, too. Now, apparently, the old man, to all appearances the most important one, had taken his own way out. Proof of conspiracy! These high-placed Romans, the people who have always stood in my light, the centurion told himself furiously, always have friends in high places to help and warn them, even after the State in its wisdom has marked them down as traitors. The woman at least is somewhere out there in the field – the woman Carthage wants. Make sure of her, and I may still get my step in rank. If I lose them all, that might break me.

A step in rank – and marry the widow? Inimicus put a consoling hand on Cornelia's forearm, and did his best to smile.

Before an expeditionary force was sent out from Rome in the year 397 to crush him, Gildo and his followers had tried to bring to life a hopeless dream. Turn the vast and far-too-often uncultivated estates of the absentee rich into small farms for the landless poor. Africa a self-governing province, with just taxes.

Circumcelliones and Donatists alike – men who worked with their hands and followed the prompting of a radical religion – joined Gildo's rising. Owners of large property had been terrified. But so long as Rome needed corn and oil in large amounts to light her lamps and feed her plebs, the rich in Africa would have to put up with these gangs of migrant pickers, moving across the countryside as crops ripened, and stubbornly nourishing ideas of their own.

The Circumcelliones, though they might suppose themselves free, were kept under police observation. This woman Clara

Cantora, who privately admitted to a name that was an echo of Gildo's, turned up at Cornelia's and the trap was sprung because Cornelia's household was already under suspicion.

For one thing, the *agentes in rebus* had their eye on the poet, Claudian – a sick man, living a long way off, yes, but notoriously a friend of Stilicho's. There had been reports, too, of a wrynecked child, in age and appearance too much like the one sought in vain at Samnium. Even in an Empire grown decadent, the police still functioned – the arm of the state could still reach a long way.

The boy, thought Inimicus, can hardly have gone far. He can be found. He is the least of my worries. The old penman, the husband, has escaped me – I must simply report him dead, and that's that. I must now make sure of the singer. The singer of sedition – and one who greatly intrigues them, to judge by my orders.

A trumpet sounded the command to mount, and Inimicus led his six horsemen in a double line, jogging slowly under the lintel of the gate, and more briskly away from the house towards the olive grove. The older women among the Circumcelliones began to jeer. Had not their men often beaten such frontier cavalry, years before, in fair fight? Had they come here asking for the same again?

Inimicus's men were picking their way circumspectly behind him, past the cistern, and under the treacherous lines of olive trees, at a walk, shoulder to shoulder. Inimicus shouted an order, and unenthusiastically they began to trot, crouching to avoid branches. Inimicus told himself: *I must make sure of the woman.* He raised and emphatically pointed his right hand. The riders converged on Gilda at a canter.

They possessed themselves of her by a parade-ground trick. Slowing to a trot, the first pair of horsemen took Gilda simultaneously by the wrists, so that she was dragged behind them. The second pair bent down a long way from the saddle for her ankles. She was carried off spreadeagled between four horses, screaming from surprise and pain. This had been too much like what happened to her as a girl, it had broken her defences. Abuse poured out of her mouth.

A shower of stones followed them, thrown by the quickerwitted among the Circumcelliones' women. One young soldier got his head cut open, and that was that. The riders were gone back to the house, the gate was closed behind them. It had all been done so fast that Gilda's friends had no time to think. Inimicus as he rode back at the head of his men was overjoyed.

Gilda astonished the slaves by the insults she was screaming. They took their prisoner downstairs, and the centurion made sure of her by bolting Gilda in a cellar store-room. In her anger she had made no attempt to deny her real name. A gift for Heraclian thought Inimicus, and certain promotion for me.

Inimicus despatched a quick-witted man on a good horse down the highway, to keep an eye open for the boy and his nurse, and order up more reinforcements from the fort. He knew what he would soon have to face. Circumcelliones never let one of their number be taken without attempting a rescue.

After sunset they would attack in their predictable fashion. Set some part of the manor house afire, and carry it by storm. Let them try, thought Inimicus. Their singer of sedition would cook alive in the cellar. Inimicus had seen it all before. Circumcelliones never let themselves be taken alive, never abandoned one another, and in the old days, so the tale went, rather than be captured, they would jump over the nearest cliff, shouting *Laus Deo*! as they fell.

Cornelia, emerging distraught from Claudian's room, had heard downstairs a tirade of yells and Latin vituperation, as four soldiers carried Gilda down to the cellar, and bolted her in. What in her calm and ordered house was happening? As she leaned over the bed where her dead husband lay, Cornelia's hair had come loose. At the top of the stairway she paused, to fit the knot of hair into the comb. Let at least one thing be in order.

Cornelia set exactly the right look upon her face, unsmiling, sad at heart, and went downstairs, to confront whatever was happening. If only, she thought, Lucas were here – but instead the centurion came forward to explain and console, and Lucas's not being here did not after all matter so much.

Out in the olive grove, the Circumcelliones were bawling their songs, and working themselves up to a high pitch of fearlessness by prayer and exhortation. Cornelia had heard tell of the Gildonic War, she knew what came next without being told. When they had worked themselves up for long enough, they would attack the big house with fire-pots and flaming brands.

Now that the traitress was safely his prisoner, Inimicus felt more confident. *The lady Cornelia is glad to have me to turn to. Let her discover once again who matters around here. Drive off the Circumcelliones first. That boy can hardly have gone far. Even show a little heroism. Women love a little heroism. And all else will follow.*

As he rode his well-behaved gelding back desultorily to the manor house, Lucas heard the roar from the olive grove, and soon grasped what it must mean. The courtyard gate was shut against him, so Lucas dismounted under the two caryatids, leaving to the slave who nervously opened the wicket when he hammered with his fist, the chore of easing the lathered beast through the narrow aperture. Inimicus, hands on hips in the midst of the courtyard, was very much in command. Cornelia's household slaves usually moved with lazy nonchalance, but with the centurion shouting at them they sped this way and that, carrying heavy vessels that slopped water.

Cornelia was waiting for Lucas with an oddly serene and even gratified face. Her fit of conventional sorrow had quickly worn off, the present excitement thrilled her. She had found time, though, to go upstairs and change into a widow's dress, dating from when her previous husband died. This was a dress she had kept handy in the clothes chest, not too far from the top. Mourning flattered her.

'Claudius Claudianus is gone at last.'

Lucas took the news like a blow in the face. The matter-of-fact way she had of telling him made it a worse shock. With Inimicus watching him closely Lucas strove against the tears that were trying to fill his eyes. Claudian's death had been long expected, but this loss, now it had come, never to hear his voice again, enjoy his wit, had an appalling finality.

'Where have you put him?'

'In his room – where else?'

'Then I think I should like to see him.'

Halfway up the stairs Lucas glanced back, to see if Cornelia would follow, but she had turned away, and was shouting instructions to a maidservant who had been too extravagant in tearing up linen for bandages.

That thing stretched out rigid, with copper coins blank on its eyes, was not the poet Claudius Claudianus, but a withered old dummy.

Lucas stood there for a while, but there was nothing to do or say. No more tears came. The old man had had no religion – there was no ritual to observe. The coins on the eyes – the coins to cross Styx – were a meaningless old custom. He went out of the room again, sad, numb, inert, as if the provincial insensibility which down here had been growing upon him might from now on become an inevitable part of him, his damnation.

Latterly Claudian had often enough teased him, for becoming plump, and growing bald, and being slow off the mark. But Claudian when living had also been his stimulus, the one person in the world whose insights illuminated, whose good opinion he valued. Lucas told himself firmly, I must be true to him, but could not quite tell as he stood there what being true to Claudian would mean, or if, indeed in the long run it would mean anything.

The woman he had once loved intensely was underfoot, in the cellar, a prisoner, but Lucas was never to know. Inimicus had prudently avoided telling Cornelia that he had the dangerous firebrand Gilda locked away.

Nor had Lucas ever known that Gilda was Iynx's mother. No instinct had informed him that he himself in the course of nature was Iynx's father. He had always treated Iynx just as he would have treated any small boy who was bright and charming, that is to say, at least as well as a father who assumed authority would have done, and perhaps better indeed. Ever since Claudian had revealed to him – mistakenly – that Stilicho was the boy's father, Lucas had felt slightly differently about Iynx, more remote from him. The boy was special.

Inimicus with a flattering word to mollify him sent Lucas up to the flat roof, well out of the way, where no heroic action he might commit was at all likely to be noticed by the lady Cornelia. A couple of slaves, who would much rather have done duty elsewhere, were made to follow Lucas upstairs, staggering under the weight of a water barrel. A common tactic of the

Circumcelliones was to shoot fire arrows upwards and drop them on the roof. Lucas and his two slaves had been stationed there to quench them as they came over.

Looking out from the roof at the night sky, acutely aware of the slaves' timidity, and Claudian stretched out dead in his room, Lucas felt desolate. What if this whole house burst into flames under his feet. Would it matter?

Suppose those vociferous and ignorant men out there did divide up the land, as in the Gildonic War they had so loudly threatened. Then educated people, Lucas told himself glumly, would themselves be out there in the heat of the day, in broken straw hats, picking olives, while ragamuffins lounged their way through this splendid house, lighting the kitchen fire with manuscripts. Things will be essentially the same for me from now on, and yet different. Iynx and I are Claudian's joint heirs. Are we not?

The foremost of the Circumcelliones, a handful of them, fire in hand, were emerging from the trees in a ragged line. Burning arrows began coming up and over, like fireflies, most of them falling short. The roof-tiles were under Lucas's sandalled feet. He sensed the solidity of the house, its actuality, and for the first time felt possessive. When they try to light fires, those people, he thought, I shall put them out, as best I can. He would defend his own.

Jacob did not care all that much for Roman generals. A Roman general had obliterated the holy city of Jerusalem, and dispersed the Jews into lands not their own. Claudian however had been Flavius Stilicho's close friend, and had written admirable poems which praised him, and Claudian had one day, by intention, passed on a certain secret about the boy's horoscope. The boy might well be the by-blow of a Roman general, and liable to suffer for it. But he was also Iynx. Simply because he was Iynx, he must be safely got away.

Jacob had then seen and heard Gilda being carried downstairs by guffawing soldiers, and had admired the eloquence of her amazing low-Latin insults. Who else could she be but the one they were looking for, the woman mentioned in Claudian's deathbed message, the mother?

And is that woman any of your business either? Jacob then

asked himself, as he wound parallel edges of bandage with scrupulous precision around the scalp of the young soldier who had been hit by the flying stone. You have a chance at last, haven't you, thanks to your brother, of escaping from the oasis? A chance that has taken a long time to organise? Then why be a fool? Exactly the kind of political fool you were, once too often, in Alexandria?

Jacob moved away from his patient, and washed his hands of blood. You are trying to stifle conscience, he riposted to himself severely. The fact, is you are already committed. You wish to save the boy – you feel for him as a son? The prisoner down in the cellar – who may before the night is out be burnt alive, as may we all – is the woman who, if they can make her blab, will lead them to the boy, incriminate him. And thence, from the boy to you. Once you put Iynx on the donkey's back, you committed yourself. He is Claudian's legacy – you are in this up to the neck. Just try not to think of the punishments they might inflict on you – the tyrant always works on his victim's imagination – but do what has to be done.

You renewed your friendship with Claudian – you need not have done. And took benefit from it. Well aware as you did so that all those years of fruitful nullity as an exile at the oasis would come to an end. Friendship brings obligation. You are back in the world of men, and therefore obliged to act. Don't wriggle. Choose your moment, and outwit them.

Jacob sighed. We live in a terrible world, he told himself, where at times a wise man must act like a fool.

He shrewdly waited until the vanguard of the Circumcelliones were making their attack, filling the night with a hullabaloo of cries and the spectacular tumbling of fiery arrows. The soldiers had something else to think of. Every armed man available had been called on to resist the attack. No one saw Jacob take the voluminous camel-rider's cloak from its peg, and step down quietly to the cellar. Even the sentry on the cellar door had been called away. Jacob wished himself luck as he slid back the heavy bar, and went inside. Suppose this woman turned out to be impossible?

Gilda lay in a heap, recovering her wits. The way those horsemen had taken her up, bodily, brutally, had been an ugly reminder, but the sense of outrage was fading. Vocal in her head were the louder, more barbed, and more painfully memorable insults she had not been given a chance to use. As the pattern of violent verbiage faded from her mind, Gilda tried by an effort of will to ready herself for the questioning she knew was bound to come – the disconcerting alternation of sympathy and cruelty for which the *agentes in rebus* were notorius. I will give them wrong answers or none, she promised herself, for as long as flesh and blood will stand it. By then with luck the boy will be a long way off.

When Jacob opened the door and tossed her a cloak, saying, 'Pull that over your head. As you follow me out of here, not a word,' Gilda baulked. This was the man, grey hair, thick eyebrows, hooked nose, who had carried off Iynx. What trick was he up to now?

'The boy – don't you want to see him?'

'Where is he?'

'Follow me and find out. If you stay in here much longer, you will never see daylight again. And nor shall I.'

Could this be the other kind of secret policeman – not the brute, but the cunning and seemingly-friendly one? Looking at his quizzical, impatient face, Gilda decided: I know men and this is a good one. Even so, she could not feel quite sure.

The long homespun robe dropped from shoulders to feet, and with a tug and a little shuffle Gilda transformed her appearance. She pulled the hood forward to conceal her face and to Jacob's admiration walked out of the cellar with a camel-rider's gait – a roll like a sailor's. As he watched her go across the cellar floor to the stairway, his confidence flowed back.

The pair of them walked through the agitated mansion like two ghosts. They were irrelevant, they were superfluous. A war was going on around them with which they had nothing to do. The Circumcelliones had lit a few arrow-fires here and there in the fabric of the house, and then backed off. The soldier standing watch on the gate, a self-important man, was not at all sure that the enemy were not still close enough to rush back. He knew the *medicus* – but who was this other one?

'The man who owns the camel. Can't you see that for yourself?'

If the Circumcelliones, in their attack, had carried off the racing camel, which he had been obliged to tether outside, or casually cut its throat, they were lost anyway.

'Did I see him come in?'

'Or would you rather I sent for your centurion?' exclaimed Jacob, simulating anger. 'Can't you use your eyes? We are being sent out with an important message.'

'Message? What for?'

'Reinforcements. As he will soon tell you when he gets here.'

That clinched it. Who wanted the rough edge of the centurion's tongue? With a bad grace the soldier slipped back the bolt of the wicket gate, and pushed the two of them hurriedly outside, as if he would rather lose them.

'Have you ever ridden a camel?'

'*Nunquam.* Never.'

'This is when you learn.'

Gilda in her unfamiliar enfolding robe climbed gingerly astride the broad leather saddle, with Jacob's arm almost accostingly tight around her waist. She snuggled against him, a declaration of confidence. The racing camel whickered like a haughty virgin, and staggered to her feet. Gilda, higher in the air than she had expected, was moving away from all this at a speed that pushed the night air fresheningly against her face. Freedom was something real, and the world outside that cellar was enormous.

Lucas on the roof turned away from dousing a fallen wad of smouldering tow, to see a camel striding away from the house with two up: Jacob, and who else?

Would he ever come back here again, the *medicus*, now that Claudian was dead? Lucas had not always relished Jacob's company. Talk with him could be too much like a gladiatorial combat. Jacob knew so much, and yet he argued to win. But, on the other hand, thought Lucas, he is now the only educated man around here, another stimulus. It was being borne in on him, as he stood there, how much he was going to miss Claudian.

War on even the smallest scale is full of yawning pauses, and now came one. The Circumcelliones having tested the defences of the manor house were pulling back to prepare their main onslaught. Until the time more fire arrows came dropping down on him – to his own surprise he had found the first attack not frightening but exhilarating – Lucas lounged there on the tiles, dreaming of what his life would be after all this was over, as Claudian's heir, his adopted son. The pang of loss had been sharp when it came, like drawing a tooth and leaving a hole. He had been aware at first of nothing but the loss. Now he began to think of the practical advantages.

For one thing there could, in canon law, be no question of his marrying Cornelia: his adopted father's wife, a prohibited degree. And lucky for me, thought Lucas, realizing as he stood there how exorbitant her demands might have been. Had Claudian in his quiet malice thought of that? Very likely. And saved me. I should have been Cornelia's servant all day, and all night too.

Standing there on the roof, looking out towards the hostile flames and hot glows bobbing to and fro under the olive trees, Lucas told himself, the way to treat her henceforward is with invariable respect, as a close member of the family. Cornelia would never turn him out, not now. We shall stay good friends, and live in peace. As he rubbed together his smut-stained hands, and eased his aching muscles and wished the night was over, or anyway, this tedious waiting, to Lucas peace seemed more than ever the one good thing in life. Peace to enjoy what now he had.

There was, to begin with, Claudian's large and extremely valuable library. Lucas so far had read only around the edges – now arrived his chance to plunge in, and become a learned man too. The manuscripts Claudian had so light-heartedly passed on to Jacob – Lucas had a list of them – must all come back where they belonged. Another thing: the old man deserved a worthy tomb. Would the local sculptor – son of the man who had carved the caryatids – be up to the job? I can at least trust myself to compose a fitting Latin inscription, thought Lucas – decent, laconic, not effusive. Claudian never cared for verbal excess. Simple and dignified. Claudian dead was becoming the most important of all Lucas's possessions.

And during the years to come, day by day, year by year, as an act of piety, copy out Claudian's entire opus, in good plain penmanship, on materials of the best quality. A tribute to friendship. Copies for the libraries of Alexandria and Carthage, where they would be safe for ever. And once this trouble with Alaric was over, a set of the later poems for the library in the Roman Forum – they lacked them. A labour of love.

From the parapet, Lucas saw the Circumcelliones come forward once again, from the dark line of trees. There were many more of them this time. He called a warning down into the courtyard, but the man on the gate had already been alerted by the approaching cries of *Laus Deo*! A long crescent line was advancing, men and women, the intermittent glow of stinkpots and torches, the fence of spears. That flickering, variegated light made them look more than ever alarming. They were singing some kind of dreadful hymn.

'Smoke 'em out!' exclaimed one loud voice, carrying on the night air, in an interval between verses.

When the first fire arrows once again began coming over, Lucas was no longer in the least afraid. To all he could see, underfoot and around, he shared a lawful right. This broad property, this civilised way of life, he would defend as best he could. He spoke sharply to the slaves; irresolutely they began pouring water from barrel into bucket, in readiness.

Jacob risked the imperial highway south, speed mattered, but three milestones along he ran into a couple of dozen border cavalry, coming the other way at a half-hearted trot. The decurio leading the column raised his hand and, as his men reined in and breathed their horses, he walked his own charger forward, easing sabre in scabbard, as though the gesture itself were a question.

Gilda heard Jacob speak out, with fake loud confidence, in not quite the tone for the occasion: an actor unsure of his lines.

'A mob, setting fire to the lady Cornelia's house!'

'I know, and who are you?'

'I have a message from your centurion. If you come up at the gallop, he says, you should be in plenty of time for the fun.'

The *decurio* glared hard at Jacob, as if a blink or a stammer or a hostile gesture might incriminate him, but in the end could think of nothing better to say than, 'At a gallop? On these old nags?'

The *decurio* let blade drop back into sheath. The *medicus*, riding back to the oasis on a camel. Nothing much wrong there. He raised his right first to his shoulder in the Roman salute, and inclined his fist forward in an oblique punch – the order to advance.

'Off we go, lads. In plenty of time to save the centurion's sweetheart.'

One man laughed. They pounded away up the highway at the same spavined trot, no faster than they had come. Jacob more fearful now than while it lasted, turned in the saddle to watch them go. His body, as Gilda could tell, was covered with the sweat not of effort but anxiety. His arm was too tight against her ribs, she could count the bones. She eased it away, but made herself consolingly comfortable against him. After what she had just seen and heard, she had more confidence in this man. The soldiers were his enemies too. Only, why was he doing all this? Who was he?

'My little boy, Iynx,' she began 'he knows you – I saw you with him –'

At last, thought Jacob, she has decided to begin talking. Now she will probably never stop.

'He is riding through the night on a donkey. By this time tomorrow I hope we shall have him out of here. And you too.'

Gilda dropped her voice, as if even in the silence of this dry and empty countryside there might be spies.

'Are you by any chance a friend of Flavius Stilicho's? You acted as he used to. Cleverly. Quickly.' Not that on Stilicho's body, thought Gilda, I ever once felt the sweat of fear.

The camel was lifting up its pads from the ungrateful road with a look of disgust, and slapping them down again, covering distance. Jacob spoke to the beast in a strange tongue, before answering.

'Stilicho? I have never met him. I was an old friend of Claudian's. Stilicho warned him, and Claudian then put me up to all this. Don't worry, Gilda. If your name really is Gilda.'

'Oh yes, it's Gilda.'

'Then let's change it, because down here Gilda is not a name but a death warrant. When others are about I shall call you Rachel. And you must go in disguise. Not just your clothes. Even your mind disguised.'

Gilda laughed. 'That is what I have been doing all my life.'

Jacob, deadly tired, had begun to wonder when this woman

who called herself Gilda, and appeared surprised that one had never heard of her, would stop chattering.

'I must admit that in Rome, Claudian never much liked me. He didn't like women, particularly Stilicho's women. Are you one with the Circumcelliones? I am. Now I have got to know them, I approve of them. Those soldiers, though – what will they do with them?'

Why should Stilicho's former mistress, wondered Jacob, be so anxious about a bunch of Circumcelliones?

'Do to them? Less than you think. You saw for yourself how half-hearted those soldiers were. Troops down here on the African frontier are spread out thin, they don't go looking for trouble. Carthage will eventually be told at great length how their promptness and their gallantry saved the lady Cornelia's life and property. The way they compose their report to headquarters matters, more than the real facts. I have sometimes helped the centurion touch up his reports. All this night's work may end in a few beatings and hangings, but I think not. By the day after tomorrow your friends will have drifted off, and joined other gangs, and begun all over again'.

The camel jogged forward, with its swaying, obstinate, rapid motion. Gilda, though still excited, fell silent. Into her head were coming so many unanswerable questions, that the mere endeavour to sort them out dropped her off into sleep. Jacob held her body close to his own, a warm, breathing bundle. As he headed the camel fast, down devious ways, through the chill of the desert night he began to revive, forgetting his fatigue. It was a long time since he had held a woman in his arms, even one swaddled in clothes.

Gilda awoke lying on the ground, her mouth puckered with thirst. An early morning sun was burning her face, and as she turned, there was the oasis, palm trees, green vegetation, set in a waste of brown nothing. Today, she told herself, you must answer to the name of Rachel.

Rachel. Rachel.

'And what does Rachel mean?' she asked Jacob's face, which had just appeared between herself and the sky.

'Mother of Israel. It also means sheep.'

'Or wolf in sheep's clothing?' That made him laugh. She had

managed, actress-like, to catch and throw back his mocking tone.

A great many pack-camels had forgathered under the palm trees, and were drinking the muddy pond of water dry. Once the last of the stragglers had come in, the caravan would journey north-east, across sand and shale, to Leptis Magna on the Libyan coast. Leptis in the past had been a busy mart for traders bringing spices, drugs and emeralds over from Egypt, and for caravans crossing the Sahara from black Africa with gold dust, ivory, ostrich feathers and slaves. There was still enough business to keep the city more or less alive.

Iynx had been sleeping in Jacob's mud hut, and Sara, the dumb nurse, hissed the two of them away until his eyes were properly open. She was greedily protective. Gilda had hardly been expecting to play mother right away, but her chagrin at being chased off was bitter and sudden. She had grasped by now the fact that she had no right. This woman Sara, she tried telling herself, has looked after Iynx since the night he was born of my body. I must somehow win back my natural right over him, little by little. By kindness, by cleverness, by guile. But she is clever, too.

Jacob meanwhile as if this morning nothing else signified, went on boasting to her about a case he had lately been treating. The caravan captain suffered from desert boils, and could find no relief. And here he was with joy in his face, to announce that they had healed up.

'Others before me used infusions of rosemary. But I mixed powdered sulphur with the fat from a sheep's fleece clarified –'

'And where do you get sulphur from – your mud hole, I suppose?'

'Sulphur comes from the craters of volcanoes – Etna, Vesuvius, Stromboli,' he answered. 'Think of sulphur as thy hot and dry – the essence of fire. It follows, since a boil is a fiery complaint, that I am treating fire with fire. What harms, says Hippocrates, will cure. Sulphur I always have by me. Indispensable in one's search for the elixir of life. And believe me, all joking apart – *Rachel*! the cure has come at the right time. Just look at that cheerful expression. This morning I had expected an argument, perhaps a refusal, but now that his boils are better, he will do anything I ask of him. Even take you women to Leptis Magna, not to mention the boy.'

The caravan captain took Jacob's proferred hand, and placed it first on his own forehead, then on his heart. They were rapidly exchanging words in a baffling Berber dialect – the caravan captain, with a seamed face made spuriously noble by the unending harassment of life in the desert, and this learned, vain, polyglot, humorous, sarcastic, grizzle-haired Jew, gabbling at each other, two of a kind.

Gilda caught her own new name in their talk: Rachel. The caravan captain so evidently respected Jacob that Gilda, despite his little outburst of professional vanity, found herself respecting him too. Though why was he doing all this, taking such enormous chances – a political exile, and this oasis his prison? Had this man Jacob perhaps been paid to put a knife to their throats, hers and the boy's, somewhere out if the sullen anonymity of the desert? If they had killed Stilicho by a trick, they could kill anyone.

Iynx and the nurse were emerging at last from the hut, hand in hand. A lop-sided head, yes, but in him that was no disfigurement. What held you were those two bright, rapidly-turning eyes that took in everything. The boy saw her and raised a hand: the singer! He gave Jacob a broad smile. The caravan captain smiled at the boy, but turned his back on the women. They might as well not have existed, yet Gilda hardly minded, because he had gone across to Iynx, palm held out, and was treating him like a little prince: an equal in this male world.

'He will take you, Rachel, and the nurse and the boy to my brother, Julius, in Leptis Magna,' said Jacob over his shoulder, in Latin, in a matter-of-fact voice that brooked no quibble. 'I have simply told him that the Romans are after you. All of us in the desert hate the Romans. And he will take no payment,' Jacob added with a chuckle, 'just another pot of my ointment.'

'What is your brother doing in Leptis Magna?'

'How do you suppose that I get my sulphur? He is in business there.'

'Is he a doctor too? An apothecary?'

'You will find out when you get there.'

Gilda for a reason she could not yet fathom felt a shiver go down her spine at Jacob's reticence.

Sara herself was already suspicious of Gilda as she was of all rivals, women who could talk, women who shone. As Jacob strode off with the caravan captain Sara followed him with her eyes, and Gilda could see at a glance that she adored him. For Sara, Jacob had unlocked the silence inside which the mountain bandits had imprisoned her when they severed her tongue – he had given an opening to Sara's intelligent but cruelly-frustrated mind. What I must try, decided Gilda, is to learn some of her chopped-up, choked-off lingo too – it will only take time and effort. That will make three of us inside her private world, and she can no longer go on ignoring me. I will give her no reason to hate me – I will move slowly. How can I take Iynx away from her? He is not a material possession, but a human creature with a mind of his own. Sooner or later, Sara will lose him anyway. Doesn't she know that?

The caravan would move when the moon came up, and travel all night to avoid the blinding impact of daylight heat. Already they were lashing up the last bales, and whipping in the laggards. With futile self-importance, the caravan dogs went barking around the camels' feet, as loaded, groaning, complaining the tall beasts stood erect.

When the sun was low and the time of departure coming close, Jacob had taken Gilda by the arm with no explanation, and led her off to the cane-brake on the remoter edge of the oasis. A thicket of whispering canes, where no one could see what happened. He has fetched me over here, Gilda decided gloomily, to take his payment. I have done this with men so often with my eyes wide open and my heart not in it, but my body sedulously obeying me. This time I rebel. Though if I make an enemy of him, where else do I go? There is nowhere to go, except with him. I must submit, as I did to that first one, that sea captain out of Marseilles, when I was only a child.

'At last, a place where it's safe for me,' said Jacob with a chuckle, as the enclosing canes parted, sprang back, hid them, 'to call you Gilda.'

'Don't bother,' she said curtly, watching him as a small animal watches a predator. I shall bruise him, she decided, where it hurts. And if I have to do what he wants, in the end, I shall give him a bad time he will remember.

'All day I have been watching how clever you are, with the boy and his nurse,' Jacob announced. 'Iynx is yours, no doubt of it, even if you have no way of proving it, though she wouldn't believe me if I told her so. I was afraid you might grow angry with her, when a squabble could spoil everything. But no you are too clever a woman for that –'

One of the other kind, thought Gilda grimly, one of those who prefer a little friendly talk, a few flatteries first, or confidences. Then take you and rape you. Who enjoy it all the better – perhaps can only enjoy it at all – if you come their way half-willing.

What Jacob said next came as a surprise.

'Are you really sure you want to burden yourself with the boy?'

'He is still my son, whatever happens,' Gilda said obstinately. 'Nothing can change that.'

Jacob sighed. She had given him the answer he was expecting.

'I have achieved most things in life,' he said, 'but never a son. So what if we simply consider what that means: your son. We have plenty of time before the light fades and they blow the ram's horn for departure. They blow three times, and the first has not yet sounded. Those words of yours "my son" are meant to make my heart bleed. That I know. But Sara has been a mother to Iynx for as long as he can remember. Let us also consider,' Jacob went on briskly, as if this were Alexandria, the marble steps outside the temple of Serapis, philosophy in the sun, 'what, by this time, must be Iynx's unusual conception of the word, "mother". He has already had other women wanting to be that to him. Cornelia. But you never met Cornelia –'

'I saw her.'

'– would very much have liked for Iynx to accept her as his mother. And how splendid for him. A rich and childless widow. Her husband – Claudian – even adopted the boy. Did you know that? There are times too, moments when even I feel towards Iynx as a father. No son of my own – and perhaps we met too late, you and I.' He nudged her, and chuckled.

Here it comes, thought Gilda, the seduction at last. Though has he time before the ram's horn blows? But the talk went on.

'Not that I am his father – or could be – except insofar that fatherhood, much more so than motherhood, is a voluntary relationship. The Christians with their cult of the Virgin Mary are clever about this one. Joseph for father, an old Jew with the fire died down, and a grown family of his own. An optional, voluntary, celibate father. As for optional motherhood, or even shared motherhood, well, we shall see, and it will be interesting. What was I saying?'

'Far too much.' Gilda, having by this time no reason to believe in the likelihood of rape, was laughing. In her first days among the Circumcelliones she had fought for her physical integrity like a tigress: they soon learned to let her alone. Gilda was a little shocked, here in the evening amid these whispering canes, and after all this talk, to find that she had, at last, encountered a man she fancied.

'Is the lecture over?'

Jacob laughed. 'My great failing – I know it. So many years here, on this oasis, alone, carrying on learned discussions exclusively with myself. Or disquisitions, perhaps, or in this case, digressions. Where was I? Ah yes.'

'I listened to everything you just said, about being a mother or a father, and most of it I had already thought about,' she told him. 'In the long run it changes nothing.'

Jacob sighed. He had not expected to convince her. And what if she were right?

'Here.' He thrust a small packet into her hand. 'A letter for my brother Julius. Take care of it please. And let me tell you in advance, you won't like him. I don't like him myself, even though this once, anyway, he is doing what a good brother should.'

The letter was folded small, and heavily sealed. 'I see you don't want me to read it.'

'I have written it in Hebrew – and who reads Hebrew? But yes – a woman's curiosity – let me tell you the nature of this letter. That after all is why I brought you here, before we got distracted. In this affair I am bound to mistrust my brother – a terrible thing to say, but I have to take into account his character as I know it, and the nature of his business. Therefore, to protect you, Gilda, and Sara, and the boy, I have been obliged in this letter to tell him one or two little lies. I hate lying, as I dare say you do too, but you would oblige me by keeping up the pretence. For all our sakes. Gilda, forgive my presumption, but I have written to say that the child is yours, the nurse the child's nurse, and you yourself the woman I am going to marry. In this letter I have called you Rachel.'

He even looks a little frightened, thought Gilda, of being taken too seriously. Has some other woman hurt him?

'He is my younger brother, but always jealous. In the past I have needed to control him, and it was never easy. Among us Jews a family sentiment is sacred, and I hope that this is still true for Julius. What else will restrain him, except the thought of money? I am lumbering him up with more people than were in the original bargain. For him less profit, more risk. He set up in business in Leptis Magna so as to help me – get me away from here if he could –'

'What business?'

'He is a business man – a merchant. He buys and sells.'

'Yes, they all do,' Gilda persisted, 'but tell me.'

'He deals in slaves.'

Iynx caught his first glimpse of the city – Leptis Magna – in the early morning of a clear hot day, the sun rising on the caravan's right hand, the dome of the sky lit up fleetingly with lemon yellow and duck-egg green, before it emerged as a clear daylight blue.

Distinct in the Mediterranean light beyond the desert's brown fringe, and further on, towards the sea, was a Roman city, girdled about with the green of irrigated vegetable-gardens. Leptis Magna had walls only on the desert side. The seaward face of the city was open to the breezes, unfortified, as if nothing hostile could ever reach it from the sea.

'Good?' Gilda asked the boy, her own face merry. The desert ride had been rather too much continual nothing, and now this astonishing sight at dawn. She had carried Iynx in her arms since after midnight, while Sara slept.

The boy was open-eyed but silent, taking it all in, then he chuckled.

The camels had been checked so that the halt and lame trailing behind could catch up. They all descended together in an animated, excited mass to the green plain, between desert and sea, the camels becoming restive at the smell of water. The thought came to Gilda that Rome meant the city. After the long-drawn-out nothingness of the desert, a city was what she had craved. Leptis Magna in its small way was like any other Roman city, buildings for government and worship, a stadium for races, a semicircular open-air theatre, not too big, she thought, and not too small. There would be a forum. There would be a library. Small and provincial, yes, lost along this desert coast, slowly decaying commercially – but a city. Romans built cities.

'What does it remind you of?' she asked Iynx. He was beginning to quite like Gilda, because with her he could have interesting conversations, but when overmuch strangeness came down upon him he clung to Sara.

With the sun risen and the camels restless, Iynx was a young prince again, conducting this caravan from his place on the broad saddle all by himself, his small bare feet dangling. Houses, he was thinking, buildings, too many of them, and over the flat roofs white sea-birds and black garbage-birds, competing. He best of all liked the glittering sea, and the white birds. He had heard tell of the sea from Claudian, but there was more of it than he imagined.

'Alexandria!' he exclaimed, to Gilda's bewilderment.

Julius, full-bearded, darkly sullen where his brother was smiling and, where Jacob was learned, cunning, was yet physically a man with a clear family resemblance – large eyes, hooked nose, broad shoulders. He examined these two shabby women and their bare-foot brat with an evident scowl, and took the letter. Before breaking open the seal with his thumbnail, he lifted a scrutinising eye. Gilda could feel him appraising her merely as so much commercial flesh and bone – she knew that look of old.

His eye brightened as soon as he had read the letter, and his manner changed. When Gilda introduced herself as Rachel he even achieved a crooked, conventional, condescending smile, as for a brother's future wife. Though he mostly kept his eye, Gilda noticed on Iynx.

Julius led them upstairs, to a raftered apartment built on the roof itself, and separate from the house underneath.

'No one else in Leptis will see you.' he assured them. 'I shall wait on you myself.'

After a while he came up again, with a flap of bread, goats' milk, fruit, hard cheese, a copper bowl of warm water, a clean towel. He had the manner of someone who had already done a great deal for them. They would not be left to starve, but until Jacob arrived, thought Gilda – if he ever did – they must not expect too much.

3

King Alaric reached down the claw-like nails of his left hand to scratch between the ears of his wolfhound, Filimer, big as a calf, brave as a lion. Filimer had run nobly at the heels of his charger all the way from Pannonia to Rome. Now that the city was at Alaric's mercy, the hound dozed all day at the King's feet. And perhaps, thought Alaric, feeling his ribs, was getting fat – too much flesh for a hunting dog. They hunt best when they feel hunger. Never feed up a hound until his ribs go from sight.

'Feed Filimer no more than once a day,' he said over his shoulder for his body-servant to overhear, and was amused that the blonde woman who stood before him so composed, should be startled by the irrelevance of what he said. Alaric stared back at her.

'You are clever enough to see for yourself, Princess ,' he pointed out 'that I can do with you whatever I choose. My men took you prisoner – you are enemies who fell into my power. The other one is the Emperor's sister – what better political hostage? But who are you, Princess? You ran away from us, your kinsmen before the great battle of Pollentia – to help your friends, the Romans.'

'My friends in those days perhaps. But let me tell you, my friends no longer.'

'I could chop you into bits, here and now, with this long sword of mine, and feed you to Filimer.' Hearing himself spoken of, the huge dog growled. The blonde woman's expression had not changed. Among Visigoths, brutal practical jokes were current coin. Her inward shudder behind her impassive face, had a thread of pleasure. What were men, in fact, but animals?

As calmly as she knew how, Veleda replied, 'Did you say Filimer? The name, surely of one of our ancient kings.'

'A king's name for a kingly hound.'

Alaric felt, with his fingertip, for the soft, tender and responsive part under the hound's jaw. Drawing back teeth from lip, Filimer rolled an eye in voluptuous acknowledgement. Alaric in fact was not displeased that he should have failed either to frighten Veleda, or to cajole her.

'Make dog's-meat of a Gothic princess?' she went on, in her haughty fearless voice. (She feels fear, thought the King, yet hides it). 'And what, King Alaric, will our people say of you for that, in years to come?'

An insolent yet a clever answer, since what in the end governs us, thought Alaric, is what other Goths will think of us, when we are gone.

'Were you not at one time General Sarus's woman?'

Alaric had hoped to abash her, and his jibe made Veleda bite her lip. But she came back at King Alaric incisively enough.

'Let me make one thing clear, King Alaric In fact your men did not take us prisoner, whatever you may have been told. We left Ravenna because we chose to leave, and we came directly to your camp. To put ourselves under your protection.'

The wolfhound, Filimer, rose like a sleepy giant from his place at Alaric's feet, to plod across the carpeted floor of the tent, and snuffle speculatively around Veleda's ankles. Lifting his huge head, Filimer licked her hand. My hunting hound, thought Alaric superstitiously, does not mistrust her. Speaking in a different voice, as though to an imprudent young kinswoman, Alaric said cordially, 'I begin to see why Sarus ruined himself for you.'

A blush this time passed from Veleda's cheeks to her forehead – but it might have been irrepressible rage.

'And if I let you keep company in my camp with your mistress, Galla Placidia, will you continue to spy on me? For the Emperor, her brother?'

The coarse provocation turned Veleda all barbarian. She spat between her feet on to the carpet.

'I spew Honorius out of my mouth.'

No Roman or Romaniser, he thought, would have done that. Speaking softly, Alaric said, 'I once saw your father spit exactly like that, when someone spoke of his enemy. Of course, his enemy in those days was Rome.'

The last of Veleda's patrician facade gave way at those words, as if it were almost beyond credence that her father, whom she hardly remembered – but in his heyday yes, he too had fought Rome – should after all this time still inhabit the memory of this ageing, important man. And do I, she asked herself, still copy his mannerisms? Still carry my father within me? Like a child unborn?

'Well then,' Alaric asked her caressingly, now that his chance had come. 'Are they as much in love as people say?'

'I am not here to spy for Honorius. Nor am I here to spy on his sister for you.'

'Even so, if you wish to stay here, I shall expect you to watch and to tell. If Galla Placidia and my brother-in-law, Ataulf, are as wildly in love as they are said to be. He with her, she with him. Then I shall need someone to tell me if they are making fools of themselves. A pair of experienced eyes, Princess. In a clear head.'

Alaric for emphasis ran large forefinger, large thumb, right and left along his enormous moustaches. She looked at the drooping mass of hair along his upper lip, and that alone was different, intimidating, unRoman.

'If only you warn me in good time of any act of folly, I can befriend them both.'

The morning Galla Placidia fell in love with Ataulf, thought Veleda sadly, I lost her. Glances, a few words, a lightning stroke. If I have occasion, by chance, to say the mere name *Ataulf*, she tightens her mouth and looks prim, yet her eyes gleam fire.

'Or else?' Veleda began, though with this man – this King – she already knew there could be no bargaining.

'Even being chopped into dog's-meat is something you might not fear, since one death is much like another. But this is worse. I shall keep your mistress here, and send you back under escort to Ravenna.'

The blandly-attentive smile beneath the drooping moustaches became saturated with cruelty. She could not refuse, none of them could ever, and therein lay the exquisite pleasure of being King. Galla Placidia's brother the Emperor is stupid. I think, however, that she is not. But if Honorius found his sister was dishonoured?'

Veleda had been trying to blot out of her mind mental pictures of the outrageous and abandoned way she had behaved with Sarus. Shame made her answer with a vehemence which Alaric found convincing.

'Galla Placidia is not Honorius. Ataulf is not Sarus. This love of theirs is a tremendous thing – a gift of the gods. Ataulf has ideas – he is overflowing with them –' Alaric nodded: yes, Ataulf had ideas. 'But let me tell you that they are the self-same ideas that Galla Placidia in Ravenna often discussed with me – even the self-same words –'

'Ideas?' Alaric was wary.

'The renewal of Rome by us barbarians. When Galla Placidia talks like that – and I heard her say these things before she even met Ataulf – you would say she was his echo. They are the two halves of the same egg.'

'What follies are they committing?' asked Alaric abruptly. And Veleda saw, at last, what was in his mind. If he sent the Roman Emperor's sister back pregnant, after keeping her hostage? Treaties have been broken, and wars declared, for less. Veleda, surmounting her own embarrassment, gave him a firm answer.

'You mean to ask me, King Alaric, is Galla Placidia a virgin? To the best of my belief, indeed she is. And wants, I am sure, to come to her wedding night a virgin, as a Gothic woman should.' (As I myself never can, thought Veleda: a Roman did that to me!) 'Believe me, King Alaric, she would stick a knife in any man who attempted her. You know Ataulf as I know Galla Placidia. They are burning, I would say, with a love that consumes both their bodies and their souls – *animae, saivalos* – his for her, hers for him. And yet they keep themselves in such a grip. It is both terrible and splendid.'

Even though she mixes Latin with her Gothic, thought Alaric, she has found her true tongue at last. I must make use of her.

The giant dog gave a grumbling growl and went towards the tent door, as if this conversation, now chopped meat was no longer mentioned, were no longer of the slightest interest.

'I ask of you nothing unworthy,' said King Alaric, getting to his feet. This was dismissal. 'I am not asking you to bring me tales about your mistress and my brother-in-law Ataulf. I do not listen to tale-bearers. But should you ever notice something dangerous to the Visigothic cause – dangerous to their happiness – then come straight here and tell me. I like talking to you. And Filimer likes you, he won't bite you. I shall give orders to my guard to pass you through to my presence without question.'

'Octavian Curtius was also making himself noticeable,' reported Veleda.

'Octavian Curtius?'

'An enormously rich money-lender. You will know him by his red nose. He afterwards gave a silly speech.'

Ataulf lifted a finger, and the young confidential, clean-shaven Arian priest, quiet in the corner, dipped his reed pen in the liquid lamp-black he wrote with, made a quick note of the name, the nose, the riches, the foolish speech, and waited for other comments. The young priest was Ataulf's memory. The priest had been a Catholic once, but won over, so he claimed, to Arianism. Veleda was never convinced by his smile. The smooth-faced priest spoke a gentle reminder.

'When Rome had to be ransomed, and the Senate agreed to a voluntary levy for *honestiores*, Octavian Curtius claimed that he had had great losses.'

Ataulf wanted to know why Veleda laughed.

'You will find the strong-room, down there in the cellar of his mansion, piled to the very roof-beams with bullion. Always a locked door – an iron door and an armed guard. That, though, is not all. No one ever unlocks that door and goes through but Octavian himself. He goes in his cellar carrying a leather money-bag, and wearing high leather boots and leather gloves. Why? Because he lets poisonous snakes breed in his cellar, to guard his money.'

Ataulf found Veleda useful and intelligent and frank with him. She was a splendid source of information about the rich of Rome, because she despised them. But he could never like her, because Veleda had been so intimate with Galla Placidia, in the old days. He wanted Galla Placidia entirely to himself.

'About Octavian Curtius you sounded very sure,' Ataulf remarked.

Veleda answered, uncomfortably, truthfully, 'At one time I knew his son.'

I could now send the two-faced priest out of the room, thought Ataulf. I could first mock her about her scandalous adultery with my *arbifijandsof* Sarus – and then about her sordid affair with this money-lender's son. I could shock her by letting her see I know that she is Alaric's spy. I could squeeze her to pulp.

Instead, in a particularly friendly tone, Ataulf asked, 'And what else can you tell us about this man, that might be useful?'

'But why do these people have to be *fed*?' King Alaric exploded, and impatiently he put down his drinking-horn. Without a word, Ataulf filled it to the brim again, from the cask. Horns had been filled and drunk between them, filled and drunk, Visigoth fashion, one serving the other, turn and turn about, until their minds were right for seeing things in a new way: the wisdom of drunkenness. What had sunk from sight into their minds was openly being said. Goths believed in the authority of drink, as a way of arriving at the truth.

'This fertile, sunny country of theirs – this Italy – look at it!' said Alaric. 'Rough grazing where there could be corn and vineyard. And you sit there, Ataulf, and dare tell me we can never be sure of Rome until we have also conquered Africa. Simply because the plebs here – the idle plebs – must needs be fed. Tell me this, clever man. Why should not the plebs of Rome live as Holy Writ says that all men must – by the sweat of their brow?'

'You mean enslave them? A thousand thousand slaves, all tied to one long chain, marching out at dawn into a field called Italy, with hoes in their hands? We should begin by needing a thousand thousand hoes. And a thousand thousand manacles.' Ataulf was giving back sarcasm for sarcasm – keeping the King's thought loose and moving, by touches of the goad. 'Or would you rather give them a small farm each, and each of them a basket of seed-corn? If you gave the Roman plebs seed-corn, they would do with it what their Emperor does – feed the birds.'

Alaric was silent; the beer which sometimes provoked spirited eloquence in him was making him gloomy. His every way of escape from the decision with which Ataulf had confronted him was being blocked off, as soon as he thought of it, by his clever, broken-nosed brother-in-law.

'If the Romans did it, in the days of Hannibal, so can we,' said Ataulf quietly. He had asked Princess Veleda to explain Africa to him, and she had told him about Hannibal.

'The Goths have never gone to war on ships,' said Alaric. 'You mean leave behind our horses?'

'Take our horses with us.'

Heraclian was sitting pat in Carthage, and by an embargo on shipments of corn he could strangle Rome at will. King Alaric poured another hornful of the brew. This was brown, the sea no certain colour, but blue or grey or green, according to the light. This was good to drink – if you drank the sea, you died.

'And how many hundreds of ships should we Visigoths need, even for our horses?' the King grumbled. 'How many of our splendid horses would arrive on the coast of Africa fit to ride?'

Ataulf knew, when the King's talk took this practical turn, that in his heart at least, the essential decision was taken, and Ataulf rejoiced, because far-fetched though an invasion of Africa might sound, what else could the Visigoths do, if they meant to keep Rome? Alaric, when it came to the point, understood necessity.

'To answer your question properly, King Alaric, must I not first begin to count ships and horses?'

'Then count them,' said Alaric, belching to feign indifference. His eyes could not as yet penetrate, except in glimpses, the gloomy forest of difficulties that confronted his people. 'Find out, then, and tell me!' Alaric's laugh as he poured the last drop from his tilted horn down his throat was deep and thick with contempt.

Retired gentlemen who had built villas in a benign climate, and were living quietly near Capua with their libraries and concubines, went out on moonless nights to bury with their own hands their spare cash, any statue or vessel made of precious metal, and even their pictures and portable mosaics. This countryside had been graciously peaceable for centuries – now terror was rampant. On the day these outrageous horsemen, clad in skins and carrying Roman weapons, arrived at the door, the rich wanted to be found living in apostolic simplicity – not worth robbing.

It never worked out. The master's favourite women would be put to the torture first, then the man himself. And even if they all kept heroically silent, under duress some household slave would blab. Opulent, cultivated sybarites hung up by the thumbs seldom failed to save their lives by renouncing their material possessions. Onwards the barbarians would ride, followed at a slower pace by a wagon loaded with the enviable objects they had extorted, having left to the *honestiores*, they would say gleefully, 'nothing but their souls'.

King Alaric, when he ransomed Rome, had been strict with his men about respecting the treasures of the church. This he had done not simply from pious motives. The Christian church in Rome would connect the conquered Romans with their new master, and become a means of government, if proof were given that he was a sort of Christian too.

This, though, was not a consideration which restrained the Visigoth irregulars who had gone further south, and were out of the King's control. And one bright morning they rode into Nola.

The actual words of the prayer that Paulinus of Nola is reputed to have uttered at the altar as the barbarians rode closer have come down to us. They hint at a truth about his character as founder of the community of St Felix – well-intentioned rather than heroic, a rich man conscience-stricken.

'Lord, let me not be tortured to reveal my gold and silver, for where all my wealth has gone, Thou knowest.'

At Nola you had only to look around to see where the money had gone. The buildings of the community – basilica, refectory, scriptorium, dormitories – were there in evidence, plain but harmonious, built and adorned as if to make life itself a work of art.

Another visible proof was the long and costly stone aqueduct, stalking across country to bring fresh water to the townsfolk of Nola, and paid for by Paulinus. His fortune had, by this time, been consumed to the last copper. The community lived nowadays off what it earned or begged, and that, Paulinus felt, was as it should be.

A dozen skin-clad Visigoths cantered into the broad, flagstoned courtyard and reined in abruptly. They had meant their arrival to come as a shock to the community, and so it did, though Paulinus had long known that nothing but a miracles could save Nola.

Dropped from a saddle like baggage, bloodstained, roped hands and feet, was a prisoner they had met on the highroad, a young man who worked in the kitchen. He had told them readily enough which way to come. People for miles around had spoken of Nola with awe – in Visigoth eyes, something important but mysterious must be going in here: how could there not be treasure? A man with a throwing-axe in his belt was apparently their leader. The horsemen dismounted, and made a joke of it as they tethered their horses to the tall olivewood crucifix which stood in the sunlight outside the basilica door. A cross displayed in public was a newfangled symbol, which meant very little to Arians.

A couple of the armed and skin-clad men glanced in at the church door, but were put off by the gloomy and incense-impregnated interior, lit by one altar-lamp, where Paulinus, dimly visible, and with his back deliberately towards them, was at prayer. Hot from their ride, others stood around the forecourt, easing their stiff legs, passing around a half-full wineskin, ignoring the whimpered appeal of the bruised and bloody prisoner they had dragged with them. They looked up at the buildings like large and greedy children who have come a long way to do mischief. After turning this way and that, they headed into the refectory.

On the refectory's longer wall, in a fresco of the Annunciation, the angel looked to them like a giant bird with a human head. From the feathered wingtips descended a ray of light, and smote the Virgin in the belly. That made them laugh. They had already seen frescoes – often titillating – on the walls of rich men's villas: Danae and the shower of gold, perhaps; Leda and the swan. The picture struck their fancy, and they stared at it. The Virgin might have been any young woman, anticipating a child. But where did the bird come in?

Halfway along the refectory's shorter wall, his feet planted apart on a trestle table, Theodorus the painter was at work, alone, on a Crucifixion. Representations of Christ on the cross – the True Cross had been dug up by St Helena in Palestine scarcely a lifetime before – were still a novelty that made Arians uncomfortable. The painter was working, with concentration, from his pattern of little perforations in the wet plaster, to depict the spear going into the victim's side.

Theodorus took no notice of the men moving behind his back. This morning they must have come in earlier than usual, to set the tables for the midday meal. Because the wonder-worker was ignoring them, the Visigoths began to suppose that he held them in contempt.

They stood unnaturally still, watching, as the image of a Roman *pilum* appeared like sleight-of-hand from the tip of the poised brush. They might have been over-excited children, held attentive by a conjuring trick. But once they had grasped how he did it, the painter's indifference provoked them.

'Hey, you – don't you know that's a blasphemy?' The Goth with the axe – the man who led them – had learned his glib impudence as a Roman slave. 'That man on the cross is only a man. You are trying to make him out the Son of God. And look at that other one – the woman. You try to pass her off as the Mother of God, but let me tell you something. We Arians know the truth. She is only a Jew woman, pregnant of a bastard. Ignorant superstition. God is God, and who else is there, beside?'

Having made this pronouncement in scurrilous street-Latin, the man with the axe turned to the others, and began haranguing them in Gothic. When a slave, he had gained the upper hand among his fellows by fanning the Arian faith. Enslaved the Goths might be, but simply by being Arians they were the Romans' superiors.

Theodorus, legs apart on the trestle top, his mind vivid with the painting, his left hand full of brushes, was annoyed at last, and turned to face his interruptors. Today's detail had not been fully worked-out, the plaster was drying, his work might be wasted.

Theodorus, given half a chance, thought in Greek. His Latin hardly did him justice. He had no particular wish, either, to argue theology with armed and angry men, but after the crude way his work had been spoken of he felt obliged to answer, in a blunt and simple Latin which, from the vantage point of the trestle, went home to them better than eloquence.

'And you call what you are doing down here Christian?' he asked. 'Bursting into houses not your own – carrying off whatever takes your fancy? You are forgetting what it says in Holy Writ. Lay not up treasure on earth, but treasure in heaven. Those who take to the sword will perish by the sword.'

Kept busy all this time at Nola, he thought wryly, day after day painting walls, and here I am, preaching at last. It must have rubbed off on me.

Visigoths, even when scallywags, were men of passionate imagination. What they heard from Thoodorus might have made them hesitate, had it not been for the man with the throwing-axe, who had so hated the picture of the crucifixion. Slavery in Rome, so he felt obscurely, had dishonoured him, and here was a man glorifying a criminal with a Roman spear thrust in his flank. His arm swung up, as if in a gesture of rejection. The throwing axe sped across the refectory, blade flashing as it passed the slope of light from the doorway.

The axe blade struck the painter full on his brow, and split his skull, as with a butcher's cleaver. Blood ran copiously down a face that was absurd in its frozen surprise. The painter's body, with the life plucked out of it, fell face downwards from trestle to floor. Theodorus, sprawled out and stone dead, still had one hand full of brushes. As if released from an inexplicable threat, the Visigoths began laughing at the excellence of that axe-throw. There was no need to say or explain: a blow told better than a word.

As if to clinch, by yet another physical gesture, the moral rightness of what he had done, the ex-slave reached down for a leather bucket full of lime-wash. When he threw the white liquid it splashed exuberantly, and trickled sideways down the wall. The shapeless patch of white had cancelled out the fresco of the Annunciation. Angel and Virgin, whitewashed, had become indistinct as ghosts. Flies had begun to buzz above the bloodstained face of the dead man, as the Visigoths went out, laughing.

Two or three of the younger brothers of the community stood blocking the doorway to the women's dormitory with linked arms, but made no great attempt to fight the barbarians off, when, still laughing heartily, they pushed a way through to get at the women. For this lack of manliness – this failure to give them a fight – the Visigoths despised them. The young men standing in the doorway were struck down, one after another, as if they had stood there offering themselves as passive targets for sword exercise. Soon from the womens quarters emanated gasps and screams as if wild animals had got in among them.

After an interval the marauders came out, bloody swords wiped and sheathed, sick grins on their faces, driving before them a flock of tousled hostages. Every onlooker knew by now what this meant. Either these unlucky women would be redeemed, before or after torment, in exchange for the community's hidden treasure. Or if the treasure were not forthcoming, they would all be sold off as slaves. They might be sold off as slaves anyway. They might be tormented for mere amusement. But first, these living creatures would be used to extract treasure.

They had found the living quarters here bleak, but that was usual. Romans these days were learning to pretend to be poor. The pots in the kitchen, the plates on the table, had been of common earthenware, and their clothes were all homespun. But one Visigoth had come across a *sacramentarium* with a gilt border, and he was waving the glittering service-book, as if in earnest of better things to come.

The Visigoths had herded their cowed prisoners into the forecourt, when out of the basilica doorway as if at a signal came the two acolytes, backing awkwardly as they carried between them a table, covered with an altar cloth. They were doing this because Paulinus told them to. They were afraid of the barbarians, but trying not to show it.

The acolytes set up the table to one side of the crucifix, clear of the hoofs of the tethered horses, as if an open-air service of some kind were about to begin, then disappeared inside the church again like frightened mice. The Visigoths were not sure what to do about all this. The basilica with its gloom and odour of incence was daunting. Sooner or later they would go inside and take whatever was worth having. Just now, they wanted to see what would happen.

Out came Paulinus himself, empty-handed, followed by the two acolytes, carrying between them a large wicker breadbasket, heaped-up and glistening in the sun: chalice, paten, silver lamps, all the multifarious vessels in precious metal of the basilica and its altar. The basket was tipped unceremoniously on to the table, a heap of treasure, and the boys scampered away.

This had all been so matter-of-fact, so deliberate, and yet so puzzling that the Visigoths were hesitant. Paulinus spread the precious objects on the table-top as though he were opening a market stall.

Long hands clasped behind his back to conceal their trembling, but with his bald and hook-nosed head held high, Paulinus then spoke to the Visigoths in the arrogant Latin of a Roman magnate, this time not even trying to temper his speech with a humility that in him never sounded natural anyway. The sin of pride, he chided himself, as he heard his own words come out of his mouth. Pride in having made myself poor.

'I want to make it clear that all this treasure you are staring at has been dedicated to the church. You are Visigoths, are you not? And Alaric your King has rightly forbidden you to lay hands on any precious object that belongs to God. All these things do. Well, then?'

His words spread confusion. The former slaves who understood Latin had heard Paulinus address them in the accents of a Roman master. They might resent the tone of voice, but could not help being overawed. Those who knew no Latin at least caught the name Alaric, and began to wonder if this brave old man might be the King's friend.

He could hardly expect to defend that pile of gold and silver with words. Was he waiting for his God to defend it? One Visigoth, having worked this much out, looked up at the clear sky, as if anticipating thunder.

'Now be frank with me. In exactly what way would you dispose of these unfortunate young women – these hostages of yours – were I not to redeem them?'

Paulinus asked his question as if expecting a sensible answer from reasonable men, and his tone disarmed them. The Visigoths looked at one another as if not sure what to reply. While ravaging that dormitory they had felt once again, here at Nola, the delicious vivifying inward roar of terror. They had always got their own way until now, without argument, because of the fear they aroused. The sunlight and glitter and faces, and this bald-headed man's calm voice were extinguishing their confidence.

At last the ex-slave who had flung the axe spoke up for them.

'Sell them to dealers in Ostia at the going price – what else do you expect?'

The holds of grain-ships that until recently had gone back to Carthage in ballast were crammed, these days, with the recently-enslaved, bought for cash and no questions asked. Men for field work, women for the brothels. There was a thriving flesh-market in Africa.

'If you know the going price,' said Paulinus, as if picking up the commercial phrase with tongs, 'I have something to tell you. The will of God came to me not long since, in a vision at the altar. Even though King Alaric forbids you taking the treasure of our shrine here at Nola by brute force, these things may be used to buy back hostages. Here is the treasure. There are your hostages. You hear what I tell you?'

The women from the dormitories, bedraggled and abused, and the youngster from the kitchen who had been caught on the road, heard him say these things with astonished joy. Paulinus carefully did not look at them, tears might have come into his eyes, but examined the baffled faces of the Visigoths.

'Fix your prices – and let them be fair prices. The eye of God is upon us all.'

The redemption of the hostages went ahead like a Roman auction. Paulinus bought them back one by one, sometimes arguing with the Visigoths, and if need be browbeating them. In all this he followed an inner conviction that sacrificing the treasure of the shrine was required of him by God. Once or twice there were surprises.

The thick blonde hair and sumptuous body of one of his nuns had long been hidden under her plain robe, and self-effacing manner. Her robe was now torn open from neck to hem, and betrayed to these men's eyes her physical beauty. The man with the throwing axe claimed for her an inordinate price. He fancied her, and there was no arguing with him, so Paulinus paid. They might be pig-headed and lustful, these Visigoths, thought Paulinus, as he handed across for the blonde woman more than anyone could suppose she would be worth. But except for odd whims like that one they are not commercial. Romans would have driven harder bargains.

As the business went forward, he began to feel a simple exaltation. The shrine's real treasures were the invocations made to the saint – the bold young soldier – over so many years, and all those daily prayers to God. The last, the very last, of the enormous fortune that once had been his was diminishing, piece by piece, before his eyes, changing to smiles on the faces of women abused against their will. Soulless gold and silver were bringing the sisters back to the life they had chosen – the life of the soul.

If that axe now flew at my own head, he told himself, all this would survive me – our buildings harmonious around this forecourt. And inside, the painted walls – books for those who cannot read. Even my poems, thought Paulinus – a poem every year in praise of St Felix. Something or other of all this is likely to survive.

Paulinus then reproached himself yet again for his besetting sin of pride – Roman pride. How difficult to convince a Roman born and bred that pride was a sin – that a Christian should accept humiliation!

By now, even the embroidered altar-cloth was gone. The wooden table lay bare, and still one captive stood there, unredeemed, the bloody-faced young prisoner they had trapped out there on the road. A kitchen boy of dirty habits. Invincibly ignorant, and with a wet-lipped leer – a young man Paulinus had always made an effort to treat considerately because he disliked him so much.

The boy's mother, a widow, had bustled out here in her apron, and her imprecations and screams when she saw her boy left to last were doing nothing to help. She had pushed her way into the space between the Visigoths and the bare table, and the more she screamed for her son, the more important and valuable she made him sound. She bent to take a handful of dust, and threw it on her own grey hairs.

The Visigoths did not really think all that much of this last prisoner. But his mother's screams had broken the spell that Paulinus had sedulously established. The ex-slave with the axe in his belt, wondering if they might all have been tricked, began to hold out for a price which Paulinus could not possibly pay.

And suppose this bald-headed old toff, the man with the axe was asking himself, had hidden the rest of his treasure?

The kitchen boy, while his mother made such a noise stood there leering. He liked being the centre of attention and his smile at last provoked the Visigoths. One who knew a way to wipe it off his face brought out a cord from inside his shirt, and began to knot up the boy's thumbs. How the old woman would caterwaul when she saw him dangling!

Paulinus lifted both hands, to implore a hearing, and still had enough influence over them for the mutters among the Visigoths to drop away. The widow stood there with her mouth wide open. There was a precarious silence.

'You have in your possession all the gold and silver,' said Paulinus earnestly, 'belonging to this shrine. We have nothing left here at Nola but a treasure your eyes cannot see.' The faces of the Visigoths became brightly expectant, but Paulinus extinguished their smiles when he went on to say, 'The hidden treasure is love.'

'No sermons!' exclaimed the choking voice of the ex-slave with the throwing-axe, who already detested Paulinus for his aristocratic mannerisms. 'Redeem the boy – or up he goes by the thumbs. And his old woman after him. By her big toes'.

Paulinus said clearly, 'There is no more treasure here – none. But will you take me instead? I will go to Ostia in his place.' He took the Visigoths' amazed silence for consent. When a dissenting rumble rose up from his own folk, he checked it with a lifted hand. In a voice which rang out uncompromisingly loud in the silence he said, 'Woman, take your son.'

She dragged her grinning son away by the wrist, grumbling at him as he went, as if to linger might be risky. Paulinus no longer saw what was in front of him. The forecourt was all golden, noontide blue. He was interested to find himself devoid of fear. The despised flesh would certainly suffer, but the soul could not be touched. He held out his wrists for the length of cord that dangled from the Visigoth's left hand. As the knots tightened, amid his strange joy a voice came to him which might or might not have been his own, saying, with your fortune gone, your own freedom was the last thing you had to give, and you have given it.

Part IX

1

Gilda very soon found that one breathlessly hot small room on the flat roof of the slave-dealer's house in Leptis Magna was a place of nightmare. Julius would not allow her out, or the boy either; there was no escaping into the fresh air. From downstairs came incessantly what she had never again expected to hear – the stink and clank and mutter of slaves held for the market. Their smell rising up the stairway was what particularly brought it all back. Close her eyes and she was a little girl again, Stridor's victim.

Sara the nurse was allowed out to fetch their water. Apart from her clumsy and puzzling manner of speech, Sara might have been friendly company for Gilda. But early on she had made up her mind that this other woman, this stranger foisted upon her by Jacob, was a rival. She had noticed the way Gilda would gaze at Iynx. She told the boy if he found himself being stared at to turn away and face the wall, for fear of the evil eye.

And that obedient turn of the head towards the wall, whenever Gilda looked attentively at Iynx and tried to find resemblances – my own child after all, she told herself, my son! even if I dare not tell him – had been painfully exasperating. There was an air of alertness about Iynx which he might well have got from Lucas. And my own mouth and chin, Gilda told herself – and, there, he has turned away again. Anyway, Iynx is the unhappiest of all three. He has never known anything like this in his life – cooped up day and night with two women, hostile to each other and hovering over him.

Julius, like his brother Jacob, had a turn for sarcasm. Physically, facially, they resembled one another, but Julius had a bad nature. In years gone by, the grotesque image of Stridor had haunted Gilda's dreams – now they were invaded by the heavy, hairy face and sarcastic voice of Julius. Large, moist mouth hidden in thick beard, a hooked nose and abhorrent greasy curls, and usually, when he spoke, that hectoring voice, as if shouting down an invisible opposition.

In one recurring dream Gilda was on stage, alone, her own voice failing her just when it was needed. And up from the invisible audience would come that other voice, Julius, loudly taunting her. She listened to the breathing of the others in the room, Iynx, her son without a doubt, and the pathetic, exasperating gurgle of the nurse, giving vent to some bad dream of her own. All three had nightmares in the little room, and Iynx's brought loud screams from him, so that both the women woke.

At first light, when the street was still quiet, Sara would go down to fill the waterpot at the corner fountain, and fetch up their food. The same food as Julius was giving his slaves, and he was not a master who fed his slaves well, even when he was offering them for sale. Stridor had shown better sense – his slaves always went to market with a well-fed gloss on them. And I even ate better than this, Gilda reflected, as she spooned cold and slimy barley gruel into her mouth, when tramping the highway with the Circumcelliones. She would lick the spoon bare, and try not to brood on those extravagant repasts she had shovelled into her mouth, unthinking, in her Roman heyday.

Whenever Sara went down alone to the kitchen, Julius would make a point of trying to talk with her. His brother in that letter must have given him some hint about how to enter the mystery of Sara's language. Gilda every morning could hear the crass, hesitant timbre of the two voices, coming up the stairway, and what they had to say to each other, day by day, more and more resembled conversation. At last, Julius attained what he had been aiming at.

Voices from the kitchen that morning deepened and grew husky, more animal. Had Iynx any idea what was going on? Children always know more than you think. Gilda did her best to distract him by making jokes. Sara eventually gave out a little caterwaul, and came up the stairs, flushed in the face, out of breath, as if the waterpot on her shoulder suddenly weighed too much. With no appetite for her food, either – not that such food as this would lend anyone an appetite. Sara tried to give what she could not eat to Iynx, and though he was hungry, Iynx refused.

Now that Julius had come close to Sara, Iynx hated him all the more. And this was early in life, thought Gilda, for Iynx to learn how to hate. Julius hates you too, she warned herself, make no mistake – the woman dumped in his lap under the transparent pretext that she was his brother's future wife. The slave dealer kept a close watch on Gilda, snubbed her, hinted that he knew her secrets, tried with great cleverness to find verbal ways of hurting her. There are a few people in the world, Gilda decided, and Julius is one, with whom no relation but hate is possible. This place is bad for me, but much worse for Iynx. When he looks away as I stare at him, he is only being loyal to his nurse. When he blames me for his being here, he is only repeating what the two downstairs have told him.

In Cornelia's establishment, Iynx had been the princeling. The grey-green olive trees might be forbidden, but he was free of mansion, courtyard, stables – and everyone in his small world made much of him. His principality had shrunk to this one small and stuffy room. Gilda watched him one morning when they were alone stand high, and pull himself up, until his eyes came level with the narrow slit of the window.

'The sea?'

'The sea!' he told her. The unusual, strange and tantalising sea, of which he could watch only one narrow blue strip. As he slid down, letting the windowsill rise above the level of his eyes and the strip of sea disappear, Iynx decided to run away. He would wait his moment, until both their backs were turned, then go down the forbidden stairs.

The shock of the vertical sun upon his head, the noisiness of the street outside, made Iynx giddy. An ox-cart squeaked by on solid wooden wheels, setting his teeth on edge. When Iynx ran across the street, too close to the wheels, the driver of the cart cracked a whip about his ears. So he turned and ran, and went on running, down a narrow alley between two blank-walled houses. This alley went a long way downhill.

But no, I am not lost, Iynx told himself, though he began to fear that he might be. Water runs downhill. The further down the hill, the nearer to the sea. He was pleased with himself for that idea. And triumphant when he came out into the bright sunlight by the harbour arm.

Lucas, in the old days, had sometimes talked to Iynx about different ships he had known when he worked at Ostia, coasters, grain-ships, galleys. They had floated toy ships together in the irrigation tank, when Cornelia's back was turned. And Claudian had once told a highly-coloured anecdote about a horrific storm at sea on his passage to Africa. Waves that ran mountain-high! Agonising thirst!

The ships here at anchor on the calm harbour water were not at all fearsome, but fat floating birds with canvas sails for wings; birds with their wings folded.

From smaller boats further along they were unloading fish. As they gutted them, the fishwives along the quay were assaulted by a squabbling tribe of white gulls. Offshore, a big corn-ship was being loaded, piecemeal, from a lighter, men hauling up corn a basketful at a time by a rope and tackle hung on a turned spar, then letting it shoot down inside the ship in a hissing, golden shower. Women with painted faces and their skirts slit high up one thigh were parading to and fro the quay, like ladies of leisure taking the morning air, and pausing now and then to chaff the sailors. Iynx felt an intense joy.

A hand gripped his shoulder, fingering implacably into flesh and bone.

'What are you doing here, young man?' The voice might have been horrible Julius.

Iynx told himself: run for it. But the hand holding tight was a man's hand, and men can run faster. He looked round and up at his captor. This was the other one, though, the brother, older and better, the *medicus*, Jacob. Dressed as a camel-man, and his face hidden by the flap that desert men pulled across to keep out blowing sand.

'Don't you know me, Iynx?'

'I know you, all right. You used to be the *medicus*.'

'Then what are you doing out here on the street? It's not safe for you on the street. Didn't they tell you?'

What was Iynx to say to that, because of course they had told him, over and over again. The man smiled. 'Or are you running away?'

'Yes. Perhaps. 'And I have not run far, thought Iynx, in chagrin.

'Have you ever run away before?'

'No,' said Iynx, glad of being given a chance at last to speak the exact truth. In Cornelia's house he had always tried to speak the exact truth. If only they would let him. He was remembering that he used to like Jacob very much. 'Though I have wanted to, often. I came to look at the sea.'

'That's a funny thing,' said Jacob, as if making of himself an accomplice. 'I wanted to see the sea again, too.'

Indeed, the memory of it had often enough taunted his eye, when penned in that arid oasis. The sea! A harbour with ships! The blue sea at Alexandria, the white Pharos on its island offshore, beyond the bristling masts! Philosophical conversation, variegated by salt smell and clear sky.

'But Iynx, we have no business down here, either of us. Do you suppose you can take me back by the way you came – to my brother's house? Can you do that? Are you still all there?'

'Yes,' said Iynx gloomily. 'All there. We never go out. Except Sara goes, to fetch the water. And I can take you there, easily. Up a passage, it's all uphill.'

Sara, utterly distraught, was screaming at Gilda in her muddled guttural Gothic, as if the disappearance of Iynx that morning had been a plot. Julius was cursing Gilda and Sara by turns, and in such a tempest of rage that he scarcely noticed his brother, in desert man's headdress, climb the stairs and poke his inquisitive head into the upper room.

In the clear, cold voice that could make listeners tremble in the back seats of a large theatre Gilda, when Julius paused for breath, said, 'And what if you stole him and sold him? Yourself? Since making away with children is your business.'

'I have no need to steal – I have money – I buy!' Julius's voice had gone up to a screech. 'How dare you accuse me. I who have hidden all three of you, and fed you. Three – was that my bargain? Fed you like my own flesh and blood – '

Iynx hid himself behind Jacob, gripping his finger. Such a peremptory, confident voice, never before heard from Gilda, had terrified him almost as much as the sudden thought that men like Julius made away with boys.

Jacob emerged, bulkily silent, in the doorway, still holding Iynx by the hand, but pushing him forward, displaying him. The diatribe told Jacob all that had been happening to them, here in this room, before he arrived. After all that shouting, the surprise of his appearance left them speechless. In a deliberately quiet voice, Jacob said, 'Here is Iynx for you, whichever of you lays claim to him.'

He pushed the boy towards not Sara, but Gilda, as if Gilda in his opinion had the better right. Gilda's heart warmed to him for that. 'Not that he ran very far. He wanted to look at the sea – as any boy would.'

Sara reached out and intercepted Iynx, taking hold of him bodily with both hands, pulling him between her knees. When folded and clutched like that, Iynx felt small again, though not sorry to be held safe. Since children could be made away with. Very soon however, his bigness asserted itself. He pulled away, with a glance towards Jacob and Gilda that asked for understanding. He wanted to take part.

'And what sort of brother are you?' Julius was bellowing, the pressure of his rage not letting up. 'To and fro on the streets of Leptis Magna as if we did not have a plan. And you with a price on your head. Putting me, your brother, in danger! A little more, a very little, and out you go, even if you have only just arrived. Let someone else save you. The boy I shall keep – I know about the boy. He belongs to no-one.' Julius paused cunningly, sure that by this threat he held them fast. 'Whose child is he? I ask myself. That dumb woman's? There is no resemblance. Yours, brother? As you would have me believe? When he has never been circumcised? I have fed him and sheltered him, haven't I? So I have as good a right to that boy as any one of you. Are you going to tell me he is yours, brother? Or your woman's either? I don't think so. Because you know I know otherwise.'

As the brothers, in this senseless way, confronted one another, grown men with their first white hairs, Gilda could see an antagonism going back all their lives. They looked so uncommonly alike, yet were utterly different. Julius was blusteringly threatening to take the boy – and Gilda knew it – not only to trick her, bully her, he had tried such tricks here before, Sara must have told him something he thought valuable, but to get some other useful admission out of Jacob. Sara, the dumb fool, was besotted by Julius – downstairs, she might have told him anything.

From the look on my face when he threatens me, thought Gilda proudly, he will have learned nothing except that I hate him.

Jacob, so far, was silent, almost as if bored. And if he now tells the others wondered Gilda, that I am Iynx's mother? Would they believe him? Would Iynx himself believe him? Perhaps not. Would it affect him? Iynx has had one woman or another around him all his short life, fussing over him, but never a mother. He likes me, on the whole, thought Gilda ruefully, but only because I make him laugh. For all his charm, he has no natural feeling for me – or Sara, or Jacob either. No tug of flesh and blood.

And why should he have? For that matter, why should I? Yet I have. I carried him inside me all those months, and I could weep to see him standing there, trying boyishly to make sense of all this loud bewilderment.

Jacob was wearing an insufferably calm smile – a smile he must have used before to disarm and yet infuriate his brother.

'You have done that much and more, Julius,' he said judiciously, as if handing out awards to all and sundry, now that the noise was over. 'More indeed than our mother would have asked of you. Almost as much, I might say, as she herself would have done. Looking after them, whether mine or not, when you could not even tell if you would ever see me again.'

Gilda pressed sharp nails into the palms of her hands. Jacob had avoided the trap about Iynx. Though to judge by the knowing look on his face, which betrayed him, Julius had been told some story of the boy's origin. 'You have treated them as your own flesh and blood. How can I ever thank you?'

'You can pay me back,' answered Julius sourly.

'So I shall, and very soon. You know I can always make money when I need it. You have had the use of my money before, Julius – remember? And will have it again. Very soon.'

'Promises,' Julius grumbled.

'Then that is agreed,' said Jacob with make-believe friendliness. 'So let us get on more quickly – shall we? You know what has to be done next. This robe I am wearing – I have not changed it for days – it stinks. Brother, in Alexandria, my clothes always fitted you – remember? I now need clothes that you, yourself, would not be ashamed to wear. And a razor, please, a comb, some tongs. Rachel, come over here to where the light is better – '

To Gilda it came as a small yet not a disagreeable shock to be called Rachel by the man who had given her the name.

'Julius, watch. She is cleverer at this than you would believe. Rachel, while my brother goes downstairs to fetch you a razor – '

'What am I supposed to do with a razor?' asked Gilda with bright impudence. 'Cut his throat?' Julius's scowl was a joy to her. And already she could guess what was coming.

'Provoking though my brother may be, not today. We still need him, and he needs us. He hasn't been paid yet, and he knows it. You are to make me look so much like him, that no one passing by on the streets of Leptis Magna could tell the difference.'

Julius had never liked this vivacious, quick-spoken, exceptional woman who called herself Rachel, but he particularly disliked her because she belonged to his brother Jacob.

His brilliant brother had been a living affront to Julius for as long as he could remember – the elder brother who made money in such easy ways, by curing rich men of the bellyache, only to fritter it away. Jacob had lived as he chose, and he deserved all the trouble that came his way for meddling in what did not concern him: religion, philosophy, even politics. Instead of working hard, every day of his life, as I do, Julius would tell himself, and at a difficult and necessary trade that nobody respects. If there were no slaves for sale, who would do the dirty work?

This woman his brother wanted others to believe was called Rachel – no Jewess either, did Jacob take him for a fool? – Julius had clearly identified from the start as a troublemaker. In his trade you watched out for them. If you had the bad luck to buy such a troublemaker, you sold her as soon as you could. Talent puts up value, but who wants trouble? Who could have predicted, though, that she could work so fast with comb and razor?

Gilda after glancing back and forth between them, much as a portrait painter might have done, was settling to work with a thumb's width of razor on Jacob's abundant beard. She has worked in a theatre, Julius told himself – and that of course puts up her price. What might be trouble in another slave is temperament in a *mima*. An actress fetches the highest price of any. He was impressed. He sat unnaturally still, conscious of being her model. And let himself drift into a reverie of carrying off this *mima* – perhaps her stage name was Rachel – from under his brother's nose.

A sweet revenge. Jacob, though clever, was the trusting type, he would never wake up to what was happening until she was gone. And then, thought Julius, be careful. You have a brother who is clever with poisons. Jacob has it badly for this trouble-making woman – look at the eyes he makes at her, while she ignores him. If I took her, and sold her when I had finished with her, he is wild enough to track me down, have me killed. Poisons. Even though to kill your brother is a terrible sin – the sin of Cain.

Would that stop Jacob? Almost Julius had made himself believe that Jacob was plotting to kill him). Jacob is no believer, the boy was never circumcised. Jacob, my brother, is an infidel. Though does that stop God from being God? Who does me an injury I will injure. This woman insulted me with the last words she spoke. Cut my throat? Yes – threatened me with death – they are both in it. Isaac's Jacob was a believer – and yet he stole his brother's birthright. My name is not Esau, either.

She is touching up the grey Jacob's beard with lampblack, making it darker, glossier, more like mine.

One thing for certain – the boy is not Jacob's. If he were, could I sell my own nephew, my own flesh and blood? Something else they think I have never seen – the yearning way this other one, this Rachel, looks at the boy. A respected Jewish name but not a Jewish character: a real Rachel, a mother of Israel, would fight tooth and nail for her child. An actress!

The woman's clever hand – give her that – cuts away the small hairs clustering high up on my brother's cheekbones. More hair than I have. And thinner than I am, because out there, in the desert, Jacob has not eaten well. I, the slave dealer, eat well every day of my life, and I have money. Then why despise me?

She is stripping Jacob to his breech-clout. Would anyone but a *mima* be so shameless? Putting on his robe for him – my second-best street robe. And lost to me now! thought Julius, with a wrench of indignation. Is teasing out the curls beside my brother's ears. Julius's hand went up beside his own ear, felt his own curls, reassured himself that they were still there.

All that I did for him was only done, Julius reminded himself, because our old mother pleaded with me, holding my hand inside both of hers. That a woman who had worked so hard should have such small hands! Shaming me until I said yes; then she let me go. A promise to a mother. But if I did say yes, it was because of what he wrote, in that first letter the caravan brought to Alexandria, about discoveries.

It may have been a piece of mystification. Or a promise – Jacob is always quick with a promise. To that oasis at great risk – great cost – I sent him the materials he needed for the great hermetic work. Losses and risks! Now let us see a little tangible return – a little gold.

To Iynx, watching all Gilda did, the transformation of his kind friend, Jacob, into the bully, Julius, was a macabre conjuring-trick. Gilda had been frizzling a row of curls across Jacob's forehead. A smell of singed hair filled the room that had been their prison, making Iynx want to sneeze. I close my eyes, Iynx told himself, and open them again, and already I can't tell one from the other.

Claudian, Cornelia, all of them, always called me Iynx. Then if Rachel's name is not Clara Cantora either but Gilda, and Jacob has been turned into Julius, is my name really Iynx? Am I me? The boy rubbed the place at the side of his neck where Cornelia's silver mirror, held up to the light, had confirmed for him that his head leaned quizzically to one side. Iynx means Wryneck. And if Iynx is only my nickname, whose child am I? Not Cornelia's. Not Sara's. Am I hers? The one with many names, the one with the curling iron, the one who can transform? Is that why she is so nice to me?

Iynx at that moment did not much want Gilda, or anyone, for a mother. He mistrusted what a mother might turn out to be. Some women – he had seen it in the village among the *coloni* – screamed at their children day and night.

'Twins,' Gilda said, prodding her little fist affectionately into Jacob's ribs. She had relished being the centre of attention, showing them all how clever she was. 'Even Inimicus would shake hands with you, looking like that. Even Heraclian.'

'Where have you been?' Julius asked her. 'Heraclian is dead.'

Gilda, holding the comb like a baton, turned to Jacob and wagged it at him. 'Don't smile at news like that, Jacob. Until you are accepted, stay in character. Only a small, sarcastic smile. That's it. Men in your brother's business do not give away their heartfelt smiles for nothing.'

'As Prefect of Africa and a man of ambition, Heraclian made one mistake,' announced Julius in the tone of one who relishes the blunders of others, and, most of all, the blunders of the great. 'All he needed, so he thought, was to land in Italy with an army, and they would all bow down and make him Emperor. We have had two Emperors already. He would make a third, a new one, the winning one. A man with an army at his back, and able to feed, or starve, Rome just as he chose? But the Emperor in Ravenna now has legions, sent by his brother in Constantinople. So they beat Heraclian, and he came scurrying back to Africa – '

' – and then? What happened to him then?' asked Gilda, betraying her concern. All the time the curly-headed brute who killed Stilicho was on the loose, she had never felt safe.

'They killed him in Carthage, in the Temple of Memory, and took away his fortune.' Julius lifted his own bearded chin, and drew a wet finger across his throat. 'You see? What you would have liked to do to me with that razor. Brother, I take no risks except commercial risks. Yet I follow politics, because for me, politics is where the profit is. Wars are terrible and yet terribly profitable. Leptis Magna is too peaceable – too safe. I hope it will be safe for you – I hope sincerely.'

He paused. Let them all make the most of his loudly-expressed hope.

'Unlike my brother here, I never meddle – I profit. Jacob would be a rich man today if he had followed that simple rule. Though, according to our mother, Jacob may soon be the richest of us all. You have your hand on the secret then – lead into gold?'

As in an undertone he threw out the trick question, Julius watched Jacob closely. His brother was clever, very clever, but ever since they were boys he had a weakness which, once you knew it, put him in your power. He could never tell a convincing lie.

'The great work has indeed gone forward, Julius. Yes, since last we met – and how many years is that? – I have made important discoveries.'

'But gold?' Julius persisted, wheedling. 'Not even a little bit of gold brought with you to show me. The size of my fingernail?'

'The search of philosophers for gold, brother, is also a search for wisdom. *Sophia* – wisdom – is gold, and, in our private way of talking, gold is *sophia*. I have made important discoveries, and I have enormous hopes – '

Across Julius's face came a broader smile than Iynx had ever seen him wear. Like the grin, thought the boy, on the face of a large fish, flopping breathless on the shore. An unnatural smile.

'So have we all brother. Enormous hopes. Tremendous hopes. We all live in hope – or how could we bear to go on living? I myself lived in hopes that you could make gold. I have some bad news, though, that I have been keeping from you. Not to spoil, too soon, the happiness of this meeting. Our mother died. Or are you so wise that you knew that already?

The dumb woman fascinated Julius. He was aware that Jacob, at some time or other, must have made love to her, even if his brother had gone no further than sweet words, so that in possessing Sara entirely he would be usurping Jacob's place, a pleasant thought.

Sara had lived a lonely, hungry life, she was more impulsive, and more grateful afterwards, than any slave woman Julius had ever known carnally. Any other slave woman, even as she gasped and writhed, might open her eyes and look at him as though she could kill him, and that was discouraging. Sara's gratefulness afterwards was a balm to him. What also fascinated Julius about Sara was the difficult language she spoke. Here at last, in Sara, he had a woman who, willy nilly, would keep his secrets. And he would find out hers.

In soft moments, afterwards, when she was tender towards him, Julius would ask Sara about the boy, though never so much at any one time as to daunt her. Very well, he told her at last, when she had confided the valuable secret. But you have been a mother to the boy, all his life. Why should not I, Julius, who have no son, not become his father? The idea set Sara alight.

Thus, in a household otherwise so at odds, the incipient love-affairs were symmetrical. Jacob, like a desert man, abstemious only when travelling with the caravan, was ready, once he had reached the city, for debauch. Jacob considered he had unfinished business with Gilda. A glance, a word, and why should she not capitulate? But Gilda, like other women who when young lived by selling the body, exuberantly, recklessly, as if there were nothing to fear, and youth and beauty would last for ever, had learned, later on, to consider carefully before she chose a man. And if I choose, she told herself, I will cleave to him. Since leaving Marcus she had formed the habit of keeping importunate men at arm's length.

Gilda thought she would have fancied a younger man. She needed reassurance – someone to remind her of the old days, before she encountered Marcus – before the rape and the barrenness and the wandering. But simply because he was there, and joking with her, companionably, ironically, and Sara every day coming upstairs saturated with love, her lineaments transformed, Jacob soon allured her.

Though the house in Leptis Magna went on crackling with the half-hidden animosity of the two brothers, so oddly similar now in appearance, they had paired off, coupled, separated as if choosing partners for a dance. Though glad he was no longer being bargained over, Iynx felt out of it. He was the only child in the house, yet instead of fussing, as once they had, the four of them had begun to ignore him. If he ran up and down the stairs shouting aloud, it no longer mattered. Only the street was forbidden him still, the harbour that he had one day glimpsed. But you will see it again, and soon, Sara had whispered.

To keep up the deception, one brother had always to stay in the house. But Jacob, whenever he was given the chance would practise being Julius, wandering around the streets of Leptis Magna at will, highly amused to be greeted gravely as a prospering slave-trader. He kept a straight face, he practised a sarcastic smile, it was hardly difficult. *Agentes in rebus* might perhaps be looking for him in Carthage or Alexandria, but who would ever come here, to this seedy and ingrown place, its trade slowly declining, and so far from the great cities? A few black slaves, lost-looking, almost naked, would be put up for sale when a caravan came in, and usually there was only Julius to buy them.

Julius though, these days, was selling, not buying, shipping out black slaves at sacrifice prices down the coast to Alexandria. 'More losses!' he would groan. The stink and noise from downstairs were diminishing, and Julius had begun to discuss taking ship for Gaul. With so much violent trouble there, barbarians, mutinous legionaries, Gaul was a promising place for new business.

'And you two will not even,' he said jocosely, 'notice that I am gone.'

Then I shall live in this house, Jacob would daydream, dressed as my brother, with the boy to educate – taking joy in his swift mind. He let his mind dwell on solitude in that mud hut, with a shelf of papyri, a box of drugs, with only fleas and flies, scorpions and casual passers-by for company. And there was Gilda. He had begun by wanting to seduce her. Now he wanted to live with Gilda at his side, all the days of his life. As for earning a living, even in a backwater like Leptis Magna, he told himself, I have as many modes of livelihood as I have fingers.

Jacob, after a night of whispering voices, real or fanciful, was still dreamily figuring out, as the light spread across the sky, what his life henceforth might be. The house was not yet astir, indeed, uncannily quiet, when this dawn hush was broken by Gilda, screaming.

Jacob rushed to find her, and the words, when they came out of her mouth, might have been half-way down her throat, and choking her. He had to hold arms around shoulders, chest solid against her breast, to help Gilda collect herself, before he could understand.

I should have known it, thought Jacob bitterly. Slyly, sideways, Julius was almost boasting to us of the wickedness he had in mind. During the night, Julius and Sara and the boy too had gone.

'And he never knew me,' Gilda sobbed. 'He would never have gone if he knew who I was.'

'Put the blame where it belongs,' Jacob told her. 'Blame Julius.' She looked back at him in mad horror, as if to accuse him, but for all the facial resemblance he was not Julius.

Jacob enfolded Gilda in his arms, and crooned to her as if she were a child in a nightmare. And where did he learn to do that? Gilda asked herself, as her head grew clearer. In childhood – with his younger brother?

All the others had gone from the council chamber.
'Ataulf!'

King Alaric's tone was ample and brotherly. He took Ataulf in a bearhug embrace. They were alone, blood kin, men who saw the joke, men who knew.

'With reinforcements from Constantinople reaching Ravenna by sea – six legions by now – how could it not be Africa?' Alaric spoke gruffly, as if seeking reassurance. He has never forgotten, thought Ataulf, how those Roman legions, undermanned as they were, chopped up our cavalry at Pollentia.

Ataulf said gravely – logic always consoled Alaric, 'Without corn from Africa, the great city we hold in the palm of our hand can be neither fed, nor governed.' Ataulf was still nursing his joy – a joy Galla Placidia would share.

'But first to pluck Rome bare,' Alaric announced, 'leaving nothing there to solace those legions, if Honorius is ever brave enough to lead them out of his little city in the marshes. I intend that the rich men of Rome shall pay, with their last gold coin, for our conquest of Africa.'

'Take the nut and leave the shell,' Ataulf agreed. His own dream – perhaps also Alaric's – of reinvigorating Rome, a city that turned out to be full of idle men living on doles, had long since faded.

Honorius, in safe Ravenna, had a secret, which would bring to his lips a private smile, whenever counsellors around him spoke gloomily of the threat from the Arian Visigoths. Who in this world was more powerful than God? And what could be more acceptable to Almighty God than an Emperor's prayers? While they all supposed he was sitting there, inert, hardly listening to what they said, silently, day and night, inside his head, Honorius prayed.

And help had come! Six legions, flung in one after another by his brother in Constantinople, until they weighed down the balance with a clang!

Honorius also extended his prayers to Galla Placidia, in heretic hands. All his life, hitherto, she had been near him, a person different from himself because feminine, and yet so specially similar, the imperial flesh-and-blood. Brooding on his sister who had always been so near him, so like him, the one in this world he could trust, the Emperor's affection for Galla Placidia grew morbidly intense.

A tough intriguer called Constantius, an Illyrian, had already stepped into Olympius's shoes. Eyewitnesses describe him as having a large head on a thick neck, with a downcast, sulky look, and large, protruding eyes that darted, they said, from left to right, full of suspicion, 'like a tyrant'. On horseback he slouched, and when drunk was full of vulgar buffoonery.

Olympius, once edged out of power, had fled to the far shore of the Adriatic, but Constantius remorselessly hunted him down, cut off his ears and had him clubbed to death. For all his piety, Honorius appeared to find this brute of a man reassuring.

The six legions which Constantius, as minister, now had at his beck and call included some of the heavily armoured cavalry – cataphracts – of which Stilicho in his day had been the advocate. And it turned out that barbarian cavalry would scatter at the massive charge of cataphracts. Constantius, with the terms of war changing at least this much in his favour, could afford to assert himself. Sooner or later – and he made no secret of it – he wanted to marry Galla Placidia, and father new Emperors.

Honorius was now making Galla Placidia's return to Ravenna, unmarried and not tampered with, the prime condition of any formal treaty – or even a sensible understanding with Alaric. For his own part, Constantius was even more implacable. Whatever Galla Placidia's own whims or wishes might be, she should not marry Ataulf, but himself – that is how Constantius saw it. And this obduracy doomed Rome.

Early on 24 August 410, before the oven heat of the Roman summer day began to blaze down on the heads of citizens and fighting-men alike, a horde of Alaric's cavalry broke through the Salarian Gate, to the east of the Pincian Hill, half a mile from the Baths of Caracalla. They streamed endlessly into Rome, as if in obedience to a plan of which they had all been made aware, diverging one way or another, to attack the mansions and palaces of the rich. Former Visigoth slaves were their guides.

Country people coming towards the city with fresh produce, on this as every other morning, saw the rising August sun irradiate the vast cloud of dust, summoned up by the hoofs of all those chargers. As they came in towards the city from their farms, they had been used to seeing Visigoths, a few here, a few there. But today the barbarian horsemen had come in enormous numbers, as if to overrun the entire city. Prosperous citizens woke from their sleep at the thunder of so many hoofs, and looked out. In the growing light their first sign of Rome being sacked was a column of fiery smoke coming from the palace of Sallust, gutted and then set alight. The fire was meant to spread terror, and it did.

The sack of the city – and this made it worse – was not recklessly impassioned, as if all these horsemen had broken through the protective walls after a long and desperate siege. They were horrifyingly systematic. When horsemen entering a narrow street were obliged to dismount, one man out of ten would hold the bridles, the other nine or eighteen or twenty-seven break into the house that had been pointed out to them. Once inside, they knew pretty much what they were looking for. Behind them in orderly fashion came empty farm-carts, held in readiness, and driven by Visigoth pioneers, to take away the plunder.

In Rome, the houses of the very rich had hitherto been inviolate. Towards Rome's previous ransom, most of them had paid out – and grudgingly – no more than a token sum. Pleasure-loving, tax-immune, domineering – today they were to be stripped of all they had. Anyone rash enough to offer a bribe, or a lie, to these soldiers about his possessions had his throat cut while the words were still hot in his mouth. Nobody, at first, could understand what was happening, much less believe it, then everyone panicked, even the poor, who in fact had very little to fear.

Lugubris, serving with the pioneers, was by this time a *decurio*, and had been given charge of a dozen carts, with their drivers. In the days that followed, running to and fro with loaded carts, Lugubris did his duty with relish. Until Veleda bought him, and made a pet of him, the Visigoth slave had suffered quite enough from the arbitrariness of the rich and highborn, so that messing up their houses, carrying off their prized possessions, ruining their lives, was a splendid solace.

Each *decurio* was vigilant, the reckoning strict. The pioneers, like the cavalrymen, were being paid off not in valuable trifles – all the treasure this time was for King Alaric – but in rape. The women of Rome were theirs for the taking. And best of all, the rich women, plump and perfumed, such as seldom came a poor man's way. Lugubris himself also got pleasure from seeing a mansion go up in smoke, often for the mere pyromaniac joy of it.

King Alaric had however given strict orders to the entire army that the many Catholic churches in Rome should be respected, most of all the basilica of St Peter's. Thus many women seeking to avoid rape had a safe place to go, if only they could get there intact – supposing that sanctuary was what they preferred.

On the second day, entering a mansion where his list said there was money, Lugubris found red-nosed Octavian Curtius on his knees before the troopers come to plunder him. The old money-lender was blubbering out one absurd offer after another – not so much bribes as despairing and ludicrous bargains. They could have half, three quarters, four-fifths of whatever they would find in his cellars. If only they would be merciful, and leave him something, some trifle, a working capital. They could have a share in his profits – they would never regret it.

'You silly old fool,' said one of them, not ungently, as if to a dotard – an old man with his mind off its hinges. 'We are here to take it all, to the last penny.'

'Would you have me start again with nothing – at my age?'

They roared with laughter, and trod on his toes to make him dance for them. Octavian Curtius had never had much dignity, and now he had none left. The soldiers and ex-slaves began to taunt him as he danced.

'You are poor now – doesn't it feel different? Naked you came into the world – strip off his clothes, boys! Now you are taking out of the world exactly what you brought into it. Everything you had the day you were born – except a mother's love.'

The Visigoths took Octavian Curtius downstairs. Despite his evident terror, they forced him to go ahead of them into the basement treasure-room. Red-nosed, naked, the old man's voice croaked as they pushed him ahead of them, and with grins on their faces closed the door, waiting for the first viper to yawn and slither and prick him with its fangs.

Bullion that Octavian Curtius had wrung implacably out of his creditors, over a lifetime, using every trick and shift of the law, was loaded like glittering rubbish into Lugubris's carts. An Arian priest, with an ink-horn and scroll, stood by to keep a tally. Ataulf would be waiting, with his guard, up on Janiculum, to take the receipt from Lugubris – from each cart as it arrived in turn – and have the list checked against what the carts contained.

Ataulf would stand back occasionally and glance up with amazement at the growing pile. To concentrate this massive accumulation of treasure, the civilised world had been squeezed by Rome for six hundred years. Today, he told himself, was the end of an epoch, the plunderers plundered.

On the eighth day the horde of barbarians moved off, wheeling away their cavalry chargers at walking pace, escorting an unending column of farm carts loaded high with plunder. Dust rose from hoofs; the summer sun glittered on the precious metals.

In the dust cloud, at the tail of the column, plodded a sad crowd of female Roman captives, some of high rank, free women only ten days ago, and now the Visigoth army's fancy-women. Galla Placidia had a glimpse of them, from a distance, and the sight made her hideously unhappy.

'We are simply doing one necessary thing,' Ataulf had told Galla Placidia, when she demanded to know the reason why.

'Making the rich of Rome pay for our conquest of Africa, because the poor of the city have been bled white.'

This answer, too, stopped her mouth, though she was too intelligent to be taken in by it. In Galla Placidia's opinion – and she watched King Alaric closely – all this had been a mania of revenge. Alaric had ravaged Rome because, when the city came to be governed, the facts were too much for him. They did not match his secret dream.

The city had been left behind, devastated, hungry, sick. Fires were still burning. Fever had broken out, and the Visigoths as they rode away took the fever with them: Rome's invisible revenge. They were heading south, to the waiting ships at Rhegium.

The news that Rome had been sacked by the barbarians arrived elsewhere in the civilised world like a thunderclap. Intellects of the first order read in the fall of Rome a portent. Jerome, in his book-lined cell in Bethlehem, was wrestling with a commentary on Ezekiel when the news belatedly reached him. The shock was almost past bearing. 'I wellnigh,' he wrote, 'forgot my own name.'

That society should go on money-grabbing in the face of this catastrophe left Jerome incredulous. To Gaudentius he wrote, 'The frame of the world is falling into ruins, yet our sin will not fall from us. There is no region where exiles from Rome are not found, churches once sacred have fallen into heaps of ashes, and yet we are still set upon covetousness.'

Africa was the only province in the Roman Empire of the West where barbarian invaders had so far not set foot. The absentee-landlords from Rome settled down, ill at ease, among the coarse-fibred provincials. They were snobbish, litigious, unpopular, sorry for themselves, a disturbing element.

Augustine in his bishopric of Hippo – a fortified city on the seacoast, west of Carthage – was the religious leader to whom those exiled from Rome were looking for clear explanations. The city that for so long had been the centre of gravity of the civilised world was cancelled out, nullified. What could possibly take Rome's place? With the familiar material world coming apart, what else could give order and meaning? Whose was the fault?

Augustine was obliged first to cope with the accusation, freely bandied about by upper-class pagans who resented their exile, that Rome fell to the Visigoths because Christianity had enfeebled the old Roman virtues.

For the next thirteen years, Augustine went on adding to his master-work, *Of the City of God*, a running argument soon rising to a pitch of eloquence and insight never before reached in Latin theology. So far from conceding that Christian believers bore responsibility for the fall of Rome, the drift of Augustine's argument was that the church itself would carry into the historical future those civilised values that the city had once nurtured. 'The City of God,' he wrote, 'abides forever, though the greatest city of the world is fallen into ruins.'

And what, Augustine was repeatedly asked, of nuns who had fallen victim to Visigoth lust? Some of them, when they lost a virginity dedicated to God, had afterwards killed themselves. But to a Christian, self-murder was a sin. Nuns who had submitted unwillingly to rape, and were trying to face life again – refurbish their vows – were being treated with scorn. For Christian women in a time of perilous carnality, answers were urgent.

The cult of chastity had been a Christian riposte to slave society, where the body of anyone sold for labour in the marketplace was also sexual provender. But when voluntary chastity in either sex had been overmastered by rape? Should the victims be despised?

'What man of good sense,' argued Augustine cogently, 'will think that he loses his chastity when his captive body has been forcibly prostituted to another's bestiality? When the body has been raped and the sanctity of the mind remains intact, so does the sanctity of the body. If the determination to be chaste is not, in any way, undermined by consenting to the evil, the rapists alone are guilty.' In a world of physical brutality, Augustine asserted, good intent was decisive – the mind, the soul, were citadels.

The ultimate victim of Rome's fall was Alaric himself.

On his way to the ships at Rhegium, the Visigoth King was no longer the man his companions had always known. On his big, bony, hammer-nosed charger King Alaric, swaying in the saddle, rode obstinately southward. The bodyguard on horseback around him could see the King clench his jaw, as if to keep his teeth from chattering. Sweat ran down his brow, and again and again he took gulps of beer from the horn his attendant held out, to quench an insatiable thirst. At his heels ran Filimer, the gigantic wolfhound, who from time to time would send up a howl, as if aware that his master was sick. Alaric would answer no-one who spoke to him, however urgent the matter, though from time to time he would mutter aloud to himself.

Through Alaric's fever-stricken mind passed many fragmentary memories of outdated arguments, and old battles. The bitter reflection came into his mind, again and again, that he should have been Rome's protector. That was all he had ever asked of Honorius, yet he had ended as Rome's destroyer. The world was awry.

King Alaric stayed in the saddle three days, but on the fourth, near Consentia, the fever became too much for him. Alaric took to his bed, and the physicians busied themselves around him at last. But they knew this was the fever that had been flaring through Rome, and none was so bold as to hold out hope.

Alaric managed however to nod – and all around saw that nod, and would swear to it – when Ataulf came to his bedside, and asked formally in front of witnesses if he should take command. Afterwards Ataulf wondered if the King had in fact nodded at some other notion altogether? Anyway, the nod signified. There were the usual grumbles from rivals, but no real dispute. In staggeringly-hot September weather, Ataulf led the army down the last stretch of the imperial highway, to Rhegium, the port on the Italian side of the strait separating the mainland from Sicily.

The sea between Sicily and Africa is famous for its sudden gales of wind, but as Ataulf and his escort rode the last mile towards the sea, with Galla Placidia, fresh-faced at his side and laughing at last, dressed in trews, like a Goth, and astride a Gothic saddle, the surface of the harbour was placid as a glittering mirror.

The harbour was crowded with shipping, and there were more ships at anchor in the narrow strait beyond. Ship's captains were happy with their charter-parties – to ship men and horses across to a designated landing-place in Africa, agains payment in gold, and lost ships to be paid for. After gutting Rome, the Visigoths had an immense abundance of gold, and were glad to buy friends.

Galla Placidia, eager, happy, delightful, never left Ataulf's side all day. Neither was sorry that King Alaric's second pair of eyes, the Princess Veleda, had been left behind at Consentia. Today Ataulf commanded, and she was his helpmeet.

That hot September night in the lamplit room, where they talked late, and from the balcony watched the assembled ships at anchor below them – more ships than Galla Placidia could believe existed in the world – was for the lovers a time of temptation. Principles of chastity, reasons of state might thrust them apart, but against that unnatural prudence beat the incessant tide of their love for one another, love, by now, both of body and mind.

Up from the harbour, as they stood watching on the balcony, came all the noises made by wooden ships at anchor, creaking of ropes, groan of block and spar. Ataulf turned to blow out the triple flame of the silver lamp, and without a word they began to kiss. They drew breath, they pulled away, well knowing this for a dangerous pastime, but the lure was too immense. Lips, limbs, touched for a second time, they were inflaming each other beyond endurance, had almost succumbed, when out of the sky came lightning and a tremendous clap of thunder.

'It can't be!' exclaimed Galla Placidia, letting go, pushing him from her. They stood to watch the lightning and the turbulent sea, Galla Placidia shivering with premonition. A wind, as hot as if someone had opened an oven door, blew in their faces. A hot wind, she thought, come to us from Africa – come to warn us.

Holding tight to the balcony rail as the gigantic wind beat against them, Ataulf and Galla Placidia saw fat-bellied ships at anchor lift and drop and break free of their moorings, like helpless lumps of driftwood. Grain-ships offshore, in ballast and high out of the water, were capsizing one after another, and going under. Some of those nearer, anchored in the harbour, broke into smithereens against the stone quay.

The gale blew a variety of human shrieks to their ears, over and above other noises. Tiles had begun crashing down from nearby roofs, open doors were slamming. They stood breathlessly still, appalled, as if nature had taken over the violence of their passion, and was using it to destroy.

'I must go down,' aid Ataulf, 'and see what can be done.' He was pretending to be calm.

'Nothing can be done.'

Ataulf pulled himself away and shouted an order. A domestic brought in a quivering taper to relight the silver lamp, then bustled about to fetch warmer clothes, Ataulf's cloak.

'By daylight,' said Galla Placidia bravely, once the servant had gone, 'you may well find it not so bad. Some will have been wrecked, some not. And what if all the ships are gone – every one? More gold will fetch us down more ships, and you have no lack of gold. In three or four weeks – '

'In three or four weeks,' said Ataulf, 'we shall have arrived at November, the month of storms. I have been given a warning. If only Alaric – ' But forcibly she interrupted him.

'What has King Alaric to do with all this, or anyone else but ourselves?' said Galla Placidia, all impatient Roman common sense.

Ataulf spoke, as if the two of them were talking about utterly different things. 'But don't you understand? That thunderclap – this storm – announced King Alaric's death.'

No argument that Galla Placidia could offer was likely, just now, to connect with Ataulf's mind. As they stood on the balcony, arms around each other, and looking seaward, Ataulf, with an inward flash of intuition as brilliant as the lightning stroke that had accompanied the first thunder, decided for himself the future of the Visigoths.

Revivify Rome? The hot wind at Rhegium had blown away for Ataulf the last shreds of that congenial dream. Were Visigoths to go out across that black sea, and spill their blood, to feed an idle mob no longer worthy of the Roman name? Rome was an old tree, once noble but now hollow at the heart, that in a storm of wind had fallen.

'In daylight it will look as you say,' Ataulf told Galla Placidia at last, 'but we should go down there now because they will expect it of us. The future is clear to me. I have thought out the next step.'

Galla Placidia told herself, whatever it is he has decided, I yield myself up to him. Yet Ataulf's next assertion came down upon her like a hammer blow.

'Find a place where I can rule!'

Quietly, calmly, in a more considerate voice, he made her a part of his plans. 'A place where we can both of us rule, unhampered by false Emperors and false pretences. Rule, the two of us, just as we see fit. Visigoth freedom, Visigoth energy, Roman law, a Roman coinage, Arian religion. Tolerance for Catholics, for pagans. Oh yes, we shall be their rulers – but they may believe as they choose. Marry you despite your brother, the Emperor, and make of that marriage a symbol that we are a people to be reckoned with. Have a son, our son, you will give me a son, to be as great a man as your father.' Ataulf's voice then dropped, as if a little afraid of his last prediction. 'Hand our kingdom over to him, and die in each other's arms.'

Their hands clutched tight, and this clutch was a vow. The practical questions she would leave to Ataulf. The King was on his deathbed, the fleet wrecked. Ataulf, though, saw his way clear, and she would follow him and sustain him. As for freedom, law, coinage, tolerance, symbol, these were all things Galla Placidia was ceasing to take too seriously. The words that went home to her had been *marry, have a son*. The rest she could take as it came.

Few had doubted that Ataulf would be the Visigoths' next king. But the old-fashioned found the speed with which he took power, foiling any possible rival, a little shocking. A galloper had brought word of Alaric's death from Consentia to Rhegium, and Ataulf's guardsmen came in a spontaneous crowd, to hoist him on a shield. Galla Placidia was not much of woman for prayer, but she silently prayed as she watched Ataulf's unsure footing on that curving shield, high above their heads. He had spread arms to balance himself, and was doing his best not to look in her direction. To fall would be bad luck – but Ataulf kept his place, and leapt down smiling. His reign had begun.

The Visigoths had plenty of treasure – too much! Ataulf's most astounding decision, which few of them had clearly understood, was to put aside only gold enough to make a full treasure chest for the army, and bury the rest with Alaric.

Ataulf had in fact decided about the treasure not out of piety but for strictly practical reasons. If the Visigoth army had to convey that vast mass of treasure it would move at the pace of a loaded farm cart, and what more would be needed to tempt those six legions out of Ravenna?

Ataulf wanted no pitched battles. To the Emperor Honorius he would yield up the empty shell of Rome, with its hungry and unmanageable population. The Visigoth cavalry vedettes he sent ahead, up the peninsula, with orders to pick a westerly route, and not get lured into fighting contact with any of Honorius's borrowed legions.

The Visigoths were glad when the invasion of Africa was called off, because the sea daunted them. They were content for the time being to do what their new king told them. Only to Galla Placidia did Ataulf reveal his deeper political hopes. I shall cross the Alps, he told her, go down into Gaul, and there I shall cut you out a kingdom. In King Ataulf, these days, there was a force that nothing could withstand.

Alaric's funeral, held in secret, was the most spectacular that any barbarian king ever had.

Pioneers working like ants with mattock and shovel had built an earth dam across the river Busento upstream. By the time Lugubris brought his wagons, one by one, down the ramp to the stony bottom, the gorgeous catafalque of the dead king was already in place, on the large, smooth-worn stones of the river bed. Beside the catafalque had been tethered Alaric's charger, restless, pawing and whinnying. Filimer the wolfhound, tied up beside his dead master, looked around with wise, large eyes, as if comprehending all that was going on, and once or twice howled disconsolately.

Around the catafalque, as cart after cart arrived, Lugubris began tipping out treasure as though it were valueless. Higher grew the mound of gold and silver, ivory and chryselephantine, emerald and amber. Masterly works of art wrought in precious metals were heaped up cheek by jowl with silver pots lifted from the kitchen of some plutocratic villa. Yet more wagons, in their fives and fifties, lumbered down the ramp, and as they unloaded the pile grew vastly higher. The river bed was changing from wet desolation into extravagant magnificence.

Under tumbled and reflected metallic brightness, the catafalque had almost disappeared.

'Am I to get these empty carts of mine out of here?' Lugubris called up to the hard-faced guards colonel, who with a nonchalant air, yet morbidly efficient eye, was supervising what went on below.

'Stay where you are, all of you. Line up your carts, until the burial service is over.'

There was a tone of knowing superiority about his answer that made Lugubris uneasy. To move the empty carts out of the river beforehand made better sense. But what else could you expect from a gaudy guardsman?

Noisily, the last iron nails were being driven into a scaffolding which stood high beside the coffin. The dais was then arrayed with a scarlet cloth. The funeral service would be spoken by the ambitious priest, who hitherto had been Ataulf's secretary, and famous for his memory. The priest came down, with a professionally sad look on his face, climbed the scaffolding, and stood there, his head bowed, as if in prayer.

'The villains are just beginning to wonder what might become of them,' the colonel remarked in a low voice to his adjutant.

'They will find out soon enough.' On the adjutant's lips was the brief compressed smile of a man in the know.

Crowding towards the catafalque, where it gleamed in the autumn sun like a jewel in an enormous setting, came the pioneers who had been working upstream on the dam, mud-stained, and carrying their tools. They were a disrespectful crowd, jostling each other to get a better view, as if this were the gladiators, and not a funeral.

Along each bank, high over all their heads, were the guardsmen, weapons in hand, dismounted from their horses. The priest began to intone the service. Alaric was to have enormous riches to honour him, an entire river bed for a grave, and this final intercession to a God he had always tried to serve. As the first words of the service were uttered, Filimer set up a poignant howl.

From upstream came a rumble, as if the dam might be giving way.

The quick-witted priest was the first to guess. Down he jumped from the platform in mid-sentence, his vestments flying.

He was scrambling up the steep bank, with Lugubris close after. Bemused by treasure and the public prayers, the pioneers were slower to move. But one by one they broke away, and surged in a mob towards the nearest bank. Lugubris, going up hand over hand, wondered why the guardsmen were not reaching down a comradely hand to help him. Then he saw that the archers, alternating along the line with the swordsmen, were flexing their bows.

An arrow, loosed pointblank, took the priest in the throat and out at the back of the neck. His memory was too good; he knew too much; he had a secret friend in Ravenna, and Ataulf knew. A second arrow hit Lugubris in the chest, a blow like a giant's fist, and then came an agony of pain. From behind him rose shouts of dismay, and screams. For the archers this was easy practice. The few that reached the river's brim, and tried to defend themselves, manfully, with their mattocks, were despatched by cut and thrust. And for the clambering pioneers the sword edge was not the only danger. Pounding down from the broken dam upstream came a wall of water.

A few pioneers, swept along by the wave, struck out for a moment, and then sank. Catafalque and treasure both were being drowned. And there, head above water, cresting the wave, paddling for his life as if he alone could see a way out, came Filimer. He made the bank and scrambled up. Guardsmen, not daring to strike out at the royal dog, let him through. Filimer shook himself, spraying water to left and right, and made upstream, at a lolloping gait, towards the wooded mountains, as if the spirit of the great king, men said afterwards, finally inhabited him.

Coffin and treasure disappeared under the rushing surface of bloodstained water. The last of the shrieks had faded. The living had joined the dead. The guardsmen wiped and sheathed their blades, and were mounting their chargers with self-conscious grins on their faces. All the pioneers who might remember to their own advantage where Alaric's body and Alaric's treasure were, were accounted for.

And could the guardsmen be trusted? Tonight they would begin their long ride north, up Italy, across the Alps, into Gaul. They had taken an oath to Ataulf, they were soldiers on campaign, they would have no possibility of turning back. The army would move faster without its great burden of treasure. There would be plenty of plunder in Gaul.

2

Waterpot and plant-cutting in hand, Gilda climbed the last of the stairs, to the room on the flat roof where, a long time ago, Iynx had lived out his imprisonment. Inside that small and stuffy room, the boy was a ghost. She could almost hear the sound of his voice.

Turning her back on the room where she and Sara and Iynx had for so long been hatefully cooped up, she put down the water-jar beside the row of flowerpots, and leant against the parapet, to breathe the fading heat of the day.

All day, a hot wind had been blowing off the desert, cracking lips, drying off the soil around potted plants, fraying tempers. Gilda began to water her flowers, being fair to each one of them. The moon was crescent and, according to Jacob, a crescent moon, when you had to plant, was propitious. Why do I bother, Gilda asked herself, to do what he says? And then smiled, because when you live with a man you fit yourself to him. With Marcus I read Scripture; with Jacob I watch for the crescent moon.

Gilda took the cutting from her apron pocket, and stuck it into a pot that had soil but no flower. Earthy grit edged its way under her fingernails; as she dribbled water, Gilda found herself praying that this piece of plant might defy the hot wind, and strike root. At least let this new flower live. Was Iynx living? Somewhere. And why should he not be living? He was vitality itself.

Why just then, Gilda wondered, did I pray? Not a question to ask Jacob, ever – his pros and cons would go on for hours, and never come to a conclusion. Jacob was religious perhaps, but only inconclusively religious. A good man, thought Gilda, smiling, who under his habitual irony takes everything about himself and me so seriously.

And do I love him? Is it real, or a deceit? I am fond of him. I admire him.

I may not love him, but I cleave to him, Gilda decided, as she cleaned the nails of one hand with those of the other. Jacob is both the explanation of the strange life I am leading here, and the explainer. Endlessly he explains. Not that I need explanations, or even understand, at times, what he is saying. About God or Aristotle or Plotinus or the zodiac or how best to cook mutton with apricots. He is a fallible man – they all are. Ludicrous at times – and so are they all. A good man, though.

Gilda, forehead blessed by a cooler gust from seaward, looked up at the stars, those bright perforations which, at one time, she had found meaningless. The patterns of the stars; the bright staring eyes of the solitary planets. Sun and moon, Jacob would say, were the guardians of our lives, more important than all the planets combined. Lowering Saturn and red-eyed Mars – know where they are but best ignore them – are no friends of mankind.

Gilda could put a name by now to a few constellations, Ursa Major and that star in Ursa around which the whole firmament revolves. Orion the Hunter, a sword dangling from his belt, as at one time from Stilicho's, when, of a morning, he had quit amorous nakedness, and buckle it on. The Scorpion. The Fish. The Moon in pagan days had been a goddess. I would like her to be a goddess still, thought Gilda. The Queen of the Night.

The sky above our heads was sublime order; all here on earth was cruel confusion. The rational order of the heavens hinted, Jacob would say, at eventual harmony down here, once heaven and earth were in accord. Might Iynx, too, at this very moment, be lifting his tilted head and looking up – a little sideways – at the stars? The same stars there as here, the same stars everywhere, from Britain to Chaldea. Is someone else, at this moment, telling him their names? If not, he will find out for himself, thought Gilda. He misses nothing.

Gilda sucked the finger which had dibbled the green sprig. She rolled the last of the earthy grit in her wet mouth, and spat over the parapet on to the street, without so much as looking where it might fall. Say it hits the top of a rich man's head? He may think it is a bird. And if my spittle lodges on the top of his cranium, unperceived, with a seed in it, a flower might grow there. Might it not? A rich man walking around Leptis Magna with a flower growing out of the top of his head, of which he knows nothing.

Left so suddenly alone in this tall, empty house, they had at first, Gilda and Jacob, been like two waifs, encountering by accident at a narrow crossway in a dark, wet forest. Or, as Jacob was more likely to put it, who had never seen a dark, wet forest, but had lived in a lucid atmosphere all his life: our conjunction was written in the heavens. I the sign of Taurus, you of Virgo. We are therefore good for each other.

Even when a little ragged slave with bare feet, Gilda had kept two private possessions, her name and her birthday. Jacob needed her birthday to cast her horoscope. Consider what your life has been, she told herself, and then remember that, astrologically anyway, you are a Virgin. Isn't that enough to make you laugh?

Gilda went quietly downstairs, holding the empty waterpot by its neck, like a club, humming an old tune from her theatre days, her good mood restored, and stood outside the door of the dome-ceilinged, first-floor chamber, the noblest room, where she took those who came directly to consult Jacob under the name of Julius. Astrology was forbidden but a wise man could give advice, and where better to look for advice than in the stars?

Halfway between jest and earnest, Gilda and Jacob had done the room up like a stage set meant to impress. The domed ceiling was decorated with constellations, and the zodiacal ring. The four walls, hung with curtains, were embellished with diagrams, pentacles, inexplicable images. The precious papyri Jacob had brought with him from the oasis were ranged in varnished honeycomb-shelving to signify learning. The lamp hanging from chains shone through a reflecting crystal, scattering lozenges of light to bedazzle.

'Let us have you looking wise,' Gilda had told him, 'even if the room makes you feel slightly a fool.'

'Not a fool, but an actor.'

'Often the same thing.'

Once in a while she burned frankincense in the room, an extravagance, but it hinted at an atmosphere of the ineffable. Little as he may care for it, reflected Gilda, I oblige Jacob to dress the part, and I am right, for this, as he says, is not a temple but a theatre. I altered his identity with a razor and curling tongs. I began to take charge of his life. I dress him in a dark blue robe, with sequins to represent the constellations, and he stands under that glittering, evasive, disconcerting lamp, an old dodge that. I have seen Stridor use it, when pimping a second-hand virgin.

These Leptis Magna bumpkins are in awe, the moment they enter. They would pay him whatever he asked. But like a man too rich to care, Jacob will point, with a certain disdain, to the silver vase into which they may drop their coin. The word is out among these provincials that here is a wise Jew indifferent to money – a man with his head in the clouds.

The coin rings like a little bell. I can hear it through the thickness of the door. That is what we need, those coins to pay the rent and eat. Jacob could be so much richer if he chose.

This is safer, he says, than practising medicine. They will be looking for a *medicus*. And every other *medicus* who practises the healing art, here in Leptis Magna, would get to know me. And envy me my skill. This house is safe, they are used to seeing Julius come out of the door. They seek out a wise man, knock discreetly. He keeps their secrets; they keep his.

By Jacob's door, Gilda put down her waterpot, and stooped with her ear to the panel. His confident, always slightly sarcastic voice was saying, 'The soul, whose essence is motion, has created out of itself the heavenly sphere – '

'But my vines – ' broke in the voice of a countryman, who had come here only to be instructed when best to plant his new vineyard.

'The soul, then – attend to me – keeps the heavenly sphere rotating, as if the firmament were pursuing the soul, but unable ever to overtake and coincide with it. The soul and the celestial sphere match each other, but never coincide. The ceaseless copulation of soul and cosmos – A top-dressing of wise words.'

'If you meant, by that, planting my new vines – '

'I have written it all down for you here.'

'But *magister* – *magus* – I never learned to read – '

'Then wear it on a string, round your neck, as a talisman,' burst out Jacob sarcastically. 'Simply wear it – until the first green bud emerges on your new vines. Then you are safe. You can take it from your neck, and put it in the fire. The land is hoed?'

'And all prepared.'

'Plant your new scions five days after the new moon. You can count up to five?'

The countryman, at that sardonic question, would doubtless be holding up his five fingers.

'Never plant in the heat of the day, or at the shrinking of the moon. But you know that. Dung well. How well? As well as you can afford. A vine is deep-rooted. Cherish the roots, and give them room. The rest will follow.'

Then came the noise Gilda was listening for, the tinkle of a coin in the silver jar, then a pause, and a second metallic clink, as if the farmer had received twice the wisdom he had first bargained on.

The man who came out was wearing his best clothes, and had been to bath and barber, but even so he smelt bucolically, of the stable yard. Demurely Gilda took him down to the front door and let him out, with a confidence-inspiring mystical mutter. She had only a bit part in this play, but she tried to play it well.

She locked the street door, and bounded upstairs again like a high-spirited girl. She went whirling on tiptoe, a dancer, into the dimly-lit, incense-odorous domed chamber, to fling her arms around Jacob's neck.

'What is all this reward for?'

'The ceaseless copulation of soul and cosmos.'

'So now, I dare not even quote a little nonsense from our interesting contemporary Macrobius, without having you overhear me, and go wild?'

'I thought you had made it up.'

Gilda spread out a handkerchief. Carefully tilting the silver jar, she tipped out the day's takings.

'Who paid in copper?'

'That countryman. Standing well between me and the jar, so that I shouldn't see. Copper makes a different noise, though – more sullen. I dare say copper was all he had.'

Gilda sighed. 'We shall never be rich.'

'On horoscopes for the propitious mating of bull and cow? I don't suppose so. This is a dull little town, that has almost come to a standstill. The desert encroaches, trade diminishes. Anxiety increases and, because of their constant anxiety, the people come at last and talk to me about what worries them, and then put coins in your jar. Sometimes copper coins, I admit. On the other hand, do I have to remind you – '

'Safe. Go on – say it.'

'Safe so far. Julius and Rachel have been here in Leptis Magna a long time. We are accepted, we are hardly noticed. They come in here gloomy, they go out feeling better. Yes, all things considered – safe.'

But Gilda, behind his back, was making the sign of The Horns with forefinger and little finger, in case his too-confident utterance brought them bad luck. She helped him off with his robe, shook out the folds, hung it on a peg. Now that the histrionic robe had slipped from his shoulders, the man himself emerged.

Jacob asked her, edgily, 'You mean you would rather live in Carthage – and go to the theatre every night?' Gilda tried to forget the theatre. The sound of applause in her ears was a craving that had almost ceased to haunt her. They would go down, now, as they did every evening, one after the other, to the kitchen, and eat whatever Gilda had prepared.

To keep no servant was another piece of prudence. Early each day Gilda pulled a scarf over her head, and went, like all the other women, to the public market, across the street from the basilica. Hers had become yet one more face, nodded-too familiarly by market women as they supplied her. Life had become simple and everyday, and thus time passed, year added imperceptibly to year, the time it had taken Jacob's beard, thought Gilda, to alter from speckled to entire grey. What has run away with my life as a woman? Gilda would, now and then, ask herself. And then provide her own answer: most women would envy me.

Jacob had tipped over the edge into elderliness; was beginning to suffer from small complaints; mocked himself for it. He did not always make love with ardour, yet in bed and out was invariably kind, considerate. And he was perceptive.

'*Molestia?*' tonight he asked gently, reading her mood. *Molestia* was dissatisfaction, boredom, a gnawing in the soul. For Gilda to be taken with *molestia* was what Jacob most dreaded –

that she might grow impatient, and one bright morning take herself off.

'A life without applause,' she answered with slow thoughtfulness, 'when from a little girl – from the horse-archers onwards – I had grown used to applause. My life though is much more peaceful. You have changed me.'

'Not to mention all that you yourself have done for me,' Jacob gave one of his irrelevant smiles, as if life were a joke of which only he saw the point, 'including hot fomentations.'

Sometimes he had gout – *podagra* – in his left foot. But Jacob had also been trying out a decoction from the root of the spring crocus, which upset the digestion, but worked like a charm. In a large and self-indulgent city like Rome or Carthage, thought Gilda, where the gouty are numbered by thousands, his remedy would make Jacob – would make both of us – a fortune. Surely by this time it should be safe?

She is all the impalpable mistresses, thought Jacob, that my imagination summoned up to share the pallet in that mud hut through the boring years of exile. Gilda is an obsession – a benign infection no remedy can cure. She is the child I never had – nor did Julius, except the child he stole. And what is a Jew without a child?

Jacob watched her taste the soup with a beechwood spoon. Who else could make an elegant drama – a laugh – out of the act of burning her tongue? And decided: she arrived too late in my life. How can a greybeard with gout possibly be all she needs? For me, though, Gilda is my wild Alexandrian youth come back. She pours out her treasures for me. A woman as good as this is wasting herself on me. Yet, so long as we stay here in Leptis Magna, she is faithful.

'Listen – I have a question,' said Gilda, as they faced each other across a scrubbed wooden table, and worked through their platefuls of plain food – the gouty must not eat richly. 'The stars overhead – I was up there, looking at them. The stars we see are divine reason – right? They are remote, yet they command us. They, not ourselves, decide what we shall do. Have I got all that right? The stars overhead are law and order – '

'Law, order – like Roman power when Rome was Rome.

Now that Rome is crumbling at the edges, the stars if you like are all we have left. Or so I tell people, if ever they ask.'

But do you actually believe it? Gilda would have liked to ask him. Do you ever believe anything – wholly, furiously, as one should? But held her tongue, for, if she asked, he would answer, with that anxious and imprisoned look on his face, 'My love for you.'

Jacob filled his mouth again, insipidly, with vegetables. He longed for red meat but dare not. With innocent, emphatic clarity Gilda had begun bouncing back at him words that once were his own.

'The stars are our destiny. But Jacob, for argument's sake, just suppose that I find a way to escape my destiny. When I was in Rome, the great general's woman, we won't even mention his name, I would sometimes have the same impulse. To escape both from Rome, and from his embraces – the strongest man in the empire. One of the best. And sometimes I did.' With Lucas, for example, she remembered with a pang. With Lucas – when Iynx was conceived. To lose Iynx – had that been ineluctable? 'If I tried again now – would the stars prevent me?'

'No reason for you to stint yourself, just because I do. This is a very long argument. Take some more wine.'

'And another thing of the same kind, Jacob. When I pray – as I found myself doing, not long ago, upstairs, on the roof, under the stars – not that I pray very often, hardly at all. But that time I prayed without thinking.' Gilda was trying to bring back to mind the mood of invocation, when she planted the cutting. 'To whom do I pray? Not to the stars – because that surely would be absurd, if they already control my destiny. The stars will not diverge from their courses because I implore them – '

'Of course not.' Jacob, as he wiped his mouth and filled her winecup, neglecting his own, looked at Gilda with respect. Not new ideas, of course. How could they be? So few are. Then a panic struck him: is she growing away from me?

'Or might it not be that I pray,' Gilda went on soberly, 'this is the idea that came to me when I stood there, not to the stars themselves, but to whatever set them in motion? I mean a power, Jacob – some great power,' she went on with rising excitement, as she saw her own ideas more clearly, 'that can alter the influence of the stars, even cancel out the stars, and so save us from our destiny? A God who can set us free as a master manumits a slave?'

The sense of her old life as a slave – its enormity – had come back to her like a weight fastened to the nape of her neck.

'And afterwards be free, is all I mean. Act for good, of course. Yet make free choices.'

'Plotinus observes – ' began Jacob with a superficial sigh, brushing the crumbs from his beard. But Gilda tonight was not to be fobbed off with Plotinus.

'You think I care what your Plotinus observes, or our interesting contemporary Macrobius, or the Babylonian Talmud either? I simply want to hear for once what Jacob himself has to say.'

'You were almost on the verge of arguing like a Christian – did you know that? Of course it is in the air – but you have almost invented Christianity'.

In none of these long evenings of endless talk had Gilda told him – a strange reticence – about the island of Cuneus. A celibate marriage – her? How he would have mocked her. But that was not all. Since Cuneus – since Marcus – she had in some way lost control of her life.

'Yes, we must talk more of this when we have time – thrash it out.' He smiled wryly, no longer letting his mind play around the ideas which had so excited Gilda. His own secret anxiety rose to the surface. 'This new Christian bishop they have in Leptis Magna is no friend to astrologers – did you know that? People these days would rather go for justice to a Christian bishop than a Roman official. But where in the world will a Jew get justice? A Jew and an astrologer? He is energetic, this bishop, and my turn will come.'

Of Christians and their beliefs – had they not engineered his exile to the desert? – Jacob only ever spoke ironically.

Gilda said, 'What makes you believe all this nonsense about the new bishop?'

'I am, after all, in the same line of business as the bishop of Leptis Magna. A competitor, another magician – '

Jacob was joking a little too much, and his inept jokes did nothing to hide the gloom settling into his face. I shall give him, thought Gilda, one of my best and bravest smiles, and see what happens. The smile Jacob gave her back was half-hearted.

Early one autumn morning, when Gilda was out at her marketing, the lictor and his men came to their tall, narrow, private house in Leptis Magna and carried off Jacob. They took away in a handcart all his books, and also the wall-hangings and diagrams from the domed room with the pattern of stars on the ceiling, where people came to consult him. He was being taken away, one of the lictor's men told an inquisitive neighbour, to the city prison.

Gilda stood outside her ruined front door, with a full basket, while other neighbours watched from doorways and windows. Nothing whatever showed in her face as she listened. Heartless, the neighbours muttered, hard as a stone. The door hung, uselessly, on one hinge where the lictor's man had burst in. Gilda left her full basket of shopping on the threshold, where anyone could have pilfered it, except that the people in this street were not like that. They were hungry to see a sign of emotion from Gilda, but she did not oblige them. Her hand appeared at the doorway, she snatched the basket inside, and came out dressed as she always was on the street, pulling the drab scarf down over her forehead, looking straight in front of her. Crumpled in her hand was the scrap of a message Jacob had found time to scribble, before they took him away.

Jacob had been denounced for witchcraft – always illegal in the Roman West, and nowadays, under Christian government, a grave crime. His denouncer was the dung-smelling countryman, who had come to him for advice on planting his vines.

Gilda walked ahead, on the other side of the street, well in view, though never once looking round. If Jacob still had eyes in his head, he must notice her, and take hope. It was plain enough where they were taking him: downhill, to the harbour. I need helping angels, thought Gilda, to come down from heaven. Marcus, at times, had prayed for helping angels. There was no trick of art or even of brute force her mind could turn to, except hopelessly fantastic ones, angels, that might wrest Jacob from the grip of those armed men, familiar with their work, who were bundling him along between them, like a bullock led blindly to the slaughter.

A smell of sea, the noise and swoop of the gulls, the quay. Tied to a bollard was a large sailing-boat, with a deck cargo of sealed olive-oil jars, and the mainsail tumbled loose. They were making Jacob stand there on the edge of the quay and wait, while the lictor entered into a long and serious conversation with the ship's captain.

Though not gaudy enough for a port harlot, Gilda sauntered in the way they did, making herself more flagrant, more conspicuous. Surely by now Jacob must have seen her? His eyes were cast down, his shoulders drooped as if crushed. Not as crushed, though, as his guards might think. Jacob's head came up a cunning finger's-breadth, and their eyes met.

He gave her a little shake of his head, hardly enough to catch the attention of the men holding him by each arm, and what it plainly said was, go away quickly! My case is hopeless – save yourself!

The captain of the coaster, now that he had an official duty to perform, was becoming more self-important in his demeanour. He stepped aboard and raised his voice. Two seamen came briskly aft, rope in hand. They were lashing Jacob to the mast by wrist and ankle, joking with him as they did so – a fellow in misfortune – yet making a good job of it.

One of the lictor's men did his small officious bit, casting off the loop of the mooring cable. Pulling on long sweeps, the two seamen began laboriously and almost imperceptibly moving the loaded coaster out into the midst of the harbour. There was Jacob, bound to the mast, cut off from all help, surrounded in this new exile by water instead of desert sand. And I can't get near him, I can't touch him, thought Gilda desperately. I don't even have a knife to cut him free. Into her mind came that night when she was a prisoner in a cellar, and the Circumcelliones fought for her. In her own extremity, Jacob had rescued her.

The painted port-women were beginning to close up on Gilda and exchange insults with her, as an interloper. There was not help for it; she turned to go. With the mast jammed into his back and his wrists and ankles pinioned, Jacob, sick at heart, watched Gilda walk away. That backward glance she was giving him, the wave of the hand, were meant to keep up his courage: Not a chance, thought Jacob. The best of all is for her, as I said in my message, it to go away from here before they catch her too. Go and forget me. If she ever can. I shall never forget her.

'The boat with the Jew on board? Bound for Alexandria? Already cleared the harbour.' A plump, elderly, preoccupied man was beginning to unlash the sloping plank that linked the deck of his small vessel to the quay.

'Won't you take me with you?' Gilda said to him, in a voice of forced gaiety, as if to an old friend she had only just recognised.

'No time tonight, dearie, even if I cared for it, which you know I don't,' answered the man, wagging the podgy finger of a reproving father. 'We are off, before the breeze drops. And nothing is going to stop us, not even you.'

'If nothing will stop you, then take me along.'

'Keep your knees together, dearie – save yourself a backache.' He was turning his own back upon her.

The bleak thought came into Gilda's mind, if I fail to charm this old man I am lost, I am dead. Between them, she felt an impervious sexual barrier, as if her voice, her body, her physical nearness could have upon him no effect whatever.

'I'm not asking you to pay me anything. I'll pay you.' Let you do anything you like with me she told herself, desperately – anything your imagination may suggest. Only, take me!

'If she'll pay for it, then take her along,' spoke up, petulantly, a boy's half-broken voice from aft, at the steering oar. 'Don't mind me, you never do. Make sure she has it on her, though. And take her. Make use of her. Why should I have to do it all?'

'Quarrelled with your husband, dearie?' asked the old man cautiously.

He had the lashing from the gangplank coiled in his hand, but had not yet bent over to pull up the plank itself.

'I want to get out of here before he catches me. Yes, I'll pay you. I'll work for you. Just take me.'

Only then did Gilda identify the stink from the open hold, ordure from horses and humans, and, incongruously mixed with it, the musk perfume in which the boy at the steering oar was drenched.

'What I mean to say is this, pay in money?' inquired the old man with a libidinous chuckle. 'The other is no fun for us.'

'She's a thing,' echoed the boy, 'and what use to us is a thing like that? Unless she has money. Unless she can cook.'

Gilda scrabbled in her purse. A weight of coin passed from hand to hand.

'This the best you can do?' said the old man, feeling at them in the darkness with his forefinger.

'There's silver there. Haven't you noticed?'

'She hasn't even bothered to ask. She doesn't even care where we are taking all this shit,' said the boy at the steering oar contemptuously.

'Oh yes,' declared Gilda, wrinkling her nose. The smell had begun to suffocate. 'I can cook for you.'

'And scrub the hold out for us, when we shift cargo?' asked the perfumed boy, with a skitter of equivocal laughter.

Laughing too, but less maliciously, the old man handed her aboard. Up came the gangplank, after, and as the gap between wall and boat grew wider, Gilda felt safe.

'Take a good whiff. You had better get used to it. Out in nightsoil and manure from Leptis Magna. Scrub out the hold, a job he hates, you heard him, though I keep telling him he had better get used to it. Scrubbing out the hold is not the captain's job. Back to Leptis Magna, grain below, straw on top, or how else would they feed and bed their horses? Nice, clean straw on deck, and a sweet-smelling cargo, if ever you want to go back to your husband. How do you suppose they keep their city clean? Because there are mucky people like us, moving about the harbour at the dead of night. Smells sweeter than me, don't he? Dousing himself with the stuff to make me love him better. And a double dose, now you are here, to make me jealous, I'm quite sure. I'm not the one who minds the smell, nor should he be, nor should you, if you are coming with us. It's my living, and how would others live, if the shit piled up to the housetops? Why I should mess with a woman like you, I can't imagine, except that I like husbands even less.'

He looked at her hard, in the glimmer of light reflected off the moving water. He gave a precipitous heave to the main sheet. The big square sail filled.

The boat full of dung was pulling away, very slowly, from

the shore, towards the defensive tower at the end of the harbour arm.

'Get your head down. Yes, down - below in all that shit. And learn to love it. Before some busybody over there claps eyes on you. Don't upset my boy. He'll be jealous enough anyway, but don't upset him. Put up with it. If you can't cook better than the last woman we took on board, the useless bitch, we'll drop you over the side. As we should have done with her.'

Part X

1

Stonemasons until lately employed along the walls of Carthage had met in a crowd outside the city gate for their long tramp along the coast, looking for work. All carried tools and possessions, some had their womenfolk and growing children. Marcus himself carried a large enough bundle, though less heavy than most. The bulk of his bag was his papyrus Testament. He was only a hod-carrier – a poor man by the standards of the masons around him, who tolerated his company on account of his goodness and strangeness.

'Here comes Old Gospel at last!' an impatient youngster had shouted. You could safely tease Marcus to his face. An older man, with a hot loaf of that morning's bread in his hand, broke off a large piece, and shoved it towards Marcus's mouth, as if feeding a pet, and thus Marcus broke his fast. The thought that they were glad to have him made him break into a smile. Not that I have ever shoved my beliefs down their throats, he told himself, as my old mate just shoved that bread. Even though, in Carthage, in these years of anxiety, religion is becoming as popular as the circus.

Any man standing on a street corner with an idea in his head could attract a crowd of earnestly-attentive working men, even though his theme might be some long-discarded heresy. Wage-workers in Carthage took questions of religion at least as seriously as their own well-being.

The essential conflict was between Donatist and Catholic – between democratic dissenters, who had dreamed of some kind of separate independence for Africa, and those thinking in terms of the City of God, unified, unanimous, orthodox, able to resist. Marcus in the great debate had privately taken sides – the City of God! – yet he never preached at those who thought otherwise. Even the Donatists respected him.

Those stonemasons also admired Marcus for another knack he had. Quietly, and without making the man who asked him the question look a fool, he would solve any problem in solid geometry that might be too much for a working mason – and sometimes beyond the grasp of the incompetent military engineer.

Old Gospel no doubt had a past, but they let him be and never inquired. An educated man who worked with his hands had a right to a past. Stonemasons whose fathers had been stonemasons before them, fierce and clannish men, contemptuous of those who lacked their skill, made an exception for Marcus. He was Old Gospel, who carried a hod, lived in one sordid room and, when not doing his job up scaffolding, would be found in some back street, helping the unlucky.

Their leader – the Father of the Guild – waved his stick in the air as a signal.

'Hippo Regius – here we come!'

Only children big enough to walk the distance were travelling with the gang, and they ran on ahead, shouting, not yet weary. Masons with smaller children had left their families behind in Carthage. Rumour went that there might still be work in Hippo Regius. And if not in Hippo, then somewhere else. They would trudge on until they found it.

Marcus's prayers for his workmates had started that morning as soon as he opened his eyes. He was managing these days to achieve, as a hod-carrier, what on Cuneus he had only striven for, though nearly gained until Gilda broke in upon his life: a state of uninterrupted prayer. As he took his first step of the day's journey, amid his workmates, he told himself: as a labourer, your life is blessedly simplified.

By nightfall they were fifteen miles along the coast, and bone-weary. Someone had heard tell of a tavern kept by the widow of a stone-cutter. They were given a welcome, but the place was poverty-stricken. The men would have to sleep in straw, under the lee of a wall. The Father of the Guild – the first day was too soon to be careful with money – gave the widow something to buy them wine and a piece of meat. From a dead mule, some swore, when they came to eat her stew.

After the meal, and before closing their eyes, the stonemasons had a singsong, and began to feel more like what they always called themselves: brothers. Their songs were different from those of the Circumcelliones. They were about feats of strength, or grief at parting, or a beautiful girl, glimpsed once and never spoken to. No satire, some sadness.

Work on the walls of Carthage had slowed down after Heraclian's attempted rebellion and violent death with an occasional flurry when an inspection was due, or a contract up for renewal. Taxes were harder than ever to collect, there was less money to spend on repairs. A few old mistakes were put right, but more gross errors of judgement were committed, and at last the money ran out. The long years I worked there, thought Marcus, cogitating on the tramp, as one leg moved past the other along the imperial highway towards Hippo Regius, have at least taught me a little about fortress design. I understand siege warfare (*Kingdom not of this world! Perish by the sword!*). I should not have been dreaming of sieges, but meditating upon God. Shall I never break the chains that bind me to this sinful world?

Carthage, to all appearance, was the same as ever. The richer refugees, fleeing from plundered Rome, hardly believed their luck in having reached a city where every impulse was still catered for. Seeing them carried in their litters to the baths, with barber and masseur and often pathic in attendance and even identifying a few of them by name and face, Marcus found himself perplexed that God should not have touched their hearts.

For Marcus, year by year, his bare, back-street room was his Cuneus. The glances of the painted women on the street, to others with wages in their pocket, tongues of flame which ignited them, never touched him. With God's grace he had overcome the folly of the flesh. This mania to gratify their bodies to the full – to make the most of life on earth, once Rome had fallen, and they themselves accidentally or mercifully had survived – all this Marcus could only explain as the work of the devil. Why harden their hearts to God's grace? With earthly disaster impending everywhere, the only refuge was eternity.

'What is your opinion, then, Gospel – will there be work for us in Hippo?'

'Am I a prophet?' – the question had been asked by one of the masons who left his family behind until he could send for them. At the start, he had felt light-hearted like a man who has thrown off a dragging weight. After a night in the straw he was missing the prattle of his young ones, his wife's consoling arms.

'I pray to God that there will be. What more can I say?'

'That's right, Gospel, you just keep on praying – we'll keep on tramping.' Even among the least pious of the masons there was an obscure feeling that Old Gospel's prayers could only bring them luck.

'Ever met Augustine?' asked a cheeky youngster. Marcus shook his head, smiling discouragement. But the youngster persisted. 'I've seen him. He comes to Carthage now and then. And they listen to him in Hippo – believe me. They listen to him in great crowds. Only an ordinary countryman, black-complexioned, nowhere near your size. You could simply go up to him, couldn't you, and say, being you, I am Old Gospel, and here are all my mates. They are here in Hippo looking for work.'

'That's never how it is,' broke in an older man, who had been on the tramp before in his life, and today was resenting it. 'They never give work to masons as a favour. Masons cost money. If there's work in Hippo, there's work. If they are short of stonemasons they will be all over us, rejoicing. And if there's nothing doing in Hippo, and very likely not, they will set their dogs on us. They will be glad to see the back of us. They want us only when they need us.'

'It stands to reason that somewhere in Africa,' answered a man who was missing his family, 'there must be work for a man who knows his trade.'

'Why should there be?' said the disgruntled older man.

'There's got to be,' said the younger.

Even with no wages coming in, and hunger not all that far around the corner, they clung jealously to their freedom as craftsmen. They were men who knew a trade. It was better to starve on your feet than cringe on your knees. They would have laughed the idea to scorn if someone suggested that they might be better off as slaves. In time of peace there was building in stone – there always had been – temples and palaces. In time of war there was yet more building in stone – defensive walls. If I tried to tell them, thought Marcus, that their way of life existed only because Rome existed, none of them would either understand or believe me. With civilisation shrinking away, unless we grasp after something new – unless we seek the City of God – then building in stone like the writing of books will come to an end.

On the second day the stonemasons did not make such good going of it. Their tools of trade, as they were not slow in pointing out, weighed heavier than Marcus's papyrus. And they had never learned, as he had, the art of marching. So Marcus had the blistered feet of others to care for, and their daunted spirits to rally. I might as well, he told himself wryly, be their *decurio*. Next morning they were slow to start, and Marcus, who was an early riser, had washed himself at the leather water-bucket and gone for a stroll long before they were packed and ready.

Local people were trailing to work, in the first light, with hoes and wicker baskets – the field-work here was market-gardening. Marcus as he strolled along, limbering his legs, caught sight of a tall and powerful man, over sixty, who had spent yesterday tracing his irrigation channels in parallel lines across a patch of fine tilth. About his stance there was something familiar – something different. With the broad-bladed hoe, the robust old man was trickling his share of water out of the main ditch, from one channel to the next, with a precision that was a delight to watch.

The man moved with more vitality, thought Marcus, than if he had spent his entire life bending, to break up the clods underfoot. He worked his best standing erect, as if his back did not bend easily. He might be a boy, thought Marcus, playing at mud pies. And then recognised him.

A sense of fitness made Marcus wait before speaking, until the last of the valuable water from the irrigation ditch had trickled through the channels, and for the old man the game was over. The man closed the entry with a skilfully-hoed wedge of earth, and the water ran further down the ditch, towards his neighbour's patch. Wondering as he raised his voice if he might be making a fool of himself, Marcus shouted, 'Paulinus!'

The gardener scratched his cropped grey poll, as if this were a name he had never expected to hear again.

Meropius Pontius Anicius Paulinus!'

The old man's face lit up. He waved an arm. A man born a slave, thought Marcus, would have been more circumspect.

'The sun is in my eyes as I stand here. Who is it?'

'Marcus Sextius Curtius.'

'Once upon a time at Nola?'

The old man, swinging his hoe like a toy, respectfully skirted the watered patch, newly planted with onions, before putting one grimy hand on the boundary wall.

'Marcus! What are you doing here?'

Paulinus's voice still had a spice of its one-time aristocratic arrogance, but the old tone was almost gone, worn away by servitude.

'Tramping westward with a gang of stonemasons, looking for work. And you?'

'I,' said Paulinus, lifting his chin as though this were a badge of honour, 'am legally a slave.'

'Does a man with your name, and your many friends, have to remain a slave?'

'Does a military tribune called Marcus Curtius have to tramp the roads? My many friends do not know, because I have not told them.' Paulinus smiled grimly. 'How much do you propose to give for me?' He paused, they looked at each other with similar smiles. 'Could you not do more good elsewhere with the price of my ransom?'

'When last we saw each other face to face like this, there was talk of making you bishop of Nola.'

'*Nolo episcopari!*' intoned Paulinus jokingly – the Latin expression of unwillingness that by tradition a priest uses when his fellows make a move to promote him bishop. At the pun – Paulinus had a weakness for bad puns – they both laughed. The joking answer had brought back the old days.

'But the most influential man in Africa – the man with whom you used to exchange letters, Augustine – is only fifty miles away.'

Paulinus, as if called upon to examine his conscience, made a serious effort to explain.

'Nothing, as you say, would be simpler than to send word to Augustine, and wait for him to redeem me. Or ought I, perhaps, to accept with patient gladness the humiliation that I was impelled by God to lay upon myself? Or is it merely that I am enjoying myself a little too much on this vegetable patch: life simplified? Ever since I was born I have taken, now I am giving back – even if only giving back a crop of onions.'

Marcus laughed, and nodded. 'I know what you mean. I have been giving back hods of mortar.'

'I am working out this question rather deliberately in my mind,' said Paulinus, gazing at the horizon as if Marcus's were a voice coming to him from very far away. 'Meantime, I keep busy with my hoe. I am worth the money they gave for me – I can earn my own living at last. I do not prey on others – I give. What an extraordinary thought. And true for you, too, Marcus, I suppose.' At last he looked Marcus directly in the eye, man to man.

'Sometimes I wonder,' said Marcus, unsmiling, 'if all this that we have spoken of may not be false pride.'

'You are a long way from Cuneus.'

'The island served its purpose.'

'And the scriptures we gave you?'

'Are in this bag on my shoulder. No one was ever better served by his friends than I by that gift.'

The stonemasons and their families were ambling along the road that lay by Paulinus's field, having made their start at last. One of them shouted ahead, 'We were looking for you.'

'I came across a friend. I'll catch you up.'

'The hoe is all very well. One can pray with the hoe – but there are shades of meaning I find it does not express. There are times when I regret my pen.'

'Especially on the anniversary of our patron,' said Marcus with a genial smile. For the birthday of the brave young soldier, St Felix of Nola, Paulinus would write the community a poem. Is he too, as I am, Marcus asked himself, even if slightly ashamed of the thought, beginning to be irked by the predictable conversation of working men?

'I have thought much of this,' Marcus continued slowly,

speaking with care – Paulinus in the old days had been both friend and master. 'Work done not as servility but as a form of worship. The obligation both to man and to God of work well done. Does that sound absurd? Work in this world is necessary, but those who do it are despised. Can this be God's will? With Rome no longer Rome, think of the necessary work that will be neglected – piping water, draining marshes, building bridges for travellers. Work necessary to mankind that does not profit the covetous, and so will never get done!'

When shoddy work was expected from them on the wall around Carthage, the men he worked with had been sick at heart. 'Work I mean,' he added shyly, as if the thought put into words were a strange one, 'done to the glory of God.'

'And whenever you say so, they look on you as mad?' asked Paulinus. 'I have had similar notions about money – I who once had uncountable millions, and now have none, not even the price of my freedom. There were men in my time, your father was one, who thought of money as the essence of freedom. But what, I now say, if holy poverty, voluntary poverty, were true freedom?'

Marcus had pulled a face, as if biting accidentally on an aching tooth, and Paulinus accused himself for having made mention of the old money-lender.

'I have tried all my life,' Marcus answered bluntly, 'not to think about money.' Yet the fact was that Marcus usually no longer fretted himself about his father, as a personage. Prayer had rinsed out his mind. But Paulinus had taken him by surprise.

'Here comes my master,' Paulinus muttered, and the shadow of an uncharacteristic anxiety passed across his face. A fat peasant leading a mule loaded with panniers was waddling down the track, wearing on his broad face a look of false good-nature. A tolerable master, Marcus decided, only by fits and starts. He was a man who would screw the last farthing out of any bargain, a man who would go too quickly from smiles to blows.

'Work? Yes,' said Paulinus, reaching for his hoe, 'if by that you signify, work for God alone.'

'I must catch up with my friends.'

Marcus himself was only too familiar with the cloud cast across the sun by the glance from the eye of the man who has bought your time. 'Unless you forbid me, in Hippo I shall speak of this to Augustine.'

Paulinus gave a half-smile, an indecisive shake of the head that was hardly discouragement, as if glad, at last, to have the responsibility taken from him. Slavery had been God's intention, but perhaps not slavery for life, since God had also sent this face from the past, this spontaneous offer. The old man, once immensely rich, struck with his hoe at a clod. If too much fuss, he was thinking, is made over my redemption, the price will go sky-high. I can gain my freedom only by taking from the church, and that means robbing the poor. The same money – and Augustine should have this pointed out to him – would redeem a younger man with all his life before him. He began attacking the clods, as if they were false arguments to be pulverised, less to placate his master, who came nearer, than to drive the thought of the price his carcass might fetch out of his mind.

His brother-and-sister life with Cornelia on her country estate, this quiet rural existence as a literary man, could erupt for Lucas into explicable anxiety, and never more suddenly than on a morning when she burst into the *bibliotheca*, hair coming loose, to tell him in a voice that toppled into hysteria, 'All our horses are gone!'

'Then tell someone who understands horses to go and fetch them back,' said Lucas, with the stolidity which to Cornelia might be infuriating, but often calmed her down. Lucas was by this time all curved surfaces – a forehead that shone where his hair had receded, cheeks shaven smooth, almost before his eyes opened, by the slave who attended him. The white line of the long-healed scar across his hand was the only visible sign of the man who once had wandered the roads and killed with a knife. A bookish existence, and successive good dinners, had left Lucas rotund, and his manner was deliberate, especially when dealing with Cornelia. The younger, thin, alert, humorous self was buried invisibly inside this well-fleshed man coming closer all the time to middle age.

Avoiding Cornelia's distraught gaze, Lucas's eyes swivelled anxiously, back and forth, along the honeycomb bookstack, where papyri were stored in small fat tubes. He knew exactly what each roll contained – could find his way around the library blindfold, authors, titles; doors into a safer, yet heightened, world. Why was life these days with Cornelia becoming such a strain?

She was standing there now, on the mosaic pattern in the centre of the room, feet planted apart. Persephone and Ceres – this room had been Claudian's, but he had died before the luxurious compliment of that mosaic floor could be offered him. Cornelia began to raise her voice, as if to lift Lucas out of torpor. And not all her fault, either, Lucas told himself magnanimously. Out there, beyond the loggia, in the world they would like to make believe is the real world, she must undoubtedly be facing some kind of practical crisis.

In the years that made Lucas plump and smooth, Cornelia herself had grown fat and loose, though her mass of slack flesh was inhabited by the same unawakened girl as had been married off, against her will, to two men older than herself, one rich, one famous – old men who were no good to her. Cornelia in normal times could perfectly well have run the estate single-handed, and cossetted Lucas too. Both her husbands, in their day, had been men who liked to be left to their own amusements. But would times ever be normal again?

'Riding a horse is not exactly what I do best,' said Lucas, good-naturedly. 'But if you want me to ride off after them, I will.'

Cornelia felt calmer. In real trouble, Lucas would always do his best for her. They still had their old, friendly, workable alliance – 'my late husband's adopted son' – even though for years they only met for meals.

Cornelia gave a sigh, let all her abundant hair down in a mass, wagging her head to and from like a mare with a long mane shaking off flies. In front of her late husband's adopted son there was no need for reticence. Once Cornelia began to think about her appearance, as Lucas was well aware, she was forgetting about her worries. This time she fastened her hair up properly, firmly, matronly, with brooch and comb. Cornelia wiped her cheeks with her flat and heavily beringed hands, dinting the rings into her cheeks, inflicting on herself that mild torture as if to wipe away the marks of non-existent tears. She spoke to him as if explaining to a child.

'Perhaps, Lucas, you don't understand how serious it is.'

Lucas had put down his pen, and folded his arms, bracing himself against this inevitable waste of time.

'Then tell me.'

'Simply this. And do try to consider what it means. The desert men – there must have been fifty – came to the stud in the night and took all the horses. All. Every one.'

'Most of them are unbroken,' said Lucas reassuringly. 'The desert men might very well drive them away in a herd, but as for mounting them and raiding us – '

'Try telling that to the slaves, and see if they will believe you. They won't keep watch. They are refusing to keep up the patrols between the towers. All they can think of is the desert men, by fifty and a hundred, on horseback, with swords, coming down on them as they trudge between one tower and the next, on foot, and with nothing but a long pole to defend them – '

'They take every last penny in taxes for the army, they take our corn and fodder,' said Lucas, giving her the usual answer in a complacent voice, so as to have time to think. 'And when you need soldiers, where are they?'

Since the border garrison had been pulled out to join Heraclian in his attempt on Italy, the forts and towers that served as a defence in depth to Africa's desert frontier had become empty shells, manned here and there by superannuated veterans commanding slaves who had no heart for the work.

Had I myself been Heraclian, wondered Lucas, idle, distant, sedulously preserving to the last his bookish dream, should I have made an attempt on the imperial throne? It was an essay question in rhetoric: Heraclian, rewarded with the governorship of Africa, declares, when he invades Italy with his army, that he has come to save the Empire ...

If I don't, this morning, do my own uncomfortable duty, then why should Heraclian do his? Do I actually have a duty? Who defines it? Does Cornelia? What is Cornelia to me? My true life, all these easy years, has been perusing and copying those books ranged in their orderly pigeonholes along the wall. That indefinable Roman thing, duty, about which Claudian wrote so much, is dragging me forth. What do I know of duty – how can I perform it? Since perform it I must. Are there answers in the books?

Rome for six hundred years had known how to protect her

own. But, lately, the probing intruders found that between the desert and the sown there was nothing to stop them but the shadows cast by empty fortifications.

To desert oasis, and poverty-stricken mountain village, the first raids brought back trinkets snatched from the dead bodies of share-croppers, live goats, girls shocked out of their wits, who had not been quick enough to hide. It had not taken the men beyond the frontier long to grasp that all the rest was theirs, too – large stone houses filled with enviable possessions, barns crammed with tall, fat jars of corn, bedrooms with tender women, and better even than women: horses. Once they were on horseback the desert folk could arrive in a night, and move off with the plunder before anyone touched them. Yes, the loss of even fifty unbroken horses was grave.

'Very well,' said Lucas, rolling up with extended fingertip the papyrus he had been copying, and sliding it into its vellum case. 'What if we take a lesson out of Xenophon?'

To reassure Cornelia he kissed her on the bare shoulder a little but only a little more warmly than a brother might have done. Make amends, make an effort, if only to reassure the slaves.

Lucas said, 'If the horses from the stud are gone, what do we have left?'

Cornelia's moist eyes gleamed greedily. This was how she liked best to see Lucas, listening to what she had to say, kissing her filially, making an effort to please her.

'In our stables here? The carriage horses, the riding hacks – '

'The *coloni* have their mules. And there must be any number of donkeys about the place.'

Xenophon had led the Greeks out of Persia to the shores of the Black Sea. And when he badly needed cavalry, Lucas remembered with rising excitement, he mounted his men on anything with four legs that would go faster than walking pace.

'Donkeys!' answered Cornelia, wrinkling her nose with contempt.

'Even donkey patrols between the towers would move faster than a slave with a stick, plodding on foot. And if he kept his wits about him, he would be safer. Listen, Cornelia, I leave this part to you. Have the *coloni* send their unmarried sons to the courtyard – the unruly ones. We need at least a few men who are not afraid of their own shadows. Enlist every household slave who does not already have a pot belly.' Lucas gently rubbed his own protuberance, and smiled ruefully at her. 'The time has come, don't you think, to unlock the sealed door down in the cellar. Yes – issue our weapons, or what is the point of having them?'

'But my father always told me – '

'Swords and spears anyway. Aiming straight with a bow is too much to ask of any of them.'

'My father warned me,' insisted Cornelia, 'that if you armed your slaves they would cut your throat. As they did around here, in Gildo's time.'

'If we don't arm them now, we shall get our throats cut anyway.'

Cornelia could almost wish she had not stirred Lucas up like this. Arm the slaves? And the *coloni* too? Up here in this airy room with his books – with all Claudian's books – at least you could put your hand on him. He was always there. Cornelia had a sudden, stupid fear of losing him. In her mind's eye she could see Lucas, dead, a desert man's spear-blade driven into his chest, and stuck out, bloodstained, between his hunched shoulders.

And who was Xenophon anyway, Lucas asked himself in high spirits, but a bookish Greek, who, when leadership was thrust upon him, found out one day that he had a gift for warfare?

'The raiders are fighting a ghost – the ghost of Roman power – and it frightens them. So what if we give that ghost a little flesh and blood? Man every tower with somebody, armed somehow. Weapons will give them confidence.' (As my knife, he thought, did me.) 'Run patrols – if only of hot-blooded young men kicking their heels into the flanks of donkeys. The raiders will see them from a long way off, and go away from here, and trouble others – '

The glow of fancying himself an African Xenophon sustained Lucas for several days. What wore down his high spirits – his *afflatus* – were the petty little difficulties.

Knocking such men as these hard-working, thick-headed *coloni*, and timid, cunning, idle slaves into a fighting force was like trying to build a wall with sand. Never in their lives had they been allowed to handle weapons. If they were not actually and visibly afraid of sharp edges, then the sword hanging from the belt was simply an emblem of power. A sword transformed a slave from a coward to a bully – it did not teach him to cooperate, or to obey. And why should it? Lucas asked himself, in a patiently reflective moment, between flashes of anger. We should first have given all of them something of their own to defend.

Every man with a weapon saw himself on horseback – no one wanted to ride a donkey. But they knew as little about horsemanship as of weapons, and were indisposed to learn, even had Lucas been the man to teach them. Lucas solved the problem in the simplest way, by putting his smallest men on donkey-back, and that made them sullen. The horses were skittish. The mules would turn around and bite one another. They could not form up into a straight line even on foot, much less when paraded astride a quadruped.

Uncertain in his own mind whether he was making himself a hated tyrant or a universal laughing-stock, Lucas had managed to line up his mounted men in column of three, to lead them out on their first patrol, when from between the pair of bare-breasted women, the sculptures which held up the cortyard gate, came the derisive blast of a trumpet. Horses whinnied and bucked, donkeys brayed, mules kicked to right and left. From behind Lucas's back came a noise which struck him between the shoulders with the impact of a weapon: a huge guffaw.

He turned, livid with anger, and there was Inimicus at the head of regular troops – but an Inimicus promoted to military tribune, transformed. On his porcine face the loud and vulgar laugh was freezing to a sneer. Cornelia ran out of the house, arms extended towards him, screaming with joy.

2

He feels each single thing that happens, thought Marcus, more distinctly and much more deeply than I do. He is so much quicker that I feel slow-witted. He has intellect, it pushes out towards me like invisible delicate fingers as I listen, as I speak. He has wisdom: *sapientia*.

And so much else to occupy his day besides talk to me: a wandering stonemason's labourer. I told him where to find Paulinus, and how to buy him free, and wasn't that enough? Why go on talking to me like this, for half an hour, for nearly an hour, stretching me, astonishing me, with black-robed men coming in deferentially to whisper, each time more urgently, that litigants were waiting for him in the *secretarium*.

Waving them away with a gentle smile, as though on a morning when he had Marcus Curtius to talk to, a hod-carrier, all those rich, perhaps immensely rich, litigants could bide their time. The rich are fond of bringing their lawsuits before a famous bishop like Augustine – in the hope of a quick, cheap and no doubt just compromise. From his gesture, the last time he whispered, 'Later,' Augustine clearly regards these lawsuits as a bore. And they must be.

This black-eyed, energetic, dark-complexioned man, with the nervous electric flow of language, the great leaps of insight, had in fact wasted little time, but brought Marcus very quickly to the serious question that was foremost in his mind. With Augustine, one's deeper preoccupations soon emerged.

'The rich refugees in Carthage, wallowing in their fleshpots,' Marcus had heard himself saying (an ungentle way, though, for a Christian to speak) 'and with Rome, the Rome of which they were the beneficiaries,' he added more thoughtfully, 'in ruins around them, why should they not fall on their knees, and listen to God?'

'The flesh is good,' answered Augustine – to Marcus an astonishing remark. The flesh good? Yet uttered so matter-of-factly he could not demur. 'But to leave the Creator and live according to the created good – the flesh – is, for them, where the trouble starts. The fleshpots – covetousness, gluttony, envy – those in themselves are wrong. But he that lives by God's love should hate the vice, and love the man.'

Though seemingly aimed wide of the mark – the heartlessness of the Roman refugees – this answer of Augustine's struck and pierced Marcus. His rage against the rich who had fled from Rome faded. I hate covetousness, he thought, and all it leads to. I have since a boy. It is the sin I must hate – covetousness. Not the covetous rich. Not my father.

'You were the hermit on Cuneus?' said Augustine, and smiled at Marcus's look of amazement. 'But why be surprised? The Christian world coincides with the civilized world, and that is immense. Yet a happening here prompts a vibration there. A man of your name and age, first at Nola, then on Cuneus – and before that, on Flavius Stilicho's staff?'

It had come out so quickly – the time in his life that Marcus did not intend to speak of. 'And now, you say, you have been a stonemason in Carthage?'

'A mason's labourer.'

'What then do you think of our walls, here in Hippo?' Another quick turn in the conversation, taking Marcus by surprise, yet also deadly serious. Augustine evidently wanted Marcus to answer as best he knew. Here, in prosperous provincial Hippo, they were repairing their city wall, and the clerk of the works had found work for all his mates. There would be work for him too, up there, carrying a hod.

Hippo Regius – Augustine's diocese – was the second port after Carthage on the African coast, its harbour a river mouth, protected to the westward by a bulking hill. The river, in debouching from the mountains, had laid down a broad alluvial plain now thick with crops. On the tramp inland across this plain, Marcus, while the walls approached, had passed his time, as he did so often, by envisaging a siege. So now he had an answer on the tip of his tongue.

'About the workmanship of your new walls – or your old walls, either – ' he said, 'there is nothing to complain of, except than in a siege they would all be useless, as they stand.' Augustine's black eyes widened, showing their whites. He looked more than ever African. Standing there in front of me, Augustine instantly decided, is a remarkable man, forthright, convincing, competent, Christian. Not someone to be lost.

'Well then. Go on.'

'Honest, four-square masonry, done by line and level, and skilfully designed – which is more than one can say for much of the wall in Carthage. But this city of Hippo Regius is, in a military sense, dominated by the hill over the west.' Marcus's left hand designed the circuit of the walls in the air, his right fist was the high hill. 'Siege artillery emplaced up there – '

'Our garrison commander has been known to answer that Berbers coming down from their mountains or Circumcelliones swarming in from the countryside, with their long staves, would hardly have siege artillery – '

'And if Heraclian had returned in triumph – to find the men of Hippo holding their city for the Christian Emperor Honorius?'

Augustine answered smiling, 'You were a soldier, and at times you speak like one. As I no doubt, too often, pomp on like a teacher. These early avocations are indelible.'

'I am, believe me, wholeheartedly for peace,' said Marcus with a short, hard laugh. He had been caught out. He felt a little contrite.

'Peace? And how would you define it?'

This also was something Marcus had thought deeply about, since he renounced the sword, and again he had an answer ready. 'Peace, to my mind, is not a mere absence of war – a pause between wars – but an orderly obedience to God's eternal law, performed in faith.'

'The answer of a soldier of God. Were you to ask it of me in all seriousness, Marcus Curtius, I would ordain you.'

This blunt offer took away Marcus's breath. When he dropped his eyes and muttered that he was unworthy. Augustine's smile was pure encouragement. 'Because you once lived with a woman as your wife?' Yes, the Christian world was small; he knew that too, perhaps everyone knew. 'But you have put that behind you, as, when the time came, did I. Marcus, you have your stonemasons, yes – but would you rather not be less alone in your spiritual life? They live here, the brotherhood, ordained and lay, in my house, in small rooms, cells. As at Nola indeed. No woman enters your quarters, no man ever enters the quarters where our sisters live. You will not find meat on our refectory table – as you will discover anyway, when you eat with us there, at noon, as I hope you will. And written on the wall is an epigram we all bear well in mind, about backbiting.'

Augustine recited the verse – how could he resist? – giving, Marcus noted, to each syllable, its exact value, a teacher of literature still.

'Whoever thinks that he is able
To nibble at the life of absent friends
Must know he is unworthy of this table.'

Augustine smiled. 'You wear a black robe. You live a virtuous life. You work for the church, as directed. No other rules, I think.'

Now that his scruples had been overcome by the swiftness of this man's insight, which had taken his consent for granted, Marcus felt as if a familiar and oppressive weight had been lifted from his chest. He breathed deeply, and God's air was good. Was he not being offered exactly the life he would have chosen? As if again in the army; not killing, though; bringing to life.

'I am a deplorably ignorant man,' Marcus began. The desert of his ignorance, as he contemplated it, stretched away from him in every direction.

'So was I,' said Augustine, getting up like someone who wastes no time, arranging the hang of his robe, flexing himself, pressing palms into tired eyes – thus might a famous and over-worked teacher of rhetoric have readied himself to enter his lecture theatre. 'Not long after I was ordained, I had to ask my bishop for time off, to study the Bible and get to the heart of it. I could impress the educated – but among simple people I was at a loss. Those litigants are waiting for me in the *secretarium* – the bane of a bishop's life, but the job must be done. Should Christians take their differences into an imperial court? I think not. Tonight, pray for me, and I shall pray for you. Tomorrow, come here at the same time, and if we are both of a similar mind, I will ordain you deacon. Once you have settled in, Marcus, my dear brother, I plan to use you in the back-country villages, where people have not enough land to feed themselves, and so are tempted by Donatism, or even worse. Hunger, serious-mindedness, then schism and heresy. A task for a man who knows men. Meanwhile – '

'Meanwhile?' asked Marcus, standing as he had not stood for a very long time, motionless, alert, erect, his head reaching high, as if to receive orders from the ghost of Flavius Stilicho.

'I should be glad, incidentally, when you have time, to be told what a suitable fort on the crest of that hill might look like. A simple drawing perhaps – '

Marcus wandered out of the bishop's house and past the basilica, feeling like a man whose dream and whose daily life at last have come to coincide. A discipline, he told himself, that I accept – that I embrace. The basilica where Augustine would by this time be sitting in judgement was large – good masonry. Built not long since. And crowded to the doors, he had already heard them boast in Hippo, whenever Augustine preached. Touched to the heart, the great crowd, rich and poor alike, would come out weeping.

Hippo Regius had all the appurtenances of a Roman city, forum, theatre, baths, yet Marcus found the centre singularly unRoman, not straight and squared-off, but winding, Levantine. You heard Punic in the street – a tongue, thought Marcus, I must not neglect to learn. The language hereabouts of the common people – and my smattering is not enough. Suetonius the historian was apparently born here – but apart from a monument to Suetonius, and the busts of dead Emperors, their forum is crowded with the statues of nonentities.

My men have hauled one simple catapult to the top of that treacherous hill of theirs, he told himself, measuring the range with his eye. And I have just dropped a fifty pound rock where I now stand, in the midst of the forum. After this one task-piece, though, I cease ever again to reflect on the arts of war. Hate the vice and love the man. I shall live in the light of God's love.

Making fair copies of the poems Claudian had left behind him – his life's work – had been a pleasant task, occupying Lucas for years. He had made, though, one strange discovery. Claudian, at the last, would have had Lucas believe that not a touch more was needed to his last poem, *The Rape of Proserpine*. All as he wanted it, nothing to add or amend. Yet after the poet had swallowed his last dose of opium, Lucas found the manuscript unfinished. Where was the rest of it?

Lucas scrutinised all the surviving rough copies, in vain. He went through every inch of papyrus in the library, in case the missing verses had been misplaced. Crazy possibilities tormented him. When the Circumcelliones attacked, had some malicious slave made away with a papyrus roll? Or Inimicus – out of vindictiveness, or a soldierly idea of a practical joke? The perplexity, the sense of loss, festered at the back of Lucas's mind for years, until the day of Cornelia's wedding.

That morning, in the whitewashed church, crowded with tenants and jostling soldiers, and the bridal couple up at the front before the altar, a consoling thought came to him as the parish priest, bare-headed in the apse, intoned the marriage service. By leaving his greatest poem unfinished before taking his own life, had Claudian meant to shrug off the world he had lived to see collapse? The Empire in the West no longer orderly, no longer pagan, crumbling? For a man of an ironic turn of mind, not to finish a pagan poem might have had deliberate significance. I too shall leave behind – he could almost hear Claudian say – a splendid ruin.

Lucas was standing too far back to hear the words of the ceremony distinctly, but something in their cadence, rather than their meaning, brought to mind half-remembered lines from Claudian's last poem. Ceres the sad mother, the pagan madonna, finding Proserpine's embroidery unfinished, kisses the stitches, pressing them to her breast. And had mourned her child, standing at night on Etna, torch in hand, light falling on the waters far and wide. A woman mourning for a woman. The poet who had celebrated Roman order and Roman might was sounding at the end of his life a new note, of feminine emotion, of poignant loss, the faint but possible hope of renewal. Escape from hell was not impossible. And Claudian might have left his poem unfinished – this, for Lucas, was the insight – as if shrugging off the world he had lived to see and regret.

There was the precedent of Virgil, Lucas reminded himself, another sexually-ambiguous poet, who lauded Roman power as Claudian had done, only to mislike the shape it was taking under the Emperor Augustus, and implore his friends, from his deathbed, to destroy the *Aeneid*.

Half-hearing words in a religious service that meant nothing to him, watching the backs of all those heads, cropped or shaggy, Inimicus's regimental comrades, Cornelia's tenantry, and the shawled heads of their women, Lucas told himself abruptly: to stay here in Cornelia's mansion any longer is out of the question.

Cornelia's last husband's adopted son? A man who no longer mattered? But where do I go? Lucas asked himself, How do I live? He was the penman, and down here on a frontier that had been pacified only after long and hard fighting, of what use was a man who read books and spent most of his life indoors? He was the dead old pederast's former slave. Sword-rattling Inimicus was the great personage now.

Inimicus too was filling out, and developing a jowl. His gestures were becoming slow, and portentous, his tongue more scathing. Another victim of Cornelia's food, thought Lucas, wryly aware of his own baldness and sleekness. (What had happened to his youth. While he unrolled a papyrus it had flown out of the window.) As for Inimicus, thought Lucas, as the nuptial mass proceeded, he will fill out even more, on her food, until he becomes a military tribune who needs helping into the saddle by two strong men, one on each side.

Cornelia this morning had all the flustered mannerisms of a young virgin brought, by surprise, to the altar. She had made several mistakes in dressing, from which Lucas might have saved her. The gold-flecked, black-banded dress, her compromise between the white of a maiden and the dark of a widow, was so tight across her haunches that she looked immense: a sacrificial heifer at a pagan feast.

You have saved money here, Lucas reminded himself, with the complacency of a man who in his lifetime has learned the importance of money. If I keep my nerve, how can they make me truckle? I need, though, to secure what is rightfully mine, go out with my head high. They will be glad to see the back of me.

A priest more vigorous could have made scandal by disapproving this marriage, Cornelia's third – but Cornelia, hereabouts, was the great patroness. Most of the congregation this morning had heard his words on Christian marriage a good many times before, always in the same order. The priest had sermons by heart for weddings and funerals and the major feasts of the church, enough to last his lifetime. And does he even know, by now, wondered Lucas, what the words signify? Once I have gone, that priest will be the last literate here.

This close to the frontier, only the army counts, those cropped heads, those shuffling, iron-shod feet. What was it Augustine wrote about godless power? 'Every state is a band of robbers, every band of robbers is a little state'. And there they are, the military bandits – just look at them – crowding close, as the fat, rich bride exchanges ring and kiss with the ventripotent groom. They are envying Inimicus his luck for marrying an heiress, and if not yet actually whispering aloud their lewd jokes at Cornelia's vastness, her palpitating eagerness, then thinking them. Thieves under forms of law, out for whatever they can grab, even heiresses. Who would not rather, Lucas asked himself, well knowing he did not mean it, have joined the Circumcelliones?

Then Lucas's irritation fell away, as he felt entirely distant from them, and his past life, as he stood there, became luminously distinct. He was walking at night along the shore, a young scribe with an old bishop. He heard a keel grate on the beach – but the noise was also the shod hooves of pack mules, loaded down with copper coin, going to Lugdunum under armed guard. Gilda, naked as Venus or Eve, in the room in Milan; Gilda pregnant and so proud of it. The child no doubt was dead, and very likely Gilda too. Claudian had once confided to him, gloomily, that anyone left in Ravenna who had had anything whatever to do with Stilicho was dead.

Friends killed off, one by one. The state a band of robbers. And that perhaps was what his last poem was meant to signify, the descent into hell, the abrupt breaking-off, the poignant sadness.

Only his sustained conviction of being different from the rest got Lucas through the wedding-feast. Household slaves who only yesterday had been prompt to move when he lifted a finger, waited on him slowly, clumsily, and once, behind his back, he heard an insulting whisper from an unidentifiable voice: 'Catamite!'

Cornelia, after toasts had been drunk, waddled between the tables towards him, plump, blurred with wine, arms held out, exclaiming, 'I want to kiss my stepson! Lucas – a lucky kiss from the bride!' Inimicus, crowned as he still was in his bridal garland – a pig's head, thought Lucas, stuffed into a wreath – led Cornelia off with a grip on both elbows before she could diminish herself by laying her own pouting lips on Lucas's.

In time the house grew less rowdy. The bridal couple had been put to bed, amid the vulgar facetiousness that the church discountenanced, but serving soldiers could hardly resist. Though he had drunk a great deal of wine, Lucas went up to his own bedroom clear-headed. He had deliberately been trying to remember the Lucas who once had tramped the roads of Gaul on a slave-chain and, later, killed that same slave-master with a knife. I can act if I have to, he told himself, soft as I have been living, and at last I have to. If I ought I can.

A smoking wick was filling his room with the familiar, coarse pungency of African lamp-oil. (Why had a slave not trimmed the wick?) He blew out the flame, and pinched the glow valiantly between his fingertips. Under the blanket was a clammy horror that, as it touched his bare legs, had Lucas yelping. From outside the door came raucous male laughter. From the wet smell, the slither, a live eel. A wedding joke. The man who had laughed was running full tilt down stairs – a household slave, because a soldier would have waited to make something more of it. I could have caught him had I been quicker, though Lucas exasperatedly. I should have stuffed his live eel down his throat.

The married pair, next morning, were breaking their fast later than usual, Cornelia clinging to Inimicus, and Inimicus himself not bothering to hide that, by now, he took her transports coolly. With a complimentary half-smile, Lucas went to his customary place at their table. He sat there waiting to be served, bracing himself for a disagreeable meal.

'Certain changes have been made, and there will be more,' Inimicus told him in a surly voice. 'This table is for the master and mistress.'

'If there are to be changes, we shall first need to discuss them,' said Lucas with a bleak smile. 'That is to say, if you are no longer rapt by your hymeneal transports.' He had long ago found that the way to baffle Inimicus was by using far-fetched words. 'In your present great joy you may have overlooked one small fact. I am the joint heir, with the lady you are so lucky as to have espoused – ' he gave Cornelia a wickedly-dazzling smile ' – the joint heir of my adoptive father, Claudius Claudianus.'

Into Inimicus's face came a cunning look, as though he had just caught a delinquent soldier in a trap. He hammered the table, once, loud and hard, with the flat of his hand, at this mention of Claudian's name, as if the mere percussive noise would shut up Lucas, then and there. A slave bobbed up to see what might be needed, saw the uncompromising look in Inimicus's eye, and bobbed away. When he was only a centurion, thought Lucas, no one would ever have taken him for anything but a centurion, cunning, ambitious, but always slightly deferential: a man who knew his place. Now he is a military tribune, and he behaves exactly like a military tribune. The rank takes over from the man.

'Here is something else you don't know about Claudius Claudianus,' said Inimicus in an undertone – speaking of something disgraceful in whispered accents of triumph. 'Named as a traitor – his estate forfeit to the Emperor.' And that, thought Lucas, is something he did not intend to tell me. I startled him into it. He is still drunk, the wine from yesterday slopping around loose inside his head, after the coarse raptures of the night. 'They told me so,' Inimicus whispered his boast, 'in Italy.'

'In those bad days,' said Lucas, more calmly than he felt, 'the grossest injustice was not impossible. But since the sentence was never carried out, it has fallen into desuetude.' He flung the hard word at Inimicus like a sharp javelin, and rejoiced to see him blink. 'Unless of course, dear father-in-law-by-marriage, you are proposing to stir the matter up. Then my share of the estate will be forfeited, but so, I may add, will be Cornelia's. Reflect on it.'

'Let us keep all this in the family,' said Cornelia in a mellifluous, honeymoon whisper, lifting arms to left and right as though to hug them closer. She was laying a gently-restraining hand on Inimicus's hairy wrist. Cornelia went on to talk in the same unfamiliar, sugary voice, yet in her old, hard-headed fashion, of the property, and the need to keep a grip on it, and to all stay friends. The less said the better of what anyone might think in Italy. As her alert, bright button-eyes moved from face to face, Lucas knew that she was the same woman, underneath. To what she had, she would hold on tight.

Her friendly gesture had let fall a loose sleeve, which hid last night's large bruise on her upper arm. Nothing to flaunt – she shook down the sleeve promptly, though, as it were absent-mindedly. The sight of the broad blue mark on the arm of this woman, towards whom he felt a brotherly affection, made Lucas turn from the food in front of him in disgust.

'In Italy you were a slave to the traitor – weren't you?' sneered Inimicus softly, as Lucas rose from his place. Lucas sat back heavily, angrily, prepared for combat. Inimicus was talking big, through the mask of his rank, and his new status as Cornelia's husband. The man underneath, though, was unchanged – could still be a target for blows.

'And how vividly I remember your sitting, silent as a naughty boy, here at this table in Claudius Claudianus's presence, because you were afraid not only of his eminent rank, but of his tongue. From whose hand, by the way, did you receive your promotion to military tribune? From the Emperor's?' Inimicus, poor fellow, could never fight well with words. Heraclian had promoted him and the rank had stuck. The question went home.

After saying what you have just said, Lucas told himself, you can never stay. You have said your goodbye. Don't forget his connections with the *agentes in rebus*. Inimicus's face had gone mottled, like brawn, with rage. Cornelia, who did not yet know her man, had put a hand on his cheek, to pacify him, murmuring, 'Not a quarrel – not today!', though Lucas could see that this quarrel excited her. Inimicus brushed the ring-adorned hand from his cheek, as though it had been a wasp.

'Now we come to my adoptive father's last wish before he died,' said Lucas blandly, aware that in saying this he was stretching the truth a little. But if Claudian knew, would he care? 'I have been working hard, so as to implement that wish, and at last the time has come.' Inimicus was pretending to be bored, covering a yawn with a hand, yet he wanted to know.

'The copies of his works are ready at last, and he wanted them deposited in all the chief libraries of Africa. If I leave you alone on your honeymoon, it is because I have this important literary business to transact.'

The reason he was giving rang in Lucas's ears as absurd. He looked at their blank faces. There was no sign that they believed, or disbelieved, or even understood what he had said. Inimicus, though, had begun to smile, greedily, at this news that Lucas was going away. From the look on his face, he might have won.

As of course he has, thought Lucas – for dare I ever come back? In as firm a voice as he could muster, he said, 'Later on we can discuss in greater detail the disposition of my share in the estate – '

'Go to law over it in Carthage,' said Inimicus darkly, as if he had already worked that one out, 'and see what happens to you.'

'Meanwhile I shall need a horse,' said Lucas, digging a simple little trap. He had to score just once, and then go.

'A horse? At a time like this? When every horse we can lay hands on is needed along the frontier?'

'Then I shall simply go to Carthage on a donkey. Goodbye.' said Lucas, getting up from table with a charming smile.

'Wait!'

Cornelia had detached herself bodily from Inimicus.

'You are my late husband's adopted son. You can't possibly go to Carthage on a donkey!' Donkey-back signified the men who worked the land, not those who owned it.

'Let him! It's all he's good for – the donkey cavalry!' flung out Inimicus, as Lucas sauntered away, thinking as he went, I am well out of this. How many more such meals could my digestion stand? I fought – he won. Except about the donkey. It was not much of a victory.

His exertions of the night, and this confusing row at breakfast, had left Inimicus exhausted. He wandered into the courtyard, leaned against a high pile of straw, and fell asleep where he was, half upright, half prone. He sprawled there, bare-headed, under the unfriendly African sun, his mouth wide open, the household slaves watching him from a prudent distance.

Cornelia already, on the first morning of her married life, was sketching in how she would manage matters henceforth, discreetly, prudently, behind her husband's back. She went upstairs, and found Lucas packing manuscripts into barrels.

'Are you taking every one of them?'

'It's the simplest. You will never read them.'

They looked at each other and pulled the faces of two children, intriguing against authority.

'Then what shall I do with these barrels?'

'Some day soon, when he is off and away playing soldiers,' suggested Lucas, 'send them after me, in a couple of carts, as estate produce.'

'Not to Carthage,' said Cornelia shrewdly. 'He writes to Carthage about everything. Not that I mind so much, actually. With a husband by my side who can make himself heard in Carthage, I shall be safe, and the estate too. I never guessed how much he hated you, until last night. He wouldn't believe we were only ever brother and sister. Are you afraid of him?'

'No. Really not. Are you?'

Cornelia dropped her eyes, like a girl caught out in a shameful lapse. 'Yes,' she said, 'I am afraid of him.' And looked up defiantly. 'Though all the same, I am not sorry to be married again. And this time, for a change, not to an old man. I need a protector, and so does this place. Of course you may have a horse to ride. You must. The best we have. But where will you go?'

'In case he sends word of me to Carthage? Where else is here?'

'Hippo?'

'As good as anywhere.'

In Hippo, he thought, Augustine at least, if nobody else, will have a library.

'And Lucas – what will you do once you get there?'

'I have my pen. I have a trade. I have these books, for a start. I can copy them for the rich in Hippo. If the rich in Hippo can read. If not, they will buy books for show, and make people admire the labels.' Lucas was so pleased with himself at having invented, on the spur of the moment, another way to live that he could have danced a jig.

'You mean you are glad to be going?' said Cornelia, crestfallen.

'I am sorry to leave you, Cornelia. But yes, I am glad to be going. Everything has changed. If ever he managed to get rid of me, his next idea would be to get rid of you.'

Cornelia, after an incredulously scornful glance, like a repudiated mistress in a play, gathered together her wits.

'I will order them to pick out a horse for you. And do you have money?'

'Yes, I have money.'

The military tribune was still snoring, and even the hoofbeats going past did not rouse him. At the last moment, Cornelia pressed a purse into Lucas's hand, as though it were a love-letter. Under his tunic his own money-belt was heavy with savings, but Lucas accepted her gift gratefully, taking it to be silver. Money would help. Later on, out of sight, when he reined in his horse at a crossroads, and opened the purse to see, it turned out to be gold.

Part XI

1

The big man with an iron hook instead of a left hand stood where the road forked, blocking the way. One-handedly he whistled his long Samnite sword, left and right, until loiterers gathered to watch. In the old days, when the games were still allowed, that was how gladiators, in their procession around the arena before the fights began, would whirl their swords, to gain the attention of the besotted women.

The woman who, lately, had helped this ex-gladiator shook her tambourine. She was not young, but all eyes were upon her as she began her voluptuous dance, bringing it to an end convulsively, as she knelt before the one-armed man, as if yielding to him. Her mass of white-streaked hair fell down to hide her face entirely, leaving the nape of her neck bare. Country idlers crowded closer, and there were hectic whispers. Some knew what was coming, others had only heard tell, and wanted to see.

'And this here that I stick on my hook,' announced the one-armed gladiator, 'is an apple.' He held up the green apple impaled on his hook for inspection, moving it to left and right in case some of them might never have seen a green apple.

The swordsman was placing the apple, stalk uppermost, on the kneeling woman's bare neck. He had lifted the *spatha* – the long gladiatorial sword – in his one good hand. Someone emitted a nervous laugh.

At the moment when the apple was balanced on her neck, across the woman's body had gone a faint but visible shudder, as of fear bravely overcome. A piece of acting? If so, it was convincing enough to catch and hold the crowd – a hint that his hand might slip, and her head, lopped from her body, lie there on the pavement before them in a pool of blood. Some, as they looked on, even wanted it to happen.

'And right here, now, before your very eyes,' said the one-armed, simple-minded swordsman, beginning once again to whirl his weapon, 'I will cut the apple I have put on that lovely lady's neck into two, as neatly as you yourself could cut it at home, in your kitchen, with a paring knife.' He then roared out, as if to leave them in no doubt, 'But with my *sword*! Leaving not a *scratch*!'

The tension slackened. The last whirl of his sword had been redundant, and he was saying too much. He was losing them. 'Tucco,' Gilda felt like saying, the flagstones painful under her knees, 'do it now!' Old gladiator though he was, Tucco had no sense of theatre whatever.

He struck. The weight of the blade once again thudded on her neck, stopping the heart's blood in her veins. The green apple fell in halves, to left and right. Up from the crowd came the usual muted gasp. On some days – the bad days – would I really care, wondered Gilda, if the iron blade went right on through me? Dead in the gutter?

She was on her feet, though, enormously alive, tossing back her hair. (What a thrilling gesture that had been for others, in Rome, when her curly hair was thick and dark and she herself nineteen!) Gilda went pirouetting through the crowd, a fixed smile on her face, shaking the tambourine for coppers. The sharp blade had yet again spared her life, and life on any terms was worthwhile.

The sun moved behind clouds, hinting at a wet and blustery night. The tambourine was heavy in her hand with copper coin. The crowd at the crossroads was dispersing.

'Enough for one day,' Gilda told Tucco.

'We could still work the brothels,' he grumbled.

The big old gladiator had never quite become accustomed to obeying Gilda, but in the end he always did. She was not like any other woman, fashionable or common, that he had ever known. Until he met Gilda he had hardly been able to scratch a living. She would never let him touch her. That swordstroke was as close as he ever got.

Every so often, like a mother buying a treat for her child,

Gilda would put in his palm the price of a woman, and push him off, and Tucco had to make the best of it. She knew he would always come back.

Gilda would never let him pimp her, either, however good the offer, even though when he first met her, a runaway from Leptis Magna, she had been selling her body. Nowadays there was no need, they were making enough money. In Tucco, Gilda had what all her life she had needed, ever since the mounted archers first ran off with her: an obedient, sword-carrying bully-boy of her own.

To Tucco her praise became a necessity, building up a confidence he had known years ago, as a two-fisted hero, in the arena. Tucco always got his patter wrong, dragging it out, but his tricks of swordsmanship never failed. Only in that brief moment, when his sword blade came down on her neck, was Gilda ever afraid of him.

Later in a tavern they sat opposite one another, with a loaf, a plate of sliced sausage and a jug of wine between them.

'Did you see me talking to those Circumcelliones?'

'I don't see why you should.' Tucco looked down on Circumcelliones, day-labourers who lacked the social standing of a gladiator, a man who in his time had been applauded by thousands.

'This place, Dyrin – one of them knows how to get there.'

'Beyond the frontier?'

'Then you heard.'

'Nobody ever goes beyond the frontier.' Here was the Roman Empire – a large lighted room – and he was a Roman. Out there, all was darkness.

'Tomorrow we are going.'

Tucco picked his teeth with the point of his knife, knowing that she hated that little trick of his. But a downright refusal would be no reply. Gilda was his luck. In the old days, before the games were forbidden, a gladiator could subdue almost any woman, just by being a gladiator. Only who wants a man with a stump for an arm, and a hook instead of fingers?

More than once, when drunk and randy, Tucco had thought to force her. But what if Gilda put a spell on him? Impotence? Blindness? He was glad of her. How could he live, otherwise?

'It is far?' asked Tucco humbly.

*

The roofless stone houses of Dyrin were at the far end of a flat valley, entered by a narrow gorge. Much of the valley bottom was covered with immense boulders, but the lower slopes of the foothills, beyond the deserted village, were terraced into narrow fields.

The fruit-trees had been ring-barked by Diocletian's soldiers and the crops burned; there were stumps of rotted crosses, there were bones, but a couple of the wells still held water, and higher up the slopes, beyond the fields, there was pasture for sheep and goats. A life there was possible, if man himself did not, somehow, make a hell of it.

The first bold and desperate souls to cross the frontier and reach Dyrin had been runaway Donatists, at the time when the Imperial Prefect in Africa began applying against them the law which taxed them all, rich and poor alike, down to the poverty line. These first arrivals thatched an empty stone house, ploughed and sowed a stony field, and hunted, or went hungry, by turns, until their first crop was garnered. They were poor and sad, apprehensive in the loneliness of the mountains, but glad to be free.

In the nearest Berber village, a day's march away, they argued around the fire, all winter, whether or not to make war on the new arrivals. But why raid the poverty-stricken?

'Later on they will have more,' said one old man.

'Later on they will be stronger,' said a younger man who loved warfare.

'They are enemies of our enemies,' said the wisest man of the tribe, 'so let them grow stronger. They are a living rampart between us and the Romans.'

The immediate danger had passed when the Circumcelliones arrived, tough men, used to irregular warfare, valuable men, who forced upon the Donatists the one practical decision that made this community different from any other – to cultivate the terrace fields and run the flocks, in common. In Dyrin there should be no private ownership, they argued, of common necessities, because there will be no private property in Heaven. This place, for the dissenters who arrived there and were admitted into the fellowship, was to be the Kingdom of Heaven on earth.

Their growing numbers, their toughness, their alertness

discouraged the more ruthless among the Berbers from raiding their sheep and goats. But also, the crucifixions in years gone by when the Emperor Diocletian had sent a punitive expedition to make of it a no-man's land had put a curse on Dyrin.

'Let us make blood ties,' said the same wise old man at last, 'with these enemies of our enemies. What we refrained from taking in plunder we shall help ourselves to, in bride-price'.

Young Berbers were sometimes killed on their raids, so that in the Berber villages there were too many women, whereas in Dyrin there were too many men. By this time they had a potter's kiln down in Dyrin, a forge burning charcoal and blown by a goatskin bellows, and a family had turned up whose trade was weaving cloth. As gifts to their allies, or as a bride-price to fathers, Dyrin had enviable goods to offer. The two sides were friends because it paid them. There was trouble now and then, usually about frail women or stray goats, but, by means of marriage, they were becoming kinsfolk. Beyond the frontier, Rome's enemies were coming together.

Gilda and Tucco arrived just as they were all out harvesting the second year's barley crop with sickles. One of the Circumcelliones recognised Gilda, and vouched for her. The songs she began to sing here alarmed him. What was a former member of the gladiators' guild doing in this discreditable place?

Some in Dyrin, too, were hesitant about accepting Tucco, a man past his prime, if anything a pagan, and with only one hand. But Gilda prompted him to show off with his sword – not the apple trick, though, never again the apple trick – and the vote was that an old gladiator might have his uses.

Tucco saw less and less of Gilda – she was always talking earnestly with schismatics and heretics, or reading the scriptures aloud for those who needed to know, or showing how cleverly the forest-dwelling British baked their loaves. She made her own living; she had learned to spin. Here in Dyrin she had no use for him. So a year later, Tucco decided to marry a Berber girl with cross eyes, a disfigurement considered so unlucky that her parents would let her go cheap.

Ataulf, when he came over the Alps at the head of the Visigothic army, ran into more opposition than he had expected. His first setback was before Massilia – Marseilles. He found the great southern port held tenaciously for the Emperor by a devout Catholic soldier called Boniface.

The delay made Ataulf furious. Was he or was he not commander of the army that had sacked Rome, and thus made the entire world tremble? He stood, one day, when the siege was clearly going against him, on the high hill to the eastward that overlooked the narrow landlocked harbour of Massilia. From their vantage point, the Visigoths could see, distinctly, the helmets and spears, almost the faces of the Roman defenders along the walls. They could watch one ship after another, loaded with military supplies, arrive unmolested.

Perhaps I am using soldiers, thought Ataulf, when I might to better advantage be spending gold. He sent off a messenger for the Princess Veleda.

'You must have heard of Boniface in Ravenna. Tell me about him. Can we bribe him?' He had taken the Princess to the far side of the hilltop, so others could not overhear. His tone was peremptory, his features flushed.

'Yes, I know him.'

King Ataulf might long to rid himself of this blue-eyed, cold-faced, handsome blonde woman – he wanted his betrothed, Galla Placidia, all to himself – but the day when Princess Veleda would no longer be useful to him had not yet arrived. No one in his host knew more than Veleda about Roman personalities, and Roman high politics. He is jealous of me, thought Veleda, scrutinising his clever, vehement, broken-nosed face, as only a Goth can be.

'Boniface? Let me see. Tall, thin, anxious-looking, a small head on narrow shoulders, like a crane or a heron. But intelligent. Brave too. No, King Ataulf – I don't think you or anyone could bribe him merely with gold.'

Such an answer, she knew, was exactly what Ataulf liked to hear: small, pertinent facts from which, even if discouraging, he could build up for himself a portrait of the general on the other side.

Down below, a coasting ship, under a fusillade of arrows, all of which were dropping short, entered the narrow harbour with insulting impunity. She tried not to smile. 'He is one of these new Catholic soldiers, with a sensitive conscience. Their first competent one. Stilicho was never like that. But I am quite sure that such men are climbing upwards rapidly both in Constantinople and Ravenna.'

'Not another Olympius, then? He was useless.'

'Nor even another Constantius.' She named the present favourite in Ravenna, a bully with a big head. 'Boniface might possibly be bribed, King Ataulf, with the combined empires of East and West, supposing you had them in your gift. But with nothing less, and even then he would only accept if his conscience assured him it was God's will.'

'Not gold? Unlimited gold?' asked Ataulf incredulously. Having seen what the citizens of Rome were capable of doing for gold, Ataulf had acquired great faith in its corrupting power.

'In my opinion, not for all the gold you have.' Have I, this time, Veleda wondered, been too emphatic – gone too far?

'Sarus could have been bribed with much less,' announced Ataulf, with the clumsy intention of hurting her.

'Could you have bribed Stilicho?'

Ataulf – Gothlike – thought none the worse of Veleda for that insolent riposte. To speak like that, forthrightly, when face to face with the King of the Visigoths, took courage, and courage, when allied with truth, could not be gainsaid. He gave a superior, forgiving smile which to Veleda was more bitter than an insult.

At least, reflected Ataulf, she does not flatter me. Flattery was what most poisoned being King.

'Shall I go on?' Veleda asked him, falsely demure. The others on the hilltop, important men used to being consulted, were glancing their way. Word had gone about in the Visigoth army that this unaccountable princess was a seer, consulted by Ataulf from time to time, as he might have consulted an oracle.

'You would rather have Honorius for your brother-in-law than your enemy – right? And will you endear yourself to him by besieging a city he thinks of as his own?'

'Haven't I implored him, time and again, for the hand of his sister!' shouted Ataulf, relieving his confusion of spirit by a burst of false rage. The highborn Visigoths standing not quite far enough off, began to turn their backs tactfully. The strain of waiting for his woman? wondered Veleda, with a certain contempt. Even though, as I happen to know, he assuages his body furtively with slave girls? Poor Galla Placidia!

'I have offered him the fairest of treaties!' Ataulf went on, in a bellowing voice. 'I am, myself, King of a great people, yet I am willing to serve him!

'You have a powerful rival in Ravenna,' Veleda went on firmly. 'Constantius, as well as being an ugly bully, winds Honorius around his little finger. Not everyone in the army sees why we came to Gaul – or what you intend. They are murmuring against you in the camp – do you know that?'

Italy had been a place of easy victories. So far in Gaul, the fighting had been obstinate.

'Let them murmur.' Then he looked up and gazed at her. 'Have I a choice?'

Between my betrothed and myself, Ataulf was thinking, she has always intruded, and always will – that sharp mind, those chilly eyes presuming. Veleda's voice spoke on, but in almost a whisper, 'Deliver up to Honorius, one by one, the heads of the usurpers.'

From the courtiers, still keeping their distance, came an unexpected cheer. Ataulf turned his head. A lucky fire-arrow had set the mainsail of an interloping cargo-ship on fire. Was this a game – that they should cheer?

'Including Sarus?' asked the King, his lip curling back.

'Even Sarus,' Veleda told him calmly, as if the name he repeated had not been another knife in her heart.

But Ataulf was hardly listening. He would not have been worthy to be King of the Visigoths had he not, long since, thought all this out for himself. That another should have seen it too was an intrusion upon him. Ataulf turned his back upon her without another word, as if cancelling out all her advice, and walked across with a false, public smile to his entourage.

None the less, next day he gave orders for the siege of Massilia to be raised, and the Visigoths moved westward to Narbonne – capital of a province extending across Gaul from the Alps to the Pyrenees. Narbonne fell to the Visigoth army easily enough. After this conversation at Massilia, he conspicuously avoided Veleda, and if they passed by accident would look right through her, but what she had said to him stayed in Ataulf's mind.

The King was beginning to suffer from the lover's fear that

even though Galla Placidia was to all appearances still madly in love with him, she was so much younger that if he did not soon marry her, he would lose her.

Joy flared in Galla Placidia's face when Ataulf told her they would marry in Narbonne.

'I purpose,' said Ataulf, 'to act from now on as if I were already the Emperor's brother-in-law. By sending him, for a start, the heads of all the usurpers and trouble-makers disturbing his imperial possessions, here in Gaul'.

'And that was why five regiments rode off last night in battle order?'

Ataul answered with a blank stare. Women – even Galla Placidia – were never to be trusted with military secrets. She is going away now, thought Ataulf, piqued because even on a day like this I will not trust her with my plans. She has gone, her arms dangling, to that wedge of bright sunlight where my tent flap opens, and her head, as it turns to say goodbye, is impudently sketching me a kiss from her pouting mouth. Why, as Galla Placidia goes from me, do I feel this dizzy emptiness, as of a man abandoned by his good angel?

Five thousand Visigoth cavalry rode unexpectedly out of the hills in the headwaters of the *Druentia* – the Durance – to trap Sarus and his men in a narrow-ended gulley. In Stilicho's day, the men he commanded would have made a fighting retreat, the rearguard selling their lives dearly to save their comrades. But the force Sarus had led across Gaul was held together by nothing more cohesive than the expectation of plunder. Scared out of their wits, they scattered and ran. Why stand and fight? They were swords for hire. Some other bandit in Gaul, with or without the high-sounding title of Count or Caesar or King, would take them on.

Ataulf, when he had cornered Veleda, had with her the conversation he had long avoided. He had found a task for her. 'Pick out whatever you think may be needed.'

'You mean, wedding presents?'

'Whatever you decide, Princess,' he told her, with affability. 'I know you will do it well. Let something be devised, both to delight Galla Placidia – you know her tastes, none better – and to strike the imagination of these literal-minded, hard-headed Gauls. Show them that we too are civilised. You, Princess, who lived all those years at the Roman court, must be well aware how men's sight is dazzled by ceremonial.'

'And the nuptial mass?' Veleda, having asked the most controversial question, let it hang in the air.

'No Catholic bishop in this part of Gaul will allow my presence to contaminate his altar,' answered Ataulf with a short, hard laugh. 'No matter. Our own Arian bishop will join us no less irrevocably. What God hath joined together, let no man put asunder – that is true for Arians too. No – don't go. Stay near me. This morning I need you.'

Ataulf and Veleda had been transacting their piece of business on the verge of a dusty drill-ground where, day after day through the late summer, the hoofs of army chargers at exercise had worn away the last vestiges of green. But after last week's autumnal rain green blades were emerging with miraculous rapidity out of the dust. Green for our marriage thought Ataulf. Blades of grass, and amid them, the little autumn flowers.

Others were arriving along the boundaries of the broad oblong space – soldiers, important greybeards, fashionable Visigoth women who had heard there might be something worth seeing. Thought Veleda, gloomily, I am planning my friend's wedding, and once she is married I shall lose her.

Attendants were dragging out two cushioned Roman armchairs for Galla Placidia and King Ataulf. They elbowed a way through the crowd, to place them in front, at the centre. King Ataulf signalled Veleda to stand behind his chair. Today he was being ominously friendly. The King and his betrothed took their places, and up from the onlooking Visigoths rose a twitter of expectation. Wolfish Ataulf has prepared a surprise for you – Veleda warned herself – that he knows will not be to your liking.

The entertainment for which the crowd waited was a long time coming, but Visigoths, unlike Roman plebs, knew how to wait in patience. They gossiped with one another, or gazed with curiosity at their King and his smiling, fresh-complexioned future Queen, or cleaned their fingernails with a knife point, or looked up at the clouds or down at the little flowers, so soon trampled underfoot again, and said to one another, look, flowers. All stood comfortably close, among people they knew, their own kind, in the late autumn sunlight, in the presence of their King, making the most of it.

I love my people, thought Veleda desolately, and yet I never feel part of them. Broken phrases, inanities, came to her ear, and she caught herself longing for the hard, laconic intelligence of Rome.

The thunder of hammering hoofs, and all heads turned. A squadron of Ataulf's horseguards, their lances puncturing the sky, a few of them laughing, like men taking part in a practical joke, were coming into the exercise field at a spectacular canter, reining in when their leader raised his arm, to salute the King with their spears.

Astride a great stone-horse fit to take the weight of two, their commander had his own lance slung, and was clasping both arms around a large sack, the reins held negligently, in two fingers of his left hand, while he controlled the charger with his knees. The troopers ranged themselves in line behind him, as the man and the sack came forward, at a controlled trot.

A spear-cast away from Ataulf, the cavalry-commander dropped the sack, as if yielding up a piece of tribute, and with a broad smile went back to join his men, who were fanning out in an arc to left and right. On the ground, inside the sack, was something that groaned and twisted, something alive.

'This is your turn,' King Ataulf said to Veleda, lifting himself a little from his chair to take from his belt a jewel-hilted dagger. He took the dagger-blade by the tip, and handed it to her civilly, haft-foremost.

And is well enough aware, thought Veleda, as I take a grip on his weapon, that there are times, this might be one, when I feel like thrusting the point of a naked blade under his ribs. Enjoys a danger which is no real danger, since this strange, teutonic loyalty, of which he is also aware, holds me back. Except in blood-feud, the King is the King, and sacred.

'He is more yours than mine. Go and cut him free.'

With far too many curious eyes upon her, and her heart in her breast a leaden weight, Veleda, dagger in hand, walked out in front of them all, to stoop by the sack, and saw the blade-edge against the string sewn criss-cross. The creature inside the sack wriggled; she had to be careful not to slash or stab.

In the autumn sunlight, as Ataulf and Galla Placidia watched attentively, from the sack, as from a chrysalis, emerged a crumpled man, reborn into sunlight. With the flat of one hand he felt for the ground under him. Solid earth was still there. Blinking from bloodshot eyes, he stumbled upwards to his feet. In the sack, from sweat, his hair had turned to rats' tails.

'You saved me?' But Sarus's words choked in his mouth, as one glance showed him how surrounded he was by enemies.

In the shake of Veleda's head he read everything, her rejection, his own danger. With the King's dagger held loose in her dangling hand she was turning her back on him, saying to herself, your heart has gone hard, but then, whose fault is that?

With both hands, Sarus pushed his neglected hair upwards and back from his face. He looked around like a wild creature penned in by hunters.

Into King Ataulf's face, there on his cushioned armchair, rejoicing at his enemy's downfall, came a cruel look such as Galla Placidia had never before seen him wear. Her hand was on her throat. That strange, revengeful look had given her a pang of homesickness for Ravenna.

Veleda's rebuff, the way she had turned her back, tightened up Sarus's blind rage the last twist. The audience, as if paying to watch a two-legged beast baited, gave a gasp, as Sarus gathered himself for his spring. He had overtaken Veleda as she walked away, head high, and was snatching the King's dagger from her right hand. Veleda went sprawling, a smudge of earth on her face, her cold dignity gone. His own head down, and with the dagger held out before him like a wild beast's sharp horn, Sarus ran full tilt upon the King.

Ataulf was ready for him. From his *arbifijandsof* – his humiliated blood-foe – what else should he expect? A blood–feud was pursued to the last dying breath.

The attempt at assassination was coolly transformed by Ataulf into a public display of prowess, intended to delight the watching Visigoths. Ataulf, in getting to his feet, had kicked back the chair. The ball-pommelled, cross-hilted, double-handed sword, mark of his rank, was poised in both hands. Ataulf's weight was balanced equally on his feet, he was perfectly the warrior.

And how can dagger fight sword?

A swordsman defends himself at arm's and blade's length, out of reach of cut-and-thrust. A dagger can strike but once – from close to, and best of all by surprise. Here and now there could be no surprise. Sarus had paused, just out of striking distance, as if it were not part of his plan to fling himself upon the swordpoint.

'Sarus, despicable enemy,' said Ataulf in a loud, clear, intentionally provocative voice. 'Insulter of my womenfolk. Come just a little closer, so that I may cut off your manhood, and stuff it in your mouth.'

The two men closed. Sarus made an impatient and convincing feint to the left with his dagger, hoping to duck in under Ataulf's guard, but Ataulf was undeceived. A small threatening motion with the edge of his long sword – a sword made to cleave a man in two – had Sarus stepping back quickly. From somewhere behind Sarus's back, out of an earth-stained mouth, came chilly laughter. About that laugh there was nothing accidental. Veleda, too, had begun to enjoy this barbarian revenge.

Into Galla Placidia's mind, though, came a remembrance of how incandescent had been the love between Sarus and Veleda – how they had kissed and fondled and lolled in her very presence. The touch of her friend's cold peal of laughter had prompted in Galla Placidia a sensual excitement that also revolted her. Sick of her virginity, yes, but also for one brief moment sick of her life among these cruel strangers – sick for home. But Ataulf was stepping out into the zone of danger, and helplessly she watched, as if she herself had become part of him.

Ataulf was lifting the long iron sword for the cleaving stroke. Sarus's jaw dropped, and rather than take the stroke on his body he turned and ran. From this penned-in field there was no escape; he was a dead man anyway. He would have done better to accept death at my hand, thought Ataulf, lowering his sword-point, than brand himself coward. The King stood there, both hands resting on the hilts, calmly attentive, as if come here to watch a piece of sport. Raising his voice, he gave the order for which the troopers had been waiting.

'Stick your pig, men!'

A gust of jubilant laughter went from one side of the field to the other, as the horsemen lowered their lances.

Sarus, before all men's eyes, thought Veleda, has by this cleverness been reduced to what he always was: an animal. A splendid animal then, perhaps, but not now. How fascinated I was by that glib beast, who sweats as he runs, swerving to avoid! The men on horseback were in no hurry to kill. They were prolonging their sport, and for the onlookers this was as vivid as the gladiators in Rome. And to their minds more just, because Sarus, by all accounts, deserved what he was getting. With their lances lowered, the troopers pricked at him, forcing him to dodge from one to another, pursuing him, goading him.

And were I out there, lance in hand and horse under me, wondered Veleda, in strange, sudden regret, would I not raise my lance, mercifully, and strike to kill? A merciful blow, the death of love?

He was more than an animal, his splendour, when he had it, was splendour. Spread out wide now, like wings, to keep his balance as he runs and turns; when he touched me with those hands I would shudder. Did I ever in my long and unrelenting hatred wish on Sarus so shameful a death? In and out between horses' legs, ducking, dodging, yelping when he was pricked, the blood by now running down his forehead in streams, dabbling his long, blond hair? At last some young soldier, swept away by the thrill of it, rammed a lance straight through him. The sport was over.

Ataulf, exactly as the mortal blow was struck, glanced sideways at Galla Placidia. She had looked on keenly to the last. She was licking her dry, virginal lips. Yet all this, thought Veleda, full of disgust as lance after lance, unchecked by any order from the King, rose and fell, striking into the lifeless body, is for Ataulf a bad portent: disproportionate. On the King's face were the lineaments of a man surfeited, satiate, exulting. Well, I too for a moment exulted, thought Veleda and I had every right, but King Ataulf forgets, as he lets them humiliate that piece of man-shaped, dead meat, that a Gothic blood-feud can be endless. Sarus has a brother, Singeric. He has many cousins, scattered through the Visigoth host. From now on, the Visigoths who secretly oppose the King – and all Gothic kings have rivals – will know which way to turn. Ataulf should have had Sarus killed quietly, in some anonymous affray, then the feud might have lapsed. He has brought on the entire family of Sarus a public disgrace.

To the slave market at Narbonne came the human debris of the entire province – victims torn away from their farms in the suffering countryside, petty prisoners of mimic wars between usurpers and pretenders. Why feed or even kill your victims when you can turn them into money?

Princess Veleda was becoming a figure in the crowded slave-market, examining, day after day, and usually rejecting, the young male slaves on offer. They were hobbledehoys, they were disfigured, they looked too hungry or shifty. So when she came across one that suited her – she wanted fifty and she was difficult to please – the dealer would make her pay a stiff price. Anyway, she was spending King Ataulf's money, and the King who had conquered Narbonne was rich. On the other hand, who could tell how long his army might not occupy Narbonne? So the price they made Veleda pay always fell short of being extortionate.

For the wedding ceremony, Veleda was out to buy good-looking boys, quick-witted, unspoiled, well-matched, and she wanted them quickly. A large order, even for Narbonne, not least because Veleda wanted slaves who did not look like slaves – youngsters who had about them, if possible, even a touch of unconscious nobility, for after the wedding they were to serve Galla Placidia as her pages.

I need youngsters who can be trusted to do for Galla Placidia what I myself have done for her all these years – serve her, she thought. Ataulf might hide his intentions behind a bridegroom's smile. Veleda's old instinct as courtier warned her that the King planned to get rid of her soon.

Whenever Veleda appeared, in her white robe, and with her heavy yellow hair braided high on her head, a tremor of excitement passed through the youngsters waiting there, on sale. Boylike, they had most of them quickly become used to the fact of being slaves. Many were forgetting the homes they had come from. Narbonne would be the start of a new life, and to be bought by the Princess, and enter the royal service, had more to be said for it than becoming some stranger's drudge or sordid pathic.

Two days before the ceremony, evening coming on and a light drizzle falling, Veleda was still one short of her fifty. A dealer with whom she had already done business had just offered her, yet again, and this time at a discount, a good-looking boy to whom, yesterday, she had taken an unaccountable dislike. Veleda against her better judgement was being tempted into taking him, when at the very back of the pen, by the wall, a pair of large, sad eyes looked directly at her, out of a face she had never seen before.

'That boy you are trying to hide from me – '

'Just in from Massilia. He is pulling a face, but take no notice, Princess. He is pretending to be sad, because this morning the woman he calls his nurse was sold off. And for a good price, considering she was dumb, to an old customer of mine who treats his slaves well. The boy was cheerful enough until that happened.'

And has this dealer in human anatomy happened to notice, Veleda wondered, that these days, my own face is sad?

'Why do you hide him?'

'Princess, we know each other by now. I would never waste your time. He is not quite perfect.'

'I like his face, sad or not.'

The dealer took a breath, and changed his tone. After gaining a reputation for sincerity for running down his wares, the time had come to run them up again.

'A good face. And if I am any judge, a good heart. Not a serious fault or blemish on him, no rupture, nothing like that. Can read and write, speaks Latin, speaks Gothic. On the other hand, Princess, when you take a closer look at him, this is one you may not want.'

The dealer, a past master at his trade, had already learnt that the way to make the Princess eager was to begin by discouraging her. 'I will be frank with you. He has a bent neck. Only slightly bent. Some might even think such a cock of the chin had its charms. But at a royal wedding?'

'Bring him here – let me see him,' commanded Veleda.

What had touched her about this boy was not only the sight of large eyes in a sad face, but the fact of his speaking, like herself, both Latin and Gothic. She could not help remembering her younger self in years gone by, alone, a hostage, and trying with all her might to be brave.

The slave dealer turned away. 'Hold up your head,' he whispered, giving Iynx a dig in the ribs with his elbow. 'Look happy – here's your chance!'

Upon Iynx, one catastrophe after another had fallen, until the world he knew was broken up and drifting by in a bewilderment. Julius had for a long time plied his trade in Massilia, under a false identity, then some rival informed against him for breaking the law about trading with the enemy – and they had hanged him. Sara, hiding under her long skirt every valuable she could make away with, had fled with Iynx to the countryside – she understood the countryside, she mistrusted towns. The two of them had been captured by armed horsemen, who lifted her skirt over her head, robbed her of what she had hidden there, and laughed jubilantly at the muffled, incoherent animal noises the dumb woman made, as one after another they raped her.

After, came a long and hungry time for both Sara and Iynx, as enslaved prisoners, dragged along the highroad at a horse's tail. And eventually, from this dealer in Narbonne, a baffling alternation of smiles and blows. Too many immense changes too quickly, and then the onset of utter loneliness because today Sara was sold, gone, disappeared. Iynx did not need telling that, in this new and horrible life, he would never see her again.

This blonde woman was looking him over from head to foot, but particularly scrutinising his face, his crooked neck. I must not look back too boldly, Iynx told himself; I must not look sullen. Anything to get away. The woman in the white dress with braided hair was speaking to him, in better Latin than he had heard spoken in a long while. She had hard blue eyes, but her handsome mouth smiled. And began again, speaking this time in Gothic, testing out what the dealer had told her.

Iynx replied to her politely, first in one language then in the other, and even managed to return her smile. He avoided the rough-and-ready talk of the slave-barracks, into which, lately, he had drifted and spoke up in a way that would have pleased Claudius Claudianus long ago, in that room of his so full of books. Yes. I can write too, but only Latin. Read it, of course.

'Not Gothic?' said Veleda, and truthfully he shook his head.

Practically only priests could read Gothic, and their one book was the Bible.

'What other languages can you speak, young genius?' prompted the slave dealer.

'Punic.'

'Say something to the Princess in Punic.'

Veleda listened gravely to harshly Semitic words she could not understand. 'Now tell me what all that means.'

'I was simply saying I hope so much, Princess,' said the boy, 'that you will pay whatever he asks, and take me away with you.' His eyes were larger than ever.

'All very well,' said Veleda to the dealer, with the mannered indifference that signalled to him right away that she wanted this boy badly. 'But the neck?'

Iynx as a rule resented any mention of his disfigurement. this time though, strangely, he did not mind. She was only doing what Julius's customers had done – going through the preliminaries to striking a bargain. Iynx held his head bolt upright to lessen the twist and, with one fingernail on the palm of the other hand, made the secret sign for good luck which a pagan camel-driver had once taught him.

'I have the impression that you know more about him,' said Veleda, 'than you say – that you are keeping something back.'

The slave dealer had been waiting to reveal his most impressive fact about the boy, and this was his chance to double the price. If she rose to what he had to say. His mouth was so close to Veleda's ear that she was queasily shrouded in garlic breath.

'Something that I would hardly dare repeat, Princess, to anyone but you. A man who knew it for a fact told a friend of mine in the trade, the night before he met his death at the end of a rope. That doesn't recommend him, I know – condemned to be hanged. But *in articulo mortis* – you know what the law says? – the truth is spoken. The dumb woman knew more than she would ever have given away. The boy, I dare say, will have heard them say it of him. He's a bright one.'

The slave dealer was spinning it out, like a lure that dazzles and hooks a fish. Veleda knew she was being trolled, by this man's garlicky words, and yet he had intrigued her.

'Get to the point of your rigmarole.'

'There are some people I know, who would like you to believe anything – '

'Dealers for example,' said Veleda. 'Yes?'

His whisper went lower, 'But there is little doubt about this one. The boy was Stilicho's by-blow. See how he winces at his natural father's name? He dealt harshly by the Visigoths in his day, and was, by all accounts, not quite the great man we all thought him. In most cases I would never even mention if – but to you, Princess? Interesting, eh? Good blood-lines. You can see at a glance there is quality there.'

Veleda had found herself thinking, if Galla Placidia is to have fifty pages, can't I have just one? This large-eyed boy that Stilicho left behind him? Could a smelly slave dealer invent such a thing?

Cropped beard, broad shoulders, blue eyes that met mine that day, long ago, on the Forum, and then my life began. Suppose we had been, he and I thought Veleda, shaking her head automatically as the slave dealer tried her with a price. He loved all manner of women. He might have declared his love for me – I would certainly have had him, bashful Gothic virgin though I was. Our son could have been this youngster's age. And bright as he was brave.

Iynx liked the feel of yellow silk against the nape of his neck. The loaded gold plates were heavy, though, coin in the left hand, jewels in the right, and the smaller boys were surreptitiously resting them on the floor while they waited outside, two by two, for the sign to enter. The princess, on the step under the portico, was watching for the right moment, and Iynx never took his eyes off her.

The spasm of atrocious loneliness, when Sara had been taken off, was wearing away. He once more had a centre in his life – someone to watch and respond to. Iynx knew, by this time, that Veleda also had singled him out. Yesterday, as they rehearsed she had commended him. She had rested her hand for a moment on his shoulder. To the Princess, the twist in his neck made no difference.

The mansion being used for the ceremony belonged to an enormously wealthy man called Ingenuus. Iynx judged all such places by Cornelia's house – and Cornelia's house had been simple by comparison. Amid these omnipresent mosaics, these redundant columns and pilasters, faced with coloured marbles or made vulgarly opulent with gold leaf, Iynx could tell that the Princess was ill at ease. But no Catholic church in Narbonne would admit an Arian bishop to solemnize a marriage.

Through the portico, the flute music faltered. To the boys waiting outside came the high intonation of Bishop Sigesarus, reading in Gothic from the Gospel of St Mark. '*Can the children of the bridechamber fast while the bridegroom is with them?*'

Veleda raised her hand, white sleeve falling back from white forearm. The first signal.

Picking up and balancing the weight of their heavy platters, the boys shuffled into pairs, and stood ready. January sunlight, striking down obliquely, touched the gold with meretricious glitter. Were this weight of gold that I lift, thought Iynx, all mine, then I should be rich. And first I should buy back my freedom. Only, afterwards, where could I go?

The princess was giving her second signal, motioning the double line of them forward, into the auditorium. The face of even the most mischievous boy in the procession had gone solemn. Again came flute music, a tune cadenced for them to walk to, embellished and variegated by a blazing trumpet. As the first four glittering platters, in two pairs of hands, appeared through the open double doors, from the gathering of Visigoths came a gasp. Iynx matched his step to the boy in front, following the best of the music, and tried to hold down his sickening excitement.

On the dais was King Ataulf himself, a smile on his face. Most of the onlookers had never seen the King without a sword within reach. In place of the rich furs that were the traditional Gothic wedding garb he had chosen to wear a white woollen tunic – Roman. He was trying to make of this ceremony a public affirmation that he was a Christian king, even if Arian, and by culture Roman, even if by birth a Visigoth. And moreover, rich. Let the words wing their way back to Ravenna.

At his side, her hand gently on his arm as if to make sure he would not vanish, and all this brilliance turn out to be a dream, stood his Queen, Galla Placidia, dizzy with satisfaction and expectation, her eyes alight. Across the room in a gilded alcove were the music makers – flute, trumpet, a chorus of singers.

When it came to his own turn to confront the Queen, Iynx bowed even lower than yesterday, at rehearsal, when he had been commended for his manners. He contrived to place his two heavy platters on the floor in front of her without spilling, no one so far had spilled, then lined up with the others, half the page boys on this side of the room, half on that. His crooked neck, however, had caught the Queen's eye, and she misliked it as an omen. When, soon, tonight, after the feast, she took King Ataulf in her arms, and opened up to conceive for him a child, a boy, a future King – a future Emperor – would she want any memory of imperfection before her eyes? A firstborn with a flaw?

To Ataulf's joy and her own, Galla Placidia very soon after the wedding night did conceive, though as the nine months of her pregnancy wore on, Narbonne became an uneasy place for the Visigoths to linger. The Emperor Honorius had been enraged by his sister's marriage. And among the Visigoths, the first murmurs of discontent began to be heard – orchestrated by the kinsmen of Sarus. Ataulf, after dragging them all this way from the far end of Italy – so they grumbled – should surely by this time have established all of them in a kingdom. There was a hard, cold wind at Narbonne – the mistral – which upset tempers. In genial Italy had there ever been such a wind?

The Roman Emperor was blockading Narbonne by sea and moving his legions closer.

Ataulf headed them the way that other land-hungry barbarians before him had gone – into Spain. He had his eye on the port of Barcino – Barcelona. With a seaport his, and the easily-defended passes of the Pyrenees on his vulnerable left flank – the only direction from which the legions could attack – they were not likely to shift him.

Male children of the imperial line, descendants of Theodosius the Great, like Honorius and his brother, had been weaklings. The womenfolk, though, like Serena or Galla Placidia herself, were strong, indeed formidable. It may have been this talent, or the hurried journey across the Pyrenees, but Galla Placidia's first child, a boy, was born frail. In the Catholic basilica in Barcelona they gave the sickly little creature the best start they could by christening him Theodosius, after his famous grandfather. He never kept down his food, he never stopped crying.

Only much later did news of this unfortunate child come, by hearsay, to Veleda's ears.

She had hoped, intensely to see Galla Placidia through her first childbirth, but hardly expected Ataulf to allow it, nor did he. Three days after the wedding, Veleda had been called to Ingenuus's sumptuous mansion. The room in which Ataulf transacted business in the intervals of his honeymoon was full of unnecessary luxury – the basin and ewer for washing hands were of solid gold, the curtains cloth of gold. Ataulf called a sentry, and stationed him outside the door, to make sure they were not interrupted.

Keeping upon her his bright, clever, implacable eyes, Ataulf began with a flick of flattery. 'Princess, I want you to do me a great service.' Her doom had come, and she knew it, though what Ataulf wanted of her turned out to be surprising.

'With the mistress you have served so well, and for so long, happily married at last, the thought must surely have crossed your mind, Princess, that it might be your own turn next?'

Did Ataulf think she was still of an age to breed children for one of his sweaty, clumsy Visigoth commanders?

With a calm hauteur which infuriated the King, though he kept any sign of it out of his face, Veleda answered, 'Our enemies the Romans trained me, as you know, for a great marriage. But thanks to my friend, Galla Placidia, now your Queen, I avoided such a degrading fate.'

'Yours would have been a great diplomatic marriage indeed', and Ataulf emphasised each successive compliment ironically. 'With your intellect. Your experience of great affairs. Your beauty.' When Ataulf spoke well of her, she was most afraid of him.

'Spain is a country as large as Gaul, but less fertile,' Ataulf went on, repeating with a glint in his eye the lesson she had once given him. Veleda felt the strange little shiver of one who hears her own words quoted back at her. 'And in Spain the Vandals have been the least lucky. They have only a foothold – a precarious foothold – in the mountains of Roman Baetica.

You can see from what I am saying, Princess, that I hardly know more about these Vandals than what you once told me.' He lowered his voice, glanced at the door. 'But were our eyes and ears among them – '

'A diplomatic marriage – I see,' said Veleda. 'You mean King Guntheric's wife has died? And would the widower go out of his way to marry a woman of my age – sent him by you?'

'A marriage into the Vandal royal family, certainly.' Ataulf was growing uncomfortable. Why did one always have to cajole this woman? She was of no real importance, in fact she was at his mercy. Briefly, he said, 'A marriage with the king's brother, Gaeseric.'

'His bastard half-brother.'

Veleda let her answer hang in the air. About marriageable males in barbarian royal houses there was not much she did not know.

'Of royal blood on his father's side. No one has ever disputed that. A clever man. The Vandals do not take bastardy so seriously – if others have a claim to the kingship, Gaeseric has one, too. He paused, and here came the threat. 'If we are to marry you off, Princess, and I think we must, there are worse.'

Gaeseric? A clever outsider – like myself? Into Veleda's nostrils came the stink of Hun. I have the hook in her mouth, thought Ataulf. Now to strike.

'He is lame,' the King added, enjoying the flash of discomfiture, like sunlight obscured, that went across her handsome face.

'From birth?' A picture came into Veleda's mind of a hideous twisted cripple.

'He limps. A horse threw him.' And why, Ataulf asked himself arrogantly, should I conciliate her, when Galla Placidia has already accepted the necessity of her going, and more calmly than I ever expected.

'And what am I to be, therefore, King Ataulf?' asked Veleda, trying to keep her wits about her, and yet shaken inwardly by rage. 'Wife? Ambassador? The pledge of an alliance? Or your spy?'

Veleda had spoken that last word too loudly for Ataulf's liking, and she had the satisfaction of seeing him glance, once again, at the closed door.

'Why bandy words with me like this?' answered Ataulf, irritated and merciless at last. 'You are intelligent enough to know how you are placed.'

And now that Galla Placidia is pregnant, thought Veleda dismally, she will dote on him even more. He will poison her mind against me. I have no future here. Anything he might offer me later would certainly be worse.

'Start as soon as you can,' said King Ataulf briskly, not waiting for Veleda to put her consent into more amenable words, but taking his answer from her dismayed face. 'Tomorrow would not be too soon. I beg of you, though, however prompt your departure, not to leave us without first saying goodbye to Galla Placidia. She has something to tell you.'

On Veleda's face, at being ordered to say goodbye to Galla Placidia – Ataulf's last twist of the knife – was a smile as fixed as the grin on the face of a corpse.

'So you are leaving to get married,' said the new Queen, turning with a certain embarrassment from Veleda's sad face to look out of the window at the winter hills. 'Marriage is splendid.'

And what small, clever lies, wondered Veleda, will he already have told her, to turn her mind from me?

'Of course you will write to me – write often,' the Queen went on with false eagerness. 'I shall be waiting for your letters, and my husband has explained all about it. Wide lines – and between the lines, written in milk – '

Galla Placidia's voice faltered at the thought of letters where, in the visible writing, nothing personal or intimate could possibly be said.

'Yes,' said Veleda. She had learned all these tricks long ago, from Marcus Curtius. 'You heat the papyrus and the real message appears.'

Galla Placidia went on with false animation, 'And also I have presents for you. Any amount of clothes – they say the Vandals down there in Baetica are still wearing skins. Just imagine. And please take some of my jewels. Ataulf has given me so many. Choose of the best – take anything I have.'

Wearing skins? Realisation of the barbarous place they were sending her to came down upon Veleda like a fog. 'You now have fifty pages at you beck and call,' she said to the Queen. 'Could you make do with forty-nine?'

'Seven times seven – a lucky number. And I want everything lucky about me.' Galla Placidia put hands on the pit of her stomach, as if what it contained were sacred. 'What was that you said, Veleda? The one with sad eyes, and the crooked neck? Are you sure? There are prettier ones, if you want to amuse yourself with a page. Yes, admittedly, he has good manners. Have him – I don't much care for him. I want to surround myself with beautiful things, and have beautiful thoughts, so that soon, when a young Emperor kicks in my belly – '

'I am sure he will be brave and handsome and everything good,' answered Veleda, thinking, she has coarsened.

Crossing Spain would be troublesome, so Ataulf allowed Veleda the uncommonly large escort of a hundred lances, and to impress Gaesaric favourably he chose good men. Iynx, since he left Cornelia's mansion, had never once sat in the saddle. After that first day's ride on his pony, only a moderate stage, he moved around stiffly, and the troopers made a mock of him, but the day after, gritting his teeth, he kept up with them. So far as Iynx was concerned, they could jeer all they liked. He had Veleda's horse to groom. Before she mounted, he made sure the girths were tight. He packed and unpacked her saddle bags, fetched and carried for her, tried to anticipate her every whim. He had someone to lay down his life for. He was of an age to worship an older woman's shadow.

2

Any time some interested passer-by paused outside his booth, to finger a manuscript exposed there for sale, Lucas would raise his eyes from the copying-desk in the alcove at the back, and watch. To test the customer's honesty, yes, since weeks of his work could be lost if a manuscript were filched. But quietly watching a customer was a relief from his long day of shaping letters with his pen.

In his early days he had even caught one of Augustine's younger monks red-handed, as he slipped an odd roll of Petronius under his black robe, ashamed to buy, wanting it for the smut. Lucas had been furious – the sneak-thief could have spoiled a complete set. He could see, though, looking back, how unwise it had been, here in Hippo, to denounce a monk. The Christians were influential, and the scandal had given him a bad name.

The book-lovers who came to his shop could find pagan, and even heretic, authors in the rack if they looked hard enough. The stock exposed for sale was all copied from Claudian's library – a collection deficient in orthodox theology. As a sop to the Christians, though, he made sure that the author most conspicuously exposed for sale was Tertullian – their man. In keeping shop, Lucas was circumspect – but inside his own head, in his private thoughts, defiant.

If Christians don't like my prices or the merchandise I offer for sale, he told himself this morning, as he watched a vigorous but grey-haired monk pull a secular manuscript from the rack and stick in his nose, they can go elsewhere. I am not, properly speaking, a shopkeeper. I am a skilled workman, copying Claudian's books, selling my daily labour by retail.

The man under the arcade, this baking forenoon, unrolling the papyrus between his extended hands, was one of Augustine's. And the book? Frontinus – *De Re Militari*. Why should a crop-headed, sunburnt monk, evidently in town on a visit, be interested in the art of fortification? Had some girl – some boy – slipped a love-letter for him inside the vellum cover of a book few would want to consult? Lucas had seen that happen before now. In the dim alcove, he laid down his iron pen, to watch intently.

The monk was pressing forty perhaps, short hair grizzled, robe uncommonly shabby, with a three-cornered slit at the back that nobody had mended. The face of a field-worker, large hands, yet in his demeanour – the way he had pulled papyrus from rack – the subtly-indelible arrogance of someone born a patrician. And he was handling Frontinus with respect. A gentleman born, an old soldier perhaps, but side-tracked into the church. No. Not looking for a love-letter. Waiting for someone.

And here came Augustine himself, crossing the sun-drenched forum at his usual heedless, headlong pace, bareheaded, as if African sun were his friend. He stepped in under the refreshing shadow of the arcade, and reached out a hand, to touch affectionately the shoulder of the man who was waiting. Promptly, as if called to attention, the monk put Frontinus back.

'No one about to hear us – this place, Marcus, will do as well as any other.'

'You want me to serve elsewhere? Well then – always at your disposal. Though one regrets, of course, leaving the flock one knows.'

Lucas from his inner alcove saw them against the blinding sunlight as two black shapes. With his sweet and eager voice, Augustine was expounding. Lucas, unbeliever though he was, had gone, more than once, to hear Augustine preach, simply for the pleasure of listening to the flow of his Latin – intellect and emotion conjoining at the highest pitch. The Sunday crowd in the basilica would gasp, and even weep. So long as the dark-complexioned man was fixing you with his bright eye, and never stopped talking, you found yourself believing every word he said.

Augustine had begun to explain. He always gave his men full reasons.

'When the Emperor Diocletian, a pagan and a persecutor but intelligent – Marcus, you agree? – drew back from the old, indefensible frontiers of the Empire, here in Africa, he left a tract of land between ourselves and Tingitana that now belongs to nobody.'

As everyone in Africa is well aware, thought Lucas, disappointed in his eavesdropping. He had expected to hear high secrets.

'Nobody?' queried Marcus gently. 'The Berbers beyond the frontier are sure it belongs to them.'

Marcus enjoyed – and Augustine tolerantly knew that he enjoyed – knowing more, occasionally than his bishop. Certainly about military matters. 'Diocletian,' Marcus went on, 'knew what he was doing. If the Berbers hold the passes, our cavalry can hardly touch them. A terrain up there, so the light horse used to say, where you had to watch your charger, your back, your flanks and your front all at once, and the top of your head as well, in case someone dropped a stone on it.'

Augustine laughed. 'You the soldier, I the pedagogue, Marcus, and neither of us has really changed. Then listen to my lecture. The Berbers have drawn well back, leaving a no-man's-land. Across the imperial frontier is at last a place to which malcontents may escape – a place beyond our reach, where Roman law, Catholic orthodoxy, can no longer be imposed. A gathering of the disorderly, the heretic, from everywhere in Africa – '

'People who do not fit always want a place to hide. I thought when first I heard Dyrin mentioned that they had imagined one. Then a couple in my parish – irreconcilable Donatists – put their farm tools, their mattress, five goat cheeses and a basket of stale bread into a cart, and set off – '

'Dyrin exists,' said Augustine dryly. 'What were those Donatists of yours like, as people?'

'They differed from me, obdurately, on every point of church discipline where Donatists do differ. Apart from that excellent. They had most of the Christian virtues. Hard workers, too, though exceedingly poor, like everyone else in my parish – '

'Circumcelliones also take refuge there,' went on Augustine, more briskly perhaps than he need have done, so as to avoid being led into Marcus's favourite disputation – about the morality of poverty in the midst of riches. They were poor in the back country – yes. He himself had been born there. The poor would be rich in heaven, while the hard-hearted rich gnashed their teeth in hell. 'There are even army deserters in Dyrin, so I have been told. They have formed the men into a militia. Runaway slaves, as you might expect. Even a notorious gladiator, who used to perform in the streets here, with a hook instead of a hand. A couple of Jews, one a potter, the other tilling the soil, and a Jew who tills the soil is a sight you don't often see. This, though, is all hearsay. No man whose word one can trust has ever been to Dyrin, and spoken his mind, and returned.'

'Go there, you mean, and preach to them? Hope to change their minds? Confront deserters? Argue with Donatists? Convert Jews?'

'If they will hear you, why not? Is any man's heart too hard to be touched by God's grace? And, at least, once you have been there we shall know.'

'Go to them dressed as I am?'

To adopt any disguise, thought Marcus with a sinking heart, even so much as a misleading look on one's face, would be backsliding into that life of deceit long ago repudiated.

'And another thing I should need to know from my bishop,' he said, his mouth tightening, his stance more military. 'Am I acting in this for the church – or the provincial authorities?'

Augustine, as if leaving Marcus alone to find his own answers, had reached, as it were absentmindedly, to the rack, for a papyrus that had caught his eye. He glanced at the label and pushed it back, with a mutter of regret. Augustine's memory, which should have been perpetually full of God, was crammed, as he was well aware, with secular eloquence. When he was in the pulpit, snatches of verse, even of pagan verse, would rise unbidden to his tongue. There are more urgent things to spend time and money on, Augustine chided himself, than buying a minor poet one had heard praised, yet never read. Half-yielding, he pulled the roll a finger's-breadth out of the rack, Lucas watching, then pushed it back emphatically with the flat of his hand.

Square-shouldered Marcus was keeping deliberately silent, full of doubt. I know what must be passing through his mind, thought Augustine. He must needs be argued with.

'The authorities are not concerned in this. Over there, Marcus, is the Roman frontier, and Dyrin lies beyond, in the mountains, out of their bailiwick. Do they ever, in such matters, look further than their noses?' He paused, to ask with a winning smile, 'Or does that sound uncharitable?' Marcus laughed. His answering nod could have indicated either yes or no.

'Gildo's Rising,' asked Augustine, 'were you in the army at the time?'

'I saw no service, though I studied the campaign. Flavius Stilicho did the staffwork, someone else over here, led the expedition for him. And afterwards, as we all know, Claudius Claudianus wrote it up in a poem, quite splendidly.

'What a talent!' Augustine sighed, glancing yet again at the papyrus he had forbidden himself. 'Now, Gildo in his day was not unlike Brother Marcus.' Augustine, though, had softened his astonishing remark with another smile. 'Deeply concerned with poverty in the midst of riches. Quite sincere. His plan was simple – to raise a rebellion, here in Africa, of the discontented – '

'There are plenty of them,' muttered Marcus, 'and with good reason.'

'Take possession of uncultivated imperial estates. Share out the Emperor's unused land among the poor. His idea, you will notice, was alluring but disproportionate, like a heresy.'

A heresy that attracts me too, thought Marcus with a sigh. He is rebuking me.

'And there were among his followers – there always are – a good many extremists. The poorer and madder Donatists, the Circumcelliones. They would have taken over all large estates, dividing all Africa into small farms. You approve? I see you do. Marcus, you were born in Rome, and rich; I was born in the back country, near Thagastes, on just such a small farm. In a land of drought there is no escape from poverty on a small farm. Smallholding yields no surplus of corn and oil, and Rome would have starved. Or so I was assured by those at the time who had studied the question – '

'The earth is the Lord's,' answered Marcus stubbornly, 'and the fullness thereof.' A repentant aristocrat, thought Augustine, and loves the poor as Christ loved them.

'Except when trying to do God's will,' he said gently, 'what men accomplish is seldom what they intend. The human will goes awry.'

'I can see that the rich might not think much of the idea,' said Marcus. 'When I was a rich young man myself, and officially Gildo was my enemy, I can assure you that the rich in Rome thought very little of his ideas.' They both laughed, but Augustine's voice as he continued turned grave.

'Wipe out all debts? Share the land? A Biblical jubilee? I too, had I stayed in Thagastes, and been what I might well have become, a small farmer, taxed beyond endurance – why should I, too, not have followed Gildo? Brotherhood on earth? Except that the delightful dream could be brought to pass only by destroying what little law, what little order, we have left in the world. The reflection, that is, in the lives of men, of the order and justice in God's mind. And once law has been destroyed, who will bring it again into being? Arbitrary tyranny in small villages – the sword as the sole arbiter. In laying rough hands on the city of men – '

' – with its unpardonable inequalities – ' persisted Marcus. Few dare check Augustine in full flow.

' – yes, extremely imperfect law. But law based, at least in intention, on natural justice. Need I go on? Barbarians, heretics, schismatics, who plunder the city made with men's hands, will they not destroy, if they can, the City of God? The moral order – the residuum of our hopes? You don't agree, Marcus? I see in your eyes that you don't, and why should you? This is a question we need, you and I, to consider more profoundly. In Dyrin, much may be learned. I would never ask a brother to go to Dyrin whose mind was firmly made up, one way or another. Is yours?'

Marcus shook his head, and this time meant it. He could seldom stand up against Augustine's presence, his readiness, his insight, his transparent goodness.

'Not many more than a couple of hundred there. But lately a change has come over them. They have in their midst a prophetess who knows how to put their dream into words. Even into songs. I lately came across a young stonemason, a friend of yous, up on the wall, trowel in hand, singing one of her songs. Once, only Circumcelliones in the back country sang them, at night, by their fires. Now masons in the city. Well?'

A neighbouring tradesman, who needed to change a silver piece for a copper, ducked under the arcade. Lucas came out from his hiding place, blinking deceitfully, a daylight owl, a man awakened from a doze. As Lucas began counting pennies into the neighbour's hand, Marcus and Augustine turned away from the bookstall, abruptly, and went walking in the heat across the open forum. Still animated, still arguing, but their voices diminishing.

'That song I heard? Witty. Gildo's ideas, of course – but taken further.' Augustine laid his hand on Marcus's sleeve. 'And the name of their prophetess? They call her Gilda.'

Lucas could not be sure if he overheard that last name, or dreamed it. You are becoming a visionary, he told himself, among books. You hear her name – you snatch it out of air. Even after all this time, she haunts you.

The assortment of women Lucas had known casually, since Gilda – dockside tarts, kitchen drabs, furtive scuffles behind locked doors with married women out for adventure – had always left him dissatisfied, and at times ashamed. What are all those women, he would at times pretend, but attempts to dim the memory of Gilda?

Casual flesh and blood, after Gilda herself, was second best. Helen and Nausicaa, Dido and Proserpine – the women in books – were a different consolation. Women intangible yet vividly real, women prompt at the rendezvous. By opening a book he could call them forth. And afterwards, back on the shelf, rolled up again, silent, no disappointment. Lucas picked up his iron pen with a sigh, and with scrupulous care, began to write down some other man's words.

3

Veleda, on her way, south found that even with a hundred lancers to ride out and forage for her at the day's end, she could still go hungry. Hispania – Spain – had been ruined to the point of starvation by one barbarian incursion after another. They travelled slowly because, along the paved and engineered Roman road, bandits had taken possession of crossroads and bridges and lay in ambush to exact toll. There were a couple of exciting little skirmishes, and the hotheads of Veleda's escort were looking forward to more of the same, when she firmly told them otherwise. Skirt dangerous places. Make detours. The point is to arrive.

Hers was a voice to be obeyed. She led them thereafter on short cuts, across bleak, bare mountains, jogging along with Iynx at her elbow, riding at the head of her hundred lances through obscure pine forests, and long hill tracks that descended abruptly into narrow, green cultivated valleys. As they tended always southward, into the waxing heat of the noonday sun, the treacherous anxieties of life at court dropped from her. Veleda grew thin and tanned and bold and cheerful.

She began to feel like the chieftainess of a robber band. Could I live like this always, she wondered, on horseback, by plunder?

The picture this land of Hispania made in Iynx's mind, as he passed through, was of a parchment crumpled in the hand. Mountain and lowland followed lowland and mountain, in uninterrupted succession. To the pious, Catholic country folk of Spain, after centuries of Roman peace, the approach of lancers, on the lookout for their sheep or goats or whatever else could be speared, and eaten, was a fearful apparition. The nearby cities which they supplied were dying too.

Veleda and her escort kept cities at a distance, but even here, in blighted Spain, they looked familiar, still carrying on a ghostly semblance of the Roman way of life, around bath and basilica, library, theatre and forum. I am seeing civilisation die, Veleda told herself as she rode south. And do I care?

The Vandals themselves, when she came into their country, were living off the land through which the broad and rapid snow-fed river Baetis flowed – the fertile province which, as Andalusia, has ever since borne an echo of their name. Down here in the south, the mountains were higher and more bleak, the valleys richer. The Vandals camped in mountain hideouts, and raided into the lush, green plentiful plains. And is this, then, Veleda asked herself, the Vandal kingdom of which Ataulf spoke? They are living in the hills like desperadoes.

Gaeseric, the Vandal King's illegitimate half-brother, was living with his personal followers in an abandoned, and tumbledown place in the foothills, midway between the broad valley of the Baetis, full of corn and olives and horses, and brighteyed, full-breasted women, and the unyielding, snow-capped sierras. When a hundred disciplined Visigoth lancers on worn-out horses approached, with a gaunt-cheeked, yellow-haired woman at their head, beside her a sprightly page on a hungry pony showing its ribs, up and down the single street of the ruined town arose a great commotion.

No sentries had been posted. Long-haired men in skins, looking poorer than the poorest of the Visigoths, tumbled out of half-wrecked houses, all far gone in drink, all running to see, one trailing an almost-empty wineskin which dribbled as he staggered. Some were decked out in extravagantly barbaric jewellery, others with bits of Roman plunder, an enamelled *fibula*, a seal ring carved from a gem, that went incongruously with their skins and rags.

A trumpeter began blaring away, his instrument green with verdigris, but, more than once, failed to hit the note. With my hundred sober and hungry Visigoth lancers, thought Veleda, I could have taken this place, and made these men my slaves, taught them obedience, built an army, seized a kingdom. As she waited to see who would come and speak with her, she laughed at herself. Such ambitions were for a man.

A man of middle height, with the severe face of one who has known pain, was limping down the road, using a javelin as a walking staff. He observed his drunken followers' confusion with a smile, half tolerant, half contemptuous, and paused to throw words at them like well-aimed stones. His genial insults, his commands, in a Gothic heavily accented and full of strange vowels, brought the skin-clad men, drunk though they were, into passable order, quicker, thought Veleda, that I could ever have done. He himself is not drunk, even if he pretends to be. He is Gaeseric.

Veleda ambled her horse towards the limping man, saluting him affably, as if this were a much more civilised place than it was, and he the host who was expecting her. Iynx pushed his own pony closer to her horse. Veleda had told him this morning to put on his clean tunic, had taken pains with her own appearance and sent word on ahead. And all to flatter, wondered Iynx, this bandit?

Veleda's lancers had dismounted, tethered their chargers, wiped them down, and were being led off by jocose Vandals to drink wine. Gaeseric, having given a hardly-necessary order here, another there, offered Veleda an arm to help her dismount. But Iynx, down from the saddle, and his own bridle in one hand, was ahead of him to do her that service. 'So you are the Princess Veleda! Come all this way astride a cavalry charger, wearing trousers, like a barbarian – simply to bring me greetings from King Ataulf?' He spoke in a public voice with a cutting edge, as if he wanted his disavowal of her to be overheard.

One or two of Gaeseric's followers were still hanging around, ears pricked, as if this woman who rode astride, in trousers and tunic and cloak all of cloth dyed yellow with saffron, might be even better entertainment that the abundance just now of plundered wine.

'You were expecting, no doubt,' said Veleda, throwing back at him his own tone of voice exactly, 'a wife who had to be carried in a litter.'

Gaeseric's hard, stony eyes as he spoke were stripping Veleda's body from head to foot of the exotic yellow cloth that clad her. Small high breasts, long flanks, neck and cheeks withered by her long journey. Food and rest, though they might fatten her up, would never make her young again, or fresh. A splendid Gothic woman, past her prime. Old enough, he thought, to be an elder sister. She and I are not unlike each other.

Pointing at Iynx, who stood there, the faithful page, holding their horses' heads, he asked insolently. 'Your son?'

Gaeseric snapped fingers, so that a groom led horse and pony away, but Iynx went on standing there, not unwilling, in fact, to be mistaken for the Princess's son, though wondering if he ought not, in some way, to avenge an insult that he did not quite understand. He was waiting there because Veleda might need him.

' – and what is this joke, Princess, that Ataulf of the Visigoths is trying to play on both of us. A virgin, I was led to believe – not a matron. A mother even?'

'In point of fact, my page there is the son,' answered Veleda in a confident but casual voice, so that those trying to overhear might not suppose she cared, 'of a Vandal more famous in his day even than Gaeseric.' She paused, and watched his face. Lame Gaeseric could not bear not to be told more. 'You have heard of Flavius Stilicho?'

Iynx, when Veleda asserted loud and clear this marvellous fact about himself, was shocked into a strange embarrassed joy. The secret of his birth had hitherto only been whispered, often by doubters. If the Princess said it out loud, matter-of-factly, to this fellow who leaned on a javelin and looked at her, then it must be true.

Gaeseric was tapping the butt end of his javelin against the upper of his clumsy, thong-sewn boot, trying to think of an answer. Usually, in this ruined mountain town where his followers had encamped, he was the one who gave the clever answers. But before he could find words, Veleda attacked.

'And is this the welcome a Prince of the Vandals gives to a Gothic princess of blood in no way inferior to his own, the legitimate daughter of a legitimate king, who has ridden a thousand miles to see if she will condescend to have him? What is this tumbledown hide-out of yours in the hills, Prince Gaeseric? The capital of the Vandal kingdom?'

The lame man armoured himself inside a fixed smile. When a highborn Gothic woman began a tirade such as this, you could only hear her out.

'Have you not yet discovered, you Vandals, how to batter down the walls of a city? Is that it? And who are these pathetic creatures sewn up into skins, with long, flapping ears and weak legs –' She withered the eavesdroppers with a glance; some turned away, some shamelessly went on listening. 'Your soldiers?'

As her rapid Gothic raillery mounted in the fearless succession of quick jibes that traditionally could end in unforgiving emnity or hot friendship, Gaeseric gave her a magnificent smile. It was to be friendship! Merely by curving his lips in the right way at the right moment, and achieving a glitter in his eyes, Gaeseric had thrown over Veleda the meshes of an invisible, unbreakable net, and they both knew it. He has used this charm of his, Veleda warned herself, on other women before he met you. Yet her heart had melted.

'Princess – take my arm. Let me show you to the house which has been made ready for you. Quartermaster, see to it that the gallant fellows sent us as our guests by the King of the Visigoths are properly entertained.'

And there is also something scandalous here, Veleda warned herself, of which these onlookers, with their ape faces, are already aware. Gaeseric treats me like this only because he has discovered a use for me. He is a little too much like Sarus, interested in others only insofar as they serve his plans. He has gone out of his way to charm me. I am captivating him. They have no other women down here, these Vandals, in any way like me.

With her forearm, she pressed Gaeseric's hand against her body – a sign to him. And turned her head to tell Iynx, by a quick glance, that he should follow. In the place got ready for her a surprise might be waiting which she would rather not face alone.

The house Gaeseric took her to had its roof of Roman tiles intact. Inside, the only furniture was a mattress-cover of thong-sewn deerskin, stuffed with wool. At least they did not mean me, thought Veleda, her bones stiff from so many nights of sleeping on bare earth, to bed down hard.

The bright winter sunlight of Andalusia intruded through a narrow, barred window, showing up the room's poverty-stricken bareness. Though what does it all matter, when I have turned my back, Veleda told herself resolutely, on the luxuries of a civilisation I despise?

A fire had burned all night on the hearthstone – the wind from the sierra, once the sun went down, could be piercingly cold. Gaeseric, with an impatient kick at the stub of a glowing log, made sparks spray upwards. He had used his lame leg stiffly, like a club. Permeating this house was a barbaric smell which took Veleda back – spilled drink gone stale, roast meat, unwashed and unwashable garments of skin.

A plump, fair, very pretty girl, six or seven months gone in pregnancy, came across the room from a dark corner, towards the three of them. She had been watching them come in, and without a word offered Gaeseric a horn brimful of wine. With curt indifference, as if already he had acquired the habit of deceiving her, Gaeseric said as he took and drank deep, 'I have this ambassador here from the King of the Visigoths. A Princess, with much to discuss that does not concern you. Go out into the sunshine, child.'

The girl sent to darken the door, plaits dangling, belly heavy, turned and glanced once, with dumb curiosity, across her shoulder at this self-possessed, older woman from the world outside, in her enviable garb of coloured cloth, this personage, an ambassador, a Princess, for whom the best house must be got ready. Gaeseric tipped back his head and drank the last of the wine, as if to wash an unwanted taste out of his mouth.

And does he expect me now, wondered Veleda, to reach out, another of his hand-maidens, and take from his hand the empty horn, which he holds negligently, as if ready to drop it. Iynx moved, with cold politeness, to save her from the indignity. The son of Flavius Stilicho, thought Gaeseric, is waiting on me!

'The woman you have just seen is my wife,' announced Gaeseric with the brazenness usual among Goths when obliged to tell an unpleasant truth. 'We were married, she and I, at the last full moon. I am waiting for her to bear me a son.'

Iynx, with sinking heart, asked himself, and now do we ride all that long way back? For Veleda however there could be no going back to the court of King Ataulf, and she knew it. She looked into Gaeseric's delinquent face, and speaking with a kind of hectic merriment, took the most crucial decision of her life.

'King Ataulf has played a practical joke on both of us. You expected a virgin, I a kingdom.'

Gaeseric silently took in that answer as he gazed at her face. What Vandal woman had he known who could not be led by the nose – by her superstitions or her appetites? This woman, into whose provocative eyes he gazed, was no plump and childbearing wife, but a second self.

'And if I decide to stay, Prince Gaeseric? You consider I might be of use?' His title on her lips was balm to Gaeseric.

'We could begin by teaching this youngster how to throw the Vandal javelin,' said Gaeseric, prodding at Iynx playfully with the butt end of the weapon upon which he leaned. 'Your page can read and write?'

Veleda and Iynx answered both at once, and then laughed together. Gaeseric, too, laughed ruefully.

'More than I can! We have priests who can read – the Bible, anyway – and one or two of them can even write. When Ataulf married the Emperor's sister, they tell me, Princess, you were her lady-in-waiting. Did Ataulf send you all this way to spy on me, perhaps?'

Here came the accusation Veleda had dreaded. Gaeseric's eye glittered, as if he had made the first stroke in a fencing match, which would back this woman up against the wall, and at his mercy.

Veleda, from old instinct, found the right tone to answer him, of deprecating circumspection mingled with downright honest.

'I served Galla Placidia for a long time before I ever heard the name of Ataulf.'

'You might not grieve, then,' said Gaeseric, watching her face, 'to hear that he is dead.'

An answer rose in Veleda's throat, but was choked.

'Stabbed,' went on Gaeseric, as if reporting news of no real consequence – but he watched her. 'In a blood feud, so I hear.'

'And Galla Placidia?'

'Oh, the former Queen is alive, but from what we hear, treated shabbily. We too, you notice, clad in skins though we are, have our spies.'

Veleda, as he continued to watch her, could feel herself blushing, as she had not blushed since her earliest days with Sarus. There was no regret for King Ataulf in her blush; this was another emotion. She was ashamed. Gaeseric took her hand at last, in a simple gesture that was also a declaration of friendship. He had accepted her.

'Princess Veleda, let me say this. But you must know already. You have nowhere else to go. Back to Ravenna? Where they will no doubt send Galla Placidia, to placate her dim-witted brother the Emperor? They would drown you in a sack. Or take service under Singeric? Yes, Singeric is the new King of the Visigoths. And Singeric would throw you to his dogs. Those of your escort willing to serve Gaeseric are welcome to stay. Let the others ride back, and make their peace with Singeric. As for you, Princess, and the boy – '

Veleda still felt around her own thin hand of the pressure of Gaeseric's muscular grip – his pledge of alliance. And sick to death already, thought Veleda triumphantly, of that plump and pretty wife. I can promise him, he shall never be sick to death of me.

'My half-brother, Guntheric, the bald-headed King of Vandals, is not much of a soldier,' said Gaeseric briskly, confidentially, his plans instantly made. 'He is however a very moral man. If an unmarried Gothic princess who might have been my betrothed, were to be living here with me, cheek by jowl, Guntheric would never approve. And Guntheric, let me tell you, disapproves of me enough already.'

As if what he planned for her were a trifle, Gaeseric added, 'So I shall make a bride of you, after all.'

Gaeseric had moved his mouth close to Veleda's ear, so that even Iynx would not hear what he said next. 'And then, very quickly, a widow. With us, to a widow, all is permitted.' He can't be serious, thought Veleda. This suddenness is to drive me mad.

'What happened to King Ataulf – tell me exactly,' said Veleda, a little hoarsely, as she drew away from him, changing the subject, giving herself time to think. Gaeseric's whisper, his closeness, his brutal plan for her, had inordinately excited her.

'Ataulf went to his stables every day, to look at his horses?'

'On breaking his fast – always.'

'A man called Dobbius, a groom I take it, or even an ostler – '

'Yes, I know Dobbius.'

' – stabbed him from behind. In the name of Singeric, brother of General Sarus. A blood-feud. And the last we hear is that Singeric has been hoisted on the shield – '

Gaeseric, as he spoke of these distant matters, wrinkled his eyes, much as a man does who looks a long way ahead in bright sunlight. He might be hardly literate, and only the leader, at present, of a gang of ragamuffins, but in matters concerning kingship his mind's eye saw far and grasped all.

'I do not somehow think,' he murmured – to himself, to her, there were confidants – 'that Singeric brother of Sarus will be King of the Visigoths for very long.'

They are none of them mocking me, Galla Placidia told herself. Those people, watching, are not scorning me. They are not cheering their new king, Singeric, either. They are standing there, along the roadside, to left and right, in silence.

The man riding ahead of her, out of Barcelona down the long straight Roman road – Singeric, on a splendidly groomed grey charger – kicked up dust for her to swallow. Let King Ataulf's widow, the Roman, had been his drunken idea, be led to his funeral insignificantly, on foot, in torn clothes, her hair loose. Let her be humiliated in men's eyes. The dapper grey horse in front carried the new king. Slung sideways across a plodding packhorse, which tramped behind her, was the blood-stained body of Ataulf.

Singeric, brother of Sarus, had been raised only yesterday on the shield; he considered this public exposure of Galla Placidia's grief to be part of his revenge. So hold back your tears, Galla Placidia implored herself. Head up high. Let those who look on, judge.

Today was not working out as Singeric had hoped. The people who watched were not despising her. They had come to the roadside out of curiosity, as their alien Visigothic masters went by. And who was that poor woman? Why were they making her walk in the dust kicked up, pace after pace, by that grey charger?

Galla Placidia, in her haste to keep up with the horse in front so as not to be ridden down by the funeral packhorse coming up behind, caught her foot in the torn hem of her skirt. At her stumble there was no laugh, though she went rigid inside, expecting one. They were not gloating, these people, over the pitiful state of the Emperor's sister, the dead king's widow. Hold up your head.

Ataulf was being taken to his grave in the bloodstained clothes he was wearing when Dubius stabbed him, flung like a limp sack across a packsaddle. When they took Galla Placidia out, bareheaded, and maliciously tore her fine clothes, and made her join the funeral procession, she had looked up and seen Ataulf dead, and the shock was still with her. Black flies on his dried-out wound had swarmed up and settled again, when the packhorse moved restively, like tiny evil spirits. Singeric's gang had been watching to see if she would again turn her head. But she never would.

Twelve milestones onwards, that much she knew because they had taunted her with it, to an open grave at a crossroads – a hole dug in unconsecrated ground. Thus Singeric, like a blind fool, shows his contempt for my brother the Emperor. But I too have been a blind fool. What have we in common, we Catholics, with these Arian Visigoths and their fits of inexplicable savagery? All that had happened to her since Rome fell to Alaric came up into Galla Placidia's mind as she plodded onwards in the lurid colours of a nightmare.

Next time she had to break into a shuffle, to keep up with Singeric on horseback, one fool laughed, amid a stony silence. They are perplexed, Galla Placidia told herself, and some are sorry. Do I need their pity? The day before yesterday, my husband Ataulf had dominion over all this land. These people all ran to crook the knee. And what is Ataulf now? Dead meat, flung across a saddle. Don't look round!

As her incoherent thought began forming words, the onlookers saw Galla Placidia's lips move, as if she were praying. But she was making a declaration to herself. Not mere *potestas*, she told herself, the power of office. *Dominatio*. Supreme unlimited power. This will not crush me, I shall again win power. In the very sound of the word *dominatio* – in her promise to herself – there was solace.

Another milestone went past, and she counted it off on her fingers. Three more. *Amor* – but did love bear thinking of? The body she had loved to distraction had been flung across a pack saddle, hoofs again coming up behind. *Dominatio*. Don't look round! No tears! Head high! On hurt feet, she shuffled forward.

Veleda, who would have stood by me, thought Galla Placidia, was sent away and I let her go. Though what could she have done? Would she have walked beside me?

As if a surgeon, fingering a wound, Galla Placidia, as the last weary miles arrived, was forcing herself to picture the dead child. Two handfuls of dead flesh, her own flesh passed on, in a hole in the apse of the church in Barcelona. A child in a silver coffin, pale and small, stopped crying at last.

Her own man-child who might in course of time – *dominatio!* – have been both King of the Visigoths and Emperor of Rome.

Galla Placidia's teeth were clenched, her jawbone ached with the effort of will, dry eyes burned, tongue stuck uncannily to the roof of her mouth. She asked herself, dare they kill me too? The Emperor's sister? After this, for the rest of my life, I shall make of this face of mine, which smiled of its own accord whenever Ataulf came into the room, a fixed mask. No one, after this, shall ever know what I think or feel.

Dobbius, whose hand struck the blow, had been a minor prince in an insignificant tribe swept up by the Visigoths many years before, when they overran Pannonia. Every morning of the year, a piece of bread in his hand to break his fast and theirs, King Ataulf would go round the stables and talk to his horses, offering them titbits. A brief respite, every day, from the weight of kingship; one time he need never be on his guard.

Dobbius was a man the King hardly spared a thought for.

He looked after the King's horses, and that did him sufficient honour. Ataulf, so clever in other ways, had never perceived the rankling resentment behind the habitual smile. But the blood-feud conspirators, Sarus's kinsmen, had taken note of Dobbius, prompted him, made him promises. Walking his usual, respectful pace behind the King, Dobbius had taken out from underneath his coat the knife he used for cutting chaff, and had struck upwards, beneath the ribs and into the throbbing heart. His blow, as the blade went home, was a joy to him.

Scarcely had Ataulf's heart ceased to beat, than Singeric was hoisted up on the shield by his blood-kin. They had a story ready to justify themselves – that Ataulf, for the sake of that foreign wife of his, was planning to turn Catholic.

Though such protestations did not sit well in the mouths of murderers, the possibility had been in Ataulf's own mind, now that he had a defensible kingdom, with Barcelona for his capital, and mountains on his flank. To change his religion would conciliate the people who were now his subjects, and might pacify Honorius. Spain had known barbarians, hitherto, only as plunderers. In my new kingdom, Ataulf had boasted to Galla Placidia, there will be law and order, culture, city life – all the best that is Roman. Yet along with it, barbarian chastity, a trustworthy currency, teutonic straightforwardness. A simple concession in religion, he had sometimes thought, would please my Queen and make all one. But that had been something for tomorrow.

Singeric's reign as King of the Visigoths lasted seven days.

Those who brought about his overthrow kept their plans secret, yet Galla Placidia herself sensed, from the comings and goings, and the way certain close friends were avoiding her, that there might soon be an action in her favour.

Singeric, though he looked well on a horse, and spoke up glibly enough about his fidelity to the Arian religion, turned out to be but an inferior copy of his brother Sarus. A bully and braggart, who spent much of his seven days as King in blind debauch. Even those who had lifted him on to the shield were asking if they had blundered.

Although Ataulf, with a broad-bladed knife in his heart, was unlikely to have breath for political epigrams, men opposed to

Singeric whispered to one another, during that week, Ataulf's political testament: 'Live in friendship with Rome – restore Galla Placidia to the Emperor.' It had soon dawned on the Visigoth nobility that Singeric, by wantonly insulting the Emperor's sister, was laying up trouble for everyone.

They had their eye on a quiet man called Wallia, far-sighted though simple in speech. On the seventh day, guardsmen dealt out death afresh. Singeric, too drunk to feel the blow that struck him, was buried, not like Ataulf, in an unmarked grave, but with appropriate dignity. A King was a King, however deplorable.

Galla Placidia was given good plain clothes to wear for this second funeral, decent black for a widow, and a maid-in-waiting to dress her hair. They had taken away all her jewels, declaring them a part of the royal treasure. Wallia's wife had her eye on them. That night Galla Placidia was brought in to join the feast, and at Wallia's right hand sat the new Queen, a woman with not an idea in her head, and cut emeralds around her neck that Galla Placidia once had worn. The former Queen and the present one exchanged tight little smiles, and Galla Placidia thought how ill those green stones went with Wallia's wife's complexion.

Wallia drove a particularly hard bargain. For the right to embrace, once more, his errant sister, Honorius made a gigantic shipment of corn from Africa, 600,000 measures, enough to feed all the famine-stricken in north-eastern Spain, and to dole out seed-corn for the next harvest. With the corn that Honorius shipped, the treasure Ataulf had left behind, Wallia was consolidating his rule.

I shall never in my life, allow myself to feel so much again, Galla Placidia told herself, as the first familiar squat-bellied Roman grain-ship wallowed deep-laden into Barcelona harbour, for any other man, for any other child. This body of mine is being made a trophy, for those in power to buy and sell. Very well, I too will trade with it, and cleverly. Never again will an ambitious man take advantage of my emotions. No one shall ever trick me. I am cured, I am hardened.

A Roman chamberlain, Eupletius, conducted Galla Placidia to the low pass where, at a line of cliffs, the Pyrenees met the sea:

the frontier of the new Visigoth kingdom. Jogging clumsily across the turf towards her came a man with a big head hanging, as if from its own weight, between his shoulders. Constantius, the Emperor's chief minister – and he had, pasted on to his face, an ingratiating leer. Constantius dismounted, with the awkwardness of a man with no gift for horsemanship, or any other physical grace, and came towards Galla Placidia, looking with habitual caution to right and left, as if suspicious, even here, of ambush.

Constantius was a man with clear ideas, great ambitions and no scruples. He wasted no time. That night he made Galla Placidia his formal proposal. 'You are to marry me, now you are widowed. And nothing would please your brother more.'

'What if it does not please me?' said Galla Placidia, tilting her chin. Though still young in years, almost fresh, she was older in manner than Constantius remembered her; she had acquired a mind of her own.

'You will come round in time,' he predicted, 'so why not say yes now?' There was about this man a weight of will, an imperious certainty, that might well have numbed into submission the girl she was when, impulsively, she left Ravenna. Go on playing for as long as you can, Galla Placidia told herself, the disconsolate widow.

They paused overnight in painfully familiar Narbonne. After drinking grossly of the local white wine – almost as if he found the prospect of approaching her as physically repulsive as she herself found him – Constantius broke into Galla Placidia's room, all perfumed and massaged, drunkenly virile. Does he think himself irresistible, she wondered, just because he has political power? Is power itself the aphrodisiac?

When it came to a threat of rape, Galla Placidia had herself better in hand than Constantius bargained for. With a swing of a three-legged stool, she cut his head open from ear to eye. Constantius, next day, was obliged to ride with a bandage around his enormous head, while, maliciously, Galla Placidia sympathised. Everyone else in the escort was frightened of the man. To marry his master's sister and breed Emperors is the summit, thought Galla Placidia, of his political ambition. He still intends to have me.

The journey across Gaul became a battle of wills. Constantius had staying-power. They crossed the inhospitable Alps, and descended into Italy, where everything was warmer, more golden, softer, reminding Galla Placidia of her own childhood. Her will to resist Constantius began to wane. As a possible lover, she told herself, he might be odious. But there is something morbidly fascinating in his mere stubbornness. Here was a man even more obsessed than she herself with *dominatio*. I have had my love-match, she told herself, as they rode side by side through sprouting vineyards, and how many other women in this world can say as much? This body and this face of mine may not be beautiful, but out of this unique flesh may come Emperors. The Romans will never let me rule in my own right, only through a son, and to make a son I must have a husband. The thought of Constantius still made her shudder.

Honorius was already becoming prematurely gross, sluggish, and the kisses he slobbered on his sister in public soon became the joke of the city. I am safe, Galla Placidia told herself, though not for long. They will get at Honorius; they always have.

A pliant priest, at a hint from Constantius, began to play on the Emperor's easily-awakened sense of guilt. His passion for his sister? An occasion for wicked thoughts if not of sinful acts. Those notorious public kisses? Were they brotherly – or incestuous? And when God takes you, said the clever priest – fear of death being what now most haunted Honorius – who but Constantius will be here to look after your sister, and preserve your Empire intact?

That selfsame afternoon, taking Galla Placidia fervently by the hand, as if her mere warm touch might keep death a little further off, Honorius began to court her on Constantius's behalf. 'When I am gone, remember this. Constantius will still be there to look after you.' Galla Placidia did not argue, though she pulled her hand away. They had closed in upon her.

Constantius finally bent her to his will by threatening to make a nun of her. 'For a widow who refuses to remarry, that is the proper thing.' Constantius always talked of the church as though it were a branch of the police. The thought of a perpetually cloistered life made Galla Placidia's blood run chill.

At last, with an apparent widowly reluctance that hid cold calculation, Galla Placidia took Constantius for her husband.

The court found it odd that she had held out for so long. Since my brother Honorius, she argued with herself, will never marry, I shall bide my time, and endure what I must, and when this is all over, rule the Empire through my son. Night after night she underwent Constantius's vigorous but unappetising embraces, submitting as to a grim fate. I am a brood mare, she would tell herself, as he rolled her on her back and prised her apart, being covered in a paddock, by a stallion chosen at random. All that counts is the foal I drop in the months to come. Love arrives but once. My marriage to Constantius has been sanctified by the church, as a means of procreation. And what else matters?

Once again, Galla Placidia conceived quickly. Her first child by Constantius was a girl, christened Honoria, very much like herself in appearance and character, a little creature whom Galla Placidia found it impossible to hate. Though five such daughters in a row, she asked herself sardonically – would that be a punishment from God?

The second child, born less than a year later, and after a difficult confinement, was a son, Valentinian. Galla Placidia took time to recover. When another eighteen months had gone by, and she was due to breed once more, the gross, oppressive and ambitious Constantius died. Of a fever. In swampy, mosquito-ridden Ravenna, fevers were prevalent. An enteric fever – and the symptoms were no different from those caused by eating the white powder which the Princess Veleda had once obtained, as a precaution, from an alchemist. He made it by burning a grey arsenical stone, found in sulphur deposits, and sold it to women who might have private and urgent need of it, at a very high price.

Two years later, on 15 August 423 Honorius himself died, a natural death, of a dropsy. He was thirty-five, and had not distinguished himself in any way whatever, except as a bird-fancier, though perhaps the strongest and wisest of Emperors might not have managed much better, in such disastrous times. The future of the Roman Empire in the West – what was left of it – belonged from now on to Galla Placidia. After adventures and vicissitudes, exile to Constantinople, victory in the field over rivals and usurpers, her implacable will triumphed. Her son, as Valentinian III, became Emperor in Ravenna and perhaps the most futile of the Roman Emperors in the West.

Galla Placidia's son was pleasure-loving, dissolute, simply not interested in government, and for twenty-five years she herself ruled the fragments of the Empire in his name, courageously, shrewdly, piously, with a consummate grip on power but an emptiness in her heart. Men called her the Augusta.

Part XII

1

Spinning was solitary, meditative, suitable. Another job that often came Gilda's way, after she had been tacitly accepted as prophetess, was to keep watch, ram's horn on her lap, distaff in hand, from a crevice in a high, bald rock. Gilda would sit there, spinning a thread of wool, and trying to make sense of her own past, or sometimes fitting words together for an oration or a song, and all the time keeping an eye on that dark slit in the cliff face, through which, one day, Roman soldiers might come.

A black dot, on this bright morning, had moved out of the slanting shadow that was the mouth of the gorge. A solitary newcomer, a man on his own, helping himself along, over boulders, with an iron-tipped staff.

He was coming her way in a line of march distinctly Roman, unwavering, straight across country, as if he had known discipline, and scorned obstacles. A priest in a black robe, and heading for the houses, the cultivated fields. Are there others, wondered Gilda, following on behind? For just one priest, do I blow the ram's horn, and have all our militia running in from the fields, buckling on their weapons? A figure sent from Rome, where they threw newborn children to the dogs.

When Marcus came closer she recognised him, despite the years that had gone by, cropped hair all grey now, body gone heavier, gait no less confident. Gilda's first notion was this, and it flustered her: he has come to Dyrin to claim me! To a Christian, a marriage is a marriage, and he somehow heard I was here.

Once, on Cuneus, when she asked him about his past, he had told her how he organised spies for Stilicho. Do I warn them, wondered Gilda. Do I ever admit that their prophetess was once married to this man?

Gilda stood up from her hidden place on the lookout rock to greet him – 'Welcome, Marcus!' – in a disturbing voice of theatrical power. A figure outlined against the sky, in a dazzle of light, ram's horn in one hand, spindle in the other. An apparition.

His face in the bright light was vividly clear to her, surprised by her voice, but older and less tormented. Gilda felt a pang of affection, at this first close sight of him.

Some mountain demon? Marcus wondered. Imitating Gilda's voice – and come here to tempt me? A believing man could reasonably expect the wilderness – and across the frontier was all wilderness – to be full of evil spirits. Thus had St Anthony been tempted, and even Our Lord. Would a demon though, hold a spindle, and dress in homespun? They came in rich raiment!

Gilda had let her own heavy grey hair grow out long, though the Berber women coloured theirs with henna, to hide their age. She had it gathered into a knot at the nape, and held there by a wooden comb. She looked more serene than the Gilda he had known, a figure of authority, an equal. And simply because of that, thought Marcus, a worse temptation.

Sitting down again on the rock, Gilda, as if such work had become as inevitable to her as breathing, went on pulling wool from her fleece, and spinning a thread with a twist of her fingers. Thus, Marcus remembered, spun the pagan Fates – the *Parcae*. The thread she is spinning is my life.

'And do you come here,' Gilda asked, enjoying his discomfiture, 'as our enemy?' Gilda for the first time since being washed ashore on Cuneus, felt, if not older than Marcus, then wiser.

'Do you suppose, Gilda, that I was ever your enemy?'

'But who sent you?' She had picked, right away, on the question Marcus was least inclined to answer.

This boulder-strewn valley was her place, as volcanic, empty, sea-encircled Cuneus had been his. In both places, frugality, holy poverty. And yet he could not help remembering the bleakness of their life together, in that poverty-stricken room in

Carthage – a life neither had chosen. That is what corrodes my memories of her, thought Marcus, watching Gilda as she faced him calmly. Our life in Carthage was an error. But he still did not say who had sent him, or why he was here.

'Or have you come here simply to take up married life again?' asked Gilda with provocative gaiety. When he remained silent, she prodded harder, 'Who sent you? A Roman bishop? A Roman governor? A Roman general?'

Marcus was not a man who, face to face, could tell a conscious lie without blushing. 'I came here to see for myself.'

'I think you were sent by that strange man, Augustine of Hippo,' Gilda said. 'The Christian bishop who shows his love of Donatists by persecuting them. Since you wear the uniform of his corps.'

And in the old days too, thought Marcus, there were times when she could read my thoughts. As if by witchcraft.

As if to make it easy for her. Marcus let drop his long, iron-tipped staff, his only weapon. The staff rattled against rocks as it tumbled, and there stood the man who once had bewildered her, hands folded, eyes cast down, making of his helplessness a weapon. All he had been sent here to do was false, an impossible duty not of his seeking. The theatricality of his gesture had enchanted Gilda. His contrite pose would look well on a stage – or before the altar. Yes, Marcus had become a priest.

'So you have come here hoping to preach to them? Well, I do that too, and, let me tell you, you won't find it easy. Do you suppose the Donatists will love you? Or the Circumcelliones? And did not Augustine also write against the Jews? We have Jews.'

'I perhaps have something to say to them. I hardly expect they will agree.'

'Then argue with them Marcus, if you must.'

He was shaking his head at her. These matters of which she spoke so light-heartedly, schism, heresy, Judaism, were, to an Augustinian, deadly serious. They were aberrations which could put in peril the City of God, much as the barbarian invasions had endangered Rome.

'Sunday is our weekly meal in common. Before the meal, those of us who want to, meet together on the hillside. If I vouched for you, Marcus they might give you a hearing. You might find you liked our life. And what if you decided to stay? Not as a priest, perhaps – we have no need of one. But as my husband?' She looked at him with a mischief, in which, like a tempting drug, was mingled sensuality.

'But I am a priest. So what do I want with a wife?'

'And I, Marcus, am a *vates* – their prophetess. You might wonder what I wanted with a husband, when all these people here are my children. So let us be clear on one thing. If we let you go back to the Romans alive, and you yourself find you want to, then how much will you tell them.'

'Only what my conscience bids me.'

'How many we are? The way the soldiers might take us by surprise?'

Marcus made no answer.

'I have only to blow this horn,' she said, bouncing it in the palm of her hand. 'You would hardly come a stone's throw nearer Dyrin. They would bury you within the hour.'

Marcus mumbled, overcome, 'I shall tell them nothing.'

'I will take that for a promise. Stay here with me till the end of my duty, and we can go back to the village together.'

This then was Tzoza, the husband Prince Gaeseric had picked out for Veleda – a man with a small, round, ineffectual cherry nose, a moustache which drooped when he would rather it bristled, and a vast opinion of himself, not diminished by this unexpected offer of marriage to a Gothic princess.

At last the whole tipsy room was unanimous that, for his own sake, the bridegroom should drink no more. 'You want to fall down on the job?' some joker was repeating, over and over again. Out came that battered Roman trumpet, trophy of some bygone skirmish. A tipsy Vandal, blowing unmusical blasts, conducted bride and groom to their chamber.

Someone to the rearward had begun the old song that accuses the bride of not coming to her nuptial couch a virgin.

> She knows all about it,
> She's had it all before

But he stopped abruptly. Iynx had his right hand on the dagger hilt, and had begun to lift the weapon to choke off the obscenity.

Gaeseric, though, was standing right behind him, and the song had been broken off in the singer's mouth by Gaeseric's glance. The lame man, taking the boy by the wrist, pushed his dagger back where it belonged. Close by his ear Iynx heard Gaeseric's whisper.

'None of that. Keep your head.'

Iynx felt crushed, as if by a master to whom all must submit.

Veleda was walking ahead of the blaring trumpet, white-clad and head erect, as if to a place of execution. The bridegroom tottered along behind the blaring noise, confused by it, held up under either armpit by officious friends. They were manhandling him through the doorway, had stretched him out on the thong-bound, wool-stuffed mattress, were sliding him out of his leather trousers. There Tzoza lay, naked from the waist down, groaning and flaccid.

Vandal women had arrived, in a twittering fluster, one of them Gaeseric's plump little wife. Someone gave the bride her posset, milk and honey mingled with herbs, to strengthen her against the onset. The drink tasted of fresh fields, and swallowing it, in here, was odious, but Veleda got it down with pretended relish. She threw the cup towards all the unmarried women crowding with make-believe bashfulness into the far corner, for the luckiest to catch. To Iynx, at the doorway, taking all this in, Veleda sent an inconspicuous motion of her hand which he understood to mean, 'Have no fear'.

Then Gaeseric's voice, which all men obeyed, spoke like the crack of a whip. 'All you others, outside.'

Glancing over his shoulder as he went, Iynx saw Veleda, clad in her thin white gown, Galla Placidia's last present to her, lean forward, and bring the candle flame close to her mouth. The bridal chamber was plunged into darkness. Tzoza gasped, or snored, and his snore, as the door closed, echoed the unmusical blasts of the verdigris-covered Roman trumpet, as it wended its drunken way up the street.

The same male hand that had held his wrist was reaching spread fingers through Iynx's hair, to hold him, brutally fast, across the dome of his head.

'Tomorrow at daybreak, Iynx, you and I go hunting – remember? Are you sober enough?'

'I am sober.'

'Then remember this. Bring my own horse up here, from the stable, the grey. You will ride your pony. They will have other mounts ready saddled for the bridegroom and the huntsman –'

'At daybreak. Yes.'

'Here, outside their door, promptly at daybreak'

'Yes, my lord.'

Gaeseric scuffed the top of Iynx's head much as he might have patted his favourite elkhound. Only then did it come home to Iynx that Gaeseric, too, was concerned for Veleda, in the dark behind the closed door, with that husband.

Iynx, at first light, stumbled his way, sleepy-eyed, to the ruined house, thatched with a roof of canes, where Gaeseric's own horses were stabled. A yawning groom was already tightening girths. Iynx led the grey charger and his own pony back up the street, their breath making copious vapour in the cold air. Behind came a servant in a tight cap and leathers, the huntsman. He was tugging at the bridles of two other horses, one his own, one for Tzoza, and he carried a boar-spear in his free hand.

Veleda, with a sheepskin over her thin, white gown against the chill of morning, was already on the doorstep at Gaeseric's side. In the clarity of dawn, when noises sounded larger, Iynx heard her whisper. 'So you are taking the boy?'

Out through the open door, unwillingly, into the chill air, came the bridegroom. Veleda had helped him dress – the only time she had touched him since they were left alone, man and wife, and she prayed it would be the last. The sight of the neat, silent huntsman with his boar-spear, the saddled horse held ready for him, Gaeseric with his javelin and his brisk morning smile, the boy beside the pony alert, was enough to make Tzoza lose his appetite. He shuddered, and for one weak moment held his face in his hands.

'Bed worn you out? The mountain air will give you strength,' said Gaeseric, with vindictive breeziness.

The emphatic sun of southern Spain rose higher, to dazzle their eyes and mitigate the chill. Veleda, from the open doorway, watched them trail into line – Tzoza slightly ahead, then Gaeseric and his taciturn hunt servant, riding side by side like close acquaintances, and trailing, and from time to time kicking heels into his pony's flanks so as to catch up, the boy.

So long as no harm, she thought anxiously, comes out of all this to Iynx! As for Gaeseric, it was hard to think of any harm coming to Gaeseric. He was the man who twisted the destinies of others into an invisible rope, and yoked them with it, pulling them along after him, here with a twitch, there a tug.

When, towards dusk, only Gaeseric and Iynx arrived back, idlers in the street of the ruined mountain town saw that the other horses, led behind them, bore limp burdens, and took them for dead game, perhaps venison. Soon though, in the fading light, two dead men could be distinguished, bloody with violence, hung over the saddles of the horses they should have ridden, hands trailing.

Gaeseric wore a profoundly sad look, and rode in slowly. He was always the master of his face. In a case of violent death, the greybeards would by custom decide – he sent a messenger for them at once.

When they were assembled, Gaeseric said to Iynx in a loud but serious voice, 'Tell them what happened. Truthfully, do you hear me? Tell them all'.

Gaeseric, standing near the hearthstone, stared at the sullen glow of a log, half-buried in its own ash, and as Iynx began to speak he squatted down nearby. He pulled the hood of his cloak down over his own face, as if so distressed that he could not bear to look at things.

'We were up in the mountains, along a track, with the wind blowing straight in our faces,' said Iynx, making a picture in his head, so as to describe exactly what he remembered. 'The huntsman pointed out to us the fresh tracks of a boar. The tracks were going away from us, and the others followed hotly, but my pony couldn't keep up. I was not too far behind though. Everything that happened on the bridle-path ahead of me, I saw, as clearly as I see you.'

That bright clear voice, thought Gaeseric, cut off from them by the hood pulled down on his face, is carrying conviction. What better witness for me than uncorrupted innocence?

Veleda stood, inconspicuously, her silvered yellow hair drawn severely back, the widow, convincingly sad. As she suppressed all glimmer of a smile, she asked herself, after all this, will you ever smile again?

'The boar may have heard the hoofbeats,' Iynx was saying, 'or else he picked up our scent. He had turned in his tracks and hid in some bushes, and was waiting for us, an old boar with long tusks. He put down his head and went straight for the first of us, Prince Gaeseric. The Prince had by this time taken the boar-spear, and the huntsman had the Prince's javelin –'

The old men looked at the javelin with its bloodstained blade, leant against the heartstone, a piece of evidence. They looked at once another knowingly.

'And then what happened?' asked the oldest of them, bright-eyed, as if this were a fireside tale about a day's hunting, and not the explanation of how men had died.

'The prince let the boar run at the spear and, with his first stroke, got the blade well between the shoulder-blades – a death stroke.' With unconcealed delight, the old man slapped his knee.

'Then the huntsman threw the javelin. He missed the boar altogether – he did not seem to be trying to hit the boar.' Iynx was pointing to the bloodstained javelin – a tremor had come into his voice. He had noticed the avid way Veleda was watching him, taking in his every word. 'Instead it hit the Princess's husband.'

'Tzoza.'

'Was his name Tzoza?' said Iynx stupidly. He was wishing he could forget.

'And what happened next?' asked another old man gently. But they could guess.

'Prince Gaeseric was in a rage.' The old men nodded, grunted. A princely anger. What else would one expect? 'He put his foot on the dead boar, and pulled out the spear, and then –'

Iynx had been astonished by the force Gaeseric had shown, hardly human, as he wrenched out the weapon, and stood there, his balance regained, poised to stab.

'Go on – and say exactly.' They could see the emotion in the boy's face. The point of all this was coming.

'When the Prince lifted the boar spear against him, the

huntsman reached for his skinning knife, as if he guessed what might happen. He waited, as if not sure whether to strike out with his knife, or plead for mercy. Then he went down on his knees –'

Gaeseric, at these last words, lifted the hood of the cloak from his eyes, and stood tall, as if now that the truth was out, he wished to face his accusers. The prince's gesture, Veleda noticed, had served to distract the old men, just as they arrived at the kernel of what they were to judge.

As for Iynx, he had never seen death so close, and in recollection it came even closer. The man with the little bulbous nose and sad moustache, ridiculous Tzoza, was at one instant alive and keeping out of harm's way. The huntsman's javelin whistled straight at him, and he was dead. Would never lay hands again on Veleda, never speak. The death of the huntsman, afterwards, was less of a shock, because Iynx could see it coming.

Gaeseric, leaning against the chimney piece, now had something to say.

'I admit the blood guilt. I will pay the blood-price. My heart was full when I struck, and still is, most of all for the sorrow of the Princess Veleda here, so quickly a widow. I double the blood-price.'

Among the Vandals, if in a case like this a blood-price could be offered and accepted, that would avert the endless feud that otherwise would follow.

A self-important mutter came from the old men as they put their heads together. From the very moment thought Iynx when I saw him thrust the broad-bladed spear in the huntsman's breast, Gaeseric must have known what I would say – how I would speak up for him. He has been play-acting. He has known the outcome all along. Did he do all this for Veleda?

Iynx, as he stood there, silent, insigificant, his importance over, felt besmirched. The simple and self-evident account he had given them was not the underlying truth, and now he knew it. Could he assert himself, ask to put it differently? That would make him a liar. There was, anyway, one good side to this – the Princess no longer had a husband.

He watched Veleda risk a quick sidelong glance at Gaeseric – her eyes were on fire for him. But Gaeseric's stony face checked her, and Veleda lowered her eyes again, utterly the widow. So she had known, too!

My half-brother's spy, Gaeseric was thinking with private satisfaction, is dead. I have the obedience of this splendid creature and her ready-witted page. His dreams were possible realities. Only King Guntheric stood in his way, and perhaps not for ever.

'In a straightforward case like this, prince,' asked the old men's spokesman querulously, 'why should you pay a double blood-price?'

'Gaeseric will pay a double blood-price because he has said he will,' the lame man answered grandiloquently, even a little cantankerously, as if his princely generosity were being doubted. And is already speaking of himself, noted Veleda, repressing a smile, as if he were a personage in history. If I can help him to it, so he will be.

They moved out into the street, where the dying pleasure of the day's sun was being chased off by cold air rolling down from the snow-capped sierras. Gaeseric, as if they were both schoolboys, and involved together in a plot, caught Iynx by an ear lobe, twisting it high-spiritedly to inflict a small, affectionate pain. He bent close, to whisper, 'You must learn to throw a javelin!' Iynx shivered – sudden death! – yet he was glad.

Iynx pushed a fingernail into his own skin. How much protection was there in mere human skin, when any point or sharp edge, a pin, a blade of grass, could pierce it? Here inside my skin, he thought, like wine in a wineskin, is held all my body's blood. Penetrate the skin and out spills the blood, and blood is life. Or air: the throat is choked by a rope, the heart stops pumping blood. Life is over. Iynx trembled, as he put the palms of his hands upon his own soft and vulnerable eyeballs. The point of a javelin through an eye? Goodbye sight, sense, and down to hell. Only the man in this world who moved quicker, and threw straighter, had a right to live.

From that day on, Iynx trained with weapons as if nothing else mattered. Gaeseric could not have watched over his prowess, or given him more encouragement, had Iynx been his own son. By this time Gaeseric's plump young bride had indeed borne him a son, a fat pudding, no great wonder. A legitimate son, an heir, a successor, but his plans would not wait that long.

Iynx is Stilicho's son, he would tell himself, bastardy and wry neck notwithstanding – and what better could you hope for? I shall owe him nothing, of right, and he will owe me all.

So while Veleda and Gaeseric plotted other, and more urgent matters, the capture of Seville – for how could the Vandals triumph without access to the sea? – not to mention a cleverly criminal approach to the kingship, Iynx's outdoor life day after day, until limbs ached and eyes blurred, was the javelin, the bow, the sling, the huntsman's lance, the light cavalryman's sabre, the heavy Gothic sword. The sheer weight and length, the huge double-handed grip of a Gothic sword, were at first too much for him. But Gaeseric kept him at it, knowing that as Iynx day by day put on muscle, so the weapon would imperceptibly grow lighter. He would find himself the sword's master, and so with life itself.

Iynx would come in, covered with sweat and dust, and smiling with joy, with Veleda, scrupulously, never telling him that he was neglecting his books, or that she had lacked attendance. She would send a maidservant after him, with towel and sponges, to wash him down. He liked her prettier maids; let him learn, thought Veleda, to be a man with them. And after, when Iynx was calm and serene, bring him back, to sit an hour beside her, for his penmanship and his Latin.

Someone who had plundered a villa brought her a gift that no one else would want – all but one roll of the *Aeneid*. Thus Vergil in consummate verse that lulled and charmed the ear, also spoke continually to Iynx of war. The men in the poem, Aeneas, Turnus, became models. One did not have to take one's heroes simply from the men one met. Aeneas was a little like Gaeseric, but less predictable, more noble. When he left Dido in Carthage and sailed for Italy – his destiny – he broke her heart.

Part XIII

1

A hot wind from the desert came through the pass and across the valley of boulders as if a reminiscence of Gehenna. Gilda looked down the hillside, at the staring faces of all those listeners, men and some women, and through her mind passed this unusual thought. All those who come here say they believe in God. But do they all believe in the same God?

As the words of a familiar prayer came, loudly, unreflectingly out of her mouth, she told herself, only their belief in God – some God or other – keeps this place together. If they ceased to believe – to look up, to listen – Dyrin would come to pieces. And this morning, will Marcus sow doubt?

I talk about God, but what do I really know? Is God One? Or Three-in-One as the Donatists tell you? Does each single one of them, here on the hillside see only one facet of God – as though God were a cut diamond?

'God is a diamond!' she heard her own loudly passionate voice exclaim. From the crowd came a moan of uncomprehending assent. And is that what I do for them? Gilda wondered. Does my voice concentrate, for each one of them, the fragmentary light into a splendid cone of fire?

'Intenser light!' she heard her own voice declare.

And if Marcus makes these different believers fly asunder? Does their concentrated light diminish?

There must be a God – there is! – because we have souls, and are not mere meat. Not someone else's two-legged animals, to buy and sell, rape, plunder, kill!

After the first crescendo of ejaculations as they stood there, waiting for Gilda to find words for them – to prophesy – some line of thought would always begin of its own accord to run through her head: the spirit possessing her. As Gilda gazed down at their expectant faces, the words of a more prolonged extempore prayer began to come, with piercing clarity, out of her mouth.

'A God of love. Yes – love! Of which such love as we have known in our earthly lives is only the faint image!'

And yet her mind, as she spoke, remained separate, going alongside the prayer, keeping it company as the words were flung from her mouth, an actress, going through a familiar part, and not yet lifted into self-forgetfulness.

On Cuneus he had said, a God of love, but how much did Marcus know about love, then or now? Gilda caught his eye, sitting a little way off, grey-polled, black-clad, lips compressed, eyes hooded. Yet she knew he was listening to every word.

'Sent his only son to save us. His son? And if he had sent his daughter?' What she spontaneously uttered had surprised Gilda herself. From the women present came a thrilled twitter. Why had she said that? A woman god was the goddess in Carthage. She saw Marcus flinch. And heard her own voice declare, 'A God – a Goddess – who passes understanding.'

Outreaches my own understanding, thought Gilda, feeling the prayer uplift her, and Marcus's too. Is everywhere, is omnipotent. The God these men squabble over. The God they share, and now to convince them that God is One, since here at Dyrin we ourselves are one only if God is One, in us and for us. You though, yourself – do you always feel at one with this strange place?

When the spirit leaves me, no. (It flows through me now!) In the old days, it sometimes left Marcus. And how, at the time, could I understand?

This hillside is our theatre, where once a week we can act out – but myself most of all – what we would like to think we are. Most of them will lie, this afternoon, man beside woman, better fed than usual, and reaching out contentedly the one for the other. Having been reminded out here this morning –

'And we are all His children. He uplifts us in the palm of His hand.'

– of their unity in God

Corporeally uniting with one another, in another kind of prayer.

'And we are all members, one of another – '

There came up another moan of consent.

Here, at the Sunday meeting on the hillside, the crops were never mentioned, nor the stock, nor the risk of drought. (The wind pushed a hot reminder against Gilda's cheek). Nor whether the Berbers would go on being friendly.

We are here to speak of God.

'We are here to speak of God!'

Here at Dyrin the centre of our lives –

' – of His power and His dominion – '

No one here has power over another. We bow our heads only to an All-Powerful Presence which defies our understanding. And as I sit down, after bringing them together in this first prayer, as I summon him by a gesture to take my place, what will Marcus say? They agreed last night – though not willingly – to let him speak.

On other days, from the first syllable, a spirit would fill Gilda's mouth with words, so that she spoke to them as one hallucinated. Today, with her mind full of thoughts that did not quite belong, she had done no more than act out her part of prophetess. New lines: God as diamond. Others would not have noticed her inward shortcoming, but had Marcus?

He stood up, deliberately, and moved forward, rather slowly, with Tucco jealously glaring after him. Marcus has dignity, thought Gilda. And how did Tucco picture the God of whom, at times, he could speak with clumsy fervour? A God of chances? A God who inexplicably let one man die, and another live?

Take the Circumcelliones down there, intently watching Marcus as he walks forward. Some of the Circumcelliones that morning, as if to give themselves, and him, a reminder of their past, had brought along their tall, iron-ringed poles. Circumcelliones always hung together in a group, radical, outrageous, expecting the worst. The Circumcelliones could only ever have a heroic, tragic glimpse of God – *Laus Deo!* – and leap over a cliff.

And the soldiers down there – those army deserters? Mithras, perhaps – the cult that in the army lingered on secretly: blood brotherhood. Soldiers believe in God – Gilda had seldom met one who did not. Though had Stilicho? Would anyone dare ask?

She could read the look on Marcus's face as his cropped, grey poll moved closer: he was conscience-stricken. Christ within him, Marcus had argued on Cuneus, in the sacrament, in the Holy Ghost, makes even a creature who was legally a piece of property entirely human. Gilda brought to mind her furious answer, which had smitten Marcus with that very look. 'Nothing whatever gives a slave dignity. I know. I have been one.'

As he approached the high place from which he was supposed to speak, Marcus's inner world had gone blank. As Gilda spoke, he had prayed for grace, and been denied.

Last night at the supper table, jammed on a bench between Tucco, spearing crusts in show-off fashion with his iron hook, and a grim old Donatist who detested Augustine's black beetles but was forcing himself to be hospitable, Marcus could feel all of them looking at him askance. Gilda's presence, he thought, saved me. the woman with whom I once sinned was all that stood between me and martyrdom. Why in God's name was I ever sent here? What am I meant to do and say?

On his way from the settlement to the hillside, pausing to glance at a tumbledown wall, Marcus had felt he could stay right there and although it was Sunday, mix himself a heap of mortar. The better the day the better the deed. String and stone for plumbline; make that broken wall square and good. Had walked on, though, with the spirit leaking out of him. To this crowded hillside – to these unyielding faces.

Preach only if they will listen to you with goodwill, had been Augustine's last advice, and it was good. A strange thought then assailed Marcus, as he turned to face them: what good soldiers they would make! I could stay here, he thought (or was that the devil tempting him?) Build their walls – and command them.

Marcus took his stance and looked downhill at his congregation. That sardonic old Donatist from last night was leaning on a long pole, eyeing him like a target. The man lifted his pole. He had a question to put.

' "Thou shalt give unto Caesar the things that are Caesar's" quoted the old Donatist with a glint in his eye, "and unto God the things that are God's." Expound.'

And he sat down, with the obstinate look on his face that makes it plain that the questioner known the answer already.

This peremptory question took Marcus off guard. He was no theologian, and this was the hardest of texts. Had God kept step with him all the way to Dyrin, only now to turn his back?

'When they gave Our Lord a piece of money,' Marcus said, in his slow and awkward but well-meant Punic, (all here spoke Punic, even if they knew Latin well) 'that was a provocation. They hoped to trap him. They were asking Jesus a question they expected would be too hard for the son of God! The coin they handed over bore the head of Caesar, as does any Roman coin, and with such coins in the image of Caesar, imperial taxes are paid. Thus to my mind Our Lord's reply, "Give unto Caesar the thing that are Caesar's" must have meant simply this. Be law-abiding. Live peacefully. Pay the lawful taxes. Do not meddle with money and power – the things that are Caesar's. But turn your mind instead to the things of the spirit.'

An old man among them with a small, round, white head and a neat white beard, who as a rule listened in respectful silence, was already hopping from one foot to the other in a rage, as he tore the shirt off his back. He was displaying the bare skin of his back to Marcus and to everyone, as if, written across it, they would find the truth they sought. Marcus saw for himself what had been inscribed there, and was shocked.

Did I ever before Christ entered me – Marcus tried to remember – give orders for a man to be flogged? He might have done – it was a commonplace punishment. Scars made by whip heal; the calligraphy on the skin remains. His eyes were filling with tears of shame.

'Lawful taxes!' the old man was exclaiming. 'Look, here it is, my receipt! No picture of Caesar in my purse, times were hard. What I could not pay in Caesar's image, they took out of me in blood. Here on my back, image and superscription both! Take a good look at the image of Caesar.'

To Gilda, sunk in reverie, it began to appear, through her half-closed eyes, as if everyone in sight had mutilations to show. A runaway soldier, not perfectly right in his head, was displaying an obscenely livid scar across his belly, and muttering something uncharitable about Heraclian. Tucco the gladiator had undone his iron wrist-ring to brandish the stump, and was shouting

'*Morituri te salutant* – die for Caesar? Or all die for Christ?' A big old woman who had been a whore in Carthage in her time unbared her breast, and was lifting a heavy, dangling dug in each hand as offerings, as if forgetting, in her excitement, that her neighbours now were Christian, and not votaries at the shrine of the Great Goddess.

The Circumcelliones, no doubt, bore wounds on their bodies too, but they were not bothering to expose them. With their long poles clashing metallically, iron ring against iron ring, they had begun to chant in chorus, '*Laus Deo!* Money is the root of all evil! *Laus Deo!*' A gaunt man, who had owned a shop, before the exactions of the state drove him bankrupt, began to recite, in a stentorian voice against which no other voice stood a chance, a piece he had by heart from the Epistle of St Jude. They had heard it before on other Sundays, and had never so far grasped the point, but amid this confusion it put words to their fury.

' "Clouds they are without water, carried about of winds; trees whose fruit withereth, without fruit, twice dead, plucked up by the roots; raging waves of the sea, foaming out of their own shame; wandering stars, to whom is reserved the blackness of darkness for ever!" '

The mere puzzling poetry of this recitation, booming over their heads, served to calm them down. At the theatrical moment Gilda rose in front of them. She had lifted up her arms, magnificently, so that the two sleeves of her homespun garment hung draped as if half-folded wings. Her voice rang out clear, from one mountain to the next.

'What then is not God's?'

Marcus felt a shuddering thrill run through him, yet also he was incredulous. Could these be the words of the woman who once had scrubbed his floor? Or some other voice, perhaps diabolical, speaking through her?

'Image and superscription?' Gilda was holding up between thumb and finger an imaginary coin. She mimed, and the invisible coin became the focus of their rapt glances. She felt power flow through her.

'If not God's – then the devil's! The devil of this world! Money and Emperor alike, are they not both creatures of the devil? Did God send us an Emperor, or did he send His Son?'

'His Daughter!' echoed an almost hysterical voice.

'Is the mark of a whip across a man's back a gift from God? Or the mark of the cloven hoof of the imperial devil? What of the holes made by nails through the hands of a crucified man? Any crucified man – ' She made a large gesture, as if to remind them that this valley was full of the ghosts of the crucified. 'The nails and the scourge and the spear in the side, and the soldiers who diced for the robe – are they not all Caesar's? The blood in which Pontius Pilate dabbled his fingers? Caesar's! Injustice parading as justice? Caesar's! The weariness of the man, sick at heart, who has laboured all day in the vineyard? Or the cornfield? Or the olive grove? And been cheated of his wage? Does that sickness of the heart come from God?'

Gilda's brazen phrases beat upon their minds. There was an answering vibration, and Gilda paused. Up from the Circumcelliones came the iron rattle of their poles, and one single great *Laus Deo!* exploded. All the crowd were on tiptoe. She had them.

'God is our father. God is good. Is the pain of Caesar's scourge sent from God? The pain of a woman in labour – is that from God?' (Is it? Is it? she asked herself, her mind stumbling, so that she next spoke out with only theatrical emphasis, the gift gone. But her emphasis made them tremble). 'Is man's blind and cruel lust sent from God?'

Gilda by the crescendo of her questions was establishing an absolute silence. They were all as one, her voice held them. This enraptured mood, though, had failed to impose upon Marcus. Whatever the others around him might see in her, he had known Gilda too well to regard her as simply a prophetess. He had ceased to be touched by her, once the first surprise was over.

To calm himself, Marcus had been noting, one by one, the intellectual contradictions in what Gilda was saying, his mind as precise as if collecting intelligence. He had separated himself from these people – they were strangers.

At the beginning, he told himself, a flirt with Manichaeanism, the world divided, black and white, between God and the devil. (But where did she learn about Mani? And from whom?) And fails to grasp the Incarnation, though we talked of it on Cuneus often enough. Other crucifixions were legal punishment; the one on Calvary was redemption from sin.

'*The rich get richer – and the poor get babies!*'

The poignant power of Gilda's voice, to his own annoyance had, for that once moment, made him shake. Inside his own mind, furiously, Marcus began to argue with her, as he might have done as a youngster, with his own father, had he only dared. *You mean the poor get living creatures with immortal souls, while the rich get only things? Or don't you mean that?* An image came into Marcus's mind that usually he forbade himself: a barred cellar in a Roman mansion, full of gold and venomous snakes.

He had lost the thread of what Gilda was saying. In the recesses of his own argumentative mind he was hiding from her voice. Pain in childhood, lustful pleasures in manhood, he had known them both. If lust and pain were not from God, did that mean they were from Caesar? God was life – was Caesar death? Augustine might very well know, but Augustine was a long way off. The litany of Gilda's eloquently-loud assertions might have flaws – but he too was trapped at last inside her flow of speech and emotion.

She has them, thought Marcus, as she had me; we are hers. Does God speak through her, or are we simply like those men she fascinated in her Roman heyday? He looked down the hillside at the humiliated and scarred and mutilated. Tucco had screwed his hook back on, the old whore hidden her pendulous bubs, like treasure, inside her blouse. And what, Marcus asked himself, am I doing here?

The simple workman was a mask he had once worn – the man who might have liked to linger and repair a ruined wall – and that was the secret part of Marcus attracted by the unifying passion she was arousing. She was reminding him of the man he was when she had tempted him with her consoling body. All the time, on Cuneus, in Carthage, this astounding woman, this prophetess, was there under the surface and I never knew her. I never allowed myself to know her.

But from his years as a priest Marcus had acquired the habit of pausing to consider, and one sobering thought still held him back. Her face, weary though exalted, had looked like that after each of their infrequent acts of love. And what was *eros* but untrammelled passion – loss of control? He had a terrifying vision of such men as these, broken loose from the iron collar that held the wild animal in them, raging like lions across the land.

'Come unto me, all ye who are heavy laden – '

Gilda's voice rose high. Above their heads the gospel promise hung. Gilda broke the mood she herself had created, with a tone of voice soberly persuasive.

'If property is good for the *honestiores* and the Emperor,' she told them, as if to plant a sensible and simple idea in their minds, 'then property is good for everyone. And should not each of us have his share? A piece of God's world? Let the world remain God's – let each have his portion. Share and share alike, as we do here, in Dyrin. I will show you a blasphemy – a fertile field untilled.' A growl emerged, as if bent backs and calloused hands were of themselves giving utterance. 'And another blasphemy – a hungry child. An untilled field – a hungry child!'

Her voice was again rising in pitch. 'Caesar, do you say? Caesar is the yell of a bandit in the depths of the forest. Caesar is a man in the dark, who drags an unwilling woman by her heels and hair. In the forum of every city in the empire you can see them – selling justice for gold. The justice that belongs to God! Law and order? A sepulchre is orderly. Law and order are a tomb. *But Our Lord –* ' and the very last of what she had to say hung triumphant in the air – *'has risen from the tomb!'*

Gilda lifted both hands outward, as if making them an invisible but generous gift: a blessing. Their turn now – and the Circumcelliones took their cue. They had begun roaring out couplets; Gilda, after the first line was sung, kept time for them with a stamp of the heel, a toss of her head.

'*St Cyprian has said and signed*'

More joined in at the rhyming answer, and the noise grew.

'*God's gifts are for all mankind!*'

Laus Deo! came out in such a roar that the two Latin words – *Praise God!* – were wrested, unaware, even from Marcus's lips. Gilda noticed how against his will he had yielded and gave him a comradely smile. Though am I, by a forced silence, to abstain from praising God? Marcus wondered.

'*St Ambrose these good words let fall,*
Mother earth belongs to all!'

But it was I who taught her that – who told her about Ambrose – thought Marcus, at the next *Laus Deo* holding his mouth tight shut. We were on Cuneus, arguing about taking more mussels from the reef. Who do they belong to? she asked me. She would have taken them all. And see how she twists it around. Did Gilda ever properly understand anything?

Withdrawn again, briefly, into a personal solitude, simply by not repeating *Laus Deo* with the others, Marcus could already see, in his mind's eye, the wild lions let loose, the Donatists shaking free from the Roman orthodoxy imposed upon them. Everywhere the old African schisms. Gilda's songs in everyone's mouth, putting words to her dead namesake Gildo's sedition. Such a woman as Gilda can rouse to a mindless frenzy. As when she was younger she did, with her body, to everyone she met. As once – more than once – she seduced me. Men and women, these here at Dyrin, who if ever let loose would break civilisation to bits.

In the Christian gospel, as they interpreted it, was a revolutionary venom that until today he had never tasted on his tongue. Marcus found himself stiffening, shoulder-square like a soldier. You must try to speak to them again, he told himself sternly. Even if they stone you to death for it.

Gilda yielded her place to him with a strange gesture of loving concern, as though she might be planting in his exended arms a weight too heavy for him.

'Only listen – listen! Whenever there is no law,' Marcus began, speaking simply, as if to bring them down from their elevated mood, 'then nothing you have is safe. Neither yourselves, nor what you possess. Nothing whatever. The great estates are divided up? By force? Then do you suppose that, without law, the piece of land you are dreaming of will remain your own for long? You may be strong enough to take it, but will you be strong enough to keep it? The soldiers will rule over the rest of you. Like so many bandits and barbarians.'

'And if we are all of us soldiers?' asked a sardonic, argumentative voice. The stones, thought Marcus, have not yet begun to fly. I have set at least one of them thinking.

'Because with no law, and no money, who will find it worth his while to take his goods to market? Your world gone to pieces – every man armed of dire necessity, against every other man.

That is what it will signify for every man to be a soldier. The world in pieces. Every man's hand against you. Because unless we are all of one mind in religion – bound together in orthodoxy – who will take another's word? Which of us will know for sure the right way to heaven? We shall fall to pieces, like a handful of sand.'

'There is no worse Emperor,' announced the old man with the white hair and short beard, and the scars on his back, 'than a Christian Emperor.' Into Marcus's mind came the vacuous face of the Emperor Honorius – and it struck him dumb. With a despairing shrug he yielded up his place again to Gilda. They were not listening, and they never would. They did not care, and why should they?

'Their power – and God's power!'

Gilda's words came as if forced from her throat by an energy greater than her own.

'The power of manacles! The power of prison!'

Stridor.

Inimicus.

Heraclian.

She raised both hands, as if to push such evil visions away.

'Over and against all that – and friends, believe me. The power of God. The power of love.'

Someone indistinct of face, Jewish and sceptical, Jacob, had lifted the bar of a door that held her prisoner, was leading her out into the freedom of the stark night.

'You would rather have law and order? The slave obeying the man who owns him?'

That brought a comradely shout from the group of runaway slaves, men prone to idleness and doubt, the most discontented here at Dyrin. But Gilda, once a slave herself, had yet again remembered them.

Marcus decided that, even so, he liked these people, but he could not rid himself of the bitter thought that someone else might come along and promise them heaven on earth because he proposed to use them. And they would succumb and accept. He will ride on their backs. And after they have done the fighting for him, grant them the shadow and keep for himself the substance. All this he saw with visionary distinctness, and was sad at his own helplessness.

Nor were hers the only promises. *My Kingdom is not of this world*. If he shouted that aloud, would anyone here listen?

Gilda was beginning yet another of her old songs. In the days when she was a *mima*, some shabby Forum poet had adapted this song for her from an older hymn to Venus. In pagan times this, or something like it, had been sung in the temple to the Goddess. Down the cheeks of the old Carthaginian whore copious tears were running, as Gilda's clear voice cleansed the words of all pantomime suggestiveness, and left them a pure promise.

> *Cras amet qui nunquam amavit*
>   *quique amavit cras amet*
> Tomorrow those who never loved will love
> Tomorrow those who loved will love once more.

The hymn as it soared up released all of them, even Marcus, from the thrall of argument. Afterwards, all together as they went amiably uphill, none were giving him the cold shoulder. There, in the open air, at long tables was set out their best meal of the week. Tucco the gladiator, on his way back to the village, had even clapped Marcus on the back with his one good hand. The black beetle had lost this Sunday's combat? No hard feelings. They had their own invincible champion in Gilda.

And even if I stayed here for the rest of my life, thought Marcus – even with God's grace – how much headway could I make against Gilda? She is not the *vates* they told me I should find, no commonplace prophetess. By bringing them together she puts an end to their loneliness. She holds them together when nothing else would. But one day, all this will fly apart.

Dyrin, his military acumen told him, exists on sufferance. They are not yet rich enough for the mountain Berbers to become insupportably jealous – though they are getting richer, and that day will come. They believe themselves free here, and in a sense they are. But this place is an accident.

Civilisation, Marcus told himself, is an open space of law and peace, fenced in by living flesh. Can Dyrin ring itself around by a wall of men willing to die. For how long – and how well – would this militia of theirs fight? If the Romans sent a couple of hundred infantry under a good centurion through the pass, that would be the end of Dyrin.

Not that I shall ever guide them. (Break my promise?) And unless I report Dyrin as a danger, there will be no punitive column. And since Carthage, as Augustine pointed out, is so lethargic that they can hardly see beyond their noses, perhaps not even then.

Augustine will know I am telling him only some of the truth, holding back. He will discern my motives, too, he sees deeper than any. This conglomeration of men and women, walking up this boulder-strewn hillside to their hot dinner – would he, or anyone, seriously see them as a mortal menace?

What real power have they, these people, up against Rome and its army, not to mention Augustine's intellectually impregnable City of God? They have no sanctions, no compulsion, no army, no written law. No science of the knowledge of God. What holds them here, as one, has not the strength of a spider's web.

The shepherd had killed an old ewe, past breeding, and the cut-up pieces, fat and lean, had been stewed all morning with onions and cracked wheat in one enormous pot. This cooking pot – it took four cooks to stagger with it to table – was the Jewish potter's masterpiece. He smiled broadly when he saw it arrive, and stood up with arms outspread, as if to welcome the pot and what it contained. This everyone expected him to do, whenever there was a feast. The field-workers chaffed him indulgently. It was a remarkable pot.

With virtue gone out of her, Gilda was feeling tender towards Marcus, and everyone else. The guest's plate was the first to be filled. She placed across it a wooden spoon, and as she passed Marcus his helping, teased him gently in the hearing of all.

'Today there is meat – the rest of the week we eat like monks.'

As he put the first titbit of mutton into his mouth, Marcus answered, 'In Augustine's house we never eat meat,' and Gilda riposted with a wicked smile, 'Does Augustine think that meat excites your passions? Be careful in your answer. I am watching you closely.' The mutton-fat had burnt his mouth, yet he managed to answer with a laugh, and his own laughter, mingling with Gilda's, made everyone else laugh. Do they know, Marcus wondered, that we were once man and wife? (And speaking strictly, canonically, still are?)

As the others crammed their mouths with Sunday food and slyly watched the conversation of their prophetess, some began to wonder if Gilda might not be casting a spell over Marcus. None of them agreed with what this Catholic had been trying to tell them, out there on the mountainside. But then, who expected to? He was one sort of man, they another. Now, with their mouths full and greasy, they were even sorry for him. They would stay here in Dyrin, enjoying the life their own hands had created. This man in the shabby black robe would go back to the cruel constraints of the Latin-speaking city.

After the stew came barley cakes – finer flour than had come their way on Cuneus, cooked all through and yet not burnt at the edges. How was it done? To Marcus, as he mopped up the last of his gravy, the taste of barley flour came as an exciting reminiscence. His brain was less clear than usual: drunk on meat.

Gilda leaned his way, to whisper unexpectedly, 'So the might of imperial Rome will tolerate our presence here?'

She had spoken, as it happened, in the midst of an accidental hush. Others had heard, who were not meant to hear. They were looking his way, to discover what answer he would give. But what answer was there? Marcus equivocated.

'Roman might? These days you might as well say, Roman weakness,' said Marcus with a gruff laugh. That laugh convinced them more than his actual words, but several looked unfriendly, still doubting.

And will Augustine himself, wondered Marcus anxiously, be content with the little I shall tell him? He is not an easy man to lead astray.

Gilda, who was sure that Marcus believed the answer he had given, felt stir within herself, as he spoke, a sentiment as of a sexual triumph. With blunt humour, she gave him a clincher for everyone to share.

'So you will be our friend? I know you, and I believe you. And just as well. Or our gladiator here would have had to kill you.' Tucco half stood from his seat, but grasping that the time had not yet come, sat down again, in confusion. 'Then, Marcus, you would be a martyr – would you not? Go straight to heaven?'

Gilda covered her mouth and belched, then looked at him and grinned, like a naughty girl. Yes, thought Marcus, as she says, we know each other, we are friends. The tune she had begun to hum close to his ear was *Cras amet qui nunquam amavit*. 'This afternoon,' she whispered, in a voice to make him shiver, 'most of them go to bed.'

Marcus noticed that, though Tucco could not have heard the whisper, his jealous eyes were watching.

'That archway over there,' he answered, pointing, 'will fall down soon, because someone tried to fit in the wrong keystone. You see how it strains? The next thing, it will crack. This afternoon, would you like to carry mortar?'

Helplessly, Gilda yawned. 'Work – on the Sabbath? We have all week long for that.' She was remembering how he would come back from work, white with splashes of lime mortar, and too tired even to talk.

'Such work is prayer – you remember how we used to say that, about carrying wood for the beacon?' Marcus looked down surreptitiously at his own pair of hands, less calloused than they used to be. 'Or is there anything of the same kind you would rather have me fix, while I am here?'

The others as they spoke had been pairing off and going homeward. Even Tucco had gone, fetched imperiously by his cross-eyed Berber.

'Marcus,' said Gilda in a whisper. 'Did you always find me so repugnant?'

He looked earnestly into her face, but there was no prudent answer, not for a priest.

'When you talk things over with Augustine, will you go out of your way to tell him, along with the rest of it, that you met your wife up here?'

She looked at him intently, and all the victory over him that she could discern was that very slightly, though distinctly, he shook his head.

Part XIV

1

Boniface, tall, thin and soldierly, Count of Africa, conscience-stricken Christian and the most powerful Roman official in the province, had walked on, this bright morning, through the streets of Hippo to the bishop's house with anxiety written like a map of misery across his face.

Two junior officers on his staff went half a pace behind him, in silent dread. In all the confused and stricken Western Empire, there was hardly a better soldier than Boniface, but this morning he had trouble on his mind, and they knew it. Count Boniface, years before, had made his name by keeping the Visigoths out of Massilia. He had, afterwards, been the one Roman soldier of distinction to side with Galla Placidia from the first, and do all he could to uphold her rights, as mother and guardian of the Emperor. When he arrived in Carthage to take up his appointment, the Africans had sighed with relief: an old-style Roman at last! Yet what pagan and self-confident Roman governor had ever walked with a face like that through the streets, just because his conscience smote him?

The two young staff officers knew their master well. They had studied him, they admired him, and that frown was a bad sign. It had been planted upon his face by two letters, arriving under seal from Ravenna. The first, when it arrived had spread gloom, the second evidently hinted at disaster.

Into Boniface's mind, as he stood at the door, hesitating, pondering, came a remark made by Augustine twenty years before, when I myself, thought Boniface, was a raw young military tribune down on the African frontier. I happened to remark how strange it was that I, a Roman, had spent my entire military career speaking Gothic, and commanding mercenaries.

'But the barbarians,' had been Augustine's surprising answer, 'can give us lessons in honesty. We owe our peace to the sworn oaths of the barbarians.' Would he still say the same today, after all this time?

A soldier, even a Christian soldier, so Boniface always held, had a right to be ambitious. Higher rank meant greater scope for service. Nor had it done a conscientious military man any harm to have Augustine for a friend. The bishop was a power in the land, his opinions were attended to, his friends were seldom overlooked. The essence of my problem, Boniface told himself, as at last he raised knuckles to knock, is exactly that. In fact, how far can barbarians – Vandals in this case – be trusted?

I need an army much bigger than the army Ravenna allows me, and I need it quickly. But will Vandals keep their word? From long-standing friendship, might Augustine not give me a hint? Even though he might notice right away – how can he fail to? – that, implicitly, I am asking him to sanction a certain disobedience to the foolish young Emperor in Ravenna, and to his all-powerful mother, Galla Placidia, the Augusta?

Years before, on the death of his first wife, Boniface had expressed to Augustine his wish to quit the army, so as to become a monk. Then it was that Augustine had introduced into his mind yet another idea, that had affected him deeply ever since. A man could conduct himself as a monk while doing his duty as a soldier. 'Be poor, just, celibate, defend the African frontier,' in Augustine's laconic words.

But the simple fact is, Boniface told himself, as, with a certain impatience, he rapped yet again, Augustine does not like my second wife. Augustine had caught one glimpse of her, walking with an armed attendant through the cloth market in Carthage, an Arian woman of Gothic extraction, beautiful, an heiress, called Pelagia. At the accosting roll of her hips, the red invitation of the soft mouth in her turning head, as if well enough aware that she was attracting his glance, the old bishop had felt his own flesh rise. That stirring of the flesh, though exempt from all blame, had profoundly offended Augustine. Other bodily organs, all of them, were subject to his mind and will, but, in his own words the genitals 'moved man, without order and measure, to acts condemned by wisdom.' If she does as much as this, he told himself, to a priest in the late evening of his life, who happens only to notice her stoop and examine a bale of coloured cloth, small wonder that this woman has Count Boniface enraptured.

Augustine looking down through the lattice window of an upper room, as Boniface was, by his direction, kept waiting, could well imagine what must have been in that second letter. He shared in the distress visible on the general's face, but told himself firmly, you must not be drawn into this, even by pity. Boniface is a Christian and a soldier, yes, and I am his friend and ghostly father. But the bishop of Hippo is not in the political service of the man who governs Africa.

The temptations of this ephemeral world – a blatant lust for such a woman as Pelagia, and that other, similar passion, carnality's counterpart, the lust to dominate – yes, thought Augustine, I myself have known them all. I have yielded, I too have sinned, but that was then. Boniface had brought his own tranquillity to an end. Such torment as he now lives through, standing there at my door, is what inevitably comes after. He stands in need – and knows that too – not of worldly advice, or specious consolation, but of God's grace.

From downstairs came the squeak of a hinge. The black-robed young monk, having taken his time to open the door, began to speak to the most powerful man in Africa in a voice than, from nervousness, was too abrupt.

'The bishop is not free, and can see no one.'

'I think you heard the name I gave you.' The voice of the soldier who once wanted to be a monk had, with the passing of time, become peremptory. 'Boniface, Count of Africa. I have already written to Augustine –'

'The bishop received your letter, for which he thanks you. And instructs me to tell you, on his behalf, that you will in due course receive from him a fitting reply.'

The young man, though he stumbled through these last words, had at least, thought Augustine with a smile, managed to get them out.

The faces of the staff officers on the doorstep were incredulous.

'But what is the bishop doing,' one of them exclaimed, 'when our general has come all this way in person –'

'The bishop is working with a scribe on his *Retractiones*'.

'*Retractiones*? What are *Retractiones*?'

'The catalogue of his complete works.' The monk seized his chance and shut the door in their faces.

Augustine went back, thoughtfully, into the small but well-lit room that was his own. Far too many books, he thought. In the corner, a narrow bed. On the wall near the bed, when there was enough light to write, a hinged flap.

A room, thought Augustine with amusement, organised in the shape of my mind. A lizard on the white wall caught his eye; he paused to watch it delicately climb, but even before he turned away, Augustine's lips had begun to move. He was praying. This inner calm, come down on him, verified that what had been said and done in the doorway was right. With Boniface's dilemma – the crisis of his worldly ambition – Augustine, Bishop of Hippo, had nothing to do. Prayer, yes, and, after, a well-considered letter. The God in whose presence he lived, night and day, was introducing into Augustine's mind, as he walked up and down his narrow room, the necessary words.

A simple letter, and non-political. He would take no part in this conspiracy, so cleverly designed to drive a wedge between Boniface – once Galla Placidia's most devoted supporter – and the Augusta in Ravenna. He would call for his scribe. He would advise the Count of Africa above all to love peace.

Two hundred and thirty-two papyrus rolls, comprising ninety-three works, longer and shorter – Augustine as he looked them over was seeing the work of a lifetime – had been arranged methodically down the scriptorium's long table. The man I once was, and perhaps still am, thought Augustine, lies there spread out. Reduced to papyrus, and papyrus, what is more, full of error.

'Where were we?' Augustine asked the tall, smiling, plump scribe, with very little hair, who had been waiting, pen in hand. The letter to Boniface had already been written, scrupulously reconsidered, modified – with omissions rubbed out by pumice stone – sealed and sent. The scribe was quick.

'*The Confutation of the Emperor Julian*, section two,' said

Lucas. 'Would you like me to prompt you with the last couple of sentences?'

After so many years of contending with Claudian's nervous high spirits, tantrums, black moods and giddy changes of mind, for Lucas to dip his iron pen and take dictation from Augustine was a joy. Augustine, too, found satisfaction in working with Lucas, even though his returning glance, at times, was sceptical. Here at last was a scribe not in awe of him, who understood the meanings of words, instead of copying by rote. Lucas was quick to verify literary quotations, which Augustine on some bygone day of haste had made from memory. He could even spell his way, if he had to, through the technical terms in theology.

Augustine did not mind being obliged, by the sardonic eyes of the man sitting opposite him, to think out more exactly what years ago, when writing in a hurry, he had actually meant. There was about Lucas's attitude to him a loving stringency. Lucas never turned a hair at the mistakes of others, even though, to all appearances, he himself might never make them. His copying was so legible and exact that Augustine scarcely needed to check. He had been trained to the needs of a great poet, Claudius Claudianus, and where else in these decadent days was such a scribe to be found.

Lucas's stock-in-trade – the copies from Claudian's library – had been stowed away in barrels, in the back shop of his booth under the arcade. Once installed in his place at the bishop's, Lucas found no reason to be sorry. Augustine's house, at first, had been a little quiet for him – devoid of fire and sex and fun. But he there enjoyed one rare pleasure, of hearing, day after day, this Latin – elegant, sensitive, sometimes heart-stopping.

Augustine had asked him to come and copy, one wet day, with drops of water falling off the arches of the arcade, as the bishop moved under cover, pulling off his head, with almost boyish relief, his damp black woollen hood.

'But I am not a believer,' Lucas had answered, with an unwilling honesty that had surprised him.

'I know who you are,' Augustine answered gently, now protected from the incessant drips, yet tempted to turn and watch them as they fell, one after another, from the curve of the overhang. 'It came back to me on the last fine day we had when you caught my eye, as once again I pushed a book back without buying.' They both laughed – Augustine's passion for books and his decision not to buy were no secret. 'You shared your cloak with one of my monks, after he had been set on by a mob.'

'A mob of angry women,' answered Lucas, 'and that was a long time ago. Very well. I will do my best for you.' Lucas found himself laughing inwardly at his own answer. How was it possible to deny this man? 'Not that you are the first bishop I have copied for –'

'That too came into my mind,' said Augustine. 'A semi-demi-Pelagian. Ah well – who can be more deceptive than someone who always agrees?'

Augustine, under cover of the arcade, eased off his cloak, to shake out the drops. 'You eat meat?'

'When I can get it. And I hear you never do.'

'Once, in the house of a rich man,' began Augustine, 'I was offered roast peacock.' One may legitimately find Augustine's religion a bore, thought Lucas, but hardly the man himself. 'Do you know, I took some. Merely from curiosity. I had never eaten roast peacock before – have you?'

Lucas, smiling, in recollection of all the remarkable meals that no longer came his way, shook his head. Not even at Cornelia's!

'Hardly worth committing a sin for.'

Lucas, invisibly shrugging his shoulders, renounced meat on the spot. With his day's work done, he could always go to a tavern.

What overcame his scepticism in Augustine's house was the atmosphere, as he started work on the muddle that others had left behind them. Peaceful good nature, impregnated with energy. The rule against back-biting was strict. The mood of the place, calm, and yet purposeful, seduced him. This was a strange new society, utterly discordant with the world outside: from each according to his ability, to each according to his needs. To join, though Lucas reminded himself, one needs to believe, and I never shall. What most amazed him was the amount of work this bishop, not young any more, could get through every day of the week.

All I do is work to his bidding, thought Lucas, lifting his right hand, halfway through the morning, to flex his fingers. And that's quite enough. Not only does the bishop set me going on my day's work – an employment that fills my mind entirely. He preaches on a new theme almost every Sunday, and has them weeping. He is guiding the spiritual life of all Africa. He writes long and serious letters. And sits patiently, wearisomely, week after week, as judge in his own basilica. Though he draws the line, I notice, at meddling in politics – and yet he has the politics of the Western Empire at his fingertips.

Once Augustine had dictated his confidential reply to Boniface, Lucas by reading between the lines could tell easily enough what must have been in those two sealed letters sent one after another, like thunderbolts, from Ravenna. Scribes are impersonal men, an ear that listens, a pen that writes. But Lucas knew. And would rather have had his tongue torn out by the roots than tell – since Augustine trusted him.

Had Count Boniface been cruelly tricked? Probably.

When Galla Placidia began the long struggle against odds to make her young and foolish son Emperor, Boniface had stood by her from the very beginning. His great rival Aetius, now Prefect of Italy, had in those days preferred to temporise. But Aetius was nowadays in Ravenna, on the spot, and had the Augusta's ear.

Aetius in Italy, Boniface in Africa, were considered to be high-minded men, yet both of them secretly craved supreme power. For what other reason were they in politics? Behind their affability they eyed each other warily, as rivals.

The first of the two sealed letters from Ravenna which made the brow of the Count of Africa furrow with anxiety had been brief. Aetius had written him what to all appearances was a friendly warning, in these terms, 'The Augusta is plotting to rid herself of you. The proof of her finally adopting that resolution will be your receipt of a letter from her, ordering you for no earthly reason to wait upon her in Italy.' A friendly warning – or a clever trap?

When the second letter, the official one ordering Boniface to Ravenna, arrived soon after, the agonising question became acute. Might Aetius be playing with cynical mastery upon

Boniface's habitual inner doubts? His duty and his power lay in Africa – for what reason should the Augusta want him back it Italy, except to place him at her mercy?

Augustine's curt advice to Boniface – 'love peace' – had therefore been bitter to digest. Though what better could Boniface expect? Lust for a woman and lust for dominion were two faces of the same coin.

His duty as a soldier was to obey. But suppose he did obey the Augusta's command, only to discover when he got back to Italy that Galla Placidia had turned against him? There was always the chance that the secret letter from Aetius was not a trick but a warning. Aetius was openly ambitious – but was he that much of a villain? Disobey, and the Augusta would hold him a traitor. Obey – cross the sea to Italy – and Boniface might be going to his own destruction.

There was no way out of the predicament, twist and turn as Boniface might. Whether Aetius's letter were true or a trick, he was to all appearance lost.

A lonely and mistrustful man, on the pinnacle of power, sooner or later has to tell someone. Augustine had left Boniface to wrestle with his own conscience. Boniface at last confided in his wife. Voluptuous Pelagia had no intention of becoming the spouse – or even widow – of a man dismissed from his post as Count of Africa. With a subtle simplicity she answered, as if diffidently, 'But in the end, won't the winner be the man who has most soldiers?'

Love peace! Boniface told himself sardonically. Pelagia's simple answer had opened his eyes: was he to love peace so much that he sailed away to Ravenna? Delivered himself up to the likelihood of death?

'If here in Africa I had not been starved of soldiers as a matter of policy,' he told Pelagia, a little pompously, 'those conspiring against me might have needed to think twice.' (But every Roman commander everywhere always thought he was being starved of soldiers).

'Then mustn't you get some more?'

Pelagia though an indolent and pleasure-loving woman was no fool. 'Mustn't you?' she murmured, putting her lips close to his cheek, as if he were being a great silly. She had enjoyed being the most important woman in Africa – much as Boniface, after a lifetime jogging along on regimental pay (even giving money away in alms!) had enjoyed being rich on her money. If you asked Pelagia, chastity and poverty were nonsense, she had never felt under the slightest obligation to practise either.

Ten days later – and Boniface had not yet sent a reply to Ravenna – Pelagia spoke to him again, her soft smile visibly touched by self-satisfaction.

'A woman I used to know quite well at one time,' she chattered away, 'arrived in Carthage only yesterday with a message to me from my kinsman, Gaeseric –'

She saw Boniface's brow darken, and added, a little too merrily, 'But here I am, telling you – am I not? Did you think I would keep it from you? Is King Gaeseric our enemy? He might turn out to be your friend. This old acquaintance of mine wants to talk to you. She was in her day very close to the Augusta. I ask you – what can you lose by it?' Pelagia put a restraining hand on his forearm, and in her velvet voice added impudently, 'The Princess Veleda was an attractive woman in her day. I wonder if I dare trust the two of you together?'

'And I dare say you already know what this Princess wants to ask of me?' Boniface would have liked to answer sternly, like a Roman patrician; but there was resignation in his voice. The touch of Pelagia's hand had been the cleverest of flattery.

'Of course I do. It's so simple. Gaeseric needs money and grain. He offers you mercenaries. You still need soldiers, don't you? Well then. See her. And be glad for once that you have a wife who takes care of you –'

They met during that African midsummer afternoon, in a whitewashed room in the Praetorium with a high ceiling. The room though gloomy was cooler than the world outside, because the window openings had been covered with palm-leaf mats. Every now and then a slave with a waterpot on his shoulder would tiptoe in and soak them anew.

As Boniface entered, simply dressed, his eye still blinking from the sunlight outside this cool, dim reception room, he could hardly make out the features of the tall blonde woman he had briefly kept waiting. As he came in she had risen to her feet, with exactly the measure of formal deference that a Count of Africa deserved of a Gothic princess. No clumsy Romanized barbarian this, thought Boniface. A woman of breeding, and used to great affairs. I must be careful.

A young man dressed in new clothes of the latest Carthaginian fashion was in attendance on her. From the way he walks and moves, decided Boniface, a soldier. Her spy. She introduced him: Captain Iynx, on King Gaeseric's staff. 'And let me add, Count Boniface,' she went on in her cool voice, 'in the King's confidence.' But Boniface had Iynx sent outside. While the preliminaries were discussed, he wanted no witnesses.

An accomplished young man, however, a good officer, decided Boniface, as Iynx nodded and moved towards the door. If all King Gaeseric's young officers are as good, I shall be glad of them. All through his career, Boniface had commanded barbarian mercenaries, yet could never rid himself of an obscure conviction that in some way they were inferior. It always surprised him to discover otherwise.

'I knew your wife, Pelagia, of course, in Ravenna,' Veleda told him, in the tone of one making the best of a social occasion. 'A mere girl in those days, but utterly charming. And grown into such a beauty.'

This Princess had already been told, Boniface decided, with a certain inward anger, about the two letters. An unnecessary confidence. But then, I put myself in Pelagia's hands. The soft inconsequential chatter of women's tongues was rendering him helpless. The Augusta, too, could play with you like this, if she chose.

'– yes, I am the wicked Princess Veleda, who led Galla Placidia astray,' she was admitting with a laugh. 'Yet what really happened, despite what they may have told you, Count, was that my dear friend Galla Placidia fell madly in love with a Goth – people do; you must have noticed. And a very good Goth too – King Ataulf.'

Madly in love?

Yes, a sacrificial love, such as the Augusta's must have been, was no doubt a kind of madness.

'The Romans held me hostage for years,' Veleda was telling him, 'at the imperial court. Not long after she was married, I returned to my own people – I serve King Gaeseric. It was always Galla Placidia's deepest hope as I well recall that one day the breach between Goth and Roman might be healed.

How reassuring that thought is. I am all the more encouraged to make my offer.'

This older woman is trying to overcome me, thought Boniface, not as Pelagia does, by her seductiveness, but by her suavity, her clarity, the excellence of her Latin, the rapidity of her mind.

'You talk as if you know me.'

'I saw you, years ago, keep King Ataulf out of Massilia. No Roman had been able to keep him out of Rome.'

Gross flattery, and Boniface despised himself for the way it had warmed his anxious heart. Such women as these tie you up with thread. Anyone can break a piece of thread with a tug of two fingers. Yet once it has been wound round and round you? With gentle hands and soft voices? A winding sheet!

'*Milites!*' Veleda remarked in a tone of almost masculine vigour. 'Soldiers! Can a Roman governor ever have enough of them? Well then, for the defence of Africa King Gaeseric authorises me to offer you fifteen thousand mounted auxiliaries. And for how long? Three months, or six months or a year. As you choose. Or even longer, at need. The customary rates of pay, with this distinction. Half to be paid to me now, in silver, and shipped back to Cartagena by the vessel I came in. The other half – and I daresay, Count, you will not be sorry for the favour done you by our taking payment in kind, not cash – King Gaeseric will accept in grain. Of course, in advance – '

Could this woman – this princess – be serious? The offer took his breath away. Fifteen thousand good Gothic cavalry, thought Boniface, and myself as their commander? Whatever Aetius may think he is doing, he has lost.

Once they know in Ravenna that I have this great force in my pay, I can bargain with Aetius from a position of strength. Come to a firm yet friendly understanding with the Augusta. She is a woman who recognises facts.

'Fifteen thousand,' he repeated, trying to hide his excitement. 'I am bound to ask myself if I need quite that many.'

'Knowing how you are placed, I am even beginning to wonder,' Veleda in the half-light whispered, bargaining with her intellect but also with her sex, 'if fifteen thousand might be too few.'

'I shall of course require serious guarantees – ' Boniface tried to sound forbidding, but she could tell he was wavering.

'You know Goths,' she was going on to say, frank and downright as a man, 'better than anyone in Africa. Vandals are Goths. A people, as you yourself, Count Boniface, must be well aware, who pride ourselves on keeping our word.'

I have hooked him, she thought with a spirit of delight. Her own nicely-calculated insolence while bargaining with this man of power had excited Veleda as nowadays little else did. One stroke of the gaff, she thought, and this big fish will lie before you, gasping for breath. As men did in time past, after you had subdued them with your body. Here in my hand is a poisoned gift he cannot do without.

'Very well, then. I will pay out for fifteen thousand cavalry, in advance. Three months to begin with, half in silver, half in grain.' Abstract promises meant nothing to barbarians. There was no other way of paying them than in advance. They needed to see the colour of your coin.

'Renewable?'

'At intervals of three months, as the need arises. We can agree on notice.'

'Now – shipping.' Veleda had spoken casually, as if of a detail hardly worth bothering him with. Yet this, for Gaeseric's ultimate plan, was the tricky bit. 'Living where we do, on the edge of Empire, we Vandals have access to only coastal shipping – and you know what a long sea voyage does to cavalry chargers. What we have in mind, therefore, is to take our horses directly across the straits of Tingitana. Only half-a-day's sail. Then march them along the coast.'

'A long ride,' said Boniface, unenthusiastically. He needed his Gothic horsemen here and now.

'Our cavalry will not dawdle, that I promise you. Let me tell you why. Have you not been pleasantly surprised by the readiness with which I agreed on King Gaeseric's behalf to the bargain you have driven? I am authorised to act quickly because the harvest in our country has been bad. So we need that grain of yours as soon as it can be shipped. And for the sake of my old affection for Pelagia I would rather deal with someone who has the name of being a friend of the Goths than with any other – '

Can she be trying to hint, wondered Boniface, that Aetius would like to have Gothic soldiers too? The rumour goes that he is hiring Huns. But Ravenna has no surplus of grain – we in Africa have plenty. That is my advantage over him. That, and Pelagia's cleverness.

In the darkened room, Veleda felt the caressing pressure of his long fingers on her hand – this Christian soldier with the panther wife. His touch was an insult. Rely on a man's honour – on his love? They were creatures who might for longer or shorter spasms obsess you – Marcus, Sarus, Iynx, Gaeseric. But always they moved away, and then you must brace yourself for betrayal.

'In fact I am only a woman, and I have done the best I can,' Veleda went on, in a falsely modest murmur that amused her, 'both for my King and for you, Count Boniface. The technical details – the military matters – I must ask you to settle with Captain Iynx. Who possesses, let me repeat the entire confidence of King Gaeseric.'

I must certainly stipulate, thought Boniface, horsemen who have seen action. And cleverly find out from this bright young staff officer how effective they are likely to be. I don't want duds.

'One last favour,' said Veleda. 'We need grain, you need our men, time is important to both of us. Simply to save time, it was King Gaeseric's intention that Captain Iynx make his way overland from here to Tingitana. And trace out a viable route, so that when our men are ready, as they soon will be, to cross the straits – '

Trace a route, thought Boniface, with the ruefulness of a man who sees through a piece of chicane. Let her believe whatever she has been told. But King Gaeseric sent that young officer with her to keep his eyes open, and find out all he can.

'Your Captain Iynx will of course be crossing into hostile territory,' said Boniface, in the friendliest of tone. 'Into barren lands we are happy to leave to the Berbers. We shall certainly – I insist upon it for his own safety – see that he has an adequate mounted escort all the way.'

Vandals, thought Boniface, have quicker wits than they have ever been given credit for. That works both ways, though –

because I shall soon have fifteen thousand of them. At my orders, and doing whatever I say.

Once they had crossed the frontier, and entered Berber territory, Iynx found it easy to give his escort the slip. At the darkest hour of their first night in camp, he crept past the sentry's back, leading his own good horse with hooves muffled, and with a drab Berber cloak thrown over his bright clothes.

At dawn, towering distantly in front of him, blue, bleak and a long way ahead, were the Atlas mountains. By asking here and there, as they sojourned in Carthage, he had found out more or less the location of Dyrin. He had more than a smattering of Punic, half a sack of provisions, his weapons. They would be hunting the coastal byways for a young officer gaudy as a peacock, who last night had chattered by the camp fire as if he had not a care in the world. Gaeseric's court was a good place to learn dissimilation. By the time they thought of searching inland, Iynx was long gone.

Iynx rode out of the gorge and into the rock-strewn valley of Dyrin three days later, as the first light rose in the sky. I could have led a hundred men in here, he thought, and what's to stop me? He walked his horse right up to a sentry who dozed at his look-out post on the high rock. Reaching from the saddle, Iynx with drawn sabre woke the man with a tap on the shoulder from the flat of his blade.

'With the edge of it I could have cut off your head.' That brief iron tap on the shoulder had hurt. Tucco had been roused heartlessly out of a nightmare of death in the arena. He backed off nimbly, professionally, out of reach of this horseman's stroke, and postured with his own long sword in an attitude not often seen any more: a gladiator awaiting combat.

Iynx went on amiably enough, 'The officers of the army in which I serve kill any sentry who falls asleep.'

As a gladiator, Tucco had fought for glory and applause. He had a dislike of armies; compulsion, loud commands, the centurion laying on his vine-root.

'What army would that be?'

'The army of King Gaeseric.'

'Never heard of him.'

'You soon will. I am here, in his name, to speak with your chief. So take me to him.'

Iynx lifted his sabre in another kind of salute, that was a promise not to strike. Tucco reluctantly belted his long sword.

'What makes you think,' Tucco asked, 'that at Dyrin we have a chief?'

And might not this young fighting cock, his head tipped quizzically on one side, be taken off his guard? A quick stroke, crossways, to the side of the neck where the big vein passes? Perhaps in an arena, in the good old days, with the music blaring, thought Tucco with a shrug, as he slipped his hook into the man's bridle to lead his horse. The crowd cheering, and I myself blessed with two good hands and steady nerves. Though with such a confident young man – you can always tell the good ones – perhaps not even then.

'But there must be somebody here in Dyrin who speaks up for you.'

'You mean, our prophetess.'

She lived alone, in a shack once an outhouse – a single room with a sloping roof and bare rafters. Years had gone by, yet she knew him at a glance and beyond all doubt – the tilt of the head, the same bright eye. So he had come at last to find her!

In a tone of disbelief Gilda said, 'Iynx!' But it was hardly a question.

Yet her emotion, Gilda soon discovered, was not immense. As he stood there in the doorway she looked at him with a disturbing kind of maternal delight, and yet felt calm.

Iynx, when recognition came to him, felt unmanned, as if at that one glance he had stepped out of commonplace reality into a more indistinct world of memory and possibility. Better not forget, he reminded himself, as he stood up straighter. You have come here to get a result.

Early light streamed through the doorway into the poverty-stricken hut, and there she was – the vivid singer in the olive grove. Had he not, thereafter, escaped from her on donkey-back? And after that on camel-back – a pursuit in a dream? No. When they rode on camel-back he clearly remembered having slept at night in her arms.

And then they had lived together, three in one hot room.

Two different women to fuss over him, indulge him, help him on with his clothes. Neither of them as she was now – her heavy knot of thick grey hair, that home-made, undyed, shapeless garment. He could remember those hands, that voice.

Jacob's woman. Always at odds, Iynx recalled, with Sara, my nurse, and in those days I was loyal to Sara. Gilda, who made me laugh so much, even though Sara mistrusted her. Now their prophetess at Dyrin? What a piece of luck! She has changed. But I have changed, too, Iynx decided, most of all since I found out that Stilicho was my father. In the past, with those Jews, Jacob, Julius, brothers – you would never think so – she sometimes went as Rachel.

'Gilda?' he asked, pulling off his horseman's gauntlet, offering her his hand. 'Or Rachel? I never expected to find you here.'

Tucco stood outside the door, his iron hook still tugging the bridle of a handsome but weary horse. Tucco went on watching.

'I have not much here to offer you,' Gilda was saying, oddly matter-of-fact. 'Food?'

'I still have food left, here in my sack.'

'Warm water?'

She had taken the blackened pitcher from the embers, was pouring water into a shallow earthenware bowl.

'You wash in here, while I look around for a fresh egg,' she said, with a sidelong glance at Tucco, 'if there is one.' She still likes doing things for me, thought Iynx with a smile. She hasn't changed.

'And here at Dyrin you are the prophetess?' His voice was civil enough, but his look incredulous, and Gilda laughed.

'You expected someone more impressive?'

Gilda turned to the hook-handed man outside, tugging at the horse. She would rather, Iynx decided, not be overheard.

'Take that splendid horse of his, Tucco, and give it a rub down – will you? And a good feed. This guest of ours must have come a long way.'

Her sudden laugh brought back to Iynx the day before yesterday: Leptis Magna, somewhere like a dream.

'You were very young,' said Gilda, watching him draw off his boots, itching to help him now. They were alone. 'The desert men in the caravan made a great fuss of you. Their prince! And look – so you are!' Iynx had just slipped off his Berber cloak, and stood there before her in his new clothes. He pulled a face at her compliment. Always, she had fussed him a little too much. Gilda gave herself a warning: you must no longer treat him as a child.

'The camels, jogging in a very long line – those I remember,' answered Iynx, to humour her. His feet hurt, his shoulders ached, he was saddle-sore. Gilda stooped, to move the bowl of hot water closer. Their chief person here, their prophetess, the one who, if led along properly, would do all he needed. And here she was, waiting on him, exactly as if she were his slave.

'You remember Julius?'

His bare and aching feet were caressed by warm water, and then by her hands. Gilda had not left him alone for the time it might take to hunt out a fresh egg from under a wandering hen, but she was feeding him on what she had, slicing an end of stale loaf, a piece of cold mutton. That knife of hers, Iynx warned himself, in the nervous languor of weariness, is sharp. She could easily cut your throat. All his muscles were taut, and Gilda had seen that before. Men who resent your touch stiffen like that – young men who hate to submit.

'Julius? Yes.' He spoke through a mouthful of crumbs.

'And after he turned his back on his brother Jacob, and went off with you and Sara – what happened to Julius?'

A slippery noose; a purple tongue protruding like a final insult. A neck even more lopsided than my own.

Iynx rubbed the kink in his own neck with one finger, and at that trivial gesture, unchanged since he was a boy, Gilda's heart turned over.

'Julius? I don't really know. He is someone that I hardly remember.'

'So now you serve King Gaeseric? The first step, no doubt, in a splendid career. Well, Iynx, we know each other of old, so explain. Even when they don't agree with me – and often they don't – the people here at Dyrin will listen to what I say. Why should we do your king this great service?'

Gilda told herself ruefully, whatever else, at least I know men. There was his body, before her, white under his clothing, bronzed in the face, yet an invisible hand held her back from flinging her arms around him. Though what in fact, she decided, holds back this impulsive, randy, long-starved old body of mine is not any prohibition but what he wants of us. The people of Dyrin need what he has just been proposing to me about as much as they need an outbreak of plague. But when he goes out and talks to them – and how can I stop him? – with his candid voice, and that frank smile?

She had borne him in pain; lost him; gone looking for him. They were joined together by a few names, a place or two, a crooked neck, old jokes, a charming smile. But what other claim did she have, that he or anyone need recognise? Gilda had tried to find traces of Lucas in that smile. Iynx, anyway, had his father's intelligence. And my charm, my tongue, thought Gilda, so very useful in a woman, so fatal in a man. Lucas, always clever and gentle; in his soul nobody's slave. This young man, his son, mine, though clever and charming, is ruthless.

Flesh of man and woman had blended one astounding night in Milan, and this young man in bright clothes had come of it. A boy child, lost the night he was born. And who had named him Iynx? (Most probably Stilicho – it was like Stilicho to give a child a soldier's nickname).

Suppose her child had been carried off, that night of pain, with the afterbirth, and thrown on the dustheap for the dogs. Others were; it had been the first thing she wondered. The women of Rome killed their children. And now Rome was dying of it. Gilda thrust knuckles into her mouth as she turned away from him, in case the young man saw. She was biting flesh and bone until it hurt.

An improper thought then broke up Gilda's sad mood, like a burst of merriment. In the half-dark who would see? Kick the door shut, now, with your heel, while no one is watching. Take Iynx to your bed. He has come a long way, he is ready for it. Have you ever known a young man refuse? Does he know who you are? And why should he ever find out? Show him a thing or two he will never forget. Happenings in the dark – flashes of lightning to remember, even when his bride is yelping in his arms.

And that indeed, she told herself, rejecting her own wickedness with a certain tenderness for the wild impulse itself, is the only way to understand a man: take his essence inside you. Marcus and I never got close enough, that was the trouble.

Under this dirty old gown, as he would discover, is still a dancer's body. I have softness and muscles and shape enough to pass.

When leaning closer to pour clean water, her ebbing naughtiness was drowned in an emotion close to a sob, as Gilda saw, beyond all doubt, that he had Lucas's foot, the heavy big toe, the high instep.

Our child, his and mine! Not that I ever doubted.

Gilda was holding the naked foot possessively in the palm of her hand, and had begun drying between the toes, almost like making love. Iynx took the towel from her a little too brusquely.

I would have done better, Iynx told himself, to wash and feed elsewhere, and come to see this prophetess in my new Roman clothes, clean and proper. Showing myself to her first and foremost as King Gaeseric's officer. With my boots pulled on I feel more myself. Shall I read out to her my credentials from the King? No, she would only laugh. She thinks of me as a small boy.

'You mean you have not even heard, here in Dyrin,' he began by saying, 'of Gaeseric King of the Vandals?'

Desultorily, in the past, Gaeseric and Veleda had talked over the possibility that Rome's empire could be attacked from within. With the once-eternal world of Roman certainties breaking apart so fast, why not widen the cracks? What Gaeseric principally needed was dissenters, firm in their convictions, who yet would do exactly what he bade them. The runaways from Dyrin?

'Will people who hold their faith half-heartedly,' Gaeseric had said, 'fight to the death?'

Iynx, as he poked about in Carthage, had already met such dissenters – Donatists, Circumcelliones, small men bled white by taxation, the land-hungry, and always, everywhere, the discontented slaves. On the day when Africans only shrug their shoulders at a Catholic priest telling them to resist heretic Arians, Gaeseric had said, with one of his cold smiles – and very seldom these days did he betray himself into a prediction – power will be ours for centuries.

'Not that I ever remember Stilicho,' Gilda was saying, 'speak of your King Gaeseric. Or any of your kings – then, why should he?'

The young man's mouth hangs open, decided Gilda, as if I claimed to have met Helen of Troy.

'At the time I was his slave,' Gilda went on, enjoying, as she always did the look on the face of an audience entranced. Tumbling back helter-skelter into her mind came memories of days gone by: the good old days, when Rome was real, and all the men wild about her. 'Yes, the famous Flavius Stilicho. He bought me, and I shared his bed. For years – and then he freed me. Anything else about him you would like to know?'

Diffidence kept Iynx back from the outrageous answer he might otherwise have given her: *Stilicho was my father*. Time for that, he warned himself, once our business has been transacted. After she has come over to our side, heart and soul, this prophetess, who was once my father's slave. (Did she ever wash Flavius Stilicho's feet too? Is that why the washing felt so strange?)

2

'We do all this for you,' answered Gilda, when she had heard him out, 'and what will you do for us?'

How had it come about that this woman, past her youth, apparently still fond of him, whom Iynx had expected to mould in his hands like wax, should have turned into an antagonist?

The fact was that Iynx had spoken of King Gaeseric's plans and ambitions a little too blatantly. In barbarian courts, Gilda told herself, they all like to speak like that, vaingloriously. Not the manly bluntness they had affected in Rome, but a cockiness to sweep all before it. Is this what the world outside Dyrin has become? He is my son, that I accept. But in what he has in mind for us all, does he simply not see the danger?

King Gaeseric, according to Iynx, wanted risings of the Circumcelliones in the south, near the frontier, and Donatist discontent, if not riots, in the cities. He would like the mountain Berbers well disposed towards him as he marched along the coast and, in all this, the men and women of Dyrin were to help. She did not much like what this man Gaeseric had been making of her son.

Gilda began to sense, as he spoke, the presence of a shadowy rival, this other woman who had handed Iynx over, body and soul, to the barbarian king. And was making of him a military dandy – a courageous dandy, no doubt, and quick-witted. But a man who had already learned to speak of others as if he despised their slow wits a little, as if anyone unwilling to help the Vandals conquer were no longer a human being, but an insect to be crushed.

If only Lucas and I – the thought came to Gilda with a certain bitterness – or, better still, Jacob and I, had been given a chance to bring him up. Though would Iynx have been any the better for it – bred on the edge of society, living precariously? Perhaps, by this time in his life, someone's slave?

Iynx was perceptive enough to have seen that, for some reason that puzzled him, he might have lost her. In warfare, as in life, one outflanked. Could he not if need be appeal to the people of Dyrin over her head? Their rebellious sentiments alone should prompt them to help King Gaeseric. Even in a material sense it should pay them. He decided to try out on this grey-haired woman, who had begun to turn obstinate, this last argument.

'Are you related to Gildo, by any chance? No doubt you are. Well then, King Gaeseric's policy is simply Gildo's old policy. To give out shares to the landless from the imperial domain in Africa –'

Gilda could well image this other woman, this invisible rival, putting such an argument in his mouth – like a poisoned kiss. How otherwise could he have known about Gildo? Yet whatever life may have made of him, she told herself firmly, we are one flesh. And could not deny that there was also a deep part of her that thrilled at the way Iynx spoke out, a masculine boldness that made her go weak inside until her own labouring brain hit on the right answer.

'Your King Gaeseric will give all the imperial domain in Africa to the poor – and take none for himself?'

'I rather think I said, give out shares.' Iynx spoke as if she could not have heard.

Gilda, when travelling with the Circumcelliones, had observed land-hunger at first hand. 'I doubt it. There have been many such promises in history, and what happened to them?'

'Our policy is to liberate the oppressed' Iynx went on, as if to sweep her objections away. 'King Gaeseric's own people, of course, to be freed first of all. All Gothic slaves. I'm sure there must be a great many, here in Africa –'

Gilda found herself nodding, even though she knew very well that here, in Africa, you seldom came across a Gothic slave. But what the Vandals had in mind was becoming clear. Freeing the slaves, wasn't that how Rome had been made to capitulate? Iynx is repeating his lines, she thought, and not badly. That too he gets from me.

'And that Roman power we all abhor?' he went on. 'Which taxes and oppresses? Gaeseric hates it, too.'

'And all these are things that you yourself believe?' asked Gilda with her disconcerting smile.

'Isn't that obvious?' He was smiling back, as if at a typically womanish question – silly, but with its own charm.

'If you are so strong against oppression, Iynx, why not stay here in Dyrin? We have our militia. Join us, become one of us, let us make use of your talents. We need a good soldier. Up here in the hills – in this no-man's-land – there is not much oppression. Perhaps, sometimes, man oppresses woman –' at which she smiled, remembering unlucky Tucco, still besotted by her, 'or woman, man. I hardly think, though, that we need your King Gaeseric and his army to improve on what we have here already. We even have land. We lack a good soldier, though. Well, Captain Iynx, what about it?'

Her ridiculous, and yet ironic, answer had been making Iynx uneasy. A woman who claimed to have been his father's slave, their prophetess – and the words she used had meanings quite opposite to the meanings of the same words in Veleda's mouth. Did they really call what he saw around him, freedom? Or is the confusion, he asked himself, simply in your own mind? You are weary of sitting in the saddle, and slightly stunned by all this newness. Alone with Gilda, a ghost out of the past? Why should she mock King Gaeseric?

'Stay here, in this godforsaken place?' The words burst out of him. 'Do nothing of importance with my life?'

Don't tell him how wrong he is, Gilda warned herself. You

don't have the right. Never wound a young man in his pride. Her actress voice became gentle. She laughed.

'And you have such clever arguments. But if only Flavius Stilicho were alive, and here in this room. Yes, he would listen politely to what you might have to say. With a brother officer, of whatever rank, he was never discourteous. Then turn his head, with that clipped beard and sharp blue eye, and give you an answer, in one sentence, that would take the breath out of your mouth. Only, I stand here with a bowl of dirty water in my hand, and ask myself, what is that sentence? I have the feelings, and not the words. And you are the one with all the arguments.'

As she spoke in that way, there he suddenly was her son again, the real and living young man, come out from behind the brazen face that had been stamped on his features, much as a royal profile is stamped on a coin.

'Flavius Stilicho was a Vandal too, I believe. Doesn't that make a difference?'

'Stilicho, let me tell you, would have said he was a Roman. You look amazed. And what did he mean by it? I can see the question in your eye. For him Rome was *orbis* – the civilized world, the world he knew, the world that mattered. Don't you ever feel like that?'

Gilda could tell from the way Iynx stared at her that he no longer knew what she was talking about. Rome, for any barbarian, was no longer an enviable but puzzling civilisation, but a rich cake, ready to slice. Rome was a way of life that this Vandal King had found a means of destroying from within.

But in saying that much, wondered Gilda, if only to myself, am I not denying all I have preached to them here in Dyrin. The songs of the Circumcelliones, which I sang without stopping to think what they might signify? Face to face with the son I have never really known, are my feelings so infallible?

I could go over, help him, improve on his performance. Sings songs for him too. (Have they thought of songs? They have thought of everything else). Stilicho is dead, and I have lived, since then, an utterly different life. At the bottom of my heart – she wondered – is Stilicho this boy's rival?

She went on with a different intensity, and Iynx, amused, told himself: she has begun to prophesy.

'Yes, Rome cast both of us forth, him and me. Except that, for Flavius Stilicho, the living man, whom I knew better than anyone, if Rome broke down then nothing left would be worth having. Does it utterly escape you, Captain Iynx, that a great man might feel like that? Are you finding it too difficult?'

'This place you have chosen to live in is hardly Rome.'

Iynx, to ease his bodily stiffness, stood up, ducking his head to avoid the sloping rafters, and went to her half-open door. Gilda's possessive assertion – Stilicho hers! – was still ringing in his ears. Iynx looked out, restlessly, upon what there was to be seen of this remote place, Dyrin, the huddle of mean, stone houses, the men desultorily at work in the fields. No overseer. No organisation.

Gilda spoke from just behind his shoulder, as if she, too, in her prophetic trance, were seeing this place for the first time.

'You are looking out there at Rome seen in a mirror. The Roman virtues, for Stilicho, were what kept the world alive – I mean, the civilised world. Dyrin is full of everything that Rome had no place for, and no time for. Even so, the very rebels against Rome are what Rome brought forth –'

She is entirely mad, thought Iynx. Is she trying to tell me that Rome brought forth this? But her insistent voice dragged his wearying mind a few steps further on.

'A civilisation produces its own rebels. Its own dissenters. Its Jesus Christ. No cross, no crown of glory. And tell me this – what does barbarism produce? I can give you your answer, in one word. At the very best, barbarism imitates. No Rome, no rebels, and therefore no one here in Dyrin to help you. Your King Gaeseric, had he no example to imitate, would have been living, as I did myself when I was a girl, in a forest, clad in skins.'

Iynx had been fixing on his face an arrogant mask, and in his perplexity, was staring at her from behind it.

'I sometimes manage to put into words what may be passing through their heads. And thus I have the name for being their prophetess, but let me tell you. I have no control over them whatever. Go then, and speak to them as you have spoken to me. If you would rather not stay here, and waste your life, leading us heroically, while we fight to the last man. You have failed with me because you come from a world I know. But with the people of Dyrin you might have better luck. They often dissent from what I tell them, because that is what they are – dissenters. At the court of King Gaeseric I dare say there is a terrified unanimity; here there is none. Before we met here, we all lived different lives. Mine most of all –'

Why is she making it easier for me, wondered Iynx. Can that be the slave mentality? I expected to have her fight harder than this for what she believes.

'– and before you open your mouth to answer,' Gilda went on with a harshness that surprised him, 'I shall stand up and tell them exactly what I think of your King's hollow promises. I shall warn them that when Gaeseric promises to reward them with the bits and pieces of the world they rejected – Rome – he probably means to cheat them. And the world he puts in its place will be worse than any they have known. After that you can tell them whatever you like. And why should they not believe a forthright, upstanding young man like you, rather than a tedious old woman like me?

I am an actress, she told herself. *Mima* – a word they think shameless. A former actress, become a tedious old woman. The time has come to bow out.

Iynx's face showed doubt. If only she does exactly what she says, he was telling himself, I have won. But can I trust her?

'On the other hand, Iynx, if for some reason the people here happen to disagree with you – if you fail to convince them –'

'Yes?'

'We both know what will happen, don't we? Dyrin will be crushed. It would not need many soldiers. Do you suppose I am giving you this chance for any other reason?'

A prophetess! thought Iynx, staring at her open-mouthed. To obliterate Dyrin, if it proved awkward, was Gaeseric's contingency plan. But how could she have known?

'He will send some other cavalry captain into the valley, but this time with a couple of hundred armed men behind him, and destroy us.' Marcus's warning: as she repeated it, she smiled.

Nor could Veleda herself, Iynx was thinking, have ended a discussion with such a trenchant answer. This prophetess had pierced to the very heart of the matter: she knew. Yet this woman in undyed homespun had been a slave, and Veleda was a princess. The top of his mind was already beginning to wonder, irrelevantly, trivially, if, when he spoke to the people of Dyrin, he should wear the drab robe – or give them a glimpse of the good clothes underneath.

'And did Flavius Stilicho,' Iynx found himself asking at random, in an amiable voice, to disguise the vindictiveness of his thoughts, 'have other children?'

'By his wife Serena? A son and a daughter. Who, with almost all his other friends and relatives, were killed off, when Stilicho fell.'

'So I have been led to believe. Didn't a swordsman called Heraclian chop off his head?'

'You have been told all this by someone who was there at the time?'

'A lady then very prominent at the imperial court – the Princess Veleda.'

An ox roasting whole under dusty chestnut trees; a hesitant young woman, conspicuous in white. And mad, in those days, about Sarus. Now with King Gaeseric? Not surprising. Stilicho had used her, years before, as a spy. Yet was always a friend to her, would help her whenever she would let him, even if sometimes, in my hearing, he would laugh about her. Best to say nothing. Let the boy keep his illusions.

'Flavius Stilicho never had a child by a mistress?'

'He might. Such men are apt to.'

Iynx was looking at Gilda in the brow-beating way which the inexperienced always believe will somehow extort the truth. 'He did not have a child by you?'

'You mean to say you have never been told who your father really was?'

'But I, certainly, have been told who my father was.'

Inyx was lifting his chin in a way that again reminded Gilda, irresistibly, of Lucas – a gesture come back to her from someone whom, for a very long time, she had tried not to remember.

And now what do I tell him? she asked herself. That he has never been quite as important as he supposes? Inform him that he was the child of two slaves – and lose him?

'Having Stilicho as my father,' Iynx was saying in a guileless voice, more to himself than to her, 'has always been my great example. To stay here, in Dyrin, and captain your militia? If you are not joking when you say that. But would not that in his eyes be to desert my place of duty?'

With this son of mine as our commander, thought Gilda with absurd regret, we might at least all have gone down fighting.

'Out of the question. I serve a great man – Gaeseric, the greatest Vandal of our day, as Flavius Stilicho, by all accounts, was in his.'

'Yet you admit that your King Gaeseric plans to come here, and destroy?'

'Only so as to reform. To purify. Redeem.' The words, she thought, are coming like echoes from his mouth. 'And what will you have to say when we put an end, once and for all, to the very religious persecution which drove so many of your people into these mountains?'

'If you believe everything your King Gaeseric tells you, even that, then would you believe an insignificant old woman like me –' the outrageous utterance, after being held back for so long, was coming out of her mouth so naturally '– if I told you what, once or twice, you may have wondered? That I am your mother?'

He stood with his mouth open, as though Gilda had given him the moon and stars.

'And it would be so easy for me to tell you the other thing that you want to hear – that Flavius Stilicho was your father. In the simplicity of your heart you would like it to be true – just as you would very much like to believe everything your King Gaeseric tells you. The world we live in nowadays has become a little too terrible. People would rather believe consoling lies.'

The trick with a woman who is overwrought, as Iynx knew, was to answer steadily.

'I take your word for it. If you say you are my mother, then that is something I am perfectly prepared to believe. It explains a lot. Even if, until now, I have never really known you.'

Gilda reached out for him, impulsively, at this open acceptance of her, as if to claim his body as her own. But Iynx like a subtle swordsman moved out of reach, lifting a hand – as if to warn her: not yet. She had not said quite enough.

'And my father?'

So why not, Gilda asked herself, lie to him? Her eyes were

on his expectant face. Tell him what he so much wants to hear, in the candid voice of an actress. The voice I can produce, that no one ever dares disbelieve. The lie would make him happy for the rest of his life. And make me happy too? Grow older, with that splendid gentleman to look after me? He could so easily have been Stilicho's child. Stilicho himself would have liked to believe it, until I told him otherwise.

A pit, she thought, lies open at his feet. He has entered upon a wrong life. How can he live, unless he knows the truth about himself?

'There were even some people at the time you were born – the *agentes in rebus* for instance – who thought your father might have been the Emperor Honorius.'

Gilda laughed, and Iynx pulled a face. For father, a dead Emperor, whom everyone despised? She was playing with him.

'I will tell you this much,' said Gilda. 'Flavius Stilicho would very much have liked to be your father. When you were very young, he saved your life – sent you to his great friend Claudian. Remember?'

Iynx's nod was concentrated anxiety, mingled with a spasm of anger.

'Flavius Stilicho – I will go this far – held himself responsible for you. But you couldn't have been his child. When you were conceived, he was off and away, winning the battle of Pollentia.'

And, perhaps, will the next words that come out of my mouth – the true ones – snatch him away from that white-clad princess? And from this barbarian brute he serves? Or shall I lose him for ever?

'Your father was a Roman slave.'

Iynx was aghast, then over his face came a look of clever incredulity. Could this grey-haired, quick-witted woman be revenging herself?

'I should like to know more,' he said coldly.

'I have hardly ever seen him since the night you were conceived, though I knew him for many years before. He came from Britain too, a free man at one time. And then, like so many of us, he was kidnapped –'

'A soldier?'

'A scribe.'

Gilda was poised, alertly, for Iynx to ask the name – a name he might indeed have remembered – but Iynx was closing his ears to her voice. Gilda went on calmly, as if reminding herself.

'When I was a little girl, the two of us were slaves together. He was the one who taught me to read and write.'

With a woman like this, wondered Iynx, how can you ever be sure? Perhaps she is not even my mother. And yet all Gilda had told him, lies or not, could never be unsaid. The worm in the apple would remain, and gnaw.

'I was told quite otherwise,' Iynx muttered, in a voice not his own, 'and by someone who in fact knew Stilicho very well. Weren't you an actress? Aren't you making it up?' *Mima* in this young man's mouth was a deadly insult. 'I am aware you would rather I went away from this place, and left the lot of you alone. You would like me to believe I am a nobody. You would like me to believe you were my mother.'

Yet even as he struck at her with words, Iynx knew very well that she must be his mother, and the knowledge was poisoning him. He was not, any more, a smart young soldier, but a spoiled child.

I have lost my son, decided Gilda, with an uncanny calmness – the son I never really had. I know these brutes – these Gothic charmers. They have captured him – impregnated him. In that manly voice of his, so convincing, my son will offer the people of Dyrin their revenge. And they will take it, with both hands.

Brutes have been my study in life, as books were for Lucas. He will take all they have, Gilda told herself, even their lives, in exchange for promises. Into her mind's eye came the image of a little girl, standing giddily on her head on the turf beside a forest track. A horseman arrived behind a frightening banner. He reached down to grasp her ankles, and lift her up, and take her away.

The Vandals landed on the coast of Tingitana, where the water was shallow, on the long sandy beach that runs eastward along the coast from what is now Tangier. The horsemen led their queasy chargers out of the boats, one by one, down plank ramps, and hock-deep through white, splashing water, to the shore. Once on the firm wet sand they tightened girths, and climbed into the saddle to seek out their proper formations.

The captains of a hundred – Iynx's rank – and the *millenarii*, colonels of thousands, had unrolled banners painted like grotesque animals as their rallying points. Vandal cavalrymen fell in behind the symbol they saw to be their own, and after a quick roll-call moved inshore at the trot, leaving behind them a sandy beach, scuffed by footmarks, as a place for the next arrivals. The ships, as they emptied, hoisted mainsail, turned about laboriously, and went back for another live cargo.

Hammered into shape by Gaeseric's kingcraft, and their successive victories, the Vandals were no longer a congeries of tribes, but a people who had begun to live as an army. Their man's *millenarius* or regiment was the only home that the family of a serving soldier now knew. Womenfolk were camp followers, children the children of the regiment. Spain was left behind, across the straits, and for the Vandals there could be no going back. There would be no boats to take them, there was no place to go, they had abandoned Andalusia. Their one hope was victory in Africa.

Before the Vandals made this enormous move, the King had counted their numbers. This knack of finding out the figures, before any great action, was an attribute of Gaeseric's that Veleda encouraged. She had seen King Ataulf learn to do the same – a useful knack that might as well be borrowed from the civilised. Eighty thousand men, women and children – of whom at least the fifteen thousand cavalry Boniface had been promised were first-rate fighting men.

The Vandal horsemen were armed, simply, with helmet, cuirass and lance. Unlike Alaric's invading Visigoths, they had at their back no arms factories on the Roman pattern. But they had been trained by Gaeseric to aim from the saddle what no Roman troops in Africa had yet had to withstand – poisoned arrows.

In the field, up against time-serving Roman troops used for frontier patrol, this Vandal cavalry would be hard to beat. Certain small cities that were slackly defended and demoralised in advance might well fall to them. But when the barbarian horsemen came up against the walls of any considerable Roman city – Hippo? Carthage? – defended by troops who knew their business? That was the great unanswered question.

'And afterwards,' Gaeseric had said, in Veleda's hearing though apparently speaking, as so often he did, more to himself than to her, 'my colonels are to rule the provinces of Africa for me. So long as I have colonels, instantly obedient to me, what need have we for civilian governors? Our army on the march is the skeleton of my new government.'

He has thought it all out, Veleda told herself. He is the cleverest man I have ever known. And clever, sometimes, at my expense – not that he will ever admit how much he owes me.

On the fourth trip across the straits, with the open beach in Tingitana by this time well defended, seasick Arian priests and their bishops had tumbled ashore from the boasts, in the company of seasick women. Their crossing had been achieved only just in time. The sea was rising.

Gaeseric said to Veleda, out of the corner of his mouth, as together they watched the landing, and kept smiles from their faces. 'In Africa, we shall use Catholic priests to sweep the streets.'

The oldest of the bishops was stumbling up the beach to greet, deferentially, the Vandal King, as he stood there, in breastplate and helmet, leaning on his javelin. In a loud voice that only just stopped short of being an order, Gaeseric replied, 'Before our army starts on its march – a short and appropriate prayer.'

Mustering his dignity the old man moved to higher ground, where the multitude of fighting men on their restless horses could at least see his gestures, if not hear his voice. The first words of the familiar Gothic prayer were caught up by soldiers nearby. They all knew it by heart. Those behind took over the words, in loud voices, and before the first invocation had been fully uttered, the prayer was spreading like a wave. The whole Gothic army began speaking to God, in a voice that made Veleda, swept heaven-high by all these male voices, shudder to the marrow of her bones.

Vairthai viljatheins – be done thy will – *sve in himina ana arthai* – as in heaven, yes on earth.

Veleda's own tense lips had begun moving, as if overmastered. No paternoster in Latin had touched her as deeply as this Gothic Our Father'.

Hlaif unsara thana sinteinan – loaf an the unending – *gif uns himme dage* – give us this day.

And that will be another question, thought King Gaeseric,

as the enormous repetition of words hammered against a mind deliberately cut off, so that he could privately consider his own business. Our daily bread! Once across the Roman frontier and into the farm lands where they grow corn for export, well and good. Let my army eat their corn, and idle Romans starve.

Cheap bread for the poor? Yes, here in Africa that too, and watch how the poor will welcome us as liberators, so long as the cheap bread lasts. Which will be long enough. The rations we ferried over with us – how long are they going to last? Dimly, Gaeseric knew that there would be numbers which matched these questions, but for the time being such numbers were beyond him.

As for the rebels who dwelt together in Dyrin, they were, at Iynx's urging, already dispersed as emissaries. Among the unfortunate in town and country the glad word was spreading: freedom arrives on horseback. The Donatists, so Iynx reported, had been so elated at a chance to put the Catholics in their place, that if I had promised them heaven and earth, he had said, then and there, in the palm of my outstretched hand, they would have believed me. Iynx had been brought up with Donatists at Cornelia's – he knew their provincial gullibility. Those were people, he had told Gaeseric, that you could pay with words.

The Circumcelliones, agitators of great experience, had spread across the broad lands of the south, rousing their fellows in the name of the dead hero, Gildo, and his miraculously living counterpart, Gaeseric. They were sacking manor houses, tying up the frontier force. and after they have amused themselves, with their flaming arrows, thought Gaeseric, as prayers came to an end? I need no vast surplus of corn and oil, so what need have I of migrant workers? Let them become *coloni*. And the recalcitrant among them, my slaves.

One regiment after another formed up and trailed away, passing King Gaeseric, saluting him with dipped banners, as he sat, impassive-faced, astride his charger. And we shall rebuild those gutted manor houses all the more quickly, he was thinking, since I shall also enslave all our prisoners of war, and set them on necessary work. In my African kingdom, I shall have no use for the ungovernable.

As the march began, a ration of parched corn had been

issued – the corn shipped by Count Boniface when he kept the first part of his bargain with Veleda. Men and horses began their march well-fed, and pitched their first camp, along the coast, towards nightfall. Families shared their rations around the camp fire, in mingled excitement and awe. The African moon was larger than the moon in Spain, the Pole Star stood lower down the sky.

Their endless concourse – eighty thousand souls – had marched onwards for three hundred miles before a Roman military tribune came in sight – sent by Boniface, who had been warned by ship that many more than fifteen thousand vandals had landed in Tingitana. Until now, in Boniface's experience as in Augustine's, all Goths had been men of their word.

The military tribune brought the Vandal King a formal message that Count Boniface had no further need of his mercenaries. The contract was at an end. His men had already been paid – indeed, overpaid – for the little they had done, and they should now go home. When he heard his entire people being ordered by the Romans to go back where they had come from, Gaeseric gave his great vindictive laugh.

He had the nearest cavalryman dismount from his horse, draw his sharp dagger, and cut off the man's nose in his presence, watching the man's face attentively as he winced, and bit his lip, and tried his hardest – a Roman, this! – not to scream aloud, and yet failed. Gaeseric sent the man back to Boniface with that disfigurement as his answer.

3

For all the human debris swept along the coast by the Vandal invasion, Hippo was the nearest large, walled city. The second port of Africa became a place of refuge.

In Augustine's basilica, services went on from morning to night, and the words contrition and expiation were often in the mouths of the busy officiating priests. Often they were met with an answering groan of asssent, as if the crowds from the countryside who stood there, cheek by jowl, possessing only what they stood up in, were breaking their hearts. The building never ceased to echo with the chanting of the penitential psalms.

Hundreds who had hesitated for a long time to become Catholic Christians were eager, in this repentant mood, for the assurance of baptism. Hour after hour, Augustine's black-robed priests administered the rite, with salt and chrism and holy water. Over the walls of Hippo the long shadow of the saintly Augustine was cast, making of it a stronghold.

Since he discovered how Count Boniface had been tricked into allowing the Vandals to enter Africa, Augustine had visibly aged. At first he had shown incredulous anger – rare for him. But he had a church to lead, and soon he was seeking for answers.

To Possidius, bishop of Clama, and all others like him, Augustine's advice was, 'Remain with your flocks, and share their miseries.' Might not the church, from this time of troubles, emerge purified?

King Gaeseric, however, had his plans for the Catholic church in Africa as for all else: impoverish, humiliate, degrade. Once the more obstinate Catholics had been reduced to poverty, he intended to harass their priests, incessantly, until they lost all the influence they had grown used to exercising over men of social importance. Rob, humiliate, torment, he told his captains and his colonels, but never do to death. Make no martyrs – even of those who seek martyrdom.

Give our own Arian priests the good places. A civil servant wants to keep his job? Let him convert. Any Catholic priest, not a zealot, who would rather go on with his career in the church, has only to turn Arian. One God or Three-in-One – what is the practical difference? Turn the waverers our way and meanwhile persecute – but not to death – the obstinate. Never make martyrs, because the blood of martyrs is the seed of their church. Let us instead make them poor and powerless and ridiculous.

The Vandals, as Possidius explained to Augustine, had gone first for the church treasure. They despoiled the altars of valuables, and the brides of Christ of their virginity. The most pitiable refugees in Hippo were the nuns. Oncoming Vandals had shown towards these religious women none of the scruples that Visigoths had affected in Rome. But they had lost what they had vowed to Christ *non animo sed corpore*; ravished, that is, according to Augustine's humane distinction, not in the soul, only in the unwilling and unconsenting body.

Two bishops, Pampianus of Vita and Mansuetus of Urusi, had been burned with red-hot irons to make them disclose where the treasures of the altar had been hidden. To make them speak – often when they had nothing to confess – clergy had been crushed under heavy stones, given sea water to drink, had a cord twisted around the forehead until eyeballs started from sockets. Gaeseric needed gold and silver for his coinage; he would make the church disgorge.

'What is the use of our remaining,' Possidius contended, in his answer to Augustine, 'simply to see the men slain, the women ravished, the churches burned, and then be put on the rack ourselves, to make us disclose treasure which we have not?' Other bishops, unwilling to accept the duty of staying by their flocks, were quoting back to Augustine the gospel advice, 'when they persecute you in one city, flee into another.' The great man yielded, and as his brother bishops arrived with demoralised faces could observe with his own eyes, 'that river of eloquence, now almost dried up with fear.'

The Vandals under Gaeseric, as they moved into Africa – the last safe place – were something never before seen. Other Goths had shown a certain tentative respect for Rome – Gaeseric's conquest was diabolically thorough. The crowds chanting and repenting in the basilica found it easy to accept the rumour spreading throughout Hippo that Gaeseric was the devil incarnate.

Lucas was no more than mildly exasperated by the mood of apprehensive penitence that surrounded him. Some of those now repenting had been arrogant enough – as perhaps, he thought, was I – when they had property, and the law on their side. One night he wandered through crowded streets to his usual tavern in the harbour. From time to time, at the end of the day, when his eyes were dazzled with copying, and religion had got too imminent for him, he would sit there in a favourite quiet corner with a cup of wine in front of him, and watch life go by. Tonight, for the first time in a long while, he went there to think. The calm and easy life you have had for so long, he warned himself soberly, is obviously coming to an end.

And why, Lucas wondered, as he sat gently sipping his wine, does this prospect of a change, any change, make me feel young again? When all around me, respectable people who never in their lives were kidnapped for a slave, or stuck a knife in an enemy, or were cheated of an inheritance, are living in blind terror?

A Greek-speaking Syrian known to Lucas, a clever fellow who earned a living around the wharfs as best he could, made an entrance through the doorway with a sand-tray held reverently in his outstretched hands. Ceremoniously, he placed the tray in the centre of the tavern floor, squatted, and began to write with a pointed stick, muttering a hypnotic patter that soon drew the idlers around him.

'Hey, you! My old friend! Scribe!' urged a hairy, illiterate and good-natured mariner, 'come over here and tell us all what you make of it.'

The Syrian had written out in the sand these Greek capital letters:

ΓΕΝΣΗΡΙΚΟΣ: GENSERIKOS.

'Come on, scribe – tell them,' invited the Syrian, lifting his head. Swallowing his last mouthful of wine, Lucas got up unwillingly. What the Syrian hoped for was a willing accomplice – a partner, off whom to bounce his patter.

'It's the way a Greek who knew no Gothic might spell Gaeseric.'

At the name, a deadly hush fell.

'You know Greek, I see. But do you also know number-magic?'

'Try me.'

'Gamma?'

'Three.'

'Epsilon?'

'Five.'

Under each letter of the name he had printed in the sand the Syrian wrote the number as Lucas announced it. The lookers-on stood with open mouths. They were being treated to a revelation.

'Three – five – two hundred – eight – one hundred – ten –

twenty – seventy – two hundred. Now which of us is scholar enough,' asked the clever Syrian, 'to add up that little lot?' He looked around him – whoever joined in now would pay up later. But the tavern owner had already brought across his abacus and, under his accustomed fingers, the beads were racing across the wires.

'Scribe, since you work for Augustine you have to know your Bible,' said the Syrian. 'Just remind us what the Bible tells us about that figure.'

Augustine would hardly be pleased to hear me answer, thought Lucas, uncomfortably conspicuous. But here, in my favourite tavern, I must give a reply.

'That? 666 is the number of the Beast in Revelations.'

'Put in other words?'

'That number signifies the Devil.'

'The Vandal King – and there you have him,' announced the Syrian, breaking into the hush and already beginning to take up his collection. Greek, thought Lucas, was the language of the New Testament, spoken by Our Lord, and written down by the Evangelists. But if the name had been written out in Gothic, would it have come out the same? While others craned their necks, and paid their farthings, Lucas left his own coin on the counter by his empty wine-cup, and went out into the night, his mind gone dark.

Augustine would no doubt condemn number-magic, along with astrology, and all other superstitions. Lucas, however, was tipsily gripped beyond all reason by the way the abacus totted up the evil total, from numbers that had come out of his own mouth. The magical demonstration, although he knew it for a piece of tavern trickery, had struck home harder to his sceptical mind than all the passionate effusions in the basilica.

Nearing Augustine's house, he went by the basilica's open door, and even this near midnight there were still candles and chanting. He had only ever gone in that door before when the great man himself was speaking. But now that there was the devil himself to confound, might not the only sure place be inside the Christian church? He hesitated, though, for a little too long, and from habit his legs took him past.

Endlessly busy as he was, Augustine spared Lucas a word next morning before work.

'What remains?'

'Your notes to *De Pulchro et Apto*,' Lucas answered. 'After that, some straightforward copying – not much. And then the work is done.'

'Done?' Augustine's weary and ageing face contrived a smile, and the habitual sense of driven urgency fell from him. 'I was young when I thought I knew enough to write on beauty. The poet Ausonius was Consul in Rome, and the great Theodosius ruled a united empire extending from Arabia to your own wet and distant land. My son had just been born.'

When Lucas, at what he had just heard, looked ill at ease, the bishop's smile grew broader. 'But Lucas, I thought you knew. Before I became a priest I had a son by a concubine. Had he lived, my Adeodatus would have been older than you are. And as good, I hope. This is hardly the time – and I dare say you will agree – to dictate notes on *The Beautiful and the Appropriate*, a book I don't even remember. Here is something more timely you can do for me. Write out the four Penitential Psalms of David, in your largest letters. To hang on my wall, so that I can read them as I lie in bed.'

Augustine had gone on talking easily, gently, as if he were taking a brief holiday. But he never took a holiday. When Lucas as he nodded consent still looked puzzled, Augustine rested a thin hand on his shoulder.

'I have a premonition, sent, I think, from God, that I shall soon be taking to my bed.'

Lucas looked hard at the face he had been seeing every day, and the change had come. Augustine, fountain of eloquence and energy, whose word echoed across all Africa, was old and close to death.

'The Penitential Psalms, then, in large letters,' said Lucas, making an effort to sound matter-of-fact. 'A little more plain copying, and the edition, as you planned it, will all be as you want it. Except,' Lucas added, as he caught Augustine's wry glance of complicity, and knew what was in his mind, 'for *De Pulchro et Apto*.'

'Which, we agree, does not matter,' said Augustine, as he turned away. Other business awaited him. Speaking over his shoulder he added, 'Finished – and I wonder what will become of it.'

*

Iynx had patiently explained to his missionaries from Dyrin what he would like them to say, but the words that afterwards came from them became unlikelier as they went deeper into Roman Africa.

The big-breasted old whore was back in Carthage, spreading the good word among the public women, who lately had been given a bad time by the pious. A man called Gaeseric was coming – and what a man! Catholic nuns, once he arrived, would become whores. And whores would again be what they always held they should be: nuns of the Great Goddess. Men everywhere were to grovel before women. No man but Gaeseric! A crazy excitement briefly swept the daughters of joy, and this was the least useful of all the seditions the Vandal King promoted.

His Donatist missionaries spoke earnestly to their own kind, and were more thoughtfully listened to. They used language that other Donatists could understand, and, anyway, had come back from this place across the border, Dyrin, where everything anyone ever dreamed of had already begun to happen.

The Donatist missionaries pictured Gaeseric as Gildo, come back to earth a second time. Had they not been bullied and fined to drive them back into the orthodox church? Gaeseric was arriving to revenge them. He would cow the Roman soldiers, who swaggered as they collected taxes from the poor. His plan, like Gildo's, was to divide the imperial domain among the needy. Cheap food for the poor. Peace, bread, land. Even before the first Vandal scouts came over the horizon, isolated Roman garrisons in the back country were finding that they floundered in a sea of organised hatred.

More than words were needed to give a slave hope. Indoctrinated slaves, sent out from Dyrin with a messages of salvation through work in common – freedom and a trade! – were never quite believed. About the virtues of work, Roman slaves had no illusions. The formidable Circumcelliones, however, made up for all.

Tucco, the one-armed gladiator, fell in with them joyously, and despite his earlier contempt for a soldier's life, took a hand in their fighting – for even before the Vandals arrived, the Circumcelliones had begun a guerrilla war of their own.

On the immense properties nearer the frontier, where the

commercial crops were olives and corn, labour gangs would pause in their work, as word reached them from the Circumcelliones, straighten backs and down tools. The day was nigh. Burn their mansions, Iynx had said, turning his back coldheartedly on a boyish past he could have wished different. That will terrify them. But leave the crops. The food in field and barn will be put to good use later.

The widespread insurrection of the Circumcelliones helped Gaeseric's strategy the most. They were tying up troops all along the frontier, leaving Boniface with no reserve of veterans he could call in to stiffen his meagre city garrisons. With this kind of turbulence spreading, what chance was there that Cornelia's mansion would escape?

Inimicus on a big and heavy horse only just up to his weight – the military tribune was a fat man now – and with a look like death on his porcine face, had ridden away at the head of his dwindling detachment of regulars. He was obeying orders, knowing that he left the protective towers between mansion and desert sparsely held by invalids and cripples – a token force.

Tucco reached Cornelia's mansion with ten dozen insurrectionaries at his back. Circumcelliones were organised in dozens, like the Apostles. Newcomers, eager, revengeful, had joined Tucco as he moved across country, drawn to him, as scraps of iron are picked up by a lodestone.

Tucco's men were bold as brass. All had personal affronts, enormous or trivial, to avenge. Some had brooded for years over one unjust word. They had paused on the road to visit an exemplary death of a government spy. Crucify him upside down, someone had suggested, but St Peter had been crucified upside down, so they flayed him alive.

Cornelia was now alone, and fat, and sad. As she saw Inimicus ride off heavily, clumsily, at the head of his soldiers, she had been ashamed of herself for her sudden hope that he might never come back.

She had always treated her household slaves decently. Could she not rely on their loyalty – their affection? Did her sharecroppers really have much to complain of, even in these hard times? But word had spread among Cornelia's *coloni*, like a triumphal vision, that once Gaeseric had arrived they would no longer be tied to the soil. A jubilee – all money debts forgiven, all men free, and the land shared out.

The *coloni* had told Tucco that inside the big house was a bricked-up cellar, full of weapons.

'We shall have enough for an army!' shouted Tucco as the cellar was emptied of greased swords still in their linen wrappers, shiny spear-blades never used, even breast-plates and helmets. As he came in through the courtyard, Tucco had killed the most promising-looking of Cornelia's slaves in single combat, at one blow. He was in his glory.

Cornelia, stunned, had lingered under the gate lintel, a fat woman with all her hair come down, and on each side of her a stone caryatid, who resembled her even though so much larger than herself, women with bare breasts, immobile, but carrying on their shoulders a great burden.

'You are traitors!' she was screaming, in the voice that in better days she would have kept for an urgent order. As if any of the unknown men stripping out her house were likely to take heed of her! 'All the men I have ever known were traitors!'

Tucco, now wearing a breast-plate came up to her, and Cornelia, fallen silent, glared at the stump to which his hook was strapped. Not even a man, this traitor, but a monster! Her evident fear filled Tucco with delight. This was like the old days, when women around the arena screamed. Ever since Gilda denied him her bed, Tucco had found an unaccountable but delicious pleasure in frightening women.

'You might find you like it.'

He waved the hook towards her face much as Pope or Emperor might proffer a beringed hand. 'Get down on your knees, and kiss it.'

Someone else's heavy hands, behind Cornelia, were pressing into soft shoulders, pushing her down. The drifted sand of the courtyard was gritty under her bare knees. From somewhere near came a high-spirited laugh. Onlookers, in years gone by, would laugh like that at some expert stroke, atrocious and yet funny. The laugh brought back to Tucco all the great things he had done when he was a man, and possessed two hands. The point of the hook was slowly coming closer to Cornelia's mouth.

She began moving her head from side to side, like a

passionate woman eluding a caress, but this invisible man, behind her had her by the long hair. From no wish of her own, helplessly, she tasted the iron, and their loud words were a chant.

'Kiss the hook! Kiss the hook!'

Her mouth, though, had been forced down on it, and that was disappointing, because Tucco had wanted to see this fat woman with so much hair kiss the hook – even kiss his stump – of her own free will. He pushed the sharp tip in past her tightly-clenched lips.

A twist of the wrist, and he had the hook through her cheek. The point came out through the membrane of flesh, and how long did she have to live, anyway? Cornelia was choking on her own blood, the pain accentuating so that she forgot the tug at her hair. They were leading her away from the caryatids, and towards the cistern, as a tamed animal is led, a pig or an ox with a ring through its nose, and all of them, without exception, laughing. They even let her pause, to spit out her own hot blood, before dragging her further.

'What shall we do with her?'

'Cut her up in strips.'

'Melt her down for lard.'

What was the use, she asked herself, before the pain blinded her, of being nice to them all these years?

Eventually, when they had exercised their imaginations in tormenting Cornelia to death, four of them lifted up her languid and stained body, and tossed it, with a splash, into the water where the eels bred. Eels are as glad to eat human flesh as any other.

Iynx reached what was left of Cornelia's mansion weeks later. The familiar masonry stood, but the woodwork, dried over many years in the desert wind, had burned to ash. He had been given command of a force of good cavalry – on Gaeseric's orders the frontier was to be made safe – and was working his way through the inland country, putting things back where they belonged. Runaway *coloni* were herded back to the sharecropping farms they had tried in vain to flee. Such Circumcelliones or free peasants as had not been killed in the fighting were reduced at once to the status of *coloni*. The landowner needed labour, so the labourer must not leave the land. The old, inconsistent world, with its ancient anomalies was being flattened out.

Iynx found himself wandering here and there around the ruined place, and momentarily a boy again – but how had everything become so much smaller? He found the skeleton in the cistern, gruesomely at peace under the green water he used to gaze through, but somewhat disarticulated. The bright dye Cornelia had used, for years, to hide the greyness of her long hair, had all washed out, and in the water the filaments of her hair were gently dancing. Her head was a bare, grinning skull, which no one who knew her in life could ever have identified.

One or two of the household survivors recognised Iynx, and came sniffing around him like lost dogs, in the hope of small favours. They were all of them careful, though, not to tell him what had happened to Cornelia, for fear of what he might do. He called out the *coloni* to dig a common grave, in the hard earth near the olive grove, for all the dead, indiscriminately, and Cornelia's skeleton was pitched in with the rest. An Arian priest, only yesterday a Donatist, said perfunctory prayers. Iynx was master here now – King Gaeseric was rewarding all his more trustworthy officers, and this was the estate Iynx had asked for and been given. Cornelia – whom he only dimly remembered – had evidently disappeared in the fighting, as had so many others. Africa had been swept clear of its Roman proprietors. Otherwise, everything would go on as before, with only certain exceptions. No Circumcelliones, more *coloni*, fewer holy days, One God instead of Three-in-One, no Blessed Virgin.

King Gaeseric, thought Iynx, camping like an old campaigner on his first evening in the ruined house, was perfectly right to give me what I asked for, and send me to serve him down here. Unlike Veleda – though she is always welcome – I have developed no taste for courts. I love the clean air of the desert. Along the frontier, whenever there is trouble, the King will need a commander. I shall keep my men in trim. I shall see a little action, even when the rest of Africa is at peace.

Though nearly all Roman Africa was overrun, King Gaeseric was held up at the gates of Hippo. He was to be held at bay there for a year, and never, in consequence, dared attempt the assault he had had in mind on the immensity of Carthage. His ingenious mind, instead of blazing into a blind Gothic fury, began to see that a compromise – a treaty – would work in his favour. Cut off these two formerly-flourishing commercial cities from the rich countryside that sustained them, and what would happen? Hippo and Carthage would ripen and rot, and fall off the tree.

Gaeseric, Veleda reminded herself, has a son. He is building a kingdom here in Africa for the plump woman's son, the child of his body. Iynx and I are now in his way.

'Let me tell you, Princess, what I shall do – and without the inestimable benefit of your advice. I myself, King of the Vandals, commander of the army, will own all the imperial domain. I shall own all the treasure. I shall melt down the silver to make coins with my face on them. All the prisoners we have captured shall be my slaves, and work my land. The richer Romans can run away to Italy if they choose – leaving everything that they own behind them. I myself shall take over their estates.'

He smiled broadly, a generous commander, attracting attention with a gesture of his gilded staff. Around him sat an invisible assembly of Vandal captains and colonels. 'I shall reward all my officers as I have rewarded Captain Iynx. Or do you think your favourite should be the only one? They will hold land from me, in return they shall do me service. If my officers are indebted to me, and therefore loyal to me, what do the soldiers matter?' He paused shrewdly.

To his disappointed surprise, Veleda had nothing to say. His life was beginning to lack voices which would disagree with him, even though their disagreement might enrage him.

'Did I ever promise you anything, Princess?'

'Nothing.'

'Did you expect anything?'

'No'

Veleda, behind a blank face, had been thinking wildly, I could take a hundred lances, and go back to Spain, and live as a bandit. But without Iynx?

Gaeseric got up and limped to and fro ranting on, Veleda thought cynically, more than ever like one of his own puritanical preachers.

'I predict. We shall better their morals. Flog the pederasts.

Drive the harlots out of the lupanars. No Catholic bishops – only Arian bishops. The Bible is enough – do you hear me? Take away their churches full of decoration and treasure, and purify them for our worship. Across this dry countryside, in its great houses,' he indicated all Africa with a sweep of his staff, 'we must have gardens with fountains. And another thing. Our warriors must learn to fight at sea. Let them keep their Hippo and their Carthage, and feed the lazy inhabitants. All the Roman coasts are open and naked. Land from our boats on their shores – ' His gilded staff was a long Gothic sword, ' – take from them whatever we need. Yet more gold. Yet more slaves. You Latin-speakers, with your figures and your verses and your churches and your laws, think that everything has to be difficult. But I tell you, it is all so simple. Let them be shabby, those Catholic priests. Let them be insufferably poor. Not martyrs, but ridiculous. Let them walk the streets, shame-faced and hungry, the priests of the defeated, leading a life that one of my slaves would despise. And without so much as a master to feed them. Ho you there – slave! More wine!'

A household slave who must in his time have served some eminent Roman, came in with an ingratiating smile, and a gold jar. Once his beaker had been filled to the brim, Gaeseric sat there, glowering, with his other fist around it, as if regretting already that he had said so much.

A handsome woman, he was thinking as he watched her, affronted by her silence. Showing her age, though, this Roman Goth, whose brain has served me better than her body ever could. Past child-bearing. Even so, I still have a use for her.

What if I send her off, as my confidential agent, to her old friend Galla Placidia, in Ravenna, to clear the ground for a treaty? If the Augusta wishes to keep Catholic Hippo and Catholic Carthage – at least until the day they fall into my cupped hands – then she had better make a treaty with Gaeseric the bastard, even though he may be both Goth and Arian.

And if I send this icy princess to Ravenna, will she ever come back?

Yes, she will come back.

Augustine had taken to the narrow bed in his book-lined room, with a low fever. When the lay brother who carried in his bowl of soup also tried to tell him the latest news of the siege, Augustine would answer with a muttered blessing, and go back to his meditation upon the penitential psalms, written out large, and hung where he could read the words without needing to turn his head.

Count Boniface had scrabbled an army together, to ride out and confront King Gaeseric as he approached, so as to bring him to battle, but it had been an army of spectres.

No nominal roll in the Roman army could be credited. Inimicus, for instance, had come in from the southern frontier, a heavy-bodied military tribune on a broken-winded charger, riding at the head of half a maniple. He was expected to bring in a weak cohort – so where were the others?

'Over a hundred deserters, *dux*,' reported Inimicus, with the manly false frankness, the impenetrable stare, of the promoted ranker. 'Add forty-seven invalids left behind in garrison – your own orders, *dux* – '

Boniface looked at him in bitter contempt – yet another! In this promoted centurion's command there would have been dozens of phantom soldiers – men who never existed, except as names on the roll, but whose pay their officer drew. Inimicus, rigidly impassive before his general, knew that all the others were doing the same – who didn't, except perhaps the general himself? And stood there, his face blankly uninformative, and wondered if, this time, he might be the unlucky one, to be plucked out as an example. There was always Cornelia's property to fall back upon – a comfort.

But Boniface, tall as a crane and sober as a judge, let him go with that one glance of contempt. How can I make an example of a man like that, thought Boniface, observing relief in the twitch of Inimicus's retreating shoulders, when I myself bear a much greater guilt?

Romans and vandals, if you only considered official figures, were equally matched. When they came face to face on the field of battle, Gaeseric outnumbered Boniface two to one. Gaeseric had never before engaged a competent professional soldier in the field, and the way the Romans had been drawn up in battle order at first perturbed him. Boniface was making the best of it, disposing his men ably, planning to fight his battle on the defensive, until, with luck, he had worn the Vandals down, or at least muddled them. Then counter-attack. But fighting such a battle called for a discipline his men no longer possessed. They ran.

In the old days, a Roman thus defeated might have fallen upon his sword. But Boniface, a Christian and forbidden suicide, was obliged to live out the humiliations of his life to the last breath. Boniface retreated on Hippo, with a disheartened but still faithful remnant. Once inside the city, he encountered a different mood.

As the gates opened for him, and promptly closed behind the last of his men, Boniface could see at one soldierly glance that these were good walls, efficiently manned. A hospital, until lately a church, was waiting for his wounded; they were treated there by nuns. Other churches in the city were full of suppliants, many of them women, though some of them soldiers off duty. Then he met Marcus, lean-faced, shabby, harassed by scruples – Boniface could recognise the dubious look, the bitten lip – but overwhelmingly obsessed by his new responsibility.

'There are fewer soldiers on the walls than you may have thought as you rode by.' admitted Marcus with his first smile. After so many years of secretly feeling utterly different from others, he was encountering in Boniface a man who thought as he did 'Enemy scouts notice heads poking over parapets and count them, let fly their poisoned arrows and ride off out of range. But most of what they see are the heads of marble statues.'

Marcus had ransacked the collections of the rich. The defence of Hippo, so far, had been improvisation and bluff.

Boniface answered with his own first smile for weeks. 'They must think them immortal.'

A comrade here with me, in the City of God, thought Marcus, glowing with pleasure, but he dare not as yet put the thought into spoken words.

Count Boniface would have gone to see Augustine – this time, he had the right! – but Augustine saw no one. He would not even charge his mind with any account from Marcus of his stewardship as the city's defender, though he sent both men a blessing.

Boniface, after inspecting and approving the improvised

defences, had asked Marcus a question. 'You served Flavius Stilicho, so they tell me. What would he have done?'

Marcus answered, with the simplicity which had so impressed Boniface, in which the manner of soldier, priest and working man were so oddly intermingled.

'*Dux* – the one useful precedent here is your classic defence of Massilia. Our posture, as I see it, is no different. If only Ravenna continues to support us, Hippo can be supplied by sea. Indefinitely. King Gaeseric has the ships that followed him along the coast from Spain. But I have been watching them, as they put about and try to claw offshore – and the Vandals, believe me, are not likely to learn quickly how to operate a blockade. All public stocks of food here in Hippo are well accounted for. Adequate rations are being issued, they could even be reduced. And our stocks, of course, are better than the figures show, because the rich have hoarded.' (As my father would have done? wondered Marcus, and the intruding thought, for once, left him calm.) 'I think they can, gently, be made to disgorge. For the common good. We can begin, if you like, by having sermons preached – '

Should I not do better, wondered Boniface with grim humour, to offer this black-clad, old-soldier monk my command, and beome a monk myself? Brother Marcus, though, would never accept. He had done everything for the defence of Hippo that a good general would have done, but his scruples remained. His vows forbade him to bear arms.

Sometimes, Augustine's eyes moved along the lines, sometimes they read nothing. Now and then he muttered a prayer, his dark-skinned, gaunt and feverish face overcast with contrition.

The lay brother who brought up the soup, and sat on the edge of the bed to crumble stale bread in it, fed sops into the sick man's mouth as if he were a child. Finding that war news held no interest for Augustine, he began telling the old bishop of the crowded basilica, the hundreds of baptisms. Augustine gave one sweet smile, as if all that were to be expected, and went back to his prayers. Repentance? He had errors of his own to repent – the salty sins of a hot youth, the subtler misdemeanours of his life as a priest. Augustine was making up his reckoning, but more important still, here in Hippo, he was shepherd of his flock. Until the very last moment, at least he could pray.

There was little chance inside Hippo that the Vandal King could take advantage of the cracks in civil society – between rich and poor, land-hungry and possessor, schismatic and Catholic – that elsewhere in Africa had worked so well for him. Hippo was united, not only by common misfortune, but also by a shared passion.

But why is this? Marcus asked himself. When I know, as I scrutinise the faces around me, that the city – its garrison, its townsfolk, its refugees – is as deeply divided as anywhere else? We have no monopoly of God's grace – and other godly places have fallen. We ourselves have all the vices – I have them, too – that we know by now the Vandals themselves possess. But when their vices – Vandal vices – besiege the heart, we hate the sin and love the man. I am at present the miser – though with food, not money – that my father was. To love you must understand.

In Rome under siege there had been food speculators, even cannibals. Here Brother Marcus, stalking the streets with a face from which wrong-doers averted their eyes, was enforcing a frugal equality for all. The fighting in Rome had been left to the soldiers. Here every man capable of bearing arms did service on the walls. In Rome, the woman had waited at home, passively, the barbarians' predestined victims. Here they rolled bandages, consoled the sick, shamed the laggards. The rich may at times have wondered about running away – but where could they go? And what wealth could they carry with them? Offshore bobbed the ships of Gaeseric's blockade, an obstacle, a reminder.

4

In shadow, at the back of the basilica, stood a woman who had come in from the country, to judge by the hood of a homespun robe which did not quite cover her grey hair. Others around her wore pious looks on their attentive faces, but she was listening to the preacher in amused wonderment.

Up there, his voice resonating, hesitating, groping for a word, was Marcus – more vividly than ever the Marcus she had known on Cuneus, but older, less uncertain, more manly. And have I changed, Gilda wondered, even more? Or in course of time have we both, perhaps, become the people that essentially we always were? Are we showing the face that when younger and passionate was always half-hidden?

The old directness, though, and the contempt that he had always shown for money-grubbing, was coming out with everything he said. Even though he paused, now and then, to find exact words, he spoke to them as if possessed of a certainty.

And has never yet discovered – Gilda noticed – how an actor throws his voice. And lacks my flights of fancy. What he says though, comes over as sincere. You, she accused herself, were always an actress; he is real. Could I ever have held, and convinced, a crowd like this, ordinary people, none of them rebels, as Marcus does, tonight, at the end of a working day, up there, by the light of lamps? I could have held them – but convinced them?

Evidently a man close to God. Up in the mountains at Dyrin, as I spun wool, I would meditate on God as Marcus once taught me, and try my very best to be God's mouthpiece. I was speaking to God's people, wasn't I – so it should have worked. But was it ever real? A pagan who knew her business might have done as well as I, and for all I know, a pagan is what I am. I knew the words, I know them still – Marcus taught me – but they were a part I had learned by heart. Marcus as he blunders on in that resounding voice has his unquestioning certainty – grace!

– that God is filling him and speaking through him. But that I have never known, and never shall. Filled with grace? I have had men inside me, until there is no room. At the wild thought that the total number of lovers even included that man up there, preaching, Gilda laughed aloud, and people to left and right turned their faces her way, scandalised.

Gilda had scrambled into Hippo alone, on foot, mingling with the last of the country runaways, before the gates were shut and barred. For the first week, as Gaeseric's army, hot from their victory, surged up and surrounded the city, and his blockading ships arrived, one by one, offshore, Gilda had blotted out all thought of past and future by working in the hospital. The gift other women had, especially the nuns, for nursing the wounded was a gift she lacked. So she had scrubbed floors, digesting, as the hard brush went to and fro across the tiles, her latest bitterness.

Dyrin was gone. Everything useful to Gaeseric had been taken over and used, and whatever might stand in his way had, afterwards, been cynically destroyed. For Iynx it had been so easy to split the community in two. The missionaries went forth, and the handful of dissenters who remained, Gilda among them, had been driven out of their houses and into the hills by a squadron of Vandal horsemen, who cut down or struck through the body those who did not move fast enough. They then went on to do pretty much what the Roman imperial cavalry had done in Dyrin a century before, burned standing crops, ring-barked the fruit trees, started fires, leaving behind them the shells of houses, and the bodies of the unburied dead.

Gilda, as she fled breathlessly up into the hills with the others, to escape Vandal sabre-strokes had tried at first to persuade herself that Iynx could never have known it would end like this. But of course he did. Perhaps he had never imagined what it would be like. And if he had? You gave your heart to a man without his ever knowing, and, afterwards, so often, came devastation.

Her hands, even tonight, here in church, were sore from scrubbing. (Why should that sensation remind her so much of Marcus?) She looked up into the ecclesiastical lamplight at another man she had lost. He was talking, tonight, with all the others about something simple – food-hoarding. Though in the name of God. We must all share; property is a trust from God; the poor are our brothers. And might just as well, thought Gilda, have been alone with a hungry woman on Cuneus, and arguing with her, strangely, how wrong it would be to strip that offshore reef of edible mussels, growing so earnest as he made his point, as if mussels clinging to a rock, so as to breed and maintain themselves, were also a part of religion.

Gilda glanced again at the faces that had turned her way, looking upwards now at the preacher, well-dressed women, announcing themselves as food hoarders by their shifty or defiant glances, until, eventually, into their fleshy faces came a look of shame. A look, thought Gilda, I could never have put there. And after they had heard all that Marcus had to tell them, would they disgorge? The fat woman nearest, who looked as if her god were her belly, had begun to sob.

'Love of money, brothers and sisters, is the root of all evil.'

Is that what the Gospel tells us? wondered Gilda. Is that what the church teaches? What would have become of Marcus had his father been penniless? Money means nothing to Marcus, never did, and nowadays he has a heavenly father. He is coming to his last argument, raising his voice awkwardly towards the transcendental. The rigmarole will soon be over. Shall I make myself known to him?

Here at the back, all through the service, there had been an ebb and flow of those who came and went. Gilda turned away from the brief temptation of a life she could never possibly share, and went outside with the others. Even in the night air, the church mood lingered. And that was the last good turn, thought Gilda, drawing an enormous breath, I can ever do him. My sins have never really felt like sins – can that be what is wrong with me? But if sins they be, let me expiate them by scrubbing floors.

Someone behind her, as with happiness she took that simple decision, reached out to accost her by touching her. A man's voice that was familiar, and yet quite out of the question, an intruder from the days when she was young, had begun to expostulate, 'But it can't be you?' Gilda's impulse, as when Heraclian had shouted after her in Carthage, was to turn and run. But the stranger had her by the arm, holding her, not brutally, but as if to establish a right to her – as a man just awaking, thought Gilda, might try holding on tight to a dream.

Inside they had begun some kind of chanting. Soon the people leaving would be thick enough to surround her – save her, if she wanted to be saved.

'Don't you know me?'

Tall, plump, almost completely bald. And did not even wait for her to answer, but said 'Come on!', letting go her arm, turning away, knowing she would follow. At one time, she thought, as she went after him, I doted on that voice.

Lucas in course of time had become old and bald, and thoughtful enough to pass for his own father – a man, she remembered, who had taught him his trade, a citizen of Londinium when Londinium was Roman, a man Lucas had always much admired. For the first time since, from under a mountain ridge, she had seen what was left of Dyrin go up in smoke, Gilda felt safe.

There was a bit of moon – enough to see by. With the breeze coming off the sea, Gilda pulled off the homespun hood, and let the night freshness blow in her hair. Let him see her as she had become.

'I was sure it was you,' Lucas said.

She touched both hands, in mock coquettishness, to the heavy twist of grey hair. 'Ah – but I am eternally young. I took you for your father.'

He laughed – their old jokes had begun.

But I could just as well have said, thought Lucas, regarding her silently, and smiling, that in the light of the church doorway I saw the cock of your head, the way your dancer's foot turns at the ankle, the arrogant stamp of your foot. And in the night as I smelled your smell – not your Roman perfume, your smell – I thought I had encountered a ghost. 'All at once I saw your profile,' he went on, limiting himself to the simple and believable, 'in the church against the lamplight. Not a place I go to often.'

'Not exactly my place, either, even these days,' said Gilda, sharing his confession with a laugh he had never expected to hear again. 'But Lucas, you used to be all skin and bone. And now so sleek. You are not by any chance hoarding food?' She passed a curved hand over his bald head, an impertinent caress, but how could she have resisted? 'What happened to your hair?'

They had turned into an alley, and were shrouded in comfortable darkness. Lucas reached for her hands, and there was no reason in the world to pull them away. Always, in those early days, thought Gilda, he was the tall one who knew his mind, and then I grew up, and for a while overtook him. I was famous, though not for long. Now he looks the solid one: the inevitable lover.

'They killed Flavius Stilicho, so I had to leave Ravenna.' (Simple when put like that!) 'You?'

'I was manumitted, but you knew all that. My master sent me here to Africa, and eventually he gave up the ghost. Dead for years, and I am free to practise my trade. In fact I always was – inscribed of the copyists' guild, in London. If there still is such a thing. So here in Hippo they can't touch me. I had a little business – though lately I have been working for Augustine.'

'A businessman? Is that how you put on weight?'

I hardly need ask him, thought Gilda, if he is married, and with a houseful of children. He would have told me. And he smells of wine, and surely a wife would have made him shave before she let him go to church. 'So now you love money? The root of all evil?' Gilda found to her surprise that, as she asked him that, her voice was nervous. Suppose he did? And like all the men she had ever known with money in their pockets, would amuse himself with her, and disappear?

'Don't worry. As the siege goes on we shall all get thin. I copied books – it was a way to live. Not rich, but not poor either. And only tonight I decided, I want to get out of this place. The Vandals are none of my business.'

Lucas had expected it to come out of his mouth sounding like a blasphemy, but they had moved into moonlight, and she was nodding. Gilda was the one woman who always understood:

'Had they really been out to free the slaves – ' she was explaining ' – and open the theatres, then I might have been for them. But I knew from the start they were only pretending. They were promising whatever they thought others might want – '

The decisive moments in life can surprise one by their

banality. Gilda, after a moment of confidential silence, knew she had already taken her own decision, yet she answered, slowly, as if continuing the conversation, 'There is nowhere else to go. That has always been the trouble.'

This excitement in Hippo, from men on the walls, ducking poisoned arrows, to the women scrubbing blood off a floor, had all at once become irrelevant. Shall I tell him, wondered Gilda, about Iynx – my child and his? But that kind of secret a woman is wiser to keep.

'I scrub floors in the other big church, where all the wounded are,' she said, as if cracking a joke. 'I scrub a floor until I am tired enough to fall asleep on it. And when I wake up, they hand me not quite enough food. Brother Marcus's official ration.' He was remembering the way, in Milan, that a vulgar crowd had laughed at her false pregnancy. Could this be the same Gilda? Her laugh had never changed.

'You are not an actress any more?'

'How could I be? The theatres are empty, the churches are full.'

'What did you think of the preacher tonight?'

'What did you?'

'I thought him rather simple-minded,' said Lucas, 'in comparison with Augustine.'

Gilda let go a huge breath, like a sigh, and then laughed at herself, inwardly. There was no reason, either, to tell him about Marcus and Cuneus. This was a clean new start. Or put it another way. This was to be young again, and be given another beginning.

'Women are never allowed in the bishop's house,' Lucas was telling her, as if what came next were cheerfully inevitable. 'I can't take you there – but we can use my old shop. If you don't mind discomfort.'

She was a small girl again, tall Lucas was explaining the language of poetry, as she ran alongside the other slaves buckled to the chain. He was making sense of everything no one else had ever spoken of. He was taking over her young life. Scrub floors? Only for him. Not that Lucas would ever ask it of her.

'Any kind of bed whatever,' she told him, astonished at the thirteen-year-old giggle that had risen into her throat, 'is better than a wet tiled-floor.'

A city full of the pious, he reminded himself, as they went together, soberly, a long-established couple, under the arcade. All the others in a state of exaltation, thinking of things we have decided don't concern us.

'What are in those barrels?'

'Books.'

'You sold books? Yes, I can imagine.'

'Most of them used to be Claudian's. So I hate to part with them. What will the Vandals do with books? Light their bonfires?'

All these books, she decided, pulling the homespun gown over her head, putting hands in the dark, to reassure herself, up and down her dancer's body, stretching out at full length on the old flock mattress that he pulled up to cover the barrelheads, are his children.

The Vandal siege of Hippo began late in April 430. The defending general, Boniface, Count of Africa, had in Brother Marcus a trusted helper who would never be a rival. A military situation on the face of it desperate, but the two men, reading each other's minds, agreed that the best hope of keeping the Vandals out of Hippo lay in a daring strategy of 'Attack! attack! attack!'

The enemy had hauled their shabby, but still workable, catapults uphill and down a thousand miles from Tingitana. Hardly had the first stone been hurled in its parabola at the city wall, than mounted lancers, hidden in the detached tower of new-cut stone that overlooked the city and was the key to its defence, charged out of a wicket gate torch in hand. From watchers on the wall came a cheer as thick smoke arose. From then on the surviving catapults were never left in peace, by day or night.

Not long after, at sundown, when a quick breeze came across the dried-out plain between the city walls and Gaeseric's camp, Boniface's cavalrymen, on their best horses, made an impudent sortie to his very headquarters. In the complacently undefended camp the cavalry raised fire and havoc. Yet, to the astonishment of the long-haired, blonde Vandal women, willing or unwilling, the Roman soliders never laid a hand on any one of them. This was to be an unusual kind of war.

The Vandal flotilla offshore was only slowly learning its job.

Packet boats with despatches were getting through unscathed, and the first seventy-five tonner came gloriously into port before dawn, all sails set, having run the blockade in the dark with a cargo of Sicilian wheat. Soon other blockade runners were moving back and forth like fish through the holes in a net, putting Raus, Gaeseric's admiral, in a fury.

On the first moonless night, at a hint from Count Boniface, the harbour master, after secret preparations, sent out a twelve-oared galley towing a hulk filled with tar and dry splinters and anything else that would burn: a fireship. They managed, by a piece of luck, to set alight Raus's flagship, and some swore later that, as they rowed away fast, all twelve oars going hard, they had heard the splash as the Vandal admiral jumped overboard, to save his life.

Boniface, by this time hardly ever paused to remember that he had a wife – she was in Carthage, disconsolate, and pining for Ravenna – or had ever been tempted to commit suicide. The siege was giving him back what his life had hitherto lacked – just as every successful little feat of arms put heart in the hungry citizens. These seemingly miraculous victories over Gaeseric became an occasion for hymns, sermons, breath-taking confessions, spectacular conversions.

While the city lived through this intensity of religious emotion and warlike deed, Lucas and Gilda stood to one side, out of it, lovers taking solace in each other. They did not doubt for a moment that around them something marvellous must be happening: the birth of Christendom, here in Hippo, the City of God. But this was not a future to which their origins in a distant, damp and humorous island, their past lives as slaves, had ever committed them.

From grain-speculators and money-lenders, out on the open street, tearing their expensive clothes and pouring handfuls of ashes shamelessly into their hair, they got only amusement. Or fashionable women, streaming with tears, making public confession of their adulteries. The working poor took their rations and did what needed to be done for the city, and, at times, were even swept away by the enthusiasm, but the two lovers looked on like spectators. They had feelings that others did not possess, and could not longer play upon. Had everyone else felt like this, the defence of Hippo, Lucas sometimes reflected, would have been a disaster. But everyone was not like this – and would they ever be?

The summer heats were approaching, and Augustine, for the last ten days of his life, lay entirely alone, the penitential psalms before his eyes, in hardly audible prayer, day and night, for the city of which he was bishop, and for the salvation of his own soul.

On 28 August 430 the bishop died. His body, as was the custom in torrid Africa, went into the grave on the same day. His basilica, at the burial service, was a mass of breathless flesh, the mood of religious ecstasy gripping the city making them all certain that Augustine had gone straight up to heaven, and was preparing a place for them. Some would ever swear they had seen his soul, rising up into the blue African sky, fainter than a blowing white garment, less vague than a puff of smoke. Augustine was already living in bliss, in the sight of God, and not a few craved to follow him.

This was the fourth month of the siege, and Vandal attacks continued incessantly, though fever was reported in their camp too. Only a miracle could save the city. The defenders, as they mourned the passing of Augustine, were rehearsing their own death.

Lucas, next forenoon, went to the bishop's house, and asked at the door to see Brother Marcus. His face was well enough known to them, so after the usual demur he was let through, and then had to wait, with others, in an antechamber for hours. Now and then the door opened and closed on some visitor more important than himself, and Lucas, through the open doorway, caught a glimpse of the grizzled, crop-haired man, hard pressed, on whom so much in Hippo depended.

At last, through the open door the man's tired eyes moved his way, and a hand waved in a gesture, half command, half greeting. When Lucas told her earlier that he was off to see Brother Marcus Gilda had answered with silence. Marcus, was the past she had turned her back on. Of the plan Lucas had in mind she was sceptical, but she herself could see no other way out of Hippo, so why argue? To rely in such decisions on another – to yield up even the will to the lover – was beginning to be a small delight.

'There is a treasure in the city. I know of it – many do not. Perhaps not even you.'

Brother Marcus at these opening words looked more wary than intrigued. He was used in this room to visits from crazy people. 'A treasure that should never be let fall into the hands of the Vandals.'

Could this bald, calm, intelligent man – a man he recognised at a glance, the scribe – be yet another, here in Hippo, unhinged by excitement? With a miraculous recipe of his own for victory? Blinking weary eyes, Marcus made an effort to answer gently, 'Gold? Silver? Kindly explain yourself. You were the bishop's copyist, were you not?'

'All the books Augustine cared to keep – his lifetime's work – he edited before he died. I know, because I copied them, and I have possession of them. All that remains of hims – his message to the rest of us, his continuing life here on earth after death – exists in those copies. And in no others.' Lucas lifted, as if in ocular demonstration, the right hand that had pushed the iron pen such a distance. 'If ever the Vandals lay hands on them –'

'I take it other copies exist?' Marcus interjected. He was seldom confronted these days with any real problem to which he could not quickly see a practical solution.

'Imperfect copies of one work or another all round the empire, which if they survive will serve to deform his thought.'

Why am I so concerned, Lucas asked himself, with Augustine? Why have I begun speaking to this weary man with such passion? At last, in this melodramatic siege, have I found something worthwhile?

Marcus had this time closed his eyes, and was squeezing his two large hands together, as if compelling himself with all the power he possessed not to yawn. Theology – the idle thought went racing through his mind – had never meant as much to him as it might have done. When Augustine ordained him he had even found the New Testament tough going. All day, after a sleepless night, he had been feeling the death of Augustine like the death of a loving and disinterested father: a gap in his mind and heart.

A father, though, leaves an inheritance.

'If what they tell me down in the docks is true,' Lucas went on, 'the Vandals, by this time, hold all Africa outside Hippo and Carthage. We may keep them out for long enough to strike a bargain – a truce, a treaty –'

Marcus nodded an answer through a weary smile, though these were likelihoods that no one else coming into this room had ever dared dwell upon.

'– and the Vandals, so I hear, have no use for any book other than the Bible –'

Slowly Marcus got to his feet, walked across the room, and eased his fatigue by resting his shoulders against the wall, like a weary sentry. Obstinately, he was telling himself – and what if it happens as this intelligent man predicts? Vandals come and go; the church survives.

'The Vandal King has in mind,' Marcus began slowly, feeling his way, 'to humiliate and degrade us Catholics until our church is the church of the poor, the helpless and the ignorant. What then? Are not they Christ's favourite people?' His own words, as he spoke them, exploded in his mind. With Augustine at our side – in our hand – surviving death, he began telling himself excitedly, though we may be poor, how shall we ever be ignorant? This, too, had become a sober and soldierly decision.

'And if the Vandals took possession of the two hundred and thirty-two papyrus rolls I copied out – unique in the world? Our treasure?'

Into Marcus's breast was arriving a miraculous surge of energy. God sends such founts of energy, he told himself, to the man who loyally serves. A scribe, he was reminding himself, intelligent, but not exactly devout. Augustine used him for his competence. Was I, in some small way, jealous because this scribe and Augustine were friends?

'I could run the blockade and take the books to Sicily,' offered Lucas. 'Better still, all the way to Ravenna. But I need your consent.'

'Those Vandals offshore are learning their trade,' was Marcus's cautious, serious answer. 'They are finding ways to stop even our big grain-ships.'

'But a small boat, a fishing boat –' began Lucas. Yielding to his yawn at last, seeing his way clear, taking his decision, Marcus interrupted him. 'Did you not at one time copy for Claudian, the poet?'

Marcus could see, in his mind's eye, the famous Claudian, perfumed and with greasy hair, blundering about in the basilica of St Peter. In Rome, in another age than this. And what if this scribe let Augustine's life-work drop into the sea?

'What exactly do you know about ships?' he asked severely.

'Years ago, in Ostia, I worked as a shipping clerk.'

Even in Lucas's own ears, the answer did not sound convincing. Marcus, for a moment, let the decision he had to take, one way or another, swing to and fro in his mind. 'With the help of God –' he had begun conventionally, then sharply he interrupted himself, less monk than soldier. 'Why are you so keen to save these books? Just because they are your own handiwork?'

'If there were no books,' said Lucas, with a smile – he had won! 'how would any of us know what happened, the day before yesterday? How could we discover what others, before us, thought and felt?'

Brother Marcus reached a blind hand for a reed pen that needed better sharpening. He had begun scribbling across a square of papyrus.

'Use this,' he said, handling what he had written to Lucas. 'I entrust the task to you – at your own discretion. Leave word at the door downstairs when you are leaving – and I will pray for you. Now, if you would kindly send in whoever is still waiting – the next in line –'

'If Gaeseric is doing better lately in the blockade,' said Gilda sagaciously, 'it can only be because, at last, he has his spies down there in the harbour. So why not let me be the one to look around?'

They had agreed between them that it would make no great difference if they also took along the stock – Claudian's books, Lucas's copies. And Lucas, with an unexpected breaking-in of love, would all at once see her, a woman somewhat past her best, wandering the familiar wharfs and drifting into taverns. Only she could do it. Gilda was a delight.

Gilda had been confident that she could, at least, get word of her old man. Yet it came as a surprise when there he was, confronting her, fatter, older, smelling, as always, faintly of horse manure, alone, unloading a clean cargo of grain halfway down the mole. He was scooping barley out of the hold with a wooden shovel, and making hard work of it. The grains of corn, tumbling into the heap made a noise, as Gilda approached, like distant summer rain.

He gave Gilda an appraising glance, as though he had only just run her out of Leptis Magna. 'Well,' he said, resting on his wooden shovel, 'running the blockade of Hippo is where the money is. And how are you making your fortune in the midst of all this mess? I have another shovel over there, against the bulkhead, if you know how to use one.'

The old man watched Gilda set to work, as if her willingness to help him would be a test of friendship. 'That's the idea. A shovel is better than a sword. Not that you are getting anything out of all this, either wages or a smacking great kiss. What is a woman to me?'

'And your boy?' Gilda asked softly, as barley grains fell with a hiss from her shovel-blade. 'Don't you have help?'

'When I heard you walking up behind my back, gently, craftily, he used to walk like that, I didn't turn, in case you might be him. But no such luck.' From the corner of his eye a tear was dribbling down his slack old cheek, as if the bright sunlight had become too much for him. 'Sooner or later, though, he would have left me – however much they love me, they can never stand the smell. But the Vandals got him. We ran this cargo under the lee of their biggest ship – cheeky, you see, the best way. But the wind dropped, and we had to get out the sweeps. Only a scratch on his arm, as he rowed beside me – but from one of those arrows of theirs –'

He blubbed for a moment or so while Gilda silently dug up barley for him, and then was himself again.

'Bread rationing. Cavalry horses. I could make my fortune. If they don't want horse manure to pile up higher than the walls, they must have me. Only now I've lost my boy, I've no heart for it.'

He went down, heavily, into the hold, to scrape the last shovelfuls out of the corners, as if not trusting a woman with the work.

'A trip to Sicily, on the sly?'

For answer he ducked out of sight into the hold, then bobbed up again to throw the last shovelful of grain on to the heap, before saying with dark suspicion, 'Are you another of them down here, working for the Vandal Bible-bashers?'

'For Augustine.'

'But he's dead.'

They stood there, looking at one another.

'I suppose,' the old man answered diffidently, 'he could help my boy into heaven.'

A sentry was coming along the quay, self-importantly, to take cognisance of the heap of barley, and guard it.

'Barrels weigh heavily,' he said in a peevish mutter, as she rapidly explained. 'Who is going to do all the lifting?'

'My husband,' said Gilda, shy, avoiding his sarcastic look, seventeen again.

They made their Sicilian landfall at Syracuse, and Lucas went ashore in his best clothes, to flourish Brother Marcus's chit and make connections. He came back that evening, exasperated by the harbour officials, and saying that if he was any judge, the Sicilians were more afraid of Vandals than anyone who had ever seen their helmets and lances. Sicily had been another safe place, and now, if they saw a strange sail come closer, it must be a Vandal. In their own minds, they were already conquered.

By the end of the day, Lucas had almost begun sympathising with the Vandals. He needed to get away from this mood of fear in Syracuse, their indifference to the cargo he had brought them.

'There is horse manure in Ravenna too,' Gilda told the old man, who was missing his boy worse than ever, and regretting Africa.

'I have a trade than can never fail,' he boasted uneasily. The presence on board of this couple, not past it yet though they should be, who could never keep their hands off each other, was an affront to his loneliness. But, at least their money was good, and they did their share of the work. Grumbling harder the further north he went, he headed the boatload of barrels into the Adriatic, and worked his way up the coast to Ravenna.

Down in the Classis – the harbour – Lucas went off once again to wrestle with the suspicious imperial officials. Three lines scribbed by a priest I was once married to, thought Gilda with a wry grin, as from the deck she watched Lucas go away and come back again, between two soldiers, and here I am, entering another world. She looked once again at the familiar city, the trees grown bigger, the white buildings shabbier. The arrival of a small boat from beleaguered Hippo was causing a stir. The harbour functionaries who had come back with Lucas were declaring, in loud, officious voices, that the line from Brother Marcus should also have had an *exeat*, countersigned by Count Boniface, as commander.

'Count Boniface has something better to do than sign *exeats*,' intruded Gilda tartly, in the ringing voice she might have used in the days when she had Stilicho to back her. Lucas heard the sarcastic authority in her voice, and saw the harbour officials, suddenly, pull incredulous and yet respectful faces, as if this mysterious, shabby woman must be some great personage in disguise. I have used that particular voice of mine, thought Gilda, for the last time. I am back in Ravenna, and must now become invisible.

Their barrels had been unloaded and separated from Augustine's, and carried off to the custom house. On the quay, as the three of them stood there together, marsh air and sea air mingled. There was a faint, far-off odour of pine balsam. Galleys were leaving for Constantinople.

'Pay me what you promised, and I'll head back to Africa,' said the old man. 'I never did like this place.'

'And what do I do?' Lucas asked the world at large. 'Open a shop? Take a job as a shipping clerk?'

'Or shall I make a come-back – if there still is a theatre in holy Ravenna, which I doubt? Or walk the streets with a big label round my neck, telling them who I am? We have already drawn enough attention to ourselves.'

'Those books of yours are a ton weight,' grumbled the old man. 'Why don't you sell some, and open a tavern.'

The place they bought eventually was in an obscure alley – not the first place others would come looking – but one way and another there was a living in it. The work was new to them – hard on the feet – but they gave people what they were looking for: good wine with cheap food, for one thing. And a brief dream of freedom, before midnight, in a world where, every day that went by, there more rules to be kept and dogmas to which lip service had better be paid.

As the evening went on, girls from the port drifted in, looking for men – a decent class of women, Gilda saw to that. They had their living to earn like everyone else. After a couple of skirmishes with the tall, bald man who knew long words, and carried a knife in his boot, the gaudier girls and their brash bully-boys learned to keep away. If one of the girls who used her place fell into trouble, Gilda would look after her. The place was home to them.

There were harbour police to be paid off, and whenever a government spy slunk in and sat in a dark corner, a finger would go, casually, to the side of Lucas's nose, and the conversation drop to silence, until he slid out again and looked elsewhere. It was a decent little place, and no bother to anyone. A singsong now and then, but the noisy and the combative went elsewhere.

Towards the end of a long evening, if Gilda felt the spirit rising in her, she might knock a table-top with her knuckle for another kind of silence. Then rap out a cadence with both palms, and softly begin one of her old songs. The one the girls liked best, not that they had ever quite grasped the words, or could get the tune right, came if you went far enough back from the temple of the Mother Goddess, the bronze gates of which had for so long been locked up tight.

Cras amet qui nunquam amavit
Quique amavit cras amet

Tomorrow those who never loved will love; tomorrow those who loved will love once more. Some, as they tried to join in the words, would laugh; one or two of the old ones were pretty sure to cry. Late at night, in a waterfront tavern, and no one outside in the alley, hearing the words, was likely to think of them as pagan.